SHORTGRASS SONG

MIKE BLAKELY

SHORTGRASS SONG

A TOM DOHERTY ASSOCIATES BOOK
NEW YORK

SHORTGRASS SONG

Copyright © 1994 by Mike Blakely

This book is printed on acid-free paper.

A Forge Book
Published by Tom Doherty Associates, Inc.
175 Fifth Avenue
New York, N.Y. 10010

Library of Congress Cataloging-in-Publications Data
Blakely, Mike.
    Shortgrass song / Mike Blakely.
        p.   cm.
    "A Tom Doherty Associates book."
    ISBN 0-312-85541-9
    1. Frontier and pioneer life—Texas—Fiction. 2. Cowboys—West (U.S.)—Fiction. 3. Family—Texas—Fiction. I. Title.
PS3552.L3533S5 1994
813'.54—dc20   94-12924
                                                       CIP

First edition: November 1994

Printed in the United States of America

0 9 8 7 6 5 4 3 2 1

For my mother,
Patricia Dawn Blakely,
and my father,
James ''Doc'' Blakely

ACKNOWLEDGMENTS

Five editors have left their stamps upon this work:

My first line of defense against embarrassing myself in
print—Rebecca Blakely.
Joe Vallely, who delicately suggested economy and imagery.
Bob Gleason, who inspired me to hone and define.
Dale Walker, who engaged his logic and love for the old west.
And Anna Magee, who weighed every word and phrase.

The libraries of the University of Texas at Austin proved invaluable sources of research material.

For helping me understand the discipline of fiddle playing, I am indebted to Doc Blakely, Johnny Gimble, Alvin Crow, Valerie Riles Morris, Ricky Turpin, and Ron Knuth. Doc Blakely, Johnny Gimble, Hank Harrison, and Ron Knuth were also instructive on mandolins and mandolin playing.

For sharing their passion for western music and cowboy poetry, I thank Jim Bob Tinsley, Waddie Mitchell, Rusty Richards, Red Steagall, J. B. Bowers, John Byrne Cooke, and especially Don Edwards. I will remember Elmer Kelton and C. F. Eckert for sharing their collections of cowboy balladry. A special thanks to Bess Lomax Hawes and Shirley

Lomax Duggan. And, though I never met them, I owe John Lomax, Nathan "Jack" Thorpe, and Charlie "Badger" Clark.

On songwriting, I have received instruction and inspiration from Floyd Tillman, Alex Harvey, John Arthur Martinez, and Jana Stanfield.

For continuing to let me work the roundup, I thank the boys at the Duncan Brothers Spade Ranch, near Egypt, Texas, including G. Cameron Duncan, Dr. Dwight "Thumbs" King, Robert Spitzmiller, Rollie Coy "Buddy" Reid, Henry Wobbe, Tony "Kid" Kitzmiller, Sonny Andersen, Noah Lopez, Bubba Blair, and Emmitt "M.T." Mathews. For teaching me long ago how to throw a rope and saddle-break a horse, I thank my father, Doc Blakely.

Thanks to the friendly people of Colorado, Texas, New Mexico, Oklahoma, and Wyoming.

I
WIND & GRASS

1860

ONE

N OTHING CALEB KNEW of could best his pocketknife. It was the first thing he had ever owned that he really wanted. Life and quack doctors had granted him plenty he didn't want: measles, mumps, whooping cough, croup, cramp colic, flux, bilious fever. But when he clutched the double-bladed, bone-handled, tempered-steel pocketknife in his little fist, he felt retribution for all his past ills.

His mother looked into the door of the dugout. "Caleb, come out and get some sun now," she said. "It will make you better."

Better? He had never felt as well in his life. He owned a pocketknife! The boy stepped out of the dugout and watched his mother climb the bank of the creek and disappear over the rim. His house was like a cave, carved into the brink of the dirt bank, its roof of poles and sod level with the vast plains his family had crossed by wagon.

He stood and looked at the mountains before he followed his mother. He didn't know why they couldn't live in the mountains. It would be fun to slide down them. He reckoned it would take him two days to slide down mountains that tall.

The scramble up the bank winded him a little. He panted and watched his mother carry her water bucket to the flowers she was trying to grow. She looked like a stick figure lost in a dream of dead grass. He preferred to look at the mountains.

Dirt fell into the dugout when the boy jumped on the sod-covered roof.

He heard it sprinkle the tabletop inside. He looked over his shoulder to make sure his mother hadn't seen him; she hadn't, so he dropped to the seat of his pants and let his legs dangle over the doorway to his home.

He fished out his knife, warm from his right pocket. The midday sun glinted against the brass endpieces. His father had oiled the hinges, and the folding blades swung easily from their slots in the handle. He chose the long one. He didn't really know why the knife had a short blade—couldn't think of anything he would want to stab that slightly.

From his left pocket he produced a chunk of kindling wood with a square end. He meant to whittle it into a point that looked like one of the mountains across the creek. Maybe he could give it to his mother and prove to her that he could do something besides lie around sick.

The blade sliced easily through the soft pine, and left facets smooth enough to reflect the sun. Caleb turned the blunt stob into a precious gem. He held it at arm's length to check its shape against the mountain. He smiled, then heard the handle of his mother's water bucket rattle behind him.

"Caleb," she said, "don't sit on the roof, you'll shake dirt. . . ."

The boy's every muscle flexed, snapping his little body into the air. His mother was screaming as if she had a panther in her petticoats. He could grab nothing, his hands busy with the paraphernalia of whittling. He bounced on the roof, pitched forward, saw the threshold below, where he would land. Suddenly his head jerked down and his shirt caught him under the chin.

His mother dragged him by the collar, up over the roof edge, and away from the creek bank, screaming. "Ab! Come here! Come here right now!" She pinned Caleb's wrist to the ground and took the pocketknife away.

Caleb's father was plowing a short way down the creek. He left his oxen and came running as the boy rubbed his throat and caught his breath. "Ella? What happened?" he said.

"Where did Caleb get such a knife?" she asked, shaking the bone handle at her husband.

"I gave it to him."

"Did you not think it important to ask his mother first?"

"The boy's six years old, Ella. I think it's time he had a knife. It folds up. It's not dangerous."

"He was sitting on the roof with it!" she screamed. "I caught him by the collar just as he was falling off! He would have cut himself to pieces!"

"Is he all right?"

"No, he's not all right. He's scared half to death."

Caleb tried to speak, but the coughing came instead.

"Oh, now he's shaken something loose," Ella said. "Take him into the hole. I'll get him some water."

The boy's father helped him to his feet and led him by the hand down to the door of the dugout.

"Can I have my pocketknife back?" Caleb wheezed.

His father squatted to his level and pushed his hat back, revealing his untanned forehead, reddened by the sweatband. "Where were you sitting when you were whittling with it?" he asked.

Caleb pointed to the roof of the dugout, above the door. "Up there."

"Is that a safe place to use a knife?"

"No, sir."

"No, it sure isn't. I thought you were old enough to have it, boy, but I guess you're not. I'll keep it for you, and you can have it when you learn to use it right. Now go in the house and think about that."

"But . . ."

"I said get in there, boy."

Caleb ran into the dark hole in the creek bank. He fell on his pallet, buried his face in his blankets, and cried, coughing between sobs. His mother came in and made him drink some water she had hauled up from the creek, then he was alone again in the dark.

It wasn't fair. Matthew and Pete had owned pocketknives as long as he could remember being their brother. He had seen them carve their names twenty feet up the trunks of trees, standing on limbs no bigger than broom handles. No one had ever taken their knives away. They got to do everything. They got to ride the horse. They got to chase the cows. They went hunting with their father. Caleb never did anything. His mother wouldn't let him until he got better. But he was never going to get better. She wouldn't even let him do that.

He looked under his arm at his view of the mountains, framed by the darkness of his dugout home. Through his tears he gazed at their vast, forested flanks—blue, black, and purple against the pale sky. He rolled over and sat on the dirt floor. He was tired of crying. No one was listening, anyway. Across the creek was a bald hill, and beyond that hill stood the mountains. He had seen Pete and Matthew playing on the hill just a couple of days ago. It hadn't seemed to take them very long to get there. He wondered if he could make it there and back before his mother returned to the dugout to cook supper.

While he was trying to calculate the distance, something unknown caught his eye. It passed over the treeless hill: maybe a wind ripple on the blade tips of the grasses, or the lingering dust from a dying whirlwind. It seemed to spell an invitation on the side of the mountain until his eyes focused, darting everywhere, finding nothing. The long sounds of his name moaned once on the wind, and then were lost. Something up there had called to him.

He crawled to the door and peeked out. No one watched. He clawed his way to the brink of the dirt bank and found his mother on her knees, tending her flower garden. His father was plowing behind the oxen. The boy waited until his father reached the end of the turnrow and started plowing away from the dugout. He glanced at his mother again, then slid down the bank on his rear. He planted his heels, sprang to his feet, and hurtled down toward the creek.

At the water's edge he glanced back but still couldn't see either of his parents over the bank. The stepping-stones stood too far apart to suit his stride, so he leapt from one to the other. The water ran shallow but swift around him like a gale in the treetops. At the far shore he slipped and landed on his back in the cold water. He floundered for a second, found his footing, splashed to the far bank, and pulled at the clothes plastered cold against his skin.

He collapsed and heaved under the cottonwoods lining the shore opposite his dugout. When he had caught his breath, he scurried uphill, weaving among the trunks. The bald hill above the cottonwoods was like a hump of the prairie that had broken free and crossed the creek. It was covered with the same short brown grass that bristled from the roof of his house. He left the trees behind and trudged up the grassy slope.

Suddenly, the mountains appeared over the bald pate of the hill. Caleb couldn't believe it. They seemed no closer here than from the dugout. The great peaks rose higher as the boy mounted the crest. He knelt and stared with his mouth open. He couldn't count the ridges between his bald hill and the mountains—some growing trees; some bare rock. They meshed and angled toward the peaks.

A bare and narrow trail passed in front of him and snaked into the foothills. He saw its curves passing over the high places. It looked like a very old trail, but it wasn't wide enough for a wagon. It might have been wide enough for two horses walking abreast, but Caleb wasn't sure. He didn't know much about riding horses.

He turned back to the plains. The dream of dead grass had grown larger and all but swallowed his stick-figure parents. Even the oxen looked no bigger than bugs. The furrows his father plowed were mere scratches on the world; the doorway to his house was nothing but a freckle on the face of a giant. Way beyond his parents the boy saw one of his brothers riding the horse around the cows. It was so far away he couldn't even tell which brother it was.

The mountains held for him a far greater appeal. He let the sun and the south wind dry him as he dreamed of riding the trail into the mountains someday when his mother let him get well—some distant day after his father gave him his pocketknife back.

TWO

BUSTER FIGURED HE could use the guitar for a mast and the banjo for a boom. He hated to waste all this wind. An intermittent breeze had blown from the south since he left Independence, twenty-eight days before. But today it had grown to a fair wind—a sailor's wind—the kind of blow Buster had loved to fill a canvas with on Chesapeake Bay before he changed his name and headed west.

All morning he had pulled his little milk wagon up a steady grade, the wind whipping the brim of his hat first against its crown, then down against his face. The parching air of the High Plains had so dried his black skin that he seemed sprinkled with ashes. His sweat evaporated instantly on the lined curve of his forehead.

He was not an unusually big man, but he was young and strong, well proportioned, and rounded with muscle. He had the endurance to pull his milk wagon ten miles or more a day, though it was barely big enough to rate as a wagon at all. The box wasn't much bigger than a coffin; the wheels only knee-high at the hub.

He had come to a low ridge, and the slope pitched downhill in front of him for a change. The angle was not severe, but it was sufficient to make the little wagon favor the west. For most of the trip it had seemed to balk like a jackass wanting to turn back to the trees of Missouri. He stopped on the rolling crest to survey the surrounding terrain. Except for the dark, hazy outline of the mountains on the western horizon, he could see nothing but grass and sky in every direction—trackless reaches of unpeopled plains.

He got one of his four canteens out of the wagon and took a swallow. The few maps he had studied before coming west had described this region as the Great American Desert, and the label had prompted him to carry plenty of water for his crossing to the mountains. Now he could see that it wasn't a desert at all, but a great wealth of grass. Some accounts he had read in the newspapers had described the plains as a sea, rolling in waves, devoid of landmarks, swept with storms maritime in nature; a sea of grass, a sea of loneliness, a sea of treelessness. Of course, now Buster saw that the plains had no more in common with a sea than an iceberg had with a lava flow. The ocean's surface lived and writhed. The waves and crests of the plains were corpses long covered with mats of grass.

But the winds did resemble the marine gusts Buster had sailed before on the Chesapeake. They lacked the spray and the smell of brine, but they begged for canvas.

A piece of old wagon sheet covered his musical instruments in the box of the milk wagon. He figured he could use it as a sail if he could build something to rig it on. He thought about removing the wagon tongue and stepping it as a mast, but he would need it to steer. That left only the instruments—the guitar, the banjo, the fiddle, and the mandolin. The guitar and the banjo were longest, so they would serve as mast and boom.

Buster put the stopper back in his canteen and got to work. He was not one to squander an idea. A crate in the wagon held his change of clothes, a few tools, some dried meat and apples, and a single-shot horse pistol. Besides the crate, the instruments, and the canteens, there was nothing in the wagon but the buffalo chips he used to build fires at night.

He turned his wagon around so the tongue pointed eastward; he knew how to sail only with his rudder astern. He moved the crate to the center of the wagon. It had a convenient knothole on top. He took the strap off the peg at the rounded end of the guitar. The peg fit easily into the knothole on the crate, and there he stepped his mast.

Now he needed shrouds to hold it erect. He didn't own any rope or cord, so he began taking the catgut strings off the guitar. He spliced four of the strings together in pairs, giving him two long shrouds to reach fore and aft. The other two guitar strings would reach the sides of the wagon box to the starboard and port. He threaded the catgut through cracks between the sideboards and wound them around the tuning keys on the guitar neck. To tighten them, he simply turned the keys as if tuning up for a dance. He thumped the shrouds, listening for the tone that would tell him when his mast stood firm.

He paused to look around the prairie. "Don't worry, Buster, there ain't a soul in thirty miles," he said to himself. He could only hope he was right. Some frontiersman might mistake a black man sailing a milk wagon across the plains for a lunatic and shoot him for the common good, as there were no asylums this far from civilization.

The boom proved much easier to rig than the mast. He simply stuck the neck of the banjo into the sound hole of the guitar. The drumlike head of the banjo would swing on the end of the boom, providing just that much more surface for the wind to push against. To suspend the boom, he ran the guitar strap from the neck of the guitar to the head of the banjo. The boom could only travel ninety degrees between the aft and starboard shrouds, but he would not have to jibe. The steady south wind would come across his port gunnel, and he could make the whole downhill run on a close beam reach with the boom over the starboard sideboards of the milk wagon.

The piece of wagon sheet already had dozens of holes in it, so Buster didn't mind cutting a few more to hitch his sail onto the mast and the boom. He would use the shoulder strap from the banjo as a sheet to hold his sail to the wind.

The canvas was popping like a flag in the wind as he climbed into the stern of his craft and sat down on the buffalo chips. Steering was going to be limited. The wagon tongue, sticking straight up now, had a crosspiece on the end of it that Buster had used to pull against for twenty-eight days. As a tiller, it wouldn't allow him much leverage to turn. However, since he had just one course in mind—west—steering concerned him little.

He drew the banjo-strap sheet in, and his dusty little triangular sail billowed with the crosswind from the south. The guitar-string shrouds sang with new tension. The wagon strained westward. Buster jerked his weight forward in the vessel, rocking it, but it refused to roll. He reached over the port gunnel, grabbed the rim of the wagon wheel, turned it, and shoved his craft off down the gentle grade to the west. She crept tentatively over the rough ground as Buster adjusted the sheet to take highest advantage of the wind. He was under way, sailing the shortgrass plains of western Kansas Territory.

"You're a crazy man, Buster Thompson," he muttered, an involuntary grin tearing at the cracks in his parched lips.

He had called himself by his new name often in the past weeks, to familiarize himself with it. He didn't want to mistakenly call himself by his old name and risk getting sent back to the Chesapeake. There he was known as Jack Arbuckle or—to the slave owners of the Eastern Shore—"Arbuckle's Jack." It was there he had learned to sail, but never had he dreamed he would lift canvas to the wind on dry ground, and sail among buffalo chips in a milk wagon.

Arbuckle's Jack had plied the Chesapeake so often that it must have come as a surprise to the bay people when he drowned. As the best fiddler on the Eastern Shore, Jack had spent almost every Friday and Saturday night playing at balls on the bay estates. His master, Hugh Arbuckle, let him keep the money he earned from fiddling and often sailed with him to hear his bow stroke music. Jack would cleat the boom sheet, sit on the transom of Master Hugh's sloop, steer with his foot, and play his fiddle as master and slave sailed across the bay. Master Hugh usually sat amidships and drank.

"Jack, you'll fall off and drown some night coming home from one of these bloody cotillions," he said once.

"I swim good," Jack replied.

He was Master Hugh's boyhood playmate, and Hugh had never learned to distance himself. The plantation owner gave Jack his choice of jobs, and Jack enjoyed a change every few months. He had tended fields and gardens where he experimented with new crops and methods of cultivation. He enjoyed building things in the blacksmith shop. He had worked in the mansion, where he cooked, made Hugh's juleps, and played while his master drank. Master Hugh had even taught him reading and writing, and given him unlimited access to the library.

When the panic of 1857 came, the Arbuckle Plantation suffered its worst year. Hugh had never been much of a manager anyway, but now acres slipped away to pay debts, and he stayed drunk more than ever. There were agents for the Underground Railroad moving among the slaves, urging them to escape, and Jack began to listen. Master Hugh was going to lose the plantation, and all his slaves would go on the block for whiskey money. But Jack steeled himself against panic. He would make no ill-conceived scramble for freedom. He intended to plan a foolproof escape. The slave hunters' hounds would never catch his scent.

One day at dawn a burly black woman came to the blacksmith shop and told Jack that a fugitive slave boat would leave the Choptank River near Cambridge at dusk the coming Saturday. Jack knew his time to escape had come; he had been asked to fiddle at a dance up Tred Avon that same night, and Master Hugh had already said he wouldn't attend.

After loading all his instruments into the sloop, Jack sailed for the Choptank. When he tied up alongside the fugitive boat, he began removing the canvas from the halyard. The burly woman who had come to him in the blacksmith shop was there with four men and a mother with two children.

"Hurry up!" the guide said. "What you doin', fool?"

"I'm drownin' myself," Jack said.

"What?"

He tied a rock to the sail and threw it overboard. "Master Hugh always said I'd fall out one night, fiddlin' on the transom. That's what he'll think. And he'll think somebody stole his sail and all my instruments after I fell out. He's gonna think I'm drowned. That way no slave hunters are gonna come after me. They won't advertise for me in the North, either." Jack grinned, proud of his plan. He handed his fiddle to the fugitive guide.

"You ain't takin' all them fiddles and things," she said, refusing the instruments. "You can't run with all that. Throw 'em over."

Jack scoffed. "If these things don't go, I ain't goin' either."

The fugitive guide pulled a pistol from her waistband and pointed it at Jack's head. "Just dead niggers go back, boy," she said.

Jack stood in the rocking sloop, clutching his fiddle case. "But, this here's how I'll make my way," he said.

"Throw 'em over."

Buster grunted, caught without words. The woman cocked the pistol.

"I'll carry one of 'em," said the oldest son of the slave mother.

"I'll carry that little one, there," a man grumbled, pointing to the mandolin Master Hugh had bought for Jack in Kentucky. "Don't need no shootin'."

The guide lowered her pistol as Arbuckle's Jack distributed his instruments among the fugitives.

They sailed by night up Chesapeake Bay and into the Susquehanna River. Somewhere in Pennsylvania their guide ordered them out of the boat. When Jack took his first step as a free man he shook with a joy and a glory so full that tears came to his eyes. Then he took his second step and almost buckled under his fears. He was helpless in a strange land, at the mercy of fugitive guides rougher than his former slave master. He had no idea where he was going or what he would be required to do.

The fugitives ran over forest trails for hours and finally came to a farmhouse where they slept. The examining committee, made up of white and black abolitionists, woke Jack before morning and interrogated him.

"Where did you come from? . . . How did your master come by you? . . . Did you have a wife or family? . . . Why did you escape?"

When Jack had answered all the questions to the satisfaction of the committee, the members explained that they had to interrogate fugitives to keep black spies from infiltrating the Underground Railroad.

"Where do you want to go?" asked a bearded white man.

"Canada, I guess," Jack said.

"Then you will go to Canada. Your name now is Buster Thompson. You must never mention your old name again. Never. Tell everyone you meet you were born a free Negro in Philadelphia and have never been a slave. There are slave hunters who will kidnap you to sell in the South.

"At dawn you will set across the mountains to Lewistown. The trip will take two days. At Lewistown you will buy a ticket and ride the jim crow car to Meadville. There is a farm south of Meadville owned by Absalom Holcomb. Everybody calls him Ab. He's a conductor for the Underground Railroad. He will get you to Canada. Ask for no one but Ab Holcomb. Say you are going to his farm to work as a blacksmith. Trust no one but him. Do not let anyone else take you to Canada. You must find Ab Holcomb."

With those orders, Arbuckle's Jack became Buster Thompson and started his solitary trek to Meadville, carrying his guitar and banjo on his back, and his mandolin and fiddle under his arm. South of Meadville, he asked a farmwife for directions to Ab Holcomb's farm.

"It was up the road two miles," she replied. "But Ab and Ella don't live here anymore."

Buster leaned against the porch columns to steady himself. "Where'd they go?" he asked.

"They went to the Cherry Creek diggin's in the Pikes Peak country. Sold everything and went west. Are you a fugitive slave?"

"No, ma'am," Buster said. "I was born free in Philadelphia. I came to work for Mister Ab."

"You can tell me if you're a fugitive. I'll help you find a way to Canada. I've helped Ella many times to cook for the slaves and send them north."

"I never was a slave," Buster said. "I'm supposed to work for Mister Ab." He stood on the front porch of the farmhouse, burdened with musical instruments, lost for words and lost in the world. He had already traveled farther than he ever dreamed he would have to go. And now—Cherry Creek, Pikes Peak, the Great American Desert. He trusted no one. He had no friends in his freedom. Only a name: Absalom Holcomb.

"Ella sent a letter to the Abolition Society. She told them not to send any more fugitives. Didn't they get it?"

"I don't know. I ain't no fugitive. How do I find Mister Ab? I came to work for him."

The farmwife went into her house and came out with a letter from Ella Holcomb. "This came last week. First time I've heard from her. Do you read?"

"Yes, ma'am."

"Maybe you are a free Negro at that, then. Here, read it. It tells where they live now. I don't think you'll want to go there."

Buster stepped into the sunshine and read:

> Dear Irene,
>
> Cherry Creek was the vilest place I have ever seen. I would not allow Ab to settle us there. We went south and now have a ranch on Monument Creek, at the foot of the Rampart Range. No neighbors. We have no house yet. Living in a hole. There is much work to do and yet I am glad I made Ab move us here. Caleb is better. He coughs less of the time. Pete is a good boy as always and Matthew has no trouble to get into. Pray for us.
>
> Ella

"What's your name?" Irene asked.

"Buster Thompson."

"Do you play all those instruments?"

He nodded. Irene took the letter into her house, telling him to wait. She came out and gave the letter back to him. "Here. What do you think? Will it pass for her writing?"

At the end of the page, Irene had added a postscript:

> Send Buster now. We need his help and some music.

Her hand passed adequately for Ella Holcomb's.

"I'll get you to Canada if you'll trust me," she said. "That is, if you are a fugitive. But if you must go after Ab, this letter will help you get through Missouri. There are slave hunters in Missouri."

Buster rode the colored cars to Independence and asked about the best route to Monument Creek. He was told to take the Smoky Hill Road across Kansas with the next bull train. The letter from Ella Holcomb got him past two groups of slave hunters looking for fugitives to sell in the

South. He spent his last few dollars on a change of clothes, a horse pistol, a few tools to bolster his story about working for Ab Holcomb, the canteens, and the little milk wagon to carry it all in.

The freighters welcomed Buster when they saw his musical instruments. He played an hour or two every night in camp while the teamsters took turns dancing jigs on a buffalo hide. By day he pulled his little milk wagon and was sometimes allowed to hitch on behind a freight wagon for the steep upgrades. He saw no buffalo and no Indians.

After seventeen days on the trail, the captain told him to fall out of the train with his milk wagon. The train would follow a branch of the Smoky Hill Road that veered south to Bent's Fort. Monument Creek was due west.

"Go around the heads of all the creeks," the captain said, "and you'll stay on the main divide between the Platte and the Arkansas. You'll find water about halfway there in the Big Sandy. In a week or so you'll see the mountains. Head north of Pikes Peak and you'll strike Monument Creek somewhere around Holcomb's Ranch. I ain't been there, but I hear that's about where he settled. If you run into Indians, hope they're Arapaho and not Cheyenne."

After eleven lonely days traveling west, the mountains were growing ever taller, and Buster finally started dropping into the Monument Creek drainage. That was the day the wind picked up from the south, and he began thinking of dry-land sailing in his little milk wagon. He knew he was no more than a day or two away from Ab Holcomb's ranch. He predicted that when he arrived, he would find out Ab and Ella had moved on to Oregon.

THREE

Buster's wind wagon balked now and then between gusts, and in places where the slope leveled out, but for almost half an hour he kept sailing west, singing an old work shanty called "Haul on the Bowline" when the running was smoothest. He found a nailhead to hitch the banjo strap on so he didn't have to hold it against the wind. He got moving up to ten or fifteen miles an hour on one stretch.

The plains continued to pitch more severely toward the west, causing the milk wagon to run faster and Buster to sing louder:

Haul on the bowline, the ship she is a-rollin'
Haul on the bowline, the bowline, haul.

Chesapeake Bay had nothing on the shortgrass plains. There was no lighthouse like Pikes Peak.

Over the square bow of the wind wagon, he saw a wide swale dropping off before him. With the jolting of the craft over the rough prairie, he could see only enough of the terrain to tell that the swale would give him his highest speeds yet. He grinned, adjusted the sheet, and hitched it back on its nailhead. He hoped to get rolling as fast as he could into the swale so his momentum would take him as far as possible up the other side.

The fiddle and the mandolin jumped in the forecastle with every bump the wagon wheels met. Buster settled lower in the buffalo chips. He hung his left arm over the port gunnel to better see around the sail and to keep his vessel aright in case a powerful gust tried to heel her over to the starboard. The sheet slipped an inch on its nail, so he double hitched it and started singing again.

> *Haul on the bowline, the bosun is a-growlin'*
> *Haul on the bowline, the bowline, haul.*

The wind wagon reached the steepest pitch now, diving into the swale, running faster than a galloping horse. Buster held his hat down with one hand.

Something caught his eye over the top of the mast. A ragged black slash across the sky. Two, three, four of them—circling. Buzzards! Something dead? They soared and banked low on the southern wind over the swale. He watched one of them, its wing feathers splayed like fingers, as it swooped toward the ground and then—*into* the ground. It vanished like a prairie dog! Now it shot out of the plains fifty yards over!

Buster pulled himself higher in the rattling milk wagon. Down in the bowl of the swale ahead, he could just make out the rim of a sand bluff. He was sailing headlong toward a plains canyon!

"Turn her to the wind, Buster!" he said to himself, but the wagon tongue proved useless as a tiller. He pulled against it with everything he had, but it wouldn't change the cut of the wheels.

He glanced ahead, saw the near edge of the gully, closer than he could have imagined. He had ten seconds to stop! He yanked at the sheet, double hitched on the nailhead. Finally getting it loose, the sail slacked leeward, but momentum kept him rolling. "Heel her over!" He rocked side to side, but the wagon wouldn't tip, its center too low.

Three seconds to stop, or fly over the bluff! Buster let the wagon tongue drag astern. He leapt over the transom and landed with both feet on the tongue. It cut into the ground like a harrow, raising a plume of dust. The wagon slowed, but the leading wheels reached the bluff and rolled off. The running gear under the wagon box slammed against the precipice and slid. Buster saw something below—smoke-blackened cones bristling with lodge poles—ten or twelve of them.

When the trailing wheels hit the ledge, the wagon bucked Buster off the tongue and back into the box as it plummeted down the steep bank of the gully. Children screamed and dogs barked as he pulled himself high enough to peer over the lurching sideboards. He was racing toward the tallest tepee in the camp. He would flatten it, killing its inhabitants, prompting the rest of the villagers to roast him alive over his own buffalo chips.

When his wind wagon hit, the leading wheels straddled a lodge pole and drove straight up toward the smoke hole. The vehicle died like a rock flung to its zenith, then fell back on its tongue. It bounced on its end and pitched everything out. Buster's fiddle and mandolin landed five feet away. The crate slid out from under the mast, and the boom swung down to slap him across the head with a discordant twanging of banjo strings, sprawling him among the scattered buffalo chips.

A dog snarled at his heels as buzzards circled overhead. A rank odor filled his nostrils, and he willed his eyes to focus. Strange people moved around him—men crouching low for a fight, women yanking naked children away. Through them rushed a lean warrior in breechcloth and leggings, his long, flying braids wrapped in spirals of fur, his eyes hot with love of battle. He drew a lance over his shoulder as he charged, turned sideways, and skipped, gathering his weight for the thrust.

A sharp voice barked, and the warrior with the spear loosened his grip, his palm sliding harmlessly along the shaft as his arm whipped toward his target. His startled eyes cut away from Buster, and Buster followed them.

From the lodge against which the wind wagon lay, a dark man emerged, holding back the bearskin that covered the entrance hole. Hair fell long and loose around his broad face, and a single black-tipped feather protruded sideways from behind his head. The breadth of his jaw was severe, his mouth straight and thin lipped, his nose like an eagle's beak. He wore a tawny suit of tanned skins, colored with beads, porcupine quills, and strips of fur. His voice knifed again toward the brave with the spear, and his eyes landed on the intruder.

The black man forced a grin. As the dark chief came to stand over him, Buster reached for his shirt pocket. Several warriors had gathered with spears or bows—one with a flintlock rifle—but only the brave with the fur-spiraled braids seemed ready to kill and brandished his lance again when the black man reached for his pocket. Buster produced only a harmonica.

He put the instrument in his mouth, blew a single note, and scanned his audience. He tripped up the scale. The chief smiled. Buster began playing

"Old Dan Tucker," shuffling his feet in time among the buffalo chips. He stopped on a sour note when the chief grabbed his wrist and lifted him.

"Do you speak the English?" the chief asked.

Buster nodded, felt his knees wobble under him.

"I am Long Fingers. What are you called?"

"Buster."

"Buster," Long Fingers repeated, amused at the sound of the thing. "You make music like I hear at Cherry Creek. You have a fiddle?"

"Yes, sir," Buster said.

"You will make music with that and eat some meat with us." Long Fingers turned to speak to his braves, then shouted at some squaws, who scattered.

The brave with the spear finally lowered it, growling with obvious disdain.

Long Fingers grunted at him. "Kicking Dog wants to kill you, but I will not let him," he said, turning to Buster. "I tell him your scalp is no good." He put his hand on Buster's head and felt his hair. "He calls you Buffalo Head, but I think the hair is not the same as the buffalo."

"I wouldn't know," Buster said. "I ain't seen no buffalo yet." He scratched the curly growth of his ragged beard. "Sorry about your tent," he said, pointing stiffly.

"It is your wagon turned over, not my lodge."

Men began reaching for Buster's belongings, showing particular interest in the sail on the guitar and banjo rigging.

"You have a strange way with your wagon," Long Fingers said. "Where is your horse to pull it?"

"I don't have one," Buster admitted. "Been pullin' it myself." He watched nervously as the braves rifled through his property.

"You say you pull it, but I see it going the wrong way. The back of it comes down on my lodge. And you cannot pull it from inside. Kicking Dog says he saw you inside. How do you pull it, then? Why do you fly the white flag?"

"Well, I was ridin' in the wagon," Buster explained. "And the wind was pushin' me with this sail." He pressed his palm against the piece of old wagon sheet to show Long Fingers how it would catch the wind.

The chief squinted his eyes and studied the wind wagon's sail. "How far?"

"Just two or three miles."

"You think the wind pushes your wagon. It is a hill for two miles where you come from and you go down the hill. I do not think the wind pushes you." Long Fingers gestured skyward. "The wind pushes clouds. Take the flag down and use these things to make music. That is what they are for. A wagon is not a cloud."

The Indians helped Buster put his milk wagon back on its wheels and watched as he took apart the catgut shrouds that had held his mast in place. They surrounded him, spoke in their language, laughed frequently. Kicking Dog looked into the crate and squalled when he found the horse pistol. He held it high for all the warriors to see.

A woman approached, wearing a calf-length deerskin dress and moccasins. She led a fat dog on a rope and carried a large club. She spoke timidly, her eyes on the ground. When Long Fingers grunted in approval, she raised the club. But before she could hit the animal, Kicking Dog shouted and stepped forward with Buster's horse pistol. He pointed the pistol at the animal and shot it in the head, splattering brains and blood across the sandy ground. The squaw dragged the carcass away, leaving a trail of gore.

The warrior shook the pistol in the air and laughed, then threw it back into Buster's crate.

"Kicking Dog says your gun is good only to kill dogs," Long Fingers said. "No good for hunting buffalo, or fighting."

Buster figured the dog must have bitten one of the children. The casual way in which Kicking Dog had killed it made him nervous. And now the warrior was looking at him the same way he had looked at the dog, muttering something in an accusing tone of voice.

"Kicking Dog says the black people are only slaves of the whites," Long Fingers said. "I hear this same thing in Cherry Creek. You are a slave?"

Buster hardly suspected that the Indians doubled as slave hunters. He decided to tell them the truth. Maybe they would respect him for escaping the whites. "The blacks who live in the South are slaves," he said, trying to put a string back on his guitar with shaking hands. "I lived there. I was a slave. But I escaped."

Kicking Dog drank from one of Buster's canteens as the chief translated for him. It seemed to Buster as if the chief were serving the brave.

"Now he says he was one time a slave, too," the chief said, listening to Kicking Dog boast. "The Ute catch him when he was a boy. He killed three of them when he escaped. He wants to know how many Buffalo Head killed when he escaped?"

Buster held up his finger. "One." He didn't much like being called Buffalo Head.

"How did you kill this one?"

"Drowned him."

The warriors muttered among themselves when Long Fingers translated. It was most glorious to kill one's enemies hand to hand. Kicking Dog threw the canteen back in the wagon and asked another question.

Long Fingers smiled. "Kicking Dog believes there are no more white men in the east. He believes they have all crossed our land now and there are no more of them. He does not believe there can be any more."

Buster looked Kicking Dog in the eyes. The little warrior may have been scary, but he sure was ignorant. "Tell him he ain't even seen the half of 'em yet."

When he got the answer, Kicking Dog stalked away to his tepee.

"I tell him that before," Long Fingers said. "I go across the plains two years ago to see how farming works. I see plenty whites there."

"Is that where you learned to speak English?" Buster asked.

"No. I learn long time ago. The Arapaho trade with whites. Our people stay friendly. I learn the English to trade better with whites."

Arapaho! The word lifted a load of fear from Buster's innards. But if that Kicking Dog was friendly, he would sure hate to see a hostile Indian. "Do you want your people to learn farmin'?" he asked.

The chief frowned, shaking his head. "The whites say we should learn, but our people do not like that kind of work. It is our way to live on the buffalo, but the white hunters are killing too many, and the wagons going everywhere scare the buffalo away. If the buffalo all go away, maybe so we will have to make a ranch for cattle or horses. But our people do not want to do farming. We do not like to dig up the ground. Maybe so you know about work with cattle?"

Buster smiled at a man who touched his guitar as he tuned it. "No. But I'm goin' to a ranch. Maybe I'll learn about it."

"What ranch?"

"Close to here. On Monument Creek."

"You know Holcomb?" the chief asked.

The familiar name rang in Buster's ears like a bell of salvation. "Not yet, but I'm supposed to find him."

"You will not learn about cattle there. Holcomb knows nothing about it. His cattle get away all the time. When we find them, we bring them back and Holcomb's wife trades with us. Sugar, flour, coffee. After we eat, I will show you which way to go to find Holcomb. It is half a day if you pull your wagon."

Buster nodded. "Thank you."

"Now, my boys want to hear you make music with all these things. Come into my tepee and show us how the black people make music."

Buster got up with his guitar.

"Are there tribes with the black people?" the chief asked.

"Yes."

"Which tribe are you?"

"African Baptist."

"African Baptist," Long Fingers repeated. He paused at the entrance hole to his tepee and looked toward the east. "There are many tribes of people on the earth."

Buster found the ground inside the tepee covered with buffalo robes, rolled robes forming couches. Light streamed down from the smoke hole, illuminating a pile of ashes circled by rocks in the middle of the lodge. The hide tent was surprisingly cool and well ventilated, though the rank smell of the camp wafted here, too.

He sat on a rolled hide and played, using the guitar first, then the banjo, then the mandolin. Between songs, he smoked a pipe with the warriors, though he was not fond of tobacco. He could hear giggling and the shuffling of feet outside, and knew the women and children were listening. When he started fiddling, Long Fingers put his hands over his ears and made him stop.

"Make the fiddle sing outside," the chief said. "It is too loud."

When Buster played "Old Brass Wagon" on the fiddle outside, Long Fingers called for his wife. The fiddler was amazed to see the chief and his wife square-dance together like white folks. The rest of the Indians laughed at the mockery, except for Kicking Dog, who considered white dancing scandalous.

"Where did you learn those dances?" Buster asked when he sat with the chief to eat a gruel made of corn from a tin plate.

"The whites at Cherry Creek do not have many women with them, so they like to dance with our women when we camp there, and they teach us their dances. But their dances do not mean anything."

The squaws brought meat after the gruel. It was cooked black and cut into chunks. It was the first fresh meat Buster had eaten since leaving the bull train, and he quickly finished the small helping on his plate.

"That's the first buffalo I've had," Buster said. "I didn't know it would taste so good. Kinda sweet."

Long Fingers laughed. "That was not buffalo you eat. That was the dog that Kicking Dog killed with your pistol. You eat more now?"

Buster's jaw muscles seized up on him, and he took a long drink from his canteen. "No, thanks."

"We will eat the rest if you will not," Long Fingers said. He thought Buffalo Head took to dog meat much more admirably than the white men at Cherry Creek. Some of them had actually gotten sick after he told them what they had eaten. It didn't make sense.

"My boys will help you get your wagon across this place," the chief said after they ate. "But first you will make some music with that thing you carry in your pocket. It has the most music to be so little."

"It's called a harmonica," Buster said.

Long Fingers tossed his loose hair over a shoulder with an almost feminine motion. "I know what it is called. But that is a hard word for me to say in the English."

"You can call it a harp if you want to."

"Harp?" He smiled. "I say that plenty good. Make some music on that harp. Then we will push your wagon out of this place."

After Buffalo Head played, Long Fingers ordered a few warriors to haul the little wagon up to the west side of the gully. Kicking Dog sat on the brink of the sand bluff and frowned.

"That is the mountain that guides you," Long Fingers said, pointing at the prominence of Pikes Peak. "You go to the north of it and come to the creek. Then you go up the creek and find Holcomb's Ranch on the east side of the creek. It is at our camp where our trail goes into the mountains. Holcomb does not ask us, but I think he wants to stay a long time. It is Arapaho land where he lives in his hole in the ground."

On the bluff the air smelled dry and clean and made Buster realize just how bad the Indian camp had stunk. Bad enough to attract the buzzards. But he had it figured. The Arapaho liked to move, follow the buffalo. Everything they owned would travel, even their houses. It made no sense to bother with sanitation at a camp that would soon be struck for a fresh site. Maybe next time he visited an Arapaho camp, it would be a fresh one.

"I want to give you something, chief," Buster said before he picked up his wagon tongue. "I think you can learn to play this harp. It travels good, too, because it's small. Maybe we can play some music together next time I see you."

Long Fingers took the harmonica with a strangely fearful expression. He turned the gift over a few times in his hand, then sent one of his warriors back to the camp. "Now you must wait. I also give something to you."

"Well, you don't have to . . ." Buster cut himself off short when he caught the chief glaring.

The warrior came back from camp with a skinny girl, about seventeen years old, dressed in ragged, grease-stained skins. Her eyes never looked up from the ground.

"I give you this squaw. She is called Snake Woman." He blew into the harmonica.

Buster looked horrified. "But . . . One of your people?"

"No. I get her from the Comanche. They keep her for a slave. They say they catch her in the south. Maybe so Mexico. I trade plenty skins for her. She was a slave like you. You will like her. She work hard. Now, go. You will go all day to find Holcomb."

When Long Fingers spoke to Snake Woman, she picked up the tongue of the little milk wagon, grasped one end of the crosspiece, and started to pull west.

"But . . . Does she speak English?"

"She does not speak. The Comanche cut her tongue out. She knows the hand signs. She will teach you some. Go, hurry. Your wagon goes like the wind pushes it. It goes like a cloud without you." He blew through the harmonica again.

Buster nodded, forced a smile, and ran after his milk wagon, feeling most uncomfortable about his trade. He hoped Ab Holcomb would know what to do with the former Comanche slave.

"Why did you give Snake Woman to Buffalo Head?" Kicking Dog asked as the black man ran away. "I have told you many times to trade her to me."

"I had nothing else to give to him. I would not trade him a horse for what he gave me. A horse makes better music than this harp. A horse would have been a bad trade."

"You could have given him one of your robes. We will kill some more buffalo soon, and you could have a new robe."

"I like the robes I have now. I have slept on them enough with my wife and now they feel just right. But you are not old enough to know about that."

They watched the wagon become a speck in the west.

"I would like to drive a wagon," Long Fingers said. "It is a good way to move things. Maybe so I will trade for one."

Kicking Dog scoffed and tossed a fur-wrapped braid over his shoulder. "My lodge poles are my wagons."

FOUR

ELLA HOLCOMB PUT the bucket of water down at the door of the dugout and sat on a three-legged stool to rest. She would have to catch her breath before she carried the burden up the steepest part of the cutbank.

She had her homesite chosen above, and Ab had promised to build her a cabin after he planted. She had already started her flower garden near the site. She meant to make sure the lily and tulip bulbs got enough water to take root.

She turned her ear to the door of the dugout but heard no sounds from Caleb. She figured he must have cried himself to sleep after his near-fatal fall from the roof. She decided to let the poor little thing rest.

Ella would have enjoyed a rest herself. But the flowers needed water, and no one would carry the bucket if she didn't. Ab was too busy breaking ground, while Matthew and Pete were trying to keep the cows together out on the plains. She stood, hefted the bucket, and scrambled up the cutbank, sloshing water.

As she poured the water, her eyes swept the plains for signs of her boys, or the cattle, or Indians. She saw only Ab, breaking virgin ground behind the oxen. He had given up everything he loved because of her and she knew it. Yet she wondered sometimes why she had married him. She took a broad view of the world—its cultures and its peoples. Ab saw only that which passed under his heels.

Poor Ab missed his farm in Pennsylvania. He missed his frame house and his toolshed and his forge. He missed his rail fences and his neighbors and his church. The only things he didn't miss were the roots that snagged his plowshares as he turned the soil over. There were no roots on the plains except for grass roots. There were no trees to clear, no stumps to pull. But this rootlessness was virtually the only advantage he saw to living in the West.

There was plenty of excitement in the wilderness, what with wolves killing his calves, and Indians visiting his dugout, and rough characters malingering about from time to time. But what did he need with excitement? He had left plenty of that back in Pennsylvania, harboring the runaways the Underground Railroad sent north, hiding them from slave hunters, moving them on midnight runs to the freedom boats waiting on Lake Erie. Even that excitement was more of Ella's doing than his own.

Only once in his life had Ab truly sought adventure, and that was as a young fool who joined the army to fight in the Mexican war. He hadn't intended to go to war until he made a trip to Washington, D.C., and fell under the influence of Captain Samuel H. Walker, who was in the capital recruiting men for a new company of mounted riflemen.

Walker's name was legend. He had fought Seminole Indians in Florida before joining the Texas Rangers. The modifications he had suggested to arms manufacturer Sam Colt had led to the success of the Colt revolver. After serving with the Texas Rangers in the war with Mexico, he had won a commission in the regular army and had come to Washington for recruits.

Walker's company of dragoons would not serve ordinary duty. General Zachary Taylor had commissioned him expressly to combat the brutal Mexican guerrillas menacing U.S. troops between Vera Cruz and Mexico City. Only Texas Ranger tactics would work against the guerrillas, and Samuel H. Walker was the only Texan General Taylor could trust to behave with the honor and dignity befitting an officer in the U.S. Army.

Captain Walker recruited a hundred men in Washington, and young Ab Holcomb was one of them. He trained for a month in Kentucky, then sailed for Vera Cruz. He learned to ride and shoot like he never thought possible, and kill as he had never imagined. Walker transformed the sluggish dragoons into a light cavalry of thunderbolt ferocity. They did not merely fight Mexicans. They hunted them.

In October of 1847, Ab rode with Walker's company in an attack on the army of General Antonio Lopez de Santa Anna at the village of Huamantla. Walker was killed leading his men into the town plaza. Ab wept over his captain's body, but Sam Walker was the only Texan whose corpse Absalom Holcomb would ever weep over.

Ab had learned to fight like a Texas Ranger, but he hated Texans. The men in Walker's company were regular army—Americans, not Texans. They wore uniforms. They behaved with proper decorum away from the battlefield. Walker himself had never uttered an oath in front of his men. He never drank or used tobacco or chased Mexican women.

But there were other Texans in Mexico besides Sam Walker—rangers and civilian volunteers who engaged in such atrocities against the civilian population that Ab came to hate them, his allies, as much as he hated his enemies, the Mexican guerrillas.

A particular incident in Mexico City turned him against Texans forever. A Texas Ranger was found knifed to death in the streets of a rough neighborhood of the occupied city, and the bloody Texans, not knowing whom in particular to punish, came down on the entire neighborhood in a vengeful wave of death. In one day's time, more than eighty civilians were dragged into the streets and shot.

After the war, Ab returned to Pennsylvania with a hatred of Texans in his heart, and one of the new Walker Colts under his belt. He had seen enough of adventure. He bought a farm and resolved to apply himself forevermore to the peaceful pursuits of agriculture. But the war would not die easy for Ab.

He saw the guerrillas in his dreams. He thought he spotted them spying on him from the woodlot. It was as if they had come all the way from Mexico to hunt him down. He smelled the stench of a day-old battlefield. In the dirt on his hands he saw human gore. He began to wish the Mexicans had killed him. The dead were the lucky ones. He envied their escape. He thought one day of suicide, and the idea began to appeal to him.

Then he met Ella, and the guerrillas faded away. In their places, he saw images of her. He saw a vision of himself as her husband. He thought less of death, more of life. She led him back and gave him hope. He had planned to kill himself the day he met her, but he found in her his only reason to live.

Ella first became interested in Ab because of the stories she had heard about the exploits of Sam Walker's men. She put more stock in Ab's war record than she should have. She agreed to marry him largely because of his service under Captain Walker. She thought such service practically guaranteed chivalry as his one predominant virtue. She thought she could manipulate his courage to serve her many social causes, the most passionate of which was abolition. Shortly after their marriage, she broached the subject to him.

"Ab, honey. We have got to do something about this disgraceful situation of those poor slaves. We have got to do our part."

"What slaves?" Ab asked, looking around his boundary fences as if he would find a slave on his property.

"What slaves? The ones down South! We could help them. This close to Lake Erie, we could help smuggle them to Canada."

"That's none of our concern. Let them make their own laws down South. We'll just take care of what's ours right here." After Mexico, Ab didn't care to see much of anything beyond the rails fencing his hundred acres.

It took Ella two months and a lot of questions about the war to figure out a way to convince Ab of the evils of slavery. "The Texans keep slaves," she said one day. "The Texans keep as many slaves as anybody. And they boast about it, too."

Ab hated Texans. He figured if they embraced slavery, the institution had to be destroyed. He began helping Ella in aiding the fugitives. He never really liked having the strange black people in his house, or even in his barn. He was appalled at the condition most of them were in when they arrived. They wore rags and ate as if starved half their lives. Few of them could read or write.

Once, in a fit of frustration, he asked Ella, "What are they ever going to do for us in return?"

"I suppose they'll vouch for us in the kingdom of heaven," she said.

Ab was not an abolitionist in his heart. He helped the slaves because he hated Texans and loved his wife. He had learned that Ella's causes were her vitality. To make her happy, he had to help fugitive slaves. She never looked at him or touched him with more passion than when he was leaving in the dead of night to lead a party of escapees to their next contact north. Their children had all been conceived after such expeditions.

Matthew was the firstborn. A handsome, dark-haired child, he was somewhat spoiled by his mother. He enjoyed periods of good behavior but frequently went looking for trouble like an Indian on the warpath. Fistfighting was his specialty.

Pete was towheaded and smaller for his age than Matthew, but he was vigorous in health and seemingly immune to pain. Cuts, bruises, and scrapes fazed him no more than mosquito bites. Only Pete would stand up to Matthew. He got whipped every time, but he never backed down.

There were two girls born after Pete, but each died in infancy. The losses plunged Ella into fits of despair. Ab would find her weeping on the graves at night. He thought for some time after the second girl died that Ella had truly lost her mind. She left Ab to care for the fugitive slaves and spent all her time cultivating her flower garden so she could keep fresh-cut blossoms standing over the graves of her little girls.

Caleb rescued Ella from her grief. His birth gave her a last chance at erasing the vague guilt she felt for the deaths of her daughters. She told Ab that she would not let Caleb die. She simply would not allow it. But Caleb was sickly as a baby, and his health improved little as he got older. He became short of breath, and coughed miserably most of the time.

One night Ella woke Ab from a sound sleep. "Do you hear Caleb coughing?" she asked. "I'm going to save him. I won't lose another child. I'll go crazy. I'll do whatever it takes to nurse him back, Ab, so don't try to stop me."

The next day she took Caleb to a doctor who said he suffered from asthma and possibly consumption. The boy's only chance was in the high, dry climate of the West.

"Woman, where in Hades is Cherry Creek?" Ab asked when she first came up with her idea of moving west. "What do you even know about it?"

"It's in the foothills of the Rockies. It has the most healthful climate on the continent. They've found gold there, and they need farmers to feed the miners. And all the land is free. It's a wilderness. You can have the pick of the land."

"I like this land," Ab said. "There are no wild Indians here."

"The Indians are peaceful there."

"Woman, now I know you've lost your mind. We can't just up and go west. What about those poor slaves of yours?"

"If you don't help me take Caleb to Cherry Creek," she said, "I'll have to send him to live with my cousin in Texas."

No son of Ab Holcomb's was going to live in Texas.

In Missouri he spoke to a busted prospector who advised him not to rely solely on farming for his livelihood at Cherry Creek. The rains were unreliable. He suggested raising cattle. "There's grass to graze a herd to feed the world," the prospector said. Ab had heard Texans speak of ranching during the war. He figured if a Texan could raise cattle, he could do it better.

He bought fifty head of cattle—mostly worn-out oxen, plus a few good shorthorns—and joined an immigrant train headed west in covered wagons on the Platte River Road. The entire train helped herd the Holcombs' cattle. In return, Ab supplemented the party's diet of buffalo and antelope meat with beef.

To her despair, Ella found Cherry Creek wallowing in its own squalor. The most healthful climate on the continent reeked of disease and filth. The town at Cherry Creek, called Denver City, consisted of crude log buildings, tents, and Indian tepees. Streets were staked out but otherwise unidentifiable. Prairie dogs peopled the town lots. Mules, dogs, and pigs wandered about unattended. Garbage heaps lined the banks of the creek where the residents drew their water. A sickness of wide-ranging symptoms known as mountain fever plagued the town.

"I'll go ask about finding us a place to camp," Ab said when the train pulled up.

"You'll do no such thing," Ella insisted. "Caleb certainly can't stay here, not even one night. You'll ask about finding us a farm as far away from this stinking town as we can get.''

The High Plains truly seemed to have improved Caleb's constitution. He had gotten accustomed to walking some of the day, and his fits of coughing had diminished considerably. Ella saw no reason to jeopardize his recovery by camping him in Denver's filth.

As Ab asked the locals about finding farmland, Ella looked with disgust over the Cherry Creek settlement. The town had no churches, schools, hospitals, or libraries, yet it had enough saloons to corrupt a nation. The place was fetid with debris and the rotting flesh of slaughtered animals.

But when she looked over and beyond the town, Ella believed she had done right for Caleb. The plains her wagon had lumbered over met mountains higher than any she had ever imagined. They looked close enough to reach in an hour at a casual stroll, but the captain of the wagon train assured her they stood a half day away by horseback. The thin, dry air of the High Plains only lent them an aspect of nearness.

A storekeeper in town advised Ab to settle on Monument Creek, sixty miles or more south of Denver, just northeast of Pikes Peak. There, in the shadows of the Rampart Range, he would find timber to build with, grass to graze his stock, canyons to winter his cattle in, and virgin plains lusting for the plow.

On the way south, Ella saw two small groups of men on a knoll outside of Denver. ''Ab, what are those men doing standing on the plains over there?''

''I don't know,'' Ab said. But as their wagon rolled nearer, he realized that two of the men were squaring off to shoot at each other. ''Why, they're going to fight a duel,'' he said.

Ella immediately screamed for her boys to leave the herd of cattle. ''Pete! Matthew! Get in the wagon! I don't care about the cows, do as I tell you this moment! Pete, bring Caleb.''

As the boys climbed in, Ella yanked the whip away from Ab and drove the oxen as fast as they would walk, running up and down the line of beasts like a crazy woman.

From the wagon, Matthew heard his mother screaming at the oxen. He reached into his pocket and pulled out his knife.

''What are you gonna do with that?'' Pete said.

''Shut up.'' Matthew poked the blade through canvas and cut a slit. He knew Pete would tell on him later, but he had to see that duel even if it meant taking a whipping for cutting the wagon sheet. Just as he peeked through, he saw the black smoke burst from the barrels of the pistols. One of the men fell as Matthew heard the double report.

''Wow,'' he whispered to Pete. ''One of 'em got killed.''

''You're gonna get in trouble,'' Pete replied.

* * *

A well-traveled wagon trace called the Fort Bridger Road led south from Denver City. Ab was told it would lead him past Monument Creek. The plains stretched away to their left as they creaked down the road. To the right ran Cherry Creek, and beyond stood the Rocky Mountains.

The Holcombs paralleled the creek, passing high wooded hills, until they came to a solid-pine forest that spilled down from the mountains and onto the High Plains. It was called the Pinery. Somewhere in that aromatic forest, the road rolled over the divide separating the watersheds of the South Platte and the Arkansas rivers. The Holcombs began moving downhill, much to the gratification of the trail-worn oxen.

The boys lost several head of cattle in the Pinery, but Ella would not let them wander into the trees to look for them. "We're not far from our new home. We can come back and find them some other day when we're more familiar with our surroundings."

The Fort Bridger Road snaked through the Pinery, until suddenly the forest yielded to the plains again. After a good fifty yards, Ab managed to get his oxen stopped. He climbed up to the wagon seat to look over the country with Ella.

The pines came down from the mountains, passed behind the wagon, and swept east and south in a graceful curve extending for miles into the grasslands. The Pinery was a peninsula of timber hooking into a sea of grass. The grasslands embraced by the forest sloped down to the west, to Monument Creek. Across the creek, the pinnacles of the Rampart Range rose sharply, climbing thousands of feet above the prairies. Among the foothills, Ab spotted huge red stone towers—oddly shaped columns of rock, like giant sand-castle watchtowers melted by rain.

"Those are the monuments," he said, pointing to the formations. "They mark the head of Monument Creek. The man in Denver City told me we'll find more of them along the west side of the creek toward Colorado City. They call this place Monument Park. The Pinery wraps almost all the way around it, except on the south side."

Ella took his hand. "Well, I told you I'd let you have your choice of land when we got here, Ab, honey. But I can't imagine you choosing any place over this. Everything we'll need is within our reach—land, grass, wood, and water. I don't know why we don't unhitch the wagon right here."

Ab studied Monument Park for a full minute in silence. He was in no hurry to settle in the wrong place. "I want to drive a few miles farther down the creek," he said. "I don't want our cattle forever straying into the pines. It would make more sense to get closer to Colorado City, too. The man in Denver said there's an old Indian trail that leads up to a pass in the Rampart Range. He said it would be a good place for a ranch."

They pulled off the wagon road and eased down toward Monument Creek, crunching over piles of buffalo bones left by white hunters. After another two hours of slow travel, they found the Indian trail leading across the creek, over a bald hill to the west, and into the mountains.

"It's called the Arapaho Trail," Ab said. "It leads to Arapaho Pass. The man in Denver told me we'll find plenty of game in those mountains. That will get us by until our herd grows and our crops start producing. I figure Colorado City is just a few miles down the creek." He set the brake on his wagon. "This looks like as good a place as any."

Ab and Matthew went to the Pinery to chop down enough trees for a cabin, but Ab refused to build before winter. He said the logs would need six months to cure first. He left them stacked in the forest where he cut them.

Ella and Pete carved a rectangular notch into the high bank of the creek and roofed it with stout pine limbs covered with sod. Against the back wall of the dugout, they built a fireplace of sods, extending the sod chimney above the roof so it would draw. They carried in a few articles of furniture they had hauled from Pennsylvania, and reluctantly took up residence. Ella refused to call it a house. She referred to it as the hole. Matthew and Pete slept in the covered wagon until the weather turned cold. Then the little dugout became crowded, but it was plenty warm with the mud-plastered fireplace burning.

Ella wouldn't let Caleb go out in the cold, but Ab took the older boys hunting in turns, and they bagged enough elk, deer, and antelope to get them through the winter without having to kill their own cattle. They had bought some flour in Denver, but it had been hauled in from New Mexico and had so much dirt in it that Ella was afraid the boys would grind their teeth away eating their biscuits. They had enough dried fruit and canned vegetables to keep the scurvy from killing them before spring.

The day Ab hitched his oxen to turn his first furrow, Ella said, "Ab, Caleb is better. He doesn't cough half as much as he used to. We did the right thing, coming here."

"If he's better," Ab replied, "maybe you should let him work some. Let him herd the cows for a while."

"Oh, honey, he's not ready," she said. "Give him time."

FIVE

"GOD ALMIGHTY!" MATTHEW said. "There's Indians comin'!"

"I'm tellin' Mama you said God Almighty," Pete replied.

Matthew was always sounding false alarms about grizzly bears and buffalo stampedes, so Pete didn't worry much about Indians. He just stared up at the cloudless sky, stretched out as he was along the back of Soupy, the Holcombs' old Pennsylvania mare as she grazed.

"Get off!" Matthew said. "I'm ridin' to tell Papa."

"I don't want to," Pete said, sitting up. The instant he spotted the two people pulling the milk wagon, his brother leapt and knocked him from the horse.

Matthew whipped Soupy through the herd of Missouri cows and across the plains to his father's new-plowed cornfield. "Papa! Indians!" he shouted, pointing.

Ab scanned the plains and accounted for Ella, carrying her water bucket toward the dugout where Caleb lay. His eyes kept searching until he spotted the wagon. "Where's your brother?" he asked as Matthew rode up.

"With the cows."

"Get your brother, boy! I told the two of you to look after each other!"

When Ella slid down to the hole, she reached into the doorway and took Ab's old Walker Colt from its peg. "Stay quiet, Caleb," she whispered. "Somebody's coming." She handed the revolver to her husband when he appeared on the bank above her. "What is it?" she asked.

"Somebody pulling a wagon. Matthew says Indians, but I don't think so. He and Pete will be here in a minute, then we'll wait and see who it is. Where's Caleb?"

"He's in the hole. He hasn't made a peep since his accident with that knife today. Poor thing."

When the boys arrived, Ella took them below the brink of the creek bank and waited with them beside the dugout door. Ab stayed above and watched the little wagon approach, baffled by the pair that pulled it.

When they arrived, the black man and the squaw dropped the wagon tongue beside the sod chimney sticking out of the creek bank. "Is this the farm of Absalom Holcomb?" the man asked.

"Yes," Ab said. "Just who in Hades are you?"

The black man smiled. "Buster Thompson. The Abolition Society sent me to find you."

It took Ab a moment to make the connection. "All the way to Kansas Territory?" He yelled over his shoulder: "Ella, get up here!"

Buster shrugged. "They just said find you. They told me not to trust nobody else."

"Who's that?" Ab asked, pointing his pistol barrel at the squaw.

"Her name's Snake Woman."

"I don't care what her name is—I mean, what's she doing with you?"

Ella climbed the cutbank and came to stand beside her husband.

"I traded a harmonica to Chief Long Fingers for her," Buster explained. "I didn't mean to, I just did. I figured you'd know what to do with her."

"I don't even know what to do with you!"

"Who are they, Ab?" Ella asked.

"This is Buster, one of your poor fugitive slaves, and his squaw. I thought you told the society not to send any more slaves."

"I did. Oh, but, honey, we can't just turn them away. Buster, where did you want to go?"

Buster shrugged. "Canada?"

Matthew and Pete were peeking over the bank at the strange couple. Matthew had never seen a female show as much leg as Snake Woman. It was a filthy leg, but he could see all the way up to her knee.

As Buster explained why he had chosen to go to Canada by way of Pikes Peak, Ella heard a distinctive sound rasp across the valley. "I thought I heard Caleb cough," she said.

"I didn't hear anything," Ab replied.

"He sounded so far away. Pete, is Caleb in the hole?"

Pete ducked into the dugout for a moment. "No, ma'am. He's gone."

Snake Woman understood none of the gibberish, but she read the look of insanity that crossed the white woman's face. The faint noise came again, and the white woman's eyes pulled toward the creek. There, on the far bank, a little boy was wading in. The crazy white woman saw him, screamed, and leapt over the brink of the creek bank. Snake Woman trembled, wondering what kind of terrible place Buffalo Head had brought her to now.

"Oh, God," Ab muttered. "Come on, Buster, and help me calm her down."

They met Ella as she carried Caleb to the near shore. Mother and son were drenched like muskrats from falling on the way across. To Buster's surprise, Ella put the soaked youngster in his arms as she waded out, as he was the closest one to her.

"He'll catch his death of cold," she said. "Ab, help me get a fire going to warm him up. He's nearly drowned. Caleb, don't you ever wander away like that again!"

"Miss Ella," Buster said. "He's fine."

"What?"

"The boy's fine. Just a little wet." He put Caleb down at the edge of the creek.

Ella looked at Caleb as if she didn't recognize him, then glared at the black man standing over him. "Don't you suppose to tell me whether or not my own son is fine, Mr. Thompson. Just you take him up to the hole so I can dry him out."

* * *

They ruled Canada out over supper. Too far away. Denver had too many southern men—most of them veterans of the old Georgia gold mines. A black man had been lynched there for no good reason recently. Ab suggested Mexico. It made perfect sense to him. Many Texas slaves had escaped to Mexico, and the Snake Woman had probably started out a Mexican anyway, according to Long Fingers.

But Ella said Mexico was almost as far away as Canada. Besides, she insisted, it was ridiculous to send two able bodies away from the farm when there was so much work to be done. Ab knew he was stuck with them then, and no amount of reasoning would change his wife's mind.

"Do you farm?" he asked Buster.

"I bossed a truck farm before. I can blacksmith, too."

"Well, that's something. We can't pay, you know. At least not this year."

"He's never been paid before anyway," Ella said. "He was a slave."

"You and that squaw will have to sleep in your wagon. The boys are using ours till we get the cabin built."

"They can't both sleep in that tiny wagon," Ella said. "We'll move the boys back in with us. Mr. Thompson and the Indian woman can sleep in our wagon."

"She can have the big wagon by herself," Buster said. "I'll sleep in mine. I'm afraid she might cut me up in the middle of the night."

Buster and the Holcombs looked through the dugout door at Snake Woman, squatting by the creek, eating her supper alone. No one insisted that Buster had to sleep with her.

"Hey, Buster," Pete said.

"Pete, you speak to him properly," Ella warned.

"I mean, Mr. Thompson. Will you play your fiddle now?"

"I will if you'll run get it."

Pete and Matthew tore out of the dugout and came back with all of Buster's instruments. As the fiddler opened his case, Caleb slipped away from his mother's arms and knelt in front of the mandolin leaning against the dirt wall between the guitar and the banjo. He had never seen anything as beautiful in his life—not even the pocketknife he had lost earlier that day.

It was just his size—barely half the length of the ungainly instruments flanking it. The body of the guitar was just a flat-topped box. The body of the banjo looked like an old drum. But the little mandolin had the graceful outline of a teardrop, tapered everywhere and inlaid with wooden bits of more colors than the mountain showed at sunrise. Yet, there was an intriguing violation of the teardrop form. The hollow box of the instrument grew an odd curlicue from one of its sides. The curlicue had a leather strap attached to it, and Caleb knew instinctively the strap was meant to sling over the shoulder of the mandolin player. Eight strings, stretched in pairs, gleamed yellow in the firelight.

"Mr. Thompson," he said in a timid voice, "can I have this one?"

"Caleb, please!" Ella said.

But Buster raised his hand. "Little man," he said, winking at Caleb, "if you learn to play it, you can sure have it."

Caleb looked at his mother. She smiled. At last he was going to have something he wanted. He was going to learn to play the mandolin.

SIX

THE NEXT MORNING, Buster went to work breaking ground in the creek bottom for his truck patch. He thought he might have to get Snake Woman to irrigate the patch by hand if the rains didn't come. Maybe next year he could try to dig an irrigation ditch.

"Don't you go gettin' ahead of yourself," he muttered. "You might not be here next year."

About halfway into the third morning, a rivet bolt broke on Buster's plow, so he led the oxen to the creek where they could drink and went back to the wagons to get a new rivet bolt and a hammer.

Caleb was sitting in the milk wagon, practicing his mandolin chords, when Buster came to get his hammer out of his tool crate.

"My fingers hurt," the boy said.

"They will at first. Then they get tough. Look at mine." He showed Caleb the calluses on the fingertips of his left hand. "Wrong fret," he said, moving Caleb's fingers to the correct positions.

Ella was nearby, worrying over her flower garden. She was shading the tender plants with her body, trying to keep the sun from withering them.

Buster walked over to the garden to see if he could do anything. He found the lilies lying limp across the ground. "Maybe you should plant somethin' else," he said.

"I don't have anything else," Ella snapped. It irritated her that Buster wouldn't let her alone to grow her own flower garden.

"It's gonna get awful dry," he said. "Those flowers won't grow here like they did back in Pennsylvania. You need some flowers that will stand this hot, dry weather. You need some western flowers. There's wild ones down the creek a ways. All different colors."

Ella loosened the strings of her bonnet under her chin. "Mr. Thompson, don't you have some plowing or other such nonsense to do? I don't recall asking for your advice."

"Oh. Yes, ma'am." He touched his hat brim and went back to the wagon to get the rivet bolt.

"If you're so smart, Mr. Thompson, you'll get me some seeds!" she yelled when he started back.

He knew she was right. "Buster, you've got to learn to keep your mouth shut," he muttered to himself.

That evening he walked down the creek to look at the wildflowers. He found five or six varieties in bloom. If they were like other plants he had studied, he figured they would go to seed a couple of weeks after blooming. He would just have to watch them closely, check them every other day or so.

He squatted down to study an orange variety with tiny five-petaled blossoms. Another type grew pink flowers on the ends of meandering stems. He wondered if he could transplant them to Miss Ella's garden. He decided to bring a spade next time and dig some up.

The most prolific tribe was the fire wheel. It had multiple lancelike petals, flame-red with yellow tips, leaping like fire from a central hub the size of a vest button.

A hummingbird attracted him to a stalky variety with small purple blossoms. He thought Miss Ella might like something that would attract hummingbirds. He got down on his stomach to inspect the roots.

"Buster, what in Hades are you doing?"

He jumped and retreated halfway down the creek bank before he realized it was Ab. "I'm studyin' these flowers," he admitted.

Matthew started laughing. Ab and the boys had gone downstream looking for the cattle and were herding them back toward the dugout for the evening.

"What do you want with flowers?" Ab said.

"Miss Ella needs some seeds," Buster answered.

"She's already got five gallons of flower seeds," Ab said. "Come on and help with these cows—quit wasting your time."

"Hey, Pete!" Matthew shouted. "We caught Buster looking at flowers!"

Matthew caught Buster in the wildflower patch several times in the weeks that followed. Buster spent almost every evening there, studying the plants. He tried transplanting a specimen of each to Ella's garden, but the yellow primrose was the only one that took.

As summer began, he painstakingly collected the tiny seeds shed by the different varieties. He put them in envelopes he made of paper scraps and labeled them: firewheel, butterfly weed, bird's eye, primrose, prairie aster. When the time was right, he intended to make a gift of them to Ella.

While on his last foray down to the wildflower patch, Buster happened to glance across the creek to see Long Fingers and a dozen braves watching him. The chief waved. He had seven spare horses and three Holcomb cows with him. As he led his party across the creek, he put Buster's old harmonica in his mouth and began to blow on it. He avoided the high notes and droned monotonously on three or four of the lower tones.

Buster put his paper envelopes in his pocket and stood to greet the warriors. Mounted and painted, they appeared ten times prouder than when he first met them in the stinking gully on the plains. Kicking Dog rode behind Long Fingers and carried a lance with a scalp of black hair, stiff with blood, tied to the shaft.

"Buffalo Head," Long Fingers said, "I see you and Holcomb cut down more trees. Why do you cut down that many? To build a lodge?"

"Yes," Buster said.

"A lodge of trees is better than living in the ground like a prairie dog. But I hope you do not cut down all the trees."

"We won't," Buster said. "We cut the last ones we needed today. Where'd you find those cows?"

"In the mountains. My boys want to eat them. I do, too, but they do not belong to my people. Not like the trees you cut for Holcomb's lodge."

On the way to the dugout, Buster had to explain what he had been doing with the flowers. Long Fingers wanted to know if the whites used them for medicine. When he found out that Buster was trying to grow them, he said, "Leave them alone and they will grow plenty good all by theirself."

Snake Woman was gathering firewood when she saw the Arapaho coming. A breath caught in her throat, and she dared to hope that maybe Long Fingers had come back for her. She hated living with the whites. She was so ashamed of the cloth dress they made her wear that she kept it covered with a blanket except in the heat of the day.

She had never eaten so well or worked so little, yet she knew the white people and Buffalo Head would do something horrible to her sooner or later. The crazy white woman had already started a daily torture of pulling her hair with a fine-toothed comb. She feared she would be scalped alive, but so far the white woman had managed only to rid her head of lice and nits. Now her scalp felt barren and unhealthy because nothing lived there anymore.

She hated the wagon they made her sleep in. The wind whistled under it at night. And that oldest boy kept watching her when he should have been hunting rabbits. If he came after her—she didn't care what the whites did to her—she would kill him.

But now maybe she wouldn't have to. Long Fingers was driving three cows before him. Maybe he had brought them to trade for her. She picked up one more stick of wood and scrambled toward the hole in the ground where the white people lived.

"Hey, Pete, here comes the snake lady," Matthew said as the squaw neared the dugout. "I'm gonna ask her."

"She doesn't understand English, stupid," Pete replied.

"Ask her what?" Caleb said. He missed out on everything.

Matthew approached the squaw and pulled on her sleeve as she dropped her wood on the pile. She ignored him and watched the Arapaho ride nearer over the rim of the creek bank.

"Hey," he said, pulling on her sleeve again.

She looked at him.

"Open your mouth."

She stared, her lip curling with hatred.

"Open your mouth, I want to see your tongue." Matthew wiggled his tongue at her and motioned for her to open her mouth.

Snake Woman looked away and prayed the three cows would be enough. She hated living with the whites.

"Leave her alone, Matthew," Pete said.

"Yeah," Caleb said. He didn't know what it was all about, but he usually sided with Pete.

Buster looked like a captive walking among the horses of the Indians. He waved at Ab to let him know everything was all right.

"Hello, Chief Long Fingers," Ella said, formally, when the Indians stopped near the roof of the dugout. "I see you've found some of our cattle again."

"I bring them back to you. Your children need them like mine need the buffalo."

"Chief, why don't you keep that big bull calf. We owe it to you for bringing so many of our cows back."

Ab was stunned. "What? Didn't you give them some sugar or something before?"

"Oh, Ab, one calf won't hurt. We wouldn't have any by now if it wasn't for them."

Long Fingers told his warriors to cut the bull calf from the bunch. "Now our women will be happy to see us. We have a calf to eat, and the horses we steal, and scalps of the Utes." He saw Snake Woman peering over the rim of the cutbank. "You make new clothes for Snake Woman."

"Yes. I think she likes it here."

"Maybe so she will come to our camp and cut up this calf. It is a job women like to do."

"I'll mention it to her," Ella said.

"Buffalo Head, tonight you come to our camp and play music on the thing that pushes your wagon like a cloud. The round one. I will play the harp with you this time."

Matthew was rolling on the dirt threshold of the dugout, giggling.

"What?" Pete asked.

"He called Buster 'Buffalo Head'!"

The chief and his war party drove the calf about a quarter mile downstream. As the Holcombs looked on, Kicking Dog goaded the calf into a run and killed it with his lance.

"My God, woman," Ab said. "Why did you go and give them that calf."

"I had to, honey. I was wrong before when I told you this land was free for the taking. It's their land, really, and we owe them something for using it."

"Who says it's theirs?"

"It's theirs by treaty. I read it in that newspaper you got at Denver City. We'd better stay friendly with them if we don't want them to take it back."

"I can't be friendly with a bunch of murdering savages."

"They're not murderers."

Ab gestured fiercely. "Didn't you see that scalp?"

"They're at war with the Utes. You went to war once, you should understand."

"I didn't take scalps."

"The scalps are their war medals."

Ab gawked at his wife in silence. What had brought on this sudden love for red men? Then he recognized the fiery glaze over her eyes, and he understood. There were not enough fugitive slaves in the West. Caleb was getting better, and Ella was looking for a new cause. These Arapaho seemed available.

Buster got his banjo and told Snake Woman the chief wanted her to go to the Indian camp and butcher the calf. He had picked up much of the Indian hand language from her and could communicate adequately.

Snake Woman took the news as a good sign. It would give her a chance to beg Long Fingers to take her back onto the plains. She put her blanket over her shoulders and walked to the Arapaho camp several steps behind Buster.

Long Fingers and Buffalo Head made a peculiar kind of music together with the banjo and the harmonica. The banjo picker found it hard to play the correct chords with the harp blower playing the wrong notes, but Buster pretended to enjoy it. After playing, he had the honor of eating the calf tongue with the chief, looking askance at the scalp on Kicking Dog's spear as he ate.

"Whose hair is that?" he finally asked.

Long Fingers considered his reply as he chewed a mouthful of the delicacy. "Kicking Dog kills this Ute to get the horses," he finally said. "We need more horses to hunt the buffalo now. They are harder to find. White men kill too many.''

Buster shifted his eyes to the fire and watched the flames spout from the embers.

"What do you want to say?" Long Fingers asked.

Buster looked at the chief, draped in blankets and sprawled across a buffalo robe, a feather sticking out of his hair. "I thought you said the Arapaho traded with the other tribes. Why don't you trade for your horses?"

"We have nothing left to trade with. And anyway, how will my boys prove their courage if they do not fight? They want to fight somebody, and I do not want them to fight the whites, so I take them to fight the Utes. We have been fighting Utes a long time anyway."

"Any of your boys get killed?"

"Not this time."

"Did you kill anybody?"

"No. I carry only my stick to count coup."

"What's that?"

"I show my boys I have a good heart. I go to battle with a stick. I hit the Utes with it when we fight, and that is called counting coup. It means more than taking the scalp."

"You mean, you'd rather do that than kill 'em?"

"Sometimes I kill them, then count coup. But I do not want to kill all the Utes. They are easy to steal horses from." He smiled briefly, stroked his greasy fingers across a tuft of buffalo grass. "My boys believe you can count coup on your enemy, Buffalo Head. The one you drown."

Buster was hoping the chief had forgotten that empty brag. He had only drowned Arbuckle's Jack in a figurative way and had mentioned it only as a joke to himself. He doubted the Arapaho would honor the counting of coup on a past identity. "Who else do you raid for horses?" he said, avoiding the matter of the drowning.

"We do not raid whites," Long Fingers said. "I want the whites to show us how to make a ranch. Our old ways are going, but if we try to fight the whites to keep our old ways, everything will go. You tell Holcomb we do not raid his ranch. He only has one horse anyway, and it is old."

"He wants to get more horses."

"It changes nothing. We will catch them and bring them back to him when they get away. Then maybe so Holcomb's wife will give us one of them. That is a woman with a good heart. I am happy Holcomb brings her here. She is like you, Buffalo Head. She wants to know our way."

* * *

Buster had to be back at the dugout early enough to give Caleb his mandolin lesson before bedtime. It had been decided that if Caleb could learn to play "Camptown Races" in three different keys, he could have the instrument. So he said his farewells and left not long after dark.

When he left, Snake Woman stayed behind to haggle with Long Fingers in the hand language. She asked the chief to give something to Buffalo Head so she could rejoin the Arapaho. She said Buffalo Head put little value on her and he would take almost anything in trade for her.

The chief let her know that Buffalo Head was needed to help the Arapaho stay friendly with the whites at Holcomb Ranch, and that trading to regain possession of her might insult him.

Snake Woman said she could not live with the whites much longer because the white woman was crazy and had already tried to pull her hair out several times. If Long Fingers would not take her back she would run away to join the Cheyenne.

Long Fingers said he was very good friends with all the Cheyenne and if she ran away to them he would catch her and trade her back to the Comanche, who would use her more harshly than any crazy white woman.

As she trudged back to the drafty wagon Buffalo Head made her sleep in, Snake Woman wondered why the spirits would not allow her a tribe. Between the Indian camp and the hole in the ground where the whites lived, she threw herself down violently, pulled her hair, and rubbed her face in the dirt. She prayed for a sign. She wanted to know what she had to do to be taken into a tribe and given honor. She thrashed about on the ground like a dog rolling on a carcass until she was exhausted. Then she lay on her back and stared at the sky. As she searched desperately among the stars, one of them suddenly flared and shot to the southeast, leaving a trail longer than a river across the sky.

To the southeast was Comanche range. She didn't know what it meant, but she believed the shooting star flew for only her eyes to see. The Comanche? She didn't understand. But it was only the first sign.

SEVEN

ELLA THOUGHT SHE would go crazy with "Camptown Races." Caleb played it all day and night. In the bed of the milk wagon, at the bank of the creek, on the floor of the dugout, "doo-dah, doo-dah" and "oh, doo-dah day" rang, rather haltingly, but repeatedly, from the lips of the young musician, accompanied by a somewhat rhythmical strumming of deadened strings.

Pete and Matthew got to stay with the cows during the day and only had to listen to it at night. Snake Woman spent most of her time watering the truck patch in the creek bottom. The men only heard "doo-dah, doo-dah" when they dragged the logs to the cabin site behind the oxen. Buster had the audacity to encourage the boy.

When Caleb finally played "Camptown Races" all the way through in the key of G without having to stop for his fingers to find the chords, it was a pivotal moment for his mother. Then he started practicing in the key of C, for which he had to learn a new chord, and the process renewed itself, but at least Ella got to hear the standard in a different key, and for that respite from monotony, she gave thanks.

One day when Ella was enjoying Caleb's lunch—for he couldn't play "Camptown Races" while he ate—Buster invaded her solitude by knocking on the roof pole at the door of the dugout.

"What do you want?" she said. "I hope you haven't hurt yourself. I'm in no mood to do any doctoring."

"No, ma'am, I'm not hurt. I just wanted to give you those seeds."

"What seeds?"

"The wildflower seeds for your garden." He handed her the paper envelopes, labeled with pencil and rattling faintly with tiny kernels.

Ella opened one and looked in.

"Those are the firewheels," Buster said. "I wrote what kind it is on the outside of the envelopes."

"The proper name is Indian blankets," Ella said. She shuffled the rest of the envelopes and read the names of the flowers. "If you're so smart, I guess you know when to plant them."

"I suppose now's as good a time as any. The flowers are droppin' 'em about now, and I guess they know how to grow their own sprouts. I'd put a little dirt over 'em to keep 'em from gettin' blown away or eaten up by birds. I don't suppose you'll see 'em grow till next spring though."

The strains of "Camptown Races" came from the dugout, and Ella rolled her eyes.

"I don't suppose I'll see them grow at all," she said. "Of all the notions!"

Buster wanted to hear the boy play, but he could tell Miss Ella was in no mood for company. He put his hat back on and climbed the creek bank.

He returned to work, round-notching the logs for the cabin. He had a knack for making the joints fit flush, so Ab had left all the notching to him. The next time he paused to wipe the sweat from his brow, he looked toward the creek and saw Ella on her knees in the flower garden, planting the seeds.

Ab had no intention of patterning his cabin after the models he had seen in Denver. Those poor examples of architecture were mere shells of green logs on bare ground, mud chinked and roofed with sod. They served as temporary quarters to the transient prospectors. But Ab had come to Monument Park for good. He would build to last.

To lift and stack the logs, the men rigged a gin pole in the middle of the cabin foundation. A rope ran through a pulley on the top of the gin pole. The oxen pulled the rope to hoist the heavy logs into their overlapping positions. Ella drove the oxen. The men and the older two boys guided the logs into place. Caleb sat in the shade of the covered wagon and practiced the key of C. The men chopped to the rhythm of "oh, doo-dah day."

One afternoon the music abruptly stopped. "Hey, somebody's comin'!" Caleb shouted.

Ab was six timbers high on one corner, watching Buster work a log with the drawknife. He looked across the creek, where the Arapaho Trail led from the mountains, and saw a distinctive herd of beasts following a rider toward the cabin.

An old mountain man rode up the cutbank on a chestnut gelding with a white rump, the white rump harboring chestnut spots the size of silver dollars. A mare trailing behind was white with bay spots from the shoulders back, and solid bay forward. An eagle feather stuck out of a beaver top hat. Stiff shocks of iron-gray hair bristled out from under the dusty brim, ran down the jowls, climbed the cheeks, hid the mouth, and brushed the collar of a bright red gingham shirt. The butt of a long rifle jutted from a fringed saddle sleeve.

"It's old Cheyenne Dutch," Ab said, climbing down from the corner.

Cheyenne Dutch had come west thirty years ago to trap beavers and trade with the Indians. He had kept a trading post on the South Platte for the first fourteen years, until he lost it in a game of three-card monte. Then he had killed the new owner with a Cheyenne lance and burned the place to the ground. He had wandered among the Indians since. It was rumored that he had a wife with every tribe in the Rockies.

Five dogs prowled at the heels of Dutch's gelding as he approached the unfinished cabin, one sorrowful swaybacked specimen almost dragging her teats on the ground. The old trader tightened his fur-trimmed reins when he arrived, and reached into a sack tied behind his cantle.

"Bitch whelped," he said. "Want one?" From the sack he lifted a whining puppy by the nape of the neck.

Matthew and Pete dropped their tools and raced to get their hands on the puppy. Dutch let them handle two of them so they wouldn't pull the one apart.

"Can we have 'em, Papa?" Pete begged.

Ab folded his arms across his chest. "What kind of dog?" he asked.

"Bitch's there," Dutch said, pointing. "She's hound. Other half's wolf for all I know."

"What will you trade?"

"Tobacco?" Dutch suggested.

"We don't keep tobacco here," Ella said, leaving her oxen to confront the visitor. She had an instinct for judging some people, and she didn't like this Cheyenne Dutch.

The mountain man refused to look at her, preferring to do his trading with men. "Don't you smoke, Holcomb?"

Ab shook his head.

"Whiskey?"

"That either," Ella said.

"You don't drink?"

"No," Ab said.

Dutch grinned, gold-capped teeth glinting through his whiskers. "Well, let's see. Don't smoke, don't drink. Probably ain't got no use for that squaw down there in the corn, either. Swap her, and I'll give you the whole goddamn litter."

"Sir," Ella said, "we don't bargain in human flesh. And mind your language around these children."

"Holcomb, ain't you even allowed to cuss?"

"No," Ab said. "Will you take some flour or coffee or something?"

The trader scratched his beard a moment. "Some coffee for one pup. Sugar for another. That's fair. Them dogs'll help that squaw keep the cows out of your crops."

"All right," Ab said, "we'll swap."

Matthew and Pete hollered for joy and took their pets under the wagon to play with. Caleb put the mandolin in the milk wagon and hung over Pete's shoulders to pet one of the puppies. He knew better than to get close to Matthew's dog. He wished his father would have traded for three pups, but he was afraid to ask for another, thinking his mother might change her mind about the mandolin if he got greedy.

As Ella went to the dugout to get the coffee and sugar together, Dutch scrutinized the black man up on the wall. Buster hadn't missed a lick with the drawknife since the trader arrived. He liked to work steady once he got going on something.

"Where'd you get him?" Dutch asked, pointing at Buster.

"That's Buster. He works here."

Buster paused long enough to tip his hat to the visitor, but Dutch shook off the courtesy and walked around the rising cabin walls to inspect the work.

"I sure like those spotted horses," Ab said. "What happened to the two others you had last winter?"

"Sold 'em. I'm goin' up to get some more come fall."

"Where do you get them?"

"Nez Perce. Up in the Palousey country."

"Indian horses?" Ab said. "That one's a gelding."

"Nez Perce geld 'em. That one there wouldn't sire spotted foals, so they cut him. They know about breedin'. They breed for the spots. Magic. Bulletproofs 'em.''

Buster watched the feathered top hat over the wall of logs opposite his corner. Then he caught Cheyenne Dutch looking back at him between the stacked logs, glaring from the corner of one eye. The mountain man's stare made him shudder and look away. He went back to his work with the drawknife.

Ab was studying the spotted horses. They had good muscle, sure feet, and alert eyes. The eyes had whites, like human eyes. The horses looked smart and seemed built for a saddle. They were long in the pastern for a smooth trot, short in the cannon for sound legs, and just big enough to carry a man fast.

"I've heard you rode with Sam Walker in Mexico," Dutch said.

Ab nodded.

"You'll know a thing or two about horses then."

"I'd like to buy a couple of these Nez Perce mounts from you this winter," he said, "if you're coming back this way."

"Maybe," Dutch said. "I'm goin' horselike myself."

"What?" Ab said.

"Seen it in a dream: me goin' horselike over the mountain of a night-time. Light moon. I'm part horse on a light moon. Breed my women horse-like, too." He shifted his eye toward Buster again, leering between the logs.

When Ella gave Dutch his sugar and coffee, he mounted the gelding and rode toward the creek, his mare and five dogs trailing behind.

Buster climbed down from the corner. "What was he talking about? Horselike in his dreams and all?"

"Don't pay him any mind," Ab said. "He says things like that. He's a little touched."

EIGHT

A NOISE ROUSED Buster from his sleep in the milk wagon. He didn't know at first what had wakened him. The moon was three-quarters full, and he could see well the features of the plains and the shoulders of Pikes Peak looming in the southwest. He had almost decided to go back to sleep when the sound came again. It was a voice half human and half wild. It had come from the Holcomb's covered wagon. He had never heard Snake Woman's voice before but knew it was hers.

He threw his piece of wagon sheet off, slid over the edge of the milk wagon, and ran quietly to the back of the covered wagon to listen. A violent movement and a grunt tempted him to look into the wagon bed. He saw the feather waving at the back of the beaver top hat.

Cheyenne Dutch had Snake Woman pinned facedown on her blankets. He held her arms together behind her back and kept her legs apart with his knees. He was pulling the dress Ella had made for her over her hips.

Buster grabbed a handful of iron-gray hair and gingham shirt and pulled Dutch out of the wagon backward, dropping him headfirst on the ground. Dutch tried to get up, but Buster kicked him to keep him down. "Mister Ab!" he yelled.

Snake Woman pulled a wad of cloth out of her mouth and looked out of the wagon. She saw the mountain man trying to get up. Buffalo Head kicked at him, but the old trader grabbed Buffalo Head's foot and threw him down. Dutch then sprang from the ground and dove for the black man, but Buffalo Head kicked both feet, carried the old trader on his heels, and launched him over the creek bank.

Snake Woman did not know what it meant, but it was so fantastic that she could only take it as her second sign from the spirit world.

Buster ran to the milk wagon for his horse pistol. "Mister Ab!" he yelled again. He heard Dutch climbing the creek bank. He opened the crate and found his gun. When he looked up, he found Dutch hatless at the top of the bank, a long knife in his hand. Buster aimed the pistol.

"Go ahead and shoot, you buck nigger. I'm a spotted-rump Palousey horse and bulletproof!"

"Mister, you don't go horselike around here," Buster said, trying to find some reason in Dutch's jabber. "That moon ain't full anyhow."

Dutch looked at the moon. He started speaking an Indian tongue and stalked closer to Buster with the knife as he raved.

"Hold it, Dutch!" Ab was coming barefoot from the dugout with his Walker Colt. Ella ran two steps behind. Snake Woman jumped out of the wagon and sprinted toward the half-built log house.

"Buster, what in Hades is going on?" Ab asked.

"He was in there with the Snake Woman, trying to take his pleasure."

"Oh, my!" Ella screamed. "You filthy devil! Get off of our land!"

"Woman, this place belongs to the gods of the red men. Palousey is my name, spotted horse god of the mountains! You'll catch my wind and fire and blizzard for your tongue, white woman!"

"Ab, shoot him if he won't go."

"I won't go till I kill that big buck nigger," Dutch said.

"Oh! I'll shoot you myself for saying such a thing!" She tried to pull the revolver away from her husband.

"Calm down, Ella. He's crazy as a coot."

Buster heard the half-animal squall again and saw Snake Woman pass in front of his pistol sights. She wielded the ax overhead and brought it down on Dutch's shoulder. The mountain man dropped his knife, roared like a bear, knocked Snake Woman against the wagon with his left fist, and staggered back to the brink of the creek bank.

· Buster moved in closer, protecting Snake Woman with his pistol. He could see the glisten of blood running down the gingham shirt.

"Give me that!" Ella demanded. She pulled at Ab's Colt, but he wouldn't let her have it. "Give me your pistol," she said, running to Buster. She wrenched the weapon from Buster's hand, pointed it, closed her eyes, and blew away a respectable chunk of the creek bank. "Fiddlesticks! Buster, where's your powder?"

Cheyenne Dutch leapt silently over the bank and ran for the trees across the creek, stooping for his beaver hat on the run. Ab went to the edge and watched him to make sure he wasn't trying to double back. He saw the weird gait of the wounded trader running apelike up the bald hill along the Arapaho Trail.

Snake Woman shook Buffalo Head by the elbow and made him watch her hand signs.

"What's she trying to say?" Ella asked.

"I don't know. Somethin' about a sign from the spirits. I guess she caught some crazy from that ol' Cheyenne Dutch."

At dawn Ab took his guns and went to see how many cattle had wandered off during the night. He found the two spotted Nez Perce horses hobbled and grazing with his herd. Across the white blanket on the rump of the gelding were six letters scrawled in the dried blood of Cheyenne Dutch: PARDON. The white flank of the mare bore its own grisly message: CRAZY.

NINE

MATTHEW CLAIMED THE gelding called Pard, and Pete took Crazy, the mare. They mounted every morning to round up the cattle and drive them to fresh grass before they came back to work on the cabin. Riding the spotted horses through the morning dew changed their dreary cow work to inspired excitement. Matthew took to chasing the cows when his father wasn't watching. The docile Missouri cows—the survivors that hadn't been eaten by mountain lions or wolves—had become rangy and wild since living on the plains. They now made for a lively chase.

Caleb asked his mother if he could ride old Soupy and go along with his brothers.

"When you're up to it, honey," she said.

He didn't tamper with his good fortune by pestering her. After all, when Pete and Matthew were gone, he had both puppies to himself. And when his brothers were around, he still had the mandolin to play. He had mastered G and C and was learning the third key, the key of D, the one that would make the mandolin his. In the evenings he and Buster sat out beside the milk wagon and played "Camptown Races" together—Buster on the guitar, patiently waiting for Caleb to find his chords.

The monotony of the one song lulled Snake Woman into trances as she stared at the stars, looking for signs. In everything she saw, she looked for signs. In the creek, the mountains, the plains. In the corn, the cattle, the birds. She watched Buffalo Head more than anything else. The second sign had come through him. The spirits had made him a warrior and protector who counted coup on her enemies. She didn't know exactly what it meant yet, but she expected the gods to work more signs through him.

All day Snake Woman kept regular watches on the black man, but Buster didn't realize it, absorbed as he was with notching the logs for the cabin. He made them fit together wonderfully, each notch cupping the log beneath it like a palm around a wrist.

The rectangular cabin would have three rooms—sleeping quarters for the boys at one end, the parents at the other, and a middle room for eating, cooking, and listening to fiddle music. No arrangements were made for the farmhands. Buster would move into the dugout, and Snake Woman would get to keep her wagon. In time, they would get their own houses.

Timber by timber the log walls climbed. The gables started to take shape at the two ends of the house. Buster sawed off the ends of the gable logs at an angle to match the slope of the roof that would rest on top of them. Purlins spanned the gables. For these lengthwise members, Ab used logs just as stout as the ones he had built the walls with. He wanted a roof able to handle heavy snows.

The cumbersome timbers could only be lifted to the gables by use of the gin pole, which naturally reminded Buster of a mast on a great ship. A mast of that height, he thought, could hoist enough canvas to move a Conestoga freight wagon across the plains in a fair wind. The gin pole was planted in the ground in the middle of the cabin and would be removed before the floor went in. Long guy ropes, extending to the four points of the compass, and staked to the plains, held it erect like shrouds on a sailing vessel.

When a log had to be moved to the roof, ramps made of timbers were leaned against the walls so the new member could slide up them to its place, lifted by a rope which ran through a pulley on the top of the gin pole. The oxen pulled on the rope under Ella's guidance. In this way the logs continued to mount until finally the ridge log came to rest on the peaks of the gables. After Buster rounded the notches in it, he rolled it into place, finally giving the shell of logs its backbone.

He untied the rope that had lifted the ridge log into place and let it dangle. "We won't be needin' those oxen for these logs no more," he shouted to Ella. "Shingles and floorboards is about all we got left to fix."

"And doors," Ella said, leaving the cattle yoked at the end of the lift rope. "And windows. God knows where we'll get glass."

Ab and Buster swung down from the purlins.

"Getting that gin pole out's going to be a chore," Ab said. "Hadn't thought about it till now."

Matthew and Pete joined the men at the base of the gin pole and looked up at it, boxed in now by roof timbers. It towered right past the ridge log Buster had just dropped into place. If someone were to cut the guy ropes and let the gin pole fall, it would take out half the rafters and maybe one of the walls. It would have to be removed with caution.

Ella stepped into the doorframe. "All you have to do is climb up there and chop the top off of it," she said. "Then it will be short enough for us to lean over and slide out through the door."

"What's going to happen to that piece we chop off, though?" Ab asked. "It'll fall down in here and break something. Or hurt somebody."

"We'll have to build us a big tripod that'll straddle the house," Buster suggested, "and tie the top of the gin pole to that so it won't fall when we chop it off. Then we can lower it easy."

"That will work," Ella said.

Caleb jumped into the doorway with the mandolin. "I'm ready!"

"Ready for what, honey?" his mother said.

"To play 'doo-dah day' in all three keys. Want to hear 'em?"

"You bet we do," Buster said.

"No, we don't," Matthew argued. "We heard it a million times already."

"Yeah," Pete said. "Can't you teach him another song, Mr. Thompson?"

"Let him play three more doo-dahs. I'll teach him a whole mess of songs after he wins his mandolin."

Caleb's audience sat on the floor joists, with their feet on the short-grass plains, and listened as he stood at one end of the cabin to play. First he played flawlessly in the key of G. In C, he attained near perfection. Being the least familiar with the key of D, Caleb worried about it the most. The A chord gave his short fingers fits. But he took a deep breath and launched the rendition that would make the mandolin his.

From the cornfield, Snake Woman was listening to the strange music of Buffalo Head and the white people. She liked to look across the plains at the gin pole and the guy ropes holding it up. It reminded her a little of lodge poles waiting to be covered with buffalo skins. But this time something was different about the angles of the ropes. One of them reached out too far across the plains, toward the creek. It was the one the oxen were tied to. They had wandered too far from the house of logs, and their rope was pulling against the top of the gin pole. She heard the white people clapping as the music ended.

Suddenly, Caleb saw a road of happiness ahead of him. They were applauding for him. Even Matthew. They were looking up at him and smiling. It was music. They liked him.

"It's yours now," Buster said. "You earned it."

Caleb yelled for joy and jumped into the doorframe with his mandolin. "Thanks, Buster! I mean, Mr. Thompson." He sprang out of the doorway and landed between the ramp logs used to slide timbers to the roof, dancing and singing "oh, doo-dah day," waving his new mandolin over his head.

Buster laughed at the boy until he heard the timbers creaking and the ropes popping with tension. For a moment he thought he was on a sailing ship. When he looked up at the gin pole, he saw that the knot on the end of the hoist rope had traveled all the way up to the pulley. The rope was stretched tight to the west. The oxen were walking toward the creek, pulling the gin pole down. As it leaned toward the oxen, the gin pole pushed the ridge log out of its notches and off the gables, and it thundered down the slope of the roof on Caleb's side of the cabin.

Ella shrieked with horror, leapt through the doorframe. She thought that if she pushed Caleb away, the log might still roll over him from behind. She had to grab him and throw him back toward the cabin so the rumbling shaft of timber would pass over his head.

Caleb lost his grip on his mandolin when his mother flung him at the cabin. He landed against the wall on the seat of his pants. He saw the shadow pass overhead. His mother was looking at him. His mandolin was on the ground behind her.

The timber rolled down from the house of logs, hit Ella in the stomach, slammed her against the ground, bounced over her head, and stopped in a swirl of dust.

Buster ran for the oxen. The gin pole had fallen against the highest purlin spanning the gables. If the beasts took the slack out of the rope again, they would pull the purlin from its notches, too, and send it rolling down on Ella behind the ridge log. He cut the rope from the yoke as soon as he reached the oxen, and they continued to walk toward the creek to drink.

Caleb saw his father kneeling over his mother. Beyond them, he saw his mandolin lying flat and splintered against the ground where the log had crushed it. He wasn't sure what had happened. He didn't know if his mother had taken the mandolin away from him on purpose or not. He had seen the log hit her but didn't know if she was as badly broken as his little instrument. He got up and looked at his mother first. Her mouth was open and her eyes were darting. His father was speaking her name. Then he looked at his mandolin. Only the strings were good. Not even Buster could fix the broken wood. He dropped to his knees on the splinters, looked back at his mother, and began to cry.

Ab held his wife's face in his hands. He was afraid to touch her anywhere else. Her head trembled, her eyes searched and batted. Suddenly she took a breath in, then coughed a spray of blood on Ab's shirt. He looked up at Buster. "Take the boys," he said. "Get some water or something."

Ella could see only light and shadows, but she felt her husband beside her. She also felt something moving inside, something very wrong. There was no pain, but the strange motion in her body prevented her from sitting up. She could only breathe in gasps. "Caleb," she said.

"He's fine, Ella. You pulled him back. He's just fine."

Ella's hand clutched his elbow. "Don't you let him die," she said. "You had better not let him die, Ab." She took in another shallow rush of air.

"I won't."

"Promise."

"I promise I won't, Ella. I'll take care of him. Now you lie still."

Something inside her chest was growing, taking away the room for her air. She wanted to tell Ab to make sure Caleb learned some new songs, but she didn't have the breath for it. The light faded and the shadows spread. She was so happy to be lying on the warm plains. She would have hated dying in that cold hole in the ground.

TEN

The moon rose just before dawn. It looked like an acorn resting against its crown—a silver cap under a dark round hull. From the east porch of his cabin, Ab watched it rise as he drank his coffee and planned his suicide.

Buster had finished the cabin. Buster had harvested the corn and truck crops and hauled them to Denver to trade. Buster had planted the winter wheat and killed the game that got them through the cold months. Ab had sat around the cabin and stared at Ella's grave and wondered how he would kill himself.

He had always assumed he would die first. He didn't know what to do without her. She had taken care of everything for him for so long—raised the boys almost all by herself. True, Ab had taught them what he knew about farming, but she had brought them up in every other way. She had kept Caleb alive for six years. Ab knew now what a burden it was to worry about Caleb. He saw a frail little boy when he looked at his youngest son.

He had come to know why Ella never let him ride a horse, or go out hunting, or have a pocketknife.

He couldn't sleep at night for worrying about what might happen to Caleb. In Ab's nightmares, Caleb drowned himself in the creek, stabbed himself falling from the dugout roof, or stood under the ridge log as it rolled down from the gables. Ab had always carried out Ella's living wishes, and he intended to honor her dying demand as well. As long as he lived, he had to look after Caleb. The responsibility would hang over him for a lifetime. Every little rasping cough he heard coming from the other end of the cabin at night reminded him of the promise he had made to his dying wife. He felt her presence everywhere he went. He had to make sure he died before Caleb, and the sooner the better. It was just a question of how to make it look like an accident so he wouldn't bring dishonor to his sons.

Ab never exerted his mind by making it think about more than two things at a time. In the past that had meant satisfying Ella and taking care of a farm. Now the two things he thought about most were keeping Caleb alive and killing himself—one of which would relieve him of responsibility for the other.

The dark round hull of the moon vanished, and the silver cap became a mere chalk mark on the sky. The sun cleared the Pinery and colored the dust kicked up by the cattle. Pete and Matthew were rounding them up on the spotted horses. Ab had told them to brand whatever cattle they could catch. Buster had invented the brand—a circle in a circle, which he called the bull's-eye brand. He had made a branding iron out of a couple of metal rings, one from a discarded saddle buckle and the other from a broken breast yoke.

As Ab watched his sons chase the cattle, Buster stepped up on the log porch with a basket of eggs. He had brought chickens back from Denver and converted his little milk wagon into a coop. The dogs followed him, hoping he would drop an egg. Over the winter they had grown into lumbering loafers with oversize paws, tongues, and appetites.

"Those boys caught any cows yet?" Buster asked.

"No, they don't know what to do with a rope. I sure can't show them. There's grass for a lot of cows here, but you have to know how to rope if you want to work them."

"Yes, sir. Maybe they'll learn."

"By the time they learn all the cows will be gone."

Buster laughed, as if Ab were joking. "That fellow in Denver who made the saddle I brought back for Matthew said he used to work a ranch in Texas. Maybe next time I go, I'll look him up and see if he can teach us something."

"Buster, don't you ever let a Texan teach a single thing to any one of my boys. Understand?"

Buster said he understood, but he really didn't. He didn't understand half of what Ab said anymore. "Where's Caleb?" he asked.

"Still sleeping."

"I've got some things he can do if you'll let me put him to work."

Ab remained silent.

"Nothing hard. Just fixing up some things. He can help me fetch my tools."

Buster knew there was nothing wrong with Caleb. The boy tended to catch cold every now and then, and cough and sneeze a lot, but that was common with some kids. He was short of breath, too, but that was because he needed exercise. He didn't do anything all day but sit around and play the mandolin. Buster had bought him a new one in Denver, though it wasn't as pretty as the one the ridge log had crushed. By the time Buster got back with it, Caleb was already getting familiar with the guitar, which he had taken up after the loss of his mandolin. When he played, he sat on the porch and looked across the bald hill at the mountains, his back to his mother's grave.

"I think the exercise will do him good," Buster said.

"All right," Ab replied. "For a while. Just look after him."

"Yes, sir." Buster opened the door to the cabin. "I'll go get him up."

"Buster."

He paused in the doorway. Ab was looking across the flower garden at Ella's grave. The seeds she had planted had sprouted and brought forth blooms of red, yellow, orange, purple, and blue. The day's first sunlight was just striking them. Ab sat silent on a split-log bench, looking at the flowers for a long moment. "She told me you got her those seeds," he finally said.

"Yes, sir."

"I'd be obliged if you'd get some more."

It didn't take Buster long to get Caleb out of bed and moving. Caleb looked at Ab's boots when he left the cabin to go to work, but avoided looking him in the eyes. His father hadn't said much to him all winter long. He thought Ab was mad at him for getting his mother killed. Matthew had told him that it was his fault; if he hadn't been standing under the ridge log when it came thundering down from the roof, their mother would still be alive. Caleb just knew his father felt the same way.

After Buster and Caleb went to work, Ab cut some flowers and put them on Ella's grave and wondered how he would join her. He thought about little else. Matthew and Pete rode up and said they couldn't catch any cows. He told them just to watch the calves and make sure no wolves got close enough to kill any. Then he went back to contemplating suicide. Snake Woman brought a bucket of water to pour on the vegetable garden. He told her to get another bucket to pour on the wildflowers. Drowning was one way, he thought, but there was no water around that was deep enough. Not even a well to fall into. A funny thought struck him. His sons would be raised by a fugitive slave and a tongueless squaw. Ella would like nothing better. He continued to imagine his death until he noticed the Indians coming down through Monument Park from the north.

Matthew and Pete galloped their spotted horses to the lean-to shed built of leftover logs, to tell Buster about the Indians.

"Hey, Buffalo Head," Matthew said, "here come your Indians."

"My name is Buster Thompson, not Buffalo Head," he said sternly.

"It's Buffalo Head. I heard 'em call you that."

Matthew had taken a mean streak since his mother's death. Buster suspected the streak had been there all along, but that Ella had merely constrained it.

"Mama said to call him Mr. Thompson," Pete said.

"She's dead."

"Just call me Buster. That's fine with me. But I don't much like bein' called Buffalo Head."

"You gonna get you another squaw from those Indians?" Matthew asked.

"She's not Buster's," Peter said. "She just lives here."

"He bought her."

"You can't buy people," Pete said. "Anyway, what would he want her for?"

"To do what Cheyenne Dutch did to her."

"What did he do?" Caleb asked. He had been happily handing Buster his tools from the wooden crate.

"Nothin'!" Buster said. "Now, Matthew, if you don't stop talkin' about things like that, I'm gonna have to tell your papa!"

"I don't care." He kicked Pard in the ribs and loped to the cabin.

"What did he do to her?" Caleb asked again.

"Nothin'. Just scared her, that's all. She did worse to him with that ax. Now, come on, let's go wait for Long Fingers."

Pete walked the mare beside Buster and Caleb as they went back to the cabin.

"Let me ride Crazy with you," Caleb said.

Pete hesitated, looked toward the cabin, reined Crazy to a standstill to let Caleb get on. Then he changed his mind. "No, Papa will beat my tail end if I let you. Sometime when he's not around I'll let you ride old Soupy if Buster won't tell."

"I don't know nothin' about ridin' no horses," Buster said.

"We'll wait till Matthew's not here, either. He'll tell if he sees you ridin' with me."

"He's always here," Caleb complained. "Just let me ride with you past the wheat. Then I'll get off. Nobody's watchin'."

Pete looked at the cabin again. "All right. Hurry up while Papa's lookin' at Long Fingers. Come on. Buster, help him get on."

"I told you I don't know nothin' about it." Buster walked on alone.

Pete pulled Caleb up behind him. Caleb kicked Crazy in the flank several times on the way up, but she stood calmly. She in no way deserved the name Cheyenne Dutch had unknowingly christened her with.

The view from Crazy's back reminded Caleb of the way things looked from the bald hill across the creek. He could see over the roof of the lean-to shed. He could look down on the top of Buster's head. The edge of the wheat field was too near, his ride too short. "Make her run," he said.

"No, get down," Pete ordered.

"Just a little farther."

"Caleb, get down. Papa's gonna see. Get down!"

He swung his elbow around and knocked his brother off, but Caleb caught Pete's shirt to break his fall. He landed on his feet and fell back into the corner of the wheat field.

"Thanks a lot," Caleb said sarcastically.

Pete shrugged as he kicked the mare. "I told you to get down."

Buster laughed, pulled Caleb up, and went on with the boys to the cabin.

ELEVEN

LONG FINGERS RODE at the head of his band. Behind him trailed his warriors. Then came the women and children and old folks, and the horses hauling the lodge poles and all the camp equipage. Some boys were driving two Holcomb yearlings. The nomads dragged a cloud of dust behind them as they filed past the Holcomb cabin to their campground downstream.

Snake Woman went across the creek to gather wood when she saw them coming. She had no further use for Long Fingers. She had spent the winter interpreting her signs from the spirit world and was waiting for the proper time to act upon them. The Arapaho didn't fit into her interpretations.

The chief stopped at the cabin as his people passed by. "Holcomb," he said. "I find your cows again."

"Take them," Ab said. "The boys can't rope them anyhow."

Matthew blushed with shame.

The chief ordered his men to drive the cattle to camp. "Big lodge," he said, looking at the cabin. "You make it better than they make at Cherry Creek. It will last a long time and you will not cut any more trees. At Cherry Creek their lodges fall apart, so they cut more trees all the time. They cut trees and carry them into the holes where they dig up the gold. It is no good to camp there anymore."

"You can look inside if you want to," Buster suggested, proud of his workmanship.

Long Fingers swung his leg over his mount's withers and landed flat-footed on the ground. He followed Buster into the cabin, carefully inspecting the ridge log overhead. He had heard about Ella. After touring the cabin and pushing on the walls, he went back outside and studied the Nez Perce horses. "You trade with Cheyenne Dutch," he said.

"No," Ab explained, "he went crazy here last summer and left them. Tried to get the Snake Woman, but Buster stopped him."

Long Fingers scowled. "He does not go crazy. It is a trick with him."

"I guess Ella was right," Ab said vacantly. "We should have shot him when we had the chance."

"Yes, your wife was smart about people," Long Fingers said, looking at the grave with the cut flowers on it. "Her heart was good. Next time you see Cheyenne Dutch, you shoot him, like she tells you."

Buster sat down on the porch and motioned for the chief to join him. "Where's Kicking Dog?" he asked. "I didn't see him."

The chief threw a blanket from his shoulders to the cabin porch and sat on it. "Kicking Dog is not Arapaho anymore. The Arapaho are friends to the white people. Kicking Dog takes some young braves to join the Kiowas. They attack the wagons south on the Arkansas River."

"Why did he run off with them?" Buster asked.

"The Indian agents trick us, Buffalo Head. They bring a new treaty and tell us to sign. We all sign. All Arapaho and Cheyenne chiefs. They tell us we will get a new reservation on the Republican River with buffalo to hunt. They tell us they will teach us how to make a ranch. We do not read, but we believe them, so we sign the paper. Then they send us to Sand Creek and tell us this is what we sign for. No buffalo, no cattle, no trees. We cannot live there. Kicking Dog and some other young ones go to join the Kiowa—very mad."

Ab saw a sudden vision of Caleb dying in an Indian attack. "What if they come around here?" he asked.

"Kiowa stay south," Long Fingers said. "I will tell you if they come north."

"What if you don't know about it?"

"I am Arapaho. The Arapaho nation is the mother of all tribes. A mother knows where her children go. We have traders with all the tribes, so we know where they go. If Kicking Dog brings the Kiowa, I will send one of my boys to tell you. Buffalo Head knows the hand talk. I will send one of my boys to tell Gribble, too.''

"Who?" Ab said.

"You have a neighbor now." He pointed north. "Twenty-two miles. Gribble makes a ranch there on Plum Creek. He did not know about you, but I tell him. He will come here maybe so tomorrow to see your cows."

"Well, what do you know," Buster said. "This country might settle up after all."

Long Fingers put his fingers into a fold of his deerskin shirt and had his harmonica in his hand as a magician would produce a dove. "Yes," he said. "It will settle with white people. So I play the white music." He blew into the harp. "Let me hear this little one play this time, Buffalo Head."

Caleb saw the huge red man pointing at him. He took half a step behind Pete. How did the chief know he played anything? Matthew said the Indians had magic powers. Caleb thought it was true with Long Fingers.

"Boys, go get us our instruments," Buster said.

"Okay, Buffalo Head." Matthew hooted and led his brothers at a sprint to Buster's dugout.

They played "Camptown Races," of course. And Buster fiddled "Listen to the Mockingbird" as Caleb tried to keep up on the mandolin and Long Fingers droned on the harmonica. The chief's favorite verse came from "Old Dan Tucker":

> *Old Dan Tucker and I got drunk,*
> *He fell in the fire and kicked up a chunk,*
> *The charcoal got inside his shoe,*
> *Lord bless you, honey, how the ashes flew!*

Ab knew Ella would not have approved of such lyrics at her home. But it was time to let Buster make those decisions. He would have his say soon enough.

Horace Gribble showed up about dinnertime the next day. He rode a fine Kentucky stud and carried a Remington revolver under his belt. His face was tanned, smooth with the bloom of youth, and bulging with tobacco. He made himself right at home—took his saddle off and threw it over a porch rail, poured a bucket of drinking water over his head, spit tobacco juice on the steps. Matthew admired him immediately.

"I'm alone for now," he said in answer to Ab's inquiries. "But I got two brothers comin'. Hank and Bill. They're bringin' the cows from Kentucky.''

"How many?" Ab asked.

"Couple of hundred head. I thought I'd jiggle on down here and see how y'all do your ranchin' before they show up. How come you ain't got no fences up, yet?"

"We have a corral," Buster said, somewhat offended, "and a rail fence around the crops."

Gribble fanned himself with his hat and squinted at the black man. "How come you fence in your crops?"

"We ain't fencin' 'em in, we're fencin' the cows out."

"That's backwards," Gribble declared. "I aim to fence my cows in."

Buster waited for Ab to set the newcomer straight, but, as he seemed removed from the conversation, Buster had to do it himself. "They'll eat all the grass if you fence 'em in," Buster explained.

"I reckon that's what makes 'em into beef, ain't it? Grass grows back anyhow."

"It don't grow here like it does in Kentucky. Don't rain enough. You'll have to build twelve miles of fence to feed that many cows. What do you plan to fence with?"

"I'm gonna go up in them mountains and split me a mess of rails."

"The Indians won't like you choppin' that many trees," Buster warned.

"I don't give a damn what an Indian likes. They gave up all this land in that last treaty they signed. I reckon I'll chop what I want."

"It's better just to let your cows run loose," Ab said, turning his eyes from the flower garden, "and round them up every now and then. The wolves and mountain lions will get some, but they'll find plenty of grass, and you won't have to build any fences."

"How in the hell am I supposed to know what land is mine if I don't fence it?" Horace demanded.

"Where'd you settle?" Ab asked.

"Up on the head of Plum Creek."

"Well, then, all the grass from there to the divide with Monument Creek is yours. Everything on this side of the divide is ours. There's plenty of room for two herds."

Horace rolled a wad of chewing tobacco around in his mouth for a while. "What if I catch your cows on my side of the divide?"

"Just run them back on our side. We'll do the same for you. I guess the boys are going to have to learn to rope and brand so we can keep our cows separate. Buster's made us a brand. Looks like a bull's-eye."

Horace thought a moment, then grinned. "I didn't really want to split all them rails anyhow," he said. "Just brand 'em and leave 'em run loose? I reckon I can learn a new kind of cow raisin' if that's all there is to it."

Buster got up and said he was about to cook dinner, and invited Horace Gribble to stay and eat.

"I won't turn my back on cookin'," he said, reaching into the pocket of his saddlebag. "While you cook, Holcomb here can read the paper. I brought a copy of the *Rocky Mountain News* with me. I figured you'd want to read about the battle."

Ab and Buster looked at each other. "What battle?" Ab said.

"You haven't heard?"

"Heard what?"

"My God, y'all have been out of the way too long. Haven't you heard about the battle of Fort Sumter?"

They shook their heads. "Where's that?" Buster asked.

"Where?" Horace started laughing. "South Carolina. The Confederates attacked it. The war's on, boys!"

"Between the states?"

"Yep. North again' South."

"If there's a war on," Ab said, sitting forward on his bench, "why aren't you back there fighting in it?"

Gribble let his chaw fall onto the dirt beside the porch. "Fight, hell." he said. "I ain't mad at nobody. What do you think I come away out here for?"

Ab's course became clear to him over the next several months. Speculation held that the war would spread west from the states and infest the territories. The Federals would probably blockade the entire Dixie Coast to cut off the sale of Confederate cotton. The secessionists would counter by trying to capture New Mexico Territory and California so they could ship their cotton out through the Pacific ports. The Texans would be coming up the Rio Grande to take Santa Fe. They might even come as far as Denver to claim the gold fields. There were already a good many southern men in Denver.

By May there was talk of raising a volunteer regiment to fight the Confederates. By July thousands of Texans were poised on the southern border of New Mexico, ready to strike. By August, the First Regiment of Colorado Volunteers was drilling near Denver. Colorado Territory had been formed from the western reaches of what previously had been the Kansas Territory.

It was all working out pretty well for Ab. He wanted to beat Caleb to joining Ella without disgracing the Holcomb name, and war seemed the perfect opportunity. He thought of the glory he would bring on his boys when he threw himself into the forefront of some battle. Buster would sing songs about the way he died leading a charge against a whole battalion of mounted Texans. That was the best part: fighting the Texans! They would name a fort after him.

In September he decided to ride to Denver and join the First. He got up early one morning, saddled Pard, and called Buster and the boys out after breakfast.

"I'm going to fight the Texans," he said, strapping his old Walker Colt around his waist.

Matthew beamed with pride. Pete wrinkled his nose and squinted. Caleb silently contemplated all the horses he would ride while his father was away.

"What about the boys?" Buster said.

"You take care of them. I want Matthew and Pete to look after the cows. See that they learn how to rope. If Caleb ever gets his strength back, you can put him to farming with you. Farming ought to be good enough for him. It was good enough for me."

Caleb's hopes sank. He wanted to ride the horses and chase the cows, not drag in the dust wake of a plow stock.

"You boys go on to work now. I want to talk to Buster."

"I get to ride Crazy!" Matthew said as he and Pete ran for the corral.

"She's mine! You have to ride Soupy!"

"I'm biggest," Matthew argued.

Caleb stood in front of the cabin, not having any work to run to.

"Caleb," Buster said, "you can carry my spade and pick on down to the creek. I'm gonna dig some more on the irrigation ditch today."

When Caleb had walked beyond earshot, Ab looked at Ella's grave. "Keep some flowers cut for her, Buster." He cinched the saddle tight around the spotted gelding's barrel. "And keep that flower garden growing." He put his foot in the stirrup and climbed up to the saddle. "She told me just after that log crushed her that I had better not let Caleb die. I promised her I'd look after him. I'm trusting you to keep my word for me."

Buster said nothing. He never understood all the concern over Caleb.

"One more thing," Ab said, reaching into his pocket. "This is Caleb's pocketknife. Give it to him when you judge he's old enough to use it safely."

Buster took the knife and nodded. Ab turned the Nez Perce gelding up Monument Creek for Denver, looking one last time over the grave of his wife. He expected never to return.

Buster shook his head in consternation and trudged down to the creek. He found Caleb digging ineffectually, standing on the spade.

"What did he want to tell you?" the boy asked.

"Here." He put the pocketknife in the little hand. "He told me to give you this."

TWELVE

S NAKE WOMAN HATED everything about living the way of white people. She hated the wagon she slept in, its hollow sound and cold iron fittings. She hated the buckets she carried water in and the wounded ground she emptied them on. She hated the oldest boy, who leered at her from the back of the spotted mare.

Most of all, she hated Buffalo Head. Actually, she despised all grown men, but none did she loathe more than Buffalo Head—the one who had brought her to live with the whites; the one who had told her to sleep in the wagon; the one who had made her teach him the hand language.

Yet, in the signs from the spirit world, the gods had told her how she must use Buffalo Head, and she found the thought repulsive. She tried to interpret the signs differently, but they fit together in just one way. The shooting star had shown her the way to the Comanche. Buffalo Head had counted coup on Cheyenne Dutch. The oxen had killed the crazy white woman. And now, a dream of two warriors, one white and one black, both wearing the dress of the Comanche, had wakened her under the canopy of the wagon she hated so much. It could mean only one thing.

It took her several days to steel herself to the idea. She hid in the cottonwoods across the creek and watched Buffalo Head dig the ditch to his truck patch. She watched as he taught the boy how to play the instruments. She watched as he crawled on the ground among the wildflowers, picking up seeds.

What made the spirits so cruel that they would require such a sacrifice of her to earn her own tribe?

A week after Ab left for Denver, Buster had Caleb working full days and enjoying his work, except when Matthew rode by to flaunt his saddle and the spotted mare he had taken from Pete.

"How come your mother never let you work?" Buster asked one evening when he and Caleb were carrying their tools to the shed from the creek bottom. "You can pull your weight good as anybody."

Talk of his mother mustered a nameless guilt in Caleb. "She said I was too sickly."

"Sickly? With what?"

"Consumption, asthma, flux."

Buster laughed. "Who told her you had all that?"

"Some doctors."

Buster hung his shovel blade on a catch made of a forked pine branch. "I think them doctors wanted her to keep comin' and spendin' her money. She was a fine lady. Smart, too. But I think them doctors tricked her. Ain't nothin' wrong with you."

"Papa thinks there is."

"Well, when he gets back from the war and sees how straight and strong you are, he's gonna change his mind for sure. Now, let's play a few songs before I fix supper."

"Okay," Caleb said, his eyes twinkling. He forced the vision of the falling ridge log aside and contemplated music.

"You can play the fiddle today."

"I don't know how to play the fiddle." He balled his little fist up and punched Buster in the stomach playfully. He had become more familiar with Buster than he ever had been with his father, or even Matthew for that matter.

"You mean I forgot to tell you? You play it just like a mandolin, except you use a bow, and you hold it under your chin. Shoot, you can halfway play it already and you just don't know it."

"But it doesn't have any frets!"

"You don't need frets. Your fingers know where they're goin' now without no frets."

"Really?"

The moon was so full and the sky so clear that night that under them Buster could read the headlines of the *Rocky Mountain News*. He sat in the moonlight for a while and played the banjo, but he was tired, and soon crawled into the dugout to find his pallet. He was looking at the dark wedge of a mountain against the pale sky, thinking about building a flume so he could irrigate more than just bottom land, when a figure appeared outside.

Buster tensed and propped himself up on his elbows. Snake Woman stepped into the dugout and became a silhouette against the open doorway. He saw both hands. She wasn't carrying a knife, thank God. Or an ax. Did she have a weapon concealed?

As if to answer his question, Snake Woman pulled her dress from her shoulders and let it fall to the floor. Buster was almost unconscious with disbelief. He said nothing. She wouldn't have understood whatever he might have said anyway. He made no attempt to communicate with the sign language either. What was the point, in the dark? He just scooted across his blankets and backed away from her until he was against the cool dirt wall. She knelt beside him. He tried to get up, but she held him down by the shoulders. She was strong. Her hands moved down his body to the button of his pants.

Buster didn't know much about it, but it wasn't supposed to happen this way. Master Hugh had sold most of the slave girls his age by the time he had had his first few experiences with them. None of them had ever come to him naked in the dark before.

But Snake Woman's carnal experiences far surpassed those of Buffalo Head. Her Comanche captors had often traded her services to bull whackers and mule skinners at Bent's Fort for whiskey and tobacco.

She mounted Buster as she would a horse, wedging her knee between him and the wall, pinning him against the floor with her hands on his chest. She felt hot as the coal in Old Dan Tucker's shoe on top of him, and his urges took their courses in spite of his protestations. It didn't take her long to get what she had come for, and then she rose in silence, slipped on her dress, and vanished without once looking back.

The next morning Buster was still wondering why. Was it delayed gratitude for kicking Cheyenne Dutch over the creek bank? Was it his good looks? Did it really happen? Yep, it happened. The thought of that tongueless savage forcing herself on him tormented him all morning as he went about his chores. He supposed he should have fought harder and wondered why he hadn't. Would she do it again? No, that was too terrible to consider. Or too much to hope for. He watched her all day. She did not so much as glance his way.

That night Buster had almost fallen asleep when she appeared again. He resolved to run her off. It wasn't proper for a woman to sneak in on a man like that. But this time she simply lay down beside him. She didn't even touch him, yet he could feel the warmth of her body. He made the mistake of putting his hand on her, to push her away, he told himself. But his arms rebelled and pulled her under him instead.

Five nights in a row she appeared and vanished. Buster was getting nervous. What would Mister Ab think? Or Miss Ella? If Matthew saw anything he would never let Buster forget it. Caleb would ask a lot of questions. What if she got pregnant? There would be no doubt of the baby's lineage. He was pretty sure that he was the only black man between Denver and Santa Fe. He was going to have to drive her off. It was simple as that.

The sixth night he sat outside the dugout instead of lying down inside. He intended to meet her standing up in the moonlight where she could see his hand signs. He stayed awake as long as he could, then fell asleep leaning against the creek bank. He woke shivering in the morning. Snake Woman had failed to appear.

With the next moon, a snow fell in the high country and dusted the mountains white like the rumps of Nez Perce horses. The nights came earlier, until they began catching Buster and Caleb playing songs on the brink of the creek bank.

Buster was teaching Caleb a ballad one night when he was almost moved to tears to hear the boy's little voice singing it. Caleb sang in a child's voice, but in a voice that never wavered or missed a note. "Ben Bolt" almost always made tears well up in Buster's eyes anyway. But now, when he thought of Miss Ella, and heard her son singing, it was all he could do to keep them from cascading down his cheeks.

> *In the old churchyard in the valley, Ben Bolt,*
> *In a corner obscure and alone,*
> *They have fitted a slab of granite so gray,*
> *And sweet Alice lies under the stone.*

"That's what they call waltz time," Buster said, clearing his throat and rubbing a sleeve across his face. "One-two-three, one-two-three. You better get on to the house now. Time for bed. Bar the door and pull the strap in."

"Aw, can't we just play one more?"

"Oh, all right. Somethin' lively, though."

"How about two?"

Buster held Caleb to a single rendition of "Down in Alabam' " and then sent him to the cabin. He waited until he heard the door close and then climbed off the creek bank and into the dugout.

At dawn, Buster shuffled up from the cutbank and collected what eggs the hens had left in the converted milk wagon. He knocked on the cabin door until Pete, draped in a red wool blanket like an Indian, let him in. Matthew poked his head out of Ab's bedroom, which he had taken over since his father's departure.

"Caleb up?" Buster asked.

"He's in there with Matthew," Pete said.

"No, he ain't," Matthew replied.

"Well, he's not in here with me."

Buster looked in both bedrooms for himself. Caleb was in neither. He went back outside and ran to the covered wagon. Snake Woman was gone. He ran to the shed built next to the corral. Soupy and the spotted mare were gone.

"Where is he?" Pete asked when Buster returned to the cabin.

"Be quiet. Let me think." He had waited to hear the door close the night before. He knew Caleb had made it inside. No one could have entered to take him away. It had to be Snake Woman. She had waited inside, grabbed Caleb, and stolen him.

"Matthew," Buster said. "Get Mister Ab's rifle."

"Yes, sir!" Matthew said, with rare respect.

"Pete, get you and your brother something to eat for dinner."

"What for?" Pete asked.

"You gotta walk to Gribble's place and stay there."

"Walk?"

"Yes, boy, walk! The horses are gone! Snake Woman took Caleb off to the Indians!"

Buster started Matthew and Pete up Monument Creek, then ran to his dugout for his things. He shoved his horse pistol under his belt and looped his powder flask and shot pouch over one shoulder. He rolled a blanket, wedged it under his arm. He filled a canteen and stowed some smoked venison in a piece of cloth. With a long stick he went looking for the cattle, cut two slow cows from the herd, and on foot drove them down the creek.

He made Colorado City by noon. The ugly little town had started out as headquarters for some prospectors hoping to find gold on Pikes Peak. The prospects had failed to materialize, but the town had hung on as a trading post and way station for occasional supply trains coming up from New Mexico on the Fort Bridger Road. It was peopled by hardened souls, but Buster hoped the worst of them had gone off to fight in the war.

He traded the two cows for a swayback sorrel horse, threw his blanket over the washboard ribs, and rode down the Fountain River. A grove of cottonwoods became his campground that night. He reached the Arkansas two hours into the next morning and turned east for Sand Creek, hoping to find Long Fingers there on his worthless reservation. The chief would know how to find Snake Woman.

THIRTEEN

BEFORE, CALEB HAD thought he would never tire of riding horses. Now he was so saddle sore that he never wanted to hear another hoofbeat as long as he lived. Snake Woman had grabbed him in the cabin that first night, lifted his feet from the floor, and clamped her hand over his mouth. She had carried him outside and dragged him over the plains until they came to the horses, saddled and waiting. He hollered for Buster once when he got on Soupy, but Snake Woman pulled him off, threw him on the ground, and threatened to hit him.

He lost track of the days. Snake Woman made him sleep on the ground with only his saddle blanket for cover. He drank mere swallows of water and ate only dried meat. He didn't know which way they were going, but the mountains got farther away until they vanished altogether. He missed his instruments and worried that his fingertips would soften if he didn't have them to play.

They crossed a river, Snake Woman leading Soupy behind the spotted mare. The thought of being swept away in the cold water made Caleb hang on to the saddle horn with an eagle's grip. He was glad his mother wasn't there, for the sight of him crossing the river probably would have killed her. Then he remembered she was dead anyway.

They crossed miles of grass and sand hills strewn with buffalo chips and buffalo skulls. Occasionally Snake Woman would get off the spotted mare and point the noses of several skulls in the direction she and Caleb were traveling.

Once, in the distance against a hill, Caleb saw a huge blanket of darkness rolling over the grass. Then the blanket began to break up, and he knew it was a herd of buffalo, more animals than he had ever seen at one time.

Three times they met Indians. Hunting parties with lances, bows, and rifles. Snake Woman made her signs at them and they pointed, giving her direction. One of the warriors frightened Caleb by poking him with the end of a bow, never smiling, never scowling, just staring with cold eyes and jabbing him hard with the bow.

They crossed another river, then another, and another, until Caleb thought the whole world had turned to grass, rivers, and canyons. Then, just as he began to get used to riding day after day, he saw a range of mountains looming against the horizon. He hoped they were going home.

But the next day he realized the mountains were not his own. They were not as huge or beautiful, but at least they were more interesting than the monotonous, rolling plains. They rose like tepees from the prairie. Buffalo and antelope skimmed broad carpets of tall grass stretching between them. He sensed Snake Woman's excitement and knew his trip was almost over. He wondered how soon Buster would follow. He did not doubt the black man would come for him.

Snake Woman found Laughing Wolf's camp at the place she remembered—a hundred lodges lining the creek that wound among the mountains. She asked to see Laughing Wolf, and the chief agreed to speak to her, mainly out of curiosity.

He was a young chief, arrogant in deportment, with tinkling bits of metal tied all over his buckskins and moccasins. When Snake Woman entered the lodge, he demanded to know why she had returned. Had she offended Long Fingers by running away after Laughing Wolf had traded her for six hides and two blankets? And where had the white boy come from?

Snake Woman told of the signs she had received from the spirit world. She had brought the Comanche two great warriors. The white boy came from fighting stock. His father was away right now with the blue coats, fighting the Texans. The child she carried inside her now was the son of

Buffalo Head, a strong, black brave who drowned his captors and counted coup on the crazy white man called Cheyenne Dutch who thought he was a horse god.

All of this bewildered Laughing Wolf. He gave Snake Woman and Caleb some buffalo meat to gnaw on while he conferred with the peace chief in his lodge. Caleb tore at the meat like a hungry dog, barely mindful of the Indian children who ran past him, shooting at him with imaginary bows.

When the sun had moved well west in the sky, Laughing Wolf returned to talk to Snake Woman. "If you give birth to a black son," he explained, "it will prove you are telling the truth about the spirits and the signs, and you may marry one of my warriors who will adopt the white boy and the black baby. If your child is not black, or if it is a girl, I will kill it and cook you and the white boy over the fire, or else the evil spirits will destroy us."

Snake Woman started singing her most joyous song—one given to her by a Comanche warrior who had once owned her. She left Caleb behind, and walked through the entire camp so all the members of the band would know how happy she was to be back among the proud Comanche.

Caleb listened to the weird wailings of the tongueless Indian woman fade. He felt alone and scared, but he was still hungry. He spotted a hunk of buffalo meat broiling over a fire. Two women and several children were waiting for the meat to cook. Caleb looked all around. He wasn't being guarded. It seemed he could move around the camp if he wished. He took a few cautious steps toward the cooking meat. No one objected. He walked closer. A boy about his size looked up as Caleb neared the fire. Before he knew what had happened, the little savage had leapt and knocked him down. He thought he would be scalped or tortured in one of the horrible ways Matthew had told him about.

A scowling woman picked him up and pointed to the sun, then to his shadow on the ground, and explained with gestures that it was not allowed to let one's shadow fall on meat that was cooking over the fire.

The white boy nodded and sat to one side of the fire, fearful that another Indian was going to knock him down again if he broke some other strange rule. He wanted Buster to come and take him home. He wanted his mother to fret over him like she used to.

"In the old churchyard in the valley, Ben Bolt." He caught himself singing, under his breath, and glanced at the Indian woman who had taught him the rule about the shadow. Though she didn't look at him, she smiled, and he figured singing was within the rules. "In a corner obscure and alone . . ."

It made him feel better. The Indian boy was staring at him with his mouth open.

"They have fitted a slab of granite so gray, and sweet Alice lies under the stone. . . ."

FOURTEEN

Buster stopped at Bent's Fort, a large thick-walled trading post with adobe parapets and cactus growing atop the walls to discourage intruders. An assistant to the Indian agent there told him he would find Long Fingers camped up Sand Creek.

The Cheyenne-Arapaho Reservation impressed Buster as the most inhospitable land he had seen in the West. There was grass for the horses to eat but little else to help the Indians survive. He saw no game except for a few jackrabbits. Some large cottonwoods grew at a place called Big Timbers at the confluence of the Arkansas and Sand Creek, but otherwise the reservation seemed destitute of wood. Long Fingers' camp wasn't hard to find. A wisp of buffalo-chip smoke in the air gave it away.

Most of the chief's warriors were out scouring the plains for herds, but none large enough to warrant a hunting party had been located, and little meat hung in camp.

"We will go to the mountains soon," he told Buffalo Head. "We should have more meat, but we must go before it is too cold."

"If you help me find the boy, you can come get a cow any time your people get hungry," Buster promised.

Long Fingers sent every available warrior in camp to the surrounding tribes to ask about Snake Woman. As the buffalo hunters straggled in, he sent them, too, back to the plains and mountains to search for Caleb and his kidnapper.

"I hope she does not go with the boy to the Utes," he said. "They will never trade him back to us."

As the days passed, Buster grew more anxious about Caleb's fate. The warriors were able to learn nothing from the nearest tribes. The Cheyenne, the Kiowas, the Apache, the Pawnee—none of them had seen or heard from Snake Woman. Buster knew the boy could be in Mexico by now. The poverty of the Indian camp depressed him, and each day brought him closer to disgrace and failure as Caleb's protector.

Yet, he knew Caleb was alive. Snake Woman had taken him alive for a reason—to barter her way into some tribal society. The horses and the life she cradled in her womb would serve the same purpose. Buster had figured it all out and wondered why he hadn't seen it clearly when the diabolical squaw came five nights in a row to his dugout. If he couldn't find Caleb, the boy was going to grow up a savage.

Finally, two full weeks after Buster arrived at Long Fingers' camp, a warrior came in from the southeast with positive news.

"Buffalo Head," shouted the chief, running across the camp to rouse Buster from his tepee. He leapt in through the oval entrance hole. "Snake Woman takes the boy to live with Comanche. One of my boys saw them there."

"Where?" Buster asked.

"Seven days southeast. A place the whites call Wichita Mountains."

"Will they trade for him? What do they want?"

"They will not trade anything. Not even twenty horses. They say Snake Woman is big medicine for their people. And the boy is, too."

Buster rubbed the wrinkles in his forehead. "But . . . What am I gonna do? How can I get him back?"

"I know a way. Maybe so it works. Maybe so it kills you."

Buster and Long Fingers spent the rest of the day planning. The next morning Buffalo Head left the reservation on the best horse in camp and rode to the southeast with an Arapaho guide. Six days later a norther was whipping sleet down his collar, and the Wichita Mountains were in view. His guide left him and rode back to Colorado. He would have to face the Comanche nation alone.

Buster saw the Wichita Mountains as islands of tree-speckled rock towering above the rolling plains. He looked for buzzards to lead him to the main camp. When a sentinel rode out to challenge him, he clasped his hands together in the sign of friendship. The warrior was so astounded that he thought Chief Laughing Wolf might want to see the visitor alive.

When Buster rode into camp, Caleb was playing with a bull roarer: a notched slab of wood tied to a long string of rawhide and whirled overhead to make a sound like the moan of a bull. Though it had taken a few days to get used to, Indian life was agreeing with him. He stayed in a tepee with Snake Woman, and though no one took much interest in him, he had been given the bull roarer and some other toys and had the run of the camp. He had never known the exhilarating pleasure of playing outside in a freezing drizzle. When he saw Buster's familiar face, he let the bull roarer fall to the ground.

"Hey, Buster!" he shouted, waving with joy. In return, he received the sternest look he had ever seen cross the black man's face, and he knew he should keep his mouth shut. It seemed Buster thought the whole thing was his fault. Then Snake Woman came running from somewhere in the camp, and Buster gave her the same look, so at least Caleb knew he was not the only one in trouble.

Buster lost no time letting Laughing Wolf know he could communicate pretty well in signs. He told the chief he had grown tired of living among the whites who did not treat him as an equal, so he had followed Snake Woman to live as a Comanche. He could hunt and fight. He was strong and a good shot.

The bits of metal on Laughing Wolf's garments tinkled as he signed. He pointed to the horse pistol under Buster's belt. He wanted to know if that was what Buffalo Head hunted and fought with.

No, Buster replied. The pistol was good only for killing camp dogs. But if the chief would produce a rifle, he would show the entire camp how well he could shoot. He would hit a rock as big as a man's head at three hundred paces. And then he would pick up the rock and throw it farther than any warrior in camp could throw it to prove his strength.

Children ran to all the tepees along the creek, shouting the news of the boasting black visitor. The women and the few warriors who were not out hunting began moving toward Laughing Wolf's lodge. Buster pulled Caleb behind a nearby tepee.

"Are you all right, boy?"

"Yeah, Buster. What are you doin' here? Are you gonna take me home?"

"No. Not yet, anyhow. We gotta make 'em think we want to live like Indians. Then maybe in few weeks we can sneak away. You're just gonna have to stand it that long. Understand?"

"Sure," Caleb said. "I don't mind."

Laughing Wolf appeared with an old Hawken rifle. Its wooden stock was decorated with brass tacks hammered in to form swirls and circles. It was rather worn, but looked as if it would shoot straight. The chief also had some bullets, a supply of percussion caps, and a powder flask. The flask was made of lead so it could be melted down into bullets when empty of powder.

Buster was happy to have killed so much game over the past year. His marksmanship was pretty good. "Come on, Caleb," he said. "Watch me show these Comanche how to shoot."

He carried the rifle out of the creek bottom and up to the plains. He found a rock about the size of a man's head lying on a stretch of ground with just a slight pitch to it. He paced three hundred steps from the rock. A gang of warriors dressed in buckskin shirts and leggings tagged along behind him, followed by the blanketed women and the half-dressed children.

Laughing Wolf hadn't given Buster a ramrod or a patch, so he put the bullet in his mouth before he poured in the powder. The saliva would make the lead stick to the powder and keep it packed if Buster shot quick enough. He dropped the bullet in and tapped the butt on the ground three times to tamp the load.

He sat in the grass and pulled his hat low over his brow to keep the sleet out of his eyes. He wanted to go ahead and shoot before his heart got to pounding so hard that it threw his aim off. His elbows rested atop his knees and his right eye looked along the top of the barrel. The only sound he could hear was the pitting of sleet on his brim. The Indians were silent behind him. He could only hope the rifle in his hands shot like Ab's piece, with the bead low in the rear iron.

The gun went off almost without Buster's realizing he had pulled the trigger. The recoil blurred his vision, but he saw a spray of dirt kick up at the very base of his target. Above the ringing in his ears, he could hear the Indians grumbling.

Buster turned around grinning. He poked himself in the Adam's apple with his finger to suggest that it was a very good place to shoot a man. If the rock had been a head, it might well have been ripped from its body.

Laughing Wolf nodded and declared the shot adequate, but the test of strength was still ahead. The chief introduced the strongest warrior he had on hand—a short, keg-trunked, bowlegged brave called Moon Bull who would try to throw the rock farther than Buffalo Head. Buster didn't see much muscle to the little man, but he didn't intend to take any chances. He didn't know what the Indians would do to him if he lost the contest.

Moon Bull and Buffalo Head strutted to the rifle target, followed by the entire camp. Buster saw that his bullet had actually clipped the bottom of the target, and he complimented Laughing Wolf on his excellent vision, to have seen from three hundred paces that the shot was good.

Buster had previously noted the slight pitch to the ground where the target lay. After he picked it up, he faced in the uphill direction, as if getting ready to throw. Then he looked at Moon Bull, tossed the miniature boulder to him, and dared him to throw first. Moon Bull could hardly refuse. He stepped up to the point Buster had established, facing the almost unnoticeable uphill grade, and prepared to throw. He cradled the rock on his palms at chest level, squatted deep, and threw his whole body into the effort. The rock arched admirably through the air and rolled to a standstill about twenty-five paces away.

Buster felt magnanimous enough to applaud, causing the squaws to giggle.

"Come on, Buster," Caleb shouted, "you can do better than that!"

The nearest squaw switched him with a stick she was carrying.

"Ouch!" he said.

Using his boot to scuff the ground, Buster drew a line where Moon Bull had thrown from. But he purposely made the line a few degrees off the perpendicular. It was not quite square with the flight of Moon Bull's throw. He scuffed a good ten feet across the ground.

When he went to pick up the rock, Buffalo Head turned back around to face the line he had drawn with his boot. Now he had two advantages. The slight downhill pitch would give his effort a better roll, and he would throw to the side of the boot mark that angled slightly toward him.

All the conniving turned out to be unnecessary. Buster let a mighty shout loose when he threw; braves, squaws, children, and one camp dog had to make way for the rock as it rolled among them, beating Moon Bull's throw by a good ten paces. Laughing Wolf applauded, jingling his sleeve tinklers in the sleet.

"Are we Indians now?" Caleb asked on the way back to the lodges.

"We're worse than just Indians," Buffalo Head replied. "We're Comanche."

FIFTEEN

AB HUNKERED AGAINST the wall of an adobe corral, but the wind still found him. It whipped dirt, smoke, and snowflakes in his face and around the piece of meat he held over his meager fire. He couldn't tell what cut of beef it was. The quartermaster had doled it out in random chunks, still warm from the fresh carcass.

He pulled his blanket back over his knees as he rotated the meat over the struggling flames. To get the beef cooked, he had to gnaw the roasted part away from the outside edges, then expose a raw layer to the coals. The fire was so spent by the time he got to the last bit of meat around the skewer that he had to lay it directly on the dying embers to sear it. He ate it—dirt, ashes, and all—and was glad to have it.

The blanket helped ease his shivering, but Ab knew Pard needed it more than he did. Many mules and cavalry mounts had died crossing the Raton Mountains into New Mexico, but the Nez Perce gelding hadn't missed a footfall. Ab got up and draped the cover over his horse, leaving only his old wool coat to turn back the wind. He intended to keep Pard sound enough for the charge when the time came for him to die.

The Texans were coming. Word was that they had fought past Fort Craig, overrun Albuquerque, and captured Santa Fe, three thousand strong. General Canby had ordered the First Regiment of Colorado Volunteers south to Fort Union. They would meet the bloody Texans somewhere between there and Santa Fe.

The irony of the matter in Ab's view was that most of the Colorado Volunteers were no better than the Texans they would have to fight. At Fort Wise the Firsters had broken down the sutler's door with a rock and diminished a month's provisions in a matter of days. They had raided every Mexican rancho they passed on the way south and helped themselves to horses, beeves, and daughters. B Company and K Company had almost gone to war with each other after K's drunken sergeant shot B's lieutenant.

Ab belonged to F, the only mounted company in the regiment. His fellow horse soldiers had elected him third duty sergeant by virtue of his service under Captain Samuel Walker in the Mexican war. They might have made him a lieutenant if he would drink or cuss.

The nine hundred volunteers—busted prospectors almost to a man—huddled under their blankets at a place called Maxwell's Ranch. The wagons had been abandoned crossing the mountains into New Mexico as the mules died pulling them. There were no tents and few provisions. Each man carried only a blanket or two and a Springfield rifle. Some of the cavalry troops had revolvers. There was nothing to oil the guns with but bacon grease, and a scarcity of even that.

Ab crouched against his wall and cursed the whole campaign as he looked across the wisps of smoke curling from the willow-brush campfires. How he longed to catch sight of a Texan. He fondled the cylinder of his old Walker Colt as if it were warm.

Staring into the snow-speckled darkness, he thought he saw a phantom horseman approaching camp—a spotted horse carrying the rider among the scrubby piñon pines. The image vanished behind flurries, materialized again, closer, more vivid—real. The rider wore a beaver top hat held on with a scarf that ran through slits in the brim, covering his ears, and tying under his iron-gray beard. An eagle feather waved violently in the wind. He entered camp not forty yards from Ab's place against the adobe corral.

"Pickets!" the rider shouted above the wind. "Where's your goddamn pickets?"

A private rose from a campfire. "It's Cheyenne Dutch, boys! What the hell are you . . ."

"Where's your captain?" Dutch barked.

"I'll run find him."

A crowd of volunteers gathered as the mountain man lowered himself from the spotted horse and limped to the nearest fire. Ab got up with his Colt and approached.

"Whole damn company of them Texan lancers might have rode in here and speared the lot of you," Dutch was saying. "Best put your pickets out. War's on."

"Lancers?" someone said.

The private came back with his officer.

"Captain Bonesteel, D Company," he said, extending his mitten.

Dutch refused to shake. "Where's your goddamn pickets, captain?"

"Pickets? Why, Major Chivington didn't give orders for any pickets."

"Gave orders for no pickets, did he?"

"Well, no. No orders on the subject at all."

"No orders for no pickets means pickets, captain. See to it."

The captain turned to his sergeant. "Sergeant!" he said.

"Corporal!" the sergeant said.

The corporal turned to his men: "Riley! Thomas! Flynn! And, you, whatever your name is!" He sent them grumbling into the dark woods.

"Who's got command?" Dutch asked.

"Colonel Slough."

"Find him."

The order went down the ranks until a private went to find the colonel.

"What's this all about, Dutch?" Captain Bonesteel asked. "Where have you come from?"

Moist eyes glistened through squints above Dutch's bearded cheeks. "Shit from the devil's bunghole."

"Beg your pardon?"

"Val Verde. General Canby sent me to make sure your regiment gets to Fort Union. The Texans are in Santa Fe."

"What was that about lancers?" a nervous private asked.

"Not a moon ago," Dutch said. "I was scout with the Second Colorados at Val Verde. Foot Volunteers, they called us. Left flank, the rebels charged us with two companies of mounted lancers. A hundred Texans! Blades a foot long, four fingers wide, shafts nine feet. Red guidons to sop your blood. Son of a bitch, the rebel yells! Rode right at us, never stopped. We fired, half of 'em fell. The rest came on. One got me through the leg, but I still kick!"

The volunteers looked at Dutch's thigh, swollen so that it pulled his buckskins tight. The bloody slit from the lance blade showed where the weapon had entered.

"We turned 'em, but here come the infantry behind 'em. They got shotguns, pistols, muskets. We fell back, gave 'em ground. Directly, they charged our cannon and took 'em. We had to fall back to Fort Craig, whipped. They come all the way on up to Santa Fe after that. You miners better get your sand up. Them Texans fight. Best fightin' men I ever seen. Backbone clean down to their assholes. . . ."

Ab pushed his way through a clot of D Company privates. "Shut up!" he said. "I won't listen to any man brag on a Texan. They brag enough on their own."

"Who's that?" Dutch said, squinting through snowfall.

"I should have shot you at Monument Creek like Ella said. I wish I had done it instead of listening to you brag on a blasted Texan now."

"Holcomb! You still riled over that squaw? Hell, I left the horses to settle up. Bone like to never healed where she chopped me. Couldn't be helped anyhow." He narrowed his crazy eyes. "One of them spells come on me."

"You're sane as the next man. You're a liar about those spells."

The D Company men backed away, expecting Dutch to reach for his knife in the fringed saddle scabbard.

A private ran recklessly between Dutch and Holcomb. "I found Colonel Slough, Dutch. This way."

The scout took his bridle reins in hand to follow the private. "I reckon you miners know Holcomb's wife died. He don't mean all he says." He limped stiffly away.

"God strike me down if I don't!" Ab yelled.

The next day, the First marched thirty miles south, out of the mountains, down to Fort Union on the Santa Fe Trail. At dusk Ab rode Pard over a low roll in the plains and saw the fort sprawled across the prairie floor. It looked like a colossal scar welt on the land, an eight-pointed star burned there by an impossible branding iron. The embankments were of dirt, surrounded by a dry moat. Under the dirt parapets were quarters. Ab saw adobe-brick chimneys jutting above the earthworks. The Star Fort, as it was called, had been newly and hastily erected to deal with the Confederate threat.

When F Company rode ahead to see about accommodations for the regiment, Ab looked into a few of the dirt-covered hovels. They struck him as larger versions of the dugout Ella had referred to as the hole—frames of stripped pine logs covered with dirt dug from the surrounding moat. They were supposed to be bombproof, but he could tell a few well-placed artillery rounds would reduce them to instant graves. Even now they were dank and suffocating.

"How many troops will these barracks hold?" he asked one of the foot volunteers who had seen action at Val Verde.

"About five hundred, they say, but there's already four hundred of us here and it crowds me as it is. How many boys in your outfit?"

"About nine hundred," Ab said, looking down on the man from his saddle.

"Damn. You boys'll have to camp outside."

Ab shrugged. "Suits me better than that hole you're sleeping in."

Ab languished in camp for ten days, thinking of the Texas volunteers he had known in the war with Mexico. Some of the same Texans were probably looting Santa Fe now, as he had seen them plunder Mexico City years before. It was easy to remember. He had his fellow Volunteers around to remind him of the unsavory behavior that had disgusted him in Mexico.

Some F Company privates had broken into the sutler's store and carried away cheese, crackers, canned goods, and six boxes of champagne. Many men stayed drunk day and night, fighting among themselves, feasting on canned fruit and oysters. A whorehouse in a Mexican village five miles from the fort enjoyed a lively trade. Cheyenne Dutch, however, was conspicuously absent from all debauches, as he was out scouting enemy movements.

Finally, Colonel Slough issued marching orders for the thirteen hundred troops under his command at Fort Union. Ab figured the colonel had finally realized that his regiment would destroy itself with drink if it didn't see some action.

A cheer circulated among the companies as they proceeded toward the occupied city of Santa Fe, eighty miles away. They marched south and west on the Santa Fe Trail, setting up a new camp at Bernal Springs, halfway to the captured capital.

It was on the morning of March 25, 1862, that four hundred troops, including Ab's company, received orders to cook two day's rations and be ready to march at a moment's notice. Word filtered down to Sergeant Holcomb that the force would make an assault on Santa Fe. Ab became almost cheerful and virtually sang orders to his corporals. Major Chivington was going to lead the attack—John M. Chivington, the gun-wielding frontier Methodist preacher, six feet four in his stocking feet, servant of the Lord, and hater of all godless Texans and Indians.

The order to mount came, and Ab rode anxiously near the head of Chivington's column. There he traveled all day among the low, pine-studded foothills flanking the old trade route. That night the Coloradoans reached a place called Kozlowski's Ranch, and camped near the Pecos River. Rumor of six hundred nearby Texans reached Ab through a private of A Company. At dawn a Lieutenant Nelson brought in four captured Confederate pickets, the first enemy troops Ab had seen during the entire campaign.

It was a sunny New Mexico morning, brisk and beautiful. Ab's company rode second in the column, in fine position for a charge if the Texans materialized on the road ahead, as expected. About five miles west of Kozlowski's Ranch, the column passed Pigeon's Ranch, a stage stop on the Santa Fe Trail consisting of several log buildings and pole corrals. The cattle had been driven into the mountains to keep them out of reach of the Texans.

Just past Pigeon's Ranch, the troops reached Glorietta Pass, on the divide between the Pecos and the Rio Grande. From there the road led downhill, through Apache Canyon, which wound seven miles toward Santa Fe, hemmed in by bluffs and mountains on both sides. If the Texans and the Colorado Volunteers met in Apache Canyon, a bloody clash would be unavoidable. Flanking maneuvers would be virtually out of the question. The canyon would funnel both forces together head-on.

Glorietta Pass struck Ab as a natural gate, a narrow opening between a rocky bluff to the north and a steep hill to the south. As he neared it, he saw Cheyenne Dutch galloping through the pass, toward the column of volunteers. Dutch had a few minutes' conversation with Major Chivington, then rode shouting along the ranks.

"Feel your sand, you damned Pikes Peakers! You damned tunnelin' prospectors! Texans ahead in the canyon! Give 'em hell!"

A rattle of weaponry commenced. The Volunteers slung canteens, coats, blankets, and knapsacks all along the Santa Fe Trail in preparation for the fight. Ab checked the loads in his Colt and slipped it into his holster. It was the best way, he reminded himself. He would die with Caleb safe in Monument Park, and his soul could proceed to heaven to join Ella. Honor would follow the Holcomb name into posterity.

"Sergeant Holcomb," a trembling voice said.

Ab turned to look at the pale face of a young private.

"Are you scared?" the private asked.

"Yes. But so are they. I don't care if they are Texans, they still scare."

"Can I ride alongside you?" the private asked.

"No. You follow your corporal. Do what he does. Don't ride with me. I don't feel lucky today."

SIXTEEN

THE ORDER CAME to advance double quick into the mouth of Apache Canyon. Captain Cook, commander of Ab's company, ordered his men to ride four abreast into the haunts of the enemy. Cheyenne Dutch galloped his Nez Perce horse forward to join F Company and took his place right beside Ab, who had no objection to taking Dutch with him into the thickest Rebel volley.

"They'll git your gold if you don't stop 'em, you damned 'fifty-niners!" the old scout yelled at the troops. Then he spoke to Ab: "The spots bulletproof 'em, Holcomb. I've a spotted rump myself, but they'll see nary of it!"

Ab hated to admit it, but Dutch's maniacal jabber stirred him for the battle.

The Pikes Peakers filed through the gate of Glorietta Pass and marched toward a certain clash with the enemy. As they turned a crook in the canyon, they suddenly found themselves looking down the muzzles of a pair of Texas howitzers, just two hundred yards away. Shells sang over the heads of the Volunteers and clipped tree limbs on the bluff behind them. The infantry broke to either side of the canyon, cavalry mounts bolted in every direction.

"Sergeant," Captain Cook said to Ab, "hold your men in place."

"Yes, sir!" Ab shouted as the shells sang lower overhead. "Close your ranks! Wait for orders!"

The rest of the companies scattered right and left, but F Company held its position in front of the howitzers, Sergeant Holcomb and Cheyenne Dutch flanking the men on spotted horses, shouting at them to take order by fours.

Chivington's infantry scrambled up the hills on either side of the Texas cannoneers and fired down on them. When the fire grew hot enough, the Texans hitched their caissons and retreated down the canyon. F Company followed a mile or more at a canter but did not charge. The Texans pulled the howitzers around a rocky point jutting into the canyon from the left and disappeared.

"Main Texas body's around that point," Dutch shouted to the captain.

Captain Cook halted his company behind the point and looked over his shoulder. "Wait till the major brings the infantry up," he said to his lieutenants, "then we'll charge the bastards."

The infantry came at a trot down the canyon and again began climbing the bluffs on either side, preparing to fire down on the main body of Texans around the bend to the left. The horse soldiers of F Company sat on their mounts and trembled in anticipation of the charge. Major Chivington galloped brazenly ahead, around the rocky point, to get a look at the enemy's position. The bullets of Rebel sharpshooters fell all around him until he regained the protection of F Company's point. He carried a pistol in each hand, a third under his belt.

"Captain," he bellowed, towering above the troops on his huge gray. "Your cavalry will charge those howitzers down the canyon floor. The infantry will give you cover from the bluffs on the flanks. Wait for my signal."

"Yes, sir," Cook said.

The major charged back across to set his foot soldiers.

"Dutch, what's the ground like around the point?" Cook asked.

Dutch gouged his spotted horse with his spurs and drew rein beside the cavalry leader. "Bad for a charge, captain. Rocky. That damned arroyo is deep up there, angles across the canyon floor. There's a bridge over it. Only way across. The son of a bitches'll be usin' the arroyo for cover."

A hush fell across the canyon, then Chivington's voice echoed as if preaching hellfire from the pulpit. Captain Cook led his men around the point, into a deluge of Texas musket fire.

Bullets came from both canyon walls and from the arroyo angling across the floor of the canyon. Ab heard the captain curse and looked ahead to see the Texas artillery already retreating over the bridge that crossed the arroyo, three hundred yards ahead.

Cook led F Company directly toward the bridge. The Pikes Peak infantry was shooting down at the Texans now, absorbing some of the enemy fire that had before rained down only on the cavalry unit.

A bullet hit Captain Cook in the thigh but failed to unseat him. A private tumbled from his saddle beside Ab. Another hundred yards down the canyon, Cook's horse stumbled on a rock and fell with him. Pard made a marvelous leap to avoid the fallen captain, lurching Ab almost out of the saddle, dashing on near the head of the charge. Lieutenant Nelson kept the charge alive and fired his revolver at the surrounding bluffs as he rode.

All eyes of F Company were on the bridge spanning the arroyo, the only way to cross in pursuit of the Texas howitzers. But as Ab galloped ever nearer the head of the charge, he saw the bridge timbers falling. The Confederates were pulling it down! Gunfire came thick from the arroyo on either side of the crumbling span.

The lieutenant balked and slowed his charge when he saw the bridge surface buckling, but Ab sped past him. He could see only the enemy now. His fellow volunteers rode behind him. The lieutenant would curse him for robbing the glory—a sergeant—but what was ire to a dead man?

The arroyo revealed itself as a narrow fissure in the canyon floor, only fifteen feet across but deep enough to protect the Texas riflemen. Ab slapped his stirrups against Pard's flanks, but he wasn't sure the gelding would have the wind for the test ahead. Then someone gained his left side.

He glimpsed the beaver hat just as a musket shot tore through the high crown of it, narrowly missing Dutch's head. The scout's spotted horse challenged Pard for the head of the column, and the charge became a race. The hoofbeats of the two bulletproof Nez Perce horses drummed in unison, and their nostrils vied for the wind. Pard lengthened his stride and held the lead by a nose.

The sunken bridge rushed to meet them, sailed under as they leapt. Eight hooves cut silently through the black smoke over the arroyo. Ab saw the long barrels sweeping over the Texans' heads as they drew their beads on the leaders of the Colorado charge. A blast went off below him and tore his right foot out of the stirrup. Pard lit on the far rim of the arroyo without so much as a stumble, but Ab left the saddle and slid across the rocks in the middle of Apache Canyon.

He sat up and saw his own company leaping the arroyo at him. The gamest mounts cleared the cut; one fell short and broke its neck on the brink, pitching its rider into the rocks. Others leaped into the arroyo on the Texans, their riders broadcasting pistol bullets like seed corn. The Texans fled the splintered bridge, retreating to either side of the canyon, where they found the Pikes Peak infantry coming down on them, squalling like Indians, rallied by the charge of F Company. The riders who made the jump across the arroyo continued to chase the Texas cannons toward Santa Fe.

Ab pulled his Colt from the holster but couldn't see a Texan to shoot at. He let a few rounds go into the pale blue New Mexican sky. He wanted them to think he had died fighting when they found his body and checked his weapon. Bullets sang near him.

He looked at his right leg and found a fountain of blood spurting from his knee and pouring across the gravel of the canyon floor. The bullet had struck him in the calf, traveled all the way up and through the bone, and come out under his knee. He lay back on the Santa Fe Trail and looked at the canyon walls rising on either side of him. The pain was mounting, but he would soon bleed to death. It was not such a bad way to die. He hoped no one would shoot him as he lay on the floor of the pass. The leg wound would do, if he just let it bleed.

The canyon had begun to darken as if filling up with smoke when he heard the hoofbeats. F Company was returning to the battle, having failed to capture the fleeing Texas howitzers. Ab opened his eyes and saw Cheyenne Dutch's grotesque face looking at him, bullets humming all around. He used his scarf to bind the bleeding knee, then took off his top hat and pointed at a large bullet hole surrounded by three smaller punctures.

"Look, Holcomb. The bastards are usin' the old U.S. musket loads. One ounce ball and three buckshot. They go like bees when they fly—a-hummin'. Sting, too."

"Go away," Ab said, trying to raise his revolver.

Dutch took the Colt from him. "Don't fret," he replied, calmly replacing his hat in the midst of musket fire. "Palousey's a spotted horse god and bulletproof."

The pain racked Ab's wounded leg when Dutch threw him over Pard's saddle. The scout found a path through the arroyo and led the bleeding sergeant back toward Pigeon's Ranch, ignoring the lead that pitted the ground in his path.

Ab dreamed of thunder in the darkness. Thunder so powerful that it shook the ground under him. He heard voices, too. Shouting, screaming, none saying anything discernible. It sounded to him like the storm that floated Noah's ark, and he thought the world was flooding again. Then there was the quiet contrast of moaning, grumbling, coughing. Something vague and violent happened to him then. It sapped his strength and left him in a dark and empty place.

When he woke, the frightened private from Glorietta Pass was beside him in a cabin.

"Where is this?" Ab asked. The leg still hurt.

"Pigeon's Ranch, sergeant. Hey, Doc! The sergeant is wakin' up."

Ab saw the regimental surgeon looking down at him, haggard, emotionless. The tired eyes checked the bandages around the shattered knee. "How do you feel?" he asked.

"I'm alive," Ab said. "The Texans . . ."

"They're whipped," the private said. "The day after you and Dutch jumped that bridge we fought 'em for six hours straight. They backed us up and took our hospital. You were their prisoner for two days. But while we were fightin' here, Major Chivington snuck around behind 'em through the mountains and blew their whole supply train up. They're licked and runnin' for Texas now.''

"You owe your life to Cheyenne Dutch and the Texas surgeons," the doctor said.

Ab remembered Dutch's interference. But the Texans? The Texas surgeons had saved his life? "What do you mean, the Texans?"

"They took that leg off," the doctor said. "They could have left it to rot and kill you, but they sawed it off. I don't guess you'd remember, but they said it took three privates and a one-armed lieutenant to hold you still. You almost lost all the blood you had, but you'll mend.''

Ab kicked at his right leg with his left one and felt nothing. He lifted his head and saw his leg ending in a bulb of bloody bandages at the knee. He gasped, almost exhausted by the simple task of lifting his head. "Sons of bitches," he muttered.

The surgeon put his hand on Ab's shoulder. "Try to remember, sergeant. They did it to save your life. Private, get him to take some soup."

Ab couldn't swallow much of the broth. He felt sick with anger and failure. As he slurped occasional spoonfuls of soup, the private told him about the battle of Glorietta Pass.

"All the infantry seen you and Dutch jump the bridge," he said. "It got 'em fightin' somethin' fierce, sergeant. The next day Dutch kept yellin', 'Remember Holcomb's Charge!' That's what kept us scrappin'. That's what beat the Texans."

Ab stayed at Pigeon's Ranch for almost three weeks, acquiring a deeper hatred for the Texans who had sawed off his leg and foiled his suicide. When he learned to walk on one leg with crutches, the surgeon made him get out of bed twice a day for exercise around the ranch.

After the Union Army chased the Texans south of Albuquerque, the Pigeon Ranch vaqueros began bringing cattle down from the mountains and back to home range. Only Mexican cowboys worked the ranch, and they knew their trade. The wild longhorn cattle required all their skills as riders and ropers.

One evening, as Ab was sulking under the low porch roof of the cabin that had served as the Union hospital, a pair of vaqueros brought fifty head down from the hills. Two others had a branding iron heating over a fire. The mounted vaqueros began cutting the unbranded yearlings out of the herd of fifty so the branders could apply the hot irons to their hips. The beauty of the work diverted Ab from his hatred of Texans, his agony over his lost limb, his grief over Ella, and his dread over Caleb.

The vaqueros used rawhide lariats sixty feet or more in length. The wide loops settled over horns and around necks like living snares. One vaquero could make a loop crawl under the flanks of a steer and stand on edge for a mere instant, so the animal would step in as if trying on a pair of bloomers. Then the roper would wrap the rawhide around his pommel and, with his partner's loop pulling on the opposite end of the same steer, stretch the animal out so the branders could tail him down for the burning and earmarking.

The heel roper swirled the dust with his swinging loop and whistled through his teeth at the dumb beeves. He might just as well have been netting butterflies.

For the first time in months, Ab thought of his ranch in Monument Park. He saw Matthew and Pete swinging ropes like the vaqueros. He had failed at trying to kill himself. He was not going to try again. The consequences were too horrible. He had to find a reason to live: a regimen of some kind to occupy his mind through the daily tortures. With a few good ropers, he could set his mind to building a ranch for Pete and Matthew to inherit. Caleb, of course, would be a farmer. Ella would never have approved of him riding wild cow ponies.

When the fifty cattle were sorted, penned, branded, and marked, the Mexican heel roper rode past Ab on the way to the water gourd.

"Is that your horse with the spots?" the vaquero asked.

Ab nodded.

He dipped the gourd into a cask of well water and held it before his mouth. "*Guapo, señor.* I would like to have some horses like that."

"To rope cows?" Ab asked.

"Yes. And to chase the *Tejanos* like the Pikes Peakers. I spit on those goddamn *Tejanos.*" He demonstrated.

The one-legged sergeant smiled for the first time in over a year.

SEVENTEEN

AFTER FOUR MONTHS, Buster had even Snake Woman convinced that he and Caleb had turned Indian. In fact, Caleb was becoming pretty sure of it himself. Buster had given him a horse and told him to get used to riding it. He had traded Moon Bull his old single-shot pistol for the horse, a long-tailed, silver grulla mustang with blue eyes and a Texas brand on the shoulder. Caleb knew no better-looking animal among the hundreds of horses grazing around camp.

Snake Woman was beginning to show her pregnancy, and it made Buster feel full of regret. She was going to have his child, and he would probably never see it. By the time the papoose came, he would either be back in Monument Park with Caleb, or dead. It was his own fault. He should have resisted her in the dugout.

He could feel the members of Laughing Wolf's band watching him constantly. Not because they mistrusted him anymore, but because he was supposed to be big medicine. He tried his best to fulfill the image. He hunted hard and brought down more than his share of game with the long rifle Laughing Wolf let him use. But he knew he had to do more. The Comanche expected something great of the strange black warrior who had figured in Snake Woman's signs from the spirit world.

Buster's chance came when Moon Bull began organizing a hunt. The brave had some trouble finding warriors to follow him at first. He had lost some status since Buffalo Head had beaten him so soundly in the rock-throwing contest. But when Buffalo Head said he would go with Moon Bull on the hunt, the ranks suddenly swelled with willing participants.

The day before Moon Bull's party was to attack the buffalo, Buster and Caleb rode to the top of one of the Wichita Mountains to survey the country for herds. Caleb rode his blue-eyed mustang, and Buster took Crazy.

"Are those buffalo?" Caleb asked in astonishment.

"Yep," Buster said. "Look like muddy rivers, don't they?"

Veins of bison streamed between the hills in every direction. Around them the barely visible wolf packs loitered—gray, white, and brown specks against the dried grass. Between the clots of buffalo, antelope grazed or moved like low-flying birds over the plains. The wind was cold whipping over the mountain peak, but the odd Comanche pair had buffalo robes. Cotton-white clouds raced across the winter sky, their shadows undulating over every rise and fall in the topography below.

"Is this what it looks like from the top of Pikes Peak?" Caleb asked.

"Oh, Lord, no, boy. Pikes Peak must be twice as high as this mountain. Maybe we'll climb it when we get home and you'll see."

"Home?"

"After I go huntin' with Moon Bull, I'm gonna let Crazy rest a few days, then we're gonna sneak away. You let Blue Eyes rest up, too. We'll have to ride fast. They might come after us."

Caleb pulled the buffalo robe around his shoulders and looked back across the plains at the Indian camp. He could just see the tops of some of the tepees in the creek bottom. "I thought we might stay here," he said. When he thought of home, he remembered the ridge log and his mother's grave and the guilt he felt in his father's presence.

"We ain't Indians, Caleb. If we stay here too long, they're gonna expect us to go kill some white folks. That's what these Indians do when they ain't huntin'. Besides, don't you miss your mandolin playin'?"

"Yeah," Caleb admitted.

"Well, that's where we belong, playin' music in Monument Park. Workin' our farm."

"I'd rather chase the cows like Matthew and Pete," Caleb said.

"You can do that, too. Your papa will let you when he sees how good you've learned to ride. Just let Blue Eyes rest, and don't let nobody know we're leavin'."

Caleb nodded. He didn't mind leaving so much if he could take Blue Eyes with him to chase the cattle with when he got home.

The next morning Buster found himself riding with Moon Bull and about thirty other warriors toward the largest herd of buffalo in the area. He had watched several hunts from the mountain and knew what to do. He had borrowed a lance from Moon Bull, choosing to use the lance instead of a rifle because hunters who dared to gallop within spearing distance of a buffalo earned the highest respect. It was the most dangerous way.

Moon Bull led his hunting party up a dry creek bed, out of sight and downwind of the herd. Sliding from his hunting pony, he climbed the bank and peeked over the rim, the yellow feather in his scalp lock rising only as high as the top blades of grass.

After observing the movements of the herd, he crawled silently back into the creek bed and issued his orders in sign. The hunters would spread out and surround the herd, closing around the buffalo on the upwind side last. Then they would circle the animals the way the whirlwinds blew, force them into a mill, and close in on them to kill as many as they could.

Buster nudged Crazy along the creek bed about two hundred yards, emerged on the plains, and galloped around the right side of the herd. He pressed himself low against the mare's back to keep from alarming the buffalo. As the horsemen closed the surround at the upwind side of the herd, the animals caught scent of the hunters and stampeded downwind.

The circling began, the riders moving counterclockwise around the animals. A few bison broke through the surround, but the downwind hunters managed to turn the major portion of the stampede with the circling motion. The best of all possible circumstances resulted for Moon Bull. The herd began to mill, and the hunters closed in ever tighter, pressing the terrified bison closer together, as if a whirlpool were drawing them down into the prairie.

Buster held his spear overhead and yelped like a Comanche. "You better hope the Lord forgives you," he said to himself, suddenly feeling like a pagan. He looped his reins around his left forearm and grasped the spear shaft with both hands. Crazy was running well around the herd, but Buster wondered how she would react when asked to press against the very flanks of a huge, bellowing beast.

The humped brutes were running with remarkable speed when a young bull veered from the whirlwind of bison in front of Crazy. To Buster's surprise, she almost shot out from under him in pursuit. He didn't twitch the reins or give his mount the slightest nudge with his knees to guide her. She closed quickly on the right of the errant bull and carried Buster within lancing distance.

The painted spear shaft was longer than Buster was tall. The point of sharpened rasp was eight inches and honed to shave. When he drove it between the bull's ribs, he felt Crazy leaning with him on the thrust and pulling away as he withdrew the bloody blade. She was taking Buster buffalo hunting.

The stuck bull stumbled once and turned to destroy the spotted mare. A hideous bellow rattled from his punctured lungs, his eyes rolled back in his huge head, and his twin horns hooked violently at the mare. Buster barely held his seat as Crazy sprang to safety, leaping almost like a cat avoiding a snakebite. He looked behind and saw the wounded bull drop and roll through the grass.

The slaughter mounted at every point around the milling herd. Dying beasts peeled away from the vortex of hooves and pitched headfirst into the sod, shuddering in their death pangs. Buster squinted at the herd through the dust and guided Crazy nearer with a nudge of his knee. He couldn't hear himself shout above the thunder of hooves. He drove the shaft into another body, angled away, returned for a third victim, circled, felt the warmth of the herd, smelled their cuds. He speared a fourth, a bull with a head that looked as big as a bass fiddle.

Then, with one sudden change, the entire herd broke from the swirl as if possessed of a single brain. Moon Bull was caught in the stampede for a couple of minutes as it rushed through the dry creek bed, but he managed to work his way to the edge without falling. The surviving bison fanned out and trampled a swath of earth a quarter mile wide as they left the exhausted buffalo horses behind. The squaws were already arriving on the grounds, leading old jaded horses that would pack the meat back to camp. They raced one another, laughing as they pretended to count coup on the carcasses.

Moon Bull rode like a king back to his band of hunters, whipping his heaving horse with a buffalo tail he had cut from one of his kills. He asked how many Buffalo Head had killed. The black warrior held up four fingers.

"There are four seasons in the great circle of time," Moon Bull said to his followers. "There are four points of the sky and the earth. There are four legs under our horses. Now Buffalo Head kills four buffalo. It means Big Medicine."

It was the last and most successful hunt of the winter. There was plenty of work ahead for the squaws, pounding the meat into pemmican, tanning the hides, making the robes. But for the braves there was nothing to do but lounge. Buster figured he would give Crazy about a week to recuperate fully from the punishment of the hunt before he made his escape on her.

However, three days after the hunt, a warrior rode into camp with news that started every tepee buzzing with excitement. The main winter camp of the Tonkawa had been located a hundred miles east.

The Tonkawa ate human flesh and fought on the side of the Texans. They had served the Texas Rangers as scouts on many a campaign against the Comanche. But now their treachery would turn against them. The Texans were too busy fighting the blue coats to worry about protecting the Tonkawa, who had moved to Indian Territory, weak in number and poorly supplied with weapons. The other tribes with Confederate sympathies had fled to Kansas. The Tonkawa had foolishly remained behind. They would make easy targets for Comanche arrows. There would be a glorious slaughter.

Laughing Wolf called a council in which he related that just the night before he had dreamed of wolves eating the corpses of a hundred Tonkawa. Every warrior in camp agreed to follow the chief in a raid on the Tonkawa village, including Buffalo Head.

The warriors painted their faces red and tied feathers in their horses' tails. They repaired their weapons as they talked about the coming battle. When the party was in fighting order, it assembled and paraded through the village, over a hundred warriors strong. Most of them wore buffalo horns on their heads and carried shields circled by eagle feathers.

Caleb could tell they had murder in mind simply by looking at them. It made him painfully aware of his own whiteness. His hair was getting long, but it was still brown. He had lost his shoes and woven clothing, now wearing soft tanned skins and mocassins, but he was still white under them. He didn't know who the Comanche were going to kill, but he knew they killed white people. Matthew always talked about Indians killing white people. Caleb had seen scalps of white people in camp. Some of them had long hair, as his mother had. He didn't want to be an Indian anymore.

Buster attended the war dance that night and listened to the old men stand and speak. He didn't understand the language but figured out that they were telling of their old triumphs in battle to urge the young warriors on. At last Laughing Wolf reminded the braves of their purpose: Annihilate the Tonkawa, steal their horses, burn their lodges, enslave their women and children. The party would leave before sunrise. There would be no sleep. The men were too excited.

When Buster left the ceremony, he went to his tepee to get his weapons—a knife, a lance, and the rifle Laughing Wolf let him use. He shook Caleb. The boy had tired of the war dance and had gone to sleep in the middle of the night.

"Wake up, Caleb," Buster said. "It's time to leave. We got to sneak away."

The news woke Caleb in an instant. "Are we goin' home?" It was strange seeing Buster's face painted red, the horned headdress covering his curly hair.

"All the way to Monument Creek. We got to ride fast, and we can't get caught, so be quiet and do what I tell you. Put those moccasins on."

Caleb slipped the deerskin shoes on and wrapped a soft robe around his shoulders. He followed Buster to the flap of the tepee and waited as the black man looked out.

"Remember that little waterfall I showed you the other day?"

"The one with the icicles?"

"Yeah. You think you can find your way there in the dark?"

"I know I can."

"Sneak over there after I leave. Don't let nobody see you. Especially not Snake Woman. I'll bring our horses and meet you there when the war party rides."

Caleb felt Buster's hand squeeze him on the shoulder and he took courage from it. After Buster left, he waited a minute, then peeked out of his tepee. The warriors were still milling about, moving between their horses and their lodges, lingering a few moments with their women. Caleb scampered into the shadow of his lodge and looked up and down the creek. No one was watching him. He ran a few yards up the creek bank and hid behind a boulder, pausing again to look for pursuers. The rocks rattled under his feet as he scrambled up the bank. At the brink he flung himself to the ground and looked back at the camp.

Amid the throng of Indians, Snake Woman suddenly materialized in the firelight, moving like a witch toward Caleb's tepee. He shrank into the grass and pulled the robe over his white face. She stuck her head into the lodge, withdrew it, and glanced around the Indian camp. Her eyes darted everywhere, first to the light, then to the shadows. Caleb's heart thumped hard against the ground. Snake Woman was looking up the creek bank, tracking his footsteps with her eyes. Her gaze climbed higher and higher until Caleb felt it lock on him. He shivered, afraid to even flinch, frozen like a mouse charmed by the stare of a rattlesnake.

Then Buster was there. He broke the spell that Snake Woman's eyes held on Caleb. The moment she turned to look at Buffalo Head, the boy slithered backward through the grass, out of sight, over the brink of the creek bank. He found his footing and ran for the waterfall, almost tearful with fear.

Buffalo Head told Snake Woman he would go to kill some Tonkawas now.

She took his hand and put it on her stomach. His son was hoping his father would be courageous in battle, she said in sign language.

Buffalo Head nodded and indicated by signing that he had to get his horse.

Where was the white boy?

He wasn't in the tepee?

No.

He wanted to watch the war party go.

Yes, she indicated, and turned into her lodge.

Buster took his weapons out of camp and walked to the far edge of the horse herd. He had Crazy saddled there. In a ravine about a hundred yards away, three other horses waited. Blue Eyes was among them, wearing the saddle Snake Woman had stolen from Holcomb Ranch. The two other horses were poor mounts he didn't think any brave would miss tonight.

He hoped no one would see Crazy's white flanks in the quarter moon as he rode her away from the herd. He took the reins of Blue Eyes' bridle and led the string of three horses up the ravine to the waterfall.

Caleb rose from the grass when he saw his horse. "Can we go now?" he whispered.

"Wait till we hear the war party ridin' out," Buster said. He got down to tighten the cinch around Blue Eyes and to tie the two spare horses behind his own mount. "They won't hear us if we leave the same time they do."

Caleb knew the Indians made animal sounds. Every wolf that howled or owl that hooted made him shudder with fear of an ambush. But finally the thunder of war horses rode east and it was time to leave.

"Come on," Buster said, lifting Caleb to the saddle.

They charged out of the ravine and rode along the flanks of a hill, Buster trailing the two stolen mounts behind Crazy. Caleb looked over his shoulder and saw the Comanche riding like ghosts in the moonlight.

"Don't look back," Buster said, flinging the buffalo headdress aside. "Ride fast and get behind these hills." It was a good thing Indians didn't go to war the way white men did, he thought. If they had called a muster roll they would have discovered the missing soldier and sent a detail out to fetch him. He knew his absence would hardly stand out among a hundred surging warriors in the dark, even if he was the only black Comanche in the territory.

They struck the Washita River after an hour of hard riding. Buster switched the saddles to the two stolen horses. He didn't tell Caleb, but he intended to ride them until they dropped, then let Crazy and Blue Eyes carry them into Colorado at a more reasonable pace. The Comanche would not pursue for a couple of days. Their horses and men would be worn from fighting the Tonkawas. With luck they would make Long Fingers' camp before the Comanche caught up with them.

It was dawn when they left the Washita, eating on the run from a parfleche bag full of pemmican. At dusk Buster was squinting at the Antelope Hills on the South Canadian when Caleb's horse gave out and fell. The boy jumped out of the way before the dying beast could roll over him. He had found an instinct for riding over the winter. Buster pressed Crazy and Blue Eyes back into action and crossed the river. He hoped an early spring rain might make it swell and cut the Comanche pursuit behind him.

After resting two hours, he woke Caleb and told him to get on Blue Eyes.

"You're gettin' mean as she was," he said, pushing himself laboriously from the ground.

"Who?"

"Snake Woman. She never let me sleep either." He noticed that Buster had washed the red war paint from his face.

"It ain't meanness. I just got to get you out of the Indian Territory before Laughing Wolf comes after us. Now, let's go. You always wanted to ride, so let's ride."

As he went to mount Blue Eyes, Caleb stumbled over an old buffalo skull and stopped to turn its nose in the direction he considered Monument Creek to be.

"What'd you do that for?" Buster asked.

"It'll make the buffalo follow us home so we can shoot 'em."

"Don't believe that heathen garbage. You ain't a Indian no more."

EIGHTEEN

W HEN BUSTER AND Caleb finally got home, they found Horace Gribble living in the Holcomb cabin. He and Pete had taken care of the place all winter and brought most of the stock through. Only five head had vanished, and Horace didn't know it, but Long Fingers had taken three of them in exchange for helping Buster find Caleb. The winter wheat was sprouting thick, owing to good snows and early rains. The plains were turning green, and the creek was flowing with snowmelt. Buster was tired, but there was little time to rest.

"Thanks for lookin' after the place," he said to Horace.

Horace shrugged. "Reckon y'all'd do the same for us."

Matthew had been living at the Gribble Ranch with the other two Gribble brothers, Hank and Bill, who had come from Kentucky with a herd of cattle. He had picked up some of their more highly refined characteristics such as chewing tobacco and cussing. He didn't really want to go back to Monument Creek, but Horace told him his little brother had been rescued from the Indians by "that colored boy" and made him go home.

Buster was planting cottonwood saplings around the cabin one day. He had dug them up along Monument Creek and was setting them in perfect orchard rows, envisioning the day when they would stand high enough to shade the yard. He was gently tamping the soil around the roots of one when he saw two riders coming.

He stood and whistled, and the boys rode in from the plains—Matthew on Crazy, Pete and Caleb riding double on Blue Eyes. They got to the cabin about the time their father arrived with a stranger and a herd of six horses. The stranger drove the horses into the corral as Ab rode to the cabin, pausing briefly at Ella's grave. It gave him a sudden pang of dread to see his youngest son straddling the wild-looking blue-eyed mustang.

"Caleb, get off that horse," he said.

Caleb slid down and looked at the ground. Matthew spit.

"What's that in your mouth?" Ab asked.

"Chewin' tobacco."

"Well, spit it out."

Matthew raked the chaw out of his cheek.

"Hello, Papa," Pete said.

"Hello." He nodded at Buster. "What are you doing?"

"Puttin' in some cottonwood trees for shade."

"You're looking pretty far ahead if you can see shade under those sprouts. Are we going to have any wildflowers this spring?"

"Yes, sir. They're up, they just ain't bloomin' yet."

"Good."

When he stepped down from the saddle, the peg leg landed right in front of Caleb. No one had seen it on the off side of the horse, but now it stood like a skeleton's leg in front of the boy. It was skinny as the neck of Buster's banjo. As if to show it off, Ab opened his coat and held the tails back, placing his hands on his hips.

His knee fit into a rawhide-lined socket at the top of the artificial limb, and an ungainly network of straps held it to what was left of his leg and attached it to his belt. He had to cinch the belt tight around his waist to get it to hold the leg on. The waistband of his trousers slanted to the right, as if the peg leg were trying to pull his pants down.

Ab had been a suspender man before Apache Canyon. Caleb had never even seen him wear a belt before, let alone strap a banjo neck to one and use it for a leg.

"Damn, where'd your leg go, Papa?" Matthew said with a look of astonishment on his face.

"The Texans shot it off at . . . What did you say?"

"I meant to say 'dang,' but . . . How'd it happen?"

"I'll tell you about it later. And if I hear you swear again, I'll take this leg off and use it on your rear end."

"Yes, sir."

Ab's companion rode toward the cabin, having closed the corral gate on the six horses. So unusual was his appearance that he drew even Caleb's attention away from the peg leg.

"This is Javier Maldonado," Ab said. "He's from New Mexico."

Javier swept the sombrero from his head and bowed from the saddle as if his own feet stood under him instead of his mount's. Rings of hair were plastered with sweat against his head. His skin was brown and olive and red, depending on the light it caught, and his beard, though shaven that morning, appeared drawn in charcoal. He had a crease in the middle of his chin that he seemed to flaunt. *"Buenos días,"* he said.

"Does he speak English?" Matthew asked.

Javier's eyes glinted with mirth. "Yes, I know English very well. I even know the cuss words! I learned in Texas."

"Probably learned the cuss words first," Ab grumbled. One of the Holcomb dogs was sniffing the wooden leg. He rapped it once across the nose.

Javier dismounted and became another person. Out of the saddle he looked rather comical. He was bowlegged, potbellied, and swaybacked. His legs, which had seemed proportionate in the stirrups, were too short for the rest of him on the ground.

"Glad to meet you," Buster said, shaking Javier's hand. He saw the thick coil of rawhide next to the saddle horn. "I guess you're gonna teach the boys how to rope."

"That's right," Ab said. "I brought him back to show Matthew and Pete how to work those cows. There's more to it than just roping."

"What about me?" Caleb asked.

Ab looked down at him and put his hand on the boy's head. "You, too. Whenever you get a little bigger. And learn to ride better."

"He's done a bit of ridin'," Buster said.

"He rode all the way to the Indian Territory," Pete added. "He stole Blue Eyes from some Comanche." He patted the grullo pony on the neck.

Ab gave Pete a stern look for telling such fabrications.

"He rides good," Buster said.

Caleb nodded.

"I didn't say he couldn't ride. I said he had to learn to ride better. Maybe you can practice a little on Sundays for fun, as long as you don't run too fast. But you better wait till you get big as Pete to start. Buster needs you to help him farming anyway. Right, Buster? Now, where did that blue-eyed horse really come from? And where's the Snake Woman?"

Caleb's adventure among the Comanche was never more than a story to Ab. Ab knew Buster didn't lie, but the man must have miscalculated the distances or something. He had probably gotten lost out on the treeless plains and ridden four times farther than he really had to to retrieve the boy. They had probably spent a few days with a band of starving Cheyenne on Squirrel Creek or something. But a whole winter among Comanche? A boy as frail as Caleb couldn't have survived it. He had to admit that Caleb wasn't sickly anymore. But he was still frail. Always would be. Ella had pointed it out many times, and she knew about things like that. Riding and roping were not the kinds of work for Caleb.

One evening after Javier had been at the ranch a while, Buster and Caleb broke out their instruments and began to run through their repertoire. After listening to a few songs, Javier asked if he might play the guitar. He raked the strings over the sound hole with his fingernails, drew a deep breath, and filled the entire prairie with a voice so clear and loud and perfectly pitched that it sounded like a human pipe organ. Caleb reeled back in the face of it. The singer bit off the words, rolled them in his *r*'s, and sent fits of falsetto to chase them through the air. It didn't matter that he sang in Spanish. By the end of the song, the boys were laughing and hooting with him like a den of coyotes.

Buster smiled politely, but he didn't enjoy being outdone. Before Javier could launch another Mexican song, he reached for his fiddle and tore into "Rosin the Bow" as if his grubstake depended on it. Javier countered with "Rancho Grande," and a contest of music began.

Caleb had never known Buster to play anything on the guitar the way Javier played it. The New Mexican made it sound like a completely new instrument. As Javier's fingers pounced on the strings, Caleb tried to watch them to figure out what they were doing. But they moved so fast, it seemed as if there were not enough of them on Javier's right hand to make all the noise that came out of the sound hole. And in fact, when "Rancho Grande" ended, Caleb saw that the little finger of Javier's right hand was missing!

"What happened to your finger?" he asked, as if he thought the vaquero had sawed it off with the furious strumming.

Javier held his hand in front of his face, turned it to show both sides, and grinned at it. "El Bronco got it," he said.

"A horse bit it off?" Matthew asked.

"No. El Bronco, the Wild One. It was the name of a big black creature in Mexico. A bull that lived on the ranch of my uncle in Zacatecas."

"A bull bit it off?" Pete asked.

"No, no!" Javier handed the guitar to Caleb and pulled himself forward on his bench. "Listen, and I will tell you how it happened. Have you heard about the bullfights in Mexico? Well, why do you think the bull fights the *torero?*

"To kill him," Matthew said.

"Yes, but why?"

"Because he hates him."

"No, not because he hates him."

"Because he's just mean," Pete said.

"No, that bull is not so mean," Javier replied. He looked at Caleb, who shrugged. "Because he is afraid of him, that is why he fights. And let me tell you why he is afraid.

"In Mexico, the bulls grow up on the ranch, far away from the bullfight. Far away from people. My uncle has a ranch like that in Zacatecas, and he raises the big black bulls for fighting. The ones of Spanish blood, not like the longhorns from Texas; not like your American cattle either. Big black cattle, and the bulls have horns sharp like the *bayoneta* and curved like the side of this guitar." He stroked his four-fingered hand along the curve of the guitar on Caleb's knees.

"And these bulls grow up far away from people and never look at them except, maybe once in a while, a man riding a horse. When they get big enough, the *charros* chase them into a pen made of rocks, very high so no one can look in. And on top of the rock wall are pieces of glass, so little *muchachos* like you three boys don't climb up the wall to look at the bulls. That way, all their life they never see a man standing on his own two legs. So, when they see the *torero* in the bullfighting ring, they are afraid. They have never seen anything stand up that way except a bear. And there is no place to run away in the bullring, so that is why the bull fights the *torero,* because he is afraid." Javier slapped his knees as if he had concluded, and leaned back against the log wall of the cabin.

"But what about your finger?" Caleb asked.

"Oh, yes, I forgot," he said, leaning into his story again. "You want to hear about El Bronco. Well, on my uncle's rancho there was one bull, five years old already, and no one could chase him into the rock pens. He was too wild. Oh, he ran like an antelope and jumped over the rock fences like a deer, and I saw him one time climb the side of a canyon like a mountain sheep.

"Well, there was a *señorita* on my uncle's ranch, and I wanted her to marry me, so I was going to show her how I was the best *caballero* around there and get El Bronco in the pens."

"How were you gonna do that?" Pete asked.

"I thought I could rope that bull and tie him to a tree and leave him there until he was almost dead from thirst and then I could chase him into the pens pretty easy. So, I got my best roping horse, a big mare called La Cruz because of a cross on her face, and I went out to find El Bronco.

"I looked around for many weeks and finally saw him across a valley, up in the high country. He was the biggest bull you ever did see. Big like a buffalo but much smarter. He was always watching out for danger, like a deer. I followed him, about a mile away, for three days, trying to think of a way to get close to him.

"On the third day he went down into a canyon to eat grass and I got an idea. I had a sling that I always carried with me, and I used it to throw rocks into the canyons to scare deer out so I could shoot at them. I thought maybe I could sling a rock all the way across the canyon that El Bronco was in and make him run up to me on my side of the canyon and then I would rope him.''

''You mean a sling like David beat Goliath with?'' Pete asked.

''Yes, exactly the same kind. So I got a bunch of rocks just right for the sling and I rode La Cruz very quietly to the edge of that canyon and— one, two, three—I made those rocks go far across the canyon to the other side!''

Caleb could see the sling in Javier's hand as he made the motions that sailed the rocks across the canyon. Then the vaquero reached for another imaginary prop, and Caleb knew it was his lariat.

''Right away I heard El Bronco coming up the side of the canyon, so I hid behind a big boulder on La Cruz and waited for him. He came out of the canyon not too far away, and La Cruz started to chase him. She was a very fast mare, but it took three miles to get close to that big black bull. Oh, he had a hump like a buffalo and, on his horns, do you know what I saw?''

''What?'' Matthew demanded.

''Blood. That bull had killed something. I don't know what. Probably a jaguar.

''After four miles I was swinging the rope and I had to catch him quick because he was getting close to the next canyon, and I couldn't run as fast as he could down into those canyons. So I spurred La Cruz and said, ''¡Pronto, yegua!'' and she ran as fast as she could, and got right behind El Bronco. Well, I made a big loop, and I threw it right over the bloody horns just before that black bull got to the next canyon!''

Javier's Mexican saddle was hanging on the porch rail, and he suddenly leaped onto it and wrapped his imaginary lariat around the rawhide-covered pommel, as broad across the top as the span of his hand.

''I made a turn around the saddle horn, and La Cruz stiffened her legs and stopped with dirt flying everywhere around her. The *reata* went slipping around the horn like a snake, so fast that it started smoking, and I thought the saddle tree was going to catch on fire and burn me up. El Bronco ran like he had nothing on his horns but a spiderweb; he was just about to jump down into the canyon. I held the rope tighter to make him slow down, but he made a leap and pulled my hand into the twist of rope smoking around the horn. I tried to let go, but this little finger—the one that is no longer there—it got pulled into the coil.

''¡Ay de mí! It went around so fast that the rope just cut that finger off when El Bronco jumped over the edge into the canyon. It cut right through the glove and the blood shot all over the rope as it went smoking around the horn, and then it sprayed everywhere like a mist until the rope was gone after the bull into the canyon.

''And La Cruz, the smell of all that blood scared her, and she threw me into a tree with a lot of thorns and ran away, so it took me four days to walk back to the rancho. I never got another look at my rope, or my finger, or El Bronco again.''

Javier looked sadly at the floor, swung his leg over the saddle, and went back to his place on the bench.

"Did that girl marry you?" Matthew asked.

"Oh, no," Javier answered. "She said a very cruel thing to me. She said she would have married me before, but she wouldn't do it after El Bronco, because she wanted to feel all ten fingers of the man who held her breasts."

Ab cleared his throat rather deliberately.

Javier grinned. "It is a good lesson," he explained.

Caleb didn't know what the lesson was, but the story made him tingle. It gave him escape from Holcomb Ranch. It took him to Mexico, away from the grave of his mother and the coldness of his father. It was like a song, a trip out of time and place, and he wanted to tell stories, too. He wanted people to look at him as a singer of songs and a teller of stories, instead of a boy who got his mother killed.

NINETEEN

JAVIER'S FIRST ACT as manager of the Holcomb Ranch was to change Buster's bull's-eye brand to a simple *H*, for Holcomb. The bull's-eye had caused problems. The hide inside the closed circles of the design tended to die and slough off, leaving large, round, raw wounds. Javier explained that the lines of a brand, unless it was a large flank brand, should never completely encircle a piece of hide.

He taught Pete and Matthew how to rope and throw calves on foot first, then mounted the boys on his trained cow ponies. Each horse could run down calves like a hound after rabbits.

Caleb felt terribly cheated to hear his brothers whistling and hollering at cattle while he harnessed oxen and watched Buster turn the grass upside down. One day when he and Buster were shocking wheat, Matthew rode by and threw a loop as big as a wagon wheel around the horns of a young bull.

"How come Papa doesn't like me as much as Pete and Matthew?" Caleb asked as he watched his brother drag the bull away behind his horse.

Buster had to stop a moment and wipe the sweat from his face. "What makes you think he don't like you?"

"He won't let me work with him like Pete and Matthew."

Buster sighed and fanned himself with his hat. "You were your mama's favorite child. She wouldn't never say so, because it might hurt your brothers' feelin's, but it was true. Your papa remembers that. He just wants to be careful with you so won't nothin' happen to you, because that's what your mama wanted, and sometimes it looks like he don't like you because of it. He's just tryin' to keep you from gettin' hurt or somethin'.''

"He's hurtin' me anyway," Caleb said, speaking as if with the wisdom of a grown man. Then he just went back to shocking wheat.

That evening the boy was trying to rope a sawhorse when his brothers rode in from the plains, their hands bloody from castrating bull calves. "You don't know what you're doin'," Matthew said.

Caleb threw the loop anyway, and missed.

"See, I told you. Give me that rope."

"No," Caleb said.

"Leave him alone," Pete said.

Matthew grabbed the rope and tried to pull it away, but Caleb wouldn't turn loose.

"Papa said you ain't supposed to rope nothin'," Matthew claimed.

"He can rope a sawhorse if he wants to," Pete said.

Matthew gave the rope a mighty yank. Caleb fell down but refused to turn loose the rope. Matthew kicked dirt in his face and dragged him across the ground beside the corral. Pete leapt from the saddle and tackled his big brother, and a three-way wrestling match commenced.

Before the boys knew what had happened, their father came down on them from Pard's saddle. He grabbed Matthew first, took one end of the rawhide lariat the boys were wrestling over, and popped the dust from the seat of his oldest son's pants until Matthew danced in pain. He grabbed Pete next, and the boy took the spanking with his heels on the ground, though the stinging blows made him wince.

Caleb saw his father come at him next. The peg leg landed in front of him, and the big hands reached down for him. He went limp with dread, saw his brothers rubbing their rear ends, and knew the rawhide was going to hurt.

But Ab merely turned the boy around and dusted him off, looking at him with distant eyes as he would inspect a piece of property for damage. "Don't you boys know any better?" he growled. "If you've got strength left to fight, you're not working hard enough."

Satisfied that Caleb was unhurt, he stalked toward the cabin. "You two take care of the horses," he said to his oldest sons.

Pete watched his father, the puzzlement plain on his face. But Matthew shook his fist at Caleb, and glared with eyes misted in anger. He sprang into his saddle and rode to the corral. Pete followed on foot, leading the other two mounts.

Buster, having seen the whole thing from the wheat field, followed Caleb into the shed after a few minutes and found him sulking on the tool crate. "Hey," he said, nudging the boy. "How would you like to do somethin' they can't do?"

"Huh?"

"They're all the time ropin' and ridin' and stuff you don't get to do. How would you like to ride somethin' they can't ride?"

Caleb crooked his upper lip at Buster. "Like what?" He sniffed and rubbed his palms into his eyes.

Buster stepped out of the shed and looked both ways before sidling up next to the boy and speaking in a tone of utmost confidentiality. "I'm gonna build me somethin'."

"What?"

"A wind wagon."

"A what?"

"Don't you tell nobody, and I'll let you ride in it with me. Just you. Not Matthew or Pete or nobody else. But you got to help me build it and you got to keep it a secret."

"I won't tell anybody. What's a wind wagon?"

"It's a wagon with a sail on it like a boat. I believe it'll beat horses," Buster said. "You sure you won't tell nobody?"

Caleb put his hand over his heart. "I promise."

Buster patted the boy on the back and left to make supper, but just before he made it out of the shed, Caleb called his name.

"Do you think it was my fault?" the boy said.

"What's that?"

"What happened to Mama."

"That was two years ago, boy."

"I know, but . . . She did it because of me."

Buster stepped back into the shed. "Listen, boy. It was my fault more than anybody. I shouldn't have left that log loose up there where it would roll off. I should have pegged it down. But I can't blame myself all my life for that. I wasn't tryin' to do nothin' wrong. I always try to do right. It just happened. The Lord took her. It was her time."

The boy sat in the shed alone after Buster left. He knew Buster was going to say it wasn't his fault, but it didn't really help. He didn't understand how God could just take his mother. He knew his mother could have explained it to him. She knew all about God and heaven and the Bible. But she was the one who was dead and causing him to want all the explanations in the first place. The longer he sat alone, the worse he felt.

Suddenly, he knew how to beat the sick guilt he felt. For a while anyway. He wanted to feel the strings under his fingers, see the toes tapping as he played. He left the dark shed to find his fiddle. The bow wouldn't jump lively on his strings tonight, but it would moan a little sorrow from his young soul, howl a primitive dirge over the grave of his lost mother. Oh, it would wring sad beauty from his heart.

TWENTY

"There's a farmer living on Camp Creek," Javier said when he got to the supper table. He had been riding all day, looking for strays.

"A farmer?" Ab sounded as if he had never heard of the profession.

"He says if we don't keep our cattle out of his corn, he is going to shoot them."

"Why in Hades doesn't he build a fence? Buster's got a fence around his corn."

Javier shrugged.

"What's a farmer doing on Camp Creek, anyhow?"

"He said he got a homestead. He's going to own the land."

"Own it?"

"The government is going to give it to him."

"The government doesn't give anything to anybody. Buster, what do you know about this homestead business?"

Buster raked his face with a napkin. "The paper said they had a land office up in Golden City. Said you had to file on a piece of land, pay a fee—I think fifteen dollars—and you can keep the land if you live on it five years and farm it."

"How much land?"

"A hundred and sixty acres."

"A hundred and sixty! A man can't live on a quarter section out here!"

"Maybe he can barely," Buster said. "If he irrigates. Some of them homesteaders might make out all right on the creeks."

Ab pondered the possibilities. The watercourses would fall into the hands of the homesteaders first. He could see them cropping up along Monument Creek. "I guess we ought to file on this place before somebody else comes along and wants it. Before we know it, they'll be all up and down the creek. Our cattle won't have anyplace but right here to come to water. They'll probably bring their milk cows and plow horses with them and eat all the grass in the park."

"If they get upstream of us, they can get all our water," Buster said. "Dam it up to irrigate."

Ab rubbed his head. He was suddenly thinking of homesteaders as he would have thought of termites back in Pennsylvania. "How are we going to keep them out?"

"Ain't no way to keep 'em out," Buster said. "We'd have to own the whole creek all the way to the head."

Javier waved his table knife in the air. "Why not get a quarter section for Señor Holcomb, one for Buster, and one for me, too? All of them along the creek.''

Ab's eyes brightened. ''That'll give us three times as much.'' He shook his head. ''It still isn't enough. Only three quarters of a section. How far will that go up the creek, Buster?''

''If the quarter sections have to be in a square,'' he answered, figuring in his head, ''it will only go a mile and a half up one side.''

''That won't do us much good. If we wanted to keep this whole creek to ourselves, we'd have to have I-don't-know-how-many men to file on land with us.''

''Let's figure it out,'' Buster said.

Ab kicked a piece of charcoal out of the fireplace with his wooden leg so he and Buster could make computations on the hearth. ''Figure eighteen miles of creek bank,'' he said.

''That's just one side of the creek,'' Buster replied. ''You have to double it to take in both sides.''

''Well, double it, then. Write it down.''

''What are they talkin' about?'' Caleb whispered to Pete.

Pete shrugged and sopped up some gravy with a biscuit.

Buster's arithmetic showed that no fewer than seventy-two homesteads would take up the entirety of Monument Creek.

Ab sank back into his chair and sighed. ''Seventy-two. Can you imagine seventy-two men working one ranch? How many men do we need, Javier?''

''We don't need any more men right now because we don't have very many cattle.''

''If we had enough cattle to graze all of Monument Park, how many men would we need?''

''Maybe twenty.''

Ab sulked silently in his chair for a while as Buster picked the dishes up from the table. ''We need some more cattle. Where are we going to get them, Javier?''

''Maybe we can get some in New Mexico. But not very many. The most cattle you have ever seen in your life are in Texas. That is the place to get a thousand of them at one time.''

''Not with the war going on. We'll have to wait till the Rebels are whipped, and that might take more years than it's taken already.''

''Won't be much homesteadin' goin' on till the war's over, though,'' Buster said. ''Then when it's over, all them out-of-work soldiers will come out here looking for a farm.''

''We'll have to be ready,'' Ab said. ''Soon as the war ends, we'll go to Texas for cattle. If we get more cattle, we can hire more men. With more men, we can file on more land and keep those homesteaders off of our creek. Off of part of it anyway.''

But part of the creek would not satisfy Ab. He would have to figure out a way to get seventy-two men, or however many it took, to file on every quarter section of land for him, on each side of Monument Creek, all the way to its source. Then he would control the entire park.

One possible solution had already come to him. As soon as his first batch of men proved up on their homesteads in five years, he would buy them out, fire them, and hire another twenty or so to file on another twenty quarter sections. Even at that rate, it would take twenty years to own the whole creek.

But one way or another, he was going to own every drop of water above his ranch. With no farms on the creek to bar his cattle from water, he could build a herd that would graze all the grass clear to the Plum Creek divide—sections and sections of land. He wouldn't even have to buy the grazing land or pay taxes on it. No one else could possibly use it. It was too dry to farm without creek water to irrigate. He wouldn't let anybody else's cattle drink at his creek, so no one else could start another herd in Monument Park.

He sensed that it all went against what the Homestead Act intended, but Congress didn't have sense enough to understand. A man couldn't live on a quarter section in the West. He had to have more. And the men who came first should have the most. He was only planning to do what Ella would have done. She would have found a way around the laws. She had broken statutes by the volume to smuggle her fugitive slaves through Pennsylvania. In Ab's view the Homestead Act was as much of an injustice as slavery, and if he had to defraud the government to overcome injustice, it was due to the ignorance of Congress, not any criminal intention on his own part.

"I'm going to Golden City in the morning," he said. "I'm going to see what it takes to file a homestead claim. Then the three of us can file on our quarter sections. When you two prove up in five years, I'll buy you out at a fair price. Is that agreeable?"

Javier nodded with satisfaction, but Buster looked glumly at the mathematical calculations drawn in charcoal on the hearth.

"What's wrong, Buster?" Ab asked. "Doesn't it suit you to help me build a ranch in this valley?"

"Yes, sir, but . . ."

"But what?"

"I want to build me somethin', too. I've been figurin' on makin' my own farm here. When I prove up, I want to keep my land."

Ab smirked. "Your own farm? Who's going to run mine?"

"I'll run mine and yours both," Buster said.

Ab folded his arms across his chest and studied for a few seconds. "Well, I guess you have a right to a quarter section if you want it. I suppose you'll make as good a neighbor as any."

"Thank you," Buster said. Ab didn't hand out many compliments.

* * *

While Ab was away at the land office in Golden City, a train of freight wagons arrived at Holcomb Ranch from Denver. Eight yokes of oxen pulled each of the huge Conestogas. The axles groaned for want of grease, and the bull whackers cussed hoarsely at the beasts as often as they blinked. One of the wagons carried the lumber Ab had ordered so Buster could build his irrigation flume. And behind it, dwarfed by the dimensions of the Conestoga, a black-lacquered spring buggy trundled in the dust. The bull whackers veered from the Fort Bridger Road and camped near the cabin about sundown.

"That's it," Buster said, pulling Caleb aside. "That's gonna be our wind wagon."

"That's ours?"

"Sure is. I ordered it four months ago. Came all the way from St. Louis."

As soon as the train stopped, Caleb jumped up on the buggy and tested the spring seat.

"Remember . . ." Buster warned.

"I know. I won't tell anybody. They wouldn't believe it anyway."

"They'll believe it when they see us ridin' it. But for now just let 'em think we want to pull it behind horses like regular folks."

The captain of the bull train marched back to unhook the spring buggy. He was a full-chested, hairy individual whose fingers looked like wheel spokes radiating from his palm. "Where's Holcomb?" he asked.

"Gone to Golden City."

"Who are you?"

"Buster Thompson."

"This is your buggy then. What the hell do want with a damn buggy in this country?"

"Tell him, Caleb."

"Me?"

"Tell him what we're gonna do with the buggy."

"Well . . . We're just gonna pull it behind horses like regular folks."

"Good boy, that's exactly what we're gonna do with it."

"Regular folks straddle their horses in this country," the captain said.

As Buster helped the freighters unload the sawmill lumber, Pete rode up on Crazy. He was leading Blue Eyes, who was wearing a red blanket under the saddle. "You want to ride?" Pete asked.

Caleb searched the plains. "What about Matthew? He'll tell Papa."

"Him and Javier went over to the Pinery to find some cows. They won't come back till supper."

Caleb looked at Buster.

"I don't need your help here, but I don't know nothin' about ridin' no horses either."

Caleb bounced off the blue-eyed mustang's ribs and landed behind the pommel.

"Where do you want to go?" Pete asked.

"I'll race you to the hill," Caleb answered, raking Blue Eyes with his heels.

They galloped across the plains like cavalry soldiers on a reckless charge, reining their horses back only for a second or two at the brink of the creek bank. Pete led down the slope, but Crazy was usually a little shy of water, and paused long enough before leaping to let Caleb take the lead. The horses splashed through the stream and climbed the west bank, snorting for air. Pete found a straighter path through the trees on the far bank and came out ahead on the last leg of the race.

Blue Eyes finished a neck behind Crazy, but Caleb accepted defeat with pleasure, thrilled to be holding his reins. The hill seemed twice as high from horseback, and he felt as if he could see all the way to the Comanche country from the saddle.

Then the smile slid from his face. He had turned to look at the mountains, and something had moved along the tree line. No matter how quickly his eyes darted, they could not catch it. It vanished like a bird in a thicket, but he heard the wind moan his name in the treetops far up the trail. It was calling again. It wanted him to follow.

"Let's put them last four planks down on the ground," Buster said.

"What the hell for? Why not throw 'em on the stack with the rest of 'em?" the captain asked.

"We can use 'em for a floor to clog on tonight, and I'll play some fiddle music for your men."

"You a fiddler?"

"Yes, sir," Buster said.

"Say, you're not that nigger fiddler that rode off to Indian Territory to get the boy back, are you?"

"Yes, I am."

"Where's the boy you brought back?"

Buster pointed to the hill. He could see the horses on its ridge against the Rampart Range. It looked as if Pete was teaching Caleb how to swing a loop from the saddle. "That was him on that blue-eyed horse. He plays a little music, too. I taught him."

That night, after helping Buster entertain the freighters, Caleb lay in his bed and dreamed of riding. He could feel the wind in his face and the roll of the horse under him. His dream horse ran to the rhythm of the songs he had played for the jig-dancing freighters, taking him far from Holcomb Ranch, over the mountains to glorious new places. And always before him, just out of reach, flew something he could see only from the corner of his eye. Something that lured him into mystery.

TWENTY-ONE

B USTER'S LUMBER REMAINED stacked near the cabin all winter. Some of it went toward building a bunkhouse for the cowboys who would come to work as the herd grew. The rest of it would have to wait until Buster got around to damming the creek.

At night, he and Caleb worked on their wind wagon. They wanted to have it ready for the chinooks that would rake the eastern slope in the spring. First, there was the mast to construct. Even before he ordered the buggy, Buster had picked out and chopped down the straightest pine sapling he could find in the Pinery, about the diameter of a lodge pole. Now it was cured and ready to finish. Caleb thought he would rasp the whole thing to sawdust before Buster was satisfied with its straightness and smoothness.

Buster had built a sheet-metal forge in the log shed, and used it to cast some brackets that would hold the boom to the mast. He also fashioned iron loops for the sheet and halyard to run through, and rings that would slide up and down the mast and attach to the sail.

He put hours of thought into the stepping of the mast, finally deciding that he would center it among the four wheels, to discourage strong gusts from capsizing the craft. The spring seat was in the middle of the buggy, so Buster unbolted it and moved it aft, over the rear axle. He sawed a perfectly round hole of the proper diameter in the floorboard of the buggy and bolted the foot of the mast to the coupling pole that ran between the axles. Rawhide shrouds held it firmly aright.

Next, the inventors had to rig a steering system to turn the front wheels. Buster had decided to let the turning wheels ride forward this time, instead of trying to make the craft sail backward, as his milk wagon had done when it crashed into Long Fingers' tepee. He ran thick cords of twisted rawhide from the front axle, just inside the wheels, around a system of spools, to a location just in front of the spring seat. There he wrapped them around the hub of a wheel taken from the old milk wagon, changing it to a steering wheel like that of an oceangoing vessel. The sailors would be able to steer, trim the sail, and swing the boom, all from the spring seat at the rear of the vehicle.

Most of the construction went on in secret. Not because Buster excluded spectators, but because the other Holcomb Ranch residents had better things to do with their evenings than watch a perfectly good buggy get desecrated without reason. Buster and Caleb refused to tell what the conversions signified.

"What are we gonna do with this thing when its finished?" Caleb asked one winter night. Buster was working by lantern light, and Caleb was practicing a song on the banjo.

"Ride in it," Buster said, adjusting the rawhide cables around the steering-wheel hub.

"Where to?"

"I don't know. Maybe we'll go to Colorado City and play for a couple of dances on Saturday night. Pass the hat and make some money."

"Can we carry anything in it?"

"It ain't very big," Buster admitted. "But it'll carry a little. And, if it works, then maybe I'll build us a bigger one. I'll build one out of a Conestoga that'll carry a whole ton."

"What for?"

"Go into the freight business. No oxen. No mules. No hay to buy. A man could freight between the Platte and Arkansas almost all year long the way the wind blows around here."

"Where are you gonna get a Conestoga wagon?" Caleb asked with a smirk. The Conestogas he had seen were high enough to walk under without bumping his head, and almost as big as his house. He knew Buster didn't have the money to buy something like that.

"That's what I need this little one for," Buster explained. "I can use it to show folks how a big one will work. Maybe some of those rich gold men up in Denver will put up some money for me."

"Will they put up some money for me, too?" Caleb asked.

"Sure. You're my partner, ain't you? Now, tune that thumb string up. Can't you hear it's flat?"

The wind wagon was ready to roll by February, but its captain decided to postpone the maiden voyage until the snows melted. He did not want for inventions to tinker with, however. Javier had been complaining about the wolves killing his calves, and wanted Buster to do something about it.

"Why don't you make something we can use," he asked one evening, "instead of cutting up that wagon? Make one of these." He slapped a newspaper down in front of Buster and pointed to an ad in the center column. The ad included a woodcut of a diabolical firearm called The Wolf-Getter. It was made to be driven into the ground on a steel spike. The trigger was a hook that extended forward into the path of the bullet. The idea was to bait the hook with meat, load a metallic cartridge into the breech, and leave the weapon cocked in the woods. When a wolf or another predator came along and tried to eat the bait, the gun would discharge, blasting the carnivore in the head almost point-blank.

Buster bought an old single-shot pistol from a gunsmith in Colorado City and had it bored to take a forty-five-caliber cartridge. Then all he had to do was mount a spike on the butt of the pistol and rig the trigger with an extension that ended in front of the muzzle.

Javier baited the wolf-getter with veal from a wolf kill and set it in the timber about a mile up the creek.

The first victim was one of the dogs that Cheyenne Dutch had left at Holcomb Ranch. Caleb cried for an hour.

The next victim was a white wolf. Javier made a daily point of loading and setting the wolf-getter from then on. Raccoons, foxes, and coyotes triggered the gun more often than wolves, but any dent in the predator population was welcomed by Javier.

When the snows finally melted in the spring of 1864, they joined one night with the runoff of a thunderstorm in the mountains and flooded Monument Creek. The torrent filled in Buster's irrigation ditch and ripped away the timber and rock dam he had begun to build to impound his irrigation reservoir. Then the storm roared down onto the plains, pounding the land with rain and hail. The creek ran icy cold, choked with hailstones the size of hens' eggs. It climbed high enough on its banks to lap into the old dugout nobody had used since Buster moved into the toolshed. The winter wheat was beaten flat, annihilated.

Buster was slogging through the mud, surveying the damage, when the low drone of a mouth harp reached his ears. He hadn't seen Long Fingers since he went to the Indian Territory after Caleb, two years before, but he knew the chief's musical style. He looked downstream to see Long Fingers riding alone.

"Howdy-do, Buffalo Head," the chief said. He was still wearing winter fur, and his magnificence surpassed that of any Indian Buster had ever seen. His mood, however, was somber.

"Hello, chief. Look what the weather did to us." He swept his arms to indicate the obliterated wheat field.

"It is a circle. Your tribe does not know the circle of time?"

"My tribe?"

"African Baptist."

"Oh, yeah. Well, where my tribe comes from the circle goes a different way. I ain't never seen no hail like this."

"You better learn the way the circle goes here, or it will kill you."

When they arrived at the cabin, Long Fingers merely glanced at Ab's peg leg. He shook Javier's hand and gladly agreed to join the Holcombs for supper. While Buster cooked, the chief gave the reason for his visit.

"Kicking Dog is a dog soldier now with the Cheyenne," he said. "He makes big trouble for everybody. On the beaver moon, before the winter, he took a bunch of my boys away from me and they catch a white woman at a ranch on the Platte. I think they sell her to the Sioux. He makes war for everybody. We have no buffalo. No good land. Kicking Dog believes he can kill all the whites and have buffalo again, and land. Now he is coming this way. I think he will come to get your cattle, Holcomb."

Ab regarded the chief suspiciously.

"The Comanche want that boy back." He pointed at Caleb. "The little one. Snake Woman tells them that boy is strong medicine for them. I think maybe Kicking Dog will catch him to sell to the Comanche."

Caleb knew Long Fingers was a friend, but he had a terrible dread of any Indian that looked and pointed at him that way.

"Comanche?" Ab said. He scratched his head. He had almost forgotten Buster's wild tale about the winter in the Indian Territory. "Buster, what in Hades does he mean?"

"It's Snake Woman. She thinks the spirits gave her a sign to make Caleb be an Indian. She's got the Comanche all believin' it."

Ab took the first good look at Caleb he had indulged in for a long time. He had a hard time envisioning Indians riding all the way across Colorado Territory for one scrawny boy. It didn't make sense, but he was not about to take any chances with Caleb's safety. He had Ella's ultimatum hanging over his head like the ridge log that had killed her.

"We better post a guard by day and keep the doors barred by night. Javier, you and me and Buster will take turns standing guard on that hill across the creek. You can see a long way from there."

Buster frowned. He had too much to do to spend every third day standing on a hill, looking for Indians. "Matthew could stand guard, too," he said. "He's fifteen now, and he can shoot good."

Matthew couldn't believe his ears. Ol' Buffalo Head rarely had anything good to say about him. "Will you let me, Papa?" he asked.

"Well, all right," Ab said.

After supper the boys ran to Buster's shed to get the instruments so Long Fingers could hear "Old Dan Tucker." He and Buffalo Head were alone on the cabin porch for a minute.

"What else have you heard about Snake Woman?" Buster asked. "Last time I saw her, she was gettin' big." He indicated her shape around his own stomach.

"She has a papoose now," Long Fingers said. "Very black, with hair on the head curly, like the buffalo. They say it is your son."

Buster pictured the baby, felt his remorse. He should have been strong enough to resist Snake Woman in the dugout.

*   *   *

The hailstorm pulled a chinook down from the mountains. It blustered across the plains and caused the men to walk around outside with their hands on their hats. Wind conditions were perfect for the maiden voyage of the Thompson Wind Wagon. The ground was still muddy, but Buster wanted to test the wind wagon while Long Fingers was at the ranch so the old chief could see how the wind could move a wagon like a cloud.

"Well, do you want us to come with you, or what?" Ab asked as Buster hitched a horse to the buggy. Buster and Caleb had dismasted the vehicle and covered it with its own sail so no one would figure out what it was. They intended it to surprise.

"No, sir," Buster said. "Just stand there on the porch and we'll ride back by and demonstrate. Don't let on what we're up to, chief."

Long Fingers gave the sign for silence, putting the fingers of his right hand over his thin lips.

The inventors drove south and disappeared behind a rise in the ground about a mile away.

Ab waited a quarter hour. "Pete, go saddle me a horse," he said. "I'm going to find out what they're up to."

Pete sprinted for the shed and soon brought Pard back, cinched under Ab's hull. Buster had built a socket in the right stirrup of Ab's saddle that enabled him to keep the end of his peg leg firmly seated. Just as he fixed the peg in the socket and got ready to ride, he saw Buster's buggy horse running back toward the ranch, her hooves kicking up clods of mud, her head high and cocked to one side as if fleeing from the worst order of horror.

Over the swell in the prairie a white triangle appeared. It grew until it looked as broad across the bottom as a chief's tepee. Under it a black dot appeared, rolling toward the ranch so fast that the buggy horse could barely keep her distance ahead of it.

"What in Hades . . ." Ab muttered.

Pete squinted.

Matthew and Javier stood with their mouths open.

"The wind pushes it like a cloud," Long Fingers said, pointing.

The buggy horse ran right past the cabin. Pard caught her fear, snorted, and perked his ears forward. He heard the rattle of the buggy, saw the cloud-sail billowing over it, and pulled against the reins in Ab's hands.

The wind wagon sailed past the cabin, Buster grinning at the wheel, Caleb waving with the sheet in one hand. Pard lunged against the reins until the hollering voices faded away.

Ab kicked his mount and gave chase.

With a smile on his face, Long Fingers jumped from the porch and ran for his horse in the corral.

Buster turned the wagon to the starboard to circle the ranch again.

"Jibe!" he ordered, and Caleb swung the boom across the wagon. "Beam reach. The wind's at our stern now."

Caleb followed the commands and glanced behind. "Hey, Papa's racin' us!" he said.

Buster turned and saw Ab riding in his wake, waving his hat over his head. Caleb waved back. There was no catching the wind wagon for Ab. Pard refused to approach it. The wheels kicked up chunks of mud and splattered them against the bottom of the buggy.

Long Fingers slipped a bridle bit between his mount's teeth, grabbed a handful of mane, and jumped on. He galloped through the corral gate, angling across the plains to intercept the cloud on wheels.

The wind wagon drove into an old buffalo wallow like a sloop into an ocean swell. Its wheels left the ground when it shot out, and the springs under the wagon seat almost launched Caleb overboard.

"Turnin' starboard again," Buster said. "Give me a close reach when I make the turn."

Hand over hand, he turned the wheel as Caleb hauled the sheet in. But the boy took in too much rope, and the boom swung down the center line, the stiff crosswind pushing against the sail. The wagon stalled; its right wheels quit the ground. Buster tried to correct to the port, but the wagon balanced precariously on two wheels for a long moment, then fell over sideways, the pine mast slapping against the ground.

Buster and Caleb landed on the canvas and lay there laughing until Ab rode up. Pard still didn't like the flapping white canvas but could bear to approach it on the ground.

"Buster!" Ab said, jumping down from his horse and pivoting on his peg. "What do you mean carrying that boy in that contraption? Are you trying to kill him?" He stalked toward the overturned buggy, his fists clenched in anger. "Pick him up, let me look at him!"

Buster pulled Caleb to his feet as Long Fingers arrived. Ab shook the boy, turned him around, felt his arms and legs.

"He's fine," Buster said.

Ab bent over Caleb and scowled at him. "If you ever get in that thing again, I'll take this stick off my knee and whop you with it. I'll whop you, too, Buster. You ought to know better." He hopped back to his horse and trotted to the ranch.

Caleb knew now that his father would never forgive him. He never heard Ab talk to Pete or Matthew in such a tone. His brothers could have all the fun they wanted, but he wasn't allowed to have any. He was not a full-fledged son of Ab Holcomb. He could sense that he was nothing more than a trial and a burden to his father. It had to be because of the way his mother died. He would pay for that as long as he lived at Holcomb Ranch.

Long Fingers sat stoically on his horse, as if he had missed Ab's entire outburst. "Now I learn something new," he said to Buster. "A wagon is not always a wagon. It can go like a cloud with the wind. Now you will have a new name, and it is Man-on-a-Cloud."

Buster put a hand on the Caleb's shoulder as the boy watched his father ride back to the ranch.

"Good," Buster said. "I never much liked being called Buffalo Head."

TWENTY-TWO

M ATTHEW LOVED FEW things more than the feel of a gun in his hands, and hated few things more than standing orders not to shoot. On his first two turns at guard duty, he had panicked everyone on the place by shooting at shadows in the woods. But now he hadn't fired a round in three weeks. His father had guaranteed him that if he gave another false alarm, he would scalp Matthew himself.

He was sitting on the bald hill west of the creek, holding a new Henry repeater his father had bought in Denver. Since he couldn't shoot it, he aimed and made various noises intended to resemble a rifle blast. One of his favorite targets was the dam Buster was building up the creek valley. He could imagine the water leaking out of it through a hundred bullet holes. Another favorite target was the wildflower garden near the cabin. First he would aim at the orange row, then the red one, then the blue one. When he felt particularly sure of his marksmanship, he would aim at the cut flowers on his mother's grave, though, at that distance, the bead at the end of the barrel could have covered four gravestones at once.

The sun was two hours high, and aiming at things was already a monotony. Matthew sat down on the grassy pate of the hill and watched the clouds float across the sky, slowly, the way time passed on guard duty. He watched Buster and Caleb climbing on the dam in the creek bed. He saw Javier training a colt in the corral.

Ab and Pete were working cattle somewhere. Matthew swept Monument Park with his eyes, looking for them, from the mountains to the Pinery and southward out over the open plains. He spotted a rider in the shadows along the creek bed downstream and watched for a second, trying to figure out if it was Pete or Ab. Then there was a second horseman, and he knew it had to be both of them. Then there was a third.

Those were not Holcomb horses. Those were . . . Cheyenne!

He fired his rifle in the air and ran for his horse. By the time he reached the creek he could hear the warriors whooping. A tingling sensation crept from under is shirttail and crawled all the way up into his hat. It gave him power. He rode to the top of the cutbank about the time Buster and Caleb got there on foot. He saw Pete and his father coming in off the plains, barely beating the Indians to the cabin. Javier was there, too, shooting a pistol at the attackers.

The war party had come so quickly that Matthew, Buster, and Caleb were unable to reach the safety of the house. The three of them dropped back under the rim of the creek bank for protection. Gunshots were already coming from the cabin.

Matthew dismounted. Holding his reins, he rested his elbows on top of the creek bank. He aimed at the Indians circling the house. One of them climbed up on the roof to look down the chimney. Matthew took careful aim and fired. To his surprise, the brave twisted in the air and rolled down the cedar shakes, dead.

"That's Kicking Dog on the paint horse," Buster said, crawling up by Matthew's side. "Give me the Henry, and take Caleb with you into the woods. I'll hold 'em back."

"I ain't givin' my rifle to nobody," Matthew said. "You take Caleb to the woods yourself."

"Give me the gun, boy." Buster reached for the rifle barrel, but Matthew jerked it away and pointed it at him.

"I'll shoot if you try to take it, Buffalo Head."

Buster saw a hateful glint in Matthew's eyes and considered it a possibility that the boy might really shoot him. He had no choice but to grab Caleb by the arm and run for the timber across the creek as Matthew fired again at the Cheyenne and levered a fresh round from the magazine.

Buster and Caleb crossed the creek below the dam and hid in the trees. When they turned to watch the battle, they saw Matthew retreating, riding across the creek. Four braves leapt the bank behind him and chased him into the trees. Just before the Indian ponies ran into the timber, a puff of black smoke knocked one brave from his horse, and the others turned and ran into the trees at another place farther down. The downed Indian tried to get up, but another blast of smoke erupted from the trees, and the brave rolled into the water.

"Matthew got another one," Caleb said, pointing.

"Come on," Buster said between gasps for breath. "We got to find more cover."

The gunfire from the cabin faded as Buster and Caleb retreated farther up the creek, looking for a thick stand of trees. Buster knew of a little draw that entered Monument Creek from the west above Holcomb Ranch. A thicket poured down from the foothills and filled the draw. It wasn't very big, but it was the best chance of survival for him and Caleb. He wished for a gun. Only Matthew stood between him and the three raiding warriors, and he wasn't sure the boy could hold them off long.

Two loud blasts sounded downstream, and Buster knew they had come from Matthew's repeater. He peeked out from the tree line and saw Matthew retreating again, only two Indians chasing him now. When the boy turned into the timber again, the Indians stopped and talked a moment before going in after him. One of them went through the willows lining the creek bank and rode up the hill to the west. The other charged east across the creek. They had decided to go around the boy with the repeater. They weren't after Matthew anyway. They wanted Caleb. The Comanche had probably offered a bounty of a dozen horses for his return.

Buster pulled Caleb by the arm as he sprinted toward the draw upstream. Glancing back, he saw one Cheyenne warrior riding across the creek. The thicket was just fifty yards ahead, yet he didn't know if he would reach it in time. His slick boots slipped on the slope of the creek bank, and branches whipped him as he raced. He stumbled into the draw just as the brave crossed the creek toward it.

Caleb tried to lie down in the bushes, but Buster dragged him deeper into the cover by the collar. The boy gasped for air but seemed unable to draw any. Finally, Buster dropped him between the trunks of two big trees and picked up a stick.

The gunshots had stopped firing at the cabin, and Caleb wondered if the Indians had killed or captured Pete. The sound of his own heaving slackened, and he could hear the rush of the creek, the whistle of a chinook in the treetops. Then he recognized the clop of hooves. The Indians were sneaking into the woods to get him. He was afraid of what Snake Woman would do to him if the Cheyenne took him back to the Comanche. He thanked God Buster was with him.

A warm foul smell hung in the still air of the underbrush. Caleb couldn't take a breath without it filling his nostrils. It made him wrinkle his nose. It was the thick odor of primitive death. Something was rotting.

Buster had his stick poised over his shoulder and was watching for movements of the two braves when he felt Caleb pulling on his sleeve. He brushed the boy's hand away and concentrated on the enemy, one coming from the mouth of the draw and another from somewhere above. The tugging came again at his sleeve, and he scowled down at the boy.

But Caleb wasn't looking up at him. Instead, the boy's eyes were fixed on something in the shadows just up the draw. Buster followed his line of sight. There, hammered into the ground at the base of a tree, was the wolf-getter, its trigger baited with rotten meat swarming with flies.

He put the stick on the ground and pulled Caleb across a small clearing to the wolf gun. He heard a Cheyenne horse kick a stone behind him. Carefully, he eased the hammer of the pistol down. The warriors were coming nearer; he could hear branches raking across the buffalo-hide shields they carried. He yanked the wolf-getter from the ground and pulled the rotting meat from the hook, flies singing war songs around him. He bent the hook to get it out of the way of the muzzle.

Moccasins hit the ground, and Buster knew the brave coming from the mouth of the draw had dismounted. Pulling Caleb between him and the tree, he cocked the wolf gun and turned back to the little clearing he had crossed. In seconds the warrior materialized, dappled with tree-strained sunlight, a shield in one hand and a revolver in the other. The wolf-getter spoke, its forty-five slug catching the dog soldier in the chest and knocking him back.

Buster sprinted across the clearing for the brave's weapon but saw the wounded warrior trying to muster the strength to raise his pistol. The spike on the wolf-getter was Buster's only weapon. He pounced on the brave and drove it into his chest, then took the pistol away and motioned for Caleb to run to him.

Caleb didn't care to run toward the bloody Indian, but he followed Buster's orders. He had taken no more than three steps when he sensed a presence behind him. It was as if his own echo followed in his footsteps. Buster's eyes grew wide and the captured revolver swung up. "Get down!" he yelled.

But Caleb was too afraid to drop. He glanced over his shoulder and saw the dog soldier reaching for him. Caleb's foot caught on something and he fell. The pistol fired, and the warrior collapsed beside him. Caleb scrambled back to his feet and buried his face in Buster's chest.

"You're all right, boy," Buster said. He listened. "We better go see how everybody else made out."

They caught the two Indian ponies in the draw, both of them wearing fine ranch saddles probably stolen on another recent raid. They heard horses coming, and when they ventured out of the thicket, they saw Ab and Javier riding toward them, calling their names.

Pete was riding behind Javier. "Caleb!" he cried.

Matthew was along the tree line, stooping over one of his dead Indians. Buster and Caleb rode the Cheyenne horses toward Matthew to meet the other men. When they got close, they found Matthew with the brave's hair in one hand and a knife in the other.

"How do you do it?" he asked his father. "How do you scalp 'em?"

"I know how," Javier said, sliding down from his Mexican saddle. "One time there was a bounty on Indians in New Mexico, and we scalped them to keep a count of how many . . ."

"What in Hades do you think you're doing?!" Ab said. "Matthew, get your hands off of those lousy plaits. We don't scalp. It isn't Christian."

Matthew let the dead man's hair fall in the dirt. "But, the Pikes Peakers scalped Texans at Glorietta Pass."

"Who told you that?"

"Those freighters here last fall."

"That's a lie. Even scalping Texans isn't Christian, and they're the scalpingest bunch of heathens the devil ever created. Buster, get Caleb off of that wild Indian pony before it kills him. How many Indians did you get?''

Caleb slid off of the captured horse.

"We got two," Buster said. "Caleb found the wolf-getter, and I got one of 'em with that. They're both back in that thicket."

"Who got this one?" Ab asked.

"And that other one back there?" Javier added. "It wasn't me. I missed every one I shot at."

"I killed three," Matthew said, drawing himself up like a decorated hero. "Got one on the roof and two along the creek."

Ab stared. "You?"

Matthew nodded and brandished the repeater.

"It's a good thing you had the Henry," Javier said. "They would have killed you if you had to stop to reload. You can load that Henry on Sunday and fire it all week."

Ab shook his head. "Thank the Lord your mama's not here to see you boys turn killer. That would break her heart. Let's drag the bodies together and burn them."

"I can't scalp mine?"

"No!"

As the slain braves burned under a great heap of timber, Ab and Javier took stock of the damages. "How many horses did they get?" Ab asked.

"Just two," Javier said.

"Well, Buster got two of theirs and we killed five of them on top of that. I guess we got the better of them. Which two horses did they get? Any good ones?"

"Not really," Javier said. "They got the black with the stocking feet and the one with the blue eyes."

"Blue Eyes?" Caleb said. "They got Blue Eyes?"

Javier squatted and rubbed his hand through Caleb's hair. "*Sí, muchacho.* They got your little pony. I tried to shoot the one who did it, but you know I can shoot nothing but wolves with that wolf gun Buster made for us." He shook Caleb and laughed, but the boy didn't laugh in return. "Well, maybe you can have one of the horses we got from those two that Buster killed."

"No," Ab said. "We'll get him a gentle horse when he gets big enough to ride. I don't want him riding those wild Indian ponies."

"But, you said," Caleb protested. "You said when I get big as Pete I can ride along with him and Matthew. I'm big as he was when you said it."

"Hush, boy," Ab snapped. "I said when you get big as Pete. Are you big as Pete now? No, you're not, are you? You'd better thank God you're alive and stop complaining."

Caleb opened his mouth, but no words would come to him. He would never be as big as Pete. Pete was older and kept ahead of him. He would never chase Holcomb cattle. He wasn't going to be a rancher. He was going to be a farmer's helper for the rest of his days, and plod in the dust wake of oxen while his brothers lost their hats in the wind.

He turned away from his father with tears in his eyes and looked over the bald hill at the mountains, wavering strangely through the heat and smoke of the cremation fire. Someday he was going all the way over the hill, he told himself. Someday he would go up into that high country. He would find a place where people rode horses and played music all day. A place where he could do whatever he wanted.

Sometimes he glimpsed a hint of something on that hill, heard a stray echo from some distant canyon—a vagrant chinook moaning over a lonely crag. It would sigh the soft sounds of his name like an Indian chant. Someday he would answer that call.

TWENTY-THREE

L ONG FINGERS LAY on his buffalo robe and stared up at the light of dawn streaming weakly through the smoke hole of his tepee. The warmth of his wife felt good beside him, but he had little else to comfort him. He had slept very little, and even in his fleeting dreams he had thought only of his people's precarious existence on the earth. A death song kept breaking the circle of his thoughts:

Nothing lives long except the earth and the mountains.

Long Fingers and a few other chiefs the Indian agents regarded as "reliables" had brought their bands to Fort Wise to seek peace. Even Kicking Dog had come, swayed by a majority of his dog soldiers, who were weary of fighting with blue coats and settlers. The Indians had turned over their weapons, received rations, and had been promised protection.

But the rations dried up all too soon. Starving, the Indians were given their weapons and told to disperse and hunt. The commander at Fort Wise ensured them that they were under army protection and would not be attacked by white settlers seeking revenge for recent depredations.

When they left Fort Wise, Long Fingers' band fell back to Sand Creek with White Antelope and Black Kettle of the Cheyenne. Most of the young braves were scouring the plains for game. Winter was coming, and there was not enough food. At least they were hunting instead of raiding, Long Fingers thought. At least now his people were under the protection of the white soldiers and not pitted against them.

Yet, out on the plains, not more than a mile from Long Fingers' Sand Creek camp, Horace Gribble was belching the fetor of whiskey up from his stomach and trying to clear his head for battle. He shouldn't have drunk so much on the long night march, but the Gribbles had always had a taste for whiskey.

His brothers, Hank and Bill, were in their graves, and Horace wanted vengeance. After striking Holcomb's Ranch, Kicking Dog had ridden north and found much greater success at the Gribble Ranch. Horace had been away in Denver. He had returned to find his home burned and the bodies of his brothers stripped and mutilated. When Colonel Chivington started recruiting men for hundred-day enlistments in the Third Cavalry, Horace signed on. Sand Creek was to be his first battle.

Dawn gave enough light for him to see all the way down the skirmish line Chivington had ordered the men to form. Most of the seven hundred mounted men belonged to the Hundred Dazers, as the Third was called, but two battalions of the old First Regiment of Colorado Volunteers were present, too.

Chivington trotted before the line, his baritone striking the clarion call to arms as if spouting from the pulpit. He badly needed a victory today. The fame he had won at Glorietta Pass, that which had elevated him to Commander of the Military District of Colorado, had already faded in the rash of Indian troubles.

"It is honorable in the eyes of the Lord to exterminate these heathen reds," he was saying. "Think of the farms they have left smoldering in their wake upon your prairies. You, soldier, strip that coat off. You'll get hot enough. . . ."

As the colonel harangued his volunteers, his scout loped up from the creek bed to report. "Did you ever whop the wild pigeons down from the roosts back east, colonel?" Cheyenne Dutch asked.

"Pigeons? No. What about the Indians?"

"Don't feel slighted for the sport. You'll get a taste of it this mornin'."

"A taste of what, man? Report sensibly."

"A taste of whoppin' down the pigeons. Killin' them Indians won't take no more trouble."

"How many lodges?"

"Three hundred, I'll wager."

"Who are the chiefs?"

"Cheyenne for the most part. White Antelope, Black Kettle, War Bonnet, Little Robe, and Standing-in-the-Water. I saw one band of Arapaho, too. Long Fingers'."

"Which one is he?"

"Talks American."

"Oh, yes." The big reverend soldier sneered with hatred. "How many warriors do you estimate?"

Dutch scratched his whiskered neck as he made his tabulations. "Maybe a buck in every lodge. Them squaws and boys'll fight, too, though."

The colonel nodded and told Dutch to choose his place in the line. "The Indians will fight to the death," he shouted at his men. "Take no prisoners!"

"Colonel," one of the soldiers said, "what about their women and children? Will we give them time to clear out?"

Chivington turned his huge dapple gray to face the questioner. "As an officer of the United States Army, I cannot order you to fire upon women and children. But I will offer an observation: Nits make lice. Damn any man in sympathy with the Indians. . . ."

Chivington's four howitzers found their places on the sand hills overlooking the creek, and the skirmish line moved forward. "What do you think the colonel meant about nits?" the man next to Horace asked. "Does he want us to kill the younguns or not?"

"Hell if I know. Don't reckon I'll shoot any unless they're shootin' at me."

"You'll wait one shot too late if you let them shoot at you first. Here, you want a drink of this?"

"Oh, Lordy, put it away," Horace said. He saw the bed of Sand Creek dropping off in front of him. The sooty pinnacles of the hide lodges emerged, standing among a few old cottonwood trees along the watercourse. "Wait a minute," he said. "On second thought, let me have just one gurgle." He took the bottle from his companion and turned it up on his parched lips.

Long Fingers came back from his musings of peace at the terrified shout of a squaw. He threw the buffalo robe off, startling his wife, and shoved his feet into his moccasins. From the flap of his lodge he saw the howitzers against the morning sky. Families stumbled from their lodges, waking in terror to the sights of the white man's war. A company of cavalrymen was galloping to get between the camp and the horse herd.

Kicking Dog came from his tepee with his weapons already in hand. "Now what have you brought us, old fool?" he said to Long Fingers.

"Wait," the chief replied. "They do not mean to fight us. Maybe it is an escort. They have come to take us to another place."

An officer shouted, and the main body of the force appeared over the sandy slope of the creek bank. Kicking Dog shouted for all the warriors to arm themselves and prepare to cover a retreat of the women and children up the creek bed.

"Wait," Long Fingers ordered. "They mistake us. Black Kettle, raise the American flag and tie a white flag under it."

The Cheyenne chief tied the flags to the end of a lodge pole and raised it overhead; a throng of women and children gathered at the foot of the staff for protection. But just as the banners reached a zenith, the howitzers spoke. Grapeshot ripped through the hide tents. The shrieks of women and children split the air, and Indians fled in every direction. Chivington's voice thundered. Soldiers cheered, and two thousand hooves drummed down the creek bank.

White Antelope ran at the cavalry charge, holding his hands high overhead. He yelled in English: "Stop! Stop!" His band of Cheyenne followed him, trying to surrender before the senseless battle could begin.

Horace saw White Antelope running unarmed at the Hundred Dazers, but when the old chief saw the soldiers would not obey, he lowered his arms, folded them over his chest, and met the onslaught as if it consisted of nothing more than a fair breeze.

The first pistols cracked, and White Antelope rolled under the trampling hooves of the cavalry. The whiskey drinker riding next to Horace spurred his horse in front of Horace's Kentucky stud and jumped off as he passed over the body of White Antelope.

"Damn you!" Horace said, whirling the stud around. "Don't cut my charge!" He had his Remington revolver drawn and pointed skyward, his thumb on the hammer.

The whiskey drinker didn't look up but drew his knife, and cut the leather leggings from the dead chief's hips. He cut the thong of the breechcloth and tossed it aside. He took the testicles of the corpse in his hand.

"My Lord," Horace said. "What in God's name do you mean to do?" Screams and gunfire cut through the dust in the creek bed.

"I'll take and fix me a tobacco pouch," he shouted above the racket, grinning up at Horace. He put his blade under the grisly trophy.

Horace spurred his stud away from the scene of mutilation. He would remember the soldier's face and report his atrocity after the battle. But for now he had to catch the warriors fleeing up the sand hills and along the creek bed. Somebody was going to pay for what had happened to Hank and Bill.

Squads of soldiers swarmed everywhere in pursuit, setting up a cross fire that proved more dangerous to themselves than anything the Indians had organized. The artillerymen hadn't stopped blasting, even though their own men were now in the line of fire.

Horace galloped among the tepees and the bushes, heading up the broad, sandy creek bed. Ahead, the warriors seemed to be making an attempt at fighting back, and he wanted to join the battle. His horse dodged bloody bodies as he weaved his way among the deserted tents.

Before he could reach the battle up the creek bed, he ran upon six soldiers preparing to set a tepee on fire. "Hey, soldier, give us a hand," one of them said. "They're in this one thick as fleas."

"They're fixin' to flush," another shouted.

Horace turned his horse and cocked his pistol, waiting for the braves to bolt from the lodge. The burning buffalo hide sizzled like grease, and smoke billowed from the lodge as the soldiers lined up and prepared to fire. The flap of the tepee flew aside, and a little girl tripped out. Strands of black hair covered her face. She held a stick with a dirty white handkerchief tied to it. Horace pointed his gun back to the sky and heaved a sigh of relief. "Just kids," he said.

He couldn't explain the gunfire that came next. It was too torrential for accident; too cruel for intent. The body of the little girl jerked, then crumpled and reeled under the hail of bullets. Women and children poured out of the burning lodge. Some dropped to their knees for mercy, some ran for their lives, but none escaped the deluge of lead. One wounded old woman attempted to crawl away. A soldier rode over her and fired down into her head.

Most of the soldiers rode on then, but two got down to search the bodies. When one pulled out a knife and grabbed a handful of hair, Horace holstered his pistol and turned away, choking to keep the whiskey down in his stomach.

A wounded soldier was returning from the fight in the creek bed, almost falling from his saddle for loss of blood. Horace caught the man before he fell and guided his horse back through the smoldering Sand Creek village. He looked at the bodies he had galloped past earlier. All women and children, except for one young brave.

Horace helped the wounded man to the hospital tent, then sat in the sand outside to watch the swarms of soldiers riding like vultures on the winds, looking for victims. He could hear the roar of the howitzers and the rattle of pistol shots.

"Are you wounded, too?" the surgeon asked.

Horace shook his head.

"Run out of bullets?"

"No. I didn't fire a single round, thank the Lord."

TWENTY-FOUR

LONG FINGERS' WIFE lay behind him in a pit they had scratched into the creek bank with a knife. After each volley, she poured the powder down his rifle muzzle, patched the bullet with a bit of cloth, and rammed it home with the rod. A constant rain of sand fell on them, and the grit kept jamming the lock on the chief's rifle.

After assaulting the creek from every quarter, the soldiers had failed to rout the defenders. But the Indians were running low on shot and powder, and Long Fingers knew that another wave or two of soldiers would finish them.

He caught Black Kettle's attention across the creek bed. The Cheyenne chief had dug in nearby, his wife shot several times but still living. They used the sign language to organize a final desperate maneuver.

The women and children would attempt a mass retreat up the creek bed while the warriors covered their escape. Then the men would bolt in every direction, dispersing the soldiers. Maybe some of them could escape in that way. Otherwise they would all die.

Long Fingers gave the shout, and the women and children jumped from their trenches, running up the creek bed. The warriors staggered their gunfire to hold the soldiers back, but a vast wave of white men rushed down on them.

Long Fingers fired, rolled out of his pit, and prepared to meet the attackers with his hands. He would hold back as many as he could until his wife had died or escaped. Perhaps she could hide between the sand hills and make her way north.

As he glanced over his shoulder to watch out for her, he saw white men on the creek bank above her. One of them—buckskinned and top-hatted—slid down the sandy embankment in pursuit of the defenseless women and children: ugly features, hobbling gait, iron-gray shocks of hair jutting out from under the dowdy hat. The chief whirled to protect his wife, but Dutch caught her, tackling her from behind. The scout grabbed her hair, wrenched her head back, and drew his knife.

Long Fingers was there, swinging his rifle stock. He knocked the scout's head out from under his feathered beaver hat. His wife jumped up and ran again. The chief shoved his knife between Dutch's ribs and prepared to drive the blade around to the chest, but bullets struck him in the back, and he could not finish it.

He fell on Dutch and rolled over to stare at the sky. His body would not work after the shock of the slugs. Warriors were retreating behind their families, running past him, pausing to fire, then running again. Sand and smoke blurred the sky.

A blanket fell beside him. Kicking Dog was there, rolling him onto the wool. He grabbed two corners and ordered two braves to take the others. They carried Long Fingers up the creek bank, saw the soldiers scattering in pursuit of victims. They sprinted around a bend with the chief and collapsed, dropping the blanket. One of them climbed the bank to look for the best avenue of escape.

"Why do you help me?" Long Fingers asked. "Leave me here and run."

Kicking Dog was on his knees, heaving for air. "I am taking you north," he said. "I want you to hear the scorn of your people. I want you to see them laugh at your pain."

The brave came down from the creek bank. "They are running all around, shooting at the people, but they are scattered out. Maybe we will get away if we lie down and hide when they come close."

Kicking Dog grabbed the corners of the woolen litter and prepared to run. "Now you will tell your people it is time to fight," he said.

Long Fingers shook his head. "They will kill us all if we fight."

"What do we have to live for? We have no food, no land, no honor."

"Our tribe is the mother of all people," Long Fingers said as the blanket tightened under his weight. "The children have no hope who have no mother."

TWENTY-FIVE

S OMETIMES CALEB AND Buster lost track of the time at night as they practiced in the toolshed where Buster lived. On cold nights they would build a fire in the sheet-metal forge and play for hours. If they went on too late, Caleb generally spent the night in the shed with Buster. He had a cot there that was just as comfortable as his bunk in the cabin.

Through this arrangement, Caleb had made a wonderful discovery. When he wasn't in the cabin, his father assumed that he was with Buster. And when he left the toolshed late at night, Buster assumed he was going home. If he wanted to stay up past his bedtime, all he had to do was leave Buster's shed and wander around the Holcomb homestead. Then he could sneak quietly into the cabin whenever he got sleepy.

He had no fear of the night as long as Wild Man stayed with him, and Wild Man would follow Caleb anywhere. Wild Man was the surviving hound left at Holcomb Ranch by Cheyenne Dutch four years before. He had grown into a ridge-hackled protector of considerable size, strength, and courage. He disappeared sometimes for days, then came down from the mountains, lame and bleeding from fighting with wild animals. Caleb would nurse him back to form and sneak him food at all hours.

One moonless night, Caleb left Buster's toolshed and headed toward the cabin with Wild Man at his heels. He passed by the bunkhouse where Javier lived alone. The Mexican foreman would have the place to himself until the ranch could get more cattle and hire cowboys to work them.

When Caleb reached his home, he stopped to look up at the stars. They covered the sky like sugar sprinkled thick on a soot-blackened hearth. He had tunes in his head. His fingertips still tingled from plucking music from the instruments. He sucked a measure of cold air in through his nostrils and scorned the houses of civilized men.

After quietly picking up an armload of wood from the pile, he left the cabin behind and walked toward a bend in the creek upstream. He made his fires there on cold nights, out of sight of the cabin. He would quench the fire with creek water before finally coming home, and hide the ashes under cow chips.

A twisted bundle of dead grass took the flame from his match and passed it to the kindling above, then to the sticks and split logs. He leaned back against the creek bank with Wild Man pressed to his side and pulled his harmonica out of his coat pocket. He watched the orange sparks rise as he played and studied the lines of the Rampart Range, so strange and distant in this darkness.

He played the harmonica low and mournfully until his hands got so cold that he had to shove them into his pockets. The warmth of the fire and the dog contented him, and he rested his head against the creek bank to look at the sky. The sounds of the popping fire lulled him, and the sky became blacker and filled with fanciful visions of horses and mountains.

He woke when Wild Man moved suddenly, felt the sting of smoke in his nostrils. It was as if the sun had risen under him. The prairie was on fire! The grass at his very feet was burning, and the orange rope of flame was spreading outward from his fire. He jumped to his feet and began stomping, but the fire spread faster than he could put it out. He ran desperately to the creek and filled his hat with cold water. He climbed the bank again, poured the water in the path of the grass fire. But his hat would not hold enough. A mischievous wind came down from the north and fanned the blaze toward the Holcomb cabin.

The winter had been a dry one, and the grass was like tinder. Each blade flared briefly and lit the next. Caleb thought about the firebreaks. Buster had plowed them around the ranch to keep prairie fires from burning down the buildings—three giant semicircles of plowed-under grass, one inside the next. The ends of the curves ran down to the creek, completing the ring of protection. But Caleb had built his fire inside the innermost ring. No break stood between the fire he had set and the buildings where his friends and family lived.

Frantically, he ran to the creek to fill his hat with water again, but the fire had spread beyond his control. Wild Man romped around him in confused excitement. Finally Caleb abandoned hope and sprinted to the cabin to warn his father.

"Papa!" he yelled, bursting in through the cabin door. He heard his father move in bed. "Fire!"

Ab appeared at his bedroom door, the right leg of his long handles swinging empty below the knee.

"The grass is burnin'!" Caleb said.

His father hopped to the door of the cabin and looked north. "That's inside the firebreak!" he said. He looked at Caleb. "Why are you dressed at this hour? Why aren't you in bed?"

Caleb couldn't answer.

"What in Hades have you done, boy?"

"I don't know," he said, his tears catching the orange flare of the approaching fire.

Matthew and Pete had woken and stumbled out of their room.

"Go wake Javier and Buster up," Ab ordered. "Hurry!"

Caleb tore away from the cabin.

"Get dressed!" Ab said, hopping back to his room. "Matthew, you go turn the horses out. Pete, soak some sacks with water!"

The fire had almost reached the cabin by the time all the men and boys were dressed. Ab ordered them to beat the fire out upwind of the cabin. "Let it burn around the house!" he said. "Just keep it away from the logs. Caleb!"

The boy was standing between the fire and the cabin, coughing in the smoky air. He wanted to do something, but didn't know how.

"Get in the house!" his father ordered.

Caleb looked at the fire and pointed.

"Get in the house before you choke to death!"

He ran past Matthew on the way to the cabin.

"Stupid!" his brother said.

Through the cabin window, Caleb watched them fight his fire. His tears and the uneven panes of glass blurred and bent the images into unearthly visions. He watched helplessly as they split the line of fire around the cabin. Then they beat the flames down with wet sacks in front of the bunkhouse and in front of Buster's toolshed. They couldn't save the corrals. The rails went up like matchsticks and crumbled to embers.

After the flames passed the buildings, the firefighters worked the edges, letting the grass burn itself out inside the firebreak. When they were sure it was out, they trudged back to the cabin.

Caleb lay facedown on his bed when he saw them coming. He was full of shame. He dreaded facing any of them, especially his father.

". . . but it's lucky," Buster was saying when they came in. "We would have burned up all the grass from here to Colorado City if we hadn't plowed them firebreaks."

"You mean Caleb would have," Matthew said.

"What was that boy doing?" Ab asked. "I thought he was with you, Buster."

"He left the shed. Said he was goin' home. I guess he wanted to sit out by a campfire. He didn't get to go up to the mountains with Pete and Matthew when you took 'em huntin'. I guess he wanted to see what it was like."

"I had reasons for not taking him hunting. He's not old enough, and he's not up to riding those mountain trails."

"He would have burned the mountains down," Matthew said.

"I know a place to take him hunting with no dangerous trails," Javier said. "Up on the divide where the Pinery comes out of the mountains."

"There's plenty of deer up there," Buster said. "Me and Javier could take him."

Matthew stomped his boot on the floor. "He dang near burned our whole ranch up! How come he gets to go huntin'?"

"Hush!" Ab said. "Nobody's going anywhere except to bed. We'll have to get up early and find the horses."

Caleb pretended to be asleep. Even when Matthew poked him, he lay as still as a corpse.

"Leave him alone," Pete said.

They were too tired to argue and soon went to sleep.

Caleb dreamed of fire, but when he woke, it all seemed like a vague nightmare. He felt glad to be awake as he walked groggily out to the cabin porch to pee, relieved to be free of the shame he had felt in his dream.

Then his eyes focused, and he saw the charred ground spreading all around his house. He saw the burned trunks of the cottonwood trees and was mortified to think that he might have killed them after Buster had gone to so much trouble to plant them and make them grow. He saw the black corral posts smoldering near the bunkhouse.

He was almost anxious for his punishment. He wanted to stop feeling guilty. But day after day the black ground reminded him of his foolishness, and his father refused to speak of it. He would do anything to make up for his stupidity. He would forget about riding and roping, and let the plow drag him. He didn't deserve to go hunting. He would build a new corral all by himself. He yearned to make it right.

But his father wouldn't forgive him. He wouldn't even address the subject. He wouldn't let Caleb make amends. And that was his punishment.

II
GLORY & HORROR

1871

TWENTY-SIX

C ALEB PICKED UP a half-rotten log and hefted it over his head. He dropped it in place at the top of the log wall, pieces of decayed wood shaking loose and falling in his eyes. Of all his hated jobs, building the homestead huts no one would ever live in demoralized him the most. Buster had taught him to love fine workmanship, but he was not allowed to use any of it in the rotten little log shacks or the crooked sod huts his father made him build in mock satisfaction of the homestead laws.

As he shook the wood flakes down the legs of his overalls, he saw a rider coming along Monument Creek from the north. He knew at a glance it was his oldest brother, the last person he cared to see.

Matthew loped to the square of stacked logs, his full-sleeved red gingham shirt flapping in the wind, and reined in his spotted horse. "Had any whores since I been gone?" Matthew asked, resting his hand arrogantly on the grip of his Colt revolver.

"None of your business."

"That's what I thought. How old are you now?"

"I'm four years younger than you. Can't you figure it out?"

"You're seventeen and you ain't had you a whore yet? What are you waitin' on? I had my first one when I was . . .''

"I know, when you were fourteen. You've only told me a couple of thousand times."

"Hell, even Pete got him one when he was sixteen. As often as you and Buster go down to Colorado City to play at them dances, I would think you could have had you a dozen whores by now.''

''Maybe I have.''

''Like hell you have. How's my house comin'?''

Caleb picked up another log and threw it in place. ''What difference does it make to you? You aren't gonna live in it.''

''I might want to camp out here once a year or so. Just so I can tell them up at the land office that I lived here. What's that other load of logs doin' up the creek on the next quarter section?''

''I have to build another shack there.''

''For who?''

''Some fellow named Sam Dugan that Papa just hired.''

''He's hirin' more men?'' Matthew asked.

''Just one to take Blackie's place.''

''What happened to Blackie?''

''If you stayed around here more, you'd know. Papa fired him.''

''Fired him for what?''

''Same reason he fires anybody. Blackie proved up on his claim, and Papa bought him out. Didn't need him anymore, so he fired him and hired this fellow Sam to file on more land.''

''Papa don't fire nobody just because they prove up. Blackie must have done somethin' else to get fired.'' Matthew rode around the pitiful log box Caleb was throwing together. ''Where's my door gonna go?'' he asked.

''If you want a door in it, you can saw it in yourself.''

''Saw it? I could rake a hole through them rotten logs with my spurs.''

''Well, do it, then. It's supposed to be your house anyway.''

''It's your job to build it, though, and I say it's stupid to build a house without no door.''

''I don't know why you'd even care,'' Caleb said. ''You won't ever use it except maybe to piss on, and I doubt you'll even come around to do that. You spend all your time whorin' in Denver and Colorado City while Pete does all your work.''

Caleb heard the saddle leather creak and thought Matthew was coming down after him. But Matthew had only thought of tangling with Caleb for an instant. Caleb was getting too stout from all that work he did afoot.

''You better watch your smart mouth or I'll climb down and clean your plow,'' Matthew threatened. ''I haven't been whorin' any more than you have. I have me a proper sweetheart now. I'm gonna ask her to marry me. I just went to Denver to get her a ring.''

Caleb dropped the log he had lifted and stared at his brother in disbelief. He couldn't imagine any proper girl wanting to marry the likes of Matthew. He had to admit his brother was a good-looking cuss, but he had the charm of a wounded bobcat. "Who would want to marry you?" he said.

"Her name's Amelia Dubois. Her father's one of them that owns the Denver and Rio Grande. They just built them the biggest house in Colorado Springs, a mile from where the new depot's gonna go."

Caleb continued to stare up at Matthew with his mouth open.

"I'm bringing her out to meet the family next Saturday. I hope you'll put some pants on. She doesn't know I got a brother that wears overalls."

"You don't think she's really gonna marry you, do you?"

Matthew took an old rope from a saddle string. "Soak this hemp in the creek for me. It's gone limp." He tossed the coil on Caleb. "A couple of hours in the water ought to stiffen it up. I have to find those yearlings up in the Pinery and herd 'em down to the pens. I'll need that rope this evenin' for brandin', so bring it back to the house when you come in for supper." His horse lurched forward between his spurs. "You better build that shack to last five years," he shouted as he rode away. "I aim to prove up!"

"Soak your own damn rope," Caleb muttered, kicking the lariat aside.

He envied Matthew so much that he almost hated him. His brother could saddle any horse on the place, anytime he chose, and ride wherever he wished. It rankled him almost to tears to see Matthew riding around shooting his pistol and whirling his loop. The only time Caleb got to ride was when Matthew and his father were away, and then he had barely the time to practice any roping. He was just as much of a Holcomb as Pete or Matthew. When would his father give him the same rights?

Pete always told him to be patient, and someday he would drive the cattle to market with the cowboys. But now the railroad had laid tracks past Holcomb Ranch, and his father had him and Buster building a depot where he could load cattle and ship them to market. Pete was wrong. He wasn't going to get to drive any cattle on the trail. It was already too late for that.

"Wait till you're twenty-one," Pete would say. "Then you'll be old enough to file on land, and Papa will have to let you do what you want with it. You'll be part owner of this spread then."

But Caleb was almost out of patience. He knew boys younger than he who could rope and throw cattle better than he could on his best day, and it caused him no small amount of humiliation. He kicked the rotten log at his feet, found the only solid place on it, and stubbed his toe through the thin leather of his boot.

He cussed and hobbled around for a while, then pulled a harmonica out of his pocket. He sat down on the rotten log and started to play. It was the only thing he could do that Matthew and Pete couldn't, and it was all that kept him from going crazy sometimes. He never went anywhere without an instrument within his reach. He could play Javier's Mexican songs on the guitar and even sang all the words, though he didn't know the meaning of half of them. He could play banjo, mandolin, and fiddle almost as well as Buster. He favored the fiddle more than anything.

"A man won't never go hungry if he can play a fiddle," Buster had told him.

Caleb had even taken to making up words that rhymed, though he hadn't mentioned it to anybody. As he sat on the log, he played the tune to "Sweet Betsy from Pike" on the harmonica, but he wasn't thinking of the words that usually went along with the tune. He was thinking of the lines he had made up himself. He couldn't say how or why the words had first come to him, but he knew that not even Buster could make up his own words to songs. The thought had occurred to him once or twice that the words may have come from God, or heaven, or maybe even his dead mother, but he wasn't sure he believed in such things.

The harmonica went back in his pocket and he hoisted another rotten log into place as he sang the two verses he had made up to the tune of "Sweet Betsy from Pike":

> *Raised within sight of the high mountaintops,*
> *He grew up 'round plow horses, cattle, and crops.*
> *With one older brother he carried his load.*
> *They tended the fields and the ranges they rode.*
>
> *Hardworkin' farm boys and ranchers by trade,*
> *They lived with the fortune the family had made.*
> *But the farm boy forever looked over the hills*
> *And dreamed of the mountains' adventures and thrills.*

The one older brother his song mentioned was Pete, of course. He knew it wasn't right to have denied Matthew in the lyrics, but including him would have ruined the song. He sang it a dozen times as he continued to lay up the crumbling timbers. Sometimes he sang it silently to himself when other people were around. It gave him the truest sense of accomplishment he had ever felt. No one would ever be able to take those lines away from him. They could take his horses and pocketknives and musical instruments if they wanted to, but they could never take those verses.

The only thing wrong with the song was that it didn't have its own tune. He knew he would have to make one up someday, but he had decided to wait to see if the tune would come to him naturally, out of the clouds, or up from the earth, as the words had.

He walked to the creek and threw Matthew's rope in the water to stiffen it. When he got back to the fake cabin, he saw Pete riding out of the mountains and into Monument Park behind five head of steers.

"Have you seen Buster today?" he asked, leaving the cattle to graze.

"Not since this mornin'," Caleb said. "Why?"

"He told me he got you and him a dance to play at next Saturday. A big one."

"What kind of dance?"

"They're almost finished laying the tracks into Colorado Springs, and they're going to throw a shindig for the workers. The railroad won't allow any liquor, but they said a dance would be all right."

"They usually throw a little more in the hat when they have some whiskey," Caleb lamented.

"So what? You and Buster would do it for free if they asked you to."

"Yeah, I guess so."

Pete hitched his knee over his saddle horn and pushed his hat back on his forehead. "I want to talk to you about something," he said.

Caleb lifted a log overhead and rolled it into position on top of the wall. "What?"

"What would you say if I . . . Well, if I turned preacher?"

"Preacher?" He spit a chunk of spongy black bark out of his mouth. Pete nodded.

"Where do you have to go to turn preacher?"

"You don't have to go anywhere. I figured I could just get a Bible and have a Sunday school on the ranch."

Caleb shrugged. "Well, I'd say go ahead and turn preacher, then, if that's all there is to it. What gave you the idea to do it in the first place?"

"A kind of a voice told me to."

"A *voice?*" He squinted at his brother. "What did it say?"

"It wasn't the kind of voice that used words, exactly," Pete said, glancing off toward the mountains, avoiding Caleb's eyes.

"Well, what did it sound like?"

"It wasn't the kind of voice you can hear, either. At least not with your ears. I was ridin' up over the Arapaho Trail, on that bald hill across the creek from the cabin, when it came to me. This voice, well, just told me to turn preacher. That's the only way I know to explain it."

Caleb scratched his head under the sweatband of his hat. "Maybe it was Mama's voice," he said.

"Maybe," Pete said. "Or one of those saints Javier's always talkin' about. Anyway, I was wonderin' if you'd loan me the money to buy a Bible. I gave all my pay to Matthew."

Caleb grinned. "You gonna let me practice some ropin' on Five Spot?"

All the Holcombs rode Nez Perce horses. Javier had found a couple of spotted studs in Denver and bought them to breed with Crazy, the brood mare. Five Spot was one of the best fillies Holcomb Ranch had turned out yet. She was becoming one of the finest cow horses in the territory.

"Is anybody around?" Pete asked.

"Matthew was here a while ago, but he went huntin' yearlings in the Pinery. I'll climb up on these logs and look around if you want me to."

"Don't do that—they're liable to fall in on you. Just get on." He vacated the saddle for his brother.

"You can take whatever money you need out of the hat next Saturday night at the dance," Caleb said as he put his foot in the stirrup.

"Thanks."

"You know what Matthew said? He said he was gonna get married." He felt the power of the horse under him, like a great living engine.

"I know. I gave him the money to buy the ring in Denver. That's why I need to borrow from you for my Bible. She's a rich gal down in Colorado Springs. He says her daddy is gonna get him a good-paying job at the Denver and Rio Grande depot so he can live in town."

Caleb coughed his indignation. He couldn't imagine such a thing. It riled him more than ever to think Matthew would give up ranching when he wasn't even allowed to get started in it.

"You know what that means," Pete said.

"What?"

"It means I can move up to take his place as foreman, and you can have my spot as straw boss."

"No, it means Papa will probably just hire some other fellow who's old enough to file on some land for him."

"Not this time. I mean to stand up to him." Pete had seen Caleb looking toward the mountains a lot lately and knew he was dreaming of leaving. But he liked having his brothers around—both of them, though they were very different souls—and he had made it his personal duty to make Caleb feel a part of the ranch. "It's time you had your chance in the cow business, and I mean to see that you get it," he promised.

Caleb untied the coil of rope from Pete's saddle and swung a loop into it. "You mean it?" he said.

"They can hang me if I don't. When Matthew gets married, you're gonna sit a cow horse. You'll make top hand on this outfit yet. Now, shake that loop a little wider and see if you can't rope that bald-faced yearling out of that bunch."

Caleb kicked Five Spot's ribs and started his loop whirling. He was hoping Matthew really would get married now. He saw his oldest brother wearing suits, getting paunchy, and going bald. He saw himself growing mustaches and roping wild steers. He didn't understand this thing about turning preacher, but Pete had the dangdest way of restoring his hopes. If not for Pete, he probably would have left home a long time ago.

TWENTY-SEVEN

S AWING LUMBER DIDN'T compare to cutting cattle from a herd, but it beat building the homestead shacks, and Caleb enjoyed seeing the depot take shape by his own hand. Over the years, Buster had acquired two crosscut saws, two ripsaws, two claw hammers, two plumb bobs—two of almost every tool, so Caleb could work beside him with his own equipment. The boy was becoming a first-rate carpenter.

Ab had ordered Buster to build a set of loading pens at the railroad. Buster had talked him into putting up a depot with a loading dock beside the pens so they could handle farm machinery, crops, and anything else that might come or go by rail. Ab had given his permission but had insisted on a simple, functional depot without any superfluous flourishes.

Buster and Caleb, however, indulged in all the fancy mitering and finish work they thought they could get away with. They carved out letters to spell *Holcomb* and nailed them above the depot door. They even put a widow's walk on top so they could watch for the smoke of the locomotives when the trains started running. The depot lacked only a few coats of paint and an inclined loading chute for the Texas longhorns Ab was running on his ranch.

Ab had bought five hundred heifers and cows, some already bred, from Oliver Loving after the war. Loving and Charles Goodnight had herded the longhorns all the way from Texas. The Texas beeves thrived on the free grass in Monument Park. They also killed almost every one of the old oxen and shorthorns Ab had brought from Missouri, not to mention Buster's milk cow. The Texas cattled carried a sickness known as Texas fever that would kill almost any bovine but a longhorn. It gave Ab yet another good reason to despise Texans.

Trail herds occasionally came up the Monument, along what had become known as the Goodnight-Loving Trail. Ab hated to see their herds linger on the free grass, and he hurried them along in every way he could. The hated Texas drovers did keep Ab supplied with cowhands, however. He had little trouble hiring them away from the trail herds when he needed them. He didn't like them because they were Texans, but he didn't mind using them to homestead the creek for him, knowing he could buy them out and fire them as soon as they proved up.

And actually he seldom had to buy any of the boys out. He had established a store on the ranch and given all the hands credit. The boys could buy grub, ropes, tack, and clothing through the ranch store. By the time each man proved up on his homestead after five years, he was usually so deep in debt to the store that he owed the land to his employer. Ab figured the Texans deserved what he dealt them for what they had done to his leg at Pigeon's Ranch, even though none of his cowboys had taken part personally in the fighting there.

Javier didn't like the Texans much either. They were good cowboys, but they took all the beauty out of the work. They were ''hard and fast'' men who tied the ends of their short ropes to their saddle horns, instead of taking dallies the way Javier did. They threw a variety of loops, but few of them cared for the flourishes Javier made with his noose. To his great sorrow, even Matthew and Pete had gone over to the Texas style of roping.

About noon, Ab rode old Pard to the depot to check on the carpenters' progress. His wooden leg clacked around on the hardwood floors for a few minutes, then he shouted, ''Buster, you and Caleb better go get cleaned up. Matthew's bringing that little gal to supper this evening, and I guess we ought to try looking civilized.''

He went up to the widow's walk before leaving and looked back toward the ranch. He could see the ridge log of his cabin from there. The graded bed of the Denver and Rio Grande snaked across the free-grass country to the north, ribbed with crossties and double-spined with steel rails. Somewhere out of sight to the south, the crews were still laying tracks at the rate of a mile a day.

Ab's ranching and farming interests had enjoyed moderate growth since the end of the war, but he knew the railroad would make him even more prosperous. He had sold cattle from Pueblo to Denver, and beyond. The gold mines, the Indian agencies, and the railroad construction crews had provided a steady market; the U.S. Army forts preferred to buy their beef from a former Union hero rather than a bunch of beaten Confederates up from Texas. Whatever surplus Ab had that he couldn't sell in Colorado, he had Javier, Matthew, Pete, and the hired hands herd to the cow towns in Kansas. But with the Denver and Rio Grande building right past Holcomb Ranch, he would no longer have to drive cattle across the plains. He could simply load them at the depot and be done with them.

The Denver and Rio Grande had its critics, but Ab was not one of them. He had confidence in the little locomotives that would run on the narrow-gauge tracks. He didn't know squat about railroading, but he knew of William Jackson Palmer, founder of the D & RG. Palmer was a former Union general and resident of Pennsylvania, a man of religion and an advocate of temperance. Ab was proud to have a station on General Palmer's road.

The railroad would probably bring more homesteaders to the Front Range, but Ab had found ways of keeping the nesters out of Monument Park. His cowboys had already proved up or filed on enough quarter sections to reach six miles up the creek. Many of them were due to prove up within the year, with a little help from witnesses who would bend the truth for them at the land office and swear that the cowboys had lived on and cultivated their homesteads for the duration. As he found reasons to fire those who proved up, and hired new men to take their places, Ab would gain control of more creek frontage, until he owned the whole of Monument Creek above his cabin.

It was a slow process, but Ab thought he could keep directing the homesteaders elsewhere until he tied up all the land along the Monument. He had taken on the title of Absalom Holcomb, Land Locator, and found it astounding that homesteaders would actually pay him to steer them clear of the best farming land along Monument Creek. As one of the earliest settlers in the region, and an erstwhile farmer, he was supposed to know all the best farm sites. He guided the settlers to farmsteads on Camp, Bear, and Cheyenne creeks, and even along the Monument, downstream of his ranch. But he kept them away from Monument Park above his cabin.

After Ab climbed down from the widow's walk and rode back to the ranch, Buster and Caleb loaded their carpentry tools into the buckboard and followed. The drive back to the cabin led them over a regular mat of browning grass. It had been a good year for rain, and all the old buffalo wallows were brimming with water. Hand-cut hay stood in stacks as high as houses. The rye and fall wheat were going to produce bumper harvests, and the corn cribs were jammed with full-kerneled cobs.

Ab claimed the climate was getting ''more seasonable'' as more settlers established farms. He believed the crops themselves caused the rain that sustained them. But Buster was silently cautious in his optimism. Old Chief Long Fingers had told him of the great circles of the plains and mountains. Circles of time, life, weather. He thought it possible that the year of 1871 had simply passed through the wettest curve of the rain circle.

''Come over to my house after you wash up,'' Buster said as Caleb jumped out of the wagon, ''and we'll tune everything up for tonight.''

''All right,'' Caleb said. He went into the cabin, got his best pair of pants and his newest shirt, and walked up to the irrigation flume to bathe. He opened the sluice gate enough to let the water run about a foot deep. He stripped and leapt into the flow, bracing himself against the cold, gripping the sides of the flume so he wouldn't slip along the bottom and get splinters in his butt. The irrigation ditches ran near enough to the cabin to fill a washtub, but he preferred to bathe in the gushing water of the flume, where he could lie back and let the current do all the work. When he finished his bath, he closed the sluice gate and sat in the flume until the sun dried him. Then he got dressed.

The wooden flume began at the reservoir on Javier's quarter section. Caleb followed it downstream until it reached the top of the cutbank and emptied into an irrigation ditch on his father's homestead. The ditch led near the cabin, where Caleb veered from it, passed Buster's wildflower garden, walked under the limbs of the young cottonwoods, and went into the cabin to throw his dirty clothes in a pile at the foot of his bed.

He went back outside, passed his mother's grave, and rejoined the irrigation ditch between two fields of waving wheat. Crimson paintbrushes bloomed along one stretch of the ditch where Buster had scattered their seeds. He jumped the morning glory vines that climbed the fence rails bordering Buster's claim. The ditch branched into laterals that fed a thirty-acre truck patch. Buster could grow enough there to get through the dry years, as long as it didn't get so dry that the creek quit running.

Buster always washed up with warm water and lye soap outside the one-room cabin on his homestead. When Caleb got there, he found the tub emptied and resting upside down on the ground, and heard fiddle music coming from the open cabin door.

"Come on in," Buster said, when Caleb stuck his head through.

" 'Turkey in the Straw,' " Caleb suggested.

Buster's cabin stood on bare ground, but he had hauled several loads of sawdust from Colorado City to spread across the floor. He had sewn a bunch of burlap bags together, stretched them over the sawdust, pegged them to the ground around the inside walls, and made a fine carpet of them. He didn't even have to sweep because dirt and dust filtered through the burlap and into the sawdust.

There was just enough room inside for the two pine bedsteads strung with rope, a table and chairs, a cookstove set on a flagstone foundation, and shelves where Buster kept his food, clothes, and personal possessions.

One of the shelves held a number of cloth tobacco pouches the cowboys had emptied and thrown away. In the little drawstring pouches, Buster kept different varieties of wildflower seeds, which he planted around his cabin and in the garden Ab made him keep up to supply Ella's grave with color. He had seeds in such variety that blooms opened from April to November in the garden, along the irrigation ditch, and all around his house.

Caleb entered the cabin and sat on the bunk he often slept in when he stayed too late at night practicing songs with Buster. "What do you think she'll be like?" he asked, tapping his foot to "Turkey in the Straw."

Buster lifted the bow from the strings. "Who? Matthew's gal? Well, I gather she'll be pretty. Matthew has a weakness for the pretty ones. And I reckon she'll be stuck-up—rich gal like that. What do you think?"

"I guess she'll have to be about as crazy as a coot to want to marry that hardhead," Caleb said.

Buster laughed, propped the fiddle up in its open case, and tightened the horsehairs on the bow a couple of turns. "Go out to the wagon and get that ripsaw for me."

"What for?"

"Just go get it. I want to show you something."

Caleb went out to the wagon and brought back the saw.

"Watchin' you rip those boards today made me remember somethin' I learned a long time ago," Buster said, taking the tool. He held the saw handle between his knees, with the sawteeth pointing in toward him, and grabbed the end of the blade in his left hand. He took the fiddle bow in his right hand, stroked it against the straight back of the steel blade, and arched the blade with the thumb and fingers of his left hand.

The saw began to sing. It sang higher when Buster bent the blade in a tighter arch, and lower when he curved it less. Its voice wavered like a tortured soul of the spirit world when he wobbled the vibrating steel. It sang in a tone more lonesome than the most distant wolf howling on the darkest night, and more sorrowful than the coldest winter wind whipping down a smokeless chimney.

However doleful the saw sang, though, it was still music, and music made Caleb smile. He shivered with the weird vibrations as the saw moaned "Come to the Bower."

Pete's freshly polished boots stepped onto the burlap carpet. "What in the world is that sound?"

"Buster's playing' a ripsaw," Caleb said over the trembling voice of the musical tool.

Pete eyed the saw with disbelief. "Well, I'll be danged. I would have never guessed. It sounded just like a crosscut saw." He elbowed Caleb and listened to the saw wail as if every stroke of the fiddle bow pained it like a hot iron.

Javier entered the little cabin and took off his sombrero. *"¡Válgame Dios!"* he said. "That music, it makes my heart like a bullet." He clutched his shirt in the V of his vest.

Buster ended the tune with a long, lonesome note that climbed two octaves and quavered to death on its way to the third.

"I swear, Buster," Caleb said, "I believe you could make a sledge-hammer play if you touched that fiddle bow to it."

"Y'all had the dogs howlin' all the way over to the bunkhouse." Sam Dugan, the new ranch hand, followed his voice into the cabin. "What was that god-awful racket, anyhow?"

"Buster burned hisself pissing up the stovepipe," Javier suggested with a ribald grin.

"Sounded like it." Sam leaned his lanky body against the doorframe and stuck his thumbs under his belt. "What are y'all doin' sittin' around here. There's a lady comin' to the ranch, ain't there? Shouldn't we be shovelin' up all the horseshit or somethin'?"

"What for?" Javier asked. "Matthew is going to bring her here in a surrey. She is going to have to look at a horse's ass all the way here anyway."

"Two horses' asses, countin' Matthew," Caleb said.

Sam sat down on Buster's handmade table and seemed not to care that it creaked under his weight. "I guess y'all don't appreciate the fairer sex the way I do. I'd have shoveled up all the horseshit for her. At least that around the house that she might step in."

"Hasn't anybody showed you where the shovels are?" Pete asked.

Buster put the ripsaw aside and grabbed his fiddle. "Get that guitar out and we'll tune up," he said to Caleb.

As they plucked the strings and adjusted the tuning keys, Sam said, "Buster, the fellers tell me you escaped as a slave."

Buster glanced and nodded.

"They say you rode off to the Indian Territory to rescue one of these boys."

"It was Caleb," Pete said. "The Comanche had him."

"I want you to tell me about all of that sometime," Sam said.

"That high E is still flat," Buster said to Caleb. He looked at Sam. "What for?"

"Well, I got me an idea. I've been punchin' cows too long. I'm gittin' so bowleggedy I couldn't stop a pig in a ditch. I've decided I'm gonna make a writer."

"A writer?" Javier said. "Do you know how to write?"

"Hell, yes, I know how. I went to school four winters in a row when I was a kid."

"You want to write about Buster?" Caleb asked.

"Well, see, I got me this idea. Since the war, all them slaves across the South have been allowed to go to school and learn to read, ain't they? How many of 'em you reckon there are? Well, I bet there's a hundred thousand. And once they learn readin', what do you think they'll want to read? You think they'll want to read about white folks? Hell, no, they'll want to read about their own kind. So, I'm gonna write a story about a nigger hero, and Buster, here, sounds like just the feller. I guess that ought to make a writer of me. Hell, anything's better than punchin' cows."

Buster smirked and said he would tell Sam all about his adventures some other day. "Give me the A string. Caleb!"

The boy was staring dumfounded at Sam. Anything better than punching cows? This Sam Dugan didn't have the sense of a goat.

TWENTY-EIGHT

A FTER TUNING UP the instruments, Buster went to Ab's cabin and started cooking the meal for Matthew's guest. Pete, Caleb, and some of the boys sat among the leaves that had fallen from the rows of cottonwoods and waited for the arrival of Amelia Dubois. At last they saw the one-horse surrey approaching, and got up as a body to tuck in their shirts and rake their bangs under their hats.

When the surrey arrived, Caleb knew instantly that Amelia Dubois was the prettiest thing he had ever seen. He had flirted with a few farm girls at harvest festivals and risked some glances at the painted ladies who worked the sawmill dances in Colorado City, but Amelia had them all beat. Her chestnut hair hung in ringlets around her face, and her hazel eyes batted mischievously. She didn't seem all that stuck-up or crazy either.

Matthew, on the other hand, appeared to have lost his mind. He was helping her out of the surrey like some kind of gentleman. He even dressed above his means, wearing a silk suit with a red cravat.

"Good evening, boys," he said, with Amelia on his arm.

She was trying to practice a lot of fine manners but could not hide her distaste of the rude surroundings.

"Allow me the honor of introducing you all to Miss Amelia Dubois," Matthew said. "Amelia, this is Javier Maldonado, the manager of the Holcomb cattle interests. And these are a few of the boys: Slim Watkins, Piggin' String McCoy, and Sam Dugan, lately of Texas."

"How do you do, gentlemen," Amelia said in a melodic voice.

Sam's hair fell down in his eyes when he lifted his hat.

"This is my brother, Pete, straw boss of the ranch. And this is my other brother, Caleb, the hardest-working man in the outfit. He does all the work these dumb cow punchers can't figure out. Plays a lot of musical instruments, too."

"It's a pleasure to meet you both," Amelia said. "Matthew speaks of you so often."

Pete said something to her, but Caleb felt too stunned to hear it. Had Matthew called him the hardest-working man in the outfit? Was that the same Matthew he had grown up with?

Amelia eyed the cabin with caution as she entered. Matthew introduced Ab as a hero of two wars and a noted pioneer of the Front Range. He styled Buster the household chef and general overseer of the Monument Park Agricultural Cooperative.

Before he would allow Buster to serve the food, Matthew asked Pete to say grace, after which he remarked, "Well said, Pete." Then he turned to Amelia. "Pete's going to start a Sunday school on the ranch."

Pete blushed.

"Oh, how wonderful," Amelia said.

"Buster and Caleb grow all these vegetables on the farm. Caleb, would you pass the mashed potatoes, please?"

"Huh?" Caleb said.

"Kindly pass the potatoes."

"Oh. All right." Caleb didn't know what to make of it. Matthew couldn't seem to say anything offensive.

"Matthew tells me you're going to play at the Engineers' Cotillion tonight, Caleb."

"Yes, ma'am. I mean, Miss Dubois. Me and Buster will be playin' there. And Javier, too."

"I look forward to hearing some of the regional music. But please, call me Amelia. I'm your age, you know. There's no need for all the formalities."

Caleb nodded and turned red. She didn't seem his age. She seemed more mature and worldly than he ever thought he would be.

"Will you be there also, Pete?" Amelia asked.

"Yes, I always go to the dances," Pete said.

"You must be quite a dancer then."

"I know the steps, but I can't quite step 'em like Matthew."

"Don't believe him," Matthew said. "He can shake a leg with the best of 'em."

"I'm certain he can," Amelia said with a seductive glance.

"Excuse me," Ab said impatiently, "but let's get that fried chicken started." He took a drumstick and said, "Just what is it your father does down there in that big house south of town, Miss Dubois?"

"He's the general manager of the Colorado Springs Company."

"Well, just what is that?"

"It's one of General Palmer's ideas," Matthew said. "Captain Dubois served with General Palmer in the war."

"All right, but what does he *do?*"

"He's in charge of getting the town of Colorado Springs started," Amelia said.

"Now, that's something you'll have to explain to me," Ab said. "There's already a town down there. Colorado City, the seat of El Paso County. Why did the general figure he needed another town just to the south of the one that was already there?"

"General Palmer is quite an idealist," Amelia said.

"Yes, quite," Matthew agreed.

"He doesn't approve of the saloons, nor of the mismanagement and squalor of the common frontier settlement. So he sent my father here to organize an ideal little city. We will have parks and libraries and colleges and wonderful neighborhoods.''

"Even trees," Matthew added. "Captain Dubois already hauled in a thousand cottonwood sprouts they dug up on the Arkansas and planted them on the plains where the new town is gonna go.''

"And we will have a system of waterworks and irrigation, too," Amelia continued. "In fact, I think I shall suggest to father that he send an engineer to inspect your network of ditches here.''

"I helped Buster dig 'em," Caleb said.

Buster beamed with pride at the kitchen table by the fireplace. He normally ate with the family, but he knew the Dubois mansion employed black servants, and he didn't want to upset anybody.

"What does a town need with irrigation?" Ab asked.

"The Fountain Colony has purchased ten thousand acres around the town site," Amelia said with little interest as she cut morsels from a chicken breast. "Members of the colony have the option of obtaining farmland in addition to residential lands in town.''

"Captain Dubois was the first member of the colony," Matthew said. "He built the first house in town, and the biggest.''

Ab pointed his fork at Amelia. "What kind of people are they letting in this colony?''

She dabbed her mouth daintily with a napkin and virtually recited the rules of the colony. "Any person of good moral character may become a member of the colony with a contribution of one hundred dollars and may then choose such lots and lands as are available. The members win title to their lands after making the required improvements. However, there is a clause attached to each land title that says ownership will revert to the colony if the members engage in selling intoxicating liquors as a beverage. General Palmer is a staunch believer in temperance.''

"As all men should be," Ab said, punctuating his approval with a bump of his fist on the table.

"Indeed, all men," Matthew agreed.

Pete almost choked on a chicken bone.

"You sure know a lot about it," Caleb said.

Amelia shrugged. "It's all very tedious, but father rambles on about it constantly. . . .''

With all his questions about the Colorado Springs Company and the Fountain Colony answered, Ab abstained from any further conversation around the supper table. He didn't know whether to consider the intelligence good news or not. General Palmer's railroad was going to attract more settlers than ever to the region, and with ten thousand acres removed from the public domain by the Fountain Colony, Ab was going to have trouble finding homesteads outside of Monument Park for the settlers. He figured he could pass some of them off as persons of high moral character and get them memberships in the Fountain Colony, but the majority would not have the hundred dollars needed. The general's narrow-gauge railroad was shaping up as a bag of mixed blessings.

After dinner, Matthew had to take Amelia back to town so she could get ready for the Engineers' Cotillion. As soon as the one-horse surrey rolled over the hump in the prairie to the south, Buster sat down on the porch, slapped his knee, and started laughing. "He sure forks it high for that gal!"

"Yeah, look," Caleb said, slapping Buster on the back. "Here sits the general overseer of the Monument Park Agricultural Cooperative!"

"And here goes the hardest-working man in the outfit!"

"Y'all shouldn't make light of him," Pete said, grinning all the same. "He's got it bad for that gal."

TWENTY-NINE

CALEB AND BUSTER let Matthew get a few miles down the road with his sweetheart, then piled their instruments into the former wind wagon and hitched a horse. The buggy had long since been restored to its original form, except for the holes in the floorboards where the steering wheel and mast had gone. The mast had become a roof pole for Buster's cabin, and the sail had rotted covering a stack of whipsawed lumber. The wind wagon had charted no course after its maiden voyage. Buster couldn't bring himself to sail it without Caleb.

The engineers and laborers for the Denver and Rio Grande had worn ruts in the road south, but the spring seat made the ride go easy for the musicians. Javier and Pete and half a dozen cowboys followed the buggy on their best horses. They rode past a few homesteads and beyond the rough-hewn cabins of Colorado City to the new railroad town of Colorado Springs.

Caleb played the harmonica as they traveled, his stomach fluttering with excitement. It happened every time he got ready to play for a crowd. Entertaining was routine to him by now, but still, he always felt nervous for the first two or three tunes.

The two-story Dubois house rose from the bare plains like a castle. It towered above the log Fountain Colony Building, the tents, and the small frame houses that had taken shape near the new tracks. Only furrows showed where the streets would crisscross the planned neighborhoods.

Caleb saw the one-horse surrey at the Dubois mansion but noticed Matthew's spotted mount down by the circus tent that would host the Engineers' Cotillion. There a dozen cook fires painted smoke across the twilight sky, and the smokestack of the two-ton locomotive, *Montezuma,* added its own plume of black.

"That's the puniest engine I ever seen," Sam Dugan said. "It wouldn't even hurt to get run over by that thing."

"You know what they use for a switch engine in Denver?" Piggin' String McCoy asked. "A mule! I swear, that's what the fellers said who was layin' the tracks!"

The D & RG and the Colorado Springs Company investors had brought their families from Denver to celebrate the laying of the tracks into the new town. What gave the occasion even more reason for celebration was the fact that the tracks had linked Denver with Colorado Springs exactly one year to the day after incorporation of the railroad.

The railroad investors congregated at one end of the tent. The laborers lounged under the other, talking among themselves, waiting for the feast to begin. About half of them were busted miners and the other half itinerant Mexicans. Caleb noticed that the two groups stayed far enough apart that Buster could have driven his buggy between them had he been of a mind to.

As the musicians began carrying their instruments to the small platform stage, one of the cooks lit lanterns around the inside of the circus tent, and others moved food to the serving table. A servant drove Amelia and her father to the tent in the surrey. Matthew appeared to help her step down. She wore a party dress of French organdy and a hat whose color clashed with Matthew's tie. She made him take the tie off immediately.

Captain Dubois told Buster to stick with the waltzes while the guests ate. "There will be plenty of time later for the quadrilles and gallopades," he said.

As the music started, the Holcomb Ranch cowboys fell in line to get some food. The fare included oyster soup, calf's tongue, corned beef and cabbage, venison with apple sauce, minced ham with scrambled eggs, and sweet potato pie. Piggin' String McCoy piled his plate so high that Sam Dugan was moved to remark, "Damn, String, they ought to have give you a plate with sideboards on it."

Captain Dubois made the three musicians stop playing for fifteen minutes during dinner so he could make a speech about the benefits the D & RG would bring to the Eastern Slope and about how the workers who had built the road into Colorado Springs had made history, establishing the first railroad in the region. Then he sat down to a round of applause led by Matthew, and the dancing commenced.

The railroad workers just watched. They had no women to dance with. Some of the Mexicans whirled imaginary señoritas outside the tent when the polkas played, and a few local homestead couples danced among the railroad investors. But the dance music served little purpose for anyone other than the rich folks.

Pete sat beside the stage and watched the proceedings until he saw Amelia approaching him, then he stood up and took off his hat, rolling the wide brim in his hand.

"You would enjoy yourself more if you'd dance with some of the young ladies," Amelia said, taking his arm with a surprising familiarity.

"I'm afraid I don't know any of 'em. They all came down from Denver."

"You know me."

"Well, Matthew's already claimed you."

Amelia laughed. "Claimed me? I'm not one of your homesteads, Pete Holcomb."

Pete drew his head back. "You mean, he hasn't asked you yet?"

"Asked me what?"

"He bought a ring and everything."

"He's not thinking of asking me to marry him, is he?" She didn't really seem surprised.

"I thought he already did."

She laughed again and adjusted her hat. "Your brother thinks a lot of himself. I hope he can get his money back on the ring."

Pete shoved a hand into an empty pocket. "So do I," he said. He felt a palm slap him on the shoulder and turned to see Matthew.

"What are you doin' over here with my gal?" Matthew said. "I can't turn my back on Pete for one minute. You talk about a charmer with the ladies." He snapped his fingers at the musicians. "Buster, give Caleb the fiddle and let him play me and Amelia a waltz. Make it a long one."

She winked at Pete over her shoulder as Matthew led her to the dance floor.

About ten o'clock, some of the Mexican laborers came to the stage to ask Javier to play something they would recognize. "How about 'Mujer Maldita'?" one of them suggested.

Javier yowled so loud that Caleb thought his voice would rip the circus tent. Then he started the guitar going as the Mexicans hooted like a band of Indians on the warpath. The families of the railroad investors backed away from the stage, uncertain of what the hollering represented, giving the Mexicans plenty of room to sing and carry on.

Caleb's mandolin and Buster's fiddle had played "Mujer Maldita" many times with Javier, and they even knew how to sing some of the words, though they didn't know what they were singing. All Caleb knew was that the song had something to do with wicked women. It was the sound of it that he liked. He knew the first few lines well and sang them in harmony with the Mexican laborers:

Hay mujeres ingratas en el mundo
Que se burlan del hombre y del amor,
Hay mujeres malditas sin conciencia,
Hay mujeres muy lindas sin pudor.

When the musicians had finished the song, and while the Mexicans were still cheering, Captain Dubois handed Buster fifty dollars and said, "That will be all, gentlemen."

It seemed to Caleb that the regional music had driven off the cultured people and ended the party. They were filing from the tent like cattle. Then he looked over the heads of the Mexicans and saw old Cheyenne Dutch straddling a spotted horse at the edge of the circus tent. The aged mountain man rode in under the canvas, followed by three hounds and a burro carrying two whiskey barrels.

"Heard they wouldn't 'low no liquor," he said to the road builders, "so I brung two kegs of Towse. Swap your pay over at the sawmill if you want a taste." He reined the Nez Perce stallion away and disappeared in the dark.

Amelia had been among the first to leave with her father and was now out of sight, so Matthew was aching to fall back on wilder ways. "Let's go over to Old Town," he suggested.

"We already got us fifty dollars to divvy," Buster said. "What do we want to go down to that sawmill for—with that ol' Cheyenne Dutch sellin' that Taos lightning?"

"I'm going to go over there," Javier said. "I want to play some more songs."

"There you go," Matthew said. "Don't worry about Dutch. He's too old to make trouble anymore. What about you, Pete? You goin'?"

"I don't know. What about you, Caleb?"

Caleb needed only a second to make his decision. He rarely passed up a chance to play for a gathering of people, whether they were rich railroad families or common saloon drunks. He was more than a sodbuster when he played and sang. "Sure, I'll go," he said.

"Gonna get you a whore?" Matthew asked, grinning like his old ornery self.

Caleb frowned and picked up his instruments.

"If you're goin', I best go, too," Buster said. "Somebody's got to keep you young boys out of trouble."

"Hell, let's all go. Hey, Slim! Piggin' String! We're headin' over to the sawmill at Old Town!" Matthew shouted.

THIRTY

T HE COLORADO CITY sawmill had seen almost as much whiskey and blood spilled on its floors as sawdust. The fandangos that cut loose there on Saturday nights made more racket than the saw blade did by day. Stacks of lumber served as stages for the musicians, bars for the whiskey peddlers, and benches for the whores who solicited business among the cowboys, freighters, and miners passing through town.

As soon as Caleb entered the mill, he looked around for Caroline. He didn't spot her until he and Buster and Javier were into the middle of the third song. As she came around the saw blade, Cheyenne Dutch offered her a drink of Taos lightning from one of his kegs. She refused it, floating like a cloud onto a stack of boards, settling herself carefully among the splinters. She drew her feet up to a high stack of boards, spread her knees, and pushed her dress down between her legs. She leaned forward and rested her elbows on her thighs. There she sat, listening to the music, swaying to its rhythm.

That was what Caleb liked about her. She listened. The other girls danced to the music and tossed their skirts to it, but only Caroline had the interest to watch and listen. Sometimes he could see her through the tobacco smoke, mouthing the words as he sang them.

The summer sky wasn't as blue as Caroline's eyes.

"What's wrong with you?" Buster asked when the song was over. "You're playin' the wrong chords."

"Sorry," Caleb said. Then he proceeded to forget the words to "The Little Old Sod Shanty." He couldn't concentrate while Caroline sat in front of him.

Matthew left the kegs to bother his youngest brother. "Hey, I see you eyeballin' that whore," he said, adjusting the gun belt he had buckled on after the Engineers' Cotillion. He went on to embarrass Caleb with remarks like, "There's the place for you to soak your rope," and "She'll damn sure make your hemp stiff for you."

Caleb felt relieved when Pete pulled Matthew over to a stack of lumber to talk to him.

"About Amelia . . ." Pete said.

"What about her?"

"You sure you want to marry her?"

"Why? Do you want her now? Find your own gal, Pete. That one's mine."

"No, I don't want her. I'm just not so sure she wants any of you."

Matthew drained his cup and glared at Pete. "The hell! She's probably over at her house tryin' on my name right now."

"I don't think so. Not from the way she talks."

"What did she say?"

"She said she hoped you could get the money back on your ring."

Matthew backed up a step. "Are you lyin'?"

"No, I ain't lyin'. Have you ever known me to lie?"

"No, but I ain't ever known you to lay eyes on a proper lady before, either."

"Well, I ain't lyin', and I'll tell you what else she said. She said she ain't no homestead and she doesn't belong to the first man to come along and claim her."

Matthew looked worried. He put his hand on the ring in his breast pocket and glanced around the sawmill. Then he slapped the stack of lumber and forced a laugh. "Hell, she's just waitin' for me to drive my picket in to stake my claim." He grabbed the crotch of his trousers for emphasis.

"You think she's like that?" Pete asked.

"They're all like that. It feels good for them, too, Pete. Haven't you ever pleasured any of these whores?"

Pete looked at the prostitutes dancing in the sawdust. "Not so much that I'd notice," he admitted.

"Well, sometimes they just don't let on or else you might not pay 'em if you thought they were havin' as good a time as you were." He reached into his pocket and pulled out a gold coin. "Here, give one of 'em a try and see if you can't make her holler."

"No, thanks," Pete said. "I'm done whorin'. I don't think it sits right with the Good Lord."

"The Good Lord put 'em here on earth, that's all I know. You want to go have a cup of Towse with me?"

"No, thanks. I'm gonna listen to them play."

"Suit yourself. And don't you worry about Amelia. She'll know it when I stake my claim."

Matthew passed in front of Caleb on the way to the kegs and tossed his head at Caroline, urging him on. Caleb looked away as if in disgust, but, in fact, he was wishing he had Matthew's gumption and could just walk up to Caroline and tell her he wanted to soak his rope. He slipped into the wrong key, and Buster poked him in the back with the neck of his banjo. "Sorry," he said.

Caleb resolved to throw his concentration into the music and avoided looking at Caroline. He did all right until he sensed her moving from the corner of his eye. He saw her floating down from her bench of stacked lumber, meandering through the dancers, drifting toward the stage with her eyes fixed on his. When she smiled and beckoned to him with her finger, he almost busted a string.

From his angle, looking down on her, he could see her breasts trying to push out of her dress. He smelled the fragrance of powder on her when he knelt to hear her speak. She put her lips against his ear and whispered like wind in the pines.

"I'm going to my cabin," she said. "It's the third one down toward the creek. Come along and tell me the words to that last song you sang. I want to write them down."

Caleb stood back up and watched her mane of yellow curls follow her out of the sawmill. His breath felt hot in his chest.

"What did she want?" Buster asked.

"I know what she wants," Javier said. "You better give him his part of the fifty dollars."

"She didn't want anything," Caleb said. "I have to go outside for a minute."

"What for?" Buster asked.

"What do you think?" Caleb jumped down from the rough-sawn boards and left the mill, using a different door than the one Caroline had passed through.

He ran around the outside of the building just in time to see the door close on the third cabin down the row. A drunken miner stumbled out of the sawmill and staggered up the street past Caroline's cabin. Buster and Javier struck up a Mexican song inside.

Before he knew what had happened, her cabin was standing in front of him. It seemed like someone else's fist knocking on the door.

"Come in," she said.

The stub of a burning lantern wick cast Caroline's shadow around the bulges of the log wall. She sat at the foot of her bed.

"Latch the door," she said, "so nobody will bother us."

Caleb bolted the door behind him and and took his hat off. "What song was it that you wanted the words to?"

"Don't be in such a hurry. Come sit down." She patted the bed beside her.

Caleb's legs felt wobbly, but they got him to the bed. As he sat down, she untied the ribbon that held her hair back, and it fell around her shoulders like a waterfall. The straw mattress sank deep under their weight and pulled them together.

"Was it that sad one about the dyin' prospector?" Caleb asked. His voice cracked when he spoke. "Or the funny one about them Mormon polygamists?"

"I'm afraid I lied about wanting to know the words," Caroline admitted. She stroked her fingers against the back of Caleb's neck, sending chills down his back and over his scalp. She leaned toward him and kissed him softly on the cheek. "Why don't you take your boots off and get comfortable?"

Caleb liked music, but he had never dreamed that it would lead him to getting comfortable with an experienced woman. "All right," he said and began pulling at the foot gear.

Caroline stood up to help him get the boots off, and he sank back on his elbows as she pulled. She turned the wick down on the lantern. Caleb felt too weak to move. Without even a window to let in the starlight, the cabin went dark as soot in a chimney. He heard her clothing rustle. He felt her sink into the mattress beside him. When they rolled together, he felt nothing but hot flesh.

For a long, terrifying minute, Caleb thought he had forgotten how to undress himself. His pants wouldn't come off. Then Caroline got up again to help him, pulling indelicately at the legs of his pants as if they were coming out of a wringer. She settled in beside him again.

"Well, get on," she said.

He floundered around clumsily, worried sick that his hemp would go limp before he could make us of it. When Caroline grabbed it, he worried he would make use of it too soon. Then he felt her warmth, and all his worries ended in fifteen seconds of unorchestrated rooting. His elbows buckled, and he collapsed on her, disoriented in the dark, unable to visualize his whereabouts. He didn't know the floor from the ceiling, or the foot of the bed from its head.

It was the music, he thought. She must like the music an awful lot.

Caroline chuckled lightly, almost mockingly. "You can get off now," she said. "I can't hardly breathe."

The whores and the Taos lightning were claiming dancers quicker than Buster could change chords. "I wonder what's keepin' Caleb," he said. "I better go find him."

"Just play a couple of more songs," Javier suggested. "Stop worrying about that boy. He won't take much longer."

Matthew stood beside the big saw blade, leaning against the stack of boards Cheyenne Dutch was using as a bar. As the crowd thinned out, he and Dutch ended up standing at the bar alone and he noticed the old trader staring at him.

"I know your face," Dutch said. "Just can't place it."

"I favor my father, Absalom Holcomb."

Dutch adjusted the beaver top hat. "One-legged Ab Holcomb? The hero of Apache Canyon? Ab Holcomb's your pa?"

Matthew nodded.

"Why the hell didn't you say so, damn you? Do you like a fight the way he does?"

"I'll fight that circle saw and give it two rounds head start," he boasted.

Dutch laughed hoarsely. "How much have you swapped me for this old Towse?"

"A few dollars, I guess."

Dutch pulled a leather pouch from the pocket of his fringed shirt and tossed it at Matthew. "Color of the Tarryall Diggin's. It'll fetch fifteen dollars an ounce. I'll not take pay from a son of Ab Holcomb."

"Thanks, Dutch," Matthew said, contemplating the weight of the gold dust in his hand.

Dutch rolled one of the kegs on the stack of lumber, sloshing the liquor inside. "Take my kegs, too. I'll stake you to the whiskey trade. I'm bound to swap my earnin's to that yaller-haired whore."

"I wouldn't do that," Matthew said. "I happen to know she's busy right now."

Dutch scratched his dirty fingernails through his beard. "Maybe you wouldn't, boy, but I will if I please. Take my quirt to him she's busy with and have her to myself. Palousey goes horselike a thousand miles over these mountains and studs where he pleases."

Matthew had heard of Dutch's addled jabber, and knew it put him in a mood for trouble. "Well, wait a minute before you go, and drink a toast to Ab Holcomb with me," he suggested.

Dutch paused, then filled his cup. "We rid abreast on bullet-proof horses down Apache Canyon," he said. "Here's to him."

Caleb was half asleep in the dark when Caroline rolled away from him to light the lantern. "You better put your britches on," she said. "I'll have another one in here before the dance is over."

The wick took the flame of her match, and Caleb saw her naked as the light grew. She didn't seem to care in the least that he stared at her. Matthew was right. Soaking his rope had made it stiff, and he wanted more of her. But she stepped into her dress and told him to hurry up and get out.

He put his pants and boots on and stood at the door. She hadn't asked him for any money. He didn't know whether or not he should offer her a few dollars before he left. The moment he had waited for and wondered about for so long had come and gone too quickly. Now her dress was back on, and he had hardly had the chance to look at her without it. He had scarcely taken the time to think about what she felt like under him. He wanted more. He stared at her as she tied her hair back. She was humming a tune he had sung only minutes before.

"What?" she said, impatiently, noticing his stare.

"Should I . . . Do you need any money for anything?"

She ridiculed him with her laughter again. "No, Matthew already paid for you," she said.

"Matthew?"

"Yes, your brother paid me. You don't think I'd have let you in without seeing some money first, do you? Tell 'em you're through with me when you get back in there."

Caleb didn't know how to feel as he heard Caroline bolt the door behind him. In one way it was the only decent thing Matthew had ever done for him, besides calling him the hardest-working man in the outfit. But he knew what was going to happen. Matthew was going to take credit for everything. He was going to tell everybody on the ranch he had to do it for Caleb, because Caleb didn't have the spine to do it on his own. Caleb wasn't going to let him get away with it. He was going to march back to the sawmill and give Matthew a lesson or two on what he was man enough to do.

"To Colonel Chivington!" Matthew said, tossing back another cup of Taos lightning.

Dutch raised his cup in return. "Chivington! Damn the Congress and all its investigations! If God tells a son of a bitch to kill Indians, I guess he's gonna kill 'em!"

Buster and Javier were latching the lids of their instrument cases. "What's he doin' drinkin' with that crazy old man?" Buster said. "And where has Caleb gone off to?"

"We better get out of here," Javier said. "That Dutch gets crazy when he drinks that much Taos lightning." He casually untied the thong that held his pistol in the holster.

Buster nodded. "Pete, go find Caleb," he said.

Pete added up the circumstances quickly and left the sawmill to find his brother.

"To Sand Creek!"

"The battle of Sand Creek! I'll gut the bastard calls it a massacre!" Dutch drained his cup. "Now, here goes Palousey for that filly with the yaller mane."

"One more," Matthew said. "To good old Governor Evans!"

"To hell with governors. If I drink another, my rooster won't peck." He slammed his tin cup on the lumber and took a step toward the door.

"To spotted horses!" Matthew said.

Dutch waved him off.

Matthew drew his Colt.

The old trader stopped when he heard the lock catch. He turned slowly to find Matthew's irons leveled on him.

"Matthew!" Buster shouted across the sawmill.

The few railroad workers and whores remaining in the mill ran for the doors, or dove behind stacks of boards when they saw the gun pointing at Dutch.

"Have you shot every soul that won't drink with you?" Dutch said calmly.

"You don't have to drink," Matthew said. "Just stand still until I tell you to go."

"Palousey goes when he pleases. Goes horselike, spotted rumped, and bulletproof."

"Buster, go get Caleb," Matthew ordered. "He's in the third cabin down the row. Get him in the buggy and get him the hell out of here."

Just as Buster started to move, Pete and Caleb came in, freezing as they saw Matthew aiming at the mountain man.

"Caleb, you and Pete git!" Matthew said.

"Who's this Caleb?" Dutch asked.

"My little brother."

Dutch began to laugh. "Would you shoot me for beddin' your brother's whore?" he asked.

"Of course not," Matthew said. "I just didn't want you to find him there. You said you'd take a quirt to whoever you found with her."

Dutch waved his hand. "Talk," he said. "I'd quirt no boy for whorin'."

Matthew gnawed his lips and dropped his sights to the floor in front of Dutch. "I reckon I made a mistake then. As long as you won't hurt my brother."

"No, I'll not touch a hair of him."

Matthew eased the hammer forward and watched Dutch for a second. He put the pistol in the holster. "No hard feelin's."

Dutch laughed. "No, I'll quirt no boy for whorin'. But old Palousey, he'll scalp any son of a bitch points a gun at him."

The old man yanked a revolver out from under his deerskin shirt as Matthew reached for his holster again. Pete pushed Caleb behind a stack of lumber.

The first shot hit Matthew between the eyes and pitched him dead onto his back in the sawdust.

Javier drew his pistol and put a hole in the whiskey keg five feet from Dutch. The mountain man merely turned his head toward the vaquero. Javier's second bullet caromed off the steel saw blade. His third and fourth shots ripped splinters from the lumber. The fifth bullet clipped the tip from the eagle feather on the top hat.

Dutch faced the vaquero, not even bothering to raise his weapon. "Shoot your last!" he said. "Bullets go round Palousey!"

Javier took deliberate aim down his barrel and squeezed the trigger.

The slug hit Dutch in the chest and slammed him against the lumber. His moccasins slipped, and he sat hard on the floor, sawdust settling around him. He dropped his pistol and cupped his hands to catch the blood that ran from his chest. "Goddamn Indian magic," he said. His voice gurgled in his own blood. He looked up at the spectators through the blue gun smoke in the sawmill. "There's a new face in hell tonight, boys." His head fell forward, and the top hat dropped into his lap.

A barber in Colorado City served also as the settlement's undertaker, and to this man's shop the Holcomb Ranch cowboys carried the body of Matthew. A gang of drunks followed with the corpse of Cheyenne Dutch. Pete and Caleb sat with their dead brother, staring blankly at him, while Buster and Javier went to the ranch to wake Ab.

The barber decided to wait for Ab to tell him what to do with Matthew, but he and his wife went right to work on Dutch. They chose to dress the corpse in a suit and keep the buckskins as souvenirs. As they stripped the body, they attempted to match the scars they found with legends of Dutch's exploits.

"This must be where that crazy Indian woman chopped him with the ax up at Holcomb's Ranch," the barber said.

"Oh, my Lord," the wife said, "I thought that was just a story."

"Old chief Long Fingers got him here in the side with a knife at Sand Creek."

"That's the one that almost killed him, wasn't it?"

"I heard he laid up at Bent's Fort for three months after the massacre."

They pulled off the pants and the wife said, "Oh, goodness, what got him there?"

"Confederate lancers down at Val Verde, New Mexico. They say it went clean through his leg."

"Let's turn him over and see."

When they rolled Dutch over on the table, the wife gasped and the barber just stood and stared for a minute. "Well, I'll be damned," he finally said. "Honey, go get those two Holcomb boys. They might want to see this."

When Pete and Caleb came into the room, they found Dutch's naked body lying facedown on the table. Each buttock had five solid spots tattooed to resemble the rump of a Nez Perce horse.

"I thought you'd like to see," the barber said. "He was a crazy old bastard. I guess some Indian tattooed 'em for him."

Pete walked around the body. "Papa said he bragged about his spotted rump a lot when they were down at Glorietta Pass."

"I never heard Papa tell that," Caleb said, staring at the dark spots on the pale rump of the corpse and feeling ill.

"You were fiddlin' around over at Buster's when he told us."

The bizarre scene swam before Caleb's eyes. It had happened again. Matthew had taken his place under the ridge log. People were always protecting him, rescuing him, risking their lives, giving their lives. He was more trouble than he was worth. Pete would die next, or Buster. He had never even learned to be friends with Matthew. Now it was too late.

It was his fault. He was whoring, for God's sake. Pete had told him it wasn't right. His father was going to hate him. He hated himself. He wanted to leave before he got someone else killed. The dormant guilt surfaced again, marking him indelibly. He tried to cover his shame, but it showed through, like the tattooed spots on Dutch's pale rump.

THIRTY-ONE

Caleb considered breaking virgin prairie through buffalo grass the worst form of livelihood man had ever invented. He thought it bad enough that he had to farm his father's land and help on Buster's, but Buster often hired out to work other homesteads as well, and Caleb frequently joined him. Many of the destitute settlers downstream didn't have the money to buy teams and plows, so they called on Buster, who had the best collection of draft animals and equipment in the valley. He charged two dollars an acre for plowing or traded for whatever the homesteaders could afford, and he split the earnings with Caleb when the boy came along to help.

Caleb managed to get out of some plowing by going to school. He was taking his last year of lessons at the schoolhouse in Colorado City. He didn't like school, but he hated it less than farming.

Today the schoolmarm had let classes out early, and the students had gone screaming with joy into the afternoon, except for Caleb. It only meant that he had to spend an hour longer than he had planned letting the plow handles jerk him across a homesteader's field. He didn't consider a dollar an acre fair wage for the worst work on earth.

At length the sun bedded down in the Rockies, and Buster told Caleb to load the implements in the wagon. While they were heading back to the ranch, Sam Dugan joined them on horseback. He trotted alongside, honing his roping skills on everything that stuck up out of the ground as he pestered Buster for stories.

He made the black man recount his escape from slavery, his rescue of Caleb in the Indian Territory, and his adventure with the wolf-getter gun in Monument Park.

"I sure wish it was you that shot ol' Cheyenne Dutch last fall and not Javier," Sam said. "That would have made a whole chapter by itself."

"Why don't you write a story about a Mexican hero and put Javier in it?" Buster asked.

Sam scoffed. "Because there ain't enough Mexicans can read. There ain't no market for it. Besides, it took him six shots to finally git him. What kind of a hero do you call that?" He looped the coil of rope over his saddle horn and got out the makings of a smoke, shaking the last slivers of tobacco from a drawstring pouch.

"Can I have that empty pouch?" Buster asked.

"Hell, I guess. What do you want with it?"

"I use 'em to put flower seeds in."

Sam stared at Buster so long that the cigarette paper dried and he had to lick it again. "That ain't gonna sound very good for a hero to be a posy sniffer."

"You don't have to write down everything he ever did," Caleb snapped. Sam Dugan irritated him something fierce. The man was forever complaining about having to live the life of a cowboy, when Caleb could imagine no finer existence.

When they reached Buster's farm about dusk, Pete loped over on a bay filly, all excited about something. "You'll never guess what happened," he said.

"I'm too tired to guess," Caleb replied. He wasn't really all that tired, but he had made a practicing of complaining to Pete in hopes that his brother would convince Ab to let him take up cowboying.

"Javier's uncle died down in New Mexico."

Caleb slid the wagon tongue out of the ring in the breast yoke and began stripping the big draft horses of rigging. "I don't see why that should make you so happy," he said.

"Javier's leavin' first thing in the mornin' to take over his uncle's place. He already sold his homestead to Papa."

Caleb looked over the backs of the horses at Pete's grinning face. "He's leavin' for good?"

"Yep."

"What do you want to get rid of Javier so bad for?"

"I don't want to get rid of him," Pete said.

"Then what are you grinnin' about?"

"Papa made me manager of the ranch. Startin' tomorrow."

"Oh. Congratulations. Now, help me get these horse collars loose, will you?"

"You don't understand what I'm sayin'. If I'm manager, I can run this place like I want, hire who I want. Come tomorrow mornin', you won't have to mess with horse collars. I'm hiring you on to ride a cow pony."

Caleb dropped the rigging between the horses and passed under the throatlatch of the one between him and his brother. "But I don't have any horses," he finally managed to say. "I don't even have a saddle."

"I already thought of that. You can have Matthew's saddle. And we'll put his horses and mine together and draw for 'em. About time we divvied his outfit anyway."

Caleb looked back at Buster.

"That's what you always wanted, wasn't it?" Buster said.

Caleb nodded.

"Then go ahead and holler or somethin'."

Caleb turned to Pete. "What did Papa say?"

Pete took some scraps of paper from his pocket and shook them up in his hat. "I didn't tell him. I'm not goin' to either. He told me to run the place the way I wanted, and that's what I mean to do. Here, you get the first draw."

Caleb reached into the hat and pulled out a piece of an old peach can label.

"Which one did you get?" Pete asked.

Caleb read the writing on the back of the label. "Five Spot."

"Dang it! I was afraid you might get her."

Caleb barely slept at all that night for thinking about horses and saddles and ropes. He was starved for action. His thoughts had been mired in guilt for months, and he had had no excitement to relieve his shame. Ab had forbidden him to play at any more dances, taking from him the one thing that gave him pride and identity. He was glad that Pete had finally taken a stand for him. With Pete to help him, he thought he could stand up to his father and finally take his rightful place as a Holcomb. He knew he could not do it alone.

When Caleb arrived at the bunkhouse in the morning, Javier was saying his farewells to the cowboys.

"You damned *borrachos* better not come to see me when Señor Ab gets your land and says adios. I don't want any *Tejanos* with short ropes working on my ranch."

"Hell, Javier," Slim Watkins said, "I'd go to ropin' with a piggin' string before I went to work for you again."

Javier couldn't be rankled this morning. He just laughed and shook hands with all the boys, then rode south with his three best horses, stopping only to say farewell to Buster.

As Caleb cinched his saddle around Five Spot, he heard some of the cowboys pestering Pete about something. They wanted to know who would get to fill the vacant foreman and straw boss positions.

"I don't know yet," Pete said.

"I hope you're not plannin' on makin' your little brother a foreman," Piggin' String said.

"I will if I see fit," Pete answered.

"Every man in the outfit's got time on him. He hasn't branded a single head."

"His name is Holcomb and this is the Holcomb Ranch. I'd be a liar if I told you I didn't favor him."

"I won't take a top job until you all know I've earned it."

The cowboys turned around to see Caleb sitting on Five Spot, fastening the end of his rope around the saddle horn.

"He looks like he means to go to work," Pete said. "I'd find my saddle if I was you boys."

After the men got ready to ride, they walked their horses away from the corral and started past the cabin.

"Do we have to ride by the house?" Caleb asked. "Papa might see me."

"Let him see you. He's gonna see you sooner or later."

The dread he felt of his father almost overwhelmed him. He felt as if he were going to meet someone for a fight. He had thought often of leaving Holcomb Ranch, of finding his freedom alone in the mountains. But he had rarely envisioned himself standing up to Ab. He would never have even tried without Pete's help. He looked at his brother with admiration. Pete's face showed that he was actually taking joy in the coming confrontation.

Caleb tried to keep hidden behind the other riders, but they were too strung out to give him much cover. He strained to keep his eyes on the plains, but his eyes kept straying back toward the log house. He knew his father was in there. Ab hadn't gone much of anywhere since Matthew died. The sun was streaming over the stalks of the shortgrass plains, enriching the hues of the wildflowers on the two graves and tinting the windowpanes.

Suddenly the curtain pulled open, and Ab's face emerged from the darkness of the cabin. It surfaced behind the glass like the face of a corpse bobbing up from a dark pool. Week-old whiskers caught the fire of the morning sun. Caleb tried to look away in time, but his father's eyes locked onto his and flared as the face sank back into darkness.

The cabin door burst open, and Ab hopped out onto the porch. He hadn't even taken the time to strap on his peg. The hollow length of his pants leg flailed wildly as he struggled to balance himself. "Pete!" he yelled. "What's he doing on that horse?"

"I made him a cowhand," Pete said, reining his horse to face his father.

"His job is farming. Get him off that horse."

"You told me to run this ranch as I see fit," Pete said. "I see fit to make Caleb a cowhand. He's almost a grown man, Papa. He's old enough to pick the kind of work he wants."

Caleb didn't feel almost grown, not with Pete doing all his talking for him. He felt Sam Dugan looking at him with disgust. He felt hollow and gutless. A spark of resentment flared within him, and a deep simmering rage began to move.

"Get him off that horse, or you can get off this ranch," Ab said.

"You made me manager. I say Caleb is gonna work cows now."

"I'll go draw your wages, then." Ab spoke as if addressing a common ranch hand. "I can get another manager." He hopped back toward the cabin door.

"Wait!" Caleb shouted. "You don't have to draw anybody's wages. If you don't want me workin' your cows, I won't work 'em."

"Caleb!" Pete scolded under his breath.

Ab held the doorframe and balanced on his one leg. "Now that's talking sense," he said.

"What the hell would you know about talking sense?" Caleb's ire began to boil. It felt good.

"What did you say to me, boy?" Ab growled.

"I said what the hell would you know about talking sense, old man? You don't know your sons from your wage hands."

Sam Dugan and Piggin' String McCoy traded looks. But Pete was worried. He knew Caleb was slow to anger but had a tendency to erupt once in a while over the smallest thing. He had once seen Caleb chase Matthew over a fence in a snarling rage simply because Matthew had called him a plowboy one time too many.

"You get off that horse and stand there till I get my leg on," Ab ordered.

"You can stick that leg up your ass for all I care," Caleb said. He opened a floodgate on a world of frustration he had held back for years.

"Come here!" Ab shouted, red-faced.

"Come out here and get me, you crippled old son of a bitch. I'll be in those mountains before you open the gate."

"You'll be in that cornfield by the time I get my leg on, or you'll feel my razor strap on your hind end! I won't let you run off to those mountains and get yourself killed like you did . . ." Ab caught his words in his throat but made the mistake of glancing at the graves.

Caleb let his old festering guilt turn to wrath. He advanced on his father, feeling the power of the horse through his spurs. "I didn't get my mother killed. A log fell on her. And as for Matthew, it was your old war pal that killed him. You should have shot Cheyenne Dutch a long time before Javier did. It was *your* fault." He took devious delight in turning the guilt back on his father.

Ab's leg was trembling under him. "Come here, boy!"

Caleb reined Five Spot back toward the bunkhouse.

"Caleb! I'm strapping my leg on!" Ab turned into the cabin and slammed the door behind him.

"Hot damn," Sam Dugan said.

Pete spurred his horse and overtook Caleb. "Where are you goin'?"

"I'm gonna roll some clothes up in a blanket and get some money."

"Then what?"

Caleb pointed at the Rampart Range. "I'm goin' up to see those mountains, first. Maybe I'll hire on at one of those ranches over in South Park for the roundup. Then I thought I might go up to the Palouse country and see those Nez Perce horses."

"What?" Pete said. "Now slow down and think for a minute. You're makin' up your mind too fast."

Caleb chuckled and felt a great wave of oppression gush from him. "It ain't sudden, Pete. It's a long time comin'."

"Well, how far away is the Palouse country?"

"I don't know. I guess I'll find out."

Pete grunted, trying to formulate his thoughts into words. "Well . . . Come back in a month or two. Maybe Papa will change his mind by then."

Caleb chuckled again. "He won't come to it that quick. I'll give it a year."

"A year!"

"Yeah." He looked toward the cabin. "I'll see you when Buster's flower garden starts in blooming again next spring. I don't care if Papa changes his mind or not, but I'll come back to see you and tell you what all I've done. That's a promise." He shook Pete's hand and loped toward Buster's house.

Ab's wooden leg tapped down the steps of the front porch. He stalked toward the group of mounted men as Pete returned to them. "Where's that boy going?"

"He's leavin'," Pete said.

"Well, go catch him!"

Pete looked down on his father. He had become an old man in one winter's time. "Go catch him yourself," he said. "It was you that ran him off." He spurred his horse for the open range and all the cowboys followed, not wanting to stand alone with old Ab Holcomb.

Though Buster had not heard the words, he had watched the entire confrontation from his cabin and knew something had gone wrong with Pete's plan to make a cowboy out of Caleb. "How long?" he asked, when Caleb told him he would go away.

"I promised Pete I'd come back and tell him some wild stories when your wildflowers start in blooming next spring."

"You got enough money?"

"Yeah. But I need a rifle. I'll trade you my other four horses for your Winchester repeater." He was tying his blankets and clothes in a roll.

"You can have the rifle," Buster said.

"I don't want you to give me anything. I'll trade you the horses for it."

"The rifle ain't worth that much. You can take it on loan, and my fiddle, too."

"I can't take your fiddle."

"Yes you can, and you *will* take it, too. A man who can fiddle won't never go hungry." Buster carried the fiddle and the rifle outside and tied them to Caleb's saddle. "Won't get rich, but you won't go hungry."

Caleb tied his bedroll down to the saddle's cantle strings and mounted. "Well, so long, Buster," he said. He wanted to say more, but he looked back toward the cabin and saw his father coming. He shook Buster's hand and rode around the cornfield toward Monument Creek. The mare grunted and heaved under him as she ran, feeding on the excitement she sensed through the saddle. Caleb gave her rein as he embarked upon the quest for a vision he had seen of himself: riding by day, singing by night, surrounded by admiring friends who held him at fault for nothing.

Buster stood in the shadow of his cabin and watched the young man mount the Arapaho Trail. He wanted to take Ab and shake some sense into him. He had seen friends sold south before the war. He had watched Miss Ella fall under the ridge log. He had lost touch with Long Fingers and left his own unborn child in the Indian Territory. Matthew was dead and Javier was gone. But none of it caused him the kind of despair he felt watching Caleb ride away.

He heard a splash in the irrigation ditch and saw Ab floundering across.

"Buster! What in Hades do you mean, letting him ride off like that?"

Buster watched Caleb top the bald hill across the creek. "He ain't my son."

THIRTY-TWO

IT TOOK MILT Starling about fifteen minutes every morning to work the cricks and cramps out of his legs before he could get up. The left knee and the right ankle usually gave him the most trouble. A California mule had kicked the knee in '49, and a Cherry Creek sluice box had collapsed on the ankle in '61. He was getting too old for mining camps.

Milt finally got on his feet and hobbled out of the back room, into the store and saloon he kept at the lower end of Gregory Gulch, below Black Hawk. He grabbed the sign he had painted the day before and limped to the front door.

North Clear Creek rushed under the boards of his porch, which stood on stilts in the water. A single step led down into the current, as if someone might walk up out of the creek for a cocktail. Customers normally used the steps on either side of the porch, however, where they could step onto the porch from the creek bank without getting their feet wet.

Milt looked around the side of his building to see if his men had gotten up for work yet. The back room he slept in butted up against the canyon bluffs, forcing the porch into the creek. The canyons of Gregory Gulch and North Clear Creek did not facilitate the laying out of towns, but where gold was found, men would build.

Near the bottom of the bluffs Milt found his two employees lounging in front of their tent. "Joe! Sonny!" he shouted. "Get off your tail ends and make some sawdust!"

"Wait till we finish our coffee, old man," Sonny said. "We've got lumber piled up head high anyway."

Milt hung the sign on a peg beside the front door. He would have left it hanging overnight, but somebody would probably have taken it for stove wood. He glanced at Sonny and Joe again and turned back into his saloon, cussing under his breath. It was a wonder he could make a living with the kind of help he had to rely on in a mining camp.

About the time he had finished his breakfast, someone came into the store with the sign Milt had hung out on the peg. "Here, now, put that back, boy!" he said.

"But it says carpenter needed," the boy replied.

"I am well acquainted with what it says, seein' as how I painted it myself. Now put it back."

"But, I'm a carpenter. I've come to fill the job."

Milt slammed a stove lid and went to picking his teeth with a splinter. "You're no carpenter. You've been in Gregory Gulch well-nigh two weeks, and I guess you've told about every worthless soul from Black Hawk to Nevadaville you're a cowboy looking for a ranch to work on."

"I am a cowboy."

"Two seconds ago you was a carpenter. Will you be a surgeon with the next breath?"

"I'm a carpenter and a cowboy. I've run out of money. I need work."

"And I need a carpenter to build sluice boxes. Have you ever built a sluice box?"

"No, sir, but . . ."

" 'But,' hell! I can't pay a cowboy to build leaky boxes. You have to know what you're doin' to get in my employ."

"I can build 'em so they don't leak. I've built irrigation flumes that never spilled a drop."

Milt spit the splinter out of his mouth. "Flumes!"

"Yes, sir."

"That's the same damn thing as a sluice box, ain't it? Why didn't you say so in the first place? What's your name?"

"Caleb Holcomb."

"Call me Milt Starling or Old Milt or whatever you please so long as it ain't blasphemous. Where did you learn to build irrigation flumes?"

"On a farm across the Front Range."

Milt rubbed the bald knob of his head. It looked like one of the hills around Black Hawk, merely studded where once whole thickets had grown. "You're a farmer, too?"

"Yes, sir."

Milt grumbled, paced on his rickety legs, kicked a spittoon. He placed his face in his hands.

Caleb thought he was weeping.

"I'll give you a try," the old man finally said. "A dollar a day plus board. Find your own lodgin'. Now git up and git to work."

"Yes, sir," Caleb said. "Only, I wonder if you might advance me a meal. I haven't et since the day before yesterday."

"A meal? A meal!" Milt kicked the spittoon again. "You won't expect me to cook it for you, will you? Help yourself, there's the stove! Hurry, boy, before the coals burn down. Wood's scarce."

Caleb slapped a slab of bacon into a skillet. "Where am I to build these sluices, Mr. Starling?" he asked as he licked his lips in anticipation.

"Up at the Littlefield Camp."

"Where's that?"

Milt looped an apron over his head. He smiled at Caleb with the sweet expression of a doting grandmother. "Would you like me to come along and hand you your tools as you need them?" The smile melted to a scowl, and Milt's brown teeth gnashed at his words. "Find it yourself! It's the last damn placer left in Gregory Gulch!"

After his breakfast, Caleb walked around the side of the building where Sonny and Joe were whipsawing lumber from a tree trunk resting horizontally on a trestle ten feet high. Sonny stood on the trestle with one handle of the eight-foot saw. Joe worked below. By pulling the saw through the tree trunk they laboriously turned out rough slabs of lumber.

Caleb learned from Sonny and Joe where he might find his carpenter's tools, his wagon, and his ox team. It took him all morning to collect them, as they were scattered from Black Hawk to Central City at various businesses and boardinghouses. Caleb wasn't really sure who they all belonged to but felt fairly secure in his right to use them. Sonny helped him load some lumber into the wagon and directed him to the Littlefield Camp.

"Bring the lumber from the old sluice boxes back with you," he said. "Old Milt will have you saw it up for stove wood."

"How long have you been workin' for him?" Caleb asked.

"Nobody works for Old Milt long," Joe said. "The work ain't steady enough."

"Yeah, take your time buildin' them sluices," Sonny added. "There won't be no work for you when you're done with 'em."

Caleb had never heard such a suggestion. Make a job last longer than necessary?

"Quit and take up another job if you find it," Joe said. "Milt keeps saying he's pulling stakes for Montana pretty soon, anyway."

Caleb found the Littlefield Camp on a small stream above Nevadaville. He patterned the sluices after the old boxes he found running parallel to the stream. Each box was twelve feet long, fourteen inches wide, and six inches deep. Riffles, nailed across the bottom about four fingers apart, caught the gold particles.

The Littlefield men used six sluice boxes end to end. A ditch leading from the creek conducted a steady stream of water through the boxes. The miners shoveled in dirt and gravel from either side of the sluice, the current washing away the lighter particles while the riffles caught the heavier grains of gold. The old sluice boxes were so eroded from such use that the knots stood out a quarter inch from the general surface of the lumber.

To make the work pass faster, Caleb ran a set of rhymes repeatedly through his head. The song he had started to the tune of "Sweet Betsy from Pike" was growing and had taken on a tune of its own. The new tune had a minor chord in it, which Caleb thought lent a lonesome and mysterious aspect to its sound.

> *When he came of age, he decided to roam.*
> *He said, "There's a life I must live on my own."*
> *And he promised his brother, that day, one sure thing:*
> *He'd return with his tales of adventure next spring.*

At sundown he loaded his tools and drove his oxen back down toward Black Hawk, studying the diggings harder now than he had the two weeks he had been here. As Old Milt had said, the Littlefield Camp was the last placer mine in the gulch. The rest of the miners had gone to sinking shafts and tunneling into the hillsides for gold. As he followed the oxen, Caleb counted rotten shaft houses crumbling over abandoned mines, and idle stamp mills standing in rusting hulks all over the hills. A few active mills used sluices, but there weren't enough of them to keep even a single carpenter busy.

He realized Sonny was probably right. The end of the Littlefield Camp job would bring the end of his carpentering career in Gregory Gulch. Still, there was no call for taking Sonny's advice in making the job last longer than necessary. That seemed dishonest.

"Well, this ain't what you imagined," he thought. "I'm herdin' cattle, all right, but they're wearin' oxbows."

One thought comforted him. He was going to eat tonight. Two meals in one day. But he'd starve to death before he went crawling back to his father's ranch.

THIRTY-THREE

E VERY DAY, BEFORE and after work, Caleb had to take Five Spot to water, then stake her in some fresh grass, which was difficult to find in quantities around Black Hawk. He hid his saddle and other gear in brush and slept near his horse on the bare ground every night, using a tarp to turn the occasional rainfall.

Between work and tending his horse, he found little time for anything else. But on his fifth day of working for Old Milt, he finished the Littlefield job a couple of hours before nightfall and found a spare hour to play his fiddle for Sonny and Joe.

Five customers were trading gold dust for drinks in Milt's saloon when the music started. In less than a minute, they had all vacated the place and gathered around the whipsaw trestle to hear Caleb play.

It took Milt a while to catch on and a while longer to catch up on his lame joints. "Stop!" he said when he finally got close enough to drown out the fiddle. "Stop the music! You're takin' my customers, boy. Play in the saloon if you're gonna play. Why didn't you tell me you could saw a fiddle same as a sluice box?"

Caleb put his hat upside down on the bar and played past midnight. When he looked into his hat on his way out, he found three dollars in money and maybe half an ounce of gold dust. "What will I do with the gold?" he asked Milt, plowing his finger through it in the crown of his hat.

"Let me see it," Milt said. "Looks like you have about five dollars there. Give it to me and take five dollars worth of supplies from the store."

Caleb stacked up four dollars' worth of canned goods and gewgaws but couldn't find anything else he wanted.

"Take a whiskey for the difference and leave me be," Milt said, pouring a shot glass.

The fiddler lifted the chipped glass and held it against the lantern light to inspect the color. He sniffed it. He swished it around in the glass to judge its fluidity. He had never dared to taste liquor at the Colorado City dances. Not with Buster or Pete around, or someone who might tell his father. But now he knew no one would care one way or the other. He stuck his finger in and sucked the whiskey off—the driest liquid he had ever tasted. He slurped a little over the rim of the glass. It seemed to disappear before he could swallow. It soaked right into his mouth. His nose drew the vapors into his head like a chimney with an open flue.

Leaning against the bar, Caleb sipped at his whiskey for some time. His chest warmed. Sonny and Joe were leaving just as he poured the last drop down his throat.

"Go easy on that nose paint," Sonny said.

"Yeah," Joe added, "that stuff'll raise a blood blister on a rawhide boot."

As he carried his fiddle up the hill, Caleb wondered if he was drunk. He knew he wasn't staggering drunk, but he thought he might be a little touched by the liquor. It wasn't at all an unpleasant feeling. Taking a whiskey now and again might not be an altogether bad idea.

After hearing the boy's fiddle music, Old Milt found work enough to keep Caleb around. He sent him to the nearest stand of pines with the ox wagon to haul back more tree trunks for Joe and Sonny to saw. Then he put Caleb to work dismantling old sluice boxes to bring back to the saloon.

"Saw 'em down to stove-wood size," Milt said. "Stack 'em along the wall, yonder."

"Can I chop 'em? It'll go faster."

"I said saw 'em, didn't I? Do I have to repeat everything twice't?"

Milt came out later and caught Caleb throwing the sawed-off sluice-box lumber into stacks. "Hey!" he shouted. "Did I tell you to toss 'em around like horseshoes? Stack 'em easy, or you'll shake the color loose!"

Caleb didn't always understand everything Milt said, but he generally obeyed as long as the old man was paying the wages. That evening he carried in an armload of the old lumber and carefully placed it on the floor beside the woodstove. Then he put his hat on the bar, got out his fiddle and began tuning up.

The place was just getting lively when Old Milt brought Caleb a whiskey. "One of them gents staked you to a drink," he said.

"Which one?"

Milt shrugged and hobbled back to the bar.

He finished the whiskey rather quickly and went back to playing. The next time he took the fiddle out from under his chin, he found another drink beside him. The warmth in his chest and stomach invited another swallow. He sipped the whiskey between songs, then gulped the last finger in the glass.

The liquor seemed to reproduce itself. With his concentration thrown into the fiddle playing, he didn't see Milt bringing the refills. They just appeared.

After several glasses, Old Milt's saloon acquired a kind of glow Caleb had never seen before. The rough lumber looked smooth; the hardened faces took on expressions of benevolence. The fiddle music, though beginning to slur and warble for some reason, sounded like the rhapsody of songbirds. Caleb downed a whole shot glass at once.

In the middle of "Listen to the Mockingbird," the saloon became unstable. The fiddler thought maybe the creek was washing the place away. The stool wouldn't sit level under him. The saloon patrons seemed to notice something unusual, too. He could see them staring at him as he played, but they wouldn't stand still. They kept jerking and wavering around. Suddenly he couldn't feel the fiddle in his hands anymore, but he knew it was there. It sounded far away, as if someone else were playing it. Whoever it was wasn't playing very well.

Caleb began to sweat. Milt must have stoked the stove with too much sluice-box wood. He looked for the stove but couldn't find it. He forgot what song he was playing, so he quit in the middle of it and reached for his whiskey. The stool lurched just as he turned the glass up; he dropped the fiddle; the floor swung perpendicular and hit him in the face, reminding him of the handle of a hoe he had once stepped on.

The blow to the head, though he felt no pain from it, hit him so hard that it made his ears ring and made him sick to his stomach. This was no time to be sick. He was missing something hilarious. He knew he was, because he could hear riotous laughter all around him. He tried to find the source of all the amusement, but everything he looked at blurred before his eyes. He tried to get up so he could get some fresh air outside, but the floor started spinning under him. He became ill with dizziness. His stomach twisted and cramped. Then he rose as if sucked into a cyclone, and he heard Old Milt's voice:

". . . you drunken fiddler, go sop your head in the crick!"

Some kind soul carried him toward the door so he could get some air. The night closed around him, and he seemed to sail out into it. He flew from the saloon porch, timelessly, fearlessly, until a wall of ice slammed against him.

Caleb tried to breathe but sucked in only freezing water. He lunged up from the creek, gasping for air. Above the rush of the stream he could hear the laughter. He saw the porch above him, lined with jeering miners. He coughed and heaved for breath until, suddenly, all the whiskey in his stomach came out. The acid smell of his own vomit made him heave again and again. He pulled himself to his hands and knees, shivering in the shallow creek, and threw up before the spectators.

"Drinks on the fiddler!" someone said.

Caleb was just grateful that they left him alone and went back into the saloon. He didn't care if they spent all the money in his hat. He dragged himself to the edge of the stream across from the saloon, where his stomach wrenched again, though it had nothing more to get out. He couldn't tell how long he sat there. Occasionally someone walked by and cussed or laughed at him. He was too weak to look at them. He woke himself up with his own shivering.

Finally two men picked him up by the arms. He stumbled across the stream, his boots full of water.

"Let's cover him up under the trestle and let him sleep it off," Joe's voice said.

"Didn't I tell him to go easy on that nose paint?" Sonny asked.

When daylight woke Caleb, his head ached in a place he had never felt pain in before. Milt Starling was shouting from the front porch for the men to go to work. Sonny pulled the blanket off, sat Caleb up, and waved a cup of coffee in his face. The boy took his aching head in his hands and felt a retch coming on. He pushed Sonny aside, stumbled to the creek, and stuck his head in the water.

"Here," Sonny said, pulling him to his feet. "Drink the coffee. I don't care if you want to or not. Drink it. The best thing for you is to eat breakfast and go to work. I don't care how much you hurt. You better learn that no boss is gonna give you time off to sober up."

"Hey, boy," Milt said, coming out of the saloon again, "what do you mean sleepin' to this hour? Now your breakfast is cold. You shouldn't have drank so much neck oil last night."

Caleb cradled his cup of coffee and started slowly toward the porch. "You were the one that brought it to me," he muttered.

Old Milt assumed his grandmotherly pose. "Oh, was it I, boy?" he said apologetically. Then he leaned toward Caleb and yelled in his ear. "Was it also I who took up the glass, opened your mouth, and poured it down your gullet?"

"You had 'em throw me in the creek!"

"Better you air your paunch there than on my floor! Now go eat your breakfast. There's lots of fat bloody bacon and scrambled eggs, cooked just the way you like 'em, sort of gooey and shakylike. Try to make it set."

The breakfast didn't set, and a queasy feeling stayed with Caleb all morning as he sawed the old sluice-box lumber into stove wood. He thanked God for North Clear Creek. He could dip his bandanna there and sop it across his brow to relieve some of the pain.

When the wood had burned down in the stove, Milt clanged a bucket and a shovel down on the porch and told Caleb to empty the ashes from the stove and bring them to the edge of the porch in the bucket. "And don't spill a jigger of it on the floor."

As he followed the instructions, Caleb noticed Milt limping along toward the porch with a prospecting pan in one hand.

"Over here," the old man said when Caleb brought the ashes out. "Set 'em down beside me."

Milt sat on the porch with his feet on the step that led into the water. Caleb had wondered about that step. Since last night he had assumed it existed to aid miners in throwing drunks into the creek. But Milt made another use of it. With his feet on the step, the old man could easily reach the water with his prospecting pan. He shook some ashes into the pan, let some water pour into it, and began washing the ashes over the rim of the pan.

Caleb stood and watched for a moment. A curious thing happened. Old Milt began to smile.

"What are you doin'?" Caleb asked.

"What does it look like I'm doin'? I'm pannin' for gold. I used to prospect for my wages, you know. Back in Californee. Them was the days, boy. A man could make a hundred a day with just a pan and a shovel." The ashes swirled in the water like clouds in his own little universe. "Grass Valley to Mariposa. I must have washed a fortune in dust and nuggets from the dirt." He dumped some more ashes into the pan. "I've never seen a strike like Californee, and I never will again to the day my soul roars up the flumes. Now it's all stamp mills and rebellious ores."

"But you're just pannin' ashes," Caleb said.

Milt washed the last wisps of ash over the rim of his pan. "The cracks in them old sluice boxes we've been burnin' is full of gold dust. It ain't hardly worth the time it takes to wash it, but it reminds me of Californee."

Caleb leaned over Old Milt's shoulder as he pushed the gold dust out of the pan and into his pouch. It hardly looked like gold to him at all. It had no glint or glow to it. It looked like fine sand of a rich dark color.

" 'In the days of old, the days of gold, how often I repine,' " the old man sang, gravel-voiced and monotoned. " 'For the days of old, when we dug up the gold, in the days of '49.' There's a song for you to learn, boy." Milt looked up and saw the expression of wonder on Caleb's face. With a sudden motion he filled his pan with water and splashed it on the fiddler.

"Hey, what . . ."

"Fight it, boy," Milt shouted.

"Fight what?"

"You've got the prospectin' fever, boy. The grip of the color's got you!"

"No it hasn't!"

"Don't let it get you, boy! It'll suck your pride down a prospect hole.

It'll leave your soul in a slag heap. I've seen boys like you grow old and die muckin' out a barren drift. I've seen 'em strike it rich and blow it overnight. Let them others root in the dirt for it, son. You mine it from their pockets. That fiddle music's your lode. You'll wash more dust with your hat turned up in a saloon than ever you will with a pan by the crick.''

"I never aimed to prospect anyhow," Caleb said, drying his face on his shirttail. "I'm huntin' ranch work."

"That's the spirit, boy! Don't let the prospectin' fever get you. And when you find your ranch, you'll have Old Milt to thank for it, too. Now get back to that stove. I've a mind to pan today."

But Caleb's vision of ranch life continued to elude him. No cattle barons came offering employment. He began to miss his home, but knew his returning before the year was up would represent a failure.

"Stay with it," he told himself. "Remember what it was like. Remember why you left. This ain't great, but it's better. Something right will come along."

His bankroll kept growing, but he kept whittling away at it with purchases of spurs, pistols, blankets, hatbands, and other trinkets that caught his eye. Still, he would have funds to get him out of Gregory Gulch when the opportunity to work on a ranch came.

A big Scot found him whipsawing lumber one day with Sonny, Joe having quit to work a new claim at Idaho Springs.

"Which one of you is looking for a ranch to work?" the Scot said.

"I am," Caleb answered. Within ten minutes he had collected his wages from Milt, saddled Five Spot, and was on his way to a ranch in South Park.

He wondered why a man with such a beautiful lilt to his voice didn't like to talk, but the Scotsman didn't. He had no objection to Caleb playing the harmonica as they rode though. The third night of their journey they reached a cabin just built on a wooded hill that looked like an island of trees in the moonlit park.

"How many head have you got?" Caleb asked.

"Just brought three hundred up from New Mexico," the beautiful voice said.

"Where are they?"

"Over the next ridge. You can find them in the mornin'."

After breakfast the Scotsman pointed the way for Caleb. "There's a Mexican with them now, but he won't stay this far north for the winter. You'll be top man if you'll stay year-round."

"Yes, sir!" Caleb said. He spurred Five Spot to the west to find the herd. After riding an hour he saw a column of smoke and figured it to be the Mexican's campfire. He rode through a line of trees that grew on a ridge and found the Mexican packing his tent on a burro. The camp over-looked three hundred head of bleating sheep.

"Where are the cattle?" Caleb asked.

"Cattle? There are no cattle. Only sheep."

Caleb was so disgusted that he didn't even get off his horse. His disap-pointment ran so deep that he felt like crying out in anguish. He thought something right had come along. He thought he had found a home where he would be top man and have people look up to him, like people looked up to Pete at Holcomb Ranch. No one looked up to a sheepherder any more than they did a drunken fiddler. He didn't even bother riding back to the cabin to tell the big Scot he would sooner raise yardbirds than sheep.

With money in his pocket and food in his stomach, he figured it was as good a time as any to light out for the Palouse country. Maybe somewhere along the way he would find what he was looking for, though he didn't know anymore exactly what it was.

THIRTY-FOUR

IT WASN'T UNTIL Pete stepped onto the gallery of the Dubois mansion that he thought to give thanks for his time on earth. He had taken to giving thanks for many things: rain, grass, banjo music, the taste of fried venison. But it didn't strike him to offer thanks for the time the Good Lord had chosen for him until his hand touched the lacquered banister of Captain Dubois's portico.

The rail at his palm and the milled lumber underfoot reminded him of the house he had left as a child to come to the wilderness. Now houses finer than any he had known in Pennsylvania stood in neighborhoods where, before, wind and buffalo grass had reigned for centuries un-counted. The Lord had seen fit to bring him into a time of Old Testament wonder, to a place where Amelia Dubois was unattached and of marriage-able age. For that great privilege, Pete silently and sincerely gave thanks as he knocked on the door of the Dubois house.

A house servant answered the door, and Pete asked to see Captain Dubois. The captain took his time in coming downstairs to the parlor.

"What can I do for you, young man?" he asked, when he finally ap-peared.

"Sir, I would like your permission to court your daughter," Pete said.

The captain stared for a moment, then fanned himself with a ledger sheet he held in one hand. "You come to the point quickly enough. What's your name?"

"Pete Holcomb, sir."

"Holcomb. That would make you the brother of Matthew. Are you the one that plays the violin or the one that preaches?"

"I don't exactly preach, sir. Just teach some Sunday-school lessons to the boys on the ranch."

"I see. Well, Mr. Holcomb, you have my permission to court my daughter, but I'm afraid my endorsement will benefit you very little if Amelia finds the arrangement in any way unsatisfactory. She makes up her own mind about who will or will not enjoy the pleasure of her company."

"As long as I have your permission, sir, I'll take my chances with Amelia."

"Very well. We have a picnic scheduled for Saturday at the Garden of the Gods. Come along as my guest, if you will. My guest, you understand, not Amelia's escort. She would think it rather forward of me if I chose her escort for her. Do you have any idea, Mr. Holcomb . . . Well, no, I suppose you don't. See yourself out, will you? I have quite a load of work to get through today."

"Yes, sir."

"Oh, by the way," the captain said before he mounted the stairs, "I was frightfully upset about what happened to Matthew last year. Terribly sorry I couldn't attend the funeral." He looked blankly at the ledger sheet in his hand. "I indulged in some rather pious notions about how he may have deserved what happened to him, until I recalled the younger days I spent in . . . well, shall we say, rather inappropriate pursuits? The same might have happened to me."

"He meant to do the right thing," Pete said.

"I'm sure he did. Saturday, ten o'clock."

When Saturday came, Amelia agreed to share her coach with Pete so they could ride together to the picnic. "Why didn't you bring your little brother?" she asked as the coach rattled over the planks of the Monument Creek bridge. "We should have enjoyed some music."

"He's gone," Pete said.

"Gone where?"

"The Palouse River country. He won't come back till next spring. The boys have been pesterin' Buster somethin' fierce about plantin' wildflower seeds."

"Your chef? The negro violinist?"

"He's not really a chef. He just don't mind cookin'."

"What does his planting wildflowers have to do with your brother?"

"Caleb promised he'd come back when the flowers started in bloomin' next spring."

Amelia smirked. "Hasn't anyone got a calender at that ranch of yours?"

"Papa's got one somewhere. But we generally go by the moon and the seasons unless we're writin' a letter or somethin'."

The coach crossed Camp Creek and neared the magnificent rock formations of the Garden of the Gods. The party traveled in awe through a narrow gap, three wagons wide, between two giant sheets of red stone that jutted, leaning, high above the tops of the piñon pines and red cedars. Magpies cavorted inside the curve of monoliths that embraced the garden, some spare and spirelike, some squat and bulbous. Between the towers of rock and the foothills of the Rampart Range, a beautiful carpet of grass spread, studded with evergreens.

"See that formation on the ridge?" Amelia said, pointing as she stepped down from the coach. "That's called the kissing camels."

"Well, I'll be," Pete said. "It does look like camels kissin', doesn't it?"

"And look over there. That one's called the weeping Indian."

"Son of a gun! I've never seen such a thing! That's God's own artwork."

"Haven't you ever come here before?" she asked.

"Once or twice, lookin' for cows. But I never stopped to name the rocks."

Pete found half a dozen servants cooking porterhouse steaks and lamb chops at the picnic grounds. The residents of the Fountain Colony considered him quite a curiosity. He answered spates of questions as he ate.

"I learned to read in Pennsylvania," he had to explain. "And me and my brothers went to school in Colorado City for a while, except when the Indians scared the schoolmarm off in '68."

"And your theological training?" a British investor said.

"Pardon?"

"Captain Dubois tells us you conduct sermons on your ranch."

Pete shrugged. "I have a Bible, and I know how to pray."

The colonists snickered. "Which philosophy do you embrace?" one of them asked.

"You've got me mixed up with Buster," Pete said. "He's our philosopher."

"The negro violinist," Amelia explained.

"The former slave? He studies philosophy?"

"Not that kind you read in Latin," Pete explained. "More the kind you can use in regular life."

After they ate, Pete managed to get Amelia away from the crowd for a walk among the rock formations in the garden. "Things are going good at the ranch," he mentioned. "Beef is high and the grass is, too. In a few years we could raise the money to buy the rest of Monument Creek from the government."

"Oh, please, I find business such a tedious topic of conversation."

"I only brought it up so you would know I can make do for you. I aim to ask you to marry me."

Amelia scarcely faltered. She stopped in the shade of a rock pillar and batted her eyes at Pete. "You sound as sure of yourself as Matthew did."

"I ain't like him, though. He wanted you so your papa would get him a job on the railroad. He thought you were pretty and all, but he was mostly lookin' out for himself. I like where I am on the ranch. I don't want a job on the railroad. I just want you. I knew it the first time Matthew brought you out to the ranch."

Amelia was so astounded that she blushed. "So, you think you can make a little ranch wife out of me?"

"A little ranch wife with a big herd of children."

She blushed deeper. "You don't really think you could keep me happy out there in that cabin on the plains, do you?"

"Not for a minute. I aim to build you a big house. Bigger than your papa's. I'm gonna plant trees and gardens all around it for you and have servants to wait on you from dawn to dusk. And you'll have your own buggy and team of spotted horses, so you can visit your friends in town whenever you want."

"My, my. The price of beef must be very high if you think you can manage all that."

"Once we own the creek we'll control all of Monument Park. We'll have the biggest herd in the territory. Then the ranch will start payin' dividends."

"Oh, I am so very bored with talk of dividends and stock values." She put her arm through Pete's and started him walking again. "We had better get out from behind this rock or father will question your intentions."

But before Pete escorted her back into view of the picnickers, he held her back and slipped his arm around her waist. "Just so long as *you* don't question my intentions," he said, and kissed her on the lips before she could even think about resisting.

She gasped and pushed against his chest, but Pete was so much stronger she could only trust him to turn her loose. "You have made your intentions clear," she said. "Now, please . . . Before father suspects."

THIRTY-FIVE

SAM DUGAN AND Piggin' String McCoy sat on the top rail of the corral fence where they could watch the odd procession arrive. The hunters came first, wearing red coats and white leather riding britches tucked into high top boots. They drove carriages, drawn by matched pairs, leading their thoroughbreds behind. The servants arrived next, driving wagons loaded with all the necessary foodstuffs for the feast that would follow the fox hunt. The dogs brought up the rear. A huntsman and two whippers-in kept the twenty foxhounds in a tight pack.

"Look at that feller in the claw hammer coat and the stovepipe hat," Sam said. "He must be the boss of the hunt. Everybody else is wearin' them little velvet caps."

"Them saddles ain't got no horns," Piggin' String replied.

"They're sure slick, all right. Look about as useful as a bull without a pecker."

"I ain't seen a rifle one. How are they gonna hunt without no guns?"

"Pete says they let them dogs kill the fox. The hunters just chouse along behind."

Piggin' String shook his head and forced a brown stream of tobacco juice between his lips. "Let's saddle up and ride drag. I gotta see this."

Colorado Springs had swelled with members of the Fountain Colony over the summer, many of them from England. Some of the old pioneer settlers had begun calling the place Little London.

Fox hunting had become a popular diversion among the foreigners, though the chases produced as many coyotes and wolves as foxes. A few of the residents kept stables of fine Thoroughbreds and kennels of ready hounds.

Thinking a fox hunt at Holcomb Ranch might help him cultivate acquaintances among Amelia's friends, Pete had made the plans through Captain Dubois for this Saturday morning's hunt. Ab had arranged to be out of the county on land-office business. He didn't have much truck with Englishmen.

Several of the hunters were accompanied by ladies, and so it was that Amelia, simply to aggravate Pete, had arrived with the master of hounds, the man in the black silk top hat.

"Good morning, Mr. Holcomb," she said haughtily, when Pete rode over to greet her. "I would like you to meet Mr. Wilson Chamberlain, my escort."

"Jolly good of you to invite us," Chamberlain said, tapping his silk hat down on his head. He jumped down from the buggy to tighten the saddle on his hunter that trailed behind.

It was Pete who thought to help Amelia down from the buggy. "Glad you could come," he said, winking at her.

"Wilson's hounds will be running the foxes today," she said. "He has them so expertly trained, I dare not question the prospects of the morning." It was scandalous the way she forced the hint of a British accent into her voice.

"Actually," Chamberlain admitted, "I have a man who does the training for me. That's him, the huntsman over there with the pack. He is quite the best man available, I believe. The dogs have performed splendidly in recent weeks. I call them the Colony Pack. They are ten couples.''

"That means twenty," Amelia said, looking down her nose at Pete. "Mr. Holcomb," she said, regarding his pistol and chaps, "there are strict rules concerning hunting attire. But I suppose you wouldn't have had exposure to them.''

"I don't mean to join the hunt," Pete said, hitching up his chaps. "I just want to ride along behind and watch.''

"Quite so," Chamberlain said, mounting his Thoroughbred. "I should consider our host exempt from all rules of dress. Silly-looking costumes in this country anyway, what? Shall we?''

Buster had built a walkway over the irrigation dam so the spectators could cross the creek to the bald hill over which the old Arapaho Trail ran. The hill afforded a splendid vantage for watching the action or listening to the dogs. By the time Amelia made it to the summit, the foxhounds were already on a trail up Monument Creek, and two dozen horses were thundering after them.

Pete stayed to the rear of the chase with Sam Dugan, Piggin' String, and Buster. "Keep those green-broke horses away from the Englishmen," he said to the cowboys when they started. "Especially you on that stud, Sam. You're liable to cause 'em trouble.'' Pete rode one of his finer mounts, a six-year-old spotted gelding.

Buster rode his fastest mule—a big, surefooted brute that could pace any Thoroughbred in rough country. He figured a sensible fox would avoid the open plains with a pack of hounds on its trail and make for the foothills of the Rampart Range. His mule would make better time than any horse over the steep slopes strewn with deadfalls and boulders.

The dogs worked the trail a half mile up Monument Creek, then turned west, yelping up the wooded draw where Buster had protected Caleb with the wolf-getter years before.

"Damn if they can't ride!" Sam Dugan shouted, trying to keep the foreigners in sight.

The hunting horses jumped bluffs and deadfalls without hesitation. Pete saw one gent fly from the saddle and land face first on a bed of sharp rocks. Piggin' String caught the Englishman's horse, and the bloody-faced foreigner climbed back on to rejoin the chase.

"That feller's game as a Shanghai rooster," Buster said, spurring his mule back up to speed.

From the bald hill, Amelia could hear the dogs working the trail up into the foothills. She couldn't see the riders through the trees, but the dogs kept her apprised of the course of the hunt. Their voices faded as they trailed farther into the hills, until she heard a change in the pitch of yelps. The foxhounds, even after miles of running, had taken on a new frenzy.

Captain Dubois came to stand beside his daughter on the hill. "Sounds as if they've sighted the fox," he said. "Now the chase will begin in earnest."

"Father, why don't you join the hunts?" Amelia asked.

"I prefer your Mr. Holcomb's form of hunting to Chamberlain's. I like to bring a little venison back to camp instead of that ridiculous foxtail these Britishers . . ."

"What do you mean, *my* Mr. Holcomb?" Amelia demanded.

Captain Dubois stumbled back in his thoughts, grasping for an avenue of escape. "Did I say your Mr. Holcomb? A slip of the tongue, dear. I meant *our* Mr. Holcomb. Our host, you know. That's all, darling."

The dogs led the hunters over a series of ridges and creek beds and began to swing to the south. Pete and his party of observers stopped on a ridge to let their horses breathe a few minutes, since the dogs seemed to be turning the game.

"What do you 'low they got?" Piggin' String asked.

"They're fox-huntin' dogs," Pete said, "so I reckon they're after a fox."

"Don't make no difference what they started out after," Sam said. "Many's the time I went up the trail to chouse cows and wound up chousin' Indians or whores."

"Them dogs have got a stronger will than you, Sam," Piggin' String said. "I'll wager they can hold their concentration on whatever it is they're chousin'."

Buster chuckled. "Sounded to me like they quit their first trail and picked up somethin' fresher when their yelpin' changed pitch a while back."

"Whatever they've got," Pete said, "they've turned it back east now. They're runnin' it downhill along Horseshoe Creek."

In a few minutes the dogs passed within five hundred yards of Pete and his men, but the observers couldn't get a glimpse of the prey through the trees. After they heard the hunters gallop by, the cowboys fell in behind and continued toward the plains. The yipping of the dogs reached its highest pitch, and Pete knew they were close to the quarry.

The hunters were only a few hundred yards behind the dogs now, and the cowboys were on the heels of the hunters. They crashed through tree limbs, jumped fallen trunks, plunged down creek banks. Buster was thankful to have the solid feet of the mule under him.

"They're baying!" Pete shouted. "They've got it holed up."

"Or treed!" Buster said.

A piercing yelp rang through the forest, and the dogs were on the run again.

"That ain't no fox!" Piggin' String shouted. "I think they got 'em a lion!"

"Maybe a wolf!" Pete said.

Another minute brought the cowboys to the site of the brief skirmish. They found Wilson Chamberlain on the ground, cradling the head of a badly wounded dog. The poor hound's stomach had been ripped open, and its innards were lying on the bare ground.

"Oh, no," Sam said.

"Mr. Holcomb," Chamberlain said. "Your pistol, if you please."

Pete handed over the revolver. Sam turned his head when Chamberlain used it to quiet the whining dog.

Piggin' String got down to look for tracks. "What was it?" he asked the Englishman. "Lion? Bear? I can't see nothin' but dog tracks."

"I don't know," Chamberlain replied, returning the pistol. "But I fear for the safety of my dogs. Let's get back in the chase."

The five men spurred their mounts east and closed the ground on the dogs as quickly as they could. They heard baying again, but it lasted only a moment. Suddenly the riders broke from the trees and thundered out into the open grasslands of Monument Park. Pete saw the last of the hunters go over the opposite bank of Monument Creek. The horses were white with lather, but the hunters whipped them harder than ever.

From her vantage on the hill, Amelia had seen the huge dark form burst the tree line, followed by the pack of dogs and the red-coated hunters. Then came Wilson's silk hat, followed by Pete and the Holcomb Ranch bunch.

"They've jumped a bear!" Captain Dubois shouted as the hunt emerged onto the plains. One of the dogs caught a hind leg of the beast, and the others swarmed like bees. "He'll rip the dogs to pieces!"

As Pete charged over the creek bank, he saw a dog fly out of a dust cloud and roll among the hunting horses, turning instantly to charge back into the fray. The cloud erupted in black fur, and Pete got his first look at the bear as it lunged at a dog one tenth its size. The hunters were circling, the huntsman shouting at the hounds. None of the Englishmen seemed to know what to do. The huge old black bear was whirling, snapping its teeth, swatting at dogs, turning to attack others at his tail. One hound was already on the ground dead. Others virtually climbed the bear's back to get in their licks.

"My Lord!" Chamberlain shouted. "He'll kill the dogs!"

Pete jerked the coil of hemp from the leather tie on his saddle horn. "He won't kill 'em all!" As he spurred his gelding on, he swung the loop underhanded, letting a round play out of the coil with every revolution, building the loop until it was almost big enough to take in the whole pack of dogs.

"Stand clear!" Chamberlain shouted when he figured Pete's plan. "Stand aside, men!"

The hunters heard and made a path through which Pete could join the dog-and-bear fight. His loop cut the dust over his head as he made his first pass, but the bear presented a poor target, spinning to fight the foxhounds. Pete turned his prancing horse back to the fight and kept the loop swinging, waiting for a clean throw at the bear's head.

The old bruin whirled to swat a dog, and Pete threw the loop side-armed, gathering in the head and one foreleg of the beast. The spotted gelding was taking up the slack even before the coils hit the ground. A dog straddling the rope went somersaulting over the plains when Pete's saddle horn snapped the sagging hemp straight.

The bear went over backward, roaring with rage, dredging a dust cloud behind him as the powerful gelding dragged him. Pete drew his revolver smoothly from the holster. He turned and aimed at the end of the rope stretched tight over his thigh. For a mere second, the dogs fell behind.

Far away on the hill, Amelia saw the blasts of smoke and heard the reports follow. The great black heap fell still behind Pete's horse, and the dogs milled around it in silence. A cheer rang from the spectators' hill.

Captain Dubois hurrahed among the loudest. "I hope you didn't bring young Chamberlain along to rival Pete," he said. "If so, you seem to have achieved a reverse effect!"

Amelia only heaved in disgust. What was she going to do about Pete Holcomb? Whatever did she want with a ranchman? How could she ever bear a rural life on the plains?

THIRTY-SIX

W INTER WAS GOING to come early to the Medicine Bow Range. Burl Sandeen didn't know how he could tell, but after forty years in the mountains he had learned to trust his instincts. He had hung up extra meat and ridden all the way out of North Park to Rawlins for more supplies than he thought he would need. Now he was anxious to get back to his cabin above the Michigan and get his wood chopped before the snow fell too deep. A blanket two inches thick already covered the ground, and the sky told him more was on the way.

As he led his mule up the trail, he noticed a wisp of smoke filtering through the trees in a coulee ahead. He tied the mule to a pine sapling, slipped his fifty-caliber Warner carbine from its scabbard, and stalked ahead to investigate. It was late in the year for Indians to be out hunting. He suspected a greenhorn looking for a mountain pass, but not even Burl Sandeen expected anyone quite as green as Caleb Holcomb.

Through the trees in the coulee, Burl saw a spotted mare and a young man holding a buffalo robe open to warm himself over a crackling fire. He could readily see that the kid was well muscled, for he was wearing a suit of buckskins that had shrunk to his knees and elbows and covered the rest of him like a second skin. As Burl crept silently through the powder, the spotted mare noticed him but the boy did not. The old mountain man eased up to Five Spot and scratched her on the rump. He rested his carbine over the spots on the mare's hip and aimed in Caleb's direction.

"Who are you?" he asked.

Caleb jumped all the way over the fire and ran three steps before he slid in the snow and turned with his hand on his pistol.

"Whoa," Sandeen said, "don't get your hackles up."

Caleb looked over what he could see of the man behind the horse. He wore a hat of beaver fur and hobnailed boots laced with leather thongs. A gray beard seemed to gush from the collar of his red wool coat. Black eyebrows thick as horses' manes hung over the old man's squinting eyes.

"Mister, you scared the hell out of me!" Caleb said.

Burl laughed.

"I thought you were a Ute," the boy said.

"Ute wouldn't have asked you who you were. One white man is like another to them, with the exception of Burl Sandeen." He jabbed himself in the chest with his thumb. "What happened to your britches?"

"I don't know. They got wet when I crossed the river yesterday, and they just kept gettin' tighter."

"Where'd you get 'em?"

"Bought 'em from the Nez Perce."

Burl laughed again and came out from behind the mare. "They took you for a fool, son. Them skins haven't been cured proper. Might just as well have wrapped yourself in rawhide. Better cut 'em off or they'll squeeze the liver out of you."

"But I don't have anything else to wear except for my long handles."

"I got duds I'll swap you. What do have to trade?"

"Nothin' much. I can't let go of my guns or saddle, or my coat."

"What's in here?" Burl asked, tapping his rifle barrel on the fiddle case tied behind the cantle.

"My fiddle. But I can't trade that either."

"I wouldn't know how to work it anyhow. Do me no more good than a steam calliope. But you can swap me some fiddle music this evenin' while I take up an outfit so's to fit you."

Caleb finally took his hand away from his pistol grip. "I'd be obliged, sir. I'm Caleb Holcomb." He waddled forward in his shrunken skins to shake hands.

The old man laughed at the sight. "We got two hours of light and three hours of ground. I suggest we git."

They arrived at Sandeen's cabin after dark, unpacked the supplies from the mule, and put the animals in a pole corral. The cabin stood wide as a barn but only eight logs high at the ridge pole. The roof was braced to handle the heaviest snows. When Caleb followed his host in, he bumped his forehead on a rafter in the dark.

"Why do you live so high up?" Caleb asked as he cut his shrunken deerskins off.

Sandeen was stoking a fire to cook supper. "Because I like it up here, that's why. The stars up here shoot thick as white hairs on a roan horse. They don't look like that below."

For furniture Sandeen had only a couple of sawed stumps that served as stools, or as dinner tables when the diner sat on the floor. Pegs sticking out of the walls snagged hats, snowshoes, ropes, traps, and other assorted possessions. The heavy rafters were at eye level, bolstered in the middle by posts sunk in the dirt floor. Layers of buffalo robes, bearskins, and beaver pelts made a regular carpet except for a semicircle around the fireplace where sparks tended to leap. Piles of hides made couches for sitting or sleeping.

"Don't you ever bump your head in here?" Caleb asked.

"I'd just as soon duck," Sandeen answered. "A low roof means less air to heat."

Caleb wrapped himself in a long buffalo robe and ate a roasted jackrabbit with the old man. After supper he opened his fiddle case as Sandeen produced a needle and thread to alter a pair of pants. The musician played as the old trapper tapped his toe and sewed.

"Do you know how to play 'Careless Love'?" Sandeen asked.

"No, I never heard of that one," Caleb admitted.

"Well, it's an old song. I can't carry a tune in a grass sack, but I'll tell you some of the words:

> *Love, oh love, oh, careless love,*
> *Love, oh love, oh, careless love,*
> *Love, oh love, oh, careless love,*
> *You see what careless love has done.*
>
> *I love my mama, and papa, too,*
> *I love my mama, and papa, too,*
> *I love my mama, and papa, too,*
> *I'd leave them both for lovin' you.*

"That was my Sary's favorite back in old Missouri," Burl said, after reciting.

"Who was she?"

"Should have been my wife." Sandeen pulled a few more stitches tight.

"Whatever happened to her?" Caleb asked.

"I guess she's still down there. Moved to Saint Jo last I heard. But that's been, oh, twenty-five years or so."

"How long have you been up here?" Caleb asked.

"Goin' on forty years. I left Missouri in '32. Wasn't much older than you. I had courted Sary about a year by that time. She was a keeper, I tell you. Pretty as a button. Come from a good church-goin' family. Not at all disagreeable about marryin' me."

"So how come you didn't marry her?"

"Oh, I got a idea to come out west, make a bundle in the fur trade. I asked her if she'd wait till I got back to marry me. She said if I left and went to the mountains, she wouldn't know if I was alive or stone dead. Said she wouldn't wait for me. Said she wouldn't be a widow before she was wed."

Caleb stroked a chunk of rosin against his fiddle bow. "I guess you came up here anyway, didn't you?"

"Well, that was the only way I knew of gittin' here, and I wasn't about to let no gal tell me where to go. At least not before we was married. I didn't believe her anyhow. I figured she'd wait at least a year before she took up with some other jack, and I knew I'd be back by that time."

Burl looked up from his sewing. "Son, the beaver was thick as the hair on your head back then. I threw in with a party out of Saint Lou and we took in I don't know how many pelts along the Yellowstone. One of our boys lost his own pelt to the Blackfeet, but we made good on the long haul. I was satisfied that I'd seen the wilderness, so I went back to make Sary my wife." He shook his head and let his hands fall still on the clothes he was taking up for Caleb.

"What did she say?" Caleb asked.

"What could she say? She'd married a fellow named Ludlow. That left me nowhere to go but back to the mountains. Now they call me a legend from Taos to Green River." Burl chuckled and started sewing again.

"You never got married?" Caleb asked.

"Oh, I've had me a squaw or two, but that ain't the same thing. No, there won't never be one like Sary." He massaged his black eyebrows a moment. "You haven't left you some pretty little gal down below, have you?"

"Me? No, sir."

"Well, if you have, you better get back there or some other young buck will take up with her. Now, play a couple more, son, then we'd better turn in. You'll want to get started early in the morning."

After breakfast, Burl advised Caleb to follow the North Platte out of North Park until he found the railroad, but Caleb shook his head. "I'm not goin' north, I'm goin' east over the mountains to winter in Denver. Where's the closest pass?''

"Now, listen here, son. You won't make it through any of them passes. Winter's comin' early this year. Don't try it or you'll get snowbound. You'd better get out of North Park in a week, or they won't find you till next spring.''

"But it don't make sense to head north with winter comin' on,'' Caleb argued.

"It don't make sense to head up to high country. You do as I say.''

"Yes, sir,'' Caleb said. But he had no intention of traveling north for days, when east was where he wanted to go. He was going to find himself a mountain pass. Hell, he could see a low spot in the divide as well as any old mountain man.

After the boy left, Burl took his ax down from a peg and spent the whole day cording wood, his breath turning to ice on his whiskers. The next morning snow began to fall and continued for two days. He knew it was time to let his mule wander down to the low country and winter in some canyon.

The morning he went to the corral to set the old mule free, he heard someone approaching through the woods below his cabin. It could only be the boy, he thought. No one else would be fool enough to travel this high up with winter on.

Caleb led Five Spot to Burl's cabin, slogging through drifts waist-deep. The mare was so exhausted that the boy was having to break the trail for her. When he got near enough for conversation, he looked at the old man's scowling face and said, "I didn't have nowhere else to go.''

"You tried to get through the mountains, didn't you?'' Burl asked, looking at the layers of ice caked around the boy's feet.

"I tried to, but I never found a pass. I guess I should have gone north like you said.''

"You guess!''

"I got lost. The snow covered all the trails. Somethin' got all my food. Drug it off two nights ago.''

"Didn't you tie your grub sack up in a tree?''

His knees wobbled with the cold. "Didn't think of it. I haven't et in a day and a half.''

Burl took a pole down from the corral fence and threw it into the snow. "What do you expect me to do for you? It's too late for me to take you down now. Even if I did get you down, I'd never make it back up. And I don't have supplies enough to get both of us through the winter!''

"I'll go huntin','' Caleb said.

"Shit!'' Burl threw another pole down. "Game's scarce. They got sense enough to go down below when winter comes on.'' He walked into the corral, kicking snow at his mule. He knew the boy would starve or freeze to death if he tried to get out of the mountains alone. "Take your gear off that mare," he grumbled.

"Sir?"

"Take your saddle and bridle off that mare, I say! Let her wander down below with old Katy."

"How will I ever find her?"

"She'll follow Katy. I'll know where to find 'em in the spring, if that mare of yours don't die tomorrow. Now turn her loose before I decide to butcher her for stew meat!"

Caleb began stripping his tack from the horse, feeling utterly ashamed for the trouble he was causing the old man.

"As soon as you thaw your feet out, get your rifle and go huntin'. I doubt you'll find anything alive, but we'd better try. We'll have to start short rations if we're to make it through to spring."

"Yes, sir," Caleb said. "But could I start on my rations before I go huntin'? I haven't et since . . ."

"I know, since somethin' drug off your grub sack! Go on to the cabin and I'll give you somethin' to eat."

Caleb hunted harder than he ever had that afternoon. He sat stone still in the snow for hours, though the cold felt like a thousand needles pricking his toes and fingers. When he moved, he paused a minute between each step, watching for deer or rabbits or mountain sheep or anything edible. Still, he had to trudge back to Burl's cabin empty-handed at dark.

"Did you see anything?" Burl asked.

"Just one wolf," Caleb said.

"Well, where is he?"

"Sir?"

"You said you saw a wolf. Why didn't you shoot it?"

"You can't eat wolf," Caleb said, collapsing on a couch of beaver pelts.

"The hell you can't! You can eat damn near anything that grows meat on its bones if you get hungry enough!"

"Well, he was too far away to shoot anyway," Caleb said. "If I see him again, I'll shoot him."

"You'll not likely see him again," Burl grumbled. "Every critter with a brain's gone below." He poured a meager helping of beans into a pot and cooked in silence for several minutes.

Caleb leaned against one of the roof poles, so filled with shame that he forgot his hunger. He hadn't meant to cause anyone trouble, but it looked as if he would half starve himself and old Burl before spring came. He almost wished he had stayed in the mountains alone to freeze to death. The night was hardly colder than the old man's words. He thought of spending every day of the long mountain winter with the old man's anger.

"Mr. Sandeen . . ." he said.

"What?" the gruff voice returned.

"If you'll allow me two days' rations, I'll go on down alone. I ain't got the right to make you suffer on account of what I've done."

Burl didn't reply. In a few minutes, he laid out the beans and a little smoked meat and told Caleb to eat. They sat on the fur-carpeted floor, their legs straddling the sawed-off stumps they used as tables.

"You clean up the dishes," Burl ordered when he had finished.

"Yes, sir." At least it was some relief to be of service in the cabin.

Burl threw a limb on the fire. "Son, you ain't the only damn fool to ever make a mistake. It ain't worth freezin' yourself to death over. You'll stay here with me."

Caleb was melting the snow to wash the tin plates with. "But what about food?"

"We'll ration what we've got and hunt every day we can. I'll make you some snowshoes. You play the fiddle, and I'll make the shoes." He shuffled through some skins, looking for one he could cut into rawhide strips to lace the snowshoes with. "I've made it through tougher spots. We'll make do."

The cabin was warm, and Caleb knew another couple of nights in the snow would likely kill him. Maybe Burl was right. It was like what Buster had once told him about the time the ridge log fell on his mother. He hadn't meant to do anything wrong. He was trying to do right. It just happened. No need to freeze to death over it.

THIRTY-SEVEN

IT ESPECIALLY BOTHERED Burl that he had to ration his whiskey on top of the food, but he would not deny Caleb a gut warmer after a cold day of hunting. After supper they would sip whiskey from tin cups as they played a few hands of poker, wagering with beaver pelts.

His first taste of Burl's whiskey reminded Caleb of his drunk in Milt Starling's saloon and almost made him gag. But after a few days he started looking forward to the nightly jigger. This was the proper way to use whiskey, he thought. One jigger a day.

"Where did you get that spotted horse of yours?" Burl asked one evening. He was sitting cross-legged on a mound of beaver pelts, dealing the cards.

"We breed 'em on our ranch," Caleb answered.

"Where'd you get your brood stock?"

"From an old mountain man."

"Cheyenne Dutch?"

Caleb looked up from his poker hand. "You knew him?"

"Knew him! Hell, I've fought with him and fought again' him. Me and Dutch saw some hard times and some good times together. What'll you bet?"

"A couple of pelts, I guess."

"Well, don't guess. Make up your mind, then bet."

"Two pelts then," Caleb said, throwing his wager onto the pot.

"I heard some desperado shot old Dutch last year."

"He killed my brother," Caleb said, tossing three of his cards aside. "Our ranch manager shot him for it."

"Ranch manager? I heard it was some outlaw."

"He killed my brother," Caleb repeated.

"I heard you. I guess old Dutch had it comin'. He was a careless soul. I went with him once to San Francisco back in the fifties. We'd made a good haul on hides together and went to blow it on women and whiskey. Dutch got drunk and had some tattoo artist put those spots on his butt. He put a lot of stock in those spots. Said they made him bulletproof. Anyway, he killed a Chinese girl in San Francisco, and we had to light out in the middle of the night. Never went back to California after that. I'll raise you another pelt." He dragged three ovals of dried beaver skin onto the pot and tossed a card on top of the ones Caleb had thrown down.

"Was he your friend?" Caleb asked.

"In this country you run with whoever you have to to stay alive," Burl said, dealing the new cards. "Dutch was good at stayin' alive before he got addlepated. Then he let that Indian magic get the better of his senses."

Caleb had forgotten which cards he had thrown aside, so he reached for the discard pile to refresh his memory. Burl caught his wrist and clamped it down against the fur carpet.

"Don't monkey with the deadwood," the old trapper warned.

"But, I was just . . ."

"I don't care what you were doin'. Once you throw them cards aside, you don't get another look. Some gamblers will cheat by peekin' at the deadwood. If you're to learn poker, you better learn it proper, or you'll get in trouble."

"Yes, sir," Caleb said.

He released the boy's wrist. "Your bet."

Caleb threw in another pelt, and Burl raised him with three more.

"Sorry Dutch got your brother," the old trapper said as he spread his winning hand across the fur.

They gave up hunting in the middle of the winter without having burned a grain of powder. Burl decided the exercise was draining too much energy and making them hungrier. He said they would lay up in the cabin until the weather broke again. They would keep the place warm and just lounge about like a couple of hibernating bears. The most exercise Caleb was allowed to get was sawing on the fiddle or blowing on the harmonica. Rations were so short he hardly had the energy for either. The pants he wore seem to have shed the stitches Burl had put in them to make them fit.

One night Caleb was playing "Don't You Marry Those Texan Boys" on the fiddle and singing what verses he could remember:

> *Missouri gals, come listen to my noise,*
> *And don't go marry those Texan boys.*
> *For if you do, your portion it'll be,*
> *Johnnycakes and venison and sassafras tea,*
> *Johnnycakes and venison and sassafras tea.*

"I'm hungry," he said, stopping in the middle of the song.

"Don't play them songs about food," Burl replied, rolling over on the beaver pelts.

"I can't help it. I'm starvin'."

Burl chuckled. "You don't know what starvin' is, son. You've had food in your mouth every day."

"Not very much of it," Caleb complained.

"Wait'll you go two weeks without a bite. Wait'll your gut's burnin' you for something to eat. You'll shit like a calf with the scutters and hump up with cramps like some poor ol' wormy dog. Then you'll know you're starvin'."

Caleb put his fiddle down and slumped against the roof post. "Have you ever gone that long without food?"

"Yes, I have. That long and longer. In '47 I went to Canada with some other fellows. Five of us started out. Me and Cheyenne Dutch was the only ones to come back alive. We ran smack out of grub before February. Got so hungry we ate all the fringes off our buckskins. Boiled 'em and ate 'em. We ate all the grease out of our guns, too. Had rawhide roofs on our cabins. We boiled that rawhide down so it looked like a pot of glue and ate that, too."

"Did the other three starve to death?" Caleb asked.

"Two tried to walk out and didn't make it. The other one went huntin' and got lost. Me and Dutch followed his tracks when he didn't come back. He was goin' in circles. It like to have killed us draggin' him back to camp, but I thought we ought to bury him."

"How did you and Dutch make it till spring?"

"I shot a white owl one night. Lined him up again' a full moon to draw my bead. We made that bird eat for three days. Ate everything but the feathers and beak. Cracked the bones and sucked out the marrow. The game started comin' back pretty soon after that, and we got strong enough to walk down.

"Things ain't near so bad for us, son. When you take to eatin' the catgut off that fiddle, you'll know you're starvin'. If we keep our rations down, we'll make it to spring. We might hunt some game up, too. We'll make out all right."

Burl kept up the encouraging chatter but held his doubts to himself. Things were not going to work out as well as he had led Caleb to believe— not at the rate the food was disappearing. He knew now he should have butchered the spotted horse. Both of them could not survive on the amount of food left.

It was Burl's food. Caleb was the interloper.

The first day the temperature climbed above freezing, Burl sent Caleb out to hunt. "You head down a few miles. Maybe an elk will come up. Shoot anything."

"What are you gonna do?" Caleb asked.

"I'll go up higher. Maybe I'll find an owl or somethin' up there. Now, git."

Caleb strapped his snowshoes on over the fur moccasins Burl had made for him and crunched through the crust downhill. He stopped every couple of minutes to rest and watch for game. The frozen forest looked desolate as an alkaline desert, yet there was beauty in the way the sunlight shined through the ice and illuminated the thin veils of snow on the tree branches. He was so wanting for food that he wondered whether he would be able to make the climb back up to the cabin.

He wasn't sure he really wanted to go back uphill anyway. Something was bothering Burl. There was something odd in the way the old man had ordered him out to hunt. Caleb couldn't put his finger on it, but it was there. Had they simply been snowed in together too long, or was it something more than that?

He found a beaver pond below—a level field of unbroken snow. Not a single track of bird or beast marred it. He brushed the snow from a boulder and sat down. He had been shivering there for an hour when he heard Burl's Warner carbine speak—not up above the cabin, but a mere mile or less on his own back trail. The shot made Caleb's heart leap in his chest, and he cursed his own nerves for burning energy so.

Then he realized what the single shot meant. An old saying Javier had often used came to him: "One shot, meat; two shots, maybe; three shots, no good." An old hand like Burl Sandeen could not have missed. The report was still echoing across the frozen ranges.

Caleb drew on his reserves of strength and mounted his own trail back toward the cabin. A mile up the mountain he found Burl's snowshoe tracks over the tops of his own. The trapper's trail turned away from Caleb's there and went across the mountainside.

Why had the old man followed him? He was supposed to be hunting up high. Had he lied or simply changed his mind? Caleb dug into a dime-size hole in the snow and found the rimfire cartridge Burl's carbine had emptied of powder and lead.

As he closed the distance on the old man, he fought an irrational fear that told him Burl would eat all the meat before he could catch up. He wondered what kind of meat it would be. He pictured quartered carcasses of deer and elk—huge red chunks streaked with white tallow. He was tripping through the white forest, slinging frozen crust from his snowshoes, when he finally caught sight of the mountain man studying something between his feet.

"Did you shoot?" Caleb yelled.

Burl turned around, shushed Caleb, and waved for him to approach. "Keep your voice down," he said when Caleb caught up. "Don't spook him any further than you have to."

"What did you shoot at?"

"A big wolf."

"Hit him?"

"Didn't you see the blood trail? Probably tramped on it, didn't you? Ain't much of a trail, but he's hit. Wolf's tough, though. Could go miles."

Caleb watched Burl point out mere specks of crimson beside the trail of the wounded wolf. "That rifle should have ripped him clean open. You sure you hit him good?"

"Don't know. It was a runnin' shot, two hundred yards away. That wolf was quarterin' your trail, son. He meant to make a meal of you."

They had trudged another hundred yards when Burl sank into the snow on his knees. "Look here, son."

Caleb looked into a hole in the crust and saw a clot of blood about as big as the back of his hand.

"He's hit hard in the lights," Burl said. "Coughed up a hunk of 'em with this blood." The old man took out his knife and lifted the chilled hunk of blackened blood and lungs with the blade. Smashing the gore between the knife edge and the thumb of his mitten, he cut it in two and let half fall into Caleb's waiting palm. Without even wondering what he was to do with it, Caleb tossed it down his throat and swallowed, chasing it with a handful of snow.

A quarter mile farther on, the old trapper and the greenhorn found the wolf's nose buried in the snow where he had died running.

"Big old feller," Burl said. "The other wolves will run an old one off. He probably came up here to die."

Caleb sank into the snow on his knees, took a mitten off, and ran his hand through the wolf's thick fur. Logic was starting to come back to him now with the prospect of food at his fingertips. He no longer suspected old Burl of anything sinister. Burl had only followed his trail to protect him from the wolf. He had only ordered him out hunting to break the monotony of cabin fever.

"He's cooled off so much his blood won't run," Burl said. "We'll have to warm him up in the cabin before we can drink it."

THIRTY-EIGHT

LEE FONG WAS squatting on his heels, bothering Buster with one of his stories. He had worked mines in California, cooked for lumberjacks in Oregon, built railroads in Utah, and operated a laundry in Wyoming. He knew tall tales from every corner of the West and loved to repeat them, occasionally going so far as to weave himself into them.

"I was kidnapped by Joaquin Murieta," he claimed. "You know about that Mexican, Buster?"

"Nope," Buster said as he cultivated his wildflower patch near the Holcomb burial plot.

"A very bad bandit in California . . ."

Lee wore American clothes except for his dish-shaped hat and thong sandals. Over the winter he had shuffled between the Holcomb cabin and the bunkhouse in leather shoes. But now that the weather had warmed up, he had taken to wearing the sandals. His socks looked something like mittens. The big toe had its own little sleeve to allow the thong on the sandal to slip between his toes. Buster had never known anyone who could take off and put on footwear so quickly. Lee would not enter a building with his shoes on. He could shed them or put them on without even looking down at them, almost without breaking stride.

"Joaquin kidnapped me to make me cook for him every day," Lee said.

Buster was looking for buds on his columbines, but he paused long enough to smirk at Lee.

"It's true," The Chinese man said. "How do you think I learned to cook? Joaquin was going to kill me, but the rangers killed him first. They pickled his head and put it in a saloon in San Francisco. The hair would not stop growing on his head, and it filled up the whole pickle jar!"

A drum of hooves preceded Pete as he rode down from Monument Park. He trotted his horse to the flower garden, jumped from the saddle, and let out several inches on the latigo. "Lee, walk this horse around a little, will you?" he said.

Lee rose, bowed with a jerk, and took the reins in his hand.

"And slow down," Pete said. "I want you to cool him down, not wear him out."

"He don't know how to walk slow," Buster said. "He leans into everywhere he goes like he was fightin' a blizzard."

Pete stared blankly at the flower garden. "How long till we have blooms?"

"A couple of weeks for the early ones. Don't worry. Caleb will come home in fine shape."

"I'm not worried about him. I've said my prayers for him."

"You sure look worried about somethin'. What is it?"

Pete sighed and sat down on the ground. "A homesteader's taken out a warrant on a quarter section up in Monument Park. Just north of Matthew's claim. He's up there right now, takin' sods out of an old buffalo wallow to build him a house."

Buster put his hoe aside and pushed the small of his back into place. "How come that county clerk didn't say nothin'? I thought Mister Ab had him paid to warn them homesteaders out of the valley."

"Papa ain't done no land locatin' since Matthew died. He didn't even bother to get Matthew's warrant transferred to his name. I had to do that on my own. That county clerk has probably quit lookin' out for us."

"You think that homesteader will prove up?"

"I don't know, but if we let one farmer get a crop in up on Monument Creek, the whole rest of the park will fill in with them. They're liable to start runnin' cattle and eat all of our grass."

"We better tell your father," Buster said. "Maybe it will get him back to work."

When they opened the cabin door, they found Ab in his usual place, sitting in his rocking chair, looking out through the window at the bald hill between the house and the mountains. He had spent almost every day there since Caleb left. He usually didn't even bother to put his wooden leg on in the morning.

"Papa," Pete said, pulling a chair up beside his father, "we got a problem. Some homesteader's staked a claim on the creek, right next to Matthew's quarter section."

The rocker creaked rhythmically as Ab pushed his good leg against the wall. It took several seconds for Pete's words to come through to him, then the chair stopped rocking and a look of consciousness filled his eyes. He was pallid from lack of sun, but some color seemed to come to him when he looked at Pete. "Must have read the map wrong," he said. "That fellow in the county clerk's office was supposed to tell me if anybody tried to file up there."

"You haven't dealt with him in over a year, Papa. I don't think he's lookin' out for our best interests anymore."

Ab stared out through the window and drummed his fingers on the chair arm.

"What do you want me to do about it?" Pete asked.

Ab sat like a statue for a long moment. "Right next to Matthew's claim?"

"Yes, sir."

For months Ab had been mired in self-pity, seldom leaving his house, avoiding everyone. One son had died and another had left him. Many were the times when, alone in the cabin, he would load his old Walker Colt and put the muzzle against his head. Caleb would come home to stay if he killed himself, and his sons would have the ranch together.

But now the thought of nesters trying to take Monument Park from his sons fired him with indignation. He became almost instantly drunk with anger. He had been looking for something like this to turn his fretting mind to good use. He forced back the echoes of his fight with Caleb and started thinking ranch.

"Papa?" Pete said. "What do you want me to do about it?"

"I'll take care of it myself," Ab answered. "Buster, go hitch your buggy. I want you to drive me to town. Where's my leg? What has that Chinaman done with my leg now?"

A line of land seekers led to the log building in Colorado City where the county clerk handled homestead claims. Ab stepped down from Buster's buggy and walked past every man in line. A homesteader was just leaving the office when Ab marched in.

"Bertram!" he said. "My son tells me a homesteader has filed on Monument Park. Why in Hades didn't you tell me about it?"

"I didn't think you were interested anymore," Morley Bertram said, glancing nervously at the men heading the line outside his building. "You haven't expressed any interest in that land in quite some time."

"You know what my interests are," Ab said. "I thought we had an understanding."

Bertram winced and jumped up from his desk. He was competent enough as a county clerk, but crises tended to rattle him. He grinned apologetically at the homesteaders in front of his office. "This won't take long, gentlemen," he said as he closed the door in their faces. "Please keep your voice down, Mr. Holcomb."

"Why should I?"

"These nesters are getting suspicious about the way we go about our business. Land's getting scarce. Things have changed around here."

"I'll say they've changed. Time was when you'd tell me if somebody tried to file on my valley, and I could steer them somewhere else."

"As I recall, I earned a stipend for such service, Mr. Holcomb, and stipends have not been forthcoming for over a year now."

"You'll get your stipend when you start looking after my interests again, and you can start by voiding that claim up in Monument Park."

"Too late for that," Bertram said. "The fellow's already completed his application. If he can prove up, he'll own that land."

"Not if I have anything to say about it," Ab said, his pale face flushing with anger.

"Don't take any rash actions," Bertram warned. "I tell you things have changed. If you start running men out of Monument Park, they'll take a closer look at your cowboys' claims with the rotten houses on them where nobody lives, and the little garden patches where nobody farms. These newcomers can challenge your claims, you know. Then the land office will send an investigator, and you're likely to lose everything you don't already have title to."

"Just what do you suggest I do then?" Ab asked.

"I suggest you content yourself with what you have. There's only five miles or so of the creek you haven't taken up already. Let somebody else have it."

"That five miles of creek gives me control of a hundred sections or more!" Ab shouted. "If some other cattlemen get that water, they'll fight me for every blade of free grass in the park. I set my mind to owning that whole creek a long time ago, Bertram, and I am not about to change it now."

"You'd better figure out a way to get it quick then," Bertram said. "At the rate settlers are trailing in, there won't be any of it left by the end of the year."

"How am I going to lay claim to that much land by the end of the year?"

"The only way is to buy it outright."

Ab rapped his wooden leg against Bertram's desk in anger. "I am not as rich as General Palmer," he said. "I cannot afford to purchase that much land at a $1.25 an acre."

"Then my advice is to buy as much as you can at intervals along the creek. That way your cattle will have access to the water and will still be able to graze around the homesteads."

"Homesteads!" Ab shouted. He sank into a chair and glowered at the little bureaucrat across the desk.

"It's the only way," Bertram said. "You'll have to give up hope of owning the whole park unless you can buy the homesteaders out in the future. Take my advice. Buy a few plots at intervals like I suggested. I know a way you can get one quarter section right now at no charge."

"How's that?" Ab said.

"You can use your soldier's homestead rights."

"How does that work?"

"Your time in the army satisfies the usual residence requirements. All you have to do is bring your discharge papers to prove up."

"Just like that?"

"Yes."

Ab sat forward in his seat. "Can any soldier do that?"

"Any soldier with an honorable discharge. Bring your papers and you can choose any quarter section you want."

"Why haven't you told me about this before?"

"It's a new law. I just got word from the land office last month."

Ab got up and paced across the office, his peg leg clacking against the puncheon floor. "What's the name of that homesteader that filed on my valley?" he asked.

"Mayhall. Terence Mayhall. He's from Georgia."

Ab nodded. "Bertram, you do whatever it takes to keep those homesteaders out of Monument Park. Tell them it's too far from town. Tell them the soil's no good. Tell them the creek floods in the spring and runs dry in the summer. If you can keep them out another month, you'll start seeing your stipend again."

"What do you plan to do?" Bertram asked.

Ab opened the door. "Never mind. Just do as I say."

When he climbed back into the buggy, he told Buster to take him to the telegraph office. By the end of the day he had notified the newspapers in Colorado Springs, Denver, and Pueblo that he would host a grand reunion of the old First Regiment of Colorado Volunteers at Holcomb's Ranch on Monument Creek. There would be food, music, speeches, contests of skill. Any member of the Colorado Volunteers or any other unit of the Union Army was encouraged to attend to partake of the festivities.

Buster thought Ab had lapsed into delirium. He had never known him to attend a party, let alone throw one.

"Buster, see that you invite that claim jumper to supper tomorrow. His name is Terence Mayhall."

Buster had too many things to do around his farm, so he talked one of the cowhands into riding up the creek with the invitation. He didn't meet Terence Mayhall until the man arrived on foot at the Holcomb cabin the next day for supper. Lee Fong had gone all out with steak, potatoes, turnip greens, corn, fresh bread, butter, and milk.

Terence Mayhall looked as though he had been made of wet rawhide shrunk over a stack of cobblestones. He was rather short, but he was so stout that he had to buy his clothes a size large and cuff them around his wrists and ankles. Even then, burls of muscle strained the seams.

Lee Fong's feast turned out to be a mistake. Mayhall asked if all the food had come from the Holcomb Ranch. When Ab told him it had, the nester was encouraged more than ever about the prospects of success with his homestead.

"But we've got better water than you'll have up the creek," Ab said.

Mayhall shrugged and continued to eat.

"The soil is better down here, too, and we're closer to town."

Mayhall grunted.

"It took us years before we knew we would make it. Didn't it, Buster? It sure gets dry here sometimes. We wouldn't have made it if we hadn't been able to save a few cattle."

Mayhall wiped his hand across his chin. "Cows brought you through? Guess I better get me some, too. Grass is free, anyway."

"Not for long," Ab warned. "I hear the government is going to start leasing out the range. No, cows will just be a drain on you. I sure wish you'd have talked to me before you filed your claim. I could have found you a better homestead."

"Too late for that now," Mayhall said. "I'll just have to make out with what I got."

"Maybe it's not too late," Ab said. "There are ways to improve your situation if you know the land laws well enough, and I do."

Mayhall shook his head convulsively. "Not interested," he said.

Ab pretended not to hear. "You can commute your claim after six months. That means you can buy it outright at a dollar and two bits an acre."

Mayhall laughed. "At those prices I couldn't even buy a garden patch. I'll just have to wait it out five years to earn my title."

"I can help you out," Ab said. "If you commute, I'll buy you out at a dollar and a half. That way you'll make forty dollars profit off your place and you can file on a better quarter section somewhere else."

Mayhall chewed a piece of meat and studied Ab's face. "Why would you want to do that?"

Ab shrugged. "I like to see a man make good. I don't think you have much of a chance of it up the creek. Uncle Sam's betting you a hundred sixty acres against five years of your life that you can't make a farm. The odds are in old Sam's favor in Monument Park. I think you should get yourself another claim where the odds favor you."

"Six months from now there may not be any land left to claim on the whole Front Range. This country is settling up fast. I'll take my chances with what I got. Besides, I never asked for no man's help, and I don't aim to start now."

Ab slurped at a cup of coffee and glared at the squatter. "I'll tell you what I'll do," he said. "I can get my hands on two quarter sections over on Camp Creek. The water's good there all year, and it's only two miles from town. I'll trade you those two claims for your one, even money."

Mayhall put his silverware down and leaned back in his chair, sucking his teeth. Pete and Buster glanced up from their plates as Ab waited for the reply.

"I ain't got a team to work one claim with, much less two," Mayhall said. "A man needs just so much land, and I got all I need up the Monument."

"Maybe I can get three quarter sections on Camp Creek," Ab said.

Mayhall snorted and shook his head. "Holcomb, what in hell do you want my claim so bad for?"

Ab pulled a napkin out of his shirt collar and threw it down on the table. "You wouldn't understand," he said. "You're a farmer. I'm a cattleman. I need that land. Me and the boys brought the first cattle to this valley. We've got claims on this creek the land office doesn't recognize. We fought Indians in this valley—just ask Buster. I lost a wife and a son here. I mean to own it all, and I want solid range. I won't stand for homesteaders squatting in the middle of my spread."

Mayhall pushed himself away from the table. "If the damned carpetbagger government hadn't took my farm in Georgia, I wouldn't have come here in the first place," he growled. "But damn it, I'm here to stay now, and I have as much right to government land as you have. I can't help that you got here first. You're an older man than I am, that's all."

Ab ground his teeth and snarled for a few seconds, then he turned away from his guest and stared at the wall.

"If y'all really do like to see a man make good," Mayhall said, "you'll show me how to build an irrigation ditch. How'd you learn how to do it?"

Ab said nothing.

"Buster and my little brother, Caleb, built 'em," Pete said.

Mayhall gawked at Buster. "You built 'em?"

Buster nodded.

"How'd you know how?"

Buster glanced at Ab. "Well, I read up on it," he said.

"Read up on it!" Mayhall blurted.

"And I saw some irrigated farms down on the Arkansas. It ain't hard to do. Water flows downhill. If you know that, you can figure it out."

"Who built your dam? Who surveyed your ditches?"

"Buster did it all," Pete said.

Mayhall slapped the table. "Well, I'll be damned, Buster. You must be the smartest nigger I ever heard tell of!"

Buster forced a smile. "And smarter than some white folks," he replied.

Mayhall tilted his chair back and laughed, slapping the legs of his pants stretched tight around his thighs.

Ab rose from the table, went into his bedroom, and came back with a double-barreled shotgun and a handful of shells.

Mayhall heard him break the breech open and turned to see him loading the barrels. "What's this?" the nester said.

"You better leave, mister," Buster warned.

"What does he mean, pullin' a shotgun on me?" Mayhall demanded, rising from the table.

"He don't like that name you called me."

Ab slammed the breech shut on the double barrel.

"I didn't mean nothin' by it," Mayhall protested.

Ab thumbed back the hammer behind the first barrel.

"You better git," Buster said.

Ab thumbed back the second.

"All right, I'm gittin'!" Mayhall grabbed his hat from a deer antler and slipped through the door as Ab's aim followed him. "Damn Pennsylvania Yankee!" he shouted when he was safely outside.

Ab reopened the breech and took the shotgun shells out. "As long as I live, that word won't be spoken in this house. Ella wouldn't approve of it." He went back into his bedroom to put the gun away.

Buster sighed with relief, then looked at Pete and shook his head. He might have appreciated Ab taking up for him if he didn't know the man so well. Buster thought Ab seemed certain that Buster should be ashamed of his race. He never even allowed the words *colored* or *Negro* to be spoken in reference to Buster—afraid they would embarrass him. He went out of his way to keep from reminding Buster of his blackness, as others took pains not to mention his wooden leg to him.

He was trying to do the right thing, but Buster knew he was misguided. Ab was almost hopeless when it came to dealing with other people. He couldn't get along with anybody.

"That was a good one, Buster," Pete said. " 'Smarter than some white folks.' "

"Yeah," the black man said. He pushed his unfinished meal away and went to the window to watch Terence Mayhall stalk away up the Monument.

THIRTY-NINE

The drifter rode in on a westerly breeze,
To the shortgrass country, out of the trees.
Down t'wards the meadows he galloped until
He stopped in the shadows cast long 'cross the hill.

He swung from the saddle, loosened the girth,
Dusted his clothes of the soil of God's earth,
Hung his old hat on a slick saddle horn,
Looked o'er the wheat fields and broad rows of corn.

The words came to Caleb as freely as if he had sung them a thousand times. From which cloud they had issued, he could not say. He stood on the Arapaho Trail overlooking Monument Park and sang the words to himself repeatedly to make sure he wouldn't lose them.

The song should say something about the wildflowers, he thought. From where he stood, Buster's flower patch looked like a crazy quilt staked to the ground.

They were all sitting outside—some cowboys in a group around the door of the bunkhouse—others outside Buster's cabin, listening to him pluck the banjo. An unfamiliar figure in a Chinese hat burst from the cabin and hustled past the cottonwoods. Under the eaves of the cabin, Caleb could just see the wooden leg of his father pushing against the porch rail, tilting the rocking chair.

He had cultivated a fanciful hope over the winter that Ab would welcome him home, apologize for the harsh words spoken a year ago, and install him as a foreman. It seemed suddenly very unlikely as he looked down on the familiar homestead. He knew, however, that he was not going to be the one to try patching things up. It wasn't his responsibility. None of it was his fault.

When he saw Pete riding up the creek valley from Colorado Springs, he cinched his saddle down, put his hat on, and mounted for the ride down to the ranch. He was anxious to talk to Pete again. He had some wild stories to tell. He couldn't wait to see the faces looking at him as he talked and sang.

Sam Dugan looked up from soaping his saddle and let out a shout: "It's him! Caleb's back!"

Buster's fingers tripped and fell from the banjo strings when he saw Five Spot coming down the hill. The spotted mare disappeared behind the trees lining the other side of the creek, and Buster glanced toward the Holcomb house to see Ab petrified in the rocker. When Caleb emerged on the near creek bank, Buster looked at the cabin again and saw the chair rocking empty.

Pete galloped up the road and met Caleb at Buster's cabin, shaking his hand from the saddle. "It's about time you got back," he scolded. "We've been puttin' off the roundup, waitin' on you."

"Sam's damn near soaped all the hide off his saddle," said Piggin' String McCoy.

Caleb was untying the fiddle case behind his cantle. "I left as soon as I could get over the mountains,'' he said. ''Now, if one of you boys'll put my horse away, I'll get tuned up with that banjo.''

Caleb fiddled until dark, when the men moved to the bunkhouse to get under the lantern.

''Where all have you been since last year?'' Pete asked, sitting on a narrow swaybacked bed. ''You said you were gonna tell me some stories.''

''I've got a few to tell,'' Caleb answered, and he put his fiddle aside to talk.

Lee Fong brought him some steak and beans, and a biscuit or two, but Caleb talked right through them. He told about his drunk in the saloon of Milt Starling, the ranch of the Scotsman in South Park, the trip to the Palouse country, and his winter in the cabin of Burl Sandeen. He drank in the attention they showered him with. It made the whole year worthwhile.

Buster thought he had never heard any finer stories than the ones Caleb told.

''. . . so old Burl helped me find Five Spot when the snows broke and led me through a place he called Sandeen Pass. Last thing he said was, 'Good luck, son, and don't come back.' I swear winter will never catch me in North Park again.''

''Hell, you ain't hardly done much to talk about over the past year, have you?'' Sam complained.

''I haven't finished yet. I didn't tell you about Denver.''

''When did you go to Denver?''

''I just came from there. I had to fiddle in a saloon a few nights for grub money. A dang bloody fight broke out while I was there. A couple of drunks had it out over a whore.''

''You sure you weren't one of 'em?'' String asked.

Laughter began to bathe Caleb like a balm, but Pete chose the moment somehow to spoil the fun. ''Why don't you go over to the house and see Papa?'' he asked.

The bunkhouse became silent. Caleb picked up his fiddle and plucked vacantly at one of the strings. ''I reckon he knows I'm here,'' he finally said. ''If he wants to come over and see me, I'll speak with him. But I really came back to see you and the boys, Pete. Not him.''

Pete turned immediately for the door.

Lee Fong picked up Caleb's plates and stacked them on one arm. ''You are a very lucky boy,'' he said.

Caleb regarded the Chinese man suspiciously. ''What would you know about my luck?''

''I lived at Fort Bridger. I pressed the beaver skins into bales there.

That was my job. I was there when Burl Sandeen and Cheyenne Dutch came back from Canada.''

"He told me about that. Said him and Dutch were the only two of the party to live through the winter.''

"But he did not tell you how," Lee Fong said. "Sandeen and Cheyenne Dutch killed the other three men and ate them! You are lucky he did not eat you, too.''

The cowboys exploded with laughter, but Caleb did not think it funny. In the first place, Burl had saved him from starving to death. In the second place, he did not appreciate being upstaged as a storyteller by a Chinese cook. "That's a lie," he declared. "Them others froze, that's all.''

Lee Fong shook his head and jutted his finger toward the mountains. "Some trappers went to get the bodies that summer. They found the bones of the legs and arms inside the hut. The skulls had bullet holes.''

"Don't pay that little Chinaman no mind," said Dan Brooks. "He says Joaquin Murietta's head gets a haircut once a week in a pickle jar in San Francisco.''

The cowboys' laughter erupted again, and Lee Fong stalked angrily out of the bunkhouse, leaping into his sandals outside the door.

"We'd better practice some of those old war songs," Buster suggested, trading a guitar for Caleb's fiddle. "Mister Ab is gonna have a reunion of the old Colorado First here in a couple of weeks.''

"He is?" Caleb said. The idea of his father hosting a reunion made him think maybe his year adrift had changed the old man for the better.

"Let's do 'Tenting on the Old Camp Ground,' " Buster suggested.

As the boys sang along with the musicians, Pete slipped back into the bunkhouse and took his seat. Over the fiddle strings, Buster caught his eye. Pete shook his head and looked at the floor.

Ab did not show himself in the morning when Caleb rode out with Pete and the rest of the cowhands to get the roundup work started. But after they left, he went out to apologize to Ella.

"I can't talk to that boy anymore," he said to her grave. "He won't do what I say. I've failed at what you wanted. I just can't talk to him.''

FORTY

W HEN THE BRANDING and castrating had been accomplished and the market steers herded to the Holcomb Station on the Denver and Rio Grande, Pete and Caleb took one last ride through the park, looking for strays and late calves. They took their time, combing the country thoroughly, camping out at night. Caleb played his harmonica or told stories he had heard across the divide.

One rainy afternoon he was telling Pete about the Palouse country where the Nez Perce raised the spotted horses. "You know that bald hill across from the house?" he said.

Pete nodded.

"Well, take about a thousand hills that size, all different shapes, and you got the Palouse country. There ain't a tree on one of them hills, but danged if there ain't grass to beat . . ."

Pete had stood in his stirrups and was squinting to see through the mist.

"What is it?"

"There's a cow down across the creek. See her?"

"Yeah," Caleb said. "She's calving."

"I believe you're right. Let's see how she's doin'."

They rode nearer, being cautious not to startle the cow.

"That's ol' Allegheny," Pete said. He knew the cow by name because she was the last of the original Holcomb herd, the only one of the Missouri cows to have survived the wolves and the Texas fever.

"Good God," Caleb said as they eased still closer to the cow. "Look at the size of that calf's head. It must weigh well-nigh a hundred pounds."

Pete got down from his horse, his slick boot soles slipping on the muddy creek bank. "She's gonna have trouble," he said. "We better pull it."

Allegheny was flailing her head and legs in agony, kicking mud, trying to push her newborn calf from the womb. Pete calmed her with his voice as he approached. He cleared the mucus from the nostrils of the half-born calf. "Bring your rope," he said. "At least we won't have to worry about choking the calf. It's already dead."

They put the rope around the head of the calf and pulled. The old cow bellowed and flailed her legs harder than ever. They wrapped the rope around their waists and leaned with all their weight. Pete put one boot against the cow's hip and pushed. The stillborn calf didn't slip so much as an inch from the laboring cow.

"Dang, that's a big calf," Pete said as he and Caleb paused to rest.

"That's one thing about them longhorns. They sure drop their calves easy. Never seen one have this kind of trouble. I'll pull the rope. You pull on the front feet."

They pulled another five minutes, grunting, rocking against the dead weight, but the stillborn calf would not come through the birth canal.

"Get my rope," Pete said. When Caleb brought it, Pete told him to tie a knot in the end of it.

"What for?" Caleb asked.

"Gonna have to whip her."

"What the hell for?"

"She's got to push that calf out."

"Can't we try pullin' it with a horse?"

"You could drag her a mile. That calf won't come out till she pushes it out. If we whip her, maybe she'll get the idea."

Caleb stood as if in handcuffs and leg irons, the rainwater dripping from the brim of his hat. "She's hurtin' too much. Maybe we should just put her out of misery with a pistol."

Pete took the rope from his brother. "You're sure sellin' our stock cheap. I'll whip her. You pull."

Pete tied a hard knot in the end of his rope and reared back to hit the cow. Caleb couldn't stand to watch, but the sound of the hemp slapping against the cow's flanks hurt him as much as watching would have. Allegheny bellowed, wheezed, and slammed her head against the ground in pain. The number of lashes mounted until Caleb lost count.

Pete shouted at the cow: "Come on, push it out, dang it!"

Caleb's muddy boots slipped out from under him as he pulled on the rope. He couldn't believe his brother could whip an animal so. Matthew would have done it but never Pete.

Pete paused a moment to catch his breath, but then Caleb heard hemp whistle through the air again and pop against the old cow's hide. Allegheny bellowed in anguish and moaned as if with her dying breath. Caleb looked around at her. Her eyes rolled back in her head, her tongue lolled out, and still the rope smacked against her ribs. He had to stop it. He couldn't stand another lick. He made up his mind to tackle Pete and shoot the poor cow with his pistol. But just as he loosened his grip on the pull rope, he felt the stillborn calf slipping from the birth canal. He leaned back a little harder on the rope, the cow's legs kicked stiffly, and the calf came out.

"That a girl!" Pete shouted. "I told you she could do it!"

Caleb dragged the giant calf out of the way and took his rope off of it.

Pete was rubbing the welts he had raised on Allegheny's side. "Go get your hat full of water," he said. "Maybe she can drink."

Caleb ran to the creek for the water. When he came back, Allegheny was trying to get up, but there was something horribly peculiar about her gyrations. She tried to roll to get her back legs under her, but they wouldn't obey. She moaned in protestation and fell back against the rocky ground, exhausted.

"What's wrong with her now?" Caleb asked.

Pete pursed his lips together to hold back the curses. "I don't know. Her legs won't work. I think pushing that calf out must have paralyzed her."

"Paralyzed her?"

"That's what I said! Have you gone deaf?" He shook the rain from his slicker and walked away to look at the mountains.

Caleb pushed the cow's head upright and put the hat full of water under her nose, but the poor dumb brute only sighed into it. He dumped the water out and looked back at his brother.

Pete had the bridge of his nose pinched between his thumb and forefinger, head bowed, eyes closed. Caleb had seen him in the same attitude the preceding Sunday as he conducted a cow-camp Sunday-school meeting. He knew it was the pose Pete struck when praying, for Caleb had peeked at him when he was asking God for healthy calves, good rains, and grass.

Caleb figured maybe he should pray, too, but he knew he couldn't do it as well as Pete; he didn't believe in it the way Pete did. If there really was a God, Caleb didn't want to bother him with inferior prayer, so he patted Allegheny on the head and used his hat to shield the rain from her eyes. He knew she was too dumb to appreciate it, but it was the least he could do since Pete was probably going to shoot her when he got through praying.

His brother prayed for a long time, and Caleb got impatient. What did Pete know that he didn't? He felt as if he were missing something. He pinched his nose like Pete. That didn't help. Nobody listened when he prayed. "Damn it," he thought, "that's enough praying!"

"Caleb, ride down to the ranch and fetch Buster," Pete said suddenly. "Tell him to bring that low drop-tongue wagon of his and a team of strong horses. Bring some lumber, too, so we can make a ramp and pull this cow up on the wagon."

"What are you gonna do with her?"

"I don't know, but I'll be danged if I'll whip a cow half to death, then shoot her. Maybe Buster can think of a way to get her back on her feet."

When Caleb left, he looked back and saw Pete collecting wood to burn the carcass of the stillborn calf. A lot of good all that praying had done. Allegheny was still lying flat on her side.

When Ab saw Buster stop the wagon with the prostrate cow under the doorway of the barn, his curiosity got the better of him. He didn't care if Caleb was there, he was going to find out what was going on.

Caleb was almost panic-stricken when he saw his one-legged father coming. He turned his back and pretended not to have seen him.

"Pete, what in Hades are you and Buster doing with old Allegheny?" Ab demanded.

Caleb shoved his hands into his pockets and stood as if his legs were paralyzed like the cow's.

"She strained herself calving," Pete explained. "She can't stand up."

"Well, then, haul her to the slaughterhouse—don't leave her here in the way."

"Buster thinks we can get her back on her feet," Pete said.

"Just how do you plan to do that, Buster?"

"We're gonna make some straps to fit under her belly and hang her from the barn door."

Ab looked at the cow, at the barn door, at Buster, at Pete. But he wouldn't look at Caleb.

"We're gonna let her stand on her front legs and hang her back end up for her. Buster says if we let her back end down a little every day, where she can put a little more weight on her back legs, she might get used to standin' on 'em again."

Ab smirked. "What happened to her calf?" he asked.

"It died," Caleb said. He saw his father's gaze shift to his boots. He felt the nervous stare climb up and down him a couple of times, but it would not look him in the eyes.

Ab pivoted on his peg and marched to the bunkhouse to dole out orders. He wanted fences repaired, prime beeves chosen for butchering, arbors built, cord wood piled for the barbecuing. The First Colorados—the old Pikes Peakers—were coming any day for the reunion, and he wanted them to suffer for nothing. It was a puzzle to everyone on the ranch that Ab had developed such a sudden streak of hospitality.

"I guess them old soldiers feel obliged to one another," Buster suggested as he rigged Allegheny's sling.

Caleb was furious to think that his father would invite his old war chums to stay at the ranch, yet would not welcome his own son. He was almost sure that Ab was holding the reunion to gall him. Well, he had learned to gall back. He didn't have to stay where he wasn't wanted.

FORTY-ONE

ALLEGHENY WAS STILL hanging from the doorway when the old soldiers began arriving. Some came on horseback with bedrolls to sleep on. Others rode the narrow-gauge tracks down from Denver or up from Pueblo. Some walked across plains or mountains, some brought wagons, some brought tents. Ab organized a committee among the early arrivals to designate chosen areas as campgrounds, speech platforms, and picnic grounds. The committee also approved a three-day schedule of events. Of music and food there would be no shortage.

Pete brought Amelia to the ranch on Friday, the first full day of festivities. A former infantry captain was slated to give a patriotic speech as they arrived. Amelia listened politely to an hour of it, then heard a fiddle tuning up near the barn and nudged Pete.

A bunch of old soldiers' children were feeding handfuls of grass to Allegheny as Amelia turned the corner of the barn. "My gracious!" she said. "Why have you hung that poor beast from the barn door?"

Buster and Caleb were just passing by with their instruments, on their way to join the band.

Pete shouted at Caleb. "You haven't said hello to Amelia," he reminded his brother.

Caleb removed his hat and approached. "My pleasure to see you again, Miss Amelia," he said.

"Charmed," she said, only glancing away from the swinging cow. Allegheny's back feet had been lowered just enough to scrape circles in the dust and straw of the barn floor. She seemed to like shifting her weight around on her front legs to make her tail end sway. "Charmed," Amelia repeated. "But why have you allowed your brother to suspend this poor creature here to be tormented by children?"

"She can't walk on her back legs," Caleb explained.

"Can't walk? Why in heaven's name not?"

"She had some trouble dropping a calf," Pete said.

"Dropping?"

"Yeah," Caleb added, "that calf looked like a yearling. She got it stuck halfway and couldn't push it out."

Amelia's lip began to curl in horror.

"It was a dead calf, but it was a big one," Caleb said.

Amelia glowered as Allegheny swayed in her sling, merrily eating grass given to her by the children.

"You know, I had a thought about that," Pete said to his brother.

"Since the calf was dead anyway, I was thinking maybe we should have cut it out of her. Maybe that would have . . ."

"Stop it!" Amelia shouted. She clapped her hands so suddenly over her ears that she knocked her chiffon hat off. "Stop it this instant! I won't hear another word. I'm going to listen to the musicians, Pete Holcomb. Join me when you will."

Pete handed her the chiffon hat, and she stalked away.

Buster could barely contain his amusement. "I guess we ought to let her down a notch," he said, jerking his head toward the cow.

Caleb put down his instruments to help lower Allegheny's hooves more firmly onto the ground. "Sorry if I said anything wrong," he said.

Pete lent a hand with the rigging. "It ain't you. Amelia hates ranches and cattle and all. She keeps tellin' me she'd rather die an old maid than marry me and move out here."

"*Marry* you?" Caleb said. Pete had talked a good deal about seeing Amelia, but the subject of matrimony hadn't come up.

"Said she'd marry me in a minute if I'd go to work for her father on the railroad and move to town."

Caleb watched Amelia walk away, the skirts swaying and the hair bouncing behind her, and knew that if he were in Pete's place, he would be considering working for the railroad about now. "When do you start?" he asked.

"You know me better than that. I'm a ranch man. She'll get used to the idea of livin' here, and I'll build her a big house when we get the money, and then we'll see if she won't marry me my own way." He threw a double half hitch into the rope he had let out to lower Allegheny and patted her bony hip. "I think she's usin' those legs some, don't you, Buster?"

"I don't know," Buster admitted. "But that little gal of yours sure used hers gittin' out of here." He almost tore himself open holding back the laughter. Amelia, with all her refinements, was a regular source of amusement to him.

The infantrymen held a shooting contest that afternoon, the winner shooting the neck from a bottle of Hostetter's Stomach Bitters at three hundred paces, freehanded. The fiddlers, guitarists, harmonica players, banjo pickers, and accordion squeezers rotated among the three areas designated for musicians. Children splashed in the flumes and fed Allegheny green grass and alfalfa hay. The few women who had come found lines of dancers waiting.

Ab was everywhere, flaunting his wooden leg, shaking hands, slapping backs, laughing at jokes. Buster saw lines on the man's face that had never before appeared—laugh lines. The reunion's able host seemed particularly interested in what had happened to his former comrades since the war: the places they had seen, the work they had taken on, and most important, the hardships they had suffered. He pretended not to see the occasional flask of whiskey.

That night, at one of the many campfires, Ab noticed a gambler in a frazzled derby hat and a silk cravat dealing a lively game of three-card monte. He stood for several minutes beyond the light of the campfire and watched. Finally he broke in on the game.

"Sir, a word with you," he said to the dealer.

After conversing privately for a minute or two with the host, the gambler returned to the game, straightening his cravat. "All's well, men," he said. "Sergeant Holcomb insists on low stakes, however. 'Recreational gambling,' he says. Wants no man going home broke."

The tale of Holcomb's Charge rang from every campfire that night. Though Ab had fought in only the one brief skirmish of the New Mexico campaign and in none of the Indian fights the First later engaged in, his charge at Apache Canyon had earned him high fame among the soldiers. Every assault that followed for the duration of the hostilities, every attack and maneuver, every advance, had to suffer the comparison with Ab's great dash at the enemy line. It gave rise to the war cry of the Pikes Peakers: Remember Holcomb's Charge! None who had seen it could forget.

By the same token, none could forget that two spotted horses had carried the charge. Two fearless riders had jumped the fallen bridge over the arroyo. Two had leapt into immortality at Apache Canyon. But it was also widely known that Cheyenne Dutch had killed Ab's oldest son, and so the old scout's name, when spoken, was whispered, the speaker glancing about for sign of the host before breathing the epithet.

On the second day, the old cavalrymen staged a race to the Garden of the Gods and back. Several of the old troopers came in hours late, having detoured through the saloons of Old Town.

Buster straightened some old shoes his draft horses had worn out and gave them to the men to toss at iron stakes pounded into the ground with a single jack. The children organized their own sack races. Music played, beef roasted, a few good-natured fistfights broke out, guns fired randomly, and Allegheny's dewclaws settled ever nearer to solid ground.

A mock debate took place under a brush arbor, the question being whether the properly attired gentleman should wear a fob ribbon or a watch chain. A less formal discussion on a more significant subject occurred around one of the campfires that night. The question was whether the action at Sand Creek under the command of Colonel John Chivington in the year of 1864 had been a massacre as opposed to a battle.

Taking the affirmation was Horace Gribble. Horace had fought with the Third, the Hundred Dazers, not the First. But he had become acquainted with many of the Pikes Peakers during the Indian campaign and had come to attend the reunion by personal invitation of Pete Holcomb.

Taking the negative was a former corporal of the First who had climbed Rowe Mesa behind the Confederate lines with Chivington to destroy the Texans' train of supplies. And he had later followed Colonel Chivington into battle at Sand Creek. "If it were a massacre," he asked, rubbing the stubble on his chin, "why weren't Colonel Chivington courtmartialed?"

"If it wasn't, why was he investigated by Congress?" Horace countered.

"Congress!" The old corporal spit a stream of tobacco juice through a gap in his teeth. It blackened an orange ember with an exclamatory sizzle. "Politicians ain't soldiers."

"Neither are men who kill unarmed women, or children carryin' white flags of surrender," Horace said calmly. He was squatting near the fire with his knees in his armpits.

"And what do you call heathen Injuns that kill white women and capture chil'uns?" the corporal answered. "To say not a word of rape and torture! An eye for an eye, the Good Book says."

"Don't preach to me about revenge," Horace said. "The Cheyenne killed my two brothers. That's why I joined the Third. But the Indians at Sand Creek had surrendered at Fort Wise. They were under army protection. They were lookin' to make peace."

"And what of the scalps of yaller-haired women found in their lodges?" The brown stream killed another coal.

"They were lost under the piles of scalps taken from dead squaws on the battleground that night by the likes of you."

The old corporal sprang to his feet. "Goddamn you to talk to me that way! I must have my satisfaction!" Tobacco juice punctuated the challenge as he put up his fists in the style of a pugilist.

Horace sprang from his squat, and each man tried to beat his opinion into the other's head for a couple of minutes before the two were pulled apart and made to shake hands.

The next morning, Pete organized Sunday services utilizing the talents of all the clergymen among the former soldiers. He gave the invocation himself and left it up to the others to read the scripture, lead the prayers, and deliver the sermons.

Caleb accompanied the hymns, but Pete's righteous streak was starting to vex him. His brother prayed just too damned much. He actually felt jealous of God.

Just at the close of the benediction, Captain Dubois and Amelia arrived from Colorado Springs in a three-spring surrey. The captain drove his team into the midst of the worshipers as they said amen, then stood in his buggy to make an announcement.

"Ladies and gentlemen," the captain said, "General William Jackson Palmer sends his regards to this gathering of loyal Union fighting men. The general regrets he could not attend himself. However, on behalf of the Denver and Rio Grande Railroad, the Fountain Colony, the city of Colorado Springs, and General Palmer himself, my daughter, Amelia, and I are pleased to present to this reunion of patriotic souls a grand and lavish feast! Behold!" and the captain swept his hand toward the plains.

Down the road from Colorado Springs came a regular processional of supply wagons, prompting a gasp and a cheer to issue from the crowd. The wagons were met by former troopers who galloped out to escort them to the reunion grounds. They carried chefs who would serve raw oysters, mock turtle soup, Mackinaw trout in egg sauce, boiled leg of mutton in caper sauce, roast loin of beef with oyster dressing, glazed sweetbreads, baked chicken pie, boiled potatoes, mashed potatoes, sweet potatoes, peas, tomatoes, spinach, celery, and olives. One wagon hauled nothing but watermelons. Another, the box of which was lined with ice, carried pies, cakes, puddings, and custards of every description.

The rest of the day favored the speechmakers, as the gluttons rendered indolent by the feast fell to lounging about under the arbors. And every orator who stood before his old comrades sang the praises of Ab Holcomb, generous reunion host and hero of Apache Canyon.

Yet Ab was nowhere to be found. Having appeared ubiquitous during the past three days, his presence was keenly missed. He hadn't been seen since the end of Sunday services.

"Where's Holcomb?" the guests began to ask. Some of them were planning on leaving by train that night. "Where's Sergeant Holcomb?" They wanted to thank their host. They wanted to toast him, favor him with a few bars of "For He's a Jolly Good Fellow," honor him with hip hip hoorays. "Where's Ab?" they wondered.

"Pete, where's your father?" one of the old soldiers inquired.

"I don't know," Pete said. "I haven't seen him."

"Find him. Bring him out. Drag him by that peg of his if you have to, but bring him round to the barn where the boys are playing the old battle songs. We won't leave until we hear him speak!"

On the way to the cabin, Pete passed a little gambler who jerked at the knot of his cravat and tipped his frazzled derby.

Pete found his father posturing in front of the mirror in his room. "Papa, they're asking for you out there. Some of them want to see you before they go home."

Ab stepped away from the looking glass. His hair was combed back and oiled, the gray streaks streaming from his temples like trails of smoke. He wore his best suit. A string tie closed his stiff collar. A gold watch chain draped gracefully from his vest pocket. And the leg! Had he polished it? No, he had sanded and varnished it! It shone like the banisters in Captain Dubois's mansion. And the awkward old leather straps that attached the peg to the belt had taken a fresh dose of blacking.

Ab breathed deep and nodded at his son. "I'm ready," he said.

FORTY-TWO

BUSTER AND CALEB were joining the band in a rendition of "Tenting on the Old Camp Grounds" when Ab appeared at the side of the barn. Applause overwhelmed the music, and singing voices jumped into "For He's a Jolly Good Fellow" before the musicians could agree upon a key to accompany it in.

The old soldiers patted Ab's back and passed him hand to hand like a gallon of water in a bucket brigade until they splashed him in glory on a little platform of oyster barrels and apple crates against the barn wall. There he cowered before applause and cheers until his guests would allow him to speak.

Pete pushed his way through the throng and took Amelia's arm, beaming with pride at his father's great success in his first role as host. He looked across the hat brims at Caleb, who was smirking beside Buster.

Ab held his hands high to quiet the crowd. "I don't make many speeches," he began when the shushing trailed off. "I don't feel at ease with it. I don't have much to say to you, except that I am happy every one of you could attend this reunion, and it was a pleasure to see you one and all. My only regret is that we soon must go our separate ways." He raked his hand back through his hair and wiped the oily tonic from his fingers onto his coat. "Well . . . in all honesty . . . there are other regrets, too. . . ."

He clasped his hands in front of him, tapped his wooden leg against the crate once or twice, and cleared his throat. "In talking with the men over the past three days it has come to my attention that many among us have fallen on hard times since the war. Not a few of you have told me you spent your last pennies in arriving here and have no idea where your next stake will come from." Ab slapped his palms against his breast pockets. "If I were a wealthy man, I would stake every one of you. Yet I know you all too well to think you would accept my charity."

A murmur passed through the crowd, and its members shook their heads solemnly over the hopeless, destitute conditions some of their comrades were experiencing.

"However," the speaker said, with a more hopeful lilt to his voice, "I believe that we, as men who have fought and suffered together, owe it to one another to exploit every avenue we have at our disposal to come to one another's aid. There are men among us with experience in many fields, and by swapping our ideas and exchanging advice, I believe we may all benefit and improve our situations. Allow me to make the first suggestion."

Ab scraped his polished leg thoughtfully against the platform and tucked his thumbs into his vest pockets.

"My specialty in the area of business, if I may claim one, is land speculation. Now not long ago I learned of a new law put into effect by the General Land Office that I think may benefit many of you here today. The law allows veterans to gain immediate title to homestead lands without the requirements of residing on or cultivating the land as is usual in homesteading. . . ."

A sudden vision came to Buster, and he finally grasped the scheme behind Ab's reunion. He saw the plat map in the county clerk's office. He saw his own little quarter section on Monument Creek with his name on it—Thompson—proclaiming the proprietorship in which he, as a former article of property himself, took so much pride. Then, above the Thompson Plat came the first of the squares labeled Holcomb—Ab's original homestead—then Javier's former quarter section, then those that had belonged to cowboys long proved up, bought out, and returned to Texas. The Holcomb squares flanked the creek for miles, halfway and more to its head, almost to the Pinery, where it poured from the mountain ranges onto the shortgrass plains.

Then Buster envisioned that blemish on the map, that one plat labeled other than Holcomb, that pockmark on an otherwise perfect slate: the Mayhall claim, just above the Holcomb quarter section once claimed by Matthew.

But above Mayhall's name were empty parcels, unclaimed lands, blank squares on the map, waiting for impoverished homesteaders to take them away from Ab Holcomb—twenty-odd squares lining the creek all the way into the Pinery, all the way to its source among the grotesque, red, sandstone monuments that had given name to the stream.

Now Buster saw the empty squares taking on the names of discharged soldiers—shiftless, penniless drifters aching to convert the quarter sections Uncle Sam gave them to gambling stakes or whores' wages. It all made such good, sudden sense. The land office that day in Colorado City, the telegrams sent to the newspapers, the sudden inclination toward hospitality. Old Mister Ab wasn't changing; he wasn't taking his blinders off; he was as single-minded as ever. He was thinking only of land!

In wanton disrespect to the speaker, Caleb was tuning his mandolin, rather noisily. He felt the elbow of Buster in his ribs.

"Listen, boy," the black man whispered, leaning toward him. "Your papa's gittin' you a bigger ranch."

"... so you see," Ab continued, "any one of you who has done your duty in service to the Union may take one hundred and sixty acres at no cost other than the filing fee and establish yourselves as farmers. That is my advice, and I hope some of you may make good use of it."

A murmur circulated among the listeners.

Ab went on. "Those of you interested in farming may come with me to the land office in the morning, if you want, to look at the possibility of getting land in this area. I know the best parcels for farming. I myself farmed between wars."

"What's it take to file?" asked a rawboned ex-private in overalls.

"You must have discharge papers," Ab explained. "But that is a mere formality. My word is good with the county clerk, and I will vouch for you in the morning if you want to get a farm. Are you a farmer?"

"I'm hired on a farm out of Greeley," the ex-private said. "I'd like to have my own, though."

"You'll have it before dinner tomorrow," Ab promised.

Whispers turned to talk in the audience.

"Who wants to settle alongside of him?" Ab asked. "There are parcels unclaimed along Cheyenne and Camp creeks where a dozen of you might farm as neighbors. You can share equipment, form a soldiers' colony."

"I'll take a farm!" a voice shouted from the back of the crowd.

"I'll come along, too," another said. "Maybe I'll take up farmin'."

"Sergeant Holcomb!" yelled the grinning dandy in the frazzled derby and the diamond-stuck cravat. "Some of our hands don't fit plow handles. Does Uncle Sam have a saloon or a gambling parlor we might file on?"

The old soldiers split the evening calm with laughter.

Ab appeared annoyed. "No property of that nature has been surveyed for filing," he said. "All the government has to offer is farmland or cash."

"Cash?" asked the husky voice of one of the soldiers' wives, her face reddening at her own outburst.

"That is to say," Ab explained when the tittering died down, "cash earned indirectly, through land speculation."

"What does that mean, sergeant?"

"Well, there are certain land speculators who would organize discharged soldiers to file on adjacent plots of land and then purchase the whole of them together at a set price, at pure profit to the soldiers."

"How much will they pay?" asked the man with the diamond-stuck cravat.

"Not more than a dollar and two bits per acre, for that's the government price, and quite likely half that or less. Any land speculator is going to offer as little as he can get away with.''

"You speculate, don't you, sergeant?'' The dandy tipped the derby back on his head.

"After a fashion. Land speculation and ranching: Those are my concerns.''

"Would you happen to be offering cash to soldiers in exchange for quarter sections?'' He straightened his cravat.

"Well, now, sir,'' Ab said. "It isn't my intention here to increase my own holdings. Rather, I intend to see that you men who have done your service to your country get all that's coming to you.''

"To your credit, sir, but, as a speculator, are you offering cash to those willing to sell their claims?''

Ab drummed his fingers on his chest and looked at the sky for a moment. "Well, in fact, there are certain parcels,'' he said, "not suited to farming on which I might graze a few head of cattle. But I'm afraid I can offer very little per acre. Perhaps you would earn more through another buyer.''

"How much do you offer?'' the gambler asked. "If I am not too bold in asking.''

"Not at all,'' Ab said. "My methods are open to the public. But I'm afraid I could offer no more than, say, oh, two bits an acre. For a quarter section of land that would add up to, oh, let's see . . .'' Ab pretended to make calculations with his peg leg.

"Forty dollars!'' shouted the gambler, shifting his derby.

"Is that the figure? That sounds correct, yes.''

"Might I have the forty in my pocket by the time the gentleman in the overalls has his farm? That is, by dinner tomorrow?''

Ab chuckled. "It could be arranged, sir. However, like any speculator, I prefer to buy land in larger parcels. I'm not at all sure I would be interested in buying just one claim.''

"He's got 'em now,'' Buster whispered to Caleb.

"Who needs forty?'' the gambler shouted, whirling to look the crowd over. "Forty dollars by tomorrow's dinner. And Sergeant Holcomb will be the better off for it. This is not charity, men, but business that benefits everybody. Raise your hands if you'll earn your forty dollars with me.''

By ones the hands rose. Grimy vagabond hands; soft-fingered hands of loafers and poor-farm idlers; manicured hands of swindlers and card sharks; eager, greedy, opportunistic hands that could already feel the coins pressing against their palms.

The wife who had spoken out grabbed her husband by the elbow and raised his hand for him. "That new stove,'' she said.

"Do you see what he's done?'' Pete said, shaking Amelia.

"Yes, he's very generous," she replied.

"No, not that. He's just acquired every claim left along the Monument. The creek is ours. And Monument Park. The whole danged valley! I guess you'll have to marry me now. I just became the biggest rancher in the county."

Amelia shrank from the commotion around her. How often would that one-legged man invite his old war chums after she married Pete? How many crippled cows would they hang in the doorway? How much longer could she possibly put it off? She was going to marry Pete Holcomb. She was going to become a wretched little ranch wife.

"Eighteen, nineteen . . ." The gambler shoved his way toward the platform of kegs and crates. "We have at least two dozen takers," he said. "That's a large enough parcel for any speculator. And you say we'll have forty each by dinner tomorrow?"

"I stand on my word," Ab said. "We'll leave at first light. Any man who wants a farm or forty dollars will have it tomorrow."

"I'll shake on it!" The gambler took Ab's hand and used it to pull himself onto the stage. "I have a proposal!" he shouted, squeezing Ab's shoulders in his hands. "Holcomb has worn stripes on his sleeves too long. He's fought in two wars, led us all to victory at Apache Canyon, fed and entertained us here for three days, and now he has brought us to farms and grubstakes! A promotion is in order. I say we brevet him Major . . . no, *Colonel* Holcomb!"

As the former enlisted men sorely outnumbered the officers, all opposition was shouted down with hip hip hoorays, and Ab was thrust into the crowd to the tune of "For He's the Jolly Good Fellow."

This last bit was the gambler's own device, and it took Ab completely by surprise. Imagine that! Colonel Holcomb! The king of all cattlemen between Denver and Colorado Springs. If only Ella could be here with him now.

"I told you," Buster said to Caleb. "I told you he was gonna get you a bigger ranch. Now he's gone and done it."

"It ain't my ranch," Caleb said, watching the crowd mob his father.

He turned away in disgust, left his mandolin in his seat, and trudged off. The corner of the barn dulled the sharp clamor of the celebration when he turned it, and he found Allegheny hanging in her sling in the doorway. It was something of a surprise to see her suspended there, though he had helped do the suspending. It was just such a ridiculous thing to do to a cow. But with the noise of his father's success throbbing in his ears, he decided he might as well let her down a notch, ridiculous or not.

The old cow's eyes rolled to follow him when he walked behind her to loosen the rope, and when he yanked at the knot, she kicked him. The sharp hoof of her right hind foot jerked back and caught him on the shin right above the top of his boot. He sucked in an epithet and started to kick her back or give her a good twist of the tail when he realized what she had done.

He hobbled back to the corner of the barn. "Hey, Pete!" he called. "Buster!" But there was no use in hollering. The music and commotion that surrounded Ab drowned out his voice.

At that moment Caleb knew he hated his father. Suddenly he despised old Ab Holcomb more than he ever thought possible. The man was a soulless fraud. He had no right hoarding all that attention. He didn't even enjoy it. He probably hated it. That false smile on his face was a scandal.

Caleb Holcomb was the one who deserved the adulation. He was the one who needed it, lived for it, sought it so desperately through his songs, his stories, the music within him that made his fingertips itch for the bite of catgut.

But all his life, his father had taken things from him. And now he would take this, too.

FORTY-THREE

Pete found Caleb in the corral the next morning, tying a fiddle and a mandolin behind his cantle. The ranch droned with voices and rattled with equipage being piled into wagon beds.

"Allegheny's standin' up," Pete said, cheerfully.

"I know. She kicked me yesterday."

Pete watched his brother loop the end of the latigo through the saddle ring as neatly as a silk tie. "Where you goin'?" he asked.

"I don't know. I have to hunt up some work somewhere."

Pete blinked in wonder. "Work? I'll have more work than you can stand after these old soldiers leave."

"I haven't been asked to stay on."

"I'm askin' you right now."

"I didn't mean by you."

Pete climbed over the rails, into the corral. "Well, listen, you haven't even given Papa a chance. He's had this reunion on his mind. If you'd ask him whether or not he wants you to stay, he'd tell you."

"I'm not gonna ask him nothin'. He should have thought about me before his danged old war pals. He doesn't even like any of them old soldiers. He just wanted them to file on land."

"Yeah, for us. He's buildin' us the biggest ranch on the Front Range. We'll own the whole creek after today and control every acre it drains."

Caleb shook his head. "He never did want me to be part of this ranch. I don't plan to stay where I ain't wanted. Open that gate for me, will you?"

Grudgingly, Pete lifted the sagging gate so it would swing open. "You're leavin' just to spite him, ain't you?"

Caleb paused with his foot in the stirrup. "You don't know how it feels, Pete. He doesn't look away from you when he sees you comin'." He threw his leg over his instruments and settled into the seat.

"You know what I think? It's a problem you don't want to handle, so you're just up and turnin' your tail. Takin' the easy way out."

Somehow Caleb felt he had a better argument from the saddle, looking down on his brother. "You come ride with me for a year if you think I'm takin' the easy way."

Pete couldn't find words. He tried to make them form in his mouth, but none would come. He huffed and gritted his teeth in frustration. "You're just like him," he finally said. "You're just as hardheaded as him."

They glared at each other until Caleb got tickled at the colors Pete was turning and started to laugh. "I guess I'll see you next spring," he said.

"That's fine. That will give you the rest of the year to grow some brains. I swear, you're just like him."

"Oh, settle down, Pete. There's always a chance we'll run this ranch together someday."

"When? When Papa's gone? Do you think he's gonna move back to Pennsylvania? You think he's gonna up and die for you?"

Caleb stared at his saddle horn. "All I know is, I won't stay where I ain't wanted. You don't know how that feels, so don't tell me I ain't talkin' sense."

Pete slid the latch on the gate with unnecessary ferocity. "See what I mean? You're just like him."

Caleb shook his head. There was no way he could make Pete understand. He couldn't explain why he felt more welcome among strangers than he did on his own family ranch. A year had shown him how folks would cook their best grub and spread their cleanest linen for a man with a fiddle. They would laugh at his stories and dance to his songs. The welcome seldom lasted long, but there was always another one down the road somewhere. Maybe he was meant to be adrift in the world.

"So long, Pete," he said. He nudged Five Spot to the west.

"Hey!" Pete shouted when Caleb had ridden beyond the barn. "You better come back with some more of them wild stories next spring!"

Caleb nodded, waved, and rode on. There was nothing for him here. Pete had more ranch than he had ever dreamed of owning. Pete had Amelia to marry soon, start a family. Old Ab had every last plat on the Monument Valley map, save for the one Terence Mayhall claimed, and Ab would find a way to cheat the southerner out of that one soon enough. Buster had his own quarter section and plenty of additional work to do for the homesteaders who continued to populate the creek bottoms.

Caleb Holcomb had only guilt to live with here: his mother and his brother buried together on the shortgrass plains, the indifferent wildflowers speckling the mounds of their sepulchers with bandanna colors. He caught himself indulging a sinister desire. He wished old Ab would just die, so he could come back here, burn that damned cabin, and watch the chinooks scatter the ashes of that cursed ridge log across Monument Park. What kind of son was it who would first cause his mother's death, then wish for his father's? This place, as much as he loved it, made him backslide into the worst order of contemplation. He felt small here; he thought mean thoughts. His place was among strangers.

A bugle blared amateurishly, and Caleb saw an obstreperous column of fours riding from the old soldiers' campground. His father led the rabble on old Pard. His first thought was to spur Five Spot out of the way, avoid the conflict. Then he looked back at the corrals to make sure his brother was still watching and reined Five Spot to face the oncoming soldiers' colony. Now Pete would see who was afraid of the fight and who wasn't.

When the soldiers approached, he caught a glimpse of his father's eyes, but Ab's hat brim quickly broke the line of sight between them. Bursts of laughter punctuated the general din of the party as the old soldiers reached Caleb's place in the road. Ab turned his back to his son, twisting in the saddle as if to look behind him at the column of fours. The old soldiers rode blindly all around the spotted mare, and Ab turned his eyes to the front again, his son behind him.

"Hey, watch out!" the gambler with the diamond-stuck cravat warned as Five Spot grunted and leapt forward between Caleb's spurs.

The young drifter drove hard through the ranks, circling his father. Caleb's nostrils flared with anger as he tried to make the old man look at him. He galloped ahead, placed the mare in Pard's path. Colonel Ab turned in the saddle again, guided the party off the road, around his son. Caleb fell in beside him at a walk, but the old man mounted a trot.

"What's that kid doin'?" somebody said.

It was almost comical, Caleb thought. The old man would not look at him. He would ride this close to his own son, his wooden leg only a foot from Caleb's stirrup, and still not acknowledge his presence. He laughed aloud—loud enough that his father would hear—then he reined hard to the right, his mare raising a dust plume for the old soldiers to ride through. As he galloped back toward the ranch, and the head of the Arapaho Trail, he took off his hat and waved it arrogantly at Pete, who stood motionless at the corrals.

Buster was waiting at his toolshed with a hoe when Caleb rode up. The homesteader simply nodded, his lips pursed, trying to smile. He had seen this coming. Caleb could no more stay here than a wild goose could stay north in the winter.

"I guess you gotta go," Buster said.

The drifter smiled and looked away, his eyes sidling toward the shed, settling on the old spring buggy that once had hurtled before the wind like a clipper ship. There were fine memories here, but all of them lost like vague dreams to a waking man.

"Which way you headin'?"

Caleb shrugged. "Just headin' out."

Standing there in silence, they felt as if they were strangers, yet strangers would merely have shaken hands and parted.

"You still got that pocketknife?" Buster asked, a grin turning one side of his mouth.

Caleb drew his eyebrows together, then stood in the stirrups, the well-worn leather squeaking only a little. He forced a hand into his right pocket and brought forth the knife, bone handled and double bladed.

"Let me see it," Buster said, letting his hoe handle fall away from him. He caught the knife in the air and deftly flipped the long blade from its place in the handle. With his thumb he tested the well-honed edge. "You keep it good and sharp."

"A dull knife's more dangerous than a sharp one. Ain't that what you told me when you give it to me?"

Buster folded the knife and lobbed it back. "When *I* give it to you? Colonel Ab give you that knife, boy."

Caleb smirked. "If he's a colonel, I'm a rear admiral. Anyway, you give me that knife, Buster. I remember you puttin' it in my hand."

"Maybe I handed it to you, but it came from him. That's just the way Colonel Ab gives you somethin'. Can't do it hisself."

The drifter shook his head. "I only recall him takin' it away from me."

"You ain't the only one's had things took from you, Caleb. Colonel's had things took from him, too."

He set his teeth together. "Not on account of me."

Buster sighed and stood to pick up his hoe. "This how you want it?"

"Want what?"

"You just gonna drift?"

"I'll come back next spring."

Buster laughed. "That'll make it worse. How you gonna find you a place to live if you go driftin' in and out of here every spring? You ain't gonna have no place you can call home."

"Not much I can do about it."

The homesteader twisted the hoe handle in his strong hands. "It took guts you standin' up to your father the way you did last year. But it's gonna take more than just guts to undo it."

"What do you mean?"

"Somebody's gonna have to shed their fool pride."

"You talkin' about me, or him?"

Buster shrugged and grinned. "Whichever one it is with the fool pride. Give you somethin' to think about out there."

Caleb nodded. He didn't want to think about it but knew he would. Buster had a way of putting a hold on a man's mind. "Them wildflowers sure looked pretty from up yonder on the trail when I rode in this year. You gonna keep spreadin' them seeds?"

"Every spring."

Caleb nodded his approval. He breathed deep, feeling anxious to move. He thrust his hand downward and felt the good sure clap of Buster's strong grip in his.

"Don't you go cowboyin' so rough you bust up them fiddle-playin' fingers, you hear?"

"I hear. So long, Buster."

Each touched the brim of his hat, and Caleb reined toward the creek. As he turned, a surge came over him, and Five Spot gouged the ground with her hooves as if she sensed it, too. The drifter felt a power greater than he alone could conjure. The willing horse, the tune within him, and the swift current of freedom swept him up in a glory even the old soldiers' reunion couldn't match.

Five Spot's dark wisp of mane streamed upward at him as he plummeted down the creek bank, across the water, and up to the bald hill. The high cantle lifted him like the palm of providence, until he reached the treeless crest.

He reined his mare in and turned to look eastward. It's not too late, he thought, as he looked back from the head of the Arapaho Trail. I can still change my mind. Pete's still watching. So's Buster. There's Mama and Matthew. But Papa's gone. Gone to the land office with the old soldiers.

Only the dust from the column of fours remained to remind him.

He felt the pocketknife in his hand, pressed between his palm and the slick side of a leather rein. His eyes found the place on the creek bank— just a beaten-down notch in the cutbank now—the place his mother had called the hole, where once he had whittled a mountain and dreamed of taking a mysterious trail over the hill his brothers played on. The hill he was forbidden to climb.

Now this was his hill, his trailhead; and it didn't matter who owned the deed according to the land-office ledgers. The trail was still a mystery, but it was his to explore. He saw them watching, and he smiled. They could take nothing more from Caleb Holcomb.

He drew his hand behind his head to hurl the pocketknife but balked there as if seized. It wasn't this simple. His cares could not be cast away like a hunk of metal and bone. He would carry them with him, feel their weight. He opened his fingers, holding the knife against his palm with his thumb.

They waved back: Pete and Buster—faceless miniature men.

He only leaned in the saddle, and the wise mare knew to turn. Now it was as if the world swiveled under him; instantly the old places fell behind. Ahead were new things, the mountains, the trail snaking gracefully among the foothills. The trillion unknowns, each one a solitary grain passing momentarily through the narrows.

Hooves drummed below him like the echoes of humankind's first ride; but he heard it, faintly, and it rang with familiarity: a voice he would someday hear calling down a box canyon. Caleb ducked and rode on, knowing he would not catch it here. It would slip up on him somewhere else—surprise him with a whisper or a solitary note. And one day it would consume him—fill him with the whole rapture and anguish of life in one expression.

But now it was gone, vanished like the Arapaho who had beaten this trail for a time, like Long Fingers and Kicking Dog. The trail was long. Long . . .

He let Five Spot choose her pace, slowing to a trot as she surmounted a rise in the trail. She was horse again now. Dumb honest brute. For a furlong back there she had been the engine of discovery, the vehicle of a wanderlust as old as the mind of man.

Caleb wondered if he was crazy. This wilderness had addled Cheyenne Dutch. Maybe tonight—at some camp whose site he had yet to choose—he would check his rump for spots. But now to ride.

The rhythm his mare settled into was slow and methodical, and words droned in Caleb's head. New words, yet it seemed they had always been there:

> At nights, 'round the fireside, they'd listen to tales
> Of wide-open country and hard-ridden trails,
> Of mountains so high, there the trees wouldn't grow,
> Of deserts so wide and of canyons so low.

What it would say in the end, Caleb couldn't guess. But someday he would finish that song.

FORTY-FOUR

Caleb so stroked the taut hair of horses across the stretched gut of cats that a cloud of rosin dust rose above the fiddle bridge, red-hued by firelight. He ended "Boil That Cabbage Down" with a monotoned flourish to the cadence of "Chicken in the bread tray pickin' up dough" and heard a wind moan replace the music. Holding his breath, he glanced at his one-man audience, then gazed into the darkness downwind of the campfire.

The pair of glowing wolf eyes blinked once, peered for several seconds. Then the old lobo, his age-frosted coat catching flickers from the fire of twisted grass and cow chips, sat back on his haunches, pointed his nose starward, and whistled a practiced song up his throat.

The half-dozen horses in the pole corral stirred, and the two cowboys sitting by the fire outside the sod shanty burst into laughter. Every night for a week, "Ol' Bitter Creek," as Ben Jones had named the wolf, had traded his primal song for fiddle music at the northernmost line camp of the Cimarron Cattle Company's sprawling free-range outfit. Any other wolf would have had his hide nailed to the door by now. But Caleb Holcomb could not see killing a fellow singer.

"What do you reckon he's sayin'?" the musician asked, only now taking the ebony chin piece out from under his stubbled jaw.

"Well, partner, I talk a little wolf," Ben began, "and Ol' Bitter Creek's sayin' the same damn thing I been wonderin' to myself ever since you drifted onto this godforsaken range. 'What in the hell are you doin' here?' If I could fiddle like that, I'd hole up in some whorehouse, turn my hat over to catch the double eagles, and go to swappin' them gals out of their wares. Where'd you learn to play that thing anyway?"

Caleb shrugged modestly and tightened the nut on the end of the bow. "The man that raised me up taught me."

"Raised? How old are you?"

"Just turned twenty."

"Same as me. Hell, we ain't neither one of us raised yet. What grown man in his right mind would be squattin' out here in no-man's-land when there's towns and womenfolk in the world?"

"Guess you're right." Caleb noticed a broken horsehair trailing from the end of his fiddle bow. He started to pull it off but thought he'd judge the wind by it for a spell.

Ben spread his bedroll and lay down on it fully dressed. The sky showed no sign of storm, and the line riders preferred sleeping outdoors to a night in the shanty, where rodents and snakes chased overhead in the brush-and-sod roof. Suddenly he sat back up and reached for his lariat.

"Hey, make that thing go like a wounded jackrabbit again, Caleb. Maybe Ol' Bitter Creek'll come close enough to rope at tonight."

The fiddler smiled, looked into the darkness where the wolf lurked, and put his violin under his chin. Fingering high on the E string, he began coaxing the most plaintive squeals from the instrument, and Ol' Bitter Creek leapt nervously into the full light of the fire.

The wolf stalked cautiously, ever nearer the artifice of the musician, as Ben Jones waited on his knees, the loop spread to his right and behind. He knew he would have no time to whirl the noose. He would have to throw in one fluid stroke, as if roping last year's bronc in a corral.

The wolf took courage from his empty stomach and made a deliberate advance on the fiddler as Ben Jones swooped the noose through the air. The hemp took Ol' Bitter Creek by surprise, blinded as he was by the fire, and fell perfectly on his shoulders. Ben jerked at the slack, but the lobo had already sprung, the noose just slipping free of his hind paws as he vanished like dust blown into the darkness.

"Damn, I had him!" Ben cried, rolling back onto his blanket.

They laughed and stomped the dirt, flailing on their backs like madmen, Caleb holding the fiddle protectively in the air. The rowels of their spurs made a music of their own.

"What were you gonna do once you had him roped?" the musician asked.

"Hell, I don't know. If I could think that far ahead, I'd be someplace."

Caleb sat up and squinted at the darkness, but Ol' Bitter Creek was probably a mile away. He felt suddenly lost, as a sailor must feel at sea. He looked upwind, over his shoulder, and saw the Two Buttes in the light of the half moon on the southern horizon.

It was the Two Buttes that had drawn him out onto the plains and into the range of the Cimarron Cattle Company. He had bid farewell to Pete and Buster weeks ago and had ridden into the Rampart Range on the old Arapaho Trail. Continuing west, he had made his way through South Park, looking for work, singing and playing for his room and board. Striking the headwaters of the Arkansas, he had followed it downstream, fiddling under the cottonwood sprouts the homesteaders had planted in orchard rows around their houses. The Arkansas had led him out of the high country and onto the open plains, beyond sight of the mountains.

Talk of the Two Buttes had lured him out of the settled Arkansas Valley and into the shortgrass country. They were stark landmarks on the High Plains, he had heard, visible at thirty miles or more. Caleb needed landmarks. He felt like a drunk, spinning in bed, with no mark on the skyline to fix his place in the world.

With the Two Buttes in view, he had drifted onto the ranges of the Cimarron Cattle Company, a free-grass outfit whose herds lapped over into Kansas, New Mexico, and even into the wilds of No Man's Land and the Texas panhandle. A rider at Ben Jones's line camp had quit, scared of Indians. Caleb took the job.

He lived in a sod house, ten by twelve. His only partner was Ben Jones—"Thin Ben," as he called himself, and he was whip skinny. Ben tormented himself nightly with talk of lewd women.

Ben and Caleb rode the northern fringes of the company's ranges, turning cattle back as they strayed too far north. The beeves were half-wild Texas longhorns, branded and earmarked, growing fat on the grass of the Northern Range.

For the first time in his life, Caleb was earning the wage of a cowboy. He had found his place in the cattle business. It was what he had always wanted. But it wasn't fair that he had to drive another man's beeves. Matthew and Pete had never been cast out on a lonely divide and relegated to the monotonous work of a line rider. They had been straw bosses, foremen, ranchers. But Colonel Absalom Holcomb had made Caleb a sodbuster—helpmate to the hired man.

But now his place was here, on the free range. He worked alone most days. Ben rode west from the sod camp and Caleb rode east, sometimes two days east, where the cow chips fell in with buffalo chips. There were still great herds of woollies south and east, he had been told, and bands of wild Indians to hunt them. One day he spotted a lone bull on a distant grassy rim.

Another day he saw three braves trotting across a slope, angling away. Vaguely he recollected that strange winter among the Comanche in the Territory. Another life, it seemed. Another time. Buster had come for him, his father busy with his old pals at war.

The three Indians quartered away from him, but all that day he scanned the rolls of ground around him. They would kill him for his horse, he thought. He wasn't riding his top horse that day, but Caleb suspected any horse might make an Indian murder.

Even here, at the sod house, he wasn't safe from Indians. The nearest reservation was a many days' ride, but not all the red men had resolved themselves to the government dole. Those horses in the corral had to be tempting.

He heard a chuckle and turned to see Thin Ben shaking his head, the hat covering his face. He was thinking about the wolf. Caleb wouldn't sleep with his hat over his face tonight. He would drift off with the light of stars in his thoughts. He put the fiddle away, spread his own blankets, and looked one last time into the darkness for Ol' Bitter Creek. Somehow he knew he'd never see that frosted coat again.

I'm like that wolf, Caleb thought. I'll stay and sing as long as they care to listen, but when my welcome gets worn out, I'll git. I'll vanish like dust blown into darkness. Thin Ben, you'll not know me long.

FORTY-FIVE

AUTUMN CAME. THIN Ben and Caleb were ordered south to the Cimarron. They rode past the Two Buttes, piddling landmarks compared with the peaks of the Rampart Range where Caleb had grown up, but he was happy to have the buttes. As they fell behind to the north, the riders descended into the Cimarron breaks. Running water greeted them, laughing among the trunks of cottonwoods. Two dozen boys had arrived at the headquarters on a bluff over the river. Stock pens filled with horses, bunkhouses with cowhands.

They swept dirt from the floors, beat dust from blankets, tuned up, and nearly danced the jinglebobs off their spurs. There were no women to dance with, so the cowboys drew straws on every song to see who would get heifer branded. Not even the toughest hand refused to wear the apron and dance backward. The cowboy who couldn't take a joke fell into the disfavor of the kangaroo court.

His fiddle saved Caleb the indignity of wearing the apron. Though he would never boast of it, he knew he was the best musician in the bunch, and he drew deep satisfaction from the fact. He knew songs to keep the boys entertained with fresh material for days. Most of the other hands could beat him at roping or riding green broke broncs by day. But in the bunkhouse, or by a campfire, he owned the night.

They put in the autumn months cutting hay that would keep the cattle living through the winter. The cattle would drift south with the blizzards, across No Man's Land, and into the Texas panhandle. The line riders would follow to turn them back to the north between storms. They would haul hay in wagons and curse the cattle for drifting with such purpose to the south.

Christmas Eve found Caleb forking hay from a freight wagon to two-year-old heifers standing ankle-deep in snow in the Cimarron Valley. Thin Ben was driving the team.

"You think the wind could move a wagon this size?" the fiddler asked, dancing to keep his balance on the slick wooden planks as the wagon rocked over a hump.

Ben Jones looked disapprovingly over his shoulder. He let the heifers bawl his skepticism.

"When I was growin' up, Buster took a crazy notion that he could start a whole line of freight wagons along the Front Range and rig 'em with canvas so he could sail 'em like ships on them chinooks that blow down out of the mountains."

"That Buster must be one loco African," Ben grumbled, pulling a scarf up around his ears.

"Started out small," Caleb said. "I helped him build a wind wagon out of a spring buggy to sort of practice on. We put a mast and a sail on it, and a wheel like a ship's helm where we could turn the front axle." He laughed and shook his head, remembering.

"Did it work?"

"Slicker'n deer guts. Got to goin' so fast we turned it over, and it throwed us out on the ground like bronc twisters."

"You're stretchin' the blanket," Ben said accusingly.

Caleb ignored him. "There was an Arapaho chief lived up around us then, name was Long Fingers. He was there the day we drove the wind wagon. He gave Buster an Indian name that day. Said the wind pushed his wagon like a cloud, so he named Buster 'Man-on-a-Cloud.' "

Ben slapped his reins along the back of the wheel horse, wondering how much of this the fiddler was making up. "I guess Buster's sailin' flat cars on the Denver and Rio Grande now. Probably the richest African in Colorado."

"Nope. He give up on the idea."

"How come?"

"My old man like to have had a fit over that wind wagon throwin' me out on the ground like that. Wouldn't ever let me ride in it again, so Buster just quit runnin' it."

"How come?"

Caleb shrugged. "I was his partner. He wouldn't drive that wind wagon without me."

"Just as well," Ben replied. "The railroad would have put him out of business anyway." He looked at the pale gray sky, shivered on the hard box seat. "What do you reckon ol' Sandy Claus'll bring us tonight?" he said as he drove past the last of the hungry two-year-olds.

Caleb kicked the remaining tufts of hay down to the bawling cattle. The air was cold, but under his coat he had managed to work up a sweat that would only chill him on the ride home. "I'd settle for an extra helpin' of that son of a bitch stew back at the ranch. I hope somebody has the stove hot when we get there." He wedged the spikes of his pitchfork between two boards on the wagon bed and climbed over the seat to join Ben.

"I'd settle for a letter from my sister," Ben said, "but I don't guess the freight wagons got through." He shook the reins and turned the horses in a wide circle back toward headquarters.

"I figured you'd want a whore for Christmas, as much as you talk about 'em."

"Hell, I'd burn a letter from my sister for a whore. But I said I'd settle for just the letter from my sister."

"Did I ever tell you about that whorehouse in Denver?" Caleb asked.

"Yeah, but you left out the particulars."

"Did I tell you about the brass coins?"

"What brass coins?"

"Well, you can buy these brass coins at three dollars a head, and every one of 'em has the name of a girl on it."

"Why don't you just pay her with real money?"

"Repeat business."

"Huh?"

"Some cow waddie will gallop in there like a bull moose on the prod and swear he's got to rut five or six heifers *tonight* or else he might bust. So he'll blow all his pay on them brass coins. Five minutes later, his conscience is clear, but he's still got all that brass."

Ben shook his head. "Now he's stuck with one whorehouse till the brass runs out."

"You're catchin' on, partner. Only thing is, every other whorehouse in town's got their own brass coins, too, so you can swap 'em. Hell, you can gamble with 'em, or spend 'em like money damn near anywhere in Denver. Some folks say they turn up in the church plates on Sundays, but I never went to see."

"Have you got any with you?" Ben asked.

"Hell, no. I used all mine up when I was there."

The wagon lurched over snow-hidden obstacles in the river valley as they talked about their Christmas plans. They were going to roast their toes beside the stove, lie in their bunks, and read the newspapers Boss Mose had brought back from St. Louis. Ben was going to write a letter to his sister. Caleb was going to fiddle some, sing with the guitar, and tell some stories.

The stove was hot when the hay wagon returned, and the cook had started the stew simmering. Cowboys were coming in from a short day of chores to muster some kind of holiday spirit. Some of the boys had gone hunting, brought in two antelope bucks and a half-dozen turkeys to roast for Christmas dinner. Sam Parker had stayed to split enough wood to last into the New Year.

After they stowed the harnesses and fed the horses, Ben and Caleb went to the bunkhouse. Ben rolled a cigarette, and Caleb began tuning up his instruments. Bill Frazer and José Garcia were already drinking coffee and playing cards.

"Where's the Smiley boys?" Caleb asked.

"Old Mose sent them down to the White Rock Camp with some other fellows," José Garcia said. "A lot of cows drifted down there. They took three loads of hay and their guitars."

"Them Smiley boys can't play them guitars anyway," Ben said. He thrust the end of a stick into the stove. "At least not like ol' Caleb can play. And, God A'mighty, I've never heard the likes of caterwaulin' as when they take to singin'."

"They ain't that bad," Caleb said.

"Say, Ben," Bill Frazer drawled, "don't you owe me a smoke?"

Ben took the stick from the stove and used the orange end of it to light his cigarette. "No, but, hell, it's Christmastime." He tossed his pouch of tobacco onto the blanket among the cards. "Help yourself."

Bill stared at the pouch. "You got a ten-dollar bill I can roll it in?"

Ben frowned and fished the cigarette papers from his pocket, squinting through the smoke that stung his eyes. "Do you want me to roll it and smoke it for you, too?"

Sid "the Kid" Loftus and "Silver" Lee Silvers burst through the door and stood over the stove, pulling off their gloves.

"Damn, Silver, close the door," Ben said. "You're lettin' the cold in."

"Well, I've been out in it," Silvers said.

"So have I! Me and Caleb went four miles up the valley with hay today."

Kid Loftus backed up to latch the door and prevent any more arguing. "I hope y'all ain't playin' for money," he said to José Garcia and Bill Frazer. "I saw Boss Mose ride in from the north range just now."

José and Bill didn't bother to reply, but they picked up some spare change they had lying on the blanket and slipped the coins into their pockets.

Boss Mose came in a minute later, stomped the slush from his boots, pulled a scarf from his neck, emptied the coffeepot into someone else's cup, and slurped with pleasure. The cowboys drew back in dread of him. They knew Mose as a fair boss, but he put up with no nonsense and nobody wanted to cross him. He had to be hard because he was black, and cowboys would take advantage of a black man if they could, even one who stood six two, weighed two twenty, and could shoot hurled coins from the air.

Caleb had the fiddle under his chin, sawing on it monotonously with the bow, trying to bring the E string up to pitch.

"Holcomb," Mose said.

Caleb squeaked the bow, getting it off the strings.

"I know y'all ain't playin' for money," Mose said, his eyes on the cards between José and Bill.

"Nope," Bill said.

"Gamblin' makes fights." He slurped at the coffee again. "You men been around here all day?"

"No, sir," Caleb said. "Just Sam has. He's been choppin' wood."

Sam came in the door just as his name was spoken and let an armload of wood fall on the floor. "Cold out there!" he said, dropping the ax behind the woodpile. "Got to work so hard to stay warm that you'll freeze in your own sweat."

"You been here all day?" Mose asked.

"Yep. Got a woodpile out there to prove it."

"Did the freight wagons come by?"

"Nope. No freight, no mail, and no peppermints for these poor younguns." He waved a stick of cord wood at the boys in the bunkhouse.

Mose grunted. "That's too bad," he said. He grunted again and slurped the coffee. "Yeah, that's too bad, all right."

"Too bad for who, Boss?" Sam asked. He could tell Mose had something on his mind.

"Oh, them little Hutchinson chil'rens. They won't have no Christmas."

"Who?" Bill Frazer asked, throwing down a poor hand of cards.

"Hutchinson," Thin Ben said. "Up on North Fork. Me and Caleb was cuttin' hay up there at Thanksgivin' and Mrs. Hutchinson cooked a big ol' gobbler for us."

"Sure did," Caleb said. "It was good, too. Henry Hutchinson told us they had sent off for all sorts of Christmas truck for the kids."

"How many kids they got?" Sam asked.

"A boy about eight and two little sisters," Ben said. "Doe-eyed little girls. They sure took a shine to Caleb's fiddle playin'. You should have seen 'em dance."

José Garcia stacked his playing cards and put them on a windowsill. "How far away?" he asked.

"Three hours' trot," Mose said.

"Hell, we could almost get there before dark," said Sid "The Kid" Loftus. "I got an old busted pocketknife to put in that little feller's Christmas stocking."

"Yeah, but what in the hell do you bring for little girls?" Bill Frazer asked. "We ain't got no dolls or umbrellas."

Lee Silvers pointed at the trunk in the middle of the bunkhouse. "They could have those illustrated newspapers Boss brought back from Saint Lou. They'd like lookin' at the pictures."

Thin Ben kicked open the lid to the trunk and thumbed through a few issues. "They'll have pictures to look at till Easter. We ought not to let 'em have the *Police Gazettes,* though. Little Hank's li'ble get bad ideas from all the murder stories."

"Little Hank?" Lee Silvers said, snickering. "Ben thinks he's the boy's uncle or somethin'."

"We ought to bring some eggs for the missus," Caleb added. "They ain't got no chickens up there." He was eager to make the Hutchinson family his audience. He didn't mind riding through three hours of snow to have people listen to him play. He was glad the Smiley boys were at the White Rock Camp so he wouldn't have to share the audience with them. Besides, Ben was right, they were bad caterwaulers.

José Garcia was pulling on his boots.

"Get some stew," Mose said. "Then we'll go. Better bring blankets for the horses. They ain't got no shed."

FORTY-SIX

MARY HUTCHINSON HAD put the children to bed early so she could rig something for Christmas. She stitched up the seams of her daughters' dirty little rag dolls, assembled some chipped cups and saucers for a tea set, and turned the tops of a pair of Henry's old boots into leather handbags with straps of plaited horsehair. She almost cried when she arranged the meager Christmas truck.

"Maybe we could tell them we figured wrong," Henry suggested, "and Christmas is yet a week away. Maybe the freight will come by then."

"Oh, Henry, they're not stupid. They know it's Christmas."

Mary had a way of making him feel every little inconvenience was his fault. After all, he had brought them to this land of no trees and no people. But Henry knew it was the best natural grazing land in the world, and someday they would all reap the benefits of his dreams. His herds would multiply on free government grass. He would trade the sod house for a frame mansion with three bedrooms and a parlor. His daughters would go to college back east. Little Hank would boss a hundred cowhands. And they would all brag about the hardships they had endured.

In the meantime Henry had done everything he could think of to make Christmas pleasant. He had killed an antelope to roast. He had driven a wagon all the way down to the main branch of the Cimarron and brought back a load of wood so the children could gather around a real popping wood fire instead of a smoldering blaze of cow chips and twisted grass. He had knocked a board off the wheelbarrow and was, even now, whittling it into the form of a little rifle for Hank to play with.

"Well, the stuff will get here sooner or later," he said. "Just think how happy they'll be to get treats when it isn't Christmas or somebody's birthday or anything."

Mary didn't answer. She dropped her busy hands to her lap, turned her head to one side, and stared into a dark corner.

Henry looked at her. "You hear me? I say just think . . ."

Mary shushed him and held one finger in the air. "I heard something out there."

"What could you possibly hear out there? The wind maybe."

"No, I swear. I heard singing."

Henry laughed. "Singing? By who? Christmas angels?"

But then Henry heard it, too. The voices of joy incarnate. Falsettos hooting to the rhythm of hoofbeats on the gallop.

"Who could it be?" Henry asked. He put the toy rifle down and reached for the real one on the mantel.

"It's got to be the Cimarron boys," Mary said.

Henry took his hand down from the mantel. She was right. The Cimarron boys, God bless them. No one else around. The hooves were outside now, the voices still yelping joy.

"Henry, maybe the freight got through. The boys are bringing the presents!"

She reached for the latch, but the door burst in on her. It ripped free of the leather hinges, crashed against her head, and knocked her to the floor. Behind it came a coil of cold wind and the beard—the black beard matted with tallow and dirt.

Henry reached for his rifle, but bullets carried his blood into the sod chimney.

The matted beard clambered in over the door, pressing the breath out of the unconscious woman under it. He tore the curtain down from the corner. Two beds behind it. One of the girls had jumped out of her bed, into her sister's, he thought. Good. They made better targets together. Twin shots made his ears ring.

The Indians streamed in, still hooting. They picked the door up off the woman, howled for joy, and began cutting her clothes off. Barely conscious, she moaned and groped at the cloth they tore away. One Indian accosted the matted beard, who simply sank to the hearth beside Henry's body and sighed.

A short, ugly white man stumbled in over the Indians. "Kicking Dog's mad, Angus. Wants to know why you went and killed those girls."

Angus took the rifle down from the fireplace hearth and handed it to Kicking Dog. "I told him we were after guns, not girls. Kids would just slow us down, and I hate a squallin' kid. I saved him the woman, didn't I? Tell him that."

The translator had words with Kicking Dog. "He wants to know where the rest of the guns are."

Angus picked up the carved replica Henry had made for Little Hank. He held it toward the Indian. "Here, take this one."

Kicking Dog slapped it to the floor.

"Don't make him mad, Angus. Damn it, don't rile him."

Angus laughed. "Oh, hell, Shorty, don't let him scare you. Tell him to look for the damned guns. There must be some more."

The translation was made, and Kicking Dog ordered his four braves to find the guns. They argued, for their woman was almost naked now, but Kicking Dog insisted. They tore through shelves and drawers, threw blankets out of the cedar chest.

Angus stoked the fireplace as if he lived there. "Tell Kicking Dog I was right about Christmas Eve, Shorty. George Washington attacked the redcoats on Christmas Eve. Never knew what hit 'em. Damned Indians ought to learn to fight in winter."

One of the braves hollered. He had found a revolver. But Kicking Dog was enraged.

"He's still mad, Angus. Says you promised bigger guns."

"I thought they were buffalo hunters. I didn't know it was a family. Tell him next time I'll get him buffalo guns. Who the hell does he think I am? Santa Claus?" Angus laughed at himself through his matted beard.

An Indian kicked snow into the doorway and jabbered something to Kicking Dog.

Shorty's eyes bulged. "He says somebody's comin'! Eight riders, Angus!"

"Shit!" Angus jumped up. "Tell them Indians to git back to the Territory! Who in hell is out ridin' tonight?"

Mary Hutchinson was starting to regain consciousness when two of the braves grabbed her by the feet to drag her outside.

"No, not the woman!" Angus shouted. "No time!" He pushed the braves away from her and clubbed her savagely with his rifle butt, caving her head in.

FORTY-SEVEN

CALEB KNEW SOMETHING was wrong the moment he saw the light from the open door of the Hutchinson house. His harmonica stopped playing and the singing died around him. Mose drew his pistol and spurred his horse. The cowboys charged the sod shanty and surrounded it.

Mose was the first in. Ben and Caleb went in after him, brandishing their revolvers. José Garcia and the rest of the boys stopped to check the bloody body of the woman for signs of life.

"Oh, my God," Ben said. "My God, they killed 'em all."

Caleb thought he might throw up. The inside of the sod house swam before his eyes. "Who did it?"

"Had to be Indians," Mose grumbled. "They was just here. We didn't give 'em time to scalp." He looked down on the bodies of the two girls. "They must have taken the boy with 'em."

"We've got to go after 'em," Ben said. "There must be less of them than us, if we ran 'em off. Let's go git the bastards, Boss, they got Little Hank."

"We'll git 'em. Let the moon rise so we can follow the trail. Look for the boy. He may have hid."

"I hope so," Caleb said. He avoided looking at the murdered girls and crouched between the beds to look under them.

The boy came scrambling out like a mouse, dashed for the door, then turned back when he saw the rest of the cowboys coming in. He darted around inside the house, terrified. Mose grabbed for him but missed. He turned into the corner beside the fireplace, crashing into pots and pans, cowering on the floor.

"Don't move!" Ben said. "Nobody move, you'll spook him." He eased toward the frightened boy. "It's okay now, Little Hank," he said, holding his arms open as if herding a calf. "Them Indians are gone. It's just us boys. You remember me. It's ol' Thin Ben. I let you ride my horse, remember? Look, here's Caleb. Remember the fiddle player?"

The boy shivered in the corner but glanced at Caleb and nodded.

"Come here and let ol' Thin Ben take care of you. Them Indians are plumb gone now."

The boy suddenly jumped up and ran at Ben, wrapping his arms around his neck and his legs around Ben's skinny waist.

"Cover his folks up," Ben said. "For God's sake, cover 'em up. Caleb, put a blanket over his sisters."

The boys picked up blankets from the cedar chest and covered the bloody bodies.

"It's all right now, Hank. Them Indians are far away by now."

"They weren't all Indians," the boy said in a detached little voice.

The cowboys stopped and stared in wonder at the boy.

"The big one was called Angus, and the little one was called Shorty," Little Hank said.

"Were they white men?" Mose asked. "Jones, ask him if they were white men."

"Were they, Hank?" Ben asked, patting the boy's back. "Were they white men?"

The boy nodded.

"How many Indians were with 'em?" Mose asked.

"How many, Hank? Do you remember how many Indians?"

The boy shook his head. "A lot."

"Did they say any Indian names?" Mose asked.

The boy buried his face in Ben's neck and muttered.

"What did he say?" Mose asked.

"He said, 'Kicking Dog.'"

Caleb gasped. "I knew an Indian called Kicking Dog," he said. "When I was about as big as him." He pointed at Hank. "He was Arapaho, but he rode with the Cheyenne dog soldiers."

"Maybe another Indian with the same name," Mose said. "Don't matter. We'll git 'em. Jones, you'll take that boy back to the ranch. Frazer, you and Kid Loftus go with him. Bring a wagon back here in the mornin' for the bodies."

"What about the rest of us?" Lee Silvers asked.

"Silvers, Garcia, Parker, Holcomb—you'll follow the trail with me. By God, we'll git 'em. Let's lay the bodies out straight before we leave. They'll git stiff. Better put the door back on, too. Wolves."

FORTY-EIGHT

THERE WERE NO landmarks for Caleb. Even the moon was useless, hanging directly overhead. Only stiff needles of grass stuck out of the snow.

Mose and his men had followed the trail of the seven murderers for hours at a trot. It was easy to see in the snow and moonlight. Caleb didn't know where they were, or in which direction they rode, but he assumed they were heading south and east, toward the unassigned strip of the Indian Territory between Texas and Kansas known as No Man's Land. Maybe they were already there. Thank God Mose knew the way.

What if there was a fight? What if Mose got killed? Who would lead them back? What if you get killed yourself, fool?

The one trail became seven at midnight. The raiders had scattered, leaving single sets of hoofprints.

"The two white ones will probably come back together," Mose said. "They're the ones I want. Comancheros. You boys pick a trail and follow it. See if it joins with another one. If it does, come back here where the trails fork. If you find a camp, don't do anything. Just come back here. If you don't find anything after an hour, come back here. I want every man back when the moon is three-quarters across. Understand?"

The boys nodded and split their forces.

Caleb followed the trail that went farthest to the south. It was easy to track. Five Spot seemed to sense that he was following it; she stayed just to the left of it and trotted with her neck out, head cocked, as if to watch the trail with one eye.

Caleb rode with his hand on his pistol grip, straining to see in the dark. A wolf howled, and he wondered what it meant. The howling of a wolf always had to mean something: rain, snow, trouble, death. Maybe it was an Indian imitating a wolf.

How long had he been riding? An hour yet? He glanced at the moon. No, not even ten minutes. There were no horizons. He rode across a circle of snow and grass that rolled smoothly under him minute upon minute, mile upon mile. Only twenty minutes now, at most. He would buy a watch with his winter pay. Maybe the trail would meet another. Then he could turn back to tell Mose.

It seemed closer without the boys near. But he had a blanket to wrap himself in it if it got too cold. Who had the eggs? Why hadn't he thought of it before they parted ways? Sam Parker had two dozen eggs packed in wadded newspaper in his saddlebags. He was hungry. An egg would go down easy right now. Thirsty, too. He would get down for some snow when he turned back.

Thirty minutes now? Yes, at least. An Indian must have made this trail. Probably heading for some camp in a canyon ahead. He wouldn't mind finding a camp about now. He wouldn't mind finding anything. He knew Mose would not let up until some justice had been served. How long would it take?

Thin Ben was in bed. Little Hank was probably there with him. Poor little fellow. His mother, father, two sisters. He had seen it all. That had to be worse than even his own time with the ridge log.

Caleb yanked the reins back. A trail had crossed the one he followed. The prints were those of cloven hooves. Buffalo. A little farther up, another buffalo trail crossed. Then a great tangle of buffalo tracks poured down from the north, mincing the smooth surface of the snow to mush.

He got down, pulled the mare out of his light. The hoofprints he followed fell on top of the buffalo tracks. He could continue, but the trailing would go slow. The tracks were hard to pick out. How long had he been gone? An hour? Almost. Ten more minutes would serve Mose's orders well enough.

He trailed on foot now, looking for the round curve of the shod hooves over the splayed prints of the bison herd. The moon lit the little ridges of snow like the brief shining paths of fireflies in the forest. His back ached from stooping, his eyes blurred. He couldn't find the trail anymore. It seemed his eyes were weakening.

Caleb turned to look at the moon. A thick mist had snuck under it, cutting its light in half. Even as he watched it, the mist thickened. There were no stars in the north. A storm was coming. A blizzard!

He cinched Five Spot tight in his hull and climbed aboard. His bootprints proved easy enough to follow back through the buffalo trail. An hour from his friends! Out of the buffalo tracks, he spurred Five Spot to a lope. The moon withered behind veils of clouds. The trail was harder to follow than a dream, barely visible.

A swirl of cold air crossed him: the first breeze he had felt all night. A gust whipped in from another quarter. The playful winds that rode before the storm caressed him with icy fingers. The moon? Gone. Only a silver fringe on the clouds. Three quarters of an hour from his friends, and the blizzard was about to strike. The trail: almost invisible.

The storm announced its own arrival. Caleb braced himself, held on to his hat. He heard the winds roar a full minute before they struck. Sleet spattered against his brim, and the full force of the norther hit him like a wall. Almost immediately the trail vanished in slush. But the wind had hit him directly in the face. In a cruel way, it would guide him.

Head into the wind, and you will find your friends.

The mare hated it. He had to fight her constantly to keep her going. Ten steps, then she would turn. The sleet stung her eyes. She felt compelled by some ancient instinct to drift south with the winds.

Even the snow was black now. Caleb navigated by wind direction alone. Five Spot turned with every three steps. He faced her into the wind again, spurred her. She took three steps and turned. He spurred her back into the wind. She faced it, turned the other way. He spurred her again, pulling at the reins. She refused to move.

Terror swept over him with the cold, biting wind. What now? A gunshot? Three rounds for distress. He pulled his pistol out, pointed it in the air. But the other boys were in the same fix. He had heard none of them shoot. They were too far away to hear. Besides, he might bring Indians instead of friends. He put the pistol away.

Maybe the mare, in the ignorant wisdom of animals, knew something he didn't. Would he stand there and let her freeze, or would he allow her to turn south. Yes, south. He could find cover somewhere. A rill, a creek, a canyon.

You're not going to die. You're going to be cold and miserable, but you will live. Lost and alone, yes. Dead, no.

He loosened the blanket lashed down behind the cantle, pulled it around his shoulders, and turned his back to the wind. Snow fell in stinging frozen flakes. He pulled his collar up around his ears. The leather gloves were worthless against the ice. The boots all but conducted the cold to the very bones of his toes. Five Spot had the reins. She dropped her head into the lee of her own body and trudged south.

The blanket froze stiff around him, a cocoon of ice. Warmth was something of distant memories. He had a fear of falling from the saddle, so he refused to ride without a hand on the horn. He kept the other hand under his armpit. Stiffness set in. His feet ached. He tried to move them but wasn't sure they obeyed. He knew he had to get down and walk. The exercise would thaw his limbs.

He got down and pressed himself against the mare's neck, the reins looped around one elbow. The wind howled so that he couldn't hear her footsteps, and the cold numbed him so that he couldn't feel his own.

Walking was a mistake. It made him tired. It didn't warm him at all. He climbed back into the saddle, his hands so numb they wouldn't grip the horn. The shivering started. It became an uncontrollable shudder that shook his whole body.

Am I dying? Am I freezing to death?

Five Spot stopped. He was almost unaware of it, except that the rocking motion under him ceased. He spurred her, but she wouldn't move. There was something in front of her. He dropped stiffly from the saddle, felt ahead of the horse with his boot. His foot slipped out from under him, and he landed on his rear. His feet dangled. She had found a canyon, a gully. Maybe just a ditch. Maybe there was wood. He had matches in his saddlebag.

Turning right, he searched the rim of the bank. He began to see the size of it. It was a black fissure in the mottled gray world of nighttime snow. He could see the other side, only yards away. But if it was six feet deep, just six feet, it would shelter him from the winds. The brink became a slope. He could sense it angling into the gully. He led the mare downward, probing with numb feet. Down by inches, carefully he dropped into the crack. The wind ceased to press against his pants legs, his blanket, his hat brim. He was in. Out of the wind! He came to the bottom of the prairie trench.

Just deep enough. Streams flow east here. Turn left, downstream. The gully will get deeper. Find wood.

Caleb stumbled on until his feet snagged a shrub. That will burn, he thought. He felt around with his legs. Scrub oak. Maybe cedar. It will burn. He found a steep cutbank to the north, maybe eight feet high. It would cut the wind. He was thinking of fire now. He had to stake the horse, get the matches, gather something that would burn. He heard Burl Sandeen's voice in his head: "Two dry sticks will burn a green one, son."

His hands were freezing. They gripped with the strength of an infant. His fingers grappled helplessly with the latigo. Only by using his teeth could he loosen it around the saddle ring. He dragged the saddle against the bluff, set it upright on its fork, and huddled against the horse warmth that the fleece lining held so briefly. He let Five Spot keep the saddle blanket and unfolded it to cover more of her back. She had the Palouse-country blood. She would survive the cold. She wore a stake rope around her neck, but Caleb knew he could never drive a pin into the frozen ground. He tied the rope around his waist instead.

Floundering in the dark, he gathered brush and grass to burn. The rope kept him from straying too far. Some of the scrubby bushes had gnarled bases wrist-thick. He kicked them, stomped them, clamped them in the crook of his elbow, and pulled them up by the roots. He herded the fuel up against his saddle.

He needed tinder. What will light easily? He remembered the lyrics to "Hell Among the Yearlings," written on a scrap of paper in the mandolin case.

He pulled his saddlebag and his instruments into the fleece-lined curve of the saddle. He had only one piece of paper. One chance to light the fire. He would have to plan carefully.

To block the wind he pulled the stirrups in against his legs and draped his blanket over his head. He kept the paper dry in the mandolin case, slapped the sticks together to knock the ice off, built the firewood up, small stuff on the bottom. He pulled the rope running to Five Spot over one knee to keep it out of the way. Now he would get a match ready, slip the paper under the wood, and light it.

His frozen fingers fumbled helplessly in the saddlebag. He could not feel the matchbox, let alone hold a match to strike it. He peeled the gloves off with his teeth and pushed his numb digits under his coat, into his armpits. He sat for the longest time, shivering, waiting for his fingers to warm. Finally he yanked his bare hands back into the cold, found the paper, placed it, struck a match against the box, and held it under the lyrics.

God, if you're there, give me fire.

His wind block worked well. The paper took the flame easily. A twig crackled. The initial flare from the burning paper died, but small orange flames clung to the grasses and twigs, reaching up to the bigger stuff. Caleb fed the meager flickers with blades of grass. One of them began to grow, and he let the others die to keep the one alive. It spread to a new twig, and his heart leaped. It burgeoned and began to thrive.

Cupping his hands over the flame, he began to feel hopeful again. The wood was burning slowly. It would last. He wanted to chunk up the fire to roaring but knew it would eat fuel too fast. Better to burn it slowly, catching the heat under his blanket and under his hands. They ached terribly as they warmed. He reached for another shrub and stripped a branch from it.

The flickering light made him think to look around at his gully. He couldn't see much with the blanket over his head and the firelight in his eyes. He had harvested most of the nearby brush. There were a few small rocks peeking out of the snow here and there. Rocks! He had seen red-hot rocks used to heat whole rooms before. They took in warmth, held it, released it slowly. He craned his neck to see under his blanket and grabbed every rock within reach. They were small and few, but he stacked them around the fire.

Coals began to drop among the cold stones. Wisps of smoke burned his eyes and lungs, but he put up with it by squinting and holding his breath. Feeling warmer, he stoked the fire with more brush. He touched one of the rocks. Getting warm.

You're smart, boy. You're going to make it. You're going to live. Damn, won't Pete like to hear about this one?

Suddenly a cramp seized him below the ribs, and the fire passed under him, bursting all around in a spray of orange coals. The blanket flew away and let the frigid wind cut him. The horse was dragging him! He heard a snarl and a yelp. The rope slacked, then jerked him again. A mass of soft, wet fur brushed by. Wolves! The mare bolted as he pulled at the half hitch around his waist. The knot slipped, the rope whirring against his corduroy jacket. The hooves clopped away, muffled by snowfall.

"Son of a bitch!" Caleb stood and drew his pistol. He fired a round. The horse made another pass! He could barely see the dark Appaloosa spots on her white rump. He heard the hooves lashing the brush, the hum of the rope around skinny branches, the popping teeth of the wolves. He fired again, the powder flash giving him a glimpse of two wolves in a running blur.

There was silence again. Then he saw the spots and chased after them. "Whoa, girl!" They stayed just beyond his reach in the blizzard. Something caught his ankle, throwing him down. The spots! He jumped and ran again, but the spots lurched ahead of him. Where were the wolves and the sound of hooves on the ground? Caleb stopped, panting, his lungs aching with cold air. He blinked. The spots were under his eyelids now. Snowflakes lit by the pistol blasts. The mare was gone.

"You stupid fool." His gloves were gone. His blanket, gone. Where was he now? Where was his fire?

Don't panic. Stay in the gully. The fire, the saddle, the blanket. They are all in the gully. Search one way, then the other.

Caleb found the coals barely glowing beside his saddle. He found a warm rock, cradled it in his hand for a moment. He had to work quickly. The coals had little left. He pushed a few scattered embers together with a rock, broke some twigs and stacked them on the coals. He blew until he felt dizzy. The brush was too wet. It wouldn't catch. He needed dry wood.

The fiddle case was made of wood. He clawed at the latches, took the instrument out, and bashed the case against the ground. It splintered. He put the dry flinders on the coals and blew until his lungs ached. Suddenly there was a flame. He nurtured it, piled on more fuel, found the blanket, nestled back into the cup of the saddle, covered his head, stacked the rocks.

Safe again. And lucky.

Exhaustion overwhelmed him. It was work to pick up the wood and apply it to the blaze. But the shivering ceased and the feeling came back to his hands. The feeling was mostly pain. His brush pile had scattered when the horse dragged him through the fire. There was little left. He dumped the mandolin out. Its case was leather stretched over a wooden frame. When the time came, he propped it, too, over the dwindling flames.

How long had he been in the gully? Two hours? Three? How long till daylight? Hours yet. Nothing more to burn. The saddle tree was covered with leather. Rosin! For the fiddle bow! He found the chunk and placed it on the fire. It flared fantastically, crackled, gave good heat, but didn't last. The bow! He could get another cheap. It snapped in his hands like a twig. The horsehair gave a terrible stench, but the slender length of hardwood warmed him for fifteen minutes.

He needed a barrel of rosin and a cord of fiddle bows. The fire was dying again. Hours yet till dawn.

The neck of the fiddle felt frail in Caleb's hand. He broke it across his knee with surprising facility. It was so delicate, he wondered that he hadn't broken it before. That night in Milt Starling's saloon in Black Hawk, when he got drunk, fell off the stool, and dropped it; it should have broken then.

The ebony, spruce, and maple burned hot. The rocks reddened. The neck of the fiddle was his Yule log. He fed the fire slowly, trying to make it last.

He felt warmer now, and he wanted to feel warmer yet. He wished for a guitar. He wondered how long a bass fiddle would burn. The mandolin snapped with a hollow sound and a quick slacking of vibrating strings. It reddened the rocks even more. He thought about crawling around for more brush, but he was too stiff and tired. The last flicker slipped back into the red coals. They died quickly. Hot rocks were all that stood between Caleb and freezing.

He crossed his legs, Indian style, around the rocks and sealed the blanket under him to hold in the warmth. He could hunker over the rocks and hold his hands just above them. When they cooled some, he put his hands directly on them. The wind was still roaring across the prairie above, and the blanket was taking on layers of ice. He was so tired, he didn't know whether his eyes were open or closed. He felt stiff and sore and lonely for a while. Then he felt nothing at all.

A noise woke Caleb, and he found himself almost paralyzed with cold. There was a tiny hole in his blanket that let in a dull thread of light. The sound he had heard was that of snow-muffled hooves. He tried to move but felt as if he had forgotten how. His hands felt like clubs on the ends of his arms. Summoning every morsel of strength he had, he lifted his arms and pushed the blanket up around him. Snow poured into his lap. He heard the horse grunt and leap.

"Whoa, boy," a voice said. "Damn, what the . . ."

Caleb's head and chest were poking out of the snow, the collapsed cone of the frozen blanket lying beside him.

"Hey! Here he is! Saints and angels, boys, we found him! Merry Christmas!" Lee Silvers jumped down from his horse and waded through the snow to get to Caleb. "Can you walk? Let me dig you out."

His eyes adjusted slowly to the morning light. Between his legs he found a pile of cold rocks. He looked at his hands. The tips of his fingers were discolored. Some of them white, some blazing red. The red ones looked waxy as candles.

He had fallen asleep. What a fool thing, to fall asleep without his hands tucked under his coat!

Silvers grabbed him under the arms as Sam Parker and José Garcia appeared across the little gully. "Get up, Caleb. Are you froze stiff?"

He tried to speak but couldn't. He wanted to tell someone that he couldn't feel his fingers. He got his legs under him and managed to stand with Silvers's help. He brushed his fingers against his coat and felt nothing.

"Bring the firewood down here, Sam. We better warm him up. He's so cold he can't talk."

FORTY-NINE

FOR A WHILE the early corn recuperated by night, drawing moisture from the soil, standing straight in the morning to meet the wilting sun of day. But then the dry winds parched the crops even in the dark. The drought was on. Buster could only thank God for his irrigation ditches and his truck patch.

The dry curve of the ancient circle of rain had come around. The country was not getting more seasonable as some overly optimistic settlers had claimed. But Buster felt secure as long as the creek continued to run. The hotels and restaurants in Colorado Springs would buy irrigated crops at high prices, for vegetables would become scarce. The potato bugs and cabbage worms were worse than usual, but they wouldn't get everything. He predicted he would turn a profit even in this, the driest of years he had yet seen on the Front Range.

Then the cloud came down from the north. Buster knew at a glance it was no benevolent bank of vapor, laden with mist and rainfall. This cloud swarmed; it hummed. With the rattle of a million wings it settled onto his truck patch. He waved sacks, but the grasshoppers crawled thicker than bees in a hollow tree. He could hear their jaws stripping greenery from the peas, the cabbages, the potatoes. He tried burning smudges of moistened hay, but the grasshoppers continued to rain from the sky, pitting against the brim of his hat. They crawled down his collar and up his pants legs. They crunched in dozens under every step he took, and the live ones ate the crushed ones left on his trail. At last he locked himself in his cabin and fiddled to beat the sound of the swarm.

In a day the cloud had moved south, having eaten every sprig of cultivated greenery on Buster's farm. But he would last. He had put money aside for years against such a disaster. He would have more than enough to purchase seed and start over when the rains came back. This would be his first year at a loss, however, and Buster considered it a dismal failure. He did not intend to let it happen again.

Monument Creek ran black with the excrement of insects. Willow switches along the creek bank looked as if a basket maker had stripped them of bark. The bugs had eaten every blade from the irrigated corn stalks and bent them to the ground under their weight. They had eaten the onions and turnips right into the ground, leaving hollows underfoot in the truck patch.

Walking the boundaries of his land, Buster couldn't help noticing a stark end to the devastation across his rail fences. The grasshoppers had stripped his land down to bare dirt. But the native prairie grass across the fences, though rather stunted and brown for lack of rain, had suffered little from the insects.

He sat on a top rail that he had installed lower than the others as a crossing place in the fence. There he studied the shortgrass plains for some time. The grass wasn't the only thing that lasted forever here. He found the roll in the prairie where the wind wagon had turned over years before. Wind and grass. The rain and the bugs came in cycles, the snow and the heat came in seasons, and even the wildflowers had bad years. But the winds forever bent the grasses.

He was still sitting on the fence rail, with his back to his farm, when Terence Mayhall rode up on a mule, his burly shoulders almost as broad as his mount, though he barely stood sixteen hands himself.

"I can't hardly stand to look at it either," the Georgian drawled. "I didn't have much for 'em to eat, dry as it's been, but I had me a garden patch I kept goin' with a bucket. Now I'm good as starved."

"You givin' up?" Buster asked.

"I just got one chance left," Marshall answered. "If Holcomb'll let me have some cows on credit, I believe I might hold out till it rains. Them bugs didn't eat the grass. I think what a feller needs to get by in this country is some cows. You think ol' Holcomb'll let me have a few cows on credit?"

Buster shrugged, but he knew Ab wouldn't do it.

"Where is he?"

"I saw him go in the barn a while ago."

Mayhall shifted his burly body in the saddle. "Let's you and me go talk to him. He might have that double-barrel again, and I'd rather you be there than not."

Buster grinned and jumped down from the fence rail. He, too, wanted to talk to Colonel Ab. Mayhall was right. A man should keep some cattle in these parts.

They found Ab in the barn, saddling his aging Appaloosa.

"You're old gelding's gettin' fat," Mayhall said. "Hope you'll have corn enough to keep him that way."

Ab whirled on his peg leg and watched Mayhall slide down from the mule. "Buster laid up plenty in the crib last year," he said. "We'll make out all right. What are you doing here? If my cows are on your claim again, I've told you before it's your responsibility to keep fences up, not mine."

Mayhall approached Ab but stopped six feet away. "That's not why I'm here. Where you headed on ol' Pard?"

"Just going to see you. Looks like you'll save me a trip. Buster, take that saddle off for me, will you?"

Buster nodded and led Pard back to his stall.

"What did you want to see me for?" Mayhall asked.

"Thought I'd help you out of the fix those grasshoppers put you in."

Mayhall glanced at Buster. "Well, that's neighborly," he said, surprised. "That's what brung me down here. Thought you might help me out with some cattle on credit."

"Cattle?"

"Yes, sir. Grasshoppers didn't get much grass. If you could let me have some cattle so I can start my herd, I'd make it through till it rains."

Ab put his hands on his hips and squinted. "There's a drouth on, Mayhall. Last thing I want is some other man's beeves eating my grass."

"Your grass? That's free government grass."

"If Monument Creek drains it, it's my pasture. There's no room for anybody else, especially with a dry spell on. Don't you realize I'm having to thin my herd to make the grass go around?" He began to pace as he lamented his misfortunes. "I've sold hundreds of head at a loss. The drouth and the money panic's got prices on the rock bottom. There's no room for you."

Mayhall swelled up. "If Horace Gribble would give me some cows, I reckon you'd have to make room for me. As long as I own my homestead on the creek, my cows can come to water there and graze government grass right along with yours."

Ab smiled out of one side of his mouth. "Mayhall, there isn't a rancher in the whole Territory of Colorado who would help a nester get in the cow business now. Not Horace Gribble or anybody else. Surely not with a drouth on."

Mayhall's burly muscles began to crawl under his sleeves. "You just said you meant to help me out. How do you mean to help me out if you won't let me have no cows?"

"I'll help you get a fresh start. You've been on your homestead long enough to commute your claim, so I'll give you the money to buy it if you'll turn around and sell it to me. That'll give you cash to file somewhere else and buy seed for next year."

Mayhall spit on the ground in front of Ab. "Damn it, that's all you ever wanted was my claim. You never meant to help another feller out in your life."

"Will you take my offer or not?"

"Do I have a choice in it?"

"I don't see that you do. You got no money, no crops, and no cattle. You know you can't keep that claim. Sell out to me, and at least you'll have money to start over."

Mayhall fumed and turned to his mule, but stopped halfway there. He turned back toward Ab, kicked a mound of horse dung, and let a string of cuss words fly. "All right, Holcomb. There's bound to be a better neighbor to settle with than the likes of you anyhow. I'll sell at a dollar fifty an acre."

"Dollar thirty-five," Ab said.

Mayhall's muscles almost ripped his clothes. "You told me before you'd pay a dollar fifty!"

"That was a year ago. The market's changed. There's a drouth on. Land doesn't fetch what it did last year."

"Why, that won't bring me more than . . . than . . ."

"Sixteen dollars profit. That'll pay your filing fee on a new claim, and maybe buy a little seed."

"How will I hire a team to plow with?"

"Talk to Buster about that. He's broken sod for poorer men than you."

Mayhall thought for a second about kicking Ab's good leg out from under him. Then he gritted his teeth, turned away, and climbed onto his mule. There was more than one way to bring a man down. He would have to think about it for a while. If kicking Ab's sound leg out from under him turned out to be the best way, he could always come back and do it.

"You damn Yankees think you can keep a southern man down," he said. "You'll see in the end who comes out on top."

"I'll give you today to get your things together," Ab shouted as the mule turned. "Meet me at the county clerk's office first thing in the morning and we'll transfer the claim."

As Ab watched the broke nester trot away, Buster came to stand beside him. Ab slapped him on the shoulder. "Solid range, Buster. By gosh, it took fourteen years, but I got the whole valley. The water's all mine now, and the grass goes with the water. The boys will have a ranch when I'm gone."

"Yes, sir," Buster said.

They stood and watched until Mayhall disappeared. For one of the few times in his life, Ab felt downright giddy. He felt craftier than all get-out. His joyful moments in life were few, but he felt them with great intensity, perhaps because of their scarcity.

"Did you want something?" he finally asked Buster.

"Yes, sir. I was wonderin' if you'd sell me a few heifers."

Ab stepped back and puzzled. "I just told Mayhall I wouldn't sell to him. What makes you think I'd sell to you?"

"Well, me and you, Colonel, we been workin' together too long. You know I ain't after your grass."

Ab's mouth quivered unnaturally in a smile. "How many heifers did you want?"

"Eight."

"May I ask what you intend on doing with them?"

"Gonna pen 'em up and raise 'em. I figure I better have some cattle to get me through the years when the drouths and bugs get my crops."

"Do you want a bull, too?"

"I'm gonna buy me a Durham bull up in Denver. I want to raise some good beef I can sell to the restaurants in Colorado Springs."

Ab punched his hat back on his head with a knuckle. "Where are you going to pen these fine cattle of yours?"

"Gonna file on more land," Buster said.

"You're not going to use free grass?"

"No, sir. Wouldn't want to crowd you. I'm gonna file on another quarter section."

"How do you plan to do that? A man can't have more than one homestead."

Buster laughed. "Colonel, you done got yourself about fifty of 'em all up and down Monument Creek!"

"Well, I had a plan," Ab said. "What's yours?"

"Don't need no plan. I can file under the Timber Culture Act."

"The Timber . . . ? You'll have to grow forty acres of trees to prove up!"

"Yes, sir. I'm gonna grow 'em along the north side for windbreaks. Maybe build me a new house up in 'em someday."

Ab looked toward Buster's ruined crops, trying to visualize a grove of trees next to them. "Well, all right. I'll have Pete cut you out some good stock. You better build a stout fence. Those wild two-year-old heifers will bust right through those rails you got over there if you try to pen them in."

"I'm gonna build with that new wire," Buster said. "That's supposed to turn them longhorns."

"Barbed wire?"

"Yes, sir."

"How do you plan on getting water to your stock in that pen? Are you gonna carry it in a bucket?"

"No, sir."

"You're going to build a lane down to the irrigation ditch and let them drink from there?"

"No, sir, they'd stomp the banks down on my ditches. No, I'm gonna build a windmill."

"Windmill?" Ab laughed. "Buster, when did you think up all this nonsense about barbwire and windmills and Durham bulls?"

"Just a while ago. Sittin' out yonder on that stile."

FIFTY

THE ROAD BETWEEN Colorado Springs and Denver, well-worn now, passed within sight of Holcomb Ranch. Before coming into view of home, however, Caleb left the road, crossed Monument Creek, and took a trail into the foothills.

He had several reasons for choosing this route.

For one thing, he wanted to look over the place from above, to see if any new buildings or fences had gone up. He also wanted to scout the ranch before riding in, to be sure he wouldn't blunder onto his father. And, most important, he intended a dramatic approach. He knew how a horseman on the bald hill looked from the ranch at this time of day, standing tall against the backdrop of the Rampart Range and the glow of the falling sun.

By the time he rode down the Arapaho Trail, every man on the place—except Ab—had gathered at Buster's house. He made his bay mount jump the rail fence and the irrigation ditch and loped into the crowd playing his harmonica in gloved hands.

Pete Holcomb was the first to tender a handshake as his little brother slipped his foot from the stirrup. "What happened to Five Spot?" Pete asked, after the initial round of howdies.

"Now that's a long story," Caleb said. "And a sad one, too. I'll tell you all about it if Lee Fong will whip me up some supper while I play a few songs with Buster."

The Chinese man groused in his native tongue as he turned for the kitchen.

"Where's your fiddle?" Buster asked as Caleb gave his mount some room in the saddle cinch.

"That's part of the same sad story, Buster. But, listen, I've been practicing on this mouth organ and I want to play a few songs."

They went to the bunkhouse, and a few songs were all that Caleb got played before Buster tried to hand the banjo to him.

"No, thanks," he said. "I'm through playin' the stringed instruments."

Lee Fong came in with a plate of grub, and Caleb took off his gloves to eat.

Buster looked puzzled. "What do you mean, you're through?"

Caleb held up his left hand. The tips of the first two fingers were gone. "I can't make the chords anymore. I borrowed a guitar and tried for about a week, but I just can't press down on the strings right. I can still play the harp, though."

"But can you sing to it?" Dan Brooks asked.

Sam Dugan jabbed him with his elbow. "How'd it happen?" he drawled.

As he ate, Caleb told about Thin Ben Jones, Boss Mose, the Christmas Eve murders of the Hutchinson family, and the lucky escape of Little Hank. "Lee Fong, have you ever heard any stories about an outlaw called Angus something-or-other that hides out in the Indian Territory?"

The cook searched his bank of stories, then shook his head.

"Next week," said Piggin' String, "he'll be tellin' us about how he used to ride with him."

Laughter shook the windowpanes, and Caleb went on with the story.

"The little feller also remembered what they called one of the Indians. Buster, you'll never guess who it was: Kicking Dog."

"He's still alive? I figured somebody would have shot him by now."

"That's the Injun that came near stabbin' you with a spear when you first come to this country, ain't it, Buster?" Dan Brooks asked.

"How'd you know about that?" Buster said.

"Read it in that book Sam's writin' about you."

The black man glared at Sam. "You still writin' that book?"

"Yep," Sam said.

"It ain't all that bad to read if you can wade through Sam's style of writin'," Dan said.

Caleb went on about No Man's Land, the blizzard, his instruments, the wolves, and Five Spot.

"I wouldn't have known it was her except I recognized the stripes in her hooves. Them wolves didn't leave much else of her."

"What about the outlaws?" Sam asked. "Did Mose git 'em?"

"He caught one of the Indians and killed him. Brought the scalp back. It wasn't Kicking Dog."

"Now, see, there, Buster," Sam remarked, "that Boss Mose is a real nigger hero. Why won't you git after some outlaws like that every now and then?"

"Write your book about him if you want to." He turned to Caleb. "What about your fingers?"

"Oh, I got the blood goin' in the rest of 'em," Caleb said. "But these two turned black and we had to cut 'em off."

"Who cut 'em off?" Pete asked.

"The boys got me drunk, then they all piled on me to hold me down while Boss Mose clipped 'em off with a dehorner." Caleb laughed. "They talked about brandin' me and earmarkin' me while they had me down, but I guess none of them wanted to maverick a puny head of stock like me."

The hired hands laughed, grateful that Caleb didn't expect them to mourn his lost fingertips. He didn't tell them how he had fought the cowboys to keep those fingers. They had held him down like a wild animal and clipped the pieces from him. He had screamed himself hoarse and bitten Thin Ben on the elbow. He had cried alone on the plains, sick to his stomach because he couldn't press the strings anymore. But that kind of story tended to wear a welcome thin, so he whitewashed the entire episode with a couple of jokes.

Buster couldn't manage even a smile. He saw everything he had taught Caleb about music lost to the cold plains wind. Worse than lost. Imprisoned in his brain, denied release through his fingers. Only he knew how it must have horrified Caleb to watch those fingers blacken and die.

"If I'd have froze my strummin' hand, I could have still played. I could have held a fiddle bow with it, too." He shrugged. "But, I can still blow a harp."

That was little comfort to Buster. He yearned to hear Caleb's fingers stretch the strings again. A harmonica could make just so much music.

The next day Pete and Caleb helped Buster dig the last of his post holes around his new timber-culture claim and prepared to stretch the barbed wire that had arrived on the Denver and Rio Grande. Curious homesteaders showed up to watch from time to time during the day.

Buster carried the spools of wire in the back of one of his wagons. He ran a pole through one of the spools and fastened the pole horizontally across the sideboards. After Pete attached one end of the barbed wire to the first corner post, Buster drove the wagon forward and let the wire play off the spool beside the new fence posts.

"How do you stretch this stuff?" Pete asked when they arrived at the far corner.

"You use the wagon wheel," Buster said.

He set the brake and put another pole through the spokes of the front wheels to make sure the wagon wouldn't roll back. He told Caleb to set the wagon jack under the rear axle and jack the back wheel off the ground.

With the wheel spinning freely, Buster clipped the wire and wound the end of it around the hub of the wheel.

"Now, you strong young men grab this here wheel," he said, "and the leverage of them spokes will help you stretch that wire right taut."

Pete and Caleb turned the wheel as if fighting the rudder on a great sailing ship, until the wire trembled with a strange metallic timbre when they thumped it. Another pole through the spokes would hold the wheel in place as they nailed the wire to the posts with staples.

"It's like tunin' up a great big o' banjo, ain't it, Buster?" Caleb said as they worked. "They were stringin' this stuff in places between here and the Cimarron. Mostly nesters tryin' to keep the cows out of their crops."

"That's about all it's good for," Pete said.

Caleb nodded his agreement. "Don't put any horses in this pasture, Buster. This wire will ruin a good horse."

"How's a fence gonna ruin a horse?" Buster asked.

"Well, after Five Spot got et, I bought me another mount from a horse trader—a little black mustang caught up in Nebraska, he told me. Now out on the open range that horse had cow sense to make you think his grand-pappy was a bull." Caleb measured the wire boot-high on the post and straddled it with a staple.

"But I rode up to Lamar for a tear with the boys on the way here, and we came to a homestead where some farmers were puttin' up a barbwire fence. They didn't even have the wire strung yet, but that mustang wouldn't walk between the posts to save his hide. I like to have quirted him to death. Thin Ben and the rest of the boys thought it was the funniest thing they ever saw. I had to ride clean around the line of fence posts to get that horse into town."

"What was wrong with him?" Pete asked around the staples he held between his lips.

"Well, come to find out, this mustang had been turned loose in a barb-wire pen in Kansas while he was still green broke. He took one look at that wire, and I guess it looked about like spiderweb to him, and he decided he'd run through it. He got tangled up in the wire and like to have cut himself to pieces. After that, he would never go between two fence posts for fear he'd get carved up again."

"What did you do with him?" Pete said.

"I had to trade him in Lamar for that bay I rode in on. So don't you put no horses in there, Buster, it'll ruin 'em."

"He couldn't put 'em in there anyway," Pete said, tapping another staple into a post. "That windmill he's gonna build would scare 'em to death. I'm not even sure the cows will go near it."

"They will if it pumps water," Buster said.

"We better build it stout," Caleb suggested. "Those two-year-old heifers are liable to push it down rubbin' their hind ends on it."

Once the wire stretching began, Buster's fence took shape with remarkable rapidity. Homesteaders continued to ride up the creek to investigate. They tested the barbs with their fingers, kicked the posts with worn-out boots, pulled against the staples holding the wire on.

"Looks good, Buster," said one of the farmers from just down the Monument.

"Thank you, Mister Josh. You want me to come build you one?"

Josh chuckled and took a bite from a plug of tobacco. "Them grasshoppers didn't leave me with the means to buy wire right off. Maybe in a couple of years."

The day they hung the gates, Buster reckoned they had three hours of light left, so he took the Holcomb brothers to the Pinery to dig up the first load of pine saplings. They drove their spades through the forest litter, sniffed deep the acrid sweetness of the conifers, and lingered in the shade.

"I think I'll take some of these with me," Pete said, holding a sprout by the roots, "and plant them for shade over there where Amelia's house is going to go."

"Amelia's house?" Caleb said. He had been so busy telling his stories to Pete that he hadn't given his brother a chance to tell his own.

Buster grinned. "She says she won't marry him till he builds her a big ol' house. Bigger than her daddy's house in town."

"Where are you gonna get the money for that?" Caleb asked.

"This ranch will make that kind of money quick after the drouth's over. Give me four or five years and I'll build her a place big as a castle."

"Captain Dubois said he'd give Pete the money," Buster said. "I think he wants that gal out from under his roof."

"Why didn't you take it?" Caleb asked.

"If my bride wants a house, I'll build it myself. I don't need no railroad money to do it for me."

That night, before they went to the bunkhouse to entertain the boys, Buster brought Caleb a guitar and put it in his hands. "You learn to play 'Camptown Races' in three different keys, and I'll give you that guitar," he said.

Caleb wondered why Buster, of all people, would taunt him so about his lost ability to play. "I told you I tried. My fingers won't reach like they used to."

Buster bunched his eyebrows. "Take hold of that guitar, boy. Don't you see?"

"See what?" The familiar feel of the slender guitar neck pressed against his palm. His fingers fell into a pattern on the grid of frets and strings. But the stubs of his amputated digits groped awkwardly for their places. "I see myself wastin' my . . ."

Something felt out of place. The strings under his good fingers were too thick. He strummed the guitar with his right hand. "You strung it upside down!"

"No I didn't," Buster said. "You're playin' it upside down. Turn it over."

"Turn it over?" Caleb looked at the instrument in his arms as if it had fallen from a cloud.

Buster shook his head. "Play it left-handed." He yanked the guitar away, turned it around, and put it back in Caleb's hands. "You got all your fingers to chord with on that hand, and you can still strum with the mangled one. What do you think about that?"

Caleb held the guitar as if it were a newborn baby. "I think it's like dancin' with a woman and she's leadin'. Oh, Lordy, no, I've been heifer branded!"

"You'll get used to it that way. That's the way you look in the mirror, ain't it?"

Caleb smiled sadly and shoved the guitar back at Buster. "You don't expect me to learn playin' that thing left-handed. Dang, Buster, I'll be another fourteen years just gettin' as good as I was."

"No, you won't." He refused to take the instrument back.

"Yes, I will!"

"No, you won't. All that guitar learnin' you done the past fourteen years you done with your head, not your fingers. You ever know a man could learn somethin' with his fingers? Your head still knows how to make that ol' flattop sing. All you got to do is train your hands over again. Train the right one left-handed and the left one right-handed."

Halfheartedly, Caleb fixed his untrained fingers to make a chord, strummed it, and heard the familiar combination of notes tremble from the sound hole, though it seemed someone else had made them.

"There, you see," Buster said, triumphantly. "You done learned a chord already. By the time those fingertips toughen up, you'll be playin' good as you ever did. The guitar's in your hands, but the music . . . Well, that's in your brains."

The blizzard had taken more than fingertips from Caleb. It had robbed him of identity. Anyone else could recognize him less the extremities, but he hardly knew or liked himself. He was sure that folks liked to see him coming only when he had a fiddle in his hands. His instruments were his companions between the camps and towns. Without them, he felt less significant. It was as if his stringed friends had died and he had only his harmonica left.

But now, with a left-handed hope in his grasp, he felt justification within reach again. He didn't belong on Holcomb Ranch or any other spread. He had found no home. But with his fingers on the strings and his voice in a song, he could go on with the search. People would see him coming and their eyes would brighten. And he could stay for a while and make them happy.

FIFTY-ONE

THE NEXT DAY Caleb brought the guitar with him and practiced in the wagon on the way to and from the Pinery. His fingers groped the graceful throat of the instrument with ungentlemanly clumsiness. The strings bit his tender fingertips. Dead chords thumped like clods against a wall, and misplaced fingers rendered hideous sharps and flats. But Buster was right. The knowledge of the thing was in his head, and his hands would learn their new roles in time.

To prove up under the Timber Culture Act, Buster had to grow forty acres of trees on the one-hundred-sixty-acre claim. The idea was that trees would bring rain to the plains. Buster knew the legislators who had passed the bill were mistaken. It was rain that brought trees, not the other way around. Still, it wouldn't hurt to have a woodlot handy.

He and the Holcomb brothers planted the trees along the northern quarter of the claim, outside of the new barbwire fence. Buster feared the cattle would stomp the saplings down if he raised them in the same pasture.

When the trees were all in the ground, Pete drove into the new pen on a wagon loaded with lumber for the windmill tower, and barrels of water to be used in the drilling process. Buster planned to drill the shaft near the high corner of the pasture so the well water could run down through the trees when they needed it.

"Did you bring that willow fork I cut from the orchard?" Buster asked.

"It's right here," Pete said. "What are you gonna do with it?"

"Watch," he said. "I'll show you."

Grasping the branches of the slender fork unnaturally in his upturned palms, Buster pointed the stub of the fork ahead of him and started pacing aimlessly about the pasture.

Caleb exchanged a shrug with Pete. "What are you doin', Buster?"

"Witchin' for water," he replied.

"Like hell," Caleb said. "You don't believe in that stuff, do you?"

"No. Except when I feel that stick start pullin' down." He slowed and turned to his left. "I feel a little right in here," he said.

Caleb looked at Pete and rolled his eyes.

"Gettin' stronger," Buster said. "Watch that stick go down."

As the brothers watched, the stub of the willow fork angled slowly downward, finally pointing at Buster's feet.

"You're makin' it do that," Caleb said.

"I'm tryin' to hold it back," Buster replied. "Feels like a good stream under here. Try it yourself if you want to."

Caleb jumped off the wagon and took the stick. Grasping it as Buster had, he changed the angle of his fists, making the stub of the fork point up, then down, then up again. "See, I can make it point any way I want," he said. "You're tryin' to pull one over on me, Buster."

"No, I ain't," Buster said. "You back off over there and walk this way, and see if you don't feel that stream."

Caleb sighed and shook his head but agreed try. He wore a smirk on his face, feeling like a dupe as he paced toward Buster's stream. Then, for reasons he could not explain, the stick began to twist in his grasp.

He stopped, held the willow fork tighter. It continued to angle down in spite of all the strength he employed. "Hey," he said. "By golly, I feel somethin'."

"Told you," Buster said.

Caleb walked slowly forward, trying to control the stick by angling his fists, but it only pulled downward. When he had reached Buster, the stub of the willow was pointing straight at his feet. "Yeah, there's a stream down there," he said. "Hey, Pete, come try this."

Pete grinned. "You two have planned this whole thing, haven't you?"

Buster shook his head innocently.

"No," Caleb insisted. "This really works. Come try it."

"You can witch all the water you want. I'll just stick to prayin' for it."

They built a wooden tower over the ground they had witched, and under the tower Caleb started the well shaft with a post-hole digger. He got down to about four feet, then he and Pete drilled deeper with an auger that had a crossbar for a handle. They added sections of pipe between the auger and the handle until they had drilled as deep as they could, about twenty feet, hauling dirt up the shaft a gallon at a time in the container above the auger blade.

"They call this here a cable-tool rig," Buster explained as he bolted his twenty-pound drill bit to the end of a cable. He had made the bit at his forge from a section of eight-inch pipe, cutting the bottom end at a slant and pouring it full of molten iron with an eye on top to attach the cable.

"You sure you know how to do this?" Caleb asked as he helped rig the cable through a pulley on the wooden platform above the well shaft.

"I watched them drill that railroad well down at Colorado Springs a couple of years ago," Buster said. "They didn't have to drill but fifty feet or so."

"How does it work?" Caleb asked.

"You just drop it down the hole." Buster lowered the bit into the shaft, then released the cable, letting the bit drop to the bottom of the shaft that Pete and Caleb had dug with the auger.

They took turns lifting the bit and letting it drop. One man poured water into the shaft as the sharp edge of the bit cut deeper with every fall. The water turned the loosened dirt into mud, which they brought to the top in a narrow bailing bucket.

The shaft deepened by inches.

After days of drilling, the bailing bucket started bringing up more water than was being poured in from the barrels. They had struck the water table. The well was in.

"How deep did you have to go?" a homesteader shouted across the new barbwire fence.

"Fifty-seven feet," Buster yelled. "And we got six feet of water."

Buster had ordered and received the pipe he would need to turn the shaft into a pumping well. He and his helpers hauled the pipe to the windmill platform and prepared to sink it into the shaft. First came lengths of six-inch iron casing that would line the dirt shaft and keep it stable. The well drillers stood the ten-foot lengths vertically and lowered them into the hole with their cable until six lengths were inside the shaft, end to end. The last length stuck about three feet above ground level.

Inside the iron casing, the well drillers inserted lengths of smaller-diameter pipe, threaded together at the ends to make a continuous stretch of "drop pipe," as Buster called it. This pipe would carry the water to the surface.

In the bottom of the drop pipe, a brass pumping cylinder was installed. A rod ran from the pumping cylinder all the way up the inside of the drop pipe and into view above the ground. The rod, when worked up and down, would move the piston in the pumping cylinder, whose valves would raise water to the surface through the drop pipe.

Buster went back to the forge and made a flange with a spout that would fit on top of the drop pipe and conduct the water into a trough.

All that was left was to build the windmill on top of the platform. Buster had decided to build a simple windmill of the baby-jumbo variety. It would take advantage of the chinooks that came down from the mountains during the dry seasons. He told Caleb to build a stout box on top of the windmill platform—with sides three feet high and no lid. Caleb used scraps of lumber and old coffee crates to accomplish the task.

Buster, in the meantime, built a wooden paddle wheel, six feet across with six blades. It looked as if it belonged on the tail end of a miniature stern-wheeler.

An iron brake rod from an old wagon became the axle for the paddle wheel, beaten arrow straight with a crank plate welded to one end. With ropes, the windmillers hoisted the paddle wheel to the top of the platform and fastened the axle to the top sides of the box Caleb had built. The wind would come down from the mountains, strike the blades of the paddle wheel sticking up above the box, and push them over the axle, turning the wheel. The box would keep the wind from catching the blades as they swung under the axle. The wheel would turn the axle, which would turn the crank plate, which would transfer the circular motion of the wheel to up-and-down strokes of the pump rod.

"What happens if the wind comes out of the north or the south?" Caleb asked.

"Then she don't turn," Buster admitted.

"You ought to make it so you can turn it into the wind somehow."

"Them factory windmills turn theirselfs into the wind, but I think this one here will work good enough for me. They build 'em like this in Nebraska. I read it in the almanac. Now all we got to do is connect that pump rod to that crank plate."

"Then we're through?" Pete asked.

"Pretty near."

"Thank the Lord. I've never done so much work without a horse under me in my whole life. These boots are killin' my feet."

"You better get used to it," Buster said. "Barbwire and windmills—that's the future for ranchin'."

"Not for this ranch. The future for this ranch is free grass and open range."

"If you have another dry year," Caleb said, "you ain't gonna have no grass. The cows have et about all you have now anyway."

"Except for that up on the divides," Buster said.

"Now, Buster," Pete said irritably, "that shows what you know about the cow business. The cattle won't eat that grass up on the divide."

"How come?"

"Because it's too far from water. Walkin' that far makes 'em too thirsty. All the buffalo wallows have gone dry up there."

"Then fill 'em up," Buster said.

"How? I'm not God. I can't make it rain. All I can do is pray for it."

"You can do more than that," Buster said, kicking the pipes sticking up from the ground.

"You mean, drill a well?" Pete said. "Then all the dang cows from across the divide would come over, too. Gribble's and everybody else's."

"So, stretch some barbwire along the divide," Caleb said, catching on.

Buster grinned and started climbing the windmill platform.

Pete scoffed and groused for a while as Caleb aligned the pump rod with the crank plate. But then he looked silently off toward the divide to the east. "Barbwire and windmills," he finally said. "Even if you're right, at least I'll never have to plant another forty acres of pine trees."

Buster wrapped his leg around one of the trusses of the platform to steady himself as he worked. "I bet you'll plant a hundred acres if Miss Amelia wants 'em around her mansion," he said. "I can hear her now: 'Pete Holcomb, why don't we have us a woodlot good as that negro fiddler's?' "

Caleb laughed so hard he almost hit Buster in the head with the pump rod.

"Hand me that rivet bolt," Buster said. "And the big hammer."

Caleb fetched the tools and watched as Buster flattened the head on the rivet bolt to hold the pump rod onto the crank plate.

"All right," Buster said, handing the hammer down. "I guess we can try her out. We got a west breeze today."

Pete pinched the bridge of his nose and muttered a prayer that all his work afoot would not go unrewarded.

"Caleb, prime the drop pipe with a bucket of water," Buster said. He climbed to the top of the platform to untie the ropes holding the paddle wheel steady.

"She's primed!" Caleb said. "Let her whirl!"

Buster set the wheel free, and the wind started turning it. The axle shrieked in its sockets, the pump rod groaned down the drop pipe. Buster jumped down to watch his creation work.

"It needs some grease," Pete said.

"Listen." Buster put his ear to the top of the pipe. The well sighed as if coming to life. It moaned a cool breath up its long throat with every stroke of the pump. And the moans, at first deep as canyon winds, climbed in pitch, one after the other. "The water's comin' up," Buster said.

The wooden platform trembled in its struggle to turn wind into water as Buster and Caleb and Pete, like hopeful alchemists, raised their eyebrows to one another and turned their ears to the mouth of the well. The sighs from the well shaft, sensual and plaintive, moaned higher and whispered the coming of water.

"I think I can smell it," Buster said. He looked along the length of the pump rod, down into the drop pipe. "I can see it!"

Each revolution of the windmill, each stroke of the rod, brought the water closer to the surface, the groaning voice of the well speaking higher, the hollow whisper of the pipe climbing, until, suddenly, the whisper died. In its place came a gurgle of brown, muddy water over the spout and a splattering of the pulse on the ground around the windmillers' feet.

A cheer came from a small crowd of onlookers across the fence. Buster cupped his hand and drank, in spite of the grit of the water from the new well. Pete filled his hat and splashed it on Caleb. Caleb bent before the spout and let the water, chilled by the earth, pour onto the back of his neck.

"Now," Buster said, grabbing a hoe from the wagon. "You fellas can build me a stock trough while I channel this water down through the trees.''

"Don't he ever rest?'' Pete asked, shaking water from his hair.

Suddenly Caleb felt a presence, like a dark cloud. He looked down toward the creek and saw his father standing, water trickling around his wooden leg, his eyes squinting at the baby-jumbo windmill. Ab marched to the well, cooled his palms in the water, watched the pump rod work up and down.

"Damn it, old man, why won't you look at me?'' Caleb thought. He remembered the day he cussed Ab and left home—a time of awful triumph. It was time to go again. He didn't belong.

"Buster, you take the prize,'' Ab said, shaking his head in wonder. "Good job.'' He slapped Pete on the shoulder. "I'd have never thought.'' He turned back toward the gate and hobbled away.

FIFTY-TWO

PETE TRIED TO talk Caleb into staying, but Caleb would remain only long enough to herd the heifers into Buster's new pasture. He wasn't going to live and work where he wasn't wanted when elsewhere he could feel the welcome of song-poor strangers.

"Where are you gonna go this time?'' Pete asked, as he listened to his brother struggle with the left-handed guitar in Buster's cabin.

"I thought maybe Texas. Find me a herd to drive up the trail.'' He adjusted the ungainly fingers of his right hand on the fret board.

"Good idea,'' Buster said, "as long as you stay the winter down there. It don't get so cold in Texas. The last two winters you come near to starvin' yourself and freezin' yourself. You better go south for the winter.''

"Maybe you should find Javier's place down in New Mexico,'' Pete suggested.

Caleb remembered the creased, stubbled chin and the wry grin of the vaquero. And the guitar music, the rowels like spokes on his spurs, the saddle horn big as a tin plate. "I might just do that, if I knew where his place was,'' he said.

"He said it was in the Sacramento Mountains, somewhere way down south, close to Old Mexico.''

"Maybe I'll try to find him after I knock around in Texas for a while.''

"On your way to Texas,'' Buster said. "I wonder if you'd do me a favor. I want to write a letter to the agent of the Arapaho reservation in Indian Territory. I wonder if you'd see that it gets delivered there.''

"All right, but what for?''

"I want to find out whatever happened to Long Fingers."

"I heard he got killed at Sand Creek," Pete said. "He had a knife between ol' Cheyenne Dutch's ribs when somebody shot him. Just think, if Long Fingers had killed Dutch there, then Dutch wouldn't have been around to shoot Matthew. Oh, well . . ."

"Some folks say Long Fingers got carried off," Buster said. "He might have lived."

"I doubt it," Caleb said. "But I'll take your letter for you if you want me to."

"If he's alive, I'd like to have him back this way to visit. If Kicking Dog is still alive, I don't see why Long Fingers shouldn't be. He was ten times a better Indian."

"I'll vouch for that," Caleb said. "Kicking Dog ought to be hung." His brain was doing flip-flops, trying to make his right hand use left-handed knowledge.

Pete and Caleb searched upstream the next morning to find eight healthy heifers for Buster's pasture. Caleb rode a strong, surefooted Nez Perce gelding called Powder River. From a distance he looked solid sorrel. A pattern of small white spots showed on his flanks and hips only from a near point of view. He was just three years old, and every year his blanket of specks grew thicker. Pete predicted he would look like a blizzard from the shoulders back by his tenth year.

As the brothers herded the eight heifers toward Buster's new pasture, a brindle made her first of a dozen attempts to escape. Each time, one of the horsemen ran her down and turned her back toward the herd, but she was relentless. When they were almost to Buster's place, the heifer made a break toward the Holcomb cabin on Caleb's side of the herd. He spurred Powder River and gave chase.

Ab was plucking blossoms from the wildflower patch when he heard the hooves pounding the parched ground. Dust blew away in a floating trail behind the running animals. He knew at a glance it was Caleb on Powder River, and he felt his whole body jerk tense with worry—even the missing leg. The brindle came toward him at breakneck speed, the horseman gaining her side, hollering, whistling, waving hands that should have been pulling leather.

With her tongue lolling out of the side of her mouth, the heifer bawled in anger, planted her front hooves, and tried to cut behind the horse. But Powder River was too canny; he met her dodge in mirror image. She broke back four times, looking for a way around the horse, but he stayed right with her, cutting so sharp that Caleb's hat flew off. At last the heifer turned for the herd and kicked a hind foot ineffectually at the gelding.

When she had rejoined the other heifers, Caleb galloped Powder River back toward the cabin, hung from the left side of the saddle like a lashed-on corpse, and swooped down to grab his hat. Powder River then doubled back like a cottontail rabbit as the rider pounded the dust from his hat on the white-speckled rump.

"Did you see that?" Ab said to Ella. "He does that on purpose. He does it to spite me." He leaned a bundle of flowers against her gravestone. "I swear he's trying to kill himself just to spite me. Did you know he's going to Texas? Do you know why? Because he knows it will worry me crazy."

FIFTY-THREE

THE DUST CLOUD hung in the sky like a giant plume, its wide feathery top rising in the north and its quill-like point touching the ground in the east. Long Fingers had studied it for an hour from the buffalo robe spread beside his tepee. Because it was moving south, he figured the herd that made the cloud probably consisted of trail horses returning to Texas after a cattle drive.

In the old days he had seen buffalo raise such plumes against the sky—whole wings of them. But the buffalo on the Cheyenne and Arapaho reservation were getting shy and hard to kill since the white hunters had come south of the Arkansas River in violation of the Treaty of Medicine Lodge. Hunting them was not like it once was anyway. He had to get permission from the Indian agent to go hunting. It hardly seemed worth the trouble.

He rose from his old buffalo robe and walked to the corrals he had ordered some of his braves to build. Several boys were waving blankets at some colts in a pen, to break their fear of objects that leapt or flailed about. The chief called to one of the boys who was resting his arms.

"Those cowboys will camp close to here," he said in English when the boy ran to him. He made all the young boys in his band go to the agency school to learn English. "They will probably camp down the river. Take the fastest horse you have and ride there. Run all of our horses away from the river before the cowboys get there, so they won't steal them."

The boy nodded and crawled between two corral rails to catch a horse.

Long Fingers strolled among the tepees and found several braves loafing under a brush arbor. He listened for a moment as they talked about the war that had started on the Red River—white hunters and soldiers on one side, Indians on the other. Many Cheyenne warriors had ridden south to join the fighting, but most Arapaho were remaining neutral.

"Red Hawk," the chief finally said, "take two of these braves and go talk to the white men with that herd. Ask them if they want to buy some good horses. Take a gun, but do not wave it around or they will shoot at you."

Red Hawk stared at the dust cloud for a long moment. He was a promising young man, well regarded among the youths in the lower ranks of the warrior society. He was thirty-one years old and already a leader in the Order of Club Men. In past battles with Utes, he had distinguished himself by riding ahead of his comrades to strike enemy warriors with his club, then returning to lead the general charge.

But now, with the Utes so far away, Red Hawk hardly knew how to prove himself. He had been absent from the village for some time, and it was said that he had ridden with some Cheyenne against buffalo hunters and soldiers in Texas. Long Fingers frequently put him in charge of minor expeditions on the reservation, hoping to channel his talents for leadership toward peaceful ends.

Red Hawk picked two warriors to ride with him to the camp of the cowboys. Each plunged the gourd dipper into the water bucket and drank heavily before sauntering out into the stifling sun.

On the way back to his tepee, Long Fingers passed the garden patch he had tried to establish this spring. The vegetables had withered and blown away. Weeds had taken over the crooked furrows. The agency's farming instructor had not come back to help them as he had said he would. A plow stock was lying on the ground. At least it wouldn't rot, the chief thought. Wood had to have moisture to rot, and the reservation hadn't seen rain in weeks.

Plowing had proven difficult with the small Indian ponies, ill-trained and fitted with a makeshift harness. Some of the old ones—especially among the Cheyenne—had ridiculed him as he plowed, but they did not know how to survive in these new times. The chief smiled. Some of those old ones were younger than he was. They would die "blanket Indians," as the government agents called them. Long Fingers was a progressive. His name would go down in the books of white men.

He returned to his tepee and wished for wind. Then he prayed for rain. Then he dreamed of mountains. There was no sense in wishing or praying for the mountains, for they would never appear on his reservation. But he could always dream.

The high country was the place to live during the hot season. He remembered the patches of summer snow under pine trees, where the sun never shined. He recalled the way the elk antlers, velvet covered, swept far through the cool air as the bulls turned to run. He longed for the music of water running down a mountain slope—cold water in his cupped hands, on his face, across the back of his neck. He yearned for battle with the Utes—the mounted charges across mountain meadows, the song of arrows in the air, the war cries. Long Fingers missed the Utes; they were always his enemy. They were not like the whites: some friends, some foes.

He dozed, and when he woke, the sun was setting, and the great plume of dust had settled. In its place a smaller spout of dirt had risen from the plains. The riders had who kicked it up came over a roll in the prairie, mere dots wavering in the heat, and Long Fingers counted five. The three braves and the boy were bringing one of the cowhands back with them. He rose to prepare himself for their arrival.

FIFTY-FOUR

CALEB RECOGNIZED THE chief instantly, though only a few strands of raven hair remained to streak his otherwise gray head. He sat a white stallion and a Texas saddle; wore a white shirt, a vest, and striped trousers. In his stirrups a vestige of the old life remained: moccasins, beaded and fringed. Boots and shoes hurt the chief's feet.

"Hello, chief," Caleb said, riding Powder River near enough to shake hands. "Do you remember me?"

Long Fingers took in the horse and the man. He noticed the humanlike whites in the eyes of the gelding. He remembered the Nez Perce horses on Monument Creek. Then he saw a guitar neck sticking out behind the saddle. "Holcomb?"

Caleb was astounded. "Yes! By golly, you do remember me!"

"Do you still play that song?" Long Fingers asked. " 'Old Dan Tucker and I got drunk, he fell in the fire and kicked up a chunk . . . ' "

Caleb joined the chief in reciting: " 'The charcoal got inside his shoe, Lord bless you, honey, how the ashes flew!' Yes, sir, I still play that."

"Red Hawk, get my friend a drink of water," the chief ordered. "Boy, take these horses."

Caleb dismounted with the chief and grabbed his guitar before the Indian boy led Powder River away. He had made a saddle wallet for carrying the instrument. It was an old feed sack with both ends sewed shut and a new opening made across the middle. The sack, when tied to the cantle strings, draped across the saddle skirts with the opening facing up, like a crude pair of large saddlebags with one common opening. He had made it expressly for the guitar, but it served to carry just about anything from spare ropes to buffalo chips for fuel.

"Look," Long Fingers said, reaching into the pocket of his vest. "I still have this harp that Man-on-a-Cloud gave me many winters ago." He blew a discordant combination of notes on the old instrument. "But now I say *harmonica*. I learn much more English here."

"You speak it good," Caleb said.

They sat down in front of the tepee and played "Old Dan Tucker," Caleb clumsily plucking his left-handed guitar, Long Fingers blowing notes in rhythm, if not in key. Red Hawk brought the bucket of water with the gourd dipper in it and sat down next to his chief to listen.

When the song ended, Long Fingers closed his eyes and allowed a thin laugh to pass between his lips. "What happened to your fingers?" he asked.

"Well, as a matter of fact, it was sort of Kicking Dog's fault. . . ."

Caleb entered eagerly into the story, surging through it, embellishing it, improving it over its last telling. He relished the spell he held over his listeners. It took him till sundown to tell it all. By that time the braves had killed a steer that had drifted out of some trail herd, and the women were butchering it. Caleb knew he had earned his share of it.

"I have heard of the white man called Angus," the chief said. "The Cheyenne call him Black Beard. He gets guns and whiskey for Indians who want to fight, and they give him cattle and horses they steal. And Kicking Dog, he fights with the Comanche now. He forgets that he has Arapaho blood."

Caleb nodded and dipped the gourd into the bucket again, the yarn having parched him. "Buster will be glad to hear that you all are getting on so good," he said, looking down the row of tepees. "We heard you got killed at Sand Creek."

"That was the last fight for us," Long Fingers said. "Now we stay in one camp. We try to farm, but we don't know how to do it. We need to learn how to do more work that the white man wants us to do, but nobody will show us how. Some of my boys want to buy wagons and haul things. That way, they could move around a little more, like the old days. The women sometimes tan buffalo hides for the traders—three dollars a hide—but they do not send us enough hides. We live here okay and raise good horses. Do you want to buy any?"

"The boss said he'd buy some two-year-olds at fifteen dollars a head if they're broke. Or ten dollars a head for broncs."

The chief shook his head. "No broncs. We break our horses. That gives my boys plenty of work to do. I will show your boss some horses in the morning, but I think he will pay more than fifteen dollars."

Caleb smiled. "I have a letter for you," he said, picking up his guitar. He held the instrument horizontally over his head, strings down, and shook it until he could see the envelope in the sound hole. He forced his fingers through the strings, pulled the letter out of the hollow body of the guitar, and handed it to the chief. "It's from Man-on-a-Cloud."

Long Fingers looked at the writing on the outside of the envelope, opened it, and unfolded the papers that came from it. He shuffled through the pages a few times, then handed them back to Caleb. "I do not read," he said. "You read it for me."

Caleb put the pages back in order. " 'Dear Chief Long Fingers,' " he began. He cleared his throat and tilted his hat back on his head. " 'I hope this letter finds you alive and well on the reservation. We are getting along good here on Monument Creek. . . .' "

Buster's letter went into a detailed account of things that had happened since the year of Sand Creek, and Caleb paused in the reading to add his own observations as they arose. Of particular interest to Long Fingers was the sawmill fight in Colorado City, where Cheyenne Dutch had killed Matthew Holcomb, and Javier Maldonado had killed Cheyenne Dutch.

"I had my knife between Dutch's ribs at Sand Creek," the chief said. "I am sorry I did not have the strength to finish him then. That way he would not have lived to kill your brother."

Then came several paragraphs of questions. Where was the new reservation? How was it fixed for game, water, grass, livestock, farming? How was the chief's wife? Was Kicking Dog still on the warpath?

Long Fingers answered each question aloud, as if Man-on-a-Cloud could hear through Caleb's ears. He knew Caleb would take the news back to Monument Creek.

Caleb continued reading, turning the pages to catch the light of the fire Red Hawk had lit: " 'I have not been able to find out what happened to the Snake Woman after Caleb and me escaped the Comanche in the Wichita Mountains. Do you have any news?' "

"Snake Woman stays with the Comanche, still," Long Fingers said. "She is with the Quahadi band—the Antelope Eaters. The son of Man-on-a-Cloud and Snake Woman is called Medicine Horse. He will be a warrior in three, maybe four, winters."

Caleb had been listening carefully to every reply Long Fingers made so he would be able to report accurately when he returned to Monument Creek. But the news about the son of Man-on-a-Cloud and Snake Woman bogged his thoughts beyond extrication. "Whose son?" he asked.

"Medicine Horse," the chief replied, "the son of Man-on-a-Cloud and Snake Woman."

Caleb rifled through his vague memories of the Comanche in the Wichita Mountains and of Snake Woman, a mute and wild-eyed witch. He remembered her being pregnant that winter, but for the life of him, he had never wondered by whom. He tried to picture her in union with Buster, but the image evaporated. It was impossible. Not laughing, singing Buster Thompson, the man of calm common sense, thoughtfulness, and inventive genius. Buster was beyond temptation. He didn't care about women. He avoided even looking at the whores in Old Town. Buster's hands were meant for tools and instruments. Music and work satisfied all his lusts.

And the Snake Woman! She was coming clearer to Caleb now. He saw her mouth, thin lipped and straight as if pulled taught toward her ears; dirty legs; sinewy forearms and hands, bulging with veins, lugging buckets of water. What would have made Buster do such a thing?

"He never told you," Long Fingers said, reading Caleb's confusion, "but it is true. I have seen Medicine Horse. He has dark skin—almost black like Man-on-a-Cloud's. And he has the same hair, like the buffalo."

Buster was a father! It made Caleb wonder what else Buster had never told him. He had never talked much about his slave days or his escape from the South before the war. He had never mentioned his boyhood or his upbringing. Here, far away from the farm on Monument Creek, Caleb wasn't sure he knew Buster at all.

"Go ahead now," the chief said. "Read the rest of the letter."

He ran his finger down the pen script and found his place on the page. "It just says, 'Come back to the mountains to stay with us for a while if you can. The country has changed, but you will still know it. Good luck,' signed, 'Man-on-a-Cloud.' "

"Where does it say his name?"

"Right here at the bottom." He pointed to the signature. "He sure likes that name you gave him, chief. He brags on it all the time."

A warrior approached the circle of firelight in front of the tepee and said something in Arapaho.

Long Fingers took the letter, folded it, and put it back in the envelope. "They have cooked a big meal for you," he said. "Let's go to eat it now. It is ready."

Caleb rose and walked with the chief. "Do you want me to tell Man-on-a-Cloud you're comin'? I'm goin' home myself in the spring. You can ride with me if you want to." He couldn't see Long Fingers' expression in the dark.

"I cannot leave here now," the old chief said. "I keep telling my boys we cannot move around the way we used to. We have to live here all the time now. Maybe so we can take some tepees and camp at another village for a while, but we have to stay on the reservation. If I go to see Man-on-a-Cloud, they will say I do not know how to follow my own words. Anyway, the Comanche are always trying to get my boys to go with them and kill the buffalo hunters. If I leave, they will all go, then there will be big trouble for us from the soldiers. Maybe so someday I will go to the mountains, but it will be many winters from now. Tell Man-on-a-Cloud I am coming, but I will follow a long and crooked trail."

FIFTY-FIVE

FOR DAYS CALEB herded the horses down the well-worn route to Texas. He had only thrown in with the cowboys to ensure safe passage across Indian Territory. He got free grub in exchange for his songs sung around the fire at night, but he didn't collect any wages. He didn't mind. The work went easy; the horses knew the way.

Because he had not yet mastered the left-handed guitar, he had taken to singing more ballads. He had always sung in a sure, clear voice, but in the past he had relied on his instruments to carry a song. Now he favored tunes meant for a tenor—mostly sad songs of old trails and lost loves. One that the cowboys made him sing every night was "Annie Laurie":

Her brow is like the snowdrift, her throat is like the swan,
Her face it is the fairest that e'er the sun shone on,
That e'er the sun shone on, and dark blue are her eyes,
And for bonnie Annie Laurie, I'd lay me down and die.

Even the hardest hand turned his eyes from the firelight when Caleb sang "Annie Laurie."

Ten days south of Long Fingers' village, they approached Fort Griffin on the Texas plains. When the drovers spotted Government Hill in the distance, they turned the horses onto fresh grass and argued about who would get to go to town. Caleb said he would stay and night-herd the horses since he had no money to buy drinks with anyway, but his camp mates insisted on treating him to a night of debauchery in The Flats, below the fort.

"I'll stay with the horses," a black cowboy named Nate said. "Last time I went to Griffin I had to shoot my way out and hide in a thicket all night. There was about a dozen of 'em after me."

"A dozen of who?" Caleb asked, suddenly concerned about going to town.

"They've got Negro troopers at the fort," explained a cowboy called Bandanna Dan Montgomery. "They're good Indian fighters, but some of the Old Law Mob don't like 'em drinkin' in the same saloons as white men. They run Nate out of town with a lynch rope last time we was there."

"Old Law Mob?"

"That's their vigilante outfit," Bandanna Dan said. "They're hell on rustlers, but some of 'em are old Rebels and don't like to see a black man get ahead. You'll be all right though. You're white as a lily."

Nate and two other black cowboys agreed to stay with the herd that night while Caleb, Bandanna Dan, July Pierce, and Bud Redden went to town—providing the white cowboys would bring back some refreshments and smoking tobacco for the night herders to enjoy the next day. They crossed the horses to the south bank of the Clear Fork of the Brazos River and trotted to Fort Griffin.

Sunset was kind to the ramshackle barracks where the black troopers lived. It bathed them in a fine hue. The four cowboys cut between the parade ground and the sutler's store on Government Hill, then rode down to The Flats. When they mounted the main street of the town, Caleb knew he had scarcely seen the likes of buggies, freight wagons, mules, oxen, and saddle horses in his life. They all but choked the flow of traffic in the rutted street.

Every man in town seemed to harbor a deep aversion to the rules of civilization. A cowboy spurred his mount onto the boardwalk to get around a wagon jam in the street. A buffalo hunter proudly carried a new Sharps rifle from a store, test-firing it even before he had closed the door behind him. A drunken Tonkawa brave staggered along a hitching rail, one hand on his knife handle, the other around the neck of a whiskey bottle. A mule skinner and a bull whacker cussed each other up and down in the street, then resorted to fists.

"What we need is a plan," Bud Redden said. "We want to make sure we get to the river before we run out of money."

"What are you gonna do with money at the river?" Caleb asked. "Throw it away?"

"More or less," July Pierce said. "That's where all the disorderly houses are."

"We'll have a drink at every saloon on the way to the river," Bandanna Dan said. "There's only three or four of 'em. Then, if we have any wages left over after whorin' up and down the riverbank, we can drink our way back up to Government Hill."

"Don't forget the whiskey and tobacco for Nate and them," Caleb reminded him.

The plan was agreed upon, and the four men hitched their horses in front of the first saloon. It was early in the evening, and most of the customers were still sober. A piano plinked out familiar tunes. There were girls to dance with at a dime per whirl. Most of them were drumming up business for their houses down on the river. One told Caleb that she worked in the Palace of Beautiful Sin, the swankiest den of debauchery on the Clear Fork.

After the third saloon, Caleb reached his favorite stage of drunkenness. He still had control of his faculties but felt oblivious to any prospect of danger around him. He embraced the chaos of The Flats. There was one more saloon left on the main street before he and his friends made their visit to the river.

As he tied Powder River to the hitching rail, he happened to notice the sign that hung down by chains from the saloon front. The place was called Starling's Lone Star.

"I used to know an old man named Starling," he said as he walked in through the free-swinging double doors. Just as the name crossed his lips, he spotted Old Milt shuffling across the floor, carrying a tray stacked with whiskey glasses. "Well, I'll be damned. There he is!"

"You know that old man?" Bandanna Dan asked. "See if you can get us free drinks."

Caleb pushed between two men standing at the bar and shouted at Milt. "Hey, old man! Remember me?"

Milt turned with a scowl and wiped the tail of his apron over his brow and bald head. "Who said that?!"

"I did. Remember? Black Hawk."

Milt stared at Caleb, squinted, and backed away. "I don't know what the hell you're talkin' about."

Caleb laughed. "I used to fiddle in your place at Black Hawk. Don't you remember throwing me in the creek that night I got drunk?"

Milt's eyebrows perked, then a look of relief swept his face. "By God, it is you!" He slapped his hand down on his bar. "I was fearin' somebody else. What was your name? Let's see, Cal somethin', wasn't it?"

"Caleb. Caleb Holcomb."

Milt invited Caleb to sit with him at a table. "Where's the fiddle, boy?" he asked. "Dancin' music would bring in some of them damsels of spotted virtue—whores, that is."

"I don't fiddle since I froze my fingers off," Caleb said, holding up his left hand. "I'm learnin' guitar left-handed, but I haven't got around to the fiddle yet."

"The guitar will do. How are you fixed for money?"

"Flat broke," he replied, as if he was proud of it.

"Then you could stand the weight in your pockets. Turn your hat up on the bar and pluck a few songs for us."

"Well, maybe. If you'll advance me and my friends a drink." Caleb pointed to his three acquaintances standing by the door.

The old saloonkeeper cussed, but he waved the three cowboys over to the bar and set up a round.

"Thanks, Milt," the musician said. "Say, how come you give up your place in Black Hawk for this dive?"

Milt hissed through the gaps in his teeth and covered his face in shame. "The fever got me, boy."

"The fever? You mean the gold fever?" Caleb laughed.

"I swore I was too old and smart for it, but it got me all over again just the same."

"What happened?"

"An old Californee friend of mine went broke on a prospect hole above Nevadaville. He asked me to come take a look at the place and see if I couldn't find him a buyer for his claim. I swear, as soon as I set foot on that claim, all my old broken joints started achin'. The fever got me like a vise. I could smell the ore down the shaft!"

"Did you find your friend a buyer?"

"Hell, yes, boy, I found him a right handy one! I sold my store and sunk all my money down that shaft myself. I blasted fifty feet before I went broke."

"So you left for Texas?"

"No, no, no! There was gold under that hill, boy! I could taste it in the shaft dust I'd been breathin'. There was a vein in there thick as my crippled leg." Milt leaned toward Caleb to speak confidentially. "I had a friend with a payin' mine in Central City. So I borrowed a little ore from him and had it assayed. I said it came out of my mine and got some Denver bankers to stake me."

"You salted your own mine?"

Milt shushed him violently. "Would you ruin me right here in my own home? Keep it down, boy. Yes, I salted it. Don't judge me, boy, the fever had me. It ain't like I run off with the money. I sunk it all down the shaft. I blasted a drift at seventy-five feet and worked like a fool, muckin' out the chunks, but there wasn't a sliver of color in nary a one of 'em."

"What did you do?"

"What do you think I did? Them Denver bankers wanted to see profits. When I ran out of their money, I skipped the territory. That's why you scared me so spoutin' off about Black Hawk. I thought they had sent a bounty hunter to find me."

Caleb smirked arrogantly, impressed that Milt had mistaken him for a bounty hunter. "But why in the hell did you come to this dive?" he asked. "Of all the sorry places on earth . . ."

"It's the safest place for me. Those bankers knew Old Milt Starling: veteran of Californee, Cherry Creek, Gregory Gulch. If they wanted to find me, where do you think they'd look?"

"A mining town, I guess," Caleb said.

"You guess, my ass! Of course that's where they'd look! So I thought to myself, 'Milt, where's the cheapest dirt on earth?' Then it struck me: Texas! If you sink a shaft here, you're lucky to strike a vein of alkali water. They'll never think to find me in Texas!"

"Well, at least the fever won't get you here," Caleb said.

"Hell, the fever runs here, too. That's the beauty of it. A man can still mine gold from men's pockets. But the fever here ain't for color."

"What then?"

"Buffler! They come in here with the same look in their eyes. They sit at that bar, get rich, and spend their earnin's before they even take aim at a hump. They stake their claims on the buffler range just like a miner up some lonesome gulch. They use Sharps rifles and skinnin' knives the way I used to work with a pick and shovel, and they haul back flint hides instead of gold dust, but it's the same old fever, boy, I recognize it."

Caleb felt a touch of the fever himself and eyed the patrons of Starling's Lone Star through the bottom of his glass. "Any hide hunters in here?"

"Yeah, there's Washita Jack Shea and a feller name of Frost over there by the stove. They're puttin' together a flint-hide party. Lookin' for skinners.''

The last of the jigger trickled down his throat. "Would you vouch for me?''

Milt's cloudy old eyes narrowed on the drifter. "I've warned you about the fever, boy.''

"I need work.''

The old miner sighed and got up. "Well, you're growed. Jist don't cuss me when the Comanch' pull the fresh bloody hide off'n your skull bone.'' He tossed his head toward the table of the hide hunters.

FIFTY-SIX

EVERY SUNDAY AFTERNOON, after presenting his Holcomb Ranch scripture lesson, Pete would treat Amelia to a picnic. Sometimes Lee Fong would fill a basket with fried chicken, roasting ears, corn bread, and fruit preserves. Sometimes Amelia would have Captain Dubois's chef pack roast beef, cranberry sauce, fresh-baked bread, and cake. Pete would borrow Buster's old spring buggy with the holes cut in the floorboards for the wind-wagon rigging and call on Amelia at the Dubois mansion.

Strict ritual attended his visits. He would twist the bell knob at the front door, wait for the house servant to answer, and announce his intentions of taking Miss Dubois on a picnic. The servant would then ask him to wait in the parlor until Amelia made her appearance on the staircase. She always looked stunning and stylish, and Pete always told her so, whereupon she would blush and ask the servant to tell her father that she was going on a picnic with Pete, as if the captain did not already know.

Once in the buggy, Amelia got to choose the picnic site. She might decide on the Pinery, the seven falls of Cheyenne Canyon, or the Garden of the Gods. Lately, she had wanted to get as far away from Colorado Springs as possible. The town had swelled with tuberculars hunting a healthful climate. Their constant coughing and hacking in all of General Palmer's public parks tended to detract from her enjoyment of the outing.

So it was, one Sunday afternoon in September, that Amelia climbed into the erstwhile wind wagon and told Pete she wanted to have her picnic at the ancient cliff dwellings above Manitou Springs.

"Well, all right, if that's where you want to go,'' Pete said. "I guess you haven't got much of an appetite yet. It's a slow drive up there.''

"Actually, I'm starving,'' she said, fanning herself with a scallop of lace. "But, it's been such a hot summer, I just want to picnic in a cool place. When I toured the cliff dwellings with the ladies' club, I can't tell you how refreshingly cool the little rooms felt to us in the middle of the day.''

Pete twitched the reins and drove down the street between the rows of cottonwoods that stood horse-high now after just three years in the ground. The buggy trundled across town and bounced over the narrow-gauge tracks of the Denver and Rio Grande. It passed the sanitarium, forded Monument and Camp creeks, and mounted the road to Manitou Springs.

"My goodness, it's dusty," Pete said. He slapped his brand new Stetson against his leg to knock the dirt from the sprawling brim. "One of these days some rain will come along and break this drouth."

"Please, you're not going to start . . ." Amelia said.

"I'm sorry, darlin'. No more ranch talk, I promise."

Pete let the horse take its time pulling the buggy up the grade to Manitou Springs. He drove past the health resorts in town and turned onto the narrow road leading to the ancient homes of the cliff dwellers. He was glad Amelia had chosen the cliff dwellings, even if it meant a long drive from Colorado Springs. The old cubbyholes of stonemasonry built under their protective outcropping of the Front Range held a mystical fascination for him. They reminded him of the glorious time and place God had chosen for him, leading a new and holy civilization into a land of primal sin and ignorance.

The road led along the cliff bases until the abandoned dwellings came suddenly into view. There, among the rambling fissures and jutting crags, a tiny two-story village of fitted stones filled a cavernous depression in the mountainside.

A well-crafted wall—broken by windows, doors, and mazelike passages—closed in the entire mouth of the cave. It wound in and out at perfectly square angles, extending in places to the very rim of the overhang above. In one place the curved wall of an ancient granary spanned the cave from floor to ceiling, like a great column built to hold it open for eternity. Wooden ladders led to the balconies of upper tiers. Rotting stubs of timbers formed horizontal rows between the upper and lower levels. Inside, the timbers supported the flooring of the upper apartments. The dwellings faced south and east, affording a view of mountains, plains, and every practical approach.

They left the buggy horse in the shade of a piñon pine, picked up their picnic basket, and went to explore the cool, dark recesses of the structure.

"I think this round room was where they put their corn," Pete said. "It reminds me of the silos I used to see in old Pennsylvania."

"Oh, you've lost your imagination out on that dreary ranch," Amelia argued. "It's a bastion of a castle-fortress. Now, isn't that more romantic than your silo?"

Pete looked up at the cylindrical bulge in the rock wall and stroked his chin thoughtfully.

"Come on," Amelia said, taking his hand. "Let's get into one of these cool little rooms and have our picnic."

Pete looked down on the turns of the switchback road leading to the cliff dwellings. He saw no horses or buggies coming. It wouldn't do for anyone to catch him in the little cubicle with Amelia.

She stepped over the knee-high threshold of an entryway that was more like a window than a door. It was so small that her skirt almost filled the entire opening as she pulled it in. She didn't seem to mind that Pete got a good look at her calves as she crawled through. He followed, putting one leg through the hole, sitting on the high sill, ducking under the low transom, and pulling his other leg in after him. The wide brim of his hat scraped against both sides of the portal as he went through.

Amelia made Pete hold the picnic basket as she spread a blanket on the floor, gently so as not to raise dust. The cubicle was so tiny that the blanket lapped up against the rock walls all the way around. She sat near the middle, her skirts billowing around her like a parachute.

"How did they live in these little bitty rooms?" Pete said, hunching under the low ceiling timbers. "They hardly had space to stretch out."

"I think it's cozy," Amelia said. "Come sit down and show me what that Chinese chef of yours packed for us." She patted the blanket beside her.

Pete glanced out of the square hole in the wall and checked the road again before he sat down. "Fried chicken, as usual," he said. "Lee Fong knows how to cook just so many things."

It was fairly dark in the ancient little room, but their eyes soon adjusted. Pete watched Amelia tear into a drumstick with abandon, licking her lips, sucking the crumbs from her fingertips. He had never seen her eat so voraciously. Appetite went before manners, he thought.

She drank from a flask Lee Fong had packed. "What do you think they were like?" she asked, catching a stray drop on her chin with her finger.

Pete threw a chicken bone through the entrance hole. "Who?"

"The people who lived here."

He leaned back to prop himself up on one elbow. The wall pushed his hat down over his eyes, so he took it off. "I'll bet they were little rascals."

"They must have been happy living here. It's so cool."

Pete was thinking that Cheyenne or Utes had probably run the little cliff dwellers off or killed them, but he didn't impose his suspicions on Amelia. "Well, they had a good view. They grew corn. They stayed out of the rain and the north wind. I guess they were happy."

"Will our house be like this one?" Amelia asked. She pushed the emptied picnic basket into a corner.

"I imagine the cellar might look plumb identical."

"Oh, you sarcastic devil," she said, stretching across the floor to hit him with her lace fan. "I mean the stonework." She stayed close to him, lying on the blanket on her stomach, propped up on her elbows.

"If you want a rock house, that's what I'll build you," Pete promised. "And if you want it four stories high, that's how high I'll make it."

"Two and a half will be quite high enough. Now the only question is when."

"It'll take time, darlin'. But once we get a few good seasons of high grass and high beef, I'll have money to build you a castle-fortress with a silo on every corner if that's what you want."

"But that will take years," she complained.

"Well, the drouth's got to break first. And the panic will keep beef down a while."

Amelia rolled onto her back and used Pete's thigh as a pillow. "Yes, I know. First the drouth, and then the wretched money panic. I'll be an old maid by the time you build that house. Why don't you just take the money Father offered to give you?"

"I've told you a hundred times I won't use the captain's money to build my bride's house. He's just testin' me with that money anyway. He doesn't really want me to take it."

"Then forget the house," Amelia said, suddenly pulling herself across his chest. "I just want to get married. Build a little cabin and I'll learn to like it."

"No, I've already promised," Pete said, slipping his hand around the back of her neck. "What would the captain think of me if I didn't hold to my word."

"But I can't wait any longer."

"Go marry some other fella, then."

"Oh, shut up." She whacked him with the folded fan again. "You know I won't marry anyone but you. Stop teasing me. I'm sick to death of waiting."

Pete chuckled and pulled her face against his shirt. "What's gotten into your head, darlin'?"

She rested her chin against his chest and glared into his eyes. "You have, damn you. I can't think of anything but you anymore. And I'm twenty years old and I've never lain down with a man."

Pete laughed. "You're layin' down with me right now."

"You know what I mean. Oh, I wish you had more money or less pride. These are my best years, and I'm wasting them."

"Now have some patience, Amelia. You know we have to do what's proper and wait."

"I have no more patience, and I don't care what's proper." She pulled herself up to his shoulders and kissed him. "We're going to be married anyway, so what difference does it make?"

The soft touch of her lips lingered on Pete's mouth. The room was so cool and comfortable—just the way he intended Amelia's house to turn out. He felt himself weakening, drifting toward the primal sins of the ancients. "Well, when you put it that way," he said, "I guess it doesn't make a whole lot of difference."

She pushed herself away from him, picked up his hat, and went to the little square hole in the wall. She put her palms on the sill and leaned out to look down on the road. Ducking back into the tiny room, she wedged Pete's hat in the entryway, the stiff brim holding it in place and blocking most of the light.

When she lay back down on the blanket, Pete rolled toward her and felt her trembling.

"There wasn't anybody comin'?" he asked.

"No," she whispered.

FIFTY-SEVEN

THE BUFFALO CARCASSES were still warm when the skinners arrived on the killing grounds. Caleb saw three cows suffering, lying on their sides, legs kicking, hooves gouging little arches in yesterday's mud. He drew his pistol and walked toward the nearest one.

"Oh, hell, Caleb," said his partner, Seth Corley, "leave them cows to bleed to death."

"It'll just take a minute to kill 'em," Caleb argued. "I hate to see 'em kick like that."

"Well, hurry up. Joe and Eddie have already bloodied their knives."

Caleb pointed his pistol at the cow's head and pulled the trigger. "We'll catch up," he shouted back at Seth. "You know there ain't another pair in camp that can outskin us."

"I know we'll catch up, but just once I'd like to start out ahead!" Seth stropped his skinningknife across its leather scabbard a time or two and made the first incision along the belly of the downed bison. It would have been easier if Caleb had been there to help him roll the carcass onto its back and prop it in place with the willow pegs Seth carried under his belt.

Another shot rang from Caleb's pistol.

"Two bits a hide," Seth muttered to himself, "and he's wanderin' over five acres, wastin' bullets on half-dead cows."

Caleb fired his third round and looked over the rest of the carcasses. More than twenty of them lay in the prairie mud between two low, rolling swells. Washita Jack Shea, the hunter who had downed them, had done a good job of picking off each cow that had tried to lead the herd away, and they had all been slaughtered in a small space. He wound his way through the dead animals, his blood-crusted clothes clinging stiffly to him, and tried to get a whiff of cool north air that didn't smell like offal.

He had hired on with the outfit at Fort Griffin. For five solid weeks he had followed the carnage of his camp's hunters and peeled the woolly pelts from wasted death. The hunters—besides Washita Jack—were Smokey Dean Wilson, Roy Badger Burton, and Tighe Frost. Frost didn't claim a nickname but was sometimes called Railroad Tighe because his wealthy father manufactured locomotive parts, or Red Hot Frost because he had already ruined one rifle by shooting too frequently without cooling the barrel.

There was one other hunter who worked out of the Salt Fork camp, but he worked alone, skinning his own kills, scouting for bigger herds, returning only for provisions. He was an old man named Elam Joiner.

Ten skinners and a camp rustler filled out the ranks of the party—sixteen men in all. For the first two weeks of their foray for hides, southern winds had blistered them day and night. Then the northers had started bringing blasts of cool air and rain. Now the cool periods were outlasting the hot spells. The moderate temperatures made the skinners' work a little less repugnant because the beasts didn't bloat and stink as quickly.

By the time Caleb drew his skinning knife, his partner had already slit the hide down the legs and was ready to start peeling it off.

"It's about time," Seth said. "Look at Joe and Eddie. They've got theirs half skinned."

"Don't blame me," Caleb said. "It's that damned Washita Jack and his lung shots. If he'd hit 'em in the neck like Badger does, they'd go down dead instead of kickin' a half hour."

"At least Washita knows when to quit. Next time Badger shoots more than we can skin in a day, I'm gonna shoot him. I'm sick and tired of skinnin' stiff stinkers."

The skinners worked the kill into the afternoon, when Tighe Frost rode up. He had used his family's money to stake the hunting party. He was not much of a buffalo hunter, but thought he was.

"Holcomb!" he shouted. "You and Corley get on your horses and come with me. I've killed a dozen cows for you to skin across the river."

Seth wiped his bloody hands on his shirt. "Can't it wait till we get through with these?"

"No," Frost said. "It will take you all day to finish the ones I killed. They're spread out."

"Well, why don't you get Joe and Eddie to do it?"

"You two are the fastest, aren't you? I need fast workers to get through before dark. Get your horses." Frost nudged his mount forward to bother Joe and Eddie.

"If that's our prize for bein' the best, I don't know that it's worth it," Seth grumbled as they walked to their horses.

"I'll bet he's got dead buffalo strung out from here to the Double Mountain Fork," Caleb said, "and not a one of 'em with less than three bullet holes."

"He shoots more lead into a buffalo than the hide is worth," Seth added, "not to mention the shots he misses altogether. I wish I had the likes of powder he burns in a day. I could hunt a lifetime on it."

"Red Hot Frost, the gut-shot champion of the Southern Plains," Caleb said. He and Seth laughed as they cinched their saddles tight.

At twilight they loped into the camp on the Salt Fork of the Brazos, covered with mud, blood, and hair from their day's work. They trotted past the stake ground where the hides were stretched flat and pinned with willow pickets, past the buffalo tongues drying on the pole racks, past the wood and buffalo chips the camp rustler collected for fuel. They rode to the wagons, threw their saddles down, and let their horses drink from a tub that had collected some rainwater. They briefly rinsed their hands in the same tub.

"The wagons are plumb full of flint hides," Seth said. "I guess Frost will drive them to Denison in the morning."

"I hope so," Caleb said. "I wouldn't mind gettin' shed of him for a while."

They walked between two tents made of green hides and joined the group of men sitting around the fire. Caleb noticed that old Elam Joiner was in camp, rubbing his trigger finger on the rough side of a whetstone. He claimed his Sharps Big Fifty had the hairiest trigger in Texas, and he had to keep his finger almost raw to give it the right touch.

"Where have you boys been?" asked Mort Fletcher, the camp rustler. He was always the jolliest man in the group, though he worked longer hours than any hunter or skinner in the outfit. "I had to fight these other fellers off with a ladle to keep them from eatin' all the biscuits. I've got fresh tongue, boiled tender and fried in bone marrow. Hurry up and get yourself a plate of it, so I can wash the dishes."

"Not tongue again," Seth complained. "I'd give my front teeth to taste somethin' I knew wasn't tastin' me back."

"Bring me some hump ribs tomorrow and I'll roast 'em," Mort suggested.

"If you cut it off of a buffalo, I'm sick of eatin' it," Seth replied.

They got their food and sat on rolled hides to eat.

"I met up with some soldiers three days back," Elam said, continuing the conversation he had started before Caleb and Seth arrived.

Smokey Dean Wilson was pouring measured amounts of black powder into the brass shells he had emptied during the day. "What did they know?"

"Said Colonel Mackenzie wiped out a whole village of Comanche up at Palo Duro Canyon. Burned their lodges and shot a thousand horses."

"Where the hell is Palo Duro Canyon?" asked a skinner named George Karnes.

"Don't worry, George," Seth said, spraying biscuit crumbs as he spoke, "it's away up in the Panhandle. It'll take them Indians all winter to walk down here and scalp you."

"Go to hell, Seth. I ain't scared of no Indians."

"Then you're a damn fool," Elam said. "About the time you decide you ain't scared of 'em, well, that's when they cut you into little chunks. Some Delaware scouts with them soldiers I run onto said one band has a camp up on the Pease River nearly every winter. That's not even a day's ride from here for a Comanche."

"We can do without seein' Indians," Washita Jack said, "but we need to find some buffalo. We've just about killed this range out."

"There's good herds up on the South Wichita," Elam said. "Hides as good as I've ever seen."

"Any hunters up there?" Smokey Dean asked.

"I didn't meet up with any. As far as I can tell, nobody's further west than us."

Washita Jack ran a piece of rag greased with buffalo tallow down the barrel of his Sharps Big Fifty. "How was your huntin' up there?"

"I killed and skinned about a dozen cows a day," Elam said. "I've got seventy-five hides staked and dryin'."

Tighe Frost had been listening with a cup of coffee in his hand. "What's your total now, Elam?"

The old hide hunter glanced disdainfully at Frost. "Hell, I don't know. Ask Mort, he keeps the tally."

Frost handed his cup to Mort and motioned for him to pour in some more coffee from the pot. "What's Elam's total?" he asked.

Mort set aside his knife and the willow stake he had been whittling, took the coffee cup in one hand and a chunk of buffalo tallow in the other. He threw the tallow on the fire, causing it to flare brightly. Then he poured Frost another cup. "Let's see," he said, "with seventy-five staked out, that brings Elam's total to four hundred and thirty-one hides. That's three hundred and eleven cow hides, seventy-two bull hides, and forty-eight kip hides." Mort possessed a remarkable facility with numbers.

"I believe I've shot a few more than that, haven't I?" Frost said, posing flamboyantly by the fire with his fresh cup of coffee.

Mort picked up his knife and willow stake and started whittling again.

"You've killed fourteen more than Elam, Mr. Frost, but Elam scouts and does his own skinning."

Frost glowered at the camp rustler. "Well, I have to freight the hides!"

"That's true," Mort allowed. "Smokey's shot four hundred and fifty-two. Washita's shot four hundred and seventy-five. And Badger Burton's killed more than anybody: five hundred and nine."

Seth whispered to Caleb: "That's 'cause he don't know when to quit."

"I've killed more than that," Badger said, through teeth clenched tight on a pipestem.

"Yes, but the wolves got some of those you left overnight and ruined the hides."

The skinners shadowed their faces with their hat brims and grinned.

"That brings the overall tally to two thousand, three hundred and twelve," Mort said. "Not bad for five weeks of huntin'. You boys through with those dishes yet?" He took the tin plates from Seth and Caleb and threw them into a caldron of water he had been heating over some coals beside the fire.

"I had figured two thousand hides to break even," Frost said. "That means everything from here on out is pure profit." He slung the coffee from his cup. "Have those oxen hitched by dawn, Fletcher. I want to get an early start for Denison."

"Yes, sir, Mr. Frost." Mort was the only man in camp who could take an order cheerfully.

FIFTY-EIGHT

THE THREE HUGE Murphy wagons had wheels waist-high at the hub and carried 250 hides each. Mort had festooned the rims of the wagon boxes with hundreds of buffalo tails. He hooked the three wagons together in a train and had them hitched to six yokes of oxen by daybreak.

With the wagons ready to roll, Mort roused the skinners to help him tie down the hides, stacked loosely in the beds. They threw ropes over the stacks of hides, tied the ends of the ropes to wagon wheels, and coaxed the oxen forward. The ropes wound around the wheel hubs, tightening over the cargo, until Mort stopped the oxen. The skinners then lashed the hides down with twisted rawhide thongs before untying the ropes from the wagon wheels.

In each wagon they left a space in the middle of the cargo large enough for a man to hide from Indians. With Sharps rifles, the hide freighters could hold off attackers at half a mile.

It was the third load Frost had freighted to Denison. He took the two slowest skinners with him, to help drive the oxen, and rolled out of camp about an hour after sunup.

After the ox train left, Elam Joiner took off in a buckboard for the South Wichita to find a new campsite. Badger Burton offered to go along, but old Elam said he preferred to travel alone. He knew Badger only wanted to get first crack at the thickest herds before the other hunters could arrive. Badger wanted more than anything to shoot a hundred buffalo without moving his sticks.

The other hunters and skinners were to follow Elam as soon as they could gather all the hides they had staked or rolled in various locations around the Salt Fork camp. Mort put some of the skinners to work pulling up hides from the stake ground, folding them, and stacking them. When each stack reached about seven feet, a hide was spread across the top to turn the rain, and the stack was staked under rawhide thongs. Frost would pass back through the Salt Fork camp and load the hides in the freight wagon before moving to the new camp on the South Wichita.

All the hides were stacked and tied down by dusk, and the hunters made the decision to move north the next day. They believed a fortune in hides awaited them on the South Wichita. That night, around the fire, their predictions ran as high as a hundred hides a day for the rest of the season.

"Whet your knives and brace for some real work," Smokey told the skinners. "Elam says he's never seen the likes of hides, and he's hunted longer than any man I know."

Hide fever burned in them all.

Caleb sang "Rye Whiskey" and "The Wounded Ranger" and the hide-camp favorite about old Crego, who refused to pay his skinners the wage promised:

> *The season being over, boys,*
> *   old Crego wouldn't pay.*
> *He said we'd been extravagant*
> *   and he was in debt that day.*
> *We coaxed him and we begged him,*
> *   but still it was no go.*
> *So we left his damned old bones to bleach*
> *   on the range of the buffalo.*

There was some loud talk about allowing Red Hot Frost's bones the same opportunity if he did not come back from Denison with some cash. He had deposited the money from the first two loads in his own account, claiming he had to recoup his investment before anyone received wages.

In the morning the men broke camp, loaded the rustler's wagon, and headed north. Elam's trail was easy to see in the range grass. It followed the Salt Fork of the Brazos northward until the river made a bend to the east. Here the hide hunters left the river and continued north on Elam's trail, crossing rolling plains and beautiful ranges grown green with recent rains. After noon they began to see buffalo herds on distant ridges and knew Elam had chosen well.

As evening approached, the hunters and skinners watched the rolls of prairie for signs of their scout. He had told them the trip to the South Wichita would take only a day. Toward nightfall they saw a wisp of smoke rising from a tree line in the valley of the South Wichita. Elam's wagon tracks led directly toward the place.

Powder River had wanted to run all day, so Caleb rode ahead with the hunters to join their scout. The horses smelled the river on the north breeze and stretched their necks to get to it. Washita Jack and Badger Burton let loose a few hoots to warn Elam of their approach. It looked as though the old man had chosen a good place to camp. He had found good water and ample timber for fuel, shade, and shelter.

The horses seemed compelled to race, running abreast, thundering over the ground, and the Nez Perce gelding began to pull away from the others. They followed the wagon tracks at a gallop, making a turn down the riverbank, through the trees, and into a clearing. Caleb was just getting ready to claim victory when Powder River stiffened his legs, balked, and reared. He heard one of the hunters swear, and when he got the gelding under control, he saw the horribly mutilated body of Elam Joiner tied to a wagon wheel, burned, scalped, and hacked beyond abomination.

The old man had been stripped and, dead or alive, lashed to the wheel spread-eagled. Arrows bristled from him like quills from a porcupine. His genitals were gone, a huge gouge in their place. His stomach had been ripped open and his organs removed. Deep, ugly gashes parted the flesh of his thighs. Half the wagon was charred from a still-smoldering fire, started at the base of the wheel Elam's body was tied to.

Turning away, Caleb stumbled down from his horse and fell into some bushes. He heard some of the other men gagging, but Washita Jack Shea was cussing in a fit of instant rancor. Caleb had only glanced at Elam, but the unreal image of the corpse, black and red, came before everything he looked at. He would have given anything to make the vision go away, and yet he felt a morbid compulsion to look again. For triggering that ghastly weakness within himself, he hated the Indians even more than for killing poor old Elam.

He turned, grunting his own vomit back down his throat, and saw Jack trying to cut the body from the charred wheel. The rest of the men had walked away. Washita looked to Caleb for help, so he got up to do what he could. He held Elam's body under the arms as Washita, still swearing anathemas against every Comanche ever born, cut the rawhide ties. Caleb looked beyond what he was doing when he stretched Elam on the ground. To his horror, Washita Jack began pulling arrows from the body. Caleb had to turn away again to escape the sounds of tearing flesh.

When the wagon arrived, Caleb pulled out a hide to wrap Elam in. Mort unloaded a shovel and a spade, and the grave digging began. The skinners and hunters worked silently, tense with horror and anger.

Badger Burton seemed palsied with hatred. "I should have been with him," he said over and over.

Elam Joiner was buried in a shroud of green buffalo hide with the skull of a bull for a headstone. Mort said a few words of prayer over the fresh mound of dirt, and Washita Jack Shea called for a council of war to meet at the wagon.

"Any man that doesn't want to fight," he said, standing in the bed, "can walk away right now and nothin' will ever be said against you."

Some of the skinners looked at their boots, but none turned away.

Washita nodded. "I thought you'd feel bloody. You've a right to." He sat on a pile of rolled hides in the wagon bed. "Smokey already found their trail across the river. They must have thought Elam was huntin' alone; they were careless. As soon as the moon comes up, we'll follow 'em. Elam told me the other night that the Pease River is about thirty miles north of here, and that's most likely where the red bastards are camped. It'll be a hard ride tonight, but we'll be on 'em at dawn, and then they'll suffer for what they did to Elam."

"How many of 'em you reckon there are?" George asked. "There ain't but twelve of us."

"It doesn't make any difference," Washita said. "They're ignorant of us. They won't have any guards posted. We'll surprise 'em the way we did when I served with Custer on the Washita. You all know I was there."

Caleb didn't know. It was the first explanation he had heard concerning Washita's nickname. The knowledge of it gave him a deep and sudden faith in the leadership of Washita Jack Shea.

"Besides, we've got something' Custer didn't have," Washita continued. "Sharps Big Fifties, and three of the best shots on the Southern Plains. Mort, make some coffee. It's an hour yet before the moon rises."

FIFTY-NINE

A DOZEN TIRED men sat on their horses in the moonlight, looking at the Pease River over a roll in the plains. It was a broad line of black foliage embedded in the gray plains. Slender columns of silver smoke rose from a bend in its valley.

"What do you call that gelding?" Washita said to Caleb.

"Powder River," he answered, whispering hoarsely.

"He's got a nose for human blood. He like to have boogered when we found Elam back there. A horse like that will smell murder for you."

Caleb nodded, and the men sat quiet for another minute, occasionally shifting in their seats, squeaking saddle leather.

"What's takin' Smokey so damn long?" Badger Burton asked.

"Relax," Washita said. "He's got to go slow to be quiet. We've got plenty of time till daylight."

Badger heaved impatiently, and the silence began again.

Washita reached into his saddlebag for a flask of whiskey, took a drink, and passed it to Badger. "Some of their women and children are bound to get hurt when the fight starts," he said to the men as the bottle went around. "We might kill some of 'em. Don't worry about it; there's nothin' we can do about that. Those butchers have put their families in danger by what they did to Elam, and if any of 'em get killed, it's their fault."

Caleb burned his throat with whiskey and passed the bottle on. He slumped forward in the saddle and snatched worthless moments of sleep, waking with a start every time he began to fall out of the seat.

Smokey Wilson finally returned from the river, riding at a lope toward his companions. "It looks good for us," he said, getting down from his horse. With his boot heel he drew a crooked line across a bare spot of ground. "This is the river," he said. "There's a bluff on the north side where you can see nearly the whole camp. They've got lodges set up all along the north bank." He pointed at his map as he reported.

"How many lodges?" Washita asked.

"I counted sixteen, but it was pretty dark. I may have missed a few."

"How far from the camp is this bluff you're talkin' about?"

"About a quarter mile. Easy range for the big guns. And there's hardly a tree for cover between the bluff and the camp. All the thick timber's on the south side of the river, along this bend."

"Where are their horses?"

"Grazin' in the canyons upstream, a good half mile off."

Washita chuckled bitterly and got down to draw his battle lines on Smokey's map. First he put three dots where Smokey had said the bluff was. "Me and Smokey and Badger will get on this bluff where we can shoot down on their camp." He drew triangles to represent the tepees. "We'll take two guns each and a man to load 'em for us. Mort, you can load for me. Corley, you load for Badger, and Smith, you'll load for Smokey. Bring some canteens to cool the barrels. We'll have to shoot fast."

"What are the rest of us skinners gonna do?" George asked in a shaky voice.

"You'll charge the camp from the south at daybreak, push 'em out, and stir 'em up so we can pick off the braves with our buffalo guns. We'll give each of you a revolver and a repeating rifle. Holcomb, your mount's the best in camp. You'll lead the charge."

Caleb felt the mettle of fear and pride surge through him.

"Caleb's my partner," Seth blurted. "Let George load for Badger. I want to make the charge with Caleb."

Washita looked at George, who nodded in agreement, glad to get out of the charge. "All right," Washita said. He drew Caleb's line of attack in the map. "Holcomb, your skinners will sneak up on the camp from the south through these trees. At first light, charge across the river and into the camp. Drive 'em all to the north, then we'll have at 'em with the Big Fifties in this open area between the camp and the bluff. Don't let 'em get into the trees or we'll lose 'em."

Caleb stared blankly at the map.

"Understand?"

"Yes, sir."

"Good. I'll leave it up to you when to charge. Wait till you can see to shoot, but don't wait for them to wake up. Remember, when they figure out where we are, they'll try to pick us off of the bluff. I'm counting on your men to keep up a steady cross fire."

Caleb nodded, wondering how he had come to be trusted with the attack. Was it because he owned a good horse? Because he was a hard worker? Certainly it had nothing to do with him looking like a leader of men. He was just a skinner, a drifter, a left-handed guitar player. If he had stayed home, he would have seen none of this. But he couldn't stay home. He didn't belong there. It wasn't his home. He had no home. What else could he have done? He just had to keep going.

In an hour the hunters were in position on the bluff and Caleb was leading his squad of skinners toward the tree line. He reined his mount in when they passed the first few trees. "Let's wait here till it gets lighter," he whispered.

"What for?" Seth asked.

"I don't want to get too close before it's light enough to shoot. A dog might start barkin', or the Indians might hear us comin' and get away."

Seth sighed and looked at the sky. "When the last star dies out," he said, "we'll start sneakin' through the trees until we see the lodges. Then we'll charge."

"Good idea."

They watched the sky. When the light of the morning's last surviving star had faded away, Caleb whispered his orders. "Spread out. Get about twenty yards abreast of each other, and ride at a walk through the trees. Stop when you see the tepees, and wait for me to give the signal to charge."

"And don't forget what the son of a bitches did to poor old Elam," Seth added.

"All we have to do is keep 'em out of the trees," Caleb said. "Herd 'em to the north."

The riders could barely see one another as they rode through the timber. Caleb thought they made a terrible amount of noise, stepping on limbs, kicking rocks, and raking past branches, but he hoped the sound of the river would cover their approach. The odor of smoke came to him, and he knew he was close. He pulled his revolver from the holster.

Spotting the first lodges through the trees, he stopped to take in the lay of the land ahead. The river was running swift, but the riffles told him it was shallow all the way across. Nothing stirred in the camp. Not even the dogs knew attackers were near. Beyond the bristling peaks of the lodges, the dark bluff loomed. He could barely see the three hunters there, kneeling behind their rifle rests, their loaders ready with the spare guns. He looked to both sides along the tree line to find Seth and the other skinners waiting. There was no use in putting it off any longer. He nodded and spurred Powder River.

The six bloody young men charged from the trees, jumped a small cutbank, and splashed into the river. Seth released a blood-curdling scream and Caleb fired the first shot through the peak of a tepee.

The camp came alive like a shaken hive of bees as the revolvers fired into it. Washita's plan worked horribly well. Every Indian that ran from the lodges turned north, away from the river. The openings of the tepees faced south, so the squad of skinners could see almost every Comanche who came out. Bullets punctured the cured hides all around the tent flaps.

The skinners halted between the river and the camp and pulled carbines from their saddle scabbards. Caleb saw blood on the ground but didn't know who had been hit. He could hear the cries of babies, the screams of women, the shouts of warriors. "Go through the camp!" he said to his men. "Spread out."

They moved slowly among the tepees, taking wild shots at fleeing figures in blankets. As far as Caleb knew, the Indians hadn't returned a single shot. Then a bullet cracked a lodge pole behind his head. He saw a brave with a repeater standing between two lodges. He turned Powder River and shouldered his carbine, but the warrior already had a bead drawn on him. A buffalo gun boomed on the bluff and the warrior jerked forward, bits flying from him.

Screams and shouts trebled as the Indians milled in terror. The hunters had waited patiently until almost the entire band was in the open flats under the bluff. Now they rifled balls of lead mercilessly down on the Comanche.

Caleb rode toward the dead warrior to keep the other braves away from the repeater on the ground. Halfway there, two small figures darted into the open. A shriveled woman with long shocks of hair pulled a naked, dark-skinned boy by the arm as they ran. She stooped, grabbed the rifle by the barrel, dragged it away. Caleb aimed but couldn't fire. Something in the woman's gait struck a deep chord of terror in him.

They had swept the camp of Indians and were raking them with a reckless cross fire. The Comanche were caught in the flats between the buffalo guns and the repeaters of the skinners. Few of the braves had had time to load their weapons. As the carnage mounted, the riflemen emptied their magazines and retired behind tepees to reload. The cross fire wilted, and Caleb knew he should have told his men to stagger their fire to maintain a constant barrage. The few Indians who were fighting back now turned their guns on the bluffs.

Clumsily, Caleb shifted rounds from his cartridge belt to the loading port of his Winchester, trying at the same time to hold Powder River behind a Comanche lodge. He glanced toward the flats, then at his men.

"They're tryin' to move upstream!" Seth shouted. "Come on, Caleb, let's turn 'em back toward the bluff!"

Looking between the tepees, he saw the Indians scrambling to his left, running low behind bushes, carrying dead and wounded. He turned Powder River and trotted behind the last row of lodges standing between him and the Indians. As he rode, he caught glimpses of the scrawny woman with the rifle, leading the naked boy by the arm. Some old, inexplicable disgust rose in him. The guns roared like cannons from the bluff.

"Hurry up!" Seth shouted.

He spurred the gelding to a lope, trying to flank the Indians and herd them like cattle back under the Big Fifties. Suddenly a barrage of gunfire erupted from the bushes, and Seth's horse went down.

"I'm shot!" Seth shouted as he jumped from the animal with a carbine in his hand.

The Indians had made a stand with the few weapons they owned. Caleb turned Powder River broadside and returned their fire. An arrow struck Seth's dead horse. The rest of the skinners rode up, increasing the resistance, and the warriors began to fall back. Seth crawled behind his dead horse and aimed at the fleeing Comanche.

The woman rose again, and Caleb saw her face. He knew her. She aimed the rifle as he stared in horror. Seth fired, and she crumpled behind the bushes. Then the naked boy rose with the gun, shooting it from the hip. The barrel swept across the line of white men. Caleb shouldered his Winchester, aimed at the boy, but froze. He recognized something in the dark skin, the frightened face. The boy's hair didn't grow long like an Indian's. It was curly, cropped short.

He watched the line of the rifle barrel become a point as the boy levered another round into it. He was too young for war. Caleb closed his eyes and jerked his trigger. He heard another rifle shoot. When he opened his eyes the boy was gone.

The screaming voices faded. Smoke tainted the air. The Indians had escaped into a canyon upstream.

"How bad are you shot?" Caleb asked, riding next to Seth's dead mount.

"Missed the bone," he said, holding his bleeding leg. "Got my horse in the lights, I guess."

Caleb jumped down. "Get on Powder River. I'll ride behind you if we have to make a run."

Seth stepped into the stirrup with his good leg, wincing with pain as he swung the wounded limb over. "I don't think they'll come back. They're whipped pretty bad. Let's go look at that squaw I killed. She was fixin' to shoot me." He reined the gelding toward the bodies.

Caleb followed and stood over the dead woman. She looked so old. It couldn't be her, he thought. Snake Woman was younger than Buster. This bent and wrinkled squaw looked like a great-grandmother. He grasped her lower jaw and opened her mouth.

"What in hell are you doin'?" Seth said from the back of the horse.

"She ain't got no tongue." The sickness rose in him again, but he choked it back.

Seth shrugged. "That little kid looks like he's got colored blood. I don't know which one of us it was that shot him, but it was just in time to save your brains from flyin' out the back of your head. He looked like he had a bead on you."

"It was you that shot him," Caleb said. "I missed him clean."

"Really? Damn, I just took a wild shot."

The eyes of young Medicine Horse were open and staring at nothing. He had Buster's features from the square jaw to the high forehead. A single bullet hole was centered in his chest.

"I missed him, I know I did," Caleb insisted. How could he tell Buster? What would he say? "It was you that shot him, Seth." He should have stayed in Colorado to live with Buster, instead of coming to Texas to kill his son. Why did he ever leave? Was it that bad at home? Right now he couldn't remember. He couldn't call to mind what had caused him to drift.

They heard shots in the distance upriver. Washita and Smokey were riding down from the bluff, shouting. A rumble came from the canyon, muffling screams of the Indians, and a hundred horses burst onto the flats.

"Trap the horses against the bluff!" Washita Jack shouted, riding into the squad of skinners. "Badger and Mort went around to stampede 'em through the Indians. Load your guns and kill 'em!"

"Kill the horses?"

"Yes, kill every damn one of 'em."

The skinners yelped like Comanche and spread out to herd the Indian ponies against the bluff. Seth sat on Powder River, feeling the pain of his bullet wound more sharply now. Caleb stood by him.

"How bad is that leg?" Washita asked.

"It's just a hole," Seth said. "Missed the bone."

"You're lucky you decided to charge with your partner instead of load for Badger," Washita said, looking up at the bluff.

"George?"

"Yeah, George. Some buck got off a lucky shot and hit him square in the head. I think it was a buffalo gun. Probably Elam's. It would have been you if you hadn't chose to stick with your partner and make the charge."

"Maybe," Seth said. "You never know."

The rifles had started firing into the herd of Indian horses, and Caleb looked at the ground between his feet. He was sick with the squeals of wounded horses, the death of George, and the killing of Buster's flesh and blood.

"What happened to the cross fire?" Washita asked.

Caleb looked up. "We all ran out of shells at the same time."

Washita smirked. "Next time you'll know better. Anyway, y'all fought well for greenhorns, and we slaughtered a mess of 'em. After we burn their lodges and shoot their horses, it'll be a hard winter for the ones that lived."

Ten Indians were found dead under the bluff. Only two were women, and one a child, although four of the warriors killed were scarcely older than boys. Washita estimated that the Indians had probably carried away another dozen casualties. On the battleground, among the carcasses of Indian ponies and the corpses of Comanche, Smokey Dean Wilson found Elam Joiner's buffalo gun in the death grip of a Comanche brave.

They fought the battle all over again around the campfire that night. The victors grunted sadly over the loss of George but burst into fits of laughter as Seth told his version, drunk as he was on wound-numbing whiskey.

For once, Caleb didn't mind another storyteller stealing his thunder. He felt strangely out of place among the celebrants. He tried to shovel all the credit over to Seth. "If he hadn't killed that squaw and that boy at the end of the fight, one of them would have shot one of us for sure. And wounded in the leg, too."

But Caleb was forced to share in the glory. He had, after all, led the charge on the camp and fired the first shot of the battle. As he lay under the starry sky that night, the whole bloody scene played before his eyes again. He had to keep telling himself the Indians deserved it for what they had done to Elam.

There were guards posted, but he couldn't get to sleep for worry about

Indians attacking in the night. When he imagined them coming, he saw Snake Woman leading them, impossible though it was. He finally dozed off and dreamed of dying horses.

They took George's body back to the South Wichita camp the next day for burial. They didn't intend to leave him on the Pease, where the Indians could dig him up and do what they had done to Elam.

When the party finally got back to the business of hides, Washita Jack decided he would make one of the skinners a hunter. With Elam gone, and Frost freighting hides, and the skinners becoming more efficient all the time, the party was in need of another sure shot. To determine which skinner would get the promotion, he proposed a shooting contest.

He had Mort cut circles of buffalo hide the size of dinner plates, one for each skinner, and staked them against a hill four hundred paces away. After each round of shooting, he rode to look at the targets. The skinners who missed their marks remained skinners. The ones who punctured their hide circles stayed in the contest for another round.

After only three rounds, the field had narrowed to two.

"Either way, it's gonna break up our partnership," Caleb said.

"Oh, I don't know," Seth replied. "Maybe we'll both miss."

Caleb laughed as he slid a fresh cartridge into the breech of the Sharps rifle. "I know you better than to think you'd miss on purpose for my sake. I wouldn't do it for you. I want to get out of the skinnin' business too bad. Grippin' that knife all day is ruinin' my touch on the guitar strings."

"It's ruinin' my touch for tits," Seth said, "and I ain't talkin' about milkin' no cows." He sank awkwardly to the ground, still favoring his wounded leg, and rested his rifle barrel on the tripod he had made of stiff willow switches bound with rawhide.

The muzzles licked the prairie air with quick black tongues. Washita rode back from the targets and announced that Caleb Holcomb was the camp's new hunter. He was given Elam's Sharps rifle to kill with.

Seth shook his hand. "Good shootin', partner. Now, just remember. We want all neck shots, and don't get greedy. Don't do like some hide hunters that don't know when to quit."

"I'll make you a deal," Caleb said. "If I kill more than you can skin in a day, I'll skin the leftovers myself."

SIXTY

FOR HOURS HE had listened to Badger Burton's guns rumble two miles away. The sound carried sharp through the crisp air of autumn on the plains. Badger used two guns so he could shoot one while the other cooled, and kill twice as fast. He had fired three shots for every one of Caleb's, and Caleb had already put fifteen buffalo on the ground. It sounded as if Badger had finally found his stand.

Caleb could see thousands of buffalo from his position in a clump of bushes under a ridge. The herd he had in range upwind consisted of only about a hundred animals, but across the far wrinkles in the prairie, he could see scores of black masses moving against the dead brown grass.

He leaned against a small bank of dirt cut vertically in the hill by autumn rains. The Sharps rifle lay across his lap, breech open, cooling. As the herd milled, he kept his eyes on the cows that sniffed the blood of their dead sisters. One of them would probably turn from the herd in a few seconds.

Badger sent another blast echoing across the wide valley of the South Wichita.

Touching the barrel of his .50-caliber Sharps, Caleb found it cool enough to take another round. He slipped a cartridge from his belt and slid it into the breech. He eased the barrel onto the forked prop stick he had driven into the ground two hours before and scooted an inch to his left to get a line on the most agitated of the blood-sniffing cows. In a moment she lifted her nose to the air and set out on a walk to the east. Another cow followed her, and another.

He already had the distance figured at 320 yards. The wind was quartering from the northeast but wasn't stiff enough affect the flight of the bullet. The downhill slope made some difference, but he had it figured, too, from the previous kills. He took a wisp of air into his lungs, inflating his slumped body to the proper height, changing the angle of the barrel on the rifle rest just enough to cover the base of the bison's neck with the sights. He started a slow, deliberate squeeze on Elam's hair trigger until the block fell and set off the eruption.

The cow's legs buckled, and she hit the ground dead. Caleb recovered from the jolt of the rifle butt in time to see her legs flail loosely as she rolled over. Her followers stopped stupidly in their tracks as the black cloud lifted. The hunter opened the breech and tossed another smoking shell onto his pile of brass.

His ears were ringing despite the tufts of cotton stuck in them. He woke up some mornings with his ears ringing. There were nights when he could barely hear himself change chords on the guitar. As a hunter he worried more about losing his hearing than he had worried about losing his dexterity as a skinner. But the veteran hunters told him the ringing would pass a few days after the season, so he continued to kill.

He had seen a day-old stand one morning at dawn. The skinners had harvested the hides and scavengers had ripped out the entrails. As he looked eastward, the morning sunlight had shone into the gutted cavities of two dozen carcasses, their red rib cages glowing like curved sheets of stained glass. He could not calculate the tons of meat he caused to go wasted.

Another shot rumbled from Badger's stand.

The tune to "Buffalo Gals" ran through his head. He longed to get ahold of a fiddle somewhere, string it left-handed, and start learning all over again. He was approaching his old proficiency on the guitar, but only a fiddle could do justice to a tune like "Buffalo Gals."

> *Oh, she danced all night with a hole in her stockin'*
> *And her knees kept a-knockin'*
> *And her heels kept a-rockin'.*
> *She danced all night with a hole in her stockin',*
> *Oh, she danced by the light of the moon.*

He wondered how Mort would dance to fiddle music. Almost every night the camp rustler staked a hide down by the fire and challenged all comers to outjig him. None was animated enough to succeed. He imagined Mort could well-nigh clog holes in a flint hide to fiddle music.

Badger fired again, splitting the quiet with pulses of echoing gunfire.

When he had killed twenty-two head of bison, Caleb heard a sound behind him and looked back to see Badger crawling on his belly, over the ridge, and down toward the bushes.

"How's your stand holdin' up?" he whispered, sliding in next to Caleb.

"Good. They're tame as a bunch of old milk cows today."

"They're charmed. It happens to 'em sometime. I killed sixty-three on my stand. Today's my day to make a hundred." He spread a tripod of steel rods in front of him.

"I'm about done," Caleb said. "I don't think the skinners can finish much more than I've killed already."

Badger snorted disdainfully. "It shows that you ain't been huntin' long. If you'd been at it long as I have, you'd know to shoot all you can when you can. Tomorrow these thousands of shaggies might hightail it for God knows where. Then the damn skinners would cuss you and me both for not shootin' more when we had the chance."

They argued until Badger agreed to stop at a hundred kills. Caleb soaked a rag with water and ran it through the gun barrels with a ramrod so Badger could reach his tally faster, allowing the skinners to start sooner.

Badger used a Sharps Big Fifty and a Springfield Army Model Forty-five. His hands held either rifle with the steady quality of earth, and his eyes rivaled the eagle's. To Badger Burton, picking off buffalo inside of four hundred yards was like spearing pickles from a jar with a pocket-knife.

In less than two hours Badger had made his hundredth kill for the day. The ground below the ridge was lumped with black masses of fur. Fewer than forty were left standing, stupefied by the rumble of guns.

"That's a hundred," Caleb said. "Congratulations. Now let's go get the skinners."

"Not yet," Badger answered, aiming the Springfield at the herd. He fired a round and a young bull went down bellowing, then scrambled onto three legs, limping.

"What the hell are you doing?"

"Crippling for tomorrow. A busted leg will keep 'em from wanderin' too far. Give me my Sharps."

"Like hell I will," Caleb said. He rested Badger's Sharps in the crotch of his forked stick, found the wounded bull's neck in the sights, and fired.

"Damn you, what do you mean?" Badger yanked his rifle away.

Caleb sprang to his feet, fired his own Sharps rifle into the air, and started hollering like a cowboy trying to turn a stampede. He kicked gravel and raked the bushes with his rifle barrel. The animals flinched in unison and bolted in three different directions.

Suddenly Caleb felt Badger on his back and saw the bushes coming up to meet him. They rolled down the hill, snapping branches in the brush, throwing elbows, fists, and knees at each other. Above the rumble of hooves Caleb heard Badger growling his entire vocabulary of epithets.

They rolled to a stop at the bottom of the slope, and Caleb sprang to his feet first. Badger tried to butt him back to the ground, but Caleb turned the attack with a knee on Badger's chin. The rumble of the herd, which should have grown faint by now, was getting louder, and Caleb realized some of the animals were stampeding toward him.

Badger missed with a wild swing of his right fist, and Caleb planted a quick left on his ear. They leaned into each other, trading uppercuts and rib shots as the thunder of bison came nearer. Badger turned Caleb's head with a hard blow to his jaw, and Caleb caught a glimpse of shining horns and frothing mouths. He snapped Badger's head back as the stampede ripped into the bushes on both sides of them. Dust enveloped them. They could neither see nor hear, but they felt each other's fists.

A hand grasped Caleb's collar and he was rolling again, breathing acres of dust. Badger was on top of him for a moment, but he writhed violently and pulled his opponent down into the dirt with him. The thunder of hooves grew distant. They rolled, exhausted, choking in dust, throwing feeble roundhouse blows at each other.

A shot fired from the ridge, and they looked through the settling dust, their hands clutching each other's shirts. Washita Jack and Tighe Frost rode down through the bushes as the combatants pushed each other away.

Washita started laughing. "We thought we heard three shots for help."

"I wonder which one of them it was," Frost said, grinning.

"Hard to tell. They both look like they've had the worst of it. Badger, what's this all about?"

Badger coughed and spit blood. "He ruined my stand."

"That true?" Washita asked.

"It was my stand first," Caleb said. "We agreed he'd stop shootin' when he got a hundred, but then he started cripplin', so I stampeded 'em."

Washita shook his head. "You two fellers shouldn't ought to hunt together. Your methods are too . . . What's the word, Tighe?"

"Contradictory."

Washita chuckled. "Your methods are too contradictory."

"Suits me," Badger said, looking for his hat in the bushes.

"We'll have to go catch your horse for you, Badger. He boogered when the buffalo came over that ridge." He turned to Caleb. "Yours is still there. He wouldn't pull the stake pin out. That's a damn sensible horse."

Caleb picked up his rifle and started walking up the hill with Tighe Frost and Washita Jack.

"You'd better keep your distance from Badger from now on," Washita said.

"What for?"

"Badger don't like anybody gettin' between him and buffalo blood. You're lucky he didn't just shoot you. Just keep your distance from now on."

Badger couldn't find a single civil word for Caleb after the day they made the mistake of hunting together. One day Caleb was riding back to camp to direct the skinners to his morning's kill when a slug sang past him and thumped against the hill behind his head. The guns of the other hunters had been firing all around him, so he hadn't taken much notice of where the blast had come from. He looked for black smoke, but it was a breezy day and he found none. He knew Badger could have killed him if he had wanted to.

The next day Frost ordered the freight wagons loaded for another haul to Denison, and Caleb volunteered to go along. Everyone understood why, and no one tried to talk him out of it, though they would all miss his guitar music and singing. Caleb could not stay where he wasn't wanted. He loved making people laugh and dance. When his welcome wore thin, however, he thought only of the next camp, the next town. Someone would welcome his stories and songs there. It was better than bearing Badger Burton's hatred.

When he left the South Wichita that morning, he wondered if he would ever hunt buffalo again. He thought perhaps he had had enough of it for a lifetime. Every hillside he could see for miles around was covered with rotting carcasses and bleaching skeletons. He would never forget the village on the Pease River where Medicine Horse and Snake Woman had died. He would always know the bend in the South Wichita where Elam and George were buried. Few memories filled him with the glory and horror he felt looking back on his season spent slaughtering buffalo.

Where am I going? I am twenty years old and I have no job, no business. I don't even have a steady line of work. Pete is talking of getting married, and I have never even had a sweetheart. I have wandered three years and have nothing to show for it. I have no home. Where am I going now?

Winter was coming. It was time to find Javier's ranch in New Mexico. Maybe there was something there for him.

SIXTY-ONE

CALEB AND RAILROAD Tighe Frost carved a slow trail eastward with their oxen. When the bull train reached Denison, Frost drove his hides to the depot and told Caleb he was going to negotiate with the hide buyers.

"Mr. Frost," Caleb said, before his employer could get away.

"Yes? What?"

"I have an idea on how you might come out further ahead on these hides."

"*You* have an idea?" Frost snickered. "Well, I'm always willing to listen to ideas. What is it?"

Caleb took his hat off and approached his employer. "I've been doin' some figuring, and it seems to me you could make more profit on these flint hides if you cured 'em first, then sold 'em."

"Do you have any idea how much it would cost to have them cured?" Frost said, turning for the hide buyer's office.

"Three dollars a hide."

Frost stopped in his tracks. "Three dollars? Where would you have hides cured for three dollars?"

"I know a chief on the Cheyenne-Arapaho Reservation in the Territory. He has his squaws cure the hides for traders. Name's Long Fingers. You'll find his village on the Canadian, west of Darlington."

Frost rubbed his jaw and contemplated. "And they'll do it for three dollars a hide?"

"Yes, sir. You'll have to go through the Indian agent, but they're always lookin' for ways to employ the Indians, so you shouldn't have any problems. I thought you at least might want to pull one of the wagons up there and give 'em a try, to see if it works out."

Frost was not much of a buffalo hunter, but he knew a sound proposition when he heard one. Two hundred fifty hides on a trial basis made sense. Young Holcomb was right. If he could get hides cured for three dollars apiece, he could make more profit than he could selling the skins as flint hides. "What do you want out of it?" he asked.

Caleb shrugged. "The chief's a friend of mine. His people need the work."

"What are you, Holcomb? Indian fighter or Indian lover?"

"Depends on the Indian, I guess."

After he sold two wagons of flint hides, Red Hot Frost paid Caleb for the buffalo he had killed and skinned. His earnings totaled five hundred twenty-five dollars. He had never before held such a wad. By the time he had enjoyed a couple of meals and a bath, lodged himself in a hotel, put Powder River in a livery stable, and patronized some of Denison's less reputable establishments, he had spent more than a hundred dollars. He then proceeded to lose his reserves in a game of draw poker.

Six opponents took turns fleecing him of his hide earnings. There were two professional gamblers, a drummer, a cowboy, a crooked-nosed little fellow who looked like a common drudge, and a big black-bearded brute who seemed to have just stepped into the saloon from the vilest buffalo camp on the ranges. Caleb was down to his last pot when a lone jack and a stray eight became a sudden queen-high straight by virtue of a lucky draw. He won the pot and ordered drinks for the table.

"We might as well carry the young man for a few deals if he's going to buy our drinks," the drummer said.

"I'd just as soon take his money and buy my own," replied a gambler with a gold tooth.

Caleb grinned and opened with a high bet on five cards he hadn't even looked at. He scorned the draw, raised every wager that came before him, and won the pot with three tens. The black beard and the cowboy were the big losers. The two gamblers, the crooked nose, and the drummer had folded.

The streak continued for Caleb. Though he lost an occasional hand to a gambler, he continued to bet high and buy drinks for the table. The cowboy went broke. Caleb staked him. He went broke again and left. The drummer turned in. Now the gamblers took turns with Caleb at beating the black beard and the crooked nose. Caleb won the biggest pots.

A saloon girl stood at his side, waiting for him to order more drinks, and a few spectators from the bar had gathered around to admire his carefree play. He couldn't begin to calculate his winnings at the rate they had multiplied.

Another hand and the deal fell to the black beard, who sat across from Caleb. The big man's stack of chips was low, but he assured his opponents he had the wherewithal to last another deal. He gave the deck to the crooked nose to cut.

The big dirty hands dealt the cards with familiarity. A silk-vested gambler opened, the gold tooth called, Caleb raised, the crooked nose folded, and the dealer doubled the bet.

The little man with the crooked nose cussed as he left the table, taking a small stack of chips with him. Caleb looked up and found the big man glaring at him. But the whiskey had made him reckless and he called the new wager.

With all bets in, the silk vest took a card from the dealer and sat poker-faced. The gold tooth asked for three. Caleb took a good look at his hand for the first time. Two queens, two tens, an eight. The way the betting was going, he didn't think he had a winning hand, so he sacrificed the two pairs for an outside chance at a flush—one of the queens, one of the tens, and the eight were diamonds. Even Caleb knew how slim the odds were, but he had had some fun and didn't mind losing most of what he had won.

When he tossed his two rejects onto the discard pile, he noticed that the black beard raked them together as if to neaten the table and deftly bent the corners of the cards up with his thumb.

"Hey," Caleb said, "don't monkey with the deadwood."

The dealer froze with his hand on the discard pile and squinted. "What did you say?"

Caleb pointed at the cards under the big dirty hand. "Don't monkey with deadwood. Those cards, there."

"I know what deadwood means, you little shit. Are you accusin' me of cheatin'?"

"No, sir. I reckon if you were cheatin', you wouldn't be so low on poker chips. But you still ain't supposed to monkey with the deadwood."

The spectators laughed and the jaws tightened under the black beard. "When I deal, I monkey with whatever I feel like," he said through his teeth.

"Actually," the silk vest said, "the young man's right. It goes against gentlemen's rules for you to flip the corners of those cards the way you've been doing."

The black beard moved his hand to his glass, downed the whiskey in it, and studied his hand.

"You owe me two fresh cards," Caleb said.

The big dealer belched and flipped two cards his way. When Caleb picked up his new cards, he found, to his utter astonishment, that his flush had panned out. Both of the new cards sported big red diamonds. When he placed them in rank with his three original cards, he almost fell over on the saloon girl beside him. The black beard had dealt him the jack and the nine of diamonds. He had parlayed two pairs into a queen-high straight flush.

The gold tooth read Caleb's face and folded, leaving the table.

"Dealer stands pat," the black beard said.

The silk vest started the last round of betting with an outrageous wager. Caleb cheerfully called it.

"That's too high," the black beard complained.

"There's no limit in this game," the silk vest replied.

"I don't have that much."

"You should have thought about that when you started the deal, my friend. I'm sorry, but you'll have to match the bet or fold."

"The hell I'll have to fold," he said, reaching into his coat.

Caleb heard a hammer catch and looked over his perfect fan of diamonds to see a derringer in the silk-vested gambler's hand. He had no idea where it had come from.

"Whoa, mister," the black beard said. "Put that little spittoon rattler back in your pocket." He cautiously pulled his hand from his coat, clutching a folded sheet of paper. "I'm just tryin' to call your bet."

The gambler frowned and put his derringer down on the table beside his whiskey glass. "With what?"

The dealer unfolded the paper to show it to the silk vest. "A house."

Caleb wondered why a man would carry a deed to his house around in his coat. "What if I was to win this pot?" he said. "I don't have any use for a house. I don't even live anywhere."

The spectators guffawed.

"Nor do I," the gambler said.

"It's a Cincinnati house," the black beard replied.

"That's in Ohio, ain't it?" Caleb turned to the barmaid. "Darlin', bring us another round of drinks. If I win this pot, I'll pay with the parlor and tip you the front porch."

The onlookers doubled over with laughter as Caleb tossed back half a jigger.

After scrutinizing the sheet of paper, the silk-vested gambler handed it to Caleb. "I guess I'll honor it if you will."

Caleb merely shrugged and threw the document onto the pile of poker chips in the middle of the table. "All right, as long as we don't have to ante outhouses on the next deal."

Great jolts of hilarity split the smoky air, and the barmaid delivered the new round of drinks.

"All bets even." The silk vest turned his cards. "Sevens full," he said, revealing three sevens and a pair of kings.

Caleb had never held a straight flush before, or even seen one, but he was pretty sure it beat a full house. Before he could find out, however, the black beard opened up and started laughing.

"I've got four goddamn deuces, you slick bastards." He fanned the cards out on the table and started herding stray chips into the pot.

Caleb turned his hand up and sat back in his chair. He had never played in a game with so many good hands and couldn't remember which ranked highest.

The vested gambler glanced at the straight flush, leaned closer for verification, and grabbed the black-bearded dealer by the arm. "Hold on. You haven't won yet. Look at the kid's hand."

The big man craned his thick neck and squinted at the winning spread. His face grew red, and his eyes rose to pierce Caleb's. The burly body flinched. The table jumped six inches off the black beard's knee and the gambler's little derringer fell to the floor. By the time the chips had settled, the beard had a Colt revolver in his hand, cocked, pointed at Caleb.

Bystanders scattered and saloon girls screamed. The little man with the crooked nose appeared, aiming a pocket pistol at the silk-vested gambler.

"You slick little son-of-a-bitch!" the big man said to Caleb. "How'd you do it?"

"Do what?" Caleb asked, holding his hands over the table.

"Own up, or I'll blow you open. How'd you cheat me?"

"I . . . I don't even know how to cheat, mister."

"Better own up like he says," the gambler advised, calmly.

"Shut up!" The big man grabbed the silk vest. "And let me give you some advice. Next time you point that spittoon rattler at me, use it." He rapped the barrel of his revolver viciously across the gambler's forehead, knocking him to the floor.

Before Caleb could move, the Colt was on him again. The pocket pistol of the little man with the crooked nose was also covering him.

"Fill it with them chips," the black beard said, tossing his hat at Caleb. "And cash 'em in. I won that fair and square."

"Yes, sir." He started raking the winnings back into a pile and picking up strays from the floor. He heard the hinges creak on the saloon door and rolled his eyes to see who had come in. A silver star followed a shotgun barrel into the saloon.

"Drop it, Angus," the lawman ordered.

The horrible sound of the name shot louder than the crack of the Colt or the roar of the scattergun. Caleb's belly hit the floor. He rolled, pulled his pistol from the holster, and fired where Angus and Shorty had been standing. Glass shattered, and he saw the two men leaping through a window.

The marshal scrambled back out through the door, dragging one leg.

Caleb floundered toward the broken window, slipping on poker chips. He stuck his head outside, saw Angus turn a dark corner. He jumped through the window and started running.

"Wait!" the marshal yelled. "Come back here!"

Caleb slid to a stop and turned. He saw the lawman favoring one leg.

"You don't know your way around this town! You'll walk right into him!" He stumbled as he tried to use his wounded leg. "If you hadn't jumped out the damn window after them, I could have got another shot off."

Caleb trotted back to help the city marshal walk. "With that shotgun? He was too far."

"Buckshot carries."

"Did you hit him in the saloon?"

"No, the little son of a bitch hit my leg with that pocket pistol and made me miss."

As they limped back toward the saloon door, a rattle of gunfire came from the darkness down the street, and planks splintered around them. Both men wheeled. The marshal used his second barrel. Caleb sprayed five rounds toward the muzzle blasts. They heard horses galloping as the silk-vested gambler joined them, bleeding from a gash on his head and carrying his little derringer. He and Caleb put their shoulders under the wounded marshal's arms.

"He'll be back in the Territory in an hour," the marshal said, gritting his teeth against the pain.

"Who the hell was he?" the gambler asked.

"Name's Angus Mackland. He steals stock, sells guns and whiskey to Indians."

"And murders people," Caleb added. "I've seen his work. I chased him into No Man's Land last winter."

A doctor had arrived and was looking after the marshal when the silk-vested gambler handed Caleb his winnings, converted to cash, and accompanied by the folded piece of paper that represented the Cincinnati house.

"Tell me something," the gambler said. "I know how I came by my full house in that last round, and I know how that big outlaw got his four deuces. But how in the name of the devil did you manage a straight flush?"

"Angus was cheatin'?"

"I felt the deck getting thinner every time he dealt. I knew he was lifting cards, but I couldn't figure out which ones. I started counting aces—they were all there. Same with kings, queens, on down to eights. By the time I figured out he was going after four deuces, it was too late. He was smart. He knew I'd look for deuces last. His partner, the little ugly fellow, was in on it, too. Probably had some kind of signal to let the big fellow know when he had found a deuce, and he'd leave it on the top of his hand when he folded. And the little fellow was using a false cut when the big man dealt.''

"You saw him?" Caleb asked.

"Yes."

"Why didn't you say somethin'?"

"You can't prove something like that. I was waiting to catch them at something I could prove.''

"What about him monkeyin' with the deadwood?"

"He was looking for deuces, of course. I tell you, he was slick. I couldn't catch him lifting a single card from deck. Those big thick fingers were nimble at it.''

"So, that's how he did it."

"Yes, now how did you manage that straight flush of yours?"

Caleb shrugged. "I just took a lucky draw."

The gambler grinned. "That's good. Never tell your secrets. Who taught you to play?''

"An old mountain man named Burl Sandeen."

"Mountain man. I like that. No gambler's going to call your hand on that claim.'' He dipped a linen handkerchief in a glass of whiskey and dabbed his bloody head. "Maybe we'll see each other down the line somewhere.'' He put his coat on.

"I doubt it. I think I'll stay poker-shy for a while."

"Well, if we do, just deal me a few good hands, then I'll bow out and let you do your trick.''

"There ain't no trick, mister, really. I just had a lucky draw."

The gambler winked, shook Caleb's hand, and left the saloon.

SIXTY-TWO

HE SLEPT WITH his pistol under his pillow and eight hundred dollars in the pillowcase, to say nothing of the papers for the house in Cincinnati. When the sun rose in the morning, he pulled his covers over his head and went on sleeping.

Sometime in the middle of the day, the pounding of someone's fist almost ripped his hotel door from the hinges. He leapt from the bed in his long handles, holding his pistol in one hand and the pillow full of winnings in the other.

"Who's there?" he shouted, standing beside the door.

A woman's voice answered. "Did you play poker with Angus Mackland last night?" She was angry.

He cracked the door to get a look at her, and she burst in.

"I want my money back," she said in a hoarse voice, raking a strand of greasy hair out of her face.

"Ma'am, this is my room," Caleb complained, clutching the pillow in front of him.

"And you've got my money in it. Where is it?" She had black, glaring eyes—narrow and suspicious.

"I won that money in a fair game."

"It wasn't yours to win. That was my dowry. Angus was supposed to buy us a farm with it." She held a dirty hand out, expecting Caleb to drop a roll of cash in it.

"Dowry? Are you his wife?"

"Yes, I am. Against the grace of God, I am that monster's wife. And I want the money he stole from me." She was a strong, thick-waisted, straight-backed young woman. Rather dirty but healthy.

He leered. "How do I know he stole anything from you?"

She pulled the tail of a print blouse from the waist of her plaid skirt, hiked the hem up around her hips, and leapt onto the bed. "I'm fixin' to scream bloody murder, and when folks come runnin', I'll tell 'em you tried to have your way."

"You can't do that," Caleb said. "This here is my . . ."

Her eyes took a wild glare, and she drew in a breath.

"Wait!" he shouted, fishing through his winnings in the pillowcase. "I'll make you a deal. I'll give you your house and enough money to get back to Cincinnati. That's fair enough."

"Do I look like I come from Cincinnati?" she screamed.

He pulled the piece of paper out of the pillowcase and shook it at her. "That's where your house is, ain't it?"

The young woman looked at the document for a second, threw her head back on the mattress, and shook with laughter. "Are you so green that you don't know what a Cincinnati house is? They just build the pieces in Cincinnati. You can put the thing together wherever you want it. The dang house is in a boxcar at the train yard right now." She rolled, and planted her feet on the floor. "You can keep it if you want it. I don't have no use for it. Just give me the money Angus stole from me before he run out."

Caleb put his pistol down on a washstand and opened the piece of paper in his hand. It was a bill of lading, not a deed, and it entitled the possessor to ownership of one ready-made house. "You ain't from Cincinnati?"

"No, I come from Arkansas. Now, are you gonna give me my money, or am I gonna have to holler?"

"You don't have to holler. Just sit still a minute, and we'll work out a deal. I don't aim to let a woman go around broke." He sat on a rickety chair, still holding the pillow in front of him. "How much did he take from you?"

"How much did you win from him?"

"You tell me how much he took first."

She pulled her skirt back down over the high tops of her lace-up boots and looked away. "A thousand dollars," she said in her rough, husky voice.

"A thousand! Lady, you don't lie worth a damn. You think I'll believe your papa spent a thousand dollars to get you married to an outlaw?"

Her eyes narrowed to slits. "You give me the money, by God, or I swear I'll scream." The skirt went up around her hips again.

"If you'd stop lyin' and tell me how much he took from you . . ."

She filled her lungs with air and uttered a horrible, croaking yodel, mussing her hair with her hands, and bouncing on the bed. Caleb dropped his poker winnings, grabbed the basin on the washstand beside him, and splashed its contents in her face.

She gasped, caught completely by surprise, stared at him with popping black eyes, coughed, and began to cry. Her lip curled, her face flushed, and her whole body shook in convulsions of despair. Tiny streams of mud ran down her fingers as she ground her dirty knuckles into her eyes.

Her sobs filled Caleb with shame and pity, but he didn't know what to do to comfort her. He simply sat back down on his chair and watched her cry. He watched her for a full minute. Then two. They seemed like hours. Finally he rose and approached her with caution.

"Here, now," he said, putting his hand on her shoulder. "That's enough of that." He shook her. "You hear? Stop that cryin'."

She raked her wrist under her nose and looked up at him with reddened eyes.

"You can have the money." He retrieved the pillow and dumped the winnings out on the bed beside her. "I can get along without it better than you can. Just make me one promise. You take this money and go on home to your folks and forget you ever heard of that sorry outfit, Angus Mackland."

She shook her head and wiped her face on the bedcovers. "I can't go back home," she said between sobs. "I ain't got nowhere to go."

"Oh, how's that?" Caleb demanded, getting a little tired of her sniffling. "You can't tell me your folks won't take you back in."

She proceeded to tell him just that in no few words. She said her mother would not take her in because she was dead, her stepmother because she was mean, and her father because he was so addled he no longer knew her.

She was Tess Wiley of the Ozark Mountains. She had never spent a day at school and had worked at raising hogs and chickens since she was old enough to walk. At fourteen, her cousin had raped her. By eighteen she had been used and passed over by every eligible buck in the county. Used because her cousin had a loud mouth, and passed over, she said, because she could never have babies.

Caleb didn't understand how Tess knew she couldn't bear children, but he preferred not to ask about such delicate matters, taking her at her word.

At twenty-one, her stepmother had decided she ate more than she earned, so, stealing Tess's egg money, which she had saved over five years, she paid a stranger to marry her and take her to Texas. The stranger happened to be Angus Mackland, who had come to the Ozarks to sell stolen horses, claiming he was a prosperous Texas rancher.

Tess's older brothers and sisters had pitched in to buy the Cincinnati house. They felt honor bound to see that she had something more than a dirt roof over her head but were just as happy as their stepmother to see her out of the state, as Tess was considered the ruination of the family name due to her loose ways with young men. When they wired Cincinnati for the house—a three-room frame affair costing $350—they ordered it shipped over the shortest route to Texas, which had brought the house, Angus Mackland, and Tess to Denison.

For two weeks Angus had cussed her when sober, beaten her when drunk, and forced himself on her as often as he pleased. One night outside of Fort Smith, she took her dowry money from his pockets as he lay in camp sleeping off a drunk and turned back toward the Ozarks. He caught her the next morning, slapped her around until she hit the ground, and told her he would kill her the next time.

It was late in the day when Tess finished telling her life's story, and Caleb had escorted her to a café for a meal.

"I was thinkin' about killin' him," Tess whispered, her mouth full of mashed potatoes. "He's lucky you and that marshal run him into Indian Territory, or I would have sure done it."

Caleb sipped his coffee and watched her feed. "Well, you're free of him now. You're better off forgettin' you ever knew him. And for God's sake, don't ever call yourself by his name. Just make out like you were never married."

He had bought her a bath, a new dress, a comb, and a leather handbag to carry her things in. Now people in the café were looking at them as if they were a couple. Her hair, with the grease and dirt washed out, was lighter than he had suspected, almost golden. She was not hard to look at cleaned up, except for one bad tooth in the top row.

After supper he turned his room over to her and told her it was paid up for two more days. "You can keep the money," he added. "All I ask is enough to pay my livery bill and get train fare for me and my horse to San Antonio."

She dropped her eyes to the floor. "Angus only had about two hundred dollars left when he went gamblin'. I guess that's all I got comin'."

"I'd say you've got more than that comin'. Take the whole roll, and the house, too."

"No, you have the house. I ain't got nowhere to build it anyhow. Or nobody to build it for me."

"You could always sell it."

"Angus tried to sell it for two days. Nobody wants it. You can have it. Take as much money as you need to ship it anywhere you want."

Caleb snorted. "That's generous of you."

She pursed her lips and glared at him with her coal-black eyes. But she had broken down and cried in front of him, and she knew she had little power over him. Her eyes cut away from him and flitted across the room. "Did you win that in a poker game, too?" she asked, pointing at the guitar.

"No," he said, peeling a few bills from the roll and putting them into his pocket. "It's mine."

"I can sing," she said. "My singin' used to be the pride of the family when my mama was still alive."

"Then you ought to join the church choir."

She pointed at his left hand. "It's a wonder you can play with them two cut-off fingers."

Caleb shoved the hand in his pocket. "It's a wonder you can sing through that rotten tooth." He regretted saying it immediately.

Tess pressed her lips together and looked away.

"Oh, I didn't mean nothin'," he said. "Just don't start in cryin' again."

"I ain't," she said.

He gathered his things and went to the door. "And don't let on to nobody that you've got that money, or you'll get robbed."

She nodded.

"Well, good luck," he said, opening the door.

"Good-bye, Caleb."

As he walked down the hall, he wished she hadn't said his name. For some reason it made him feel as if he was the one turning his back on her instead of Angus Mackland or her stepmother or her brothers and sisters. She must have known that speaking his name would make him feel that way, he reasoned, and had done it on purpose.

"Is there a relief society in town?" he asked the hotel clerk.

"The Baptists have got one," the clerk said.

Caleb found the parsonage near the chapel and told the preacher there about Tess. "She's a good girl, but she's had a rough time," he said, as if he had known her for years. "She needs a start, that's all."

Having taken care of Tess the best way he knew how, he went to the depot and paid to have the Cincinnati house shipped to Buster Thompson at the Holcomb Station on the Denver and Rio Grande. He figured if Pete wouldn't let Captain Dubois build him and Amelia a house, he wouldn't take one from his no-'count brother either. Buster, on the other hand, would surely jump at the chance to get out of his little cabin with the burlap carpet. He sent a message with the bill of lading:

> Dear Buster,
>   Won it for you in a poker game in Texas. See you in spring.
>   Caleb

It was after dark when he and Powder River boarded a stock car for the trip to San Antonio. The gelding was fat and rested, and that gave Caleb a great deal of comfort. He would have to cover some ground fast to get from San Antonio to the Sacramento Mountains before winter set in.

SIXTY-THREE

MARISOL ALWAYS WAITED for Javier to pass by before she went into her adobe for siesta. She always brushed her hair as she waited—a task that could keep her busy for half an hour or more, as her hair grew thick and luxurious, hanging in shiny waves and coils to her waist.

She was sure that she was in love with Javier. It didn't matter that he was old enough to be her father. She had never known her own father and recognized no particular age beyond which a man became a generation too old for her. Any man with black hair and good teeth was worth consideration, though Marisol was very discriminating in regard to the men she wasted her flirtations on.

She had always been fascinated with boys older than she was, but ever since Javier came to Peñascosa, her interests had gravitated more toward grown men. She was thirteen then. Now she was seventeen, and she had moved out of her grandmother's house, into her own room in the adobe-walled fortress-village that was Peñascosa. The room had been left vacant by the death of an old man. It was located in a perfect place in the compound, between the corrals and the alcalde's house, where Javier walked every day on his way home to eat his midday meal and take his siesta. He could not fail to see her sitting in front of her room, brushing her hair.

Many young vaqueros passed by her room, too, whether it was on their way or not. Some stopped to flirt. She didn't pretend to resent their advances, for she relished their attention. But it was Javier she wanted more than any other. He looked good on a horse, he wore his sombrero well, he sang with the voice of a wolf, and he had the most remarkable crease in the middle of his chin. He rode as well as any vaquero and was above them all in terms of social standing, held in higher regard than any other man in Peñascosa.

There was only one problem. Javier liked his women older and plump. Marisol had eaten tortillas and honey until she thought she would burst, but her figure remained like that of a busy wasp. Javier liked bumblebees. When he passed by her room on his way to the alcalde's mansion, he would nod and occasionally say *"Buenos días,* Señorita Marisol,'' but never did he look at her with any evidence of desire in his eyes.

He fascinated her. He told stories of Mexico, Texas, Colorado. He had survived fights with bad men, killed an old white devil in a sawmill somewhere to the north, and skirmished often with Indians: Comanche, Apache, Cheyenne. He led war parties against the Mescalero when they came down from the Sacramento Mountains to steal cattle, and even commanded the respect of the Texans who wanted the ranges flanking the Rio Peñasco. He was top man, and she desired him more than anything in life. She would let nothing come between her desires and Javier, not even his fat wife, Sylvia.

Marisol pulled the shawl tighter around her shoulders as a cold wind whipped down the street. She drew her brush through the tresses running over her shoulder and in front of her waspish figure. Inside her room she had a fire crackling and, warming over some coals, a bowl of chicken mole, plus a stack of tortillas and a jar of honey. She wished Javier would hurry up and pass by so she could go inside, enjoy the hot meal, and take her siesta.

Finally, she heard his spurs jingling above the whisper of wind and the rush of the Rio Peñasco, which ran cold and clear through the compound. She tossed her hair over her shoulder, sat up straight on her stool, and pulled the corners of her shawl in front of her to hide the severe curves of her waist and hips.

In a moment Javier came strutting up the dirt lane, wearing a leather riding coat, pulling at the fingers of his deerskin gloves. He tucked the gloves under his belt and breathed into his cupped hands to warm his fingers. He saw Marisol holding strangely to the corners of her shawl and stopped in his tracks. It was not unusual to see her there. She was always there when he passed by. But today was the coldest day Peñascosa had felt since the girl moved into the room vacated by the old man, and Javier hadn't expected to see anyone sitting out in the wind.

"Buenos días, Señorita Marisol,'' he said.

Her eyes came alive with hope. *"Buenos días,* Alcalde Maldonado,'' she replied with playful formality.

He took a few steps toward her and smiled. ''Why are you sitting out here in the cold wind? Don't you know a skinny thing like you could catch a cold?''

She looked down and adjusted her shawl. "I was just brushing my hair," she said, pulling her tresses over her shoulder for Javier to admire.

"You can brush your hair inside your room, can't you?" he asked.

"Yes," she said. "But . . ."

Javier chuckled. "But what?"

She felt a tremor of nervousness flutter through her tiny stomach. Finally she had her chance to tell him. "If I brush my hair inside," she began, "I cannot see who passes by on the street. I might miss seeing someone who passes by on the street every day and . . ."

Javier was still standing there, but he wasn't listening. He had turned toward the sound of a galloping horse. As alcalde, he had made a rule against riding horses through the village compound. They only made dust and left dung. But someone was breaking his rules.

"Alcalde Maldonado!" a young man shouted as he rode to Javier. "A *Tejano* is coming up the river!"

"Just one?"

"Yes."

"How near is he?"

"About a mile away."

"What is he doing?"

"He is just riding up the river toward the village."

"Just one damned *Tejano* does not give you the liberty of galloping your horse up the street!" the alcalde shouted. "Look at the people coming out of their homes! Now you have frightened the devil out of them."

"I'm sorry," the young man said, removing his hat in a gesture of apology.

Javier regained his composure, shook his head, and smiled at the guard to make up for his outburst. "Don't apologize. You did your job well. Take that horse back to the corral. I am coming to see about this *Tejano*."

He followed the horseman, neglecting to excuse himself from the conversation he had started with the skinny señorita.

Marisol stomped her foot and tossed her hair back over her shoulder. It was just like a Texan to come around and ruin her finest chance of winning Javier's affection. She stalked into her room and slammed the pine door behind her.

Caleb reined in his gelding when he saw the guards posted behind the low wall running around the village. It was not the kind of place he had expected. He had envisioned Javier's ranch as a collection of ramshackle sheds, bunkhouses, and corrals. What he saw instead was an orderly and well-fortified village between sheltering foothills of the Sacramento Mountains. Plenty of grass grew in the valleys, and forests of straight pines spilled down from the mountains to the very outskirts of the village. The Rio Peñasco, though it was narrow enough for a horse to jump without wetting a hoof, brought a constant flow of fresh water down from the high country. Just outside of the adobe walls the villagers had channeled the river into irrigation ditches that ran through fields, orchards, and vineyards. Wood smoke streamed from the chimneys, and the brown adobe walls of the houses invited him to enter. He was hoping the guards would do likewise.

"Buenos días," he shouted, raising one open hand in the air. "Is this Javier Maldonado's rancho?"

The guard at the main gate of the corrals looked back for orders, then waved the stranger in. The guns of the guards followed Caleb all the way into the compound where he found Javier poised indifferently with a heel and an elbow resting on the rails of the corral. He got down from Powder River and took off his hat. "Howdy, Javier," he said. "Recognize me?"

The stern look melted from the alcalde's face as he glanced from the man to the speckled horse to the guitar sticking out of the saddle wallet. He took a step toward the stranger and squinted. "Wait a goddamn minute," he said. "Is that you, Caleb Holcomb?"

"It's me, all right."

Javier laughed as he shook Caleb's hand. *"Un abrazo!"* he said, squeezing the new arrival in a hug. "We thought you were a goddamn Texan. You're grown up as big as your father."

"Bigger. I've got both legs."

Javier laughed loudly and gave orders for the vaqueros to take care of Caleb's horse. "I almost didn't recognize you with that mustache."

"I just started lettin' it grow in San Antone," Caleb said, following Javier out of the corrals and into the village compound. "Saves me time shavin'."

"I know better," the alcalde said. "You are wearing that to tickle the señoritas." He laughed, wide-eyed, and slapped Caleb on the back. "How about some enchiladas and tamales?"

"Sounds good. I haven't et much since I left Fort Stockton a week ago."

As they walked briskly up the dirt lane, Javier asked about Ab, Pete, Buster, and the cowhands he had known at Holcomb Ranch. Doors opened as they passed, and curious faces peered out from the warm rooms.

"Me and the old man fell out after you left," Caleb was explaining. "I've gone back every spring, but I've been mostly driftin' since I left home. How come everybody's lookin' at us?"

Another door opened, and a beautiful, slender, ample-haired girl leaned out. Javier didn't notice, but Caleb did.

"They think you are a Texan. Some of those goddamn Texans have been trying to get this valley from us. Besides, my people want to know what is going on with their alcalde," he said, thumping himself on the chest.

"Their what?" Caleb was staring over his shoulder at the long-haired señorita.

"I am the alcalde here. The *jefe,* the mayor, the boss."

Caleb's view of the girl was broken as they rounded a corner. "You mean you're the hookin' bull of this whole town?" Their boots clogged over the planks of a footbridge crossing the river.

Javier nodded proudly.

"How many people live here?"

"You know, it is a funny thing. We have exactly one hundred. Old Garcia died a few months ago, but then José Hidalgo's wife had a baby and now we have one hundred again."

"I hope you won't mind me makin' it 101."

Javier stopped at the side door of the biggest house in the village, and the highest. It looked down on the town, the river, and the arid plains to the east. "Have you come to stay with us, then?"

"Lookin' for a place to winter. Got any work for a cowboy?"

"You are welcome to stay, of course. I cannot pay you anything, but you will have food to eat and a place to stay. Anyway, as I remember, you were better with guitar and fiddle than with horse and cattle."

"Well, things change, Javier. It'll take me a while to get you caught up."

The alcalde put his hand on the door latch. "We eat first," he said. "Then siesta. Then we play some songs and you can tell me about all the things that have changed with you. I have suffered some changes myself."

When Javier opened the door, Caleb beheld a rotund, rosy-cheeked woman carrying a baby boy under one arm and setting steaming platters of tamales, wrapped in corn shucks, on a table of hand-hewn pine planks. Without even looking up, she lit into her husband in Spanish, rattling off syllables with woodpecker rapidity.

"Sylvia . . ." Javier attempted as she continued to jabber. "Sylvia . . . " he tried again.

Caleb saw a tiny girl child pull herself up to table height in one of the chairs.

"Sylvia!" Javier shouted.

She turned, scowling. Then she saw Caleb, gasped, and put on the sweetest smile and the warmest disposition. "Oh, *buenos días,* " she said, hoisting the baby to her shoulder. "Hello, hello."

As Javier explained in Spanish, Caleb picked out the few words he knew: ". . . amigo . . . Colorado . . . Caleb Holcomb."

"Welcome, welcome," Sylvia said, pulling out a chair for Caleb. She turned her face to her husband and snarled a few words at him in Spanish. Then she smiled sweetly at Caleb again. "He is late," she explained. "The food is getting cold." She hurled a few more choice Spanish expletives at her husband for emphasis.

SIXTY-FOUR

CALEB MOVED INTO a room in the back of Javier's house with its own fireplace, a door to the outside, and a patio that stood on the edge of the pine forest growing above Peñascosa. Someone in the village brought an old violin, unused for years. Caleb strung it left-handed and began to relearn the art of fiddling.

One afternoon, after fiddle practice, he saw an old woman and some children trying to herd a pig back into its enclosure near the corrals. They were having little luck, so he gave them a hand. When the pig was back in, he saw Marisol coming with an armload of pine pickets to be used in mending the pen. He became suddenly expert at fixing pigpens and stayed to see that it was done properly.

"Javier told me you speak English pretty good," he said, sharpening a pine limb with a hatchet.

"Yes. I do speak some English. But not all of it."

"Maybe we should talk more often. I could teach you English, and you could teach me Spanish."

"Of course," she said. "¿Como no?"

"¿Como no?" he repeated.

"That means 'Why not?' "

"Como no," he said. They worked together in awkward silence for a minute. "Is this your pig?" he finally asked.

"No, it belongs to my grandmother. That old woman, there."

The old lady smiled toothlessly when he looked.

"Where's your folks?"

"Folks?"

"Yes, your mama and papa?"

"Oh," she said, driving a picket into the ground. "My mama is dead. And my papa . . ." She shrugged.

From that day on, Caleb met Marisol every afternoon so they could teach each other their native languages. He brought his guitar one day to have her translate a song Javier had taught him. When he found he remembered new words better if they came in the form of lyrics, he continued to bring the guitar. He embarrassed the daylights out of Marisol by making her sing to him in English. People would stop and stare at them in bewilderment as they repeated patches of songs to each other. But Marisol soon became accustomed to the method of learning, and even the people in the village accepted it after a couple of weeks. Her singing voice was timid but pretty.

Winter brought snow to the mountains and pushed the game closer to Peñascosa. When Caleb suggested a simple hunt one day, Javier delved into a week's worth of coordinating cooks, butchers, skinners, mule packers, wood choppers, camp rustlers, and guides. When the expedition finally got under way, it included twelve men, nine hounds, six pack mules, and four canvas wall tents complete with stoves, three guitars, a fiddle, and a case of tequila.

Their base camp was a mountain meadow a thousand feet higher than Peñascosa and ten miles away by trail. Smoke from the ever-burning tent stoves filtered up through the branches of towering ponderosa pines around the camp. After ten days the party had more meat than it could carry back to Peñascosa, so the hunt was judged a success and called to an end.

"You know, this would be a good place to build a huntin' cabin," Caleb said the last night of the hunt as the men passed a tequila bottle between songs.

"A warm one with a big rock fireplace," Javier added.

"There's plenty of straight trees to build with, and water runnin' at the bottom of the meadow. A cabin would sure beat these drafty tents."

"We will build it next November when you come to spend the winter with us again."

Thus it was suggested, with no argument from Caleb, that he might spend every winter in Peñascosa—hunting, singing, learning Spanish, and perhaps even working a few cows.

The hunting party returned in glory with sprawling antlers of elk and deer lashed to every mule and fine furs from two wolves, a bear, and a mountain lion in addition to the deerskins and elk hides. The entire village began to prepare for a wild-game feast to be held that evening.

The front half of Javier's adobe mansion consisted of a single large room that functioned as a public meeting place and dance hall called the *casa consistorial*. It had cavernous fireplaces at both ends and a hearth in the middle where red-hot rocks were piled for further warmth. The adobe walls stood all of ten feet high, and overhead, huge trunks of ponderosa pine, stripped of bark, spanned the breadth of the room. Lanterns hung around the inside walls on twisted wrought iron fixtures. The entrance to the public room was an archway closed by carved double doors.

The celebration didn't get under way in the *casa consistorial* until about ten o'clock that night. Then the big room became quickly crowded with people from great-grandfathers to babies. Children ran in packs like yelping coyotes. Dogs waited outside the double doors to catch the bones tossed out by the feasters. When they had washed down their sopapillas and honey with coffee, the musicians got the dance started.

Because its economy revolved around Javier's cattle herd, Peñascosa claimed a disproportionately large number of young vaqueros. Competition for available señoritas was intense. Few of the girls got to sit out even one dance. Marisol had a particularly long line of dancing partners to deal with.

Empty wine and tequila bottles began to pile up as the night wore on. The guitar players worked in relays, so the music never flagged. Caleb made a debut with his left-handed fiddle, playing an easy waltz with great success. He also made a profound impression on the crowd by singing, in near perfect Spanish, "Mujer sin Corazon."

When finally he saw Marisol sitting in a chair and refusing offers to dance, he put his guitar aside and filled two glasses with wine.

"*Hola,*" he said, taking a seat next to her and handing her the wineglass.

"Thank you," she answered, taking a little energy from his arrival.

"I wish I could ask you to dance," he said, "but I don't know how to dance to these Mexican songs."

"I can teach you how," she said.

"You can?"

"*¿Como no?* I can teach you right now."

"In front of all these people?" Caleb said. "I wouldn't know how to take the first step."

"You are not afraid, no?" She tilted her head and let a cascade of dark, rich hair tumble over her shoulder.

"Yes, I am afraid. I'm afraid of makin' a fool out of myself. How do say it? *Bufón?*"

Marisol laughed. "Yes, that is right. *Bufón.*"

Caleb was aware that every gossipy crone and every jealous vaquero in the room was staring at him.

"You need to take your dancing lessons *privadamente,*" she suggested.

"What's that mean? Privately?"

She nodded as she lifted the wineglass to her lips.

"You're right. Private dance lessons, that's what I need."

"Give me about five minutes to get away," she said. "Then come to my room. We can hear the music from there. I will teach you how to dance." She got up, leaving the wineglass on the table. "Don't let anybody see you come in. The old women will gossip." She left without waiting for his response.

He wandered casually back toward the musicians, forcing himself to ignore Marisol. After a couple of minutes, he picked up his fiddle and strolled into Javier's kitchen. He felt his way through the dark house to his room, left the fiddle there, and went out through the door to his patio. Sneaking along the side of the house, he hid behind a woodpile and waited until the way was clear between Javier's house and the rest of the village. Then he rushed to the footbridge and crossed the river.

Walking with the closest thing he could manage to an ordinary gait, he swung down the lane toward Marisol's door. When he saw the firelight leaking out around the portal, he glanced over his shoulder and, seeing no one behind him, leapt at the door and knocked on it. It swung open immediately, and his dance instructor pulled him in.

"Did anyone see you?"

"No. Everybody's at the *baile*."

The only light in the room came from the bell-shaped fireplace that bulged from one corner. Marisol's straw-filled mattress was rolled, tied, and placed against the wall to make room for dancing.

"Stand over here out of the way and I will show you some steps," she said. "They are playing the music for the bolero. Watch."

As the musicians played, barely audible away up the hill, Marisol whirled and stamped her feet on the tiled floor, sweeping her hands over her head, striking sudden poses. Her hair enveloped her face when she spun, raked the whitewashed walls with shadows, and even brushed her student as he stood watching.

"There," she said. "Can you make those moves?"

Caleb took a step toward her. "I don't think so," he said. "Let's start with somethin' a little easier. *Más fácil.*"

"Something like what?"

"Come here and I'll show you." He put his right arm around her waist and took her hand in his. "We'll have to be real quiet to hear the music."

"I am not the one talking," she said.

They stood together for a moment, trying to hear the distant guitars above the crackling of the fire. He saw the reflections of the flames in her eyes. His heart was pounding in his ears. He couldn't hear a thing. The musicians had stopped playing. He pulled Marisol closer to him; closer, until she was looking almost straight up at him. He faintly heard the band strike up a waltz.

Instead of dancing, he kissed her. She didn't resist. In fact, she pressed herself against him. Then, after a few seconds, she pushed away.

"You did not really want to learn how to dance, did you?" she whispered.

"No. I'm hopeless at dancin'. I never was any good at it."

"Then why did you come to my room?"

Caleb stammered. He could never tell what women wanted to hear. "Because I . . . Well, I . . . I want to get to know you better." He felt her hand move on his shoulder and showed a sudden surge of foolish courage. "I mean, a *lot* better."

She slipped from his grasp and backed away. He glanced at the door latch to see how it worked, in case she had it in mind to hit him with a water bucket or a fireplace poker or something. But Marisol had no intention of driving him away. She knew what he wanted, and she knew she would not deny him. She had made her decision well ahead of time. She liked the way he sang. He said nice things to her. She had known all along that this time would come, and she was ready.

She knelt and began untying the strings around her mattress. She let the soft cushion unroll itself across the cool tiles.

III
SORROW & BEAUTY

1882

SIXTY-FIVE

THE FLURRY OF white on Powder River's hips and flanks had become a blizzard by the time he reached his ninth year. The markings that had once merely dusted his coat now formed solid white spots with roan edges. From the shoulders back he looked as if giant snowflakes had splattered on his hide. Caleb could have been no prouder of the spots had he grown them himself.

"Where did you get that horse?" asked the manager of the Double Aught Ranch, in the Davis Mountains of Texas.

"He's a Nez Perce horse. They come from up in the Idaho Territory. My brother raises 'em on our ranch in Colorado."

"I've seen a couple of other horses with spots like that. I was told they were called Appaloosas."

"Same thing," Caleb said. "They come from the Palouse River country. I reckon that's where the name Appaloosa comes from. Did you ever hear of a crazy mountain man name of Cheyenne Dutch?"

The ranch manager bit a corner from a plug of tobacco and mulled the matter over as he moistened his cud. "I've heard some tall tales about him," he finally admitted.

"Well, we got our brood stock from him. The Nez Perce had told him those spots were magic, and he took 'em at their word. He used to get crazy spells where he'd think he was an Indian god called Palousey. He had spots tattooed on his butt."

The rancher chortled and spit. "Now there you go branchin' out again."

"No, that's the truth," Caleb insisted, but he didn't have time to do much convincing. The sun was getting high, and he had a lot of ground to cover.

"Where you headed?" the ranch manager asked as the musician mounted the spotted horse.

"Got me a Mexican woman in the Sacramento Mountains."

"That's a ways from here. You got grub to get you there?"

Caleb knocked on the fiddle in his saddle wallet. "Here's my supper. I'll call on the boys at the Two Bar tonight and trade 'em a few songs for some grub."

"Well, you didn't have to up and leave all at once, you know. You've only been here two days."

"I know when my welcome's worn out. Your cook don't like me laying around in his trail all day long."

"Yeah, he's an ornery cuss, but he makes a fine apple pie."

Caleb reined Powder River north. "Then you're better off losin' me than him. You can't eat fiddle music."

The ranch manager laughed, spit, and waved until Caleb rode over the ridge.

He hadn't been gone two hours when he came upon a fence. It was getting difficult to ride anywhere in Texas without having to let down a barbwire fence every couple of days. The stuff was twining its way all over the plains. He wondered if the day would come when a man couldn't ride horseback from one ranch to the next. He had to let every strand but the bottom one down to get his gelding across. Being raised as a plains cow pony, Powder River had never been much of a hand for jumping.

At least the railroads hadn't spread as much here as they had in other places. There was just one railroad between the Davis Mountains and the Sacramentos. The lack of rails was one thing Caleb liked about his annual autumn trip to Peñascosa. New Mexico was still wide open. Colorado, on the other hand, was becoming veined with rails as if caught in some gigantic spiderweb.

In his wanderings he still found vistas devoid of fences, railroads, and windmills, but they were getting scarce. At only twenty-eight, Caleb was getting nostalgic, pining for the days before the Indians were whipped and restricted to reservations, before the buffalo were slaughtered to make way for cattle, before the steam whistles rent the quiet air of the prairies.

On the other hand, progress had served his brother well. Pete had made his fortune selling cattle to railroad crews. Windmills had gotten Holcomb Ranch through the drought. Barbed wire had enabled Pete to fence out the cattle of neighboring ranches so he could control grazing in Monument Park and improve his herd with blooded bulls. He had made enough money to build Amelia her stone house. They had been married seven months now. They had held the wedding in the spring, so Caleb could be there.

He wondered if Pete would be a father when he returned next spring. He looked forward to having nieces and nephews, but a persistent dread nagged him when he thought of becoming an uncle. What if Pete turned out to be a better father than he had been? He was, in fact, almost sure that Pete would beat him in that respect. Fatherhood had taken Caleb by surprise.

He had met his son, Angelo, when he returned for his second winter in Peñascosa. Since then, Marisol had turned them out like clockwork, one every other year, so that Caleb was now a father three times over. He adored his children, but he was only with them three or four months out of twelve.

He had told Marisol from the first that he would have to return to Monument Park every spring to see his brother. And he had promised her that if he ever smoothed things over with his father, he would make an honest woman of her and take her back with him to Colorado to live year-round. He meant it, too. Sometimes he even looked forward to it happening. Other times he was sure it never would.

During the rest of the year he drifted, found work, sent money to Marisol. Javier was glad to have him in Peñascosa for the winter but could not offer him wages without taking money from some other hand who stayed to work all year.

Caleb was convinced that he was doing all he could do for Marisol and his children. He had no place else to take them. He did well enough at fatherhood one season out of the year. Maybe not as well as Pete would, but better than his own father had done with him. Of that he was confident.

By midday he had almost contemplated himself into a headache, so he shook his head as if to cast off his worries and sang some verses he had been working on for several months:

The drifter was faithful, returned every year.
His brother was eager his stories to hear,
And he'd watch o'er the hilltop when wildflowers bloomed . . .

(He was having a devil of a time trying to find an appropriate word that would rhyme with *bloomed*.)

At nights, by the fireplace, he'd listen to tales
Of wild West adventures and hard-ridden trails,
Of mountains so high that the trees didn't grow,
Of deserts so wide and of canyons so low.

The drifter pulled a mandolin from his saddle wallet and accompanied himself as he rode alone through the desolate mountains of the Davis Range. The spotted gelding seemed to quicken his pace to match the rhythm.

SIXTY-SIX

HE ALWAYS FOUND Peñascosa the same. Still a hundred souls, give or take a few. Still all Mexican, except during the winter when the lone Anglo came to live with Marisol. Still quiet at siesta, riotous with music at night, and nestled between the hills, out of the coldest winter winds.

He arrived at twilight, left Powder River in the corrals, and walked up the lane to Marisol's home. She had moved to a two-room house, just across the Rio Peñasco from the alcalde's mansion. When he opened the door, he smelled beans frying.

"Where's the little mama?" he shouted.

A crawling baby girl looked up from a rug on the floor. A three-year-old peeked around the kitchen doorway. Then Marisol appeared and ran nimbly to the front door to kiss Caleb.

"Where have you been?" she asked. "It's almost December."

"Oh, I wound up in Houston and figured, since I was so close, I ought to go and see the ocean."

"Would you rather go look at the ocean than come here to look at me?"

"Of course not," Caleb said, hanging his hat on a peg. "But I thought I'd go get a look at it so I could tell the children about it. Now turn around and let me look at you."

She whirled as if dancing the bolero.

"You cut your hair!"

"Just that much," she said, measuring a few inches between her thumb and forefinger.

"Well, it shows."

"I have to cut it sometime," she argued. "You don't want it looking like the tail of a wild mustang."

He grabbed her and pulled her against him. "I don't know why not. I've tamed wilder fillies than you."

"Stop that!" She wrestled out of his grasp. "The children are watching."

"Is this little Elena?" He picked the baby up from the rug. She looked at him, bewildered, reached for her mother, and began to cry. Caleb gave her to Marisol. "And that must be Marta," he said, smiling at the little girl

in the kitchen doorway. "Come here, Marta." He knelt and opened his arms to her.

Marta glanced at her mother, looked back at the strange man.

"She doesn't remember you," Marisol said.

"She does so." Caleb took a stick of hard candy out of his shirt pocket. "Look what I brought you from Galveston," he said, bribing the little girl with the candy. "A peppermint stick."

Marta took a few careful steps and, seeing her mother smiling, ran to get the candy. Caleb wrapped her in his arms and kissed her cheek, scratching her tender skin with his mustache.

"Don't eat it all before supper," Marisol warned.

"Where's Angelo?"

"I don't know," Marisol said, trudging back to the kitchen with Elena in her arms.

"What do you mean, you don't know?"

"I mean, I don't know. I told him to come home before dark, but he never listens to what I tell him anymore. You better get a switch and teach him a lesson. He's making me go crazy."

"Well, it's not very dark yet," Caleb said.

"It's dark!"

"Well, honey, I can't give the boy a whippin' on my first day back."

The front door burst open and little boots clopped against the tile floor. Angelo slid into the kitchen, looking worried, until he spotted the man with the mustache. "Papa?" he said.

"You're dang right, it's your papa." He crouched and braced himself.

"Angelo, go close the door!" Marisol said.

The boy ignored his mother, jumped into Caleb's arms, gritted his teeth, and squeezed his father's neck as hard as he could in a brutal hug, his eyes popping with intensity.

"Oh, ouch, stop it!" Caleb said in mock agony, collapsing to the floor and rolling with the little boy.

Marta giggled and leaped onto the pile.

"Angelo! I said go close the door."

"Oh, let us rassle some, honey," Caleb said.

Marisol sighed indignantly and stepped over the mass of bodies on the floor to close the door herself. "Ask him why he didn't come home at dark like I told him to," she said when she came back into the kitchen.

"What's that, honey?" Caleb asked, hugging the squirming children.

"Ask him why he didn't come home on time!" she shouted.

"Oh, yeah. Hold on, you little lizards!" He stood the boy on his feet and looked him sternly in the eyes. "Angelo, your mama is a little riled at you."

"Not just a little!" she said. "I am mad enough to pinch his head off!"

"You hear that?" Caleb said, faking a fearful grimace.

Angelo laughed.

"Now listen here. You knew you were supposed to be back here at dark, didn't you?"

Angelo nodded. "But, I was playing . . ."

"Now no *buts* about it," his father warned. "If you want me to get you a little horse to ride, you're gonna have to do what your mother says."

"A horse!" Angelo cried. "Mama, I'm going to get a horse!"

Marisol lolled her head back and looked with disgust at the ceiling.

"Only if you mind your mama," Caleb warned. "Now do you promise not to come in late anymore?"

Angelo nodded energetically.

"Good," Caleb said.

The boy jumped on him again, pulling him to the ground, and began riding him like a horse, saying, *"Arre, arre!"*

Caleb squealed and bucked like a wild bronco as Marta climbed on behind her brother. Angry as she was, Marisol couldn't help smiling at them. The baby was jumping in her arms, excited by the laughter of her older siblings.

After they ate supper, the children went into the front room to eat their candy. Caleb tilted a pine-and-rawhide chair against the adobe wall and watched Marisol clean up the kitchen. When she had finished, he grabbed her, pulled her onto his lap, and kissed her. He pressed a roll of cash into her hands. Her eyes bulged as she peeled off the bills for counting.

"Now you squirrel some of that away," he ordered. "Don't blow it all on fiesta stuff like you usually do. Use some to buy Angelo a horse, and get the girls some new dresses or something."

"Angelo doesn't need a horse," she said. "There is nobody around to teach him to ride when the weather is warm enough."

"Javier will teach him. I promised the boy a horse—now don't make a liar out of me."

"It's better to have a fiesta for the whole village," she said. "Angelo would like that as much as a horse."

"Don't argue with me, just get the boy a horse. I'll teach him some ridin' before I go up to the huntin' cabin."

She tore his arms away from her and jumped off of his lap. "You're not going to that cabin again!"

"Well, honey, why do you think me and Javier built the dang cabin in the first place? If you want to blow that wad of cash on a fiesta, we'd better go kill some meat."

"You have only been here an hour and already you are talking about going away to the mountains with Javier!"

Caleb got up and tried to embrace her, but she avoided him. "I must have told you a hundred times," he said, "that if you want to be with me so bad, you can come with us."

She put her hands on her hips. "I don't want to go with a bunch of stinking *borrachos* and sit around a dirty cabin and sing songs and tell nasty stories!"

"Oh, it ain't that bad. Besides, you know it'll take Javier two weeks to get the hunt organized. That's two weeks for just you and me." He trapped her in a corner. He was the only man he knew of who could still chase his woman around after six years. It made sense to stay gone three out of four seasons, he thought. It made them yearn for each other when they came together.

Marisol was wishing Caleb would settle down and live like Javier, who came home to his wife every night. If they lived together all the time, maybe he would learn to behave himself in his own house.

"Why don't you take the children over to your grandma's house," Caleb suggested. "I'll drop in on Javier and let him know I'm back." He raked her neck with his mustache.

She moaned, half in protest, half in surrender. "I'll take the children," she said. "Just let me out of this corner."

She carried Elena and herded Marta and Angelo down the lane to her grandmother's house. The old lady was not overjoyed to see her great-grandchildren arrive at such an hour, but she dutifully took them in.

Marisol stopped at her house to brush her hair a hundred strokes. There was no hurry. Caleb would stay awhile with Javier. She only hoped they didn't pick up their infernal guitars. She freshened up, put on a clean dress, and stepped out into the cool November night. Crossing the footbridge, she saw lights on in the *casa consistorial.*

When she cracked the doors, a group of young men burst into laughter. Javier had a guitar on his thigh and was smiling at Caleb, with one hand stroking the handsome crease in his chin. Caleb had a fiddle, but they were between songs.

". . . And after that," Caleb said, "I headed west of San Antonio and fell in with a fellow named Halsey who was a tax assessor. He went around tellin' people how much their land and stuff was worth so he could tax 'em for it. Well, we came on an old Mexican on the Devil's River, and he had him a house made out of crossties. Halsey looked it over and says, 'Francisco, I'm gonna assess this place of yours at three thousand dollars.' Well, Francisco like to have throwed a fit and says, 'This house is not worth that much!' But Halsey says, 'Damned if it ain't, Francisco. You've got about a thousand crossties in this place, and they sell for three dollars apiece, conservative!' And Francisco says, 'God damnit, Halsey, you know I didn't pay no three dollars apiece for them crossties. You know I stole every damn one of them from the Texas Pacific Railroad!' "

The listeners roared with laughter. Sylvia shrieked and wrapped her arms around Javier's neck.

As she watched through the crack between the double doors, Marisol had to smile. Caleb told a fine story and loved a crowd around him. Sadly, she closed the laughter inside, turned away, and went home to wait.

SIXTY-SEVEN

BUSTER ROSE IN the dark of early morning. He needed no more than five hours of sleep a night and always got up well before sunrise. Gently, he lifted Gloria's arm and slipped out from under it. He slithered out of the bed as if he might wake her, but he knew better. In their one month of marriage, he had learned that nothing short of artillery fire could rouse her before eight o'clock in the morning.

He shivered as he stood in his long underwear at the window of the Cincinnati house. For a ready-made structure that had been won in a poker game, the little frame home was built amazingly well, but was hard to keep warm. It had no fireplace, just a single woodstove in the lean-to kitchen that jutted out from the back. A bedroom and a parlor completed the floor plan. It was a nice little honeymoon shack, but Buster knew he would have to add on soon. He intended to raise a family.

Through the bedroom window, he looked out on his grove of young pines, bathed in the light of a full moon hanging over the Rampart Range. He turned to look at Gloria's face, benign and restful on her pillow. It amused him to think of how different she had looked the first day he saw her.

Amelia had brought Gloria to the ranch after her honeymoon with Pete in Denver. There was no way Amelia, by herself, could have kept a house as big as the one Pete had built for her, so she had employed Gloria as a cook and housekeeper. The day Pete and Amelia returned from their honeymoon, Buster drove to the station to pick them up in Amelia's surrey, a wedding gift from Captain Dubois.

When Gloria appeared and started putting luggage in the surrey, Buster stared as if he had never seen a black woman in his entire life. In fact, he had seen pitifully few women of his own race since coming to Colorado, and of the few he had seen, Gloria fetched his attention quicker than any. She was ten years younger than he was, comely, and buxom. He simply sat in the driver's seat and ogled her as she loaded the baggage.

"What're you lookin' at?" Gloria said, scowling under the brim of a floppy straw hat.

"Didn't mean to stare," Buster said, tipping his hat.

"Get down off that seat and help me get Miss Amelia's bags in there."
Buster almost followed her orders but caught himself. "That's your
job. I don't work for Miss Amelia. I'm just being neighborly." He met her
glare with a smile.

After Gloria got over her first meeting with Buster, and found out that
he was as well-off as any homesteader in the county, she stopped ignoring
his attempts to call on her. Then, in a matter of weeks, she agreed to marry
him.

For the first time since coming west, Buster felt civilized. He had a
farm, a house, a wife, good neighbors, and respect—even among white
people. The country had never looked better to him than it did in the morning moonlight. He could gaze from the window of his Cincinnati house,
look through the pine trees he and Pete and Caleb had planted seven years
before, and see his old cabin near the irrigation ditches. It was still one of
his favorite places, and he used it as a private retreat, storing his wildflower seeds and other specimens there and designing new implements he
could build to use on his farm.

Turning his eyes from his old burlap-carpeted cabin, he looked upstream, across the barn and bunkhouse, past the old Holcomb cabin, toward Pete's two-story stone mansion above the irrigation reservoir.
Amelia fed pet ducks and swans there and planned to landscape the creek
bank all the way from the pond to the mansion. Upper branches of cottonwoods that Pete had planted around the site years before the home was
built were approaching the second-story windows in height.

The house had cylindrical towers at all four corners. Many Colorado
Springs residents had criticized Pete for attempting to upstage General
Palmer's mansion, Glen Eyrie, built along the order of a castle near the
Garden of the Gods. Pete and Amelia mused secretly. Only they knew that
the ancient cliff dwellings above Manitou held the true inspiration for
their home.

Just when he got ready to turn from the window and start a fire in the
stove, Buster saw a light come up in the kitchen of Pete's house. Rarely
did any of his neighbors rise as early as he did. He was intrigued but deter-
mined not to let his curiosity turn into nosiness. He pulled the curtains
together and went to start the fire, taking his clothes and boots with him so
he could dress by the warmth of the stove.

With his overalls and flannel shirt buttoned, and the stove lids warming, he could not resist taking another look at Pete's mansion through the
kitchen window. Just as he peeked through the curtains, Pete's door
cracked open and Pete came out, carrying a lantern, and walking quickly
toward the barn. Buster was overcome with curiosity. He grabbed his
scarf, a felt hat, and a sheepskin coat and went to see what Pete could
possibly be up to so early on such a winter morning.

The clean freshness of the cold air filled him with vigor, and he covered the frosty ground in long strides, the dead and frozen stalks of grass crunching under his heels. A half-Durham, half-longhorn heifer saw him from the middle of the barbwire pasture and let out a plaintive moan, begging for hay. He glanced back and saw her breath rising against the dark sky, a gray cloud in the moonlight.

Leaving the pines behind him, he marched toward the barn, where he could see Pete's lantern shining between the planks. Ab's house was silent and dark in the distance, the nearby bunkhouse merely dark: He could hear the snores of the cowboys rasping through the board-and-batten walls.

He looked in through the large doorway of the barn where, years before, Allegheny had hung in a sling, convalescing. He saw Pete throwing his saddle over a high-strung three-year-old stallion called Whiplash, a classic Nez Perce pony, black with a white "blanket" on his rump and black spots on the blanket.

"Where are you goin'?" Buster asked.

Pete almost jumped over the horse, and the horse almost pulled the barn down by the bridle reins, which were looped around a post. "Dang, Buster! You know better than to sneak up on a man in the dark like that!" Pete said, calming the stallion.

Buster laughed. "You're the one sneakin' around. What're you doin' up so early?"

"I'm tryin' to get up in the mountains before the boys get out of bed and see where I'm goin'." He pulled the fork of the saddle back onto Whiplash's withers.

"You must be goin' after that buck," Buster said.

Pete's buck had been the source of rampant speculation among the cowhands since spring. In May he had found a shed antler somewhere up in the Rampart Range—the right-hand antler from a huge black-tailed buck. It was no typical antler. It didn't follow the orderly lines of most deer horns. Instead of branching cleanly into a few slender, graceful tines, it bristled with at least a dozen points—heavy, gnarled appendages protruding at random angles.

Sam Dugan had accidentally given name to the originator of the antler. He had burned cedar brakes in Texas and, later, pulled the charred stumps out by the roots. He said the antler Pete had found reminded him of a twisted mass of cedar root. Thus, the buck who had shed the antler became known as Ol' Cedar Root.

There was much argument as to whether the single antler sported twelve, thirteen, or fourteen points. Piggin' String McCoy insisted that a point was anything a watch could be hung on by its chain, and he found ways to hang his watch from fourteen points. Dan Brooks insisted that a point had to measure one inch from its base to its apex. He could only find twelve tines that met up to his measurements. Every man agreed, however, that Ol' Cedar Root would be the kill of a lifetime for any hunter.

Pete refused to say where he had found the antler. He didn't want any of the boys beating him to the trophy or spooking the buck out of its home range. One night in September, however, he let it slip that he had actually seen Cedar Root on the hoof, from only a couple of hundred yards away, sporting his new set of hardened antlers.

"What's the left-hand horn look like?" Sam Dugan asked anxiously.

"I just got a glimpse of him," Pete replied. "I couldn't tell exactly what he looked like. But I'd say String could hang as many watches on that left horn as he could on the right one."

All through the summer and fall the cowhands had pestered Pete for some clue as to where the big buck hid out, but he wouldn't give up so much as a hint. Now that the high-country snows had claimed much of the old monarch's range, and restricted him to his lower haunts, Pete knew it was time to hunt him down.

"Yep, I've got his range figured," he said to Buster as he tied a thick roll of blankets and canvas behind the cantle. "He doesn't move far south in the winter—he just comes down low. I think I know just where I'll find him." He chuckled as he stuffed his saddlebags with biscuits and bacon.

"What's so funny?" Buster asked.

"Oh, I was just thinkin' about Sam. You remember in August, when me and him went up into the mountains to hunt that Hereford bull that got through the fence? Well, we found the bull in a canyon and was drivin' him back home when that big buck ran across the bottom of the canyon not two hundred yards in front of us, and Sam never saw him. He was rollin' a smoke. My eyes dang near bugged out of my head, but I didn't say anything to Sam."

"Is that where you're headin' to find him today?"

"Yes, but don't let on to the boys, or they'll come along and spoil my hunt."

"I won't tell 'em," Buster said. "How long you gonna stay out after him?"

Pete slipped his Winchester model 1876 into his saddle scabbard. It chambered a .45-caliber cartridge with a 350-grain bullet. It was a lot of gun for a deer, but Ol' Cedar Root was a lot of deer, and Pete anticipated having to shoot at some distance. Buster had helped him attach an extra rear sight on the wooden stock behind the hammer—an adjustable sliding leaf sight for long-range shooting. He had been practicing for months and could hit a pie plate eight out of ten times at four hundred yards with a firm rest.

"I've got bacon to last four days," he said. "I'll be back Saturday night unless I get him before then. I have to give my scripture lesson to the boys on Sunday morning. That reminds me," he said, pulling on his gloves, "can you play 'Rounded Up in Glory' on the fiddle or the guitar or somethin'?"

"Sure," Buster said. "What's the scripture lesson gonna be about?"

"Thou shalt not covet anything that is your neighbor's," Pete said. "I figure the boys will need remindin' of that when I bring in Ol' Cedar Root." He grinned and led his stallion to the doorway of the barn. "Amelia's a little rankled at me for goin' huntin' when her mare's about to foal. I told her you and the boys would be around if the old girl needed any help."

"How close is she?" Buster asked.

"She's got milk drippin' from her bag."

"Could be any time, then. Don't worry about her. I'll look after her."

"Thanks, Buster." He pulled himself up into the saddle seat and held a tight rein. Whiplash wanted to run. "I better get goin' before the boys wake up and see me. Put that lantern out for me, will you?"

"Sure. Good luck."

Somewhere out on the prairie a pack of coyotes greeted the new day with a weird vocal fanfare that sounded like the echoes of ancient war cries. Pete pulled his scarf up under his chin and held the stallion to a walk until his hoofbeats were beyond earshot of the bunkhouse. Then he let Whiplash trot across Monument Creek, lope up the bald hill, and gallop down the other side, taking the old Arapaho Trail into the Rampart Range.

SIXTY-EIGHT

By NOON, DARK roiling clouds were catching on the mountaintops. Pete looked up at them with gratitude. He knew he was in for miserable weather, but there was nothing like a norther to get the deer moving. Animals could sense coming changes in the weather—even domesticated animals. Whiplash knew the norther was coming. He tossed his head and flared his nostrils, hoping to get a whiff of crisp arctic air.

Pete stopped a moment to figure his strategy. Ol' Cedar Root's canyon was just over the next ridge. With rough weather coming, the buck would almost surely be there already, seeking shelter. The trail Pete was riding would bring him to the south rim, which, like the north rim, dropped at sheer angles to the canyon floor. There were only a few trails where a horse could get down into the canyon. A mountain deer, on the other hand, could come or go by any one of a hundred routes.

Pete decided that, once he reached the south rim, he would turn east, toward the mouth of the canyon, and ride along the rim until he found a trail to the bottom. He would set up a camp at the mouth of the canyon and spend the next few days hunting for the buck of a lifetime. If he succeeded in killing Ol' Cedar Root, not even Caleb would be able to match the story.

When he reached the south rim, blue clouds were boiling down the mountainsides, shooting blasts of frigid air into the canyon and up the sheer face of the south wall, whipping sleet and snowflakes over the brink. He paused to survey what he could see of the canyon. It wound a good three miles from its mouth to its head, flanked by cliffs along its entire length. The north rim was visible through the frozen mist, five hundred yards away. It would take days of hunting to sneak up on the wily old buck in there. A silent bolt of lightning struck a distant mountainside.

He turned eastward along the south rim of the canyon and looked into it as he rode, searching for a trail that would take him safely down. Only a few wind-whipped piñon pines clung to the rim of the canyon, but dense stands of white firs, quaking aspens, and ponderosa pines mottled the canyon floor. The buck wouldn't be as easy to find among them as the Hereford bull had been in August. It would take plenty of luck to hang those freak antlers on the parlor wall.

Whiplash tossed his head incessantly. Pete jerked the reins to settle him down, but the blue norther and the distant rumble of thunder were making him nervous. As he approached a lone pine on the trail ahead, a sudden gust shot up the cliff face and caused the little tree to flail its limbs violently. The stallion spooked and jumped sideways toward the escarpment. Pete got him settled down before he could slip, but he came so close to the edge that rocks clattered over the canyon rim and fell among the crags below.

"Whoa, boy." He stroked his shivering mount on the neck.

The stones seemed to echo forever, until Pete realized they had rattled too long. Looking over the precipice, he saw a deer bounding across the canyon floor toward the north rim, its hooves mocking the sounds of the falling rocks. He only caught a glimpse before it disappeared into the trees, but only one buck could carry such a rack. He saw it again, briefly, bolting headlong among the leafless aspens. The sprawling antlers hooked bare white branches, wrenching Ol' Cedar Root's head from side to side as he fled.

The buck vanished in the pines, but the rattle of hooves continued up the far wall of the canyon. A flash of lightning struck the nearest mountain slope, and the huge old deer vaulted into view again, above the trees. He was going to quit the canyon! He made tremendous leaps up the steep face of the bluff, five hundred yards away. Sleet pitted against Pete's hat brim as the thunder reached him.

There was no time. Once over the rim and into the cover of stunted evergreens, the buck would never show himself again. Pete pulled the Winchester from its scabbard. An impossible shot! Running? Five hundred yards? He flipped up the rear sight and adjusted it for the yardage. No time to dismount. The buck devoured the cliff face in heroic leaps. Some hunt! Some strategy! He levered a live round into the chamber and felt Whiplash trembling with excitement.

He shouldered the rifle. There was not enough time! He couldn't steady the sights on the leaping animal; the bead covered the entire buck. In the distance, through the frozen drizzle, the antlers waved strangely on the monarch's head. They were colossal, unreal. They rose like the wings of a soaring bird, to the very brink of the north rim. Another leap would win the buck his safety.

There was only one chance. Pete sucked in a chest full of cold air and forced a piercing whistle between his teeth. Whiplash flinched. Ol' Cedar Root, one leap from cover, stopped on the brink of the north rim, standing broadside, looking south.

The hunter held his sights above the target and curled his trigger finger. A deafening blast split the mountain air and flared with volcanic caliber. The stallion ramped and bucked. Pete let the rifle slip from his hands as he groped for the saddle horn. He flew, empty-handed, fire and ice below him.

Above: a glorious vision!

SIXTY-NINE

NOTHING WAS WHITER than new snow under lantern light. Surrounded by the darkness of a cloudy night, the powder flew from Buster's toes like showers of white-hot coals as he slogged through it to the barn. He had left Amelia's mare standing at midnight and didn't expect to find a newborn foal in the stall this morning.

Why did mares nearly always foal in hours of darkness? He didn't think they had the reasoning power to do it on purpose. It was probably instinctive. Probably had something to do with some signal relayed through the eye. When darkness came, the signal relaxed and told the dull brain of the mare that time for dropping the foal had come. That was Buster's theory. Maybe someday he would blindfold a mare in foal to see if she would drop in daylight.

As the lantern light filled the barn, Buster stopped short. Whiplash was standing against the door to his stall, as if trying to get in.

"Pete?" he said. He hung the lantern and looked in on Amelia's mare, still standing. No foal yet. "Pete?" he called again. There was no answer. He spoke to the stallion and looked him over quickly. He was wet but seemed sound. The saddle was cinched tight, the rifle missing from its scabbard, the bedroll tied in place. He searched the saddlebags. Bacon and biscuits all there. Pete was in trouble—cold and hungry. Buster prayed he was well.

* * *

Lee Fong came when Buster pounded on the cabin door.

"Get the colonel up," Buster said.

"I am up. What's wrong?" Ab hollered from his bedroom.

Horace Gribble had ridden down with the norther the day before to trade horses. He looked out of the other bedroom in his underwear.

Buster told Ab and Horace about Pete's horse coming back without him. "Sam knows where the canyon is. He and Pete found that Hereford bull there in August."

"Thank the Lord for that," Ab said, strapping on his wooden leg. "You better go tell Amelia. And rouse the boys out of the bunkhouse. Send Sam. Lee Fong! Breakfast for everybody. We'll ride as soon as we can see the ground."

"I'm coming!" Amelia shouted as she ran down the stairs with a lamp. "Is she all right?" she asked, opening the door.

"It ain't the mare, Miss Amelia. It's Pete. His horse came back without him, and we have to go find him."

As Buster explained, she thought about Caleb's old tale of No Man's Land and the frozen fingers. "Are you going, too?"

"Yes, ma'am."

"What can I do?" She couldn't stand the thought of waiting, idle and alone, while the men searched for her husband.

"Stay here and look after your mare. Gloria will help you if the foal comes." Buster turned and trotted toward the bunkhouse.

The boys sprang like trail hands after a stampede when Buster woke them with the news. They threatened to bring the bunkhouse down in their tumultuous attempts to dress themselves. They stomped their feet into their boots and walked briskly to Ab's cabin, pulling on their coats as they went.

"Sure, I can find it," Sam said, his mouth full of bacon and eggs. "It's a narrow canyon, out of the weather. Pete will be fine there. He carries his matches in his pocket. He must have got off that damn stallion with his rifle, and the horse run off." He slurped his coffee and shook his head. "I just can't believe Ol' Cedar Root ran right in front of me and Pete didn't tell me."

The men drained a pot of coffee and went to choose their mounts. Buster saddled his two best mules, one for himself and one for Pete. The cowboys made fun of his mules, but he knew they had good feet for the mountains. Horace borrowed one of Ab's spotted horses. He had ridden down on a gelding of Kentucky blood whose long legs were more suited to plains than mountains.

"You takin' *him?*" Buster said when he saw Ab saddling Pard.

"Why not?"

"Colonel Ab, that horse is near 'bout twenty years old."

"It's just a half day's ride. Pard will come in ahead of your mules."

Dawn came late through the cloud cover, and the rescue party left at a trot for Ol' Cedar Root's canyon.

The sky had cleared by noon, and the day became crisp and breezy in the high country. Periodic gusts whipped snow from the tree branches, stirring brief blizzards. Sam got lost once. The mountains looked very different in winter. But he rode to a bare mountainside to get a look at the country and saw the canyon from there. He followed a low trail that led to the mouth of the canyon, coming in the way he had herded the bull out in August.

"This is the place," Sam said. "There's not a doubt in my mind. This is where we found the Hereford."

An even blanket of powder covered the grass on the canyon floor, but at the bases of the cliffs it stood deep among the crags. Ab felt thankful that the canyon was narrow—a quarter mile in some places, no more than six hundred yards at its widest point. It would be easy to search. Their own tracks in the fresh snow would show them where they had already looked. If Pete was there, they would find him.

"How far up does this canyon run?" he asked Sam.

"Only about three miles."

He sat on Pard, squinting at the blinding snow. Under him the old horse was shivering in a way he had never felt. "Sam, you ride on ahead," he ordered. "Go at a walk in case he sees you and calls out. Take Buster's spare mule to bring him back on. The rest of you boys spread out and start searching the canyon. Look for him in the timber, and keep your eyes open for a cave or something he might have crawled under. Look close, but don't go too slow. We have to find him before dark."

"Call his name out," Horace suggested. "Maybe he'll hear us."

The men fanned out at the mouth of the canyon and started searching. Sam took the extra mule and rode up the floor of the canyon at a trot, calling Pete's name as he went.

Tracks of the searchers zigzagged and crisscrossed until almost every square rod they left in their wake had been trampled. When they had covered a mile, Sam came trotting back to the search party, leading the mule.

"Well?" Ab said.

Sam shook his head. "No sign. Nothin'."

Ab looked worried. He hurried back and forth between the canyon walls, behind the men, searching the thickest cover and deepest snow drifts. He had to spur Pard constantly to keep him running.

"The colonel looks damn near pale as the snow," Sam said quietly to Buster.

Another half hour passed, and then Ab heard a cowboy shout. Spurring Pard to a gallop, he rode to the site of the find, at the base of the north canyon wall. The men sat on their horses in a half circle, staring at a snowdrift in a craggy niche of the canyon wall.

"What is it?" Ab was filled with hope and dread.

"Look, Colonel," one of the hands said. "It's Ol' Cedar Root."

"We didn't want to move it until you got a look at it," Dan Brooks said.

Ab rode closer and got down. He saw only the tips of the antler points above the snow. The rest of the buck was completely covered. "Give me your rope, String. Let's pull him out." He struggled to get closer on his wooden leg and tossed Piggin' String's loop over the antlers.

String backed his horse away, tightening the noose, pulling the dead buck out of the snowdrift and down from the niche in the rocks. The carcass was twisted grotesquely and frozen stiff. Cedar Root's nose was stuck against his side, as if he were licking his shoulder. His back was humped and his legs protruded at unusual angles. His rigid carcass slid down a slope, startling the horses, and came to rest against a tree trunk. The men tied their mounts and gathered around to investigate.

"Is he gutted?" Horace asked.

"No," Sam said.

"Shot?"

"I don't know. I'm lookin'." Sam brushed snow from the vital areas of the carcass.

"What kind of shot does Pete like?" Horace asked.

"Lung shot," Ab said, clamoring down the slope to join his men.

"There's a lot of points broke off of these horns," Buster said, kneeling to inspect the antlers.

"What a buck!" Piggin' String retrieved his loop from the antlers. "I can't reach my hand all the way around the base of these horns. They've grown even bigger than last year's."

"Look here," Sam said, scraping ice from the carcass. "This looks like a bullet hole, and it's a lung shot, all right."

"Pete sure had him figured." String was in awe of the kill.

"Turn him over," Ab said. "Let's see if the bullet went through, so we can figure what angle he shot from."

They used the stiff legs as levers to turn the buck and began brushing away the snow from his other side. They found a larger hole, caked with frozen blood, where the bullet had torn through the deer.

"If you look at the two bullet holes," Horace said, "it looks like Pete was on the same level as the buck when he shot. That would put him down here in the canyon somewhere." He swept his hand in an arch to indicate the canyon floor.

"That buck wasn't down here when he got shot," Buster said. "He was up there." He pointed to the brink of the north rim, high above.

"Oh, how do you know, Buster?" String said.

"All these broke-off points. He must have busted his horns fallin' down the cliff."

"He could have busted 'em off fightin'," Sam argued.

"I ain't never seen a buck this big with that many points broke. And they all look like fresh breaks. No dirt or anything in 'em. Anyway, look at how twisted up he is. He fell from up there. It don't make sense that he would jump up into that notch in the rocks if Pete shot him down here somewhere."

"Maybe Pete put him there," String said.

Buster shook his head. "Pete would have gutted and hung him."

"I think you're right," Ab said, looking up the cliff. "If he fell from up there, Pete must have been up there when he shot. Maybe he's up there yet."

Buster left the dead buck, climbed up the slope, and started scaling the cliff.

"Buster, where in Hades do you think you're going?" Ab said.

"I'm gonna climb this bluff and see if I can't tell where he fell from."

"There's ice all over the place up there," Dan said. "You'll bust your black ass!"

"Shut up," Ab said, glowering at Dan. He turned to Buster. "Be careful," he said. "Sam, you and Horace go find a trail where you can get the mules up and meet Buster at the top. The rest of you boys go on searching the bottom of the canyon."

Ab stayed below and watched Buster inch up the cliff.

"Here's a bush he fell on!" Buster shouted. He continued to climb and shout his findings back down to Ab. An occasional broken branch or a tuft of buck hair on a sharp rock told him he was on the right path.

Sam and Horace found a trail to the top and lowered a rope when Buster was thirty feet from the brink.

"Look!" Buster shouted. "Here's one of them broken points!" He held the antler fragment up between his fingers, then put it in his coat pocket. He used the rope to climb the rest of the way up.

"He must have fell from right here," Horace said.

Buster made one of the mules stand near the edge of the cliff and tied its reins to a stob. "This mule is standin' about where Ol' Cedar Root was when Pete shot him. Let's go along the rim and look for anyplace where Pete could have got a clean shot at him."

Horace agreed. "Maybe we'll find some sign of him—an empty rifle shell or something."

"Not likely in this snow," Sam said, "but it's worth tryin.' "

They went different ways and searched every place along the north rim that was in clear view and within rifle range of the mule posing as Ol' Cedar Root. Ab watched them from below. The afternoon was getting old. Daylight grew scarce. Finally Horace, Sam, and Buster met on the north rim, nothing among them to report.

"There's one other place he could have shot from," Buster said.

"Where?"

He pointed across the canyon. "The south rim, straight across."

"Oh, hell, Buster," Sam said, growing frustrated.

"That would have been a long shot," Horace said.

"Pete's a good shot."

Horace untied the reins of the mule. "Well, let's ride over there and look. Sam, stand here where the old buck was to mark the spot for us." He mounted one mule as Buster took the reins of the other.

They took half an hour getting around the head of the canyon to the south rim. Looking across, they saw Sam waving his hat. They waved back. The sun had sunk behind the mountain peaks to the west. When they reached a point directly across from Sam, Buster pulled in on the reins and got down from his mule.

"Look at this," he said. He approached what was left of a small pine standing on the very brink of the canyon rim. It was split and charred, one limb ripped away by an unfathomable force. Looking around the tree, he found chunks of it as big as his arm lying as far as thirty paces away. "Lightning struck it," he said. "Yesterday, I'd say. Ashes are fresh. Wood's green." He shook his head. "Look's like somebody blew it up with dynamite."

He looked around to see Horace getting down from his mule, his eyes trained on the ledge of the canyon rim. As Buster watched, Horace sank to his hands and knees to reach for something on the ice-slick precipice. Then he saw what Horace wanted—a rifle barrel jutting out over the escarpment, a thin layer of snow unable to disguise its machine-straight bore.

Horace pulled it to safe ground and brushed the snow off. "This Pete's?"

Buster nodded.

"The rear sight is up," Horace said. He blew the snow away. "It's set for five hundred yards." He worked the lever once, breaking ice away. An empty brass shell flew out. He picked it up and showed it to Buster. "How many shells does this rifle hold? Twelve?"

"Yeah," Buster said. "Plus one in the chamber. But Pete never carries one in the chamber when he's ridin'. Says it ain't safe."

Horace put his hat on the ground and worked the lever until all the cartridges were in his hat. "There's eleven live rounds here. He just shot once, and he didn't even kick the empty shell out." He looked across the canyon at Sam. "Lordy, what a shot that was." He handed the rifle to Buster. "You better show Ab."

Buster balked for a few seconds, then stepped carefully to the edge with the gun. He saw Ab standing below, looking up. He raised the rifle over his head. "We found Pete's Winchester," he shouted. His echo repeated the news.

Ab warmed his hands with his breath but otherwise stood motionless. Buster waited several seconds. "Tell the boys to look under the cliff," he shouted, pointing below him. "Down here."

Ab pulled himself up on old Pard and went to fetch the men, who had worked their way some distance up the canyon. When he mounted, the horse humped his back and coughed, a cloud of vapor blasting from his nostrils.

"What's wrong with that gelding?" Horace asked.

Buster shook his head. "Colonel Ab shouldn't never have rode that old horse this far."

When Horace and Buster got back into the canyon, they found Ab standing at the bottom of the cliff, watching his men dig through drifts of snow in the recesses above him.

"Have they found anything?" Horace asked.

"No," Ab said.

"I'll go help 'em look."

"What was his rifle doing up there, Buster?" Ab asked, as if annoyed at his son for leaving a good weapon in the weather.

Buster swung down from the mule. "He must have dropped it."

Ab kicked narrow trenches in the snow with his peg leg. "What do you think it means?"

"I don't know," Buster said.

"What time do you think he got here yesterday?"

"I reckon about noon."

"That's about the time that blue norther came through."

"Yes, sir. There's a tree up there that was hit by lightning. Probably yesterday."

They stood silently together for several minutes until Buster sensed an end to the search. Dan Brooks had been clawing through drifts without a moment's rest, but now he stopped and stood looking down into the snow. "Colonel!" he shouted.

The men came to stand with Dan. Piggin' String McCoy knelt in the snow. Ab and Buster arrived as Dan pulled Pete's body from the snowdrift. Like Ol' Cedar Root, his limbs were locked in bizarre contortions. Frozen blood molded his face.

Sam Dugan trotted up, out of breath, having climbed down from the north rim. When he saw Pete, he took his hat off. He stared for a minute with everyone else, until he got his wind back. He looked up at the south rim, then across to the north. "My Lord," he said. "That was sure some shot."

"I reckon he saw that buck about the time the norther hit," Horace said.

"Ol' Cedar Root was about to hit high ground and scat, so Pete had to shoot from the saddle," String added.

"That stallion would have been spooky anyhow," Dan said, "on account of the smell of snow in the air."

"There was lightning, too. Me and Buster found a tree up there that was struck."

Dan made as if aiming a rifle. "He had both hands on that Winchester. If his horse pitched . . . He couldn't hold on."

Sam was still looking up. "That was one hell of a shot," he whispered.

Ab hadn't heard them. He stood, staring at the frozen body of his son, wondering why he should outlive so many of his children. He should have joined Ella long ago. He should have spared himself this misery.

"I got a sougan we can wrap him in," Buster said. He wanted to cover Pete. He didn't want to remember him that way.

Ab sat on the old spotted gelding as the boys lashed the frozen body to the back of Buster's spare mule. The cargo under the tarpaulin hardly looked human. Ab twirled a strand of Pard's mane around his finger, his eyes staring blankly down at the snow. The gelding was trembling worse now, but Ab hardly noticed.

When they were ready to leave, Sam said, "Let's get the hell out of this damned canyon."

They hadn't gotten far when twilight came. As they rode speechlessly up a mountain trail, old Pard suddenly balked. Ab spurred him, but he refused to move. "Come on, you lazy old cob!" He gouged the gelding fiercely with his spurs. Pard grunted and shuffled sideways a few steps but wouldn't move another inch uphill. His head dropped. Ab pulled it back up with the reins. "String, give me your quirt." With the rawhide in his hand, he belabored Pard's spotted rump mercilessly and jerked forward repeatedly in the saddle, as if momentum would start the horse up the mountain. Pard coughed, craned his neck strangely, and dropped to his knees.

Ab caught the horn as he swung clumsily down from the saddle. "What in Hades is wrong with you?" he shouted at the horse.

"He's jaded, Colonel," Buster said. "He can't go no fu'ther."

"He'll go a sight farther! He'll carry me home to bury my son!" Ab put his shoulder under Pard's neck and tried to make him stand up. Pard heaved and got one forefoot under him, but the hoof slipped and he went down again, this time all the way over onto his side. Ab yanked his head up with the bridle reins, but the Nez Perce horse was spent.

Buster got down from his mule and took the reins away from Ab. He knew the old man was addled with grief, but he had no cause to treat a dying horse that way. "Let him go. He can't climb no more mountains. He's older than your wooden leg."

The words hit Ab like an avalanche of years. Pard came before Ella went, before General Palmer brought the railroad, before Cheyenne Dutch killed Matthew. He had failed to take account of the toll of decades. To Ab, Pard would always be fleet of foot and bulletproof—the way he was at Apache Canyon. Only now did he realize what the suns, the moons, and the Indian winters had taken out of the old warhorse.

For the first time, he thought of himself as a one-legged old man. His life seemed suddenly near its end. How much longer could a man endure this agony? How many more mountains could he climb? How many sons did he have to bury?

Buster loosened the saddle to let Pard breathe easier.

Ab took the bridle off. He knelt over the head of the dying horse. "He's hurting. We can't leave him here to freeze." He stood, paused. He sighed. "Give me your rifle, Sam."

Sam reluctantly drew his Winchester from the scabbard and handed it to his boss. Ab opened the breech to make sure he had a live round in the chamber. He stood between his horse and his men and cocked the hammer. He put the weapon to his shoulder and aimed down at Pard's head. He stood motionless for a long moment as the men looked away and gritted their teeth.

Then Ab began to shudder with the gun at his shoulder. A single sob escaped his throat almost like a cough. "Damn those white eyes!" he blubbered. "You'll have to do it for me, Buster," he said, handing over the gun. He wanted to turn it on himself.

Ab stumbled down the trail, brushed the snow from a boulder, and sat down. The rifle cracked. He didn't move. Twilight had passed and the mountainside grew dark.

Buster came to Ab's side. "We better get goin'." he said. "You can ride behind me on the mule."

Ab sniffed and rubbed his sleeve under his nose.

"Colonel?"

He looked up with a world of terrors in his eyes. "Who's going to tell him, Buster?"

"Tell who?"

"Who's going to tell Caleb?"

"About Pete? You're gonna tell him. You're his family."

Ab shook his head. "I can't tell him. I can't talk to that boy anymore."

"He's a grown man now," Buster said. "And you *can* tell him."

Ab looked up, his eyes begging for pity. "You could tell him for me."

Buster wanted to pick the old fool up by the collar and shake him. "Colonel," he said, growling under his breath, "I'll be *damned* if I have to tell your own son his brother has died. I'll put your poor old horse out of misery for you, but I won't ease your conscience about the way you've treated your son."

Ab shook his head, grief-stricken, afraid, alone. "But I can't tell him," he whispered. "I can't think of any way I could possibly tell him."

"Then you had better find a way, old man." He pulled Ab to his feet by the collar, angrier than he had ever been at him. "You find a way to do it." He turned back up the trail, leaving the old man in the dark.

Amelia was giddy with relief and joy. She hugged Gloria around the neck and watched the foal wobble on spindly legs, rooting vaguely for his first taste of milk.

Gloria touched the lily-white arms squeezing her neck. The little white woman was strong! "I told you, Miss Amelia. You don't need those menfolks around here."

"Oh, hush. The old girl did it all by herself. I only watched."

"But you was here, just in case."

"Yes, I was. I never thought I'd see such a thing." She beamed with accomplishment as the foal found the bag. "Do you think it will be as easy for me when my time comes?"

Gloria bunched her eyebrows and shot questioning glances all over the barn. "Why, Miss Amelia, are you in the family way?"

Amelia nodded, blushing. "Pete doesn't know yet. I wanted to be sure."

"I s'pect I'll be right after you."

"Are you . . . ?"

"I don't know, but the way that fool man of mine comes after me of a evenin' . . . *Every* evenin'!"

"Buster?"

"Uh-huh! He tried to git me in the mornin', too, but I just roll on over. I ain't no mornin' glory!"

Amelia gasped and laughed all at once. Imagine! She relished Gloria's ribald candor.

SEVENTY

Every spring, when wildflowers began to bloom along the Rio Peñasco, Caleb knew it was time to drift north. He would hug his children and tell them to obey their mother. He would kiss Marisol and promise to return earlier next time. He would wander up through Albuquerque, Santa Fe, and Taos, stopping to play at ranches for food, or saloons for money. The vanguard of wild blossoms would follow him northward as spring advanced. By the time he arrived at Monument Creek, Buster's flower garden would be putting out colors, and Pete would be watching for him to appear where the old Arapaho Trail ran over the bald hill to the west.

He liked to appear at dusk on the bald hill and stand there in the stirrups until someone noticed him. Then he would trot down the slope, splash across the creek, and lope up to the ranch with a flourish of his hat, singing some cowboy ditty. The Arapaho Trail approach also gave Ab time to spot him and get out of the way somewhere. Caleb didn't any more want to speak to his father than his father cared to speak to him. They had built the wall of silence together. It was the only thing they cooperated in.

It was late afternoon when he came through Arapaho Pass in the Rampart Range. He had come from Leadville, where he had filled his pockets with the former wages of drunken miners. Wildflowers were breaking out in bevies on the hillsides and in the coulees flanking the trail. The open range had become overstocked in recent years, and grass had grown scarce, but nothing ate the wildflowers. If anything, they had become more prolific, claiming the former range of retreating grasses. He knew Buster's garden would be resplendent with blossoms.

It was the place he loved most on the face of the earth, where the High Plains met the Rocky Mountains. The Front Range, the Eastern Slope. He rode a little lighter in the saddle under the Ramparts. Monument Park, the Arapaho Trail. He loved the sounds of the place names.

He was going home. Would he ever stay? Was it right to stay? Was it wrong to leave? Should he be living like Pete instead of drifting like some shiftless vagabond? Would he ever bring Marisol to Holcomb Ranch? Did he want to?

Pete has a big ranch. I have a horse and some instruments. Pete works the land. I play songs. Pete does good in the world. Pete knows God. What do I do? What do I know?

He had perfected the timing over the years. At dusk he recognized the west side of the bald hill, green with new grass. Powder River knew it, too, and his hooves chopped the ground a little quicker. Holcomb Ranch, just over the hill. Caleb cocked his hat, stroked his mustache, and tucked his pants legs down into his boot tops. Home, not a mile away. He started the climb up the west face of the bald hill.

He stood in the stirrups as the trail rolled under him. He craned his neck. In a moment he would see his home spread. A tremulous breath of anticipation fluttered in his lungs. He knew which story he was going to tell first. He had practiced it well. He had rehearsed them all.

He squinted. A strange dark square had appeared on the summit, against the pale sky. Powder River looked at it sidewise, suspiciously. They approached it cautiously. It was a stray chunk of rough stone, standing on the apex of the Arapaho Trail. Beyond it, now, the dark-green penisula of the Pinery jutted into the plains. As he climbed higher over the bald swell, the gossamer rails of the Denver and Rio Grande came into view, then the windmills, the big pastures, the plowed fields, the Cincinnati house, the bastioned mansion, the cabins, and Monument Creek.

Only the chunk of stone on the trail was unfamiliar. It was quarried granite, large and imposing. The gelding gave it a wide berth as Caleb urged him around it. The side of the stone that fronted the plains had a polished face, smooth as glass, except for a few characters gouged in two severe lines. He leaned from his saddle to read it in the waning light:

PETE HOLCOMB
1852–1882

Caleb dropped from the saddle, touched the letters, drew his fingers back from the cold stone. He fell to his knees as the helplessness crawled under his flesh, like worms tunneling the dark earth. There was an empty place in the world where once Pete had stood, a dearth of life sucking a million moments into oblivion.

He had felt the vigor of Pete's handshake all day, glimpsed his sallow eyes. But now he held nothing, saw darkness. The wildflowers were blooming, the new moon rising. It was spring on the Front Range. He had come home to tell Pete some stories.

Buster could not bring himself to watch for Caleb's arrival that spring. The stone on the hill marred his view and he felt responsible for its placement there. He was the one who had told the old man to find a way to tell Caleb himself. The old man had found a way. He had buried Pete under the Arapaho Trail.

Buster didn't look forward to witnessing Caleb's return, so he avoided looking at the hill, concentrating on his fields and pastures instead. That night, however, Buster couldn't ignore the campfire that burned on the hill near the gravestone.

"What is that up there?" Gloria asked.

"It's got to be Caleb," he answered. "Nobody else would camp up there."

Gloria grew wide-eyed. "With that grave up there! You won't catch me around there at night."

"It's just Pete, woman."

She shook her head and pulled the curtains.

He debated on whether or not he should go up there, thinking maybe Caleb would come down after a while. But the fire kept burning for hours after dark, and he finally decided he should climb the hill.

He left the Cincinnati house, using Caleb's fire as his guide. Cool wind sang through winter wheat. The creek, swollen with snowmelt, laughed at him as he crossed the dam; then it gave way to the distant songs of night birds and the faint rustle of new leaves in the cottonwoods. A lone coyote howled somewhere in the mountains. They were all familiar sounds, well loved. But as he neared the top of the hill, an unexpected strain reached his ears. It was Caleb's voice.

The drifter had built his fire close to the gravestone on the Arapaho Trail, and the polished face of the stone caught the flickering light of the flames. Caleb sat on his saddle between the fire and the stone. When Buster came near enough, he could hear Caleb telling Pete a story:

". . . well, this Rhode Island gambler had never seen one before, so he asked me why I called it a stout lizard. And I says, 'Because it's so stout, you can't hold it down on the ground by pokin' your finger in the middle of its back.' Well, he just had to try it, of course, and when he poked it on the back, that scorpion lifted its tail and stung him right smart on the trigger finger so he couldn't deal off the bottom of the deck for a week. It just happened to take me about that long to win back everything he had cheated me out of . . ."

Buster smiled. The fire blurred. He listened only a minute or two, just beyond the firelight. He knew he wasn't needed. When he reached the creek, he could still hear Caleb's voice and see the flames flickering great sorrow and beauty on Pete's stone.

At dawn Buster went back up to the hill and nudged Caleb in his bedroll.

"Mornin', Buster," he said, propping himself on his elbows. He lingered for a moment in the innocence of dreams, then saw the gravestone and felt a new despair.

"I brought you some breakfast." He opened a basket, steaming with the aroma of biscuits. He pulled Powder River's stake pin from the ground and led the horse to fresh grass. When he came back, Caleb was groping around in the basket.

Buster piled wood over the coals and got the fire going again. He put a coffeepot on as Caleb ate boiled eggs, bacon, and biscuits smeared with butter and honey. He handed Caleb a tin cup steaming with coffee and they sat together silently, warming their fingers on the hot metal as the sun rose beyond the Pinery.

"I had practiced a whole string of stories to tell him," Caleb said, "and I wasn't about to let nobody stop me."

Buster nodded. "I know."

The sun clung desperately to the horizon, then lost its hold and became a perfect sphere.

"How'd it happen?"

Buster told how Pete had died in the place that had come to be called Cedar Root Canyon, though not a single cedar was known to take root there. The sun was high when he finished. The denizens of Holcomb Ranch were up and working. Gloria had walked over to the mansion to cook Amelia's breakfast. It seemed that only Ab had failed to show himself.

"Is Amelia still here?" Caleb asked.

"She sure is," Buster said, almost proudly. "I thought she'd run back to her daddy in town, but she won't leave her house. Won't leave her horses either. She's been out in the pens almost every day, tellin' the boys how to work 'em. I caught her pitchin' hay last week. Says she's gonna take up ridin' after the baby comes."

"Baby?"

"That's right. You're gonna be an uncle."

Caleb turned to grin at Pete but found only a cold stone there beside him. He clutched the tin cup, cold and empty now. "Things sure happen sudden."

"Yeah," Buster said, staring blankly, arching his eyebrows, and pressing his lips together. "You ready to come down to the ranch now?"

He nodded, threw the tin cup into the basket, and rolled his sugan.

SEVENTY-ONE

AMELIA GREETED HIM at the door and her grief began again. She had learned to conceal it, smiling through everything. Caleb tested her though. He walked with Pete's gait and wore his hat at the same angle. And there were certain lines around his mouth and eyes that they held in common. She had never noticed them in Caleb before. They didn't come from Ab. They must have come from Ella, but, of course, Amelia had never known her. There wasn't even a picture of her anywhere.

She hugged him, embracing him a little longer than she should have. "Gloria!" she called. "Some tea for our guest, please."

Caleb was a guest on his own ranch, in his brother's own house. He sat rigidly on the velour sofa and hung his hat on his knee.

Amelia sat across from him, smiling deceptively. She straightened the front of her maternity frock and sighed. "Well, I suppose Buster's told you everything."

"Yes," Caleb said. "I'm sorry I didn't know. I'd have come sooner."

"I know you would have. I sent a letter, but, of course, I had no way of knowing if it would ever find you." Her smile quivered. "This must be very difficult for you." She was staring strangely at him, smiling purposefully.

"Don't worry about me," he said.

Gloria arrived with the tea and poured Caleb a cup. He would have preferred coffee with about two fingers of whiskey. "Thanks," he said.

"That will be all, Gloria." Amelia dismissed her with a brush of her hand. "But I *am* worried about you," she said to Caleb. "I'm afraid you'll think . . . I had no idea why your father wanted to bury Pete on the hill. I surrendered all the arrangements to him. I hope you don't think it was my idea. I didn't want you to find out that way."

"It's all right," he said. "I know the old man was behind it. I don't blame nobody but him."

When Caleb slurped the hot tea, it scorched his lip. To cool it, he poured some into the saucer and blew on it. He slurped some of the cooled tea and poured the rest back into the cup, repeating the process until the tea in the cup became cool enough to gulp.

Amelia's sad smile became more forced. Pete would never drink his tea or coffee until it had been "blowed and saucered." It was a crude habit cowboys engaged in when given the luxury of saucers. She had tried unsuccessfully to break him of it.

"I'm worried about your father," she said, as Caleb cooled his tea. "He doesn't come out of his cabin very often anymore. Lee Fong says he rarely even puts on his leg, but hops about the house when he wants to move."

Caleb shrugged.

"Maybe you should go over and talk to him," she suggested.

He set his cup down rather abruptly on the saucer. "I'm the last person he wants to talk to. Pete must have told you that a long time ago."

"I never understood it," Amelia said. "What happened between the two of you?"

"We had a fallin' out over whether or not I ought to work cows." He snickered and glanced around the room. "Sounds silly, don't it?" He was looking for Ol' Cedar Root's horns. They weren't hanging in the parlor, but he didn't think it polite to ask about them.

"What was said between the two of you?"

He sighed. "I guess we said about what we thought of each other at the time."

"How long ago has it been?"

"Goin' on ten years now."

"Ten years! Well, it's time you forgave each other. Pete would like that. If nothing else comes of his death, at least you and your father can settle your differences."

He scoffed. "Not much chance of that."

"But you'll be staying here now. You'll have to reach some sort of understanding."

"I beg your pardon?" Caleb said.

Amelia stared for a moment, silently. "You will be staying, won't you?"

"What for?"

"To manage the ranch, of course. Someone will have to do it."

"Who's manager now?"

"Sam Dugan, but . . ."

"He'll do a fine job, I'm sure."

"But, it's your ranch. Your name is Holcomb."

"It's the old man's ranch," Caleb argued, "and I'm the last man in the world he wants to run it."

"But how do you know that?"

"If he wanted me to manage this ranch, he'd be over here right now telling me so."

"Why wait for him?" She pointed to the old Holcomb cabin. "Go over there and tell him you want it. You are his last surviving son. Certainly he cannot refuse."

Caleb stopped forcing the tea down his throat. He put the saucer and cup down in front of him. "Amelia, I appreciate you tryin' to look after me, but I know ten other ranches I can work on from Montana to Texas. Ranches where I'll be welcomed."

"Yes, and you'll never amount to anything on any one of them." She sprang to her feet and paced across the room. "And do you know why? Because you have to come back here every year to tell your stories and play your songs. Because this is your home."

Caleb rose and rolled the brim of his hat nervously in his hand. "This hasn't been my home since the day my mother died. It was Pete's. That's the only reason I ever came back. Now that he's gone, I don't know that I've got anything to come back for, so I might as well go on down to New Mexico and work with Javier. I'll amount to something there." He was lying, of course. Javier had nothing for him but hospitality.

"Back to your little señorita?" She shook her head at the scandal of it. "Did you ever marry her? What's her name?"

"Her name is Marisol and, no, I haven't married her yet. You can't find a priest down there in winter."

"How very convenient."

"But I reckon I could find one this time of year, so maybe I'll just trot on back down there and marry her. Javier's ranch is more mine than this one is. And my children are down there, too."

She put her hands over her stomach. "And your brother's child is here. Who will fill the role of its father?"

"The old man is here. And Buster."

Amelia gestured in disgust and slapped her palms against her hips. "I was hoping for someone a little younger and, well, not quite so colored."

"Buster did a fine job of raising me," he said defensively.

"Did he?"

Caleb rolled his hat brim tight as a cigar. "Well, the boys are all here." He gestured toward the bunkhouse.

"I won't have my child influenced by a group of foul-mouthed roughs!"

He saw Gloria peeking into the parlor from the kitchen. He put his hat on his head. "Thanks for the tea," he said and headed for the door, his spurs ringing with every step.

"Wait!" Amelia ordered. "You're needed *here!* Can't you see that? When are you going to stop feeling sorry for yourself and forgive your father?"

He stood in the open doorway. "Do you know how I found out my brother was dead? I rode over that hill and saw his name carved on a cold piece of stone. There ain't no other way to feel for myself *but* sorry, and I don't see that the old man deserves my forgivin' him. Good mornin'!" He turned his back and escaped down the steps.

Amelia stepped into the doorway. "Caleb! Don't you stalk out of here on me!" She felt Gloria's strong hand on her shoulder.

"Here, now, Miss Amelia. You know you're not supposed to get yourself upset when you have that baby. Come sit down."

Amelia allowed herself to be led back into the house. "Damn! I'm such a fool. I pressured him too quickly. I'm a fool."

"No, you're not. Don't you say that. You're just thinkin' like a mama, that's all. Makes you crazy, being in the family way."

Amelia collapsed on the sofa. "Why won't he stay?"

"You can't make him stay. He's got to make up his own mind. Now, you rest easy there and let me get you some more tea."

SEVENTY-TWO

AB NEVER SHOWED his face outside of the cabin while Caleb was on the ranch. He wouldn't even go out to the privy without reconnoitering like an old spy. Buster didn't hear any stories. The cowboys didn't hear any songs. It didn't seem proper to sing and play and carry on. To Caleb, Pete was just a few days in the grave.

He didn't stay a week. He didn't help in the roundup. It had changed since the fences had been stretched anyway and wasn't much of an event anymore. He did go over to see the boys at the bunkhouse one night, however, to get them to give him directions to Cedar Root Canyon.

"Where's the old buck's horns?" he asked.

"We left him up there, horns and all," Dan explained. "We all forgot about Ol' Cedar Root after we found Pete. The horns were busted up pretty bad anyhow."

"We've still got the horn he shed last spring though," Sam said. He took the antler down from a sparsely stocked bookshelf. "This is what got Pete huntin' after him in the first place."

Caleb held the antler and whistled in amazement. "I guess I'd have hunted for him, too."

The next morning he found Buster getting ready to hitch a team and plow the cornfield beside his irrigation ditch. Caleb had Powder River saddled, his belongings tied or stowed in the old sack behind the cantle.

"Where are you going?" Buster asked.

"I thought I'd ride up in the mountains and find Cedar Root Canyon."

"You want me to show you where it is?"

"No. I'd rather go alone."

He nodded. "What do you need all your stuff for?" he asked, pointing at the bulging saddle wallet.

"I ain't comin' back."

Buster hung his harnesses. "Leavin' a little soon this year, ain't you?"

"It ain't the same anymore. I don't feel much like stayin'."

"What about the ranch?"

"Sam will take care of it."

"You better hope he can handle it if you ever want to make this ranch your own. There's lots of talk goin' around about takin' the fences off of the government land. Some of them nesters want a law against it. Them factory windmills are sellin' cheap now. Could be nesters filin' all over this ranch pretty soon."

Caleb looked out over Monument Park, sparkling with dew under the low morning sun. "The old man's still got the county clerk on his payroll, don't he?"

"I don't know. That business don't concern me. I worry about my land."

"Let the old man worry about his. It ain't my concern either."

"What about Amelia and her baby?" Buster said.

"Oh, she'll probably marry some rich fella and move back to town. She don't need me to help with no youngun. If she needs help, you'll be here."

Buster snickered. "She don't want me teachin' her kid nothin'. Anyhow, I'll be busy with my own."

"Huh?"

"I'm gonna be a papa, too."

"Well, I'll be damned. You don't waste time, do you?" He slapped Buster's muscle-knotted shoulder and smiled, but he was swamped by an old festering shame. He had never mentioned the Pease River fight. Buster had fathered a child before—a son he would never see.

"Can't waste time," Buster said, grinning. "Gettin' old."

"Oh, fiddlesticks. You're as sound as old Powder River." He slapped the gelding on the rump.

Buster took his hat off and ran his hand over his hair, molded by the hatband. "Gettin' almost as many white hairs as him, too."

"Looks good on you. What are you? Forty?"

"Forty-two."

He slapped the gelding again. "And just as sound as old Powder River."

"Sounder," Buster replied. "I still got my balls."

Caleb laughed. "Say, before I go, have you got any of them old tobacco pouches filled up with those flower seeds? I'd like to spread some on the hill around Pete's grave."

"Sure I do. I've got seven or eight different kinds. Come on over to the cabin and I'll get you some."

Buster not only gave Caleb some seeds but followed him up the hill to make sure he spread them evenly.

"You think they'll come up?" Caleb asked.

"With good rains they will. Some of 'em will come up next year. Some may take two. When you come back next spring, we'll spread some more."

Caleb stood silently, looking at the gravestone.

"You're comin' back next year, ain't you?"

Caleb shrugged. "Don't know that there's anything to come back for. Pete's gone."

Buster thought he would wilt like a lily in the desert. Nothing to come back for? What about the man who had taught him to play five instruments, taught him to work, to sing, to laugh? He knew Caleb didn't mean to be cruel, that he spoke too often without considering the toll his words would take. But it hurt anyway.

"I wish I could have seen him again," Caleb said.

Buster felt suddenly selfish. Who was hurting more? "We'd all like to see him again. That's what makes you feel bad. But if you believe in heaven, you know he's in a better place and you *will* see him again." He grimaced inwardly. He had promised himself he wouldn't use any of the stock phrases people rattled off at times of death.

Caleb shifted his feet and looked out over the plains. He cleared his throat. There was a cool breeze climbing the hill, but he felt sweat around his collar. He felt as if he had drunk too much whiskey. "I'm afraid I might not."

"Might not what?" Buster said.

"I'm afraid I might not believe."

"What do you mean?"

He jutted his thumb at his brother's stone. "Pete always believed. He could see somethin' I couldn't. I'm afraid I'll never see it."

"Afraid? Afraid of what?"

Caleb contemplated, then looked at Buster. "Afraid of goin' to hell." He was serious.

Buster smirked, puzzled. "Who you think's gonna send you to hell?"

He struggled. "God, I guess." He wasn't like Pete. It embarrassed him to utter the name of God outside of an oath.

"Why? Because you don't believe in him?"

"Yeah."

Buster laughed. "Don't you know what it means to be God fearin'? If you're scared God is gonna send you to hell, then you *must* believe in him. Ain't no way you can be afraid of somethin' you don't believe in."

Caleb had never understood religion in all of its small, silly intricacies: the Bible telling him what to do, the power of prayer. The Bible was written by men, not God. Prayer was talk wasted on vapor. Yet, he had feared God, dreaded hell. Pete had told him once that all he had to do to get into heaven was to believe in God. He had hoped there was no God, afraid he would never believe. But now he knew. To fear *was* to believe. Not just to profess belief but to *feel* it! To fear God was to believe in God. To believe in God was to fear nothing.

He rose like a hawk on the wind. It was so commonsensical that only Buster Thompson could explain it. Suddenly God was laughing at him from on high. Ridiculous mortal! He who feared God! Pete had known it all along.

He might never own Holcomb Ranch, but he would know the kingdom

of heaven. He felt a soul within. Of course he believed! He had always
believed because he had always feared. He was no less holy than the next
man. The cold weight of dread lifted from his heart.

He should have known it long ago. The words that came to him came
from somewhere. From God or God's angels: maybe Ella or Matthew. Or
Pete! Hadn't he thought of a new verse just two weeks ago? He had made
the words rhyme without effort. They had fallen into place, in perfect cadence, set to music. They were not his. He was only the carrier of the song.
He was the voice, the player, the drifter.

"Hey," Buster said. "You feel all right?"

Caleb felt the hand on his shoulder. "Huh? Yeah, I feel fine."

Buster told him to come back next spring—or summer, or winter, or
fall. Caleb made no promises. He seemed dazed.

He mounted and followed the Arapaho Trail into the Rampart Range.
He had the presence to wave but hardly saw Buster when he looked back
at him. Maybe he would never be moved to turn preacher, like Pete, but he
had religion. He was going to Cedar Root Canyon. Beyond that he knew
no destination other than the Great Reward.

SEVENTY-THREE

MAJOR EARL STANLEY Bannon walked the streets with purpose. He
needed horses, Indians, crack shots, fancy ropers, trick riders. He had just
come from the Dodge City stockyards, where he had purchased two dozen
longhorn steers, each with horns spanning six feet or more, to be used in
his tent-show stampede. The drunken cowboys, the cattlemen, the gamblers, the merchants, and the ladies of easy virtue surged aimlessly around
him, but Bull Bannon's path was ramrod straight. He had direction.

As his pale green eyes swept the bustling street for prospects, he spotted a wide-brimmed hat above the crowd. He leaned casually against a
storefront and watched. The horseman rode a huge dapple gray that carried him a head above the surrounding riders. Bannon glimpsed a Colt
revolver belted around the rider's waist and a sea-grass rope tied in a coil
to the saddle. The cowboy rode stone sober in the midst of drunkenness.

"Hey!" the major shouted. "You! Cowboy! Yes, you. Come over
here."

The cowboy guided the dapple gray between other horses and around
wagons, sizing up the man on the board sidewalk as he approached. He
noted the long waves of silver-blond hair flowing out from under the perfectly creased felt hat; the immaculate mustache swept back to the side-
burns; the full-sleeved shirt, vest with conspicuous watch chain, black

leather holster with pearl-handled pistol, striped riding trousers, black boots, silver spurs.

"What do you want?" the cowboy said, directly but respectfully.

"What's your name?" Bannon asked.

"Who wants to know?"

"I'm Major E. S. Bannon—Bull Bannon to most." The cowboy smiled skeptically with one side of his mouth. "Are you really him?"

"Why do you doubt me?"

"They make you out to be taller on them theater posters."

Bannon smiled, a perfect row of white teeth appearing under the silver and yellow mustache. "I'm six feet even. I simply made sure nobody else in the cast stood over five seven. Creates an illusion through relative size. That's quite a mount you're riding."

The cowboy leaned forward on the saddle horn. "Oh, he cuts a pretty good outline, but he ain't crazy about dust and sweat."

"Maybe that's what I saw in him. We're kindred souls. How's your marksmanship with that Colt?"

The cowboy paused, then answered cautiously. "Fair."

"How's your roping?"

"Can't be beat. I'm top hand."

"How would you like to show off your stuff from here to New York City?"

"Sir?"

"I'm organizing a traveling tent show. Calling it Bull Bannon's Extravaganza of the Western Wilds. First show's in Saint Jo, two weeks from Saturday. I need a top hand."

"New York City?"

"Yes, and Cincinnati, and Philadelphia, and all points in between. What's your name?"

"Cole Gibson." He shook the major's hand, calloused but manicured.

"Got a nickname?"

"No, sir."

"Better get one."

"How come?"

"Back east they think everybody out west has a nickname. Let's make yours to have something to do with roping. Like 'Loop' Gibson or . . . How about 'Lariat' Gibson? . . . " The showman glanced at the rope coiled on the cowboy's saddle. "I've got it! Cole 'Seagrass' Gibson."

Gibson reeled back, propping his hand on the dappled rump. He tried the name on, snickering. "Seagrass Gibson."

"It's got a ring to it."

"I don't hardly use this grass rope, though, except for heel ropin'."

"Doesn't matter. The folks back east won't know the difference. They don't know grass from gut line any more than they know sit from sic 'em. Get six of the best ropers you can find in Dodge City and have them report to the station this afternoon. No drunks. See my assistant, Captain Singletary.''

"Well, hold on a minute," Seagrass said. "What's the pay, and for how long?''

"The show will run at least through the summer. As for pay . . ." He stroked his mustache and tossed a golden curl of hair over his shoulder. "What do you make as top hand on the trail?"

"Forty a month."

"I'll double it. But the men you hire will only get fifty a month. Plus a tent or a boxcar to sleep in every night. Do we have a deal?"

Seagrass mulled it over for a second. "Yes, sir."

"Good. Get to work."

The dapple gray turned toward the stockyards, its rider entertaining fanciful visions of Cincinnati, Philadelphia, and New York.

Bannon bit the end off of a cigar as he scouted the street. He fished a match from his pocket, struck it on his boot heel, lit his smoke, and strode briskly down the boardwalk.

Coming to a corner, he heard a fiddle wailing across the way. He spit a flake of tobacco. The intersection was deep with mud and his boots were shiny, but the music intrigued him. He sprang from the boardwalk to the tailgate of a passing wagon, rode across the mire, and jumped to the saloon front across the intersection.

The music rang cleanly through the smoky air. A few modestly dressed saloon girls danced with some old veterans of the trail. Bannon spotted the fiddler in a corner, sawing on a dusty instrument he held propped against his right shoulder. He couldn't see the musician's face, leaning into the fiddle tune as he was, his hat brim low over his eyes. The bow moved too fast to follow. It hopped from string to string, raked harmony from them in pairs, and jittered like dragonfly wings.

Bannon put his elbow on the bar and his heel on the brass rail as he watched the ladies whirl the old trail bosses. The fiddler finished his tune with a flourish, jerking the bow so quickly that his whole body shook. A small, short burst of applause rang from the dancers. As the fiddler bowed and brandished his hat, a trail hand dropped a coin in and pulled him down from the soapbox he was standing on.

"Sell me a whiskey, will you?" Bannon said to a harried little man behind the bar.

"Keep your shirt on." The barkeep looked up once, then did a double take. "Say, you're not . . . No, you're not Bull Bannon?"

"Thirsty Bull Bannon to you. Where's my whiskey?"

The fiddler had switched to guitar. He strummed a lively rhythm as the old trail hand standing next to him started singing "Utah Carroll," gravel voiced but on key.

> *"And now, my friends, you ask me, what makes me sad and still,*
> *And why my brow is darkened like the clouds upon the hill.*
> *Run in your pony closer, and I'll tell you the tale*
> *Of Utah Carroll, my partner, and his last ride on the trail."*

The major sipped his whiskey once, then cupped it in his hand for show as he looked over the barmaids. He knew the song. When the last verse started, he began weaving his way between the poker tables, toward the soapbox. The musician harmonized with the drover in singing the last two lines. His voice sounded smooth as honey compared with the grating of the trail boss.

> *"Then on his funeral mornin' I heard the preacher say*
> *I hope we'll all meet Utah in the roundup far away."*

Bannon flipped a silver dollar into the upturned hat. "How many instruments do you play?"

"I don't know," the musician said. "How many fiddles, guitars, banjos, mandolins, and harmonicas you reckon there are in the world?"

Bannon snorted. "You've answered that one before. Do you know these girls who work here?"

"Most of 'em."

"Tell them I'd like to hire them. I need some authentic saloon girls for a traveling tent show. No funny business, just serving drinks in the beer garden and playing in the saloon scene in the show."

"Why don't you tell 'em yourself?"

Bannon ignored the suggestion. "I could use a western singer, too. What would you say to thirty a month plus all the money you can collect in your hat?"

"To do what?"

"Sing these old cowboy songs in the beer garden, maybe chase a steer or two in the tent show."

The musician seemed interested. "Where'bouts?"

"Missouri, Illinois, Indiana, Ohio, Pennsylvania, and New York."

He put the guitar on a table, moved the money from his hat to his pocket, and put the hat back on his head. "Who are you?"

"Major Bull Bannon."

"You sure you're the *real* Bull Bannon? Where's your fancy buckskin suit with all the furs and beads sewed onto it?"

"I wear store-bought off the stage. Who are you?"

"Caleb Holcomb."

"Got a nickname?"

He fell a step behind in the conversation. "They used to call me the Colorado Kid."

"Who did?"

"Buffalo hunters in Texas."

"Who'd you hunt with?"

"Washita Jack Shea, Badger Burton, Smokey Dean Wilson, and old Elam Joiner, before the Comanche butchered him. And a fellow from back east that we called Red Hot Frost."

"Red Hot Frost!" Bannon released a burst of laughter. "That's one of the best I've heard. I fought with Jack Shea on the Washita, scouting for the Seventh. Hunted with Smokey Wilson in Kansas. Never met Joiner, but knew of him." He pulled the watch from his vest pocket, glanced at it, and returned it without missing a word. "Always hunted alone, I heard. That was his downfall. Badger Burton was a fool from what I saw of him. Anyway, Colorado Kid won't do. Let's see . . . Fiddlesticks . . . Rosin . . . Catgut! 'Catgut' Caleb Holcomb. That's appropriate. Has a good ring. Carries the hard *c* sound through it."

Caleb still hadn't caught up with the major's line of thinking. "Am I supposed to call myself that?"

"Once I print it on the program, you'll never hear the end of it back east. Bring the gals around to the station before nine o'clock in the morning." He leaned close to speak confidentially. "No soiled doves, just honest barmaids." He offered his hand to seal the deal.

Caleb still wasn't ready to shake. "What'll I tell 'em their pay will be?"

"Same as yours. Dollar a day and tips. They'll have their own tent and their own sleeper car. No funny business, on my honor."

He felt the tight grip of Bull Bannon's hand.

"See my assistant, Captain Singletary," the major shouted over his shoulder as he left.

SEVENTY-FOUR

W HEN THE TRAIN came to a stop at St. Joseph, "Catgut" Caleb Holcomb and Cole "Seagrass" Gibson jumped from their boxcar and headed for their horses, several cars back. On the way they met Bull Bannon, stepping from his bright-red Pullman coach with fancy yellow letters on the side spelling BULL BANNON'S EXTRAVAGANZA OF THE WESTERN WILDS.

"Where are you two going?" the major asked.

"To get our horses," Caleb said. "I've got somebody to look up in town."

"I'm goin' with him," Seagrass added.

"No you're not. Neither one of you. We have ten boxcars to unload and five tents to erect."

The cowboys looked at each other.

"You never said nothin' about unloadin' trains or puttin' up tents," Seagrass complained.

"Did you think they would erect themselves?"

"Well, the first show ain't for five days yet," Caleb said.

"What show?" Bannon roared. "We have no show! We need rehearsal! Unload the cars, set up the tents, then we'll rehearse!"

A short, husky bear of a man stepped from the red coach, rolling his sleeves up on his hairy forearms. He held a whittled-down pencil between his teeth and carried a leather-backed notebook under one arm.

"Captain Singletary," the major ordered, walking away to inspect the show grounds, "put these men in charge of livestock."

Singletary eyed the two men as he opened his notebook and licked the point of his pencil. "Seagrass Gibson and Catgut Holcomb," he mumbled as he jotted their names down. "Build your pens downwind, gentlemen. One for horses, one for longhorns. You'll find the troughs and fence rails in the third boxcar." He walked toward the head of the train, muttering to himself as he scribbled.

"I'm damned if I ever thought I'd take pay to put up circus tents," Seagrass said. "I've got half a mind to saddle my horse and ride on back to Texas."

"I've got the other half. We might just make a whole mind, partner."

Gibson nodded indignantly. "Maybe we ought to wait till payday though," he said after some reflection.

Caleb felt his empty pockets. "I guess so. Where'd Singletary say them fence rails were at?"

It took them all of the first day to rehearse the two-hour show just once. The second day, they got through it three times. The third day, Bannon marched them through six rehearsals with military precision, railing at the oncoming darkness when the sun set.

Caleb played bit parts in the main show, herding longhorns, shooting blank cartridges at Indians. His real responsibility was performing in the western saloon reconstructed inside the beer-garden tent. Bannon ordered him to sing and play for the cast there every night after rehearsals.

The third night he approached the stage and said, "Catgut, I haven't heard you repeat a single tune in three days. How many songs do you know?"

"How many?" Caleb said. "Hell, major, I know 'em all!"

On the fourth day of rehearsal, Captain Singletary pulled Caleb out of the grub line, where he and Cole Gibson were waiting to get supper. The show manager handed the musician a stack of sheet music.

"What's this?" Caleb asked, staring at the hieroglyphics.

"Major Bannon's repertoire."

"His what?" Cole asked.

"That's what he's going to sing for tomorrow's matinee."

"Matinee?" Caleb said.

Singletary frowned. "The afternoon show."

Caleb blew a sigh through his mustache. "I didn't even know he could sing."

"Of course he can sing. He's taken voice lessons."

That night Bannon ordered Caleb to the beer garden to rehearse. "Where's your sheet music?" he asked when the accompanist arrived.

"I don't read chicken scratchin'," Caleb said, "but I know all them songs anyway. Which one you want to start with?"

" 'Home on the Range,' " Bannon said.

Caleb stepped onto the stage beside the major and started the waltz time. He didn't see why they had to rehearse this stuff at all.

Bannon grabbed the neck of the guitar, deadening the music. "This is fine for your part of the show," he said pointing to the floor of the stage. "You can stand wherever you want. But then when you get the crowd warmed up, you'll ask Bull Bannon to sing a song or two. Not Earl Bannon, not Earl Stanley Bannon, not E. S. Bannon, and not Major Bannon, but *Bull* Bannon. I'll make out like I'm modest, but you'll insist and get the crowd behind you until I step up on stage. Then," he pointed to a dark corner of the stage, "you'll step back there and play softly while I sing. Understand?"

This Caleb did not care for. "All right," he said through clenched teeth. "But, major, if you ever want to stop the music again, I'd just as soon you grab *me* by the neck instead of my guitar."

He took his place in the shadow and listened to the major sing, coming quickly to the conclusion that the man had wasted whatever money he might have spent on voice lessons. Caleb had played songs for men who could stutter off-key with more feeling than Bull Bannon sang with. He hit all the pitches, but there were no guts in anything he said.

After a tense two-hour rehearsal, Bannon let Caleb go. He saddled Powder River immediately and rode to town. He had been trying to get into St. Joseph for four days, but rehearsals had kept him busy. Bannon was probably expecting him to practice his own routine for the cast again tonight, but Caleb had taken enough orders. He had business of his own to attend to in town.

He asked a few people on the streets if they had ever heard of a woman named Sarah Ludlow. Finally, an old gentleman scratched his head, stared at the stars, and brought her to mind.

"Ludlow, Ludlow," he muttered. "Sounds familiar. Yes, come to think of it, there's an old lady named Ludlow who runs a boardinghouse at the end of Hall Street. I don't know if her name is Sarah. Everybody calls her Widow Ludlow."

Caleb tied his reins at a hitching rail in front of the run-down two story. There were lights on in most of the rooms, so he didn't think it too late to call. When he knocked on the door, an old man answered.

"I'm looking for Mrs. Ludlow," he said.

The old man left the door open, disappearing into another room. Caleb waited on the porch until a stooped, shriveled, gray-haired woman appeared.

"We don't have any rooms," she said curtly, closing the door in his face. "Good night."

He blocked the door with his hand. "Wait, ma'am! I'm not lookin' for a room."

She looked him over suspiciously. "What do you want, then? You're not a drummer."

"No, ma'am. I'm a friend of a friend. That is, if your name is Sarah Ludlow."

"It is, but you're obviously mistaken. I don't have any friends."

Caleb felt suddenly awed by the ravages of time. Burl Sandeen had described his Sarah as the prettiest thing in Missouri. But that had been fifty years ago.

"I met a friend of yours ten years back," he said. "He helped me out of a bad spot. I've always wanted to make it over to Saint Jo and tell you he's still thinkin' of you."

"Young man, what on earth are you talking about?" She pursed her lips and glared at him. The old man had wandered back into the parlor behind her and was cupping his hand behind his ear.

"I'm talkin' about Burl Sandeen. He's a friend of mine."

The widow's eyes grew wide and she stepped back from the door.

"What'd he say?" the old man shouted.

The Widow Ludlow whirled as if starlted by the voice. "Go to bed, Mr. Hazelwood, it's none of your concern!" She walked out onto the porch with Caleb and closed the door behind her. "Sit down, young man," she said, pointing at a rocking chair on the porch. She sank into a porch swing facing the rocker. She seemed quite aggravated. "Now, tell me what you know of Burl Sandeen."

"Well, he saved me from freezin' in the Medicine Bow Range ten winters ago. Let me stay with him in his cabin. We nearly starved, but we made it on wolf meat and beans."

"And what did he tell you about me?" she demanded.

"He said he wanted to marry you a long time ago. Said he went on a trip to the mountains and when he came back, you had married some other fellow named Ludlow. Said it nearly broke his heart, and he moved back to the mountains. He said the last he heard of you, you had moved to Saint Jo. That's how I found you. I wasn't sure you'd still be here, but I thought I'd try lookin' you up. I thought you'd like to know where old Burl is at.''

"I would at that," the old lady said, shaking as she rose. "I most certainly would. I would like to dispatch a marshal to arrest the old *bastard*. There is no statute of limitations on murder." She had become hateful, her voice vindictive.

"Ma'am?"

"Count yourself among the luckiest fools on the face of the earth, young man. Thank God for your life. If you wintered with Burl Sandeen, you might as well have survived a season in hell with the devil!"

He was sure she was a crazy woman now. The dark porch and the old creaking house began to spook him. "Are we talkin' about the same Burl Sandeen?"

"The old fugitive obviously forgot to mention that I never wanted nor intended to marry him in the first place. It was the happiest day of my life when he left to go trapping in the mountains. I hoped Indians would scalp him. He was the vilest boy I had ever known and hadn't given me a moment of ease since I was sixteen. He *disgusted* me. I don't suppose he told you that."

"No, he didn't tell it quite that way," Caleb agreed.

"I don't suppose he told you that when he returned from the mountains, and found me married, that he flew into such a rage that he murdered Mr. Ludlow in our own home!" She put her hand over her mouth.

By the light from a window, Caleb saw a tear sparkle in her wild old eye. "No, ma'am," he said. He was stunned. No one had treated him with more kindness than Burl Sandeen.

"That horrible devil will never cease to torment me!" she murmured. "To think of him speaking my name . . . Haven't you heard the stories?" she demanded.

"I just couldn't believe . . ." he said.

"Believe it, young man. He's a bloody murderer who eats human flesh!" She staggered back and clutched her chest, heaving.

Caleb thought she would collapse. He jumped from the rocker to grab her bony elbow and felt the cold, loose flesh of her forearm. "Are you all right, ma'am?"

She jerked away from him. "Don't touch me!" She glowered at him, her face half shadowed by the light from the window. The one eye glistened, the only living part of her dried and wrinkled face. Crisp stalks of gray hair stuck up around her head and caught the light like a shattered halo. "He should have eaten *you*," she hissed.

Caleb remembered tracks in the snow: Burl's over his own. Following him. Hunting him? He backed away, stumbled down the porch steps. "I'm sorry," he said.

The old man opened the door and looked out as Caleb mounted. "Who is it?" he shouted, cupping his hand behind his ear.

Widow Ludlow watched Caleb ride away. She screamed: "Go to bed, Mr. Hazelwood!"

SEVENTY-FIVE

HE THOUGHT HE would feel relieved to reach the show grounds again and to be among his new acquaintances. But he didn't really know any of them. He thought he liked Seagrass Gibson, but what did he know about him? No more than he had known about Burl Sandeen. He wondered about every man he had ever met, from Milt Starling to Washita Jack Shea to Bull Bannon. He didn't really know any of them. Not even Javier Maldonado. Not Horace Gribble nor Chief Long Fingers. Who were they?

He knew only Pete and Buster. Pete was dead.

This was the drifter's life. Loneliness. He knew more about music than he knew about people. He knew his horse better than his friends. He barely knew his woman. He didn't know his children at all. He was wasting his life. A saddle tramp. He should have stayed. Amelia wanted him there. Buster Thompson was the one man he knew. He should have stayed home.

"Hey, Catgut!" someone said, stepping out of the glowing beer-garden tent. "The girls'll dance if you'll fiddle for us. Will you?"

He held the gelding back. "Will I? Hell, that's all I'm good for. I *reckon* I will."

So he carried his fiddle into the tent and leaned his bow hard on the strings, escaping in song. He made the instrument moan and sing; he made it drone like a bagpipe he had once heard played by a Scottish ranch manager. He stomped music from his boots, sweated harmony from his pores.

And he played his crowd as well as any song or hollow box with strings, soaking in the applause, filling for a time the loneliness inside. When he sang, the air he breathed was pure elixir. They took turns looking up at him in wonder and envy, and Major Bannon could hardly tear his admiring eyes away. Finally Bull had to stop the music and send the players to bed.

But the great power continued to engulf Caleb as he traveled alone through the darkness of the tent city. Tunes merged in his head as he went about the motions of removing his saddle and turning Powder River into the pen. He carried his weightless tack to his canvas tepee and dropped it inside. He fell on his bedroll, almost exhausted.

Then, before he could sleep, the helplessness returned, rushing down on him like an avalanche. The crowd was gone, its memory worthless. He was suddenly sick and hollow. Glory forsook him like a bullet and discarded him, a smoking empty shell. He lay in his tent, desperate and vacant. He had no one, felt nothing. Cold blowing winds seemed to echo inside of him. Stones falling in hollow canyons, blasts of faraway lightning. Every breath hurt like black smoke. What was the use? Pete was dead. What was the use of anything?

It should have been me, he thought. Oh, why couldn't it have been me?

Then the words began to whisper. They sang down to him, and he breathed them in like oxygen. He lay limp, absorbing the lyrics like a tree taking life from sunlight. They formed the essence of everything he knew, all that had gone right and gone wrong in his past and all that would move him into the future. He sang them, soundlessly, again and again in his head. It was the end of something he had started years before under the Rampart Range. It was the beauty and sorrow of his life in song.

There was a guitar somewhere in the tepee. He rolled to all fours and crawled around in the dark, feeling. His knuckle thumped against the box and knocked a chordless sound from it. He pulled the instrument across his lap and placed his calloused fingertips over the strings.

Bull Bannon was walking from the darkened beer garden to the shiny red Pullman car when heard the singing. He stopped, tossed a golden curl back from his ear, cocked his head to one side, and listened. He stayed for a verse or two, then shrugged and walked away as the strange sad words faded behind him. That Catgut Caleb Holcomb knew songs he had never even heard of.

The next day, after the opening performance of his Extravaganza of the Western Wilds, Major Bannon caught up with Caleb on his way to the beer garden. The showman was beaming over the reaction of the audience to his first show. He strode long in his famous buckskin suit, well pleased with his success.

"Come on, Catgut," he said. "I'll introduce you. I know just the tune to grab the crowd's guts."

When they entered the tent, Caleb made his way among the saloon girls to the stage, Bannon falling behind, being swamped by admirers. The fiddler began tuning up, hoping he wouldn't disappoint Bull. He didn't know if he was in much of a mood for playing today.

When he finally reached the stage, the major turned to the city gents in the beer garden and said, "Gentlemen, your attention please. Our own Catgut Caleb Holcomb—authentic minstrel of the western wilds, Rocky Mountain troubadour, a cowboy of no small renown—will now favor us with a song." He gestured so pointedly that the fringes on his buckskin suit almost shook themselves into tangles. "Catgut!" he cried. "Play the 'Shortgrass Song'!"

Caleb raised his fiddle but only gawked at Bull. "Sir?"

"The 'Shortgrass Song.' You know, the one about the drifter. He comes riding down from the mountains, out of the trees, and into the short-grass country. I heard you practicing it last night in your lodge, son. The 'Shortgrass Song.' "

Caleb balked. Some of the words were not even a day old. Others he had known for years. He put his fiddle down, picked up the guitar, and put the strap of rattlesnake skin behind his head. "I'll give it a try," he said. "But I only just learned it here lately."

Bannon laughed. "Such modesty!" he cried. "They only make them like this out west, gentlemen!" He urged Caleb to play with a flourish of his hand.

The minstrel of the western wilds stepped to the edge of his platform and looked over the audience. He had never intended to play this one for anybody. It was like doing "Camptown Races" the day his mother died. He thanked God they didn't know he had made it up himself. To them, it was just another western ditty. He started strumming with his short-fingered left hand and entered uncertainly into a thing Major Bannon had termed the "Shortgrass Song."

The drifter rode in on a westerly breeze,
To the shortgrass country, out of the trees.
Down t'wards the meadows he galloped until
He stopped in the shadows cast long 'cross the hill.
He swung from the saddle, loosened the girth,
Dusted his clothes of the soil of God's earth,
Hung his old hat on a slick saddle horn,
Looked o'er the wheat fields and broad rows of corn.
Indian blankets grew 'round the gravestone.
Paintbrushes, too, where their seeds had been thrown,
And his home was not even a mile out of sight,
But he'd throw down his bedroll and stay for the night.

He rode in from the West,
Down from the Rockies and onto the plains
To the land he loved best,
Where he could never remain.

Born within sight of the high mountaintops,
He grew up 'round plow horses, cattle, and crops.
With his older brother, he carried his load.
They tended the fields and the ranges they rode.
Hardworkin' farm boys and ranchers by trade,
They lived with the fortune the family had made,
But the drifter forever looked over the hills
And dreamed of the mountains' adventures and thrills.
When he came of age, he decided to roam.
He said, 'There's a life I must live on my own.'
And he promised his brother, that day, one sure thing,
He'd return with his tales of adventure each spring.

And then he rode into the West,
Up to the Rockies, away from the plains,
From the land he loved best,
Where he could never remain.

The drifter was faithful, returned every year.
His brother was eager his stories to hear,
And he'd watch o'er the hilltop when wildflowers bloomed,
'Til the drifter rode down through the air they perfumed.
At nights, by the fireplace, he'd listen to tales
Of wild West adventures and hard-ridden trails,
Of mountains so high that the trees didn't grow,
Of deserts so wide and of canyons so low.
The brothers, together, would ride o'er the plains,
Bound by the blood that ran red through their veins,
And they'd savor each moment together until
The drifter would saddle up, bound o'er the hill.

And then he'd ride into the West,
Up to the Rockies, away from the plains,
From the land he loved best,
Where he could never remain.

Early one mornin' while coyotes cried,
The elder son went for a deer-huntin' ride,
For he'd saddled his pony and loaded his gun,
And was off with the first eastern glow of the sun.
The stallion was nervous to smell of the snow
Whistled in by a norther beginnin' to blow,
When across a box canyon, the hunter, in luck,
Leveled his sights on a wide-antlered buck.

The cloudy sky rumbled, the Winchester roared,
The cow pony stumbled, the freezin' rain poured,
The wide-antlered buck and the hunter both fell
Into the box canyon, as deep as a well.

He died there in the West.
Over the prairies, the drifter rode on.
When they laid him to rest,
None could bear sayin', 'He's gone.'

So they buried him under the homecoming trail
That the drifter returned on each year without fail.
When he read the inscription, he got down and cried,
For he knew from the gravestone his brother had died.
And his home was not even a mile down the hill,
But he stayed for a promise he had to fulfill.
He camped there that evenin', and he camps there each year
To tell his wild stories for his brother to hear.
And now every year when the drifter rides west,
He carries a package of seeds in his vest.
And he stops on the hill, throws 'em all 'round the tomb
And each spring a new wildflower memorial blooms.

And then he rides into the West,
Up to the Rockies, away from the plains,
From the land he loves best,
Where he can never remain.

The drifter found Bull Bannon alone that night and told him he couldn't go east with the show.

"Not you, too, Catgut," the showman cried, throwing his hands into the air. "Seagrass was just in here to tell me the same damn thing. Said he didn't want to miss the cattle drive from Texas. Says there might not be many more of them. I hope you have a better reason."

"I believe I do," Caleb said. "I have to marry the mother of my children and take her home so's I can run my pa's ranch."

Bannon shook his head. "You boys are fools for the cow business." He tried to change the young man's mind, but he could tell it was no use. He was going to have to find another tent-show fiddler. Oh, but there would never be another like Catgut Caleb Holcomb.

SEVENTY-SIX

SAM DUGAN DIDN'T understand the principles of delegation. As manager of the Holcomb Ranch, he could have taken up a life of easy riding, making the rounds on the spread, looking after his subordinates. But Sam still roped, branded, castrated, and earmarked with the cowboys on the bottom of the payroll.

He even did fence work, a job so demeaning that Sam couldn't bear to force it on anybody else. He did almost all of the fence riding on his own, and lately there had been plenty of it to keep him busy.

The sentiment against fences on public land had been growing. Holcomb Ranch, as one of the most flagrant fence outfits on the Front Range, was a constant target for retaliation.

Ab didn't own most of the land he fenced. The only plots he held exclusive title to flanked Monument Creek. The rest of the range he claimed was public land. But since he owned the nearest water, Ab figured no one else could use the grass.

His argument had held up before Pete had ordered several wells drilled on the divide to the east of Monument Creek. A windmill at each well pumped just enough water to keep a trough full. The troughs allowed the cattle to better use the grass up on the divides. They didn't have to walk all the way down to Monument Creek to get water between feeds. They didn't walk off as much weight.

But because the windmills were on public land, some nesters thought anyone's cattle should be able to use the water they pumped. They didn't see how Ab had the right to fence the range in for his own personal use. Maybe he owned the windmills, but he didn't own the land or the well water.

So occasionally some small-time farmer would buy a few head of cattle, cut the Holcomb fence, and let his herd graze the public lands and drink from the wells Pete had drilled. Ab took a dim view of such practice. Any stray cow that showed up on his ranch would be drawn mysteriously into the mountains, and perhaps never found.

Most of the old nesters feared and respected Colonel Holcomb, even if they did disagree with him on the fencing issue. Only the newcomers attempted to break his monopoly of Monument Park, and none of them had the resources to fight long.

In his own mind Ab knew he was right in claiming everything inside his fences. It was not just a matter of legal ownership, private or public land. He was first in Monument Park. He had fought Indians and defended Colorado against the Confederates. He had beaten droughts and plagues.

He had worked hard and buried loved ones. He knew what was rightfully his.

Sam Dugan, as ranch manager and head fence fixer, knew as well as anybody how powerful the antifencing sentiment had grown. He was not at all surprised one morning in midsummer to see all five strands of the south fence curled back like whiskers where once they had met between two posts.

The thing that did surprise him was the size of the herd that had been turned into the Holcomb pasture—the biggest incursion of beeves that had taken place yet. Hooves had turned the ground to bare sand at the hole in the fence. Sam decided to hunt up the cattle and run as many of them as he could find back out through the hole before fixing the fence.

The tracks told him that the cattle had scattered after entering the pasture, probably spooked on purpose by the fence cutters, to make them harder to round up. He headed for the nearest windmill, following a trail left by about a dozen beeves. A half mile from the well, he spotted a scrawny bovine taking in grass on a prairie ridge. It looked at first like a skinny heifer or a young dogie steer. Upon closer examination, however, Sam saw that the stray was actually a bull—though a pitifully flaccid excuse for a breeder.

Colonel Holcomb wasn't going to like this at all—a mongrel bull undercutting his imported herd sires, corrupting his Hereford and Durham bloodlines. As he topped the ridge on which the puny bull grazed, Sam came into view of the windmill. Around it stood the sorriest gathering of bulls he had ever seen dangle a set of testicles, and Sam had seen his share. The bull on the ridge seemed like a prizewinner by comparison.

He loped northward, in search of more trespassing cattle. He found nothing but spindly legged, ridge-backed, ewe-necked bulls. Someone had set out to ruin the Holcomb pedigrees. Someone wanted war with Colonel Ab.

Before he reached the next windmill, Sam saw a derrick towering over the plains in a new place. Riding to a high roll in the prairie for a better view, he saw a collection of wagons bearing well-drilling tools, lumber, fencing, and farm implements. Half a dozen men were at work, two of them marking off corners. In the middle of them all stood a short, stout man with his hands placed on his hips in a stance of determination, a rifle hung from one shoulder by a leather sling. Sam recognized him instantly.

When he arrived at Ab's cabin, his horse was frothed with more sweat than Sam had caused any mount to produce in years. He didn't bother knocking on the door. It was almost midday, and he knew where Ab would be—sitting in his rocking chair, one legged, staring at the gravestone on the bald hill.

"Colonel," he said, out of breath. "You ain't gonna believe this, but Terence Mayhall is back."

The rocker creaked. Ab craned his neck to look at Sam. His eyes swiveled in the slack, pale skin of his face. "What do you mean, he's back?"

"Looks like he's stakin' a new claim, up near the divide, about a mile from the Pinery. He's got men with him. They're drillin' a well and buildin' a house."

Ab turned back to the window.

"That ain't all," Sam said. "They cut your fences and run in about a hundred head of the wormiest little bulls I ever seen. He's out to get your goat, colonel."

Ab sighed. He was tired. He had been sitting there wondering if the history books would ever mention his name. They might describe him as a hero of two wars, pioneer of the Front Range, cattle king, land baron. They might paint his life as a glory or a triumph. They would never know how many days he had spent mired in depression, his mind numb with confusion, unable to sift through the complexities of living, his body almost paralyzed, detached from his brain and his will. He knew he was not like other people. Others did not dwell on death the way he did, hour after hour. No history would ever say how many times he had fought his way back from the tempting brink of self-obliteration.

But now, as he gathered Sam's words, one thought began to stray from the swarm. He lost his memories of Pete, Matthew, and Ella. He released the vexing specters of cattle, water, war. Children, grandchildren, wage hands, crops, and railroads—all intertwined—streamed away to some remote chamber of his mind. Caleb remained, plunging into a million horrors from here to Texas. But there was room for one other thought: land. Terence Mayhall, that worthless Georgia cracker, had no business coming back to Monument Park.

"Lee Fong," he said. "Lee Fong! Where in Hades is my leg?"

When Mayhall saw the two men coming, he cocked his rifle and rested it on his burly shoulder, his finger on the trigger. For years he had worked toward this moment. He was going to show that Pennsylvania Yankee that a southern man would not be held down. Three men joined him as he gloated, waiting for Ab to arrive.

The colonel rode uneasily; he hadn't been in a saddle for months. "You're trespassing," he said when he rode up with Sam.

Mayhall's muscles bunched under his tight shirtsleeves. "*You* are," he replied. "You see those stakes you passed back yonder? That's my property line."

"This is my ranch," Ab said.

"This is public land, and I've filed on it. So have my brothers. Meet Joe, Frank, and Edgar Mayhall." He tossed his head sideways to indicate his kin. "We've filed under the Homestead and Timber Culture acts.

That'll make us owners of better than twelve hundred acres when we prove up. Plus we have all this free range around us."

"This is not free range. You cut my fence to get in, didn't you? You can't go cutting a man's fence whenever it suits you."

"I damn sure can. If a man fences public range, I have a right and duty to cut his fences."

"And I have a right to notify the county sheriff."

"Go ahead and notify him. But you ought to know that I cut your fence under the advice of the U.S. marshal."

"Did he advise you to ruin my herd with your worthless bulls, too?"

The Mayhall brothers chuckled. "No," Terence said, "that was our own idea. We must have hunted all over the state of Colorado for those bulls. You know, it's hard to find a sorry bull when you go lookin' for one."

"They'll be harder to find once they get up in those mountains," Ab said, pointing his thumb toward the Rampart Range.

Mayhall glared at Sam. "Anybody we catch rustling our cattle into the mountains will get a bullet through the head." He lifted the rifle barrel from his shoulder and propped the butt against his hip. "We're prepared and authorized to kill stock thieves caught in the act of rustling."

"You can't run that many bulls on the free range!" Ab shouted. "I'll notify the cattlemen's association!"

"The cattlemen's association can be damned and go to hell. I already sent them a letter telling them those bulls will stay on this range until you and all the others take down your illegal fences. Me and my brothers are not alone, Holcomb. Don't think you can outgun us. We can muster a hundred settlers on any day."

"A hundred settlers! When I came here, there were no settlers!"

"Uncle Sam never said the first could have it all."

Ab chewed his lip. "I'll fence the creek! Don't let your U.S. marshal tell me I can't fence the creek! I own it. I'll keep your herds from water."

"We'll use the windmills," Mayhall said.

"Those are my windmills. I'll tear them down."

"Can't you see us drillin' our own?" He angled his rifle barrel toward the wooden tower where the well drillers were working. "We'll drill more, too. We'll have plenty of water without your cotton-pickin' creek."

Ab fumed. "You won't prove up."

Mayhall shrugged. "Maybe not. Won't be the first time, will it? But I'll still take you down a peg or two. Now that we're here, others will be comin'. There's men filin' on Monument Park land today. You're gonna see a land rush, colonel. Meanwhile, my little ol' bulls will be breedin' your prize cows faster than you can . . ."

"Shut your mouth!" Ab shouted. "You've made your point." He reined his horse away from the newly established Mayhall Ranch.

Sam followed. "What are we gonna do, colonel?" he asked.

"You send the boys out," Ab said. "Have them ride all the fences. I want to know how many have been cut. Don't fix any yet, just get back to the ranch and tell me how bad it is. I'm going to ride into town and see the county clerk."

"Yes, sir," Sam said.

SEVENTY-SEVEN

AB FOUND A line of land seekers at the county clerk's office. He stormed past all of them.

"Good morning, colonel," one of them said with a self-assured grin.

Morley Bertram and a homesteader were looking over the county map when Ab burst in.

"Get your fingers off my land," he said. "I see where you're pointing!"

Bertram frowned. "Mr. Smethers, would you excuse us, please."

The homesteader smirked and saw himself out.

"What do you mean letting Mayhall file on my ranch?" Ab demanded.

Bertram shook his head and sat on his desk. "It's not your ranch, colonel, and you know that as well as I do."

"Have I not supplemented your salary for fifteen years in order to gain exclusive ownership of Monument Park?"

"Colonel, how many times have I told you over the past three or four years that if you want to own Monument Park, you had better start buying it from the government? Merely fencing the land is not good enough. I've told you that a hundred times."

"You were supposed to keep the settlers out!" Ab said.

"And I did keep them out, sir, as long as I possibly could. But there have been numerous complaints sent in to the land office, the state capitol, Congress! The Front Range is settling too fast, colonel. I simply can't keep the homesteaders out anymore. They have a legal right to file on Monument Park."

Ab pointed a threatening finger at the little functionary. "Don't you quit on me now, Bertram. I'll see that you are ruined along with me. I'll tell them about your stipend."

Bertram scoffed. "I'd rather take my chances with you than with them." He nodded toward the land filers beyond his door. "I can deny your charge. It's your word against mine. And, frankly, colonel, you're not as popular a figure in this county as you once were. The fence cutters are gaining control. Besides, if I did continue to work with you, the land office would come out here to investigate, and they would find both of us guilty of fraud. They're cracking down, colonel.''

Ab couldn't think of anything else to say. He held his breath, turned red, grunted, and began to pace.

"It's the windmills," Bertram said. "They've tipped the odds. Times have changed.''

Ab's wooden leg continued to clack against the floor.

"It's not as bad as it looks," Bertram said. "You still own every plot on both sides of the Monument, all the way from your ranch to the head of the creek. That's valuable land. You control the water rights. The Appropriation Doctrine entitles you to as much water as you need to irrigate all the land you own. You were first to build ditches. That gives you priority. And there's still time for you to buy more land. As much as you can afford. Come look at the map. Show me what you want to buy.''

"Look at the map?" Ab roared. "Is that what you think you're giving away to these claim jumpers? Squares on a map? Why don't you come look at the land instead of the map?'' He stomped his peg down on the floor and stormed out, pushing his way through the homesteaders who would soon acquire his kingdom.

Sam collected intelligence from the fence riders and sauntered to the cabin about sundown to break the news to Ab. "It ain't good," he said, standing on the porch, talking to his employer in the dark doorway. "They've cut the wire to every pasture, even the cross fences. There's already another homesteader drivin' stakes around your number-four windmill.''

"Using my well?" Ab said, as if wounded.

"Yes, sir. Says you can tear the windmill down if you want to, but you can't legally close the well. He says he can build his own windmill or buy yours from you. Either way, he has claim to the land.''

Ab glanced nervously across his fragile domain. He could feel them digging post holes, breaking sod. Their plowshares might as well have been turning his own flesh.

"Mayhall organized them," Sam said. "They planned to move in today and all this week, together. They say there's a dozen men ready to stake their claims tomorrow.''

Ab's eyes were still sweeping the prairies.

"What do you want us to do, colonel? You want us to run those sorry bulls into the mountains? We could stampede some through Mayhall's place. We'll make it hard on 'em. That homesteader up on number four has already plowed a firebreak. We could set fire inside of it. Burn his grass.''

"No," Ab said.

"The boys are with me," Sam said. "If this ranch goes, our jobs go."

"No," Ab repeated. "It isn't worth getting yourself killed. Mayhall meant what he said today. He'll put a bullet through your head. You dumb Texans can never tell when you're whipped."

Sam straightened up and stepped back. "Wouldn't be no Texas if we did."

"And the whole nation would be better off. Just leave those nesters alone. There's nothing you can do."

Sam left, angry and worried, and trudged back to the bunkhouse. He liked the Front Range. He had planned on working there the rest of his life.

Ab dragged his rocker out onto the porch and watched the stars come out.

"You want your supper, colonel?" Lee Fong asked.

Ab waved him away. "Give it to the dogs, Lee Fong." He rocked, his mind getting tired again.

A light came up in Buster's little cabin. What in Hades was that black man up to now? Always working on something, always tinkering, inventing. Nigger rigging! Ab chuckled. ("Forgive me, Ella. Just a thought.") Always improvising. Always thinking.

He left the rocker and walked down the porch steps. Pausing, he looked up at the stars. He followed the irrigation ditch, gurgling with life-giving water. The trail was well-worn. Buster had forgiven him for burying Pete on the hill. Buster forgave everything. His was true wisdom.

It was over. The ranch was lost. He felt almost relieved. He wanted to laugh. He wanted so badly to feel the release of laughter.

When he got to the door, he found Buster working on an experimental wildflower seeder.

"Evenin'," the inventor said, looking up from his work table. "Come in."

Ab made for the old bunk, his peg leg leaving craters in the burlap carpet as he walked. He sat quietly and watched Buster trying to fashion a funnel from an old sheet of tin.

"What did that little county clerk tell you?" Buster asked.

Ab sighed. "I'm whipped, Buster. They've got my ranch now."

"What are you gonna do?"

Ab leaned back against the log wall. "What would you do?"

Buster tapped a single rivet and pushed his new contraption away. He tilted back in his chair and propped his feet up on the table. "I'd get my good name back."

"What in Hades does that mean?"

Buster smiled. "Ol' Mayhall has made hisself the hero. Made you look like the goat. Them new settlers, they don't know you tamed this place. They don't know you fought the Indians, brought in the first cattle.

You got to start all over makin' your reputation with them. They think you're just a greedy old rancher fencin' the public range.''

"I'm greedy for what's rightfully mine: Monument Park.''

Buster scratched his curly beard. "There's more than one way to own land.''

Ab waited. He squinted. "Are you going to tell me what you mean?''

"Get 'em on your side instead of Mayhall's.''

"How?''

"Let 'em have your ranch. They're gonna get it anyway. Tell 'em they're welcome to it. Sell 'em the wire off your fences. Sell it cheap. *Help* 'em settle. Sell 'em your cattle, too.''

Ab sat up, tense and hopeful. "Go on.''

"Take the money you make and buy as much land as you want around the ranch here. You can keep raisin' your horses and maybe a few beef steers.''

"How am I going to make my living off of a few horses and beef steers?''

"You can make your livin' off land and water. You own all that land along the creek. Hold on to it. Lease it out to them farmers. Sell 'em the water. You own the water rights. I'll help you build a new reservoir upstream, just as long as I get enough down here to grow my crops. We can irrigate this whole valley.''

"You think they'll buy water from me? They'll just drill the park full of wells.''

"They can't pump enough out of a well to wet more than a couple of acres. They can grow enough to get by but not enough to make money. They want to make money. They'll buy your water.''

Ab sank back against the wall again. "Maybe. But that's one poor way to own this valley. They'll reduce me to opening sluice gates and turning spigots.''

"I ain't through yet,'' Buster said. "You need to buy yourself a quarter section beside your railroad pens and your depot.''

"What for?''

"Start yourself a town. Holcomb, Colorado. Cut it up in lots and sell 'em. Build yourself a general store. Them farmers will need supplies and tools. Might as well buy 'em there. It's closer than Colorado Springs. Give 'em credit. Help 'em make good.''

"Credit?''

"Yes, sir. You've got to get 'em started. You want 'em to prove up.''

"I do?''

"Some of 'em. There's good farmers and there's bad farmers. About half of 'em will prove up. Then they'll want to buy out the farms of the other half, the ones that don't make it. And that's where you really make your money. That's where you start to own this valley all over again, in a whole new way.''

"Buster . . .'' Ab rubbed his temples, trying to make sense of the advice. "What are you talking about?''

Buster let his feet fall from the table to the burlap. He leaned forward in his chair. "Make yourself a banker.''

"A banker!'' Ab actually laughed at the notion. It felt good to laugh.

"They're gonna need to borrow money to buy more land. You loan it to 'em. They're gonna mortgage their farms, colonel. If you want to own Monument Park, that's the way to do it. Repossess it!''

Ab fell sideways on the bunk, kicked his wooden leg, and released his cares in laughter. "Oh, Buster, you've got more big ideas! Where am I going find the funds to start a bank?''

"Think like bankers think. Start with a little of your own money, then go see Captain Dubois. Go courtin' investors.''

"This isn't Wall Street. Where am I going to find investors?''

Buster stomped his foot on his burlap carpet. "Start right here.''

Ab couldn't sit up for laughing. "You? Buster, you have no idea how much money it takes to start a bank, do you?''

Buster grinned and got up. He walked to the open door, looked out both ways, closed the door, and latched it. "Help me move this table over,'' he said.

Ab shook his head and pushed himself up from the bunk. He lifted one side of the table and helped set it aside. Buster knelt on the burlap and found a flap that had been under one leg of the table. He pulled the flap back to reveal the sawdust underflooring. Carefully, he parted the sawdust with his hands as Ab bent over him. Under four inches of wood shavings he came to the lid of a wooden box. He opened the lid. Ab gasped. Buster began removing bundles and bundles of government bills, neatly sorted and tied.

"My Lord, Buster! How much have you got down there?''

"Almost ten thousand.''

Ab staggered back to the bunk and sank onto the quilt. His face darkened. "Where did you get that much money?'' he asked.

"Been farmin' twenty years now. Never bought nothin' I didn't think I couldn't make money with. I grow my own food. I grow feed for my stock. I just been savin' it. It ain't enough to start a bank with, but it's somethin'.''

Ab stared with admiration at the pile of bills on the table. "You need to put it in a bank, all right. But you know how people are. No offense, but if folks heard I was starting a bank with the wages of a Negro homesteader, they'd laugh me all the way back to Pennsylvania.''

"You don't have to say where all the money comes from. Nobody will laugh at Captain Dubois's name. I know he'll help you. He doesn't want you goin' broke and losin' Amelia's share of the Holcomb fortune.''

Big ideas just came naturally to Buster. There *was* more than one way to own Monument Park. How long had he been thinking about it? Ab grabbed two bundles of cash, squeezed them, smelled them. He looked up, sadly.

"I just wanted a ranch," he said. "Not for me. For the boys."

"They're all gone, now. Except for Caleb. And if he wanted this ranch bad enough, I guess he'd be here fightin' for it."

Ab cringed. He knew Caleb hated him. The awful guilt came over him, and the fear. Where was Caleb? Why did he live that way? To spite me, Ab thought. Some day Buster was going to come to him, stone faced, and tell him Caleb was gone, too. Ella would curse him from on high. A father should leave his sons living. Death stalked Caleb, like a hawk hovering over him.

"You've got to look after what *you* want," Buster said. "Caleb's made his own choices."

SEVENTY-EIGHT

AB MADE DAILY trips to the railroad station to oversee the surveying of his town. He had to ride past sod huts, frame houses, sheds, cottonwood sprouts, and windmill towers that stood where once his cattle had roamed. The old free range that had been his ranch was now crisscrossed with dirt lanes running between the homesteads.

One of the roads ran right past the cornfield Buster farmed for Ab on shares. One day while riding by, the colonel noticed that some parties unknown had been pilfering sundry roasting ears from his field. He saw several sets of footprints leading from the road to the edge of the cornfield, where he found bare corn stalks, stripped of ears. He whipped his mount to a gallop and found Buster supervising the building of the Holcomb General Store near the train station.

"Buster!" he shouted, getting down from his horse. "Come down here!"

Buster climbed down from the corner of the building, and took the square-shanked nails from his mouth.

"Who in Hades has been stealing my corn?" he demanded.

Buster shrugged. "Probably starvin' homesteaders. They don't take much. They got to eat."

"I want you to do something about it." He hitched up his belt, encumbered as it was by the leather rigging of his wooden leg. "They won't get away with stealing my crops in addition to my land."

"What do you want me to do?"

"I don't know. Think of something. You're always thinking of things."

Buster twirled his clawhammer in his hand. He shook his head. "I just don't how you're gonna stop 'em, colonel. You can't stand out there and guard the cornfield. It ain't hardly worth it for a few ears of corn."

Ab frowned and stomped away to sit on a stack of lumber in front of the store.

Buster went back to framing the building with the carpenters Captain Dubois had hired through the Holcomb Town Company. He glanced down at Ab every now and then and found him in deep study, solving the problem of the corn thieves.

After almost an hour he heard a saw hacking furiously at a plank and saw the old colonel cutting a length of board. Ab cut three pieces in all, each about two feet long. Then he found a hammer and some nails and fastened the three boards to a four-foot stake he had sawed to a point at the bottom end.

"Buster!" he shouted. "Where's the paint?"

"What color?"

The old man threw his saw down. "In the name of the devil! I don't care what color!"

"There's some buckets of white paint in the depot. Some red over there in the wagon."

Ab shouldered his blank placard and stalked to the wagon. He found a paintbrush, spent a few minutes slathering his message on the sign, then stepped back to admire his handiwork.

Curiosity got the better of Buster. He put his tools down and walked over to the wagon to read the sign. It was scrawled in gangling red letters across the three boards Ab had nailed to the stake. He had applied the paint rather liberally; it ran down from the letters like blood. The message was just as ghastly:

> ONE OF THESE EARS OF CORN
> IS POISONED. CAN YOU
> GUESS WHICH ONE?

He planted the sign in his cornfield, facing the road. The pilfering came to an abrupt end. "That will teach these nesters what's theirs and what's not," he bragged to Buster. He drew a feeling of omnipotence from the sign every time he rode past.

One morning, however, just a couple of days before Buster planned to harvest the corn, Ab glanced approvingly toward his sign and, to his astonishment, found another one driven into the ground right next to his:

NOW THERE ARE TWO.
YOU GUESS.

Buster had to laugh when he heard.

"What do you find so funny about these land grabbers poisoning my corn?" Colonel Holcomb railed.

"I thought you poisoned it yourself," Buster said.

"No, I didn't poison my own corn! I had no cause to. The sign only made them *think* there was an ear poisoned in there."

Buster almost tore himself open trying to hold his laughter back. "Maybe now they just *think* there's two," he said.

Ab thundered away at a gallop. He rode to the Mayhall Ranch and found Terence picking his own corn with the strap of a sack looped over one solid shoulder.

"Mayhall!" he shouted, swatting stalks aside as he limped between the rows.

"Good mornin', colonel," Terence said, taking his hat off to fan himself.

Ab stopped a few feet away. "I have never seen the likes of thieves and vandals as those you brought into this valley! You have turned my peaceable ranch into a hive of ne'er-do-wells. I want to know who poisoned my corn!"

Mayhall scratched his head. "Why, colonel, I was told you poisoned it yourself."

"Who put that sign in my field?"

"Sign? What sign?" Mayhall wrinkled his nose and squinted quite convincingly.

Ab shuddered with anger. He turned around and marched back down the furrow.

"Wait, colonel."

The old man stopped.

"If it's good safe corn you want, why don't you just say so. I'll be neighborly. Here." He tossed an ear at Ab. "You can have some of mine."

Ab caught the ear and threw it back.

Mayhall ducked, laughed, and began tossing ears at Ab as he stalked away. "Hope you don't have any trouble sellin' that poisoned corn!" Mayhall shouted.

Ab pulled the signs up and threw them away, but it was too late. Someone had notified the newspapers. One Denver editor, a rabid opponent of public-land fencing and, as such, an old enemy of Ab Holcomb's, made great sport of the tainted-corn fiasco. He even had the audacity to refer to Ab as "a colonel of poisoned corn."

No buyer would accept a single ear of Ab's corn that summer, and the Denver and Rio Grande would not ship his crop to another market where he might find a willing buyer. The newspapers had sources in Monument Park who kept a close eye on the colonel's produce. He was stuck with wagonloads of corn.

"Now what are we to do?" he asked Buster. "Let it sit out in the weather and rot? Let the bugs get it?"

"I'll build us a big corn crib," Buster said. "We can fence in a stock-yard and feed it to the cows. They can't read no signs."

Ab sighed as he looked out over the remnants of his ranch. "I never thought I'd see the day when my own cattle would stomp this park into a stinking stockyard," he said.

SEVENTY-NINE

THEY WERE TOTAL strangers—he a line rider for the Seven Stars, she a common whore of Seymour, Texas. They inspected each other only briefly before they went upstairs.

He looked familiar. She wondered. No, she would have remembered that mustache—two mops hiding his mouth. The rest of his beard looked about two weeks old. He needed a haircut. He had been out at some line camp for a while. At least he had taken a bath. No, he was not a regular. He was new. Maybe he would be the one to take her away. She would work a little harder for this fare—the way she did with all the new ones that didn't just outright disgust her.

She looked familiar to him, too. He couldn't figure out why. He had seen his share of whores, that was why. They were starting to look alike. No, he didn't know her, and that was the way he liked it. He knew whores had it tough, but he didn't want to hear about it. He just wanted to see her smile, feel her soft skin, and get his money's worth. If he didn't some other jack would. He would treat her kindly. He was doing her a favor.

She closed the door and started taking off her dress. He pulled his boots and pants off and sat on the bed. She pulled the curtains together to dim the afternoon sunlight and came to him, wearing only a frilly pair of bloomers. She was not particularly big breasted, but what she had was firm, and he felt the guilt giving way to the old recurrent longing. She had the build of a railroad trestle: straight and strong. He didn't speak.

She smiled. She was painted like a porcelain doll, her mousy hair piled up in ringlets. She lay on the bed and touched his arm. He rolled onto her. She closed her eyes. He nestled his mustache against her neck, touched his lips to her skin, and smelled the powder on her shoulders.

She felt his rough hand touch her above the waist of the frilly bloomers and move across her heaving stomach. A peculiar touch. Over her ribs gently. He almost tickled her, but there was something strange in his tender grip. His left hand found her breast and squeezed, as if to pick up a melon.

Her eyes opened. With her right hand, she put her fingers over his. The first two felt odd. No fingernails. Too short!

"Caleb?" she said in a husky voice, feeling his frost-shortened digits.

His breath stopped short in her ear. He pushed himself up to look at her. "How did you know? . . ." He pushed farther away, kneeling between her thighs. "Who the heck? . . ." His hemp sagged.

Her eyes glistened. She pushed herself up on her elbows and smiled. "Don't you remember? Denison, Texas. I'm Tess Wiley."

He turned apple red. "Oh, for the love of God!" He jumped off the bed and hid on the floor, the edge of the mattress shielding him from her view. He shoved his feet desperately into his pants. "They said your name was Candy!" He peeked over the edge of the mattress.

She was sitting cross-legged, confused. "That's just my sportin' name. What's wrong with you?" She scooted to the edge of the bed.

He jumped up, retreated, turned his back, fastened buttons. He studied her face. Too pretty. He couldn't believe it was her. He advanced on her suddenly, held her face in his hands and pulled her upper lip away from her teeth.

"Hey!" she said, swatting his hands away. "I ain't no horse!"

"I thought you had a bad tooth!"

"It got rotten. I pulled it out with a pair of tongs." She removed one of her front teeth. "This one's carved out of an old piano key."

In shame, he sensed the eyes of God drilling him like skewers. His angel-mother turned her haloed head in humiliation. Pete scowled. Matthew laughed. He cussed and picked up his boots.

"Where are you goin'?"

"I'm gettin' out of here!"

"Why? There somethin' wrong with me? Ain't I good enough for you, now that you know where I come from? I hope you don't want your money back!"

He shoved his foot into a boot. "No, I don't want the damn money." He raised his eyes to her, looked quickly away. "For God's sake, put some clothes on!"

She sighed, exasperated, and sprang from the bed.

"Didn't that preacher come see you in Denison? I told him to look after you."

She gasped. ''So you're the one sent him. He took care of me, all right. About once a week, till his wife found out. Them church-goin' biddies liked to have tarred and feathered me!''

He stomped his other boot on. ''What did you do with all that money I gave you in Denison?''

''You didn't give me nothin'!'' She shook her dress down over her head. ''That was my money that Angus stole from me.''

He glanced to make sure she was dressed. ''Well, what did you do with it?''

''I bought me a farm, that's what.''

''What did you want with a farm?'' He propped his hands on his hips and stared at her as if she were the most ignorant child on the face of the earth.

''I wanted to grow corn, stupid.''

''You? Alone?''

''Well, why not? I grew up with a hoe in my hands. I can grow corn.''

''If you can grow corn so damn good, what's makin' you whore for your keep?''

''Don't you git snotty with me.'' She fastened buttons and glowered fiercely. ''The man that buys a whore ain't no better than she is.''

Caleb tucked his shirt in. He didn't answer. He knew she was right.

''Anyway, I had me a good corn crop. I was livin' with some settlers. We all had farms until the ranchers ran their cattle into our fields. The folks I was stayin' with got scared and left, and I didn't have no money, so I had to turn to sportin'.''

''You're lyin'. I've seen acres and acres of corn around this town. Them farmers ain't left.''

''The ranchers gave up on runnin' 'em off.''

''Then how come you won't go back to your farm?''

''I ain't got no house to live in.'' She sat on the bed and pouted.

''Won't any of them settlers take you in again?''

She shook her head. Her eyes were getting puffy, but she wouldn't cry in front of him. ''Not since I turned to sportin'. I ain't good enough for 'em. Or you neither, I guess.''

He frowned. She had an excuse for everything. ''I don't believe you ever had a farm. Farmers work on their feet, not on their backs.''

Tess fixed her eyes on a pitcher of water on the nightstand next to her. ''Well, you think you know everything,'' she growled in her hoarse way. ''I don't always do it on my back. Some of my regular customers have more fancy ideas than you.'' As she spoke, she slid her fingers around the handle of the pitcher. Suddenly, she jumped up and splashed the water at him.

He had seen her reach and knew what she was up to. She owed him one. When the water came at him, he jumped aside and only got sprinkled.

He started to laugh at her failure until the pitcher bounced off the top of his head and broke against the wall. The seat of his pants landed in the puddle on the floor. "Damn your hide . . ." he began. But the basin came flying next, and he considered flight wiser than talk.

Scrambling, he got to his feet and threw the door open as Tess searched for something else to bounce off his skull. He heard the door slam behind him and didn't look back until he reached the bottom of the stairs. She wasn't coming after him.

Several men looked up from their drinks or their poker hands or their conversations with the harlots. Caleb looked down his nose at them, but the wet spot on the seat of his pants took some of the swagger out of him. He rubbed his head. He just wanted to leave.

"Through already?" the buxom madam said, smirking. "Sounds like you had a row up there. I hope you didn't hit my girl."

He took his hat and gun belt down from the pegs on the wall by the front door. "She spilt some water." Gingerly, he positioned his hat around a knot the pitcher had raised on his head, and walked out.

He heard them laughing after he closed the door. He took his bridle reins from the hitching rail. Before he mounted, he looked down the street. He could see corn stalks behind fences on the edge of town.

He shook his head and put a foot in the stirrup. Matthew would have gotten his money's worth whether he knew her or not. What the hell do you care? Why can't you be more like Matthew? He put his foot back on the ground. He couldn't believe himself. Matthew had been only twenty-one when he died, and he was still thinking of him as an older brother.

It wasn't right to leave her there. Not after what he had said to her. But, damn it, it was not his fault. He put his foot back in the stirrup. The joys of his younger days were not joys anymore. Time was when he could use a whore and never care. He was growing a conscience. That preacher in Denison never should have treated her that way. He slipped his foot from the stirrup again.

He had changed. He was fighting the change, but it was coming anyway. Since Pete died, Caleb looked at things differently. These were supposed to be his wildest oats, this his last summer footloose before he married Marisol and took his children back to Holcomb Ranch to live. But he kept hearing Pete telling him he was living all wrong. He burst back into the whorehouse and stormed across the floor to the bottom of the stairs.

"Wait a minute!" the madam yelled. "Your guns, mister."

He ignored her and sprinted up the stairs. He blundered into Tess's room and found her sopping water up from the floor, crying.

"Come on," he said. He grabbed her arm and pulled her to her feet.

"You take your hands off of me," she said, struggling.

"Shut up." He dragged her out of the room.

"What are you doin' with me?"

"I'm gonna teach you how to make a livin' on your feet. I want to have a look at that farm of yours. And it better be there, or I'll put you over my knee."

They scuffled all the way down the stairs. When he made for the doorway, Caleb saw the madam loading shells into a shotgun. He drew his pistol and pointed it at her.

"Lady," he said, "I've never shot a whore before, but I've shot squaws, and as far as I can see, a whore is just the next rung up." He hoped she couldn't read a bluff. He wasn't about to shoot her.

The madam froze and looked him over. "If you don't want to go with this saddle tramp, I'll give him both barrels," she said to Tess. "I won't have it said that I don't look after my gals."

Tess's eyes darted between the two of them. She swallowed hard. "It's all right. He thinks he's tryin' to help me." She yanked her arm from his grasp. "Just ain't got no manners, that's all."

The madam lowered her shotgun. "You sure it's all right?"

"Yes, ma'am."

Caleb eased the hammer down on his Colt.

"Well . . ." The madam tossed the shotgun onto the bar. "You come on back whenever you want."

"She ain't comin' back," Caleb said. He reached for the polished brass doorknob.

They rode double, two miles out of town.

"Did Angus Mackland ever come back after you?" Caleb asked as they plodded along.

"No. They sent a bunch of lawmen into the Indian Territory to find him after he shot that town marshal in Denison. They flushed him out, and he went down to Old Mexico. I don't know whatever come of him down there."

"No good, more than likely."

Some farmer was using Tess's land to graze his milk cows. She owned a hundred hardscrabble acres in the Brazos bottoms, a few stunted trees on the highest corner.

"We'll build your house there," Caleb said. "That'll give you some shade."

She snorted. "Build it with what?"

"We'll buy some lumber."

"I ain't got no money."

"Well, Lordy, girl, you got three dollars a customer. What did you do with it all?"

"Old Rose got to keep most of it."

He shook his head. "But she won't have it said that she don't look after her gals."

"She did look after us."

"Well, now you can look after yourself."

She snorted again. "With what? I ain't got no house, no plow, no mule, no seed. I ain't got nothin'."

"We'll buy everything you need."

"I told you I ain't got no money."

"I've got enough to buy a wagon and team of mules."

She could see a woman looking at them from the porch of the nearest farmhouse. "I thought you were gonna make me a farmer. Now you're gonna make me a mule skinner."

"We have to earn enough money to buy the stuff you need for this place. With a wagon we can do it."

She felt her sweaty dress sticking to her. The backs of her hands were going to burn crisp as cracklings working outdoors. Her skin hadn't seen much sun in the past few years. "What are we gonna haul?"

"Bones."

EIGHTY

THEY MADE FIFTEEN miles the first day in a secondhand Studebaker freight wagon. Their two mules, one brown and one gray, didn't like each other. The second morning it took thirty minutes of cussing and flogging to get the team in harness. By the time they left camp on the Salt Fork, the mules were already worn out from kicking and biting each other. Tess had stood back and laughed.

For lunch they ate canned beef and stale biscuits on a blanket spread under the wagon. A hot breeze blew in from the south. They were on the divide between the South Wichita and the Salt Fork of the Brazos. They could see a lot of open country. Caleb was trying to cheer Tess up, telling her about the Extravaganza of the Western Wilds.

"... So, anyway, when I left, Captain Singletary talked me into taking a horse as part of my pay. He had this herd of paint ponies for the Indians to ride in the show, and he had taught 'em this trick where, after we killed all the Indians, we'd round up the horses and shoot our guns in the air and they'd sit back on their haunches and paw the sky."

"What for?" Tess asked.

"I don't know. I never did figure out the meanin' of it. The crowd liked it though. Anyway, this one little paint colt never could get it right. He thought every time a gun went off, he was supposed to sit down right there and start pawin'. It didn't make any difference to him whether the show was goin' on or not. So Captain Singletary traded him to me to make a cow pony out of.''

"How come you didn't bring him with you?'' she asked. "I like paint horses.''

"Well, I took to ridin' that colt to spell ol' Powder River, and I just happened to be on him the day I rode into Dodge City. Some boys there were havin' some fun, tearin' down the street, shootin' their irons, and that dang colt just sat down right there in town and went to pawin' the air. I slid right off his rump and landed in the mud.''

Tess laughed, throwing her head back, showing the gap in her smile. "What did you do with him? Sell him to some poor ignorant cow waddie?''

"No, I took him down into the Indian Territory and gave him to old Chief Long Fingers. The chief thinks I'm a pretty good white man ever since I got Red Hot Frost to send his squaws all them buffalo hides back in '74. I 'magine he's probably butchered and ate that little paint by now.''

Tess looked across the desolate ranges, the smile falling from her lips as she remembered where she was. "How do you know we'll find bones out here?'' she asked.

"I hunted buffalo out here on the narrows. I remember where we made our biggest kills. They say you can get eight dollars a ton for buffalo bones if you haul them to the railroad. A hundred buffalo skeletons makes a ton. Hell, we killed a hundred a day. Badger Burton killed a hundred all by himself one day. I figured it out. We can get eight cents for every skeleton. It'll be like pickin' up pennies.''

"Which railroad are we gonna haul 'em to?'' Tess asked.

"The Fort Worth and Denver is at Wichita Falls now.''

"How far is that?''

"About seventy miles, I reckon.''

"Oh, my God,'' she said. She had already had enough of riding in the wagon. "How many tons can this wagon carry?''

"About half.''

"Half a ton?'' She sat up so quickly that she almost bumped her head on the running gear. "Four dollars a trip?''

He was unconcerned. "I can make a trip a week while you stack the bones. I'll go in on Saturday so I can earn some fiddlin' money on top of the bone money. In a month or so, we can buy a bigger wagon. Maybe a train of 'em, and a team of bulls. By wintertime you'll have enough to build you a little shack on your farm and get you through till spring.''

Tess fell back on the blanket. "You're gonna leave me alone out here to pick bones while you drive to town every week?''

"A friend of mine named Cole Gibson is workin' a line camp near here. I'll have him check on you every now and then. Of course, you could drive the wagon if you want, and I'll stack the bones.''

She covered her face with her hands.

Caleb finished his lunch and took a drink from a canteen. He nudged her with it. She took the canteen, tilted it over her face, and let some water trickle on her brow.

"You know," he said, looking out from under the wagon, "when it rains here on the narrows, the water runs off two different ways."

Tess wasn't interested.

"On the south side of this divide it goes into the Brazos and runs all the way down to the Gulf of Mexico. On the north side it runs into the Wichita, then into the Red, then into the Mississippi, then into the Gulf. So two drops of rain, fallin' an inch apart, could end up hundreds of miles away from each other."

"Like you and me done," she said hoarsely. " 'Cept, somethin' done washed us together again." She closed her eyes. "Two drops of rain."

They arrived at the South Wichita before dusk. Caleb drove the wagon into a line of trees near the riverbank. They had just enough daylight left to set up a camp. He built a stout tent of the wagon sheet, held erect with straight green oak limbs and staked with willow pickets. He hobbled the jaded mules and turned them loose to graze.

"Caleb!" Tess shouted from a stand of brush. "Look! I found some already!"

"Don't mess with those," he said, coming to her side.

They stood over two old buffalo skulls, bleached and crumbling, gnawed by rodents, overgrown with bushes.

"Those are grave markers. That's where we buried Old Elam Joiner and a kid named George somethin' or other."

"What kilt 'em?"

"Indians."

"There ain't no more Indians around here now, are there?"

He chuckled. "Nope. Long gone. We cleaned 'em out in '74. The army and us buffalo hunters."

She breathed a sigh of relief.

"I better go see if I can shoot a coon or a rabbit or somethin' to eat. Can you imagine that all these plains used to be covered with game?"

He seemed to recall that she had once bragged on her singing, so Caleb got Tess to sing some songs that night after supper. She preferred hymns—"Amazing Grace" and "Shall We Gather at the River." The husky quality of her voice carried over into song. She hit every pitch without a hint of any wavering or vibrato in her voice. Caleb harmonized and strummed a mandolin.

The next morning they went in search of bones. Caleb drove the wagon among the ridges, scanning the far horizons for landmarks. After a couple of hours he stopped and stood on the wagon seat.

"That's it," he said. "Over that next ridge." He sat down, shook the reins, and growled at the mules.

Tess was riding Powder River. "What is it?"

"That's where me and Badger Burton killed sixty buffalo in one morning. Two miles down is where he killed sixty-three by himself the same morning. We'll make our first load there."

When they topped the ridge, Caleb recognized the clump of bushes where he and Badger Burton had fallen out. He rode the brake down a precarious grade and trundled into the slaughter grounds. Bleached bones cropped up everywhere through the short clumps of grass.

He drove the wagon from pile to pile until he and Tess had filled it up. Then he unhitched and hobbled the mules. They started stacking the skeletons that were left in one central pile so they could be easily loaded on the next trip.

They took their dinner break during the heat of the day, in the shadow of the wagon. Tess napped while Caleb carved a sign on a piece of sideboard that had broken off. He fastened it to a stake with a strip of rawhide from his saddle wallet. He woke Tess and told her to stake her claim on the bone pile with the sign: T. WILEY.

"Nobody'll bother it now," he said.

"Nobody's fool enough but us," she replied, climbing down from the small stack of bones.

They left the loaded wagon, rode double on Powder River to Badger's old stand, and starting stacking the bones there. They situated the main pile in the middle of the kill. The afternoon was hot and still, and the work was monotonous. Tess remembered Arkansas: the hard labor, the scorching sun in the fields, the good days before her mother died.

As they finished one skeleton, she walked a few steps ahead to the next. "What do they do with all these bones?" she asked.

"Fertilizer," he said, straggling along behind her, dabbing his face with a bandanna. "You may be spreadin' some of it on your farm someday. They also use it to refine sugar with, but damned if I know just how."

She bent to gather a handful of ribs and heard a short dry sizzle down in the bones. She knew the sound, but it was too late. From under the flaking skull of a long-dead buffalo bull, the huge head of a rattlesnake jabbed her in the shin. It hit so hard that she lost her balance and fell onto the skeleton. She rolled, screaming, out of the way.

Caleb was already sending bullets into the bones. The flat ugly head lunged again, and he blasted it before it could find cover in the shade of the skull. The rattling died, but Tess screamed on.

"I'm killed!" she said, holding her leg and rocking on the ground. "Oh, my God, it's killed me!"

Caleb lifted her hem and checked the wound. "You're not killed," he said. "He just got you with one tooth." He put his mouth on the puncture and sucked but could draw nothing out. The wound was a tiny point of blood on Tess's shin.

"I can't feel it!" she screamed. "I can't feel my leg."

Caleb spit and took the bandanna from his neck. "Well, I can feel it, and it's still there." He tied the bandanna tight under her knee.

"Ouch!" she cried.

"I thought you couldn't feel it."

"Go to hell, Caleb Holcomb!" A hateful rattle accompanied her usual coarse tone.

"Now hold still and keep your leg low so the poison won't come up."

He sprinted for Powder River and rode back. When he knelt over her again, he was chewing furiously on a large quid of tobacco.

"This is a hell of a time for a chew!" she said.

He grinned as he untied the bandanna. He took the moistened wad from his mouth and slapped it firmly on the snake bite, lashing it in place with the bandanna.

"Is that gonna save me?" she said. "What about my leg? Are they gonna cut it off?"

"Of course not. Have you ever heard of a one-legged . . . farmer?"

"You were gonna say *whore,* weren't you?" Tears were running down her cheeks.

"No, I wasn't gonna say *whore.* Let me show you something." He pulled his skinning knife from his gun belt and used it to spear the rattler behind the head. He lifted the snake, still writing in torpid convulsions.

Tess grimaced and turned away.

"My stars, if he ain't a big one!" Caleb declared. "He must go over five and a half feet."

Powder River held his head high and backed away.

"Well, look at him," Caleb said. "How am I gonna show you anything, if you won't look at him?"

She risked a glance.

"See how fat he is right here in his neck?"

"Snakes are all neck, stupid," she said.

"I mean right here behind his head. He just swallowed somethin'. Probably a big ol' rat. Them rats come to chew on these bones, and he was layin' for 'em."

"I don't care what a snake eats!" she moaned. "You're about to make me sick to my stomach!"

"You'd feel a lot better if you'd listen to me. This snake didn't have hardly no poison in him if he just bit him a big ol' rat." He pried the bloody mouth open with his pistol barrel. "And look, he ain't got but one fang in his head. Must have broke the other one off in that rat."

Tess looked cautiously at her leg.

"It ain't stuck in you," he said. "I already looked."

"But it hurts!"

"Oh, it'll hurt. Maybe swell up some. But you and your leg will make it all right."

He stepped on the head of the snake and cut it off. Then he turned it over and began slitting it up the belly in short strokes. The snake, even headless, tried continuously to right itself.

"Let me skin him right quick, and I'll take you back to the wagon," he said.

Tess moaned and fell back on the ground. "I don't think I can ride."

"I'll hold you on. The saddle's the best place for you. It'll keep your leg low, keep the poison from comin' up."

She listened to the knife hack away at the belly of the rattler. "Damn you for bringin' me out here," she said.

He didn't take it personally. "You better learn to poke around in those skeletons before you go pickin' 'em apart." He finished slitting the snake's belly and separated the skin from the body around the bloody stub where the head had been. Then he took the body in one hand and the scaly skin in the other and pulled them cleanly apart with a steady motion.

The sound made Tess grimace. The pungent smell of butchered snake almost turned her stomach.

"Yep, it was a big old rat," Caleb said.

She rolled onto her knees and thought she was going to throw up, but she merely gagged a couple of times.

Powder River remained calm, though he quivered about the nostrils and rolled his white-ringed eyes to follow the folded skin as Caleb put it into his saddle wallet.

He helped Tess into the saddle and rode behind her to the wagon. He made her sit in the saddle until he had taken the snakeskin from his sack, unfolded it, and pressed its sticky inside surface to the seat of the wagon.

"It'll stick there like it was glued," he said.

"What did you put it there for?"

Caleb shrugged. "To show it off, I guess."

He helped Tess from the horse to the wagon seat and gave her a canteen. He went to harness the hobbled mules as she stretched out on the fresh skin of the beast that had so recently poisoned her. The load of bones in the wagon bed loomed above her.

The mules smelled snake and showed fight. They went to kicking and biting. The gray busted his rawhide hobbles loose and dragged Caleb about fifty yards.

Her leg hurt bad, but Tess smiled.

EIGHTY-ONE

"STRATEGY, SHORTY." ANGUS Mackland struck a match on the checkered stock of the Marlin carbine sticking out of the saddle boot under his left leg. He lit his cigar. "How many times do I have to tell you?"

Shorty looked at him, half cross-eyed, strands of oily hair sticking to his temples. "I guess about a thousand times, 'cause your strategies don't never make no sense to me. I would have lived to be an old man in Monterrey, and died there happy. Had me a good fat woman and all sorts of stepchildren workin' for me."

"You might have died, Shorty, but you wouldn't have lived to be an old man. After all these years, I'd think you would learn to trust my higher intellect. As I recall, you didn't want to leave your squaw when I pulled you out of the Territory nine years ago. If I hadn't took you to Mexico then, them marshals would have hung you."

"So why the hell are we goin' back there now? Headin' north with winter comin' on. It don't make no sense!"

He shifted the cigar in his black beard. "They've forgot who we are in the Territory. It's safe for us there now. Damn sight safer than Mexico. Those *federales* would have splattered our guts against the wall by now if I hadn't gotten us out."

"If you wouldn't have shot that one in Matamoros, we wouldn't have had to get out."

"If I hadn't have shot him, he would have sold us to the Texas Rangers."

Shorty wrinkled his ugly bulbous nose, set like a crooked walnut on his pockmarked face. "Now then, here's where your strategy keeps slippin' by me. If you didn't want the Texas Rangers to get us, why in the hell did we cross over into Texas right after you shot that *federale?* What the hell kind of strategy is that? Your kind of strategy has had the U.S. marshals, the Mexican *federales,* and the Texas Rangers takin' turns doggin' our asses for nine years."

"Nope," Angus said. "My kind of strategy has kept 'em from catchin' us."

"We ain't out of Texas yet," Shorty said. "The rangers could catch us before we get to the Territory."

"We've only got the Wichita and the Red left to cross, then we're back in our old stampin' grounds. Trust me, Shorty. Once you bone up on your Injun, we'll round us up a gang of renegade Cheyenne and Comanche and Kiowa and such and go to playin' hell with the damn Texas Rangers."

Shorty spit. "There ain't no more renegade Indians in the Territory from what I hear. Uncle Sam gave 'em all farms and reservations. I've a good mind to head west right now and hide out in New Mexico."

Angus reined his horse in. "All right, I guess I might as well tell you," he said.

Shorty stopped his mustang and turned in the saddle to look at Angus. "Tell me what? For the love of Jesus Christ, what have you got planned now?"

Angus clenched the cigar stub in his teeth and grinned with conceit. "Remember that Kickapoo I told you I met outside of Laredo? The one that spoke English?"

"Yeah. What about him?"

"He told me an old friend of ours was on his way back to the Cheyenne-Arapaho reservation in the Territory."

"Who's that?"

"Kicking Dog."

Shorty's mouth dropped open under his wispy mustache. "Oh, no. I thought Kicking Dog was dead."

"Nope, he never was dead. He joined the Northern Cheyenne and ran with the Sioux for a while way up north, gutted some of Custer's boys at the Little Bighorn. But the Indian Police got after him, so he left, headin' for the Territory. At least that's what that Kickapoo told me."

"How the hell would a Mexican Kickapoo know what Kicking Dog was up to?"

"The Injun telegraph, Shorty. It ain't got no wires or operators, but it gets the message home. Besides, it makes sense that Kicking Dog would head back to the Cheyenne-Arapaho reservation. He started out a Southern Arapaho."

"He started out loco," Shorty said, bug-eyed, "and got worse with every scalp he ever took. That Indian scares the tar out of me, Angus."

Mackland tapped his horse with his spurs and motioned for Shorty to continue north with him. "That's what you always say, Shorty. You're always scared till we get a posse on our rear ends. Then your face takes on the dangedest expression of happiness I ever saw."

"That's 'cause it feels so damn nice and warm in my britches all of a sudden."

Angus laughed. "I've seen you grin like a possum in a fight. You're like a big ol' boar coon, Shorty. You're a coward till you're cornered, then you turn grizzly and whip ass."

Angus chuckled as he rode on, and Shorty, honored, quit complaining. He only hoped they could get out of Texas without running onto rangers. And, once into the Territory, he hoped they wouldn't find Kicking Dog. He hoped the Indian telegraph had picked up a false rumor. Kicking Dog truly frightened him.

They rode in silence, the dry north wind blowing cool in their faces. September rains had brought the green luster back to the rocky swells. Frost would kill it brown soon, but for now it was a time of rich beauty on the Southern Plains.

As they topped the divide between the Brazos and the Wichita, they held the brims of their hats against the wind whipping over the ridge and scouted for any form of trouble that might lie in their path. All they saw were a few white pyramids rising from the greenery, far scattered across the valley.

"What are them white things?" Shorty asked. He squinted, his eyesight poor. "Tents? Looks like they got flags on top."

"Those are buffalo bones. Some fool's been gatherin' 'em to sell. They put their name on a sign on top of the pile to stake their claim on it. I saw them doin' it in '74, when the marshals ran me into Colorado. If you didn't have me to take care of you, Shorty, that's the kind of work you'd have to do to make your livin'."

Shorty snorted. "That's a lie. If I hadn't throwed in with you, I could have been an honest interpreter in the Territory."

The big outlaw started down into the broad valley of the South Wichita. "That's what you were tryin' to do when I found you starvin', remember? Come on, let's go see if the name on that pile is whose I think it is."

"What? Whose name? What do you mean?"

"Come on, you'll see."

They angled a mile to the nearest stack of bones to read the sign. The front of it faced north, so they couldn't see the letters until they got around it. Angus jerked his reins in and squinted. "T. Wiley," he muttered.

"Never heard of him," Shorty said. "Come on, let's get down in them trees along the river and make a camp out of this wind. It gives me an earache."

Angus was laughing; roaring with mirth. "By God, it's her, all right!"

"Who?"

"Tess Wiley. What the hell would she be doin' out here stackin' bones?"

"Who's Tess Wiley? Some whore you knew?"

Angus guffawed and tugged at the long black beard. "Watch what you say, Shorty. Tess Wiley was my wife. Don't you remember the one I brought out of Arkansas?"

"How'd you know she was pickin' bones away out here?"

"I make it my business to know shit like that."

In reality, Angus had come by the knowledge by pure luck. On the way north from Mexico, he and Shorty had found an old compatriot tending bar at a road ranch outside of Brady City. Hank Gibbitts, who had gone straight except when it came to fencing the occasional stolen horse, mentioned that he had made a trip horseback to Wichita Falls recently and had seen Tess Wiley in a bone camp with some fiddling drifter. Shorty had missed out on the intelligence only because he had been in a drunken stupor.

Now Angus took the cigar butt from his teeth and flicked it at Tess Wiley's carved sign. "Looks like the little bitch has gone and dishonored me by takin' her maiden name back. Seems she needs remindin' of her vows."

EIGHTY-TWO

T HE WIND KEPT shifting in the trees around the old buffalo camp. Tess couldn't keep out of the smoke. She had beans and bacon cooking in a skillet, sourdough biscuits in a Dutch oven. She had stacked a lot of bones that day. The snakebite had swollen some and kept her off her feet a day or two, but hardly left a scar. Caleb was away, freighting a load of bones to Wichita Falls. It was almost dark. She planned to eat her supper and go straight to the tent to sleep. When the smoke came around on her again, she simply closed her eyes and held her breath. She was too tired to keep shuffling in a circle around the fire.

When she opened her eyes again, she saw movement in the bushes near the old skull-marked graves. A runty little man materialized. She found a burst of energy and sprinted for the Studebaker wagon. Grabbing Caleb's Winchester, she thumbed the hammer back and swung the barrel around on the intruder.

"Whoa, lady," Shorty said, raising his hands. "I don't mean you no harm."

"What are you doin' here?"

"My horse throwed me about five miles south. I was wonderin' if you'd seen him."

"No, I ain't seen no horses."

"He's a little bay mustang, wearin' an old beat-up slick-fork saddle and a . . ."

"I said I ain't seen no horses. Now, git!" Tess shouldered the rifle and found the little man in the sights.

She felt a weight strike her on the shoulders. The rifle pulled against her trigger finger and fired. The ground rushed at her, illuminated briefly by the muzzle blast. A hand pushed the side of her face into the dirt. She tried to scream, but another hand, foul smelling, covered her mouth.

"Hold your tongue, woman, or I'll break your neck."

She recognized his voice and felt sick.

Shorty came running. "Damn it, Angus, you almost had her shoot me!"

Angus ignored him. He eased his hand from her mouth. While sitting on her, he turned her onto her back and pinned her arms. "Happy anniversary," he said. He wheezed with laughter and looked at Shorty. "I'll be damned if it wasn't October when her folks paid me to marry her. Eight years ago." He turned his horrible face back on Tess. "What day was it, honey?"

She choked with fear as she spoke. "You better get out of here. My husband is comin' back."

"If you've got a husband, why are you markin' your bones with your maiden name?" he wheezed with cruel joy.

"We ain't church married yet."

"Check it out, Shorty." He tightened his thighs on her.

"Some cowboys are comin' back with him," she said, gasping. "And some bone buyers. You better git."

"One bedroll in the tent," Shorty shouted. "Eats for one on the fire."

"You ain't got nobody comin'," Angus said. He looked up at Shorty. "Keep a watch out just in case." He looked toward the tent. "Get up," he ordered, rising over her and pulling her up by her wrists.

Tess made a sudden lunge and snapped at his knuckles, but he was too strong and kept his hand beyond her teeth. He slapped her and began dragging her to the tent. She kicked and screamed. He hit her again. Tess writhed. She wasn't going to go willingly, but Mackland felt very little put out at dragging her.

Shorty knelt by the fire and stirred the beans. The tent shook, and he heard Angus hit her again. He lifted the lid on the Dutch oven to check the biscuits. He used the brim of his hat to grab the hot skillet handle and pull it from the fire. He helped himself to Tess's supper. He was pretty sure she wouldn't have the stomach for it after Angus got through with her.

When Angus came out of the tent, Shorty had another batch of beans cooking for him. He had water boiling for coffee.

"I spared you a biscuit," Shorty said.

Mackland sat across from the fire so he could watch the tent. He brooded. He despised her for stacking bones. He had his own view of dignity, a twisted and pitiless way of gauging people. Tess ranked low. She would get what she deserved for getting in his way after eight years.

Shorty handed Mackland a cup of coffee and glanced toward the tent.

"Them beans are ready," he said. He looked at the tent again, a little more lingeringly.

Mackland took the coffee. "Go ahead," he said, barely loud enough to be heard. "Take your turn with her. I'm just gonna sell her to Kicking Dog anyway."

EIGHTY-FIVE

THE EMPTY MURPHY wagons barely encumbered Caleb's oxen. He had to walk at a brisk pace to keep up with the train. He had invested a lot of bone money in the six-yoke team and the three big freight wagons, but the investment would soon pay off. Now he could haul several tons of bones a week, instead of just half a ton. He could haul them faster than Tess could stack them. He was thinking of hiring someone to help her.

The quick pace kept him warm in the crisp morning air. He figured four or five more trips to Wichita Falls would earn Tess plenty of money to start her farm. By then he would be needing to get into the Sacramento Mountains where he would tell Marisol and his children to enjoy their last winter in Peñascosa. He would be practically broke when he arrived, but he would feel good knowing he had turned Tess onto a better path.

For the first time in his life he felt he was doing something Pete would have looked up to him for. He was helping someone worse off than himself. Sometimes he felt so bad off himself, adrift and homeless in the world, that he couldn't imagine how low Tess felt on her worse day. At least he could play a few songs to lift his spirits. Tess had nothing.

He was sure that what he was doing for Tess was right, but it was hard work. And it was causing him problems. She was dropping hints. Without saying it in so many words, he knew she wanted him to stay with her on her farm near Seymour.

Caleb made it a point to mention Marisol every so often, but Tess tended to ignore her existence. As he jogged along beside the bull train, he suddenly figured out where he had gone wrong. He had received aid and kindness from many individuals in his life, and it now felt good to be returning it to someone. But his mistake was that he had chosen a woman to help. He would never be free of her. Women had a way of clinging.

"Get over!" he shouted at the lead yoke. He trotted to the head of the team and tapped the leaders with a long stick. He looked beyond the oxen, to see where he was on the bone-market trail he had blazed weeks before and saw a rider coming.

Seagrass Gibson came galloping up to the bone wagons, his horse covered with sweat.

"It's Tess," he said. "She's gone. So is your horse and a lot of food and stuff out of the wagon."

"Gone where?" Caleb asked.

"I don't know. I found some tracks leadin' into the river. Three riders. But . . . Aw, I ain't no kind of tracker. I never found where they came out."

Caleb stopped. The oxen lumbered past him.

"I'm sorry," Seagrass said. "I told you I'd look after her. I just . . . I couldn't be with her all the time."

"It ain't your fault. I'll find her."

"I'll help you," Seagrass said. "I got some of the boys out lookin' right now."

"Good. Help me set these bulls loose, and we'll go get some fresh horses."

You did right, he thought. It would have been a sin to leave her in that whorehouse. A sin? What do you know about sins? You ain't no preacher. You can't quote the Bible. Maybe messing with other people's lives is as big a sin as leaving them in a whorehouse. Where has it gotten her? Where is Tess now? Wherever she is, it's your fault.

EIGHTY-SIX

THE BANDANNA DROPPED from Long Fingers' hand, and the hooves thundered away, churning up sod as they left the starting line. It was a fine time of the year to race.

His long gray hair touched the ground as he stooped to pick up the bandanna. The course was three miles. The racers wouldn't be back for a few minutes. The chief turned away from the horses to behold his people—the old ones clinging to the old ways, and their rotting deerskin clothes—the young ones wearing the dress of white people. They were all smiling.

It had been a pretty good year. Things would continue well unless the whites succeeded in getting the reservation. He had heard talk of some white people called boomers who wanted to get the Cheyenne and Arapaho land. Thinking of it, he smiled. *Boomers* was a funny-sounding name for a tribe. There were many tribes among the whites. It was wrong to think of them as one people.

The quality of his stock was improving. His people were getting good prices for their best horses. He was glad the white agents let them keep horses. Some of the youngest braves, who had never known battle, considered breaking horses the best way to prove themselves.

Long Fingers was no young brave, but he needed ways to prove himself, too. The young men didn't remember his glory on the battlefields. They had their own ideas about which directions the tribe should be taking. Some of them wanted to break ties with the whites and guard the borders of the reservation to keep them out. The chief spoke against it, but with no more battles to fight or hunts to lead, he sometimes found himself wondering how he would maintain their respect in his old age.

He was still quick and strong, but there were others who were quicker and stronger. They would have to take over someday soon, but they were not quite ready.

Red Hawk was almost ready. In the year of the Red River war, he had gotten into trouble with some Comanche and Cheyenne and had been sent away to prison in a place called Florida. There, and later at the Carlisle School in Pennsylvania, he had learned to speak the English as if he were a white man—even to read and write it. Now he was a captain of the Indian Police and an interpreter at the fort. He knew white men, he had learned patience, and he possessed leadership qualities beyond his years.

But if Red Hawk was going to lead the people down the path Long Fingers was marking for them, they would have to remember Long Fingers as a great chief. What would leave them with such a memory? He was constantly looking for ways.

His eyesight was not what it had once been, but it was strong enough to see the pretty, smiling faces of the Arapaho women—the most beautiful women on earth—and clear enough to catch the movement behind them. He saw two men loping toward the racetrack from his village. He recognized one of the riders. He had been expecting him all day.

Caleb Holcomb and Seagrass Gibson arrived about the same time the racehorses completed the circle. The winner was a glossy chestnut stallion whose jockey crossed the line whooping a victory cry, both hands in the air, shirtsleeves flapping. The gamblers settled their wagers as Caleb jumped down from his tired horse and shook the chief's hand.

"I know why you come here," Long Fingers said. "You would not sell that horse you call Powder River."

His eyes brightened. "What do you know about my horse?"

"Who is that man?" The old chief pointed at Seagrass.

"This is Cole Gibson. He's a good man."

Seagrass tipped his hat and took in the old leader's getup: headband, shirt, pants, suspenders, and moccasins.

"Do you know who has your horse?"

"No," Caleb said. "I was hopin' you would. I'm lookin' for a woman too. Her name's Tess Wiley."

A few of the young warriors had come near to listen. They knew Caleb, liked his music. But he had no instruments with him today.

Long Fingers raised his gray eyebrows. "I did not know the woman was yours."

"She ain't mine, exactly. I'm just lookin' after her. Where is she? Is she all right?"

"She is alive."

"Where?"

"Do you remember the Comanchero called Black Beard? The whites called him Angus. He has your horse and the woman."

The visions of Mackland's violent work came back to Caleb. He remembered the horrible Christmas Eve on the Cimarron, the slain Hutchinson family, the blizzard, the wolves, and the bitter cold. He remembered the Denison poker game. Tess was in the most unspeakable kind of trouble, and he couldn't figure out whether or not it was his fault. Doing good things came natural to some people, like Buster, or Pete, but Caleb's good deeds always seemed to turn sour.

"Angus Mackland?" Cole said. "I thought he went to Mexico years ago."

"He has come back from the south. The little ugly one is with him, Man-of-Many-Tongues. And Kicking Dog is with them."

"Kicking Dog?"

"Yes." The chief pointed north. "He comes back here from the Sioux lands. I would not let him stay in our village. He wanted to buy a horse, so I sold him that one you gave to me in the spring." He smiled. "The one that sits down when it hears guns shooting."

"Well, where are they now?" Caleb asked. "They stole that woman. I've got to get her back."

"Kicking Dog went to the Washita. Red Hawk took some boys to watch him. One of them came here yesterday to tell me that Black Beard and Man-of-Many-Tongues comes with the woman and your horse. Now they are with Kicking Dog. I have been waiting for you."

"Where is this place they're at?" Caleb asked. "What's it like?"

"A cabin on the Washita. Many years ago Black Beard met the Comanche there to bring them guns and whiskey. It is falling down now. The top of the cabin is gone, but they are staying in it anyway."

"Will you tell us how to get there?"

"I will take you. I have horses ready. We will be there before the night comes." The old chief could hardly wait to get started. He was always looking for ways to win glory in the eyes of his people.

EIGHTY-FIVE

THEY LED THEIR mounts under the rim of the Washita's bank: Caleb, Seagrass Gibson, Long Fingers, Red Hawk, and a young Arapaho brave named Tommy White Fox. Red Hawk paused now and then, climbed a few steps up the bank, stretched his neck like a wild turkey to peer over the rim. He led the party around a bend to the north and motioned for the rescuers to crawl up next to him at the top of the bank.

When Caleb raised his hatless head above the weeds, he saw the dilapidated cabin some three hundred yards away across an open prairie. Red Hawk had brought them around for a western approach, so the sinking sun would be at their backs. Smoke trailed from the stone chimney of the roofless log structure. Powder River and three other mounts, including the trick paint, stood in a corral made of rotten logs, about forty paces from the cabin. The door to the cabin opened to the east, so Caleb could see nothing inside. A few small trees grew around the cabin, but they would not provide much cover for a rescue.

He studied the lay of the land until he realized that the Indians were looking at him. They were waiting. It was his fight. They expected him to come up with a plan. He slid a few feet down the bank.

"What are we gonna do?" Seagrass said.

Caleb looked into Cole's anxious eyes. Hell, I don't know what to do, he thought. He wished suddenly for Washita Jack Shea to step out of the bushes and make a battle plan. This wasn't unlike Shea's Pease River fight, come to think of it, where Caleb had led the charge of the hide skinners, forcing the enemy out under the buffalo guns. There was just one big difference. This was a rescue; the Pease was a revenge fight.

"We've got to get them away from the woman," he whispered, surprised to hear himself speak. "They'll kill her if we just charge in there."

Long Fingers nodded.

"How are we gonna do that?" Cole asked.

Caleb tugged at the end of his mustache and stared blankly at the ground. "Their horses. Chief, can one of your boys sneak up there and take a rail down to let their horses out?"

"I can," said Tommy White Fox. He was about seventeen years old and stealthy as a cat.

The chief nodded again.

"Make sure they hear 'em runnin'," Caleb said, "so they'll come out of the cabin to catch 'em. But don't let 'em see you, or you're one dead Indian." He looked at the chief. "Who's the best shot?"

Long Fingers put his hand on Red Hawk's shoulder.

"All right, you sneak around to the northeast, Red Hawk, so you can see the cabin door. Once they're all out of the cabin, don't let 'em back in where they can get at Tess. The rest of us will charge out of the sun and get 'em. Seagrass, you hold off shootin' till we get in close."

"How come?" Gibson demanded.

"We'll stagger our fire that way, and won't get caught with all our guns empty at the same time."

They looked at him.

"We better do it now," he said, "while we've still got the sun in their eyes."

Long Fingers motioned to the young brave, who padded quickly back down the riverbank, disappearing in the brush. Red Hawk took his rifle and a cartridge belt and swung around the other way, to get northeast of the cabin. The rest of the men mounted to wait and watch over the rim of the riverbank from horseback.

After a few minutes, Long Fingers pointed, and Caleb saw Tommy White Fox slipping through the bunchgrass like a coyote. Shorty's bay mustang saw the boy and began darting around nervously inside the corral. The other horses merely perked their ears and watched the brave approach on all fours.

Caleb searched beyond the cabin and caught a glimpse of Red Hawk as he crawled through a narrow shaft of orange sunlight and disappeared under the low limbs of a scrubby post oak, in perfect position.

You should have left her in the whorehouse, he thought. What business do you have trying to fix other people's lives? Fix your own. You're life's a joke. But, hell, if you had left her there, you'd be regretting that now, too. You never should have gone into that whorehouse in the first place. What do you know about anything?

Tommy White Fox crawled up to the corral and reached to take a rail down. The skittish mustang shied to the other end of the corral, reared, and came down with his belly on the top rail, breaking through the rotten barrier as if he knew he was supposed to escape. Tommy ran like a deer back toward the river, dropping to the ground after about fifty strides, and crawling furiously for cover.

As Powder River, the trained paint, and Mackland's sorrel stepped out of the corral, the mustang circled the cabin and swung to the south of the corral in a head-high lope, looking for the Indian who had crawled up to the pen. The other horses milled calmly and ate grass between the corral and the cabin.

Kicking Dog appeared. Caleb still recognized him, though he had grown grizzled before his time due to years of war and privation. He carried a bridle in one hand and had a carbine slung across his back with a rawhide thong. The rifle sling crossed a cartridge belt slung over the other shoulder.

Angus came around the corner with his bridle and stood beside the old renegade. He pointed, and Kicking Dog moved swiftly around the cabin to get on the west side of the horses. He and Angus moved in on the animals, waving their arms, pressing the three horses back into the pen. The mustang continued to prance through the grass to the south.

"It ain't gonna work," Seagrass said, leaning toward Caleb. "The other son of a bitch won't come out of the cabin."

"Just wait. They still have to catch that mustang. It might take all three of 'em."

Kicking Dog put his bridle on the trick paint that Long Fingers had sold to him, mounted bareback, and circled wide to herd the nervous mustang back toward the corral. Angus stood near the pen to make sure the other horses didn't try to get back out. The mustang showed no signs of going willingly back into the pen but didn't seem to want to leave the other horses either. He made galloping passes at the corral but doubled back every time, eluding Kicking Dog.

The sun was sinking fast behind the treetops.

Angus put his bridle on Powder River. "Shorty!" he shouted. "Get your ass out here and help us catch your mustang!"

From the riverbed, the rescuers heard the order.

"Get ready," Caleb said. "As soon as the last one gets to the corral, we'll go."

Shorty emerged from the cabin, scratching himself, and walked to the corral.

"Get on my horse," Angus ordered as he pulled himself onto the stolen Appaloosa gelding. "Let's go help Kicking Dog run that damn wild mustang of yours back over here."

"That damn wild mustang's got better bottom than any horse you ever . . ." Shorty choked the words with his throat and looked west, shading his eyes. Hooves had come rumbling out of the red setting sun. Long shadows almost touched him, three riders in a blinding ball of fire.

"Get the girl," Angus said, kicking Powder River. As he rode bareback past his saddle on the corral fence, he pulled his Marlin repeater from the scabbard. He galloped past Shorty, who was sprinting as fast as he could on foot, until the first bullet from Red Hawk's rifle hissed between them and cracked a corral timber behind them.

"Shit, how many of 'em are they?" Shorty said.

"No tellin'."

They took cover on the south side of the cabin and faced the charge from the west.

* * *

Long Fingers had come out of the riverbed first, and now shook his old vocal cords with a horrifying war cry. He smiled as he saw the trick paint horse sit on his haunches, Kicking Dog sliding off gracefully, confused for a moment at the antics of the paint. Holding on to the reins, the renegade slung the rifle down from his shoulder to face the chief.

Long Fingers had gotten a good look at that rifle the other day at his village—a Springfield trapdoor carbine that Kicking Dog had picked up on the Little Bighorn battlefield after he had helped massacre Custer's troops. It was a single-shot arm, but the chief knew Kicking Dog could reload and fire it at the rate of fifteen times a minute, without even looking at the weapon. The stock had been broken off at one time, to make it easier to hide under squaws' skirts on the reservations. Wet rawhide, wrapped around the break, held the two pieces of the stock together.

Now, as he charged, Long Fingers noticed a new addition to the rifle: an eagle feather dangling from the barrel by a string. He brandished his Winchester and angled to his right, away from the cabin and the corral, toward the renegade who had forgotten his tribe.

The charge rattled Shorty so much that he tried once more to get around the southeast corner of the cabin, into the door. Red Hawk's rifle drove him back. "We're pinned down!" he yelled. "We ain't got no cover."

Angus dropped from Powder River and led the gelding to the cabin wall. He pulled his pistol, put the barrel against the horse's head. He fired, and the great hulk of horseflesh dropped between him and the attackers. "There's your cover," he said, falling behind the dead horse.

Caleb felt his fear turn to anger. He drew his Colt and fired at the men using Powder River's carcass as their bulwark. Long Fingers had angled away to do battle with Kicking Dog. Seagrass was still to his left, two strides back. He saw the blasts from Mackland's rifle, heard the reports. Cole's horse fell under him. He charged on alone.

When he had used all six rounds in his revolver, the drifter swung to the left and got behind the corner of the cabin. He jumped to the ground holding his rifle and let his horse go. His hands shook with great surges of excitement as he squatted with the Winchester across his knees and tried to reload his pistol.

Looking south for his friends, he saw Seagrass limping for the corral, bullets flying all around him. Caleb forgot about reloading the pistol and ran to the southwest corner of the cabin. Holding his rifle around the corner, he began shooting.

The overlapping log ends splintered in his face, driving him back. A piece of wood had hit him in one eye, but through the other he saw Seagrass collapse behind the cover of the old corral. Cole was hit bad. He didn't rise to fight.

* * *

Kicking Dog tried to aim at Long Fingers, but he was holding his reins along with the Springfield, and the paint pony was lunging behind him, throwing his bead off the chief. He let a wild shot go, reloaded. The chief thundered down on him, holding a Winchester high in one hand: an easy target, but the paint continued to tug at his reins.

Long Fingers was feeling the old glory. They would remember him for this. And though his eyes were young no longer, there was wonder in what they saw. The young paint stud was working good magic against Kicking Dog. He drew strength from the sounds of battle, and the guardian spirits filled him with abandon. It was one thing to kill one's enemy, to feel the glory of the charge. It was another thing—a thing of far greater courage— to count coup on a living foe.

Kicking Dog saw his irons between the chief's suspenders. He pulled the trigger as the paint made another unexpected lunge behind him. The bullet hit Long Fingers' arm, but the old chief came on, the rifle waving high in the air. The renegade dropped the reins and reloaded, but it was too late. Long Fingers was there.

The barrel of the Winchester clubbed him on the ear, sprawling him on his back. His head rang, and he felt the familiar warmth of blood. He took a desperate shot at close range, saw Long Fingers land limp on the ground near him.

As the chief fell, Kicking Dog rocked dizzily back, his shoulder blades hitting the ground. And now he saw the bleary image of the paint pony towering over him. The front hooves pawed against a colorless sky. The last ray of sun found a gap in the trees to the west, struck the rearing pony on the white of the belly, and glinted in his black eyes.

The orange death horse brought his front hooves down on Kicking Dog's chest, then rose to paw the air again. Kicking Dog tried to scramble away, stricken with utter terror to think of Long Fingers' soul leaping into the horse. He heard the lever rattle on the Winchester and saw Tommy White Fox holding the chief's weapon. He heard the crack of the rifle as the hard hooves of the spirit horse came down on him again.

Caleb saw the paint pony doing the tent-show tricks over the body of Kicking Dog. Tommy White Fox was coming up behind the corrals. Long Fingers? Gone.

He braced himself as Tommy began a deliberate fire. He figured the outlaws would either come around the corner in front of him or risk Red Hawk's aim to get at Tess in the cabin. If they came his way, he was deter- mined to stand his ground.

* * *

Angus Mackland felt a bullet tear his thigh open. He jumped up and hobbled for the southeast corner of the cabin, trying to get around to the door, to the woman. A bullet caught him in the chest when he made the turn. The Marlin carbine flew from his slack grip and landed six feet away.

Shorty bolted like a rabbit. He screamed some Pawnee words as he dashed for Mackland's body. A shot creased him, but the little man stayed to pick up the Marlin carbine and shove Angus's Colt revolver under his belt. A bullet tore through his ribs, and he ran along the south wall of the cabin, bits of wood flying all around him from the fire of Tommy White Fox.

Then the ugly little man jumped up on the ribs of the dead Nez Perce horse and faced the corral. The slack skin of the dead animal shifted under his boots, making his stance unnatural. He ignored the bullets that came at him, railed in the tongues of a dozen tribes. He found Tommy White Fox in the sights of the Marlin and drove the young Indian down behind the rotten logs.

The rifle clicked. He dropped it, sprang from the carcass, and turned the southwest corner, carrying Angus's revolver in one hand and his own in the other.

Caleb was ready. His Colt blew Shorty's hat away and took a hunk out of one shoulder, but the bloody little man only staggered back a step.

Tommy White Fox mounted his barrage again, and Shorty trained a pistol on each point of attack, a Cheyenne death song wavering from his punctured lungs. He fired in turn—right, then left, then right—looking from one target to the other. Even in the core of the fusillade he made his bullets fly true enough to force the Indian down behind his barrier and drive the musician around the northwest corner of the old cabin.

Caleb was thankful that Red Hawk didn't mistake him for an outlaw when he came around to the north wall. He wondered what Shorty was doing. Dying? Reloading? One way to find out. He finished replacing the empty cartridges, took in a breath, and swung back around the corner.

He fired blindly, his shot hitting Shorty's boot. The little man was streaming with blood, climbing up the overlapping log ends at the corner of the old cabin. Caleb fired his revolver and saw his shots hit flesh with horrible impact, but Shorty held on and kept climbing. Tommy White Fox made his shots count, too, and Shorty's blood fell like raindrops.

Caleb heard Tess scream as the outlaw fell in through the open roof. She wailed in terror as Caleb ran for the door. He expected to see Shorty dead but found the little man wrestling with Tess! She was his match in size and strength—she exhausted from rough treatment and he wound weakened—and they flung each other against the walls as if in a violent dance. Shorty started to moan the death song again, which, accompanied by Tess's hoarse screaming, raised the hairs on Caleb's neck. He used his pistol like a club on the little man's blood-spattered head until he tore Tess from the outlaw's grasp.

She clung to him from behind, sobbing. Caleb leveled his revolver on Shorty. To his astonishment, the bullet-torn man pulled himself from the dirt, blinded by the flow of his own blood, gurgling with every gasp for breath. Shorty drew a knife from a scabbard on his belt and staggered at Caleb. The drifter's last round slammed Shorty against the wall and left a red smear where he slid to the ground.

The ringing and the dull throb in his ears muffled Tess's gasps. He felt her trembling embrace, and then the sharp sting of wounds. He looked down at his bullet-ripped clothing, tested himself for broken bones. The frame was sound, but the flesh was torn at the right calf, the right hip, and the left shoulder.

He heard the faint shuffling of moccasins. Tommy White Fox appeared in the twilight beyond the doorway, a body over his shoulder. The young Indian eased Cole Gibson to the ground, turned the sightless eyes to the sky, and straightened the arms and legs.

Caleb stepped through the doorway, Tess still clinging to him. He put his arm around her. Red Hawk was coming with Long Fingers. The chief's head was hanging, but his legs were wobbling under him, a bullet having creased his skull.

Tommy White Fox looked excitedly at Caleb. "Did you see the old man counting coup?" he asked.

"No," the musician admitted.

Tess had stopped crying, and she was looking at the bodies. "Are they all dead?" Her speech sounded choked. She had Shorty's blood on her face and all down the front of her dress.

"The bad ones are all dead," Caleb said, not sure whom she was asking about.

She sniffed and wrapped her arms around her own waist. "I want to wash myself off."

"The river's cold. You'd better wait." He was trying to give thanks. It was hard. Cole was dead. Dead without firing a shot.

She shook her head. "I don't want to wait."

Caleb went with her toward the Washita. They passed the body of Angus Mackland, turned the corner, and saw the dead horse.

"Caleb," she said.

"What."

"You ain't gonna make me pick no more bones, are you?"

"No," he said. "Of course not."

"Please don't make me go back to that farm. I don't want to stay there all alone." She started crying again as he led her to the river.

EIGHTY-SIX

THE FENCE RAN for miles over the rolling New Mexico plains, catching tumbleweeds and coaxing whistles from the wind. Five tight strands, without a gate in sight. The pony Caleb had bought from Long Fingers didn't care much for high stepping. He had to let down every strand but the bottom one to get the horse across.

He remembered the days when he could ride from San Antonio to the Sacramento Mountains without crossing a single fence. Now cattlemen had parceled the open range into pastures. It would never be the same. It was just as well that he was settling down. It was time to wed Marisol and take her home to Holcomb Ranch. Then, like the song said, he could camp by the gravestone every spring to tell Pete some wild stories.

He would have some to tell this spring, what with that fight on the Washita to talk about—Shorty with eleven bullet holes in his body, Long Fingers returning to his village in glory.

He wondered how Tess was getting along. She would be at the ranch when he arrived with his family. He had sent her with a letter addressed to Buster, and another to Amelia, asking them to find some work for her. He had made her swear on her life not to tell how they had met at Seymour.

Yes, he would have some stories to tell this year. But what about the spring after that? And the one after that? What kind of adventures would he have raising a herd of children on the ranch? Oh, well, it was just a song. He didn't have to live it out.

Dread swept him up as he mounted the horse. He would have to face his father. If he was going to stay at Holcomb Ranch, he would have to arrive at some kind of truce with the old man. It was going to be harder than making the charge at the Washita.

But he would have to do it. Caleb was twenty-nine years old and knew no home. He was torn between Holcomb Ranch and Peñascosa, the mountains and the plains, the campfire and the stove. His style of life had aged him beyond his years. Creases marked his face like branches of a canyon. Seasons in the saddle had so strained his leg joints that he could hardly climb a staircase.

It was time. He was going to marry Marisol and take her back to Holcomb Ranch.

His mount stepped nervously over the wire and waited as he tapped the staples back in with a rock. It was Indian summer in southern New Mexico. Dazzling sunlight streamed over the peaks of the Sacramentos. He spurred the horse and headed for the last barbed wire gap between him and Peñascosa.

The next fence was one Caleb had helped build a few winters ago. When first he saw it, he thought he noticed a man standing along the fence line on the side of a hill. But when he got closer, he could see it was just a dead antelope hanging by one hind foot.

He had seen it happen with deer and antelope many times. Jumping a fence, they usually tucked their hind feet against their bellies, hooves pointing forward. Oh, if they were really pressed by something, they'd clear a fence all stretched out, with the hind hooves pointing straight back. But usually they'd just hop over with legs in the tucked position, and sometimes they didn't hop high enough.

All it took was for one hind hoof to get hooked under the upper strand, then the leg would act as a lever as the weight of the animal carried over, and the second highest strand completed the fatal twist. It had happened here, to this buck antelope.

As he rode near enough, the drifter could see the upper two strands twisting together around a leg stripped of hide. The buck had thrashed around some time before coyotes came to rip out the tender spots. They would return for the rest tonight.

He remembered stretching that top strand. "Sorry, ol' buck," he said and rode on down the fence line to the gap.

He had to get down to open it when he got there. The vaqueros had recently rebuilt the gap, stretching its strands taut as banjo strings. It consisted of nothing more than five short lengths of wire between two cedar poles that stood on top of the ground. Wire loops held the cedar poles to the fence posts set in the ground at either side of the gap. In place, it looked much like any other section of fence. Unhitched, it served as a limp wire gate that could be swung to one side, wide enough for a wagon to drive through.

Caleb had to lean his shoulder into the cedar pole to slip the wire loop over the top of it and open the gap. He wished Javier's vaqueros wouldn't string their gaps so tight. It was a contest among them to see who could build the tightest one and still be able to open it.

Closing the gap was more difficult than opening it. After leading his horse through, he positioned the bottom of the cedar pole in the lower wire loop and tried to push the top of the pole near enough to the fence post to slip the upper loop over it. He had to put his left shoulder against the pole and pull toward the fence post while his right hand groped at the wire loop and tried to slip it over the top of the pole.

He finally succeeded but pinched the first two fingers of his right hand under the tight wire loop. "Ouch!" he yelled, jerking his fingers out of the bind and startling his horse. "Damned bobwire," he muttered, sucking his injured fingers. They were going to hurt when he made his chords with Javier in the alcalde's mansion tonight.

That's where he would break the news to them. He would get down on one knee and propose to Marisol in the *casa consistorial.* Sylvia would shriek with joy, then weep with sorrow to think of Marisol leaving. Some of the children would mutter about having to leave, but Angelo would be ready. He had always wanted to go to Colorado. It would be an image they would long remember in the village of Peñascosa: Caleb on one knee, asking the mother of his children to join him in marriage.

The village came into view as he rounded the last curve in the river valley. No one saw him arrive. Javier had done away with guards since the Mescaleros had settled down on their reservation and the honest cattlemen had pressed the outlaw Texans out of the country. He turned his horse into the corral and hung his saddle.

As he walked up the lane, he heard a grinding noise and saw an old farmer named Salo pushing ears of corn into a hand-cranked mill that stripped the kernels from the cobs. He shouted, but the old man could not hear above the noise of the machine, so he walked over to the corncrib and put his hand on Salo's shoulder.

The old man turned. His eyes opened wide.

"Howdy, Salo," Caleb said with a grin. "Where's my little *mamacita?*"

Salo didn't answer. He grabbed another ear of corn, pushed it into the mill, and turned the crank with new vigor.

"Hey," Caleb said, nudging the old farmer again.

Salo ignored him. Something was wrong.

Caleb left the corncrib behind and took quicker strides toward the alcalde's house. He rounded the crook in the lane and came to Marisol's door. Just as he put his hand on the latch, he looked across the footbridge toward the alcalde's mansion and saw her there. Her back was turned and she was kneeling at the woodpile, but he recognized her thick mane of long, black hair. Relief swept over him. She was safe.

She looked around at him when she heard his boots clogging across the footbridge, spurs ringing with every step. She rose, holding her armload of stove wood in front of her.

"*Hola, querida,*" he said, smiling and putting his hand under her chin. He stooped over her to kiss her on the mouth, but she turned her cheek to him.

"Hey, what's wrong?" he asked.

She would not look at him.

"Here, give me that wood and come tell me what's wrong." He put his arms under the load of fuel.

"No, please," she said, but he lifted the burden from her arms anyway. She brushed her hair away from her face and looked away.

Caleb got the wood situated and turned for Marisol's house. He sensed after a few steps that she wasn't following. "Well, come on," he said, looking back. He froze, his mouth hanging open. Marisol was pregnant.

Caleb had never seen her pregnant with any of their children. They had each come into the world between August and October, while he was gone. But now it was late November and she was pregnant yet. The sight bewildered him. He thought back to the spring of the year. He had left Peñascosa in March. But she was not *that* pregnant. Not eight months. Maybe five or six. She clasped her hands in front of her stomach and looked at the ground beside her with an expression of utter shame.

He continued to stare at her, openmouthed, until the load of wood began to tire his arms. He tried to speak, but his voice wouldn't work until he cleared his throat. ''Who?''

She didn't answer, but she cast her eyes a little higher, and glanced at the alcalde's mansion.

''Javier?''

Marisol looked at him, tears welling in her eyes. ''Sylvia is dead,'' she said. ''She got sick and died just after you left in the spring.''

''Was it Javier?'' Caleb said.

She covered her face with her hands.

He dropped the load of wood and stalked toward Javier's door, anger and shame boiling up in him.

''What are you going to do?'' she asked as he passed. He didn't answer, but she saw him put his hand on the butt of his revolver. ''No!'' she screamed, grabbing his arm.

He shook loose, pulled the Colt out, cocked it, marched for the kitchen door of Javier's house. Above Marisol's screaming, he heard singing coming from the kitchen. Holding the pistol in front of him, he opened the door and flung it hard against the adobe wall.

The singing ended and children screamed. Caleb saw Javier sitting in a chair at the kitchen table, children of all sizes around him, some hiding behind him. Some were Javier and Sylvia's children. Some were Caleb and Marisol's. Angelo was sitting on the table in front of Javier, a guitar in his hands. Javier was teaching him. They had all been singing.

Marisol pulled at him from behind, but Caleb hardly felt her.

''Put that pistol away,'' Javier said. ''You are frightening the children.''

Caleb pointed the revolver at the ceiling and eased the hammer down. He let the weapon hang at his side, cold in his grip. Marisol squeezed by him to get inside. She rushed to Javier's side to protect the children. Marta was standing at the fireplace, staring at him in disbelief and fear.

''Take the children in the other room,'' Javier said, getting up. ''Take them!'' he repeated.

She herded them away.

''Come outside,'' Javier said to Caleb.

They stepped out, and Javier closed the door to the kitchen. He walked to the woodpile and turned around to face Caleb. "If you want to shoot me, do it here. Not in front of the children."

"Go get your gun." He seethed with rage. Javier was remorseless.

"No. I don't care if you want to kill me, but I will not try to kill you. I would rather die than shoot at you, my old friend."

"Don't 'old friend' me, you son of a bitch. You've dishonored me and my woman."

"I have honored her where you would not. I married her. Marisol is my wife."

Caleb staggered back. "You married *my* woman?"

"Not your woman. My wife."

"The mother of my children!"

"And I will care for them as if they were my own. You will never have to worry about them. You can still come to see them if you wish. But they will stay here with their mother and me."

The shadows of the mountains were on Peñascosa now, and a breeze chilled the sweat on Caleb's forehead. "What are you tryin' to say?" His anger turned to sick fear.

"I am telling you that if you want Marisol and the children, you must kill me now. That is the only way I am going to let you have them." He lifted his eyes to the mountains, held his creased chin high, and awaited Caleb's decision.

It was unthinkable. Caleb had never considered that Marisol might quit him for an aging don like Javier, who was growing gray haired and paunchy. Seven winters had gone wasted. Amelia was right. He should have married her long ago.

He was late again. He had let one year too many pass. He could have had them all with him under one roof. Now he was expected to turn his back on his children. He did truly love them. He thought about them often, bragged on them all over the shortgrass plains, cuddled and wrestled them when he was with them. That they would so quietly, so readily, adopt a new father stung him hard.

It was like that winter on the Cimarron, when the cowboys held him down and clipped his dead fingers off with the dehorner. He could feel his own flesh and blood tearing away from him again, leaving him huddled and shuddering in pain and disbelief.

"You can visit them, just like always," Javier said. "But they live under my roof now, and Marisol is my wife."

Meekly, he slipped his pistol back into the holster. He grasped for something to salvage from Peñascosa. He felt like a dog sniffing for scraps.

It was worse than the Cimarron. He could visit his children, but he would sleep alone in a dusty Peñascosa adobe while Javier warmed himself with Marisol's body. There would be no more hunts in the mountains, no more songs sung in the *casa consistorial.*

"Now I think you better go away and cool down someplace," Javier said. "Do you want some food to take with you?"

"Hell no, I don't want no food from you! If I want food, I'll go shoot somethin'!"

Javier shrugged.

Caleb shuffled in his tracks. "Well, I'd like to tell 'em so long."

"I will tell them for you. I think it is best that you come back to see them when you are not so mad."

"What about Marisol?"

"I will tell her you said *adios."*

He felt the remorse in his stomach. There was nothing he could do but go. He wasn't going to shoot Javier. He walked toward the footbridge, avoiding the black eyes of the old ranchero as he passed. He reached the woodpile, then stopped. "I thought you liked 'em big," he said.

Javier smiled a sad, sympathetic smile. "I have seen her big many times. Big with your children. And now she is big with mine. I have been here when you have not."

He started again and didn't look back. He took an agonizing stroll across the footbridge, down the lane, to the corrals. He saddled up and went to spend a lonely night on the prairie ground. He would be cold, hungry, and alone. He would probably get the mandolin out and play a couple of the saddest songs he knew. Certainly he would play the "Short-grass Song." With a musical instrument in his hands, Caleb could make a kind of celebration even out of agony. He found beauty in sorrow. The music was his only refuge. The fiddle would drone and wail, and gush high clear melody like tears from his eyes.

EIGHTY-SEVEN

"SHORTY HAD ELEVEN bullet holes in his carcass." Caleb leaned back on his old saddle, its stirrups spread-eagle on the ground between the fire and stone. "Looked like a chunk of rat cheese. I whitewash that story when I tell anybody else, Pete, but I'm here to tell you it was the bloodiest mess I ever seen. It was almost as bad as the time we found poor old Elam butchered by the Comanche."

He sighed, looked out over Monument Park, speckled as he had never seen it with the lantern lights of homesteaders where once he and Pete had ridden together on unfenced range.

"What's happened to the ranch, Pete? You're not a year in the ground, and it's busted to pieces. Damn, I had some big ideas about bringin' Marisol and the kids here, and takin' things over." He threw a chunk of wood on the fire. "Hell, I don't know what I'm gonna do now."

He listened to the fire pop and caught himself looking at the dim light shining from Ab's cabin. "I wish I could patch things up with the old man."

He fell back on his saddle and looked at the stars twinkling in the clear winter sky. "What do you do up there all day?" he said, watching his breath cloud take an orange light from the fire. "Maybe turn them longhorn devil-critters back from the pearly gates, and chouse 'em back to hell." He smiled. "That would make a pretty good song, wouldn't it?"

He closed his eyes, heard tunes, saw memories, and fell off to sleep.

The next morning Caleb saw the Rampart Range in its full cloak of snow for the first time in ten years. Buster was waiting for him in the Cincinnati house when he came down. Caleb met Buster's newborn baby, Frederick, then walked to the mansion to get a look at his new nephew, Pete Holcomb, Jr.

"My stars," Amelia said, hugging him. "What are you doing here this time of year?"

"I've come to see Little Pete."

She puffed her cheeks with a sigh. "Oh, please, not now. He's been up all night with the colic, and I just got him to bed. Come back tonight for Sam's farewell dinner."

He left the mansion, and Buster drove Caleb to town in the old spring buggy. Looking under the seat as they drove, Caleb saw the hole in the floorboard where once he and Buster had stepped the mast. How old had he been that day they drove through Monument Park on the wind wagon, the triangular sail billowing before a chinook? Ten? Eleven?

They stopped at the Holcomb depot the two of them had built together. Nearby stood a new store, a bank, a café, a livery, a laundry, and a few other businesses. Caleb went into the boardinghouse to see how Tess was getting along.

"How come you to end up workin' here?" he asked.

"The colonel give me the job," she said. "He read your note to Buster and asked me if I wanted to work here."

Caleb merely shrugged. "The old man sure knows how to throw a town together quick."

That night Caleb and Buster were arguing lyrics in Buster's old cabin when Ab burst in without knocking.

"Buster!" he shouted. Then he saw Caleb, but it was too late. He looked away from his son and glared at the black man. "Where were you today when the stovepipe caved in at the café and filled the place with smoke?"

"Me and Caleb was up tendin' the ditches, colonel. I don't know when things are gonna break."

"Well, why won't you come by my office every afternoon to see if I need anything done?"

"Because if you don't need anything done, I've wasted a ride to town."

Ab stomped his peg leg ineffectually on the burlap carpeting. "Once was the time, Buster, when I'd holler and you'd come running. What's gotten into you?"

"Nothin', colonel. You're just more spread out now. Used to be all the work you needed done was right here on your farm. Now you've got that town and those ditches and they're spread over miles."

Ab hissed and turned toward the door. "Tell Amelia I won't be able to make her dinner tonight. I've got books to go over."

Caleb drew a breath. He wanted to thank the old man for giving the boardinghouse job to Tess. But he let his father get out of the cabin before he could bring himself to speak.

"He's been like that ever since he built that town," Buster said. "You ain't never seen him so ornery in your life."

"Hell, that's the way he shows his joy," Caleb said. "He likes that town."

Buster chuckled. "I guess you're right. Come on, we'd better pick up and get over to the big house."

They carried their instruments together in the twilight, past the grove of pines on Buster's timber-culture claim, under the cottonwoods around Ab's cabin, and up the lane toward the mansion Pete had built for his bride. "I can't figure Amelia," the drifter said as they walked. "She never did like Sam Dugan, and here she is throwin' him a farewell dinner."

"She ain't as particular as she used to be since she took to workin' them horses," Buster said. "A while back Dan come in all bloody from castratin', and she didn't even turn her lip up when she seen him."

The other guests had gathered at the mansion by the time the musicians arrived. The cowboys looked out of place sitting in the parlor drinking coffee, but they seemed at ease.

"Sam," Caleb said as he sat on the sofa. "You never did show much good sense. Here you are, finally manager of this ranch, and you're gonna up and leave us."

Sam shrugged. "Well, when them homesteaders took over the park, the colonel told me I could pick one man to help me run the place and fire the rest. I just couldn't do it. I've about had a bellyful of punchin' cows, anyhow. Dan and String are gonna stay and run the outfit. I'm goin' to New York to sell my book.''

Amelia and Gloria brought in a silver serving set and refilled the coffee cups.

"You finally get that thing writ?'' Caleb said. "What's it called?''

" 'Thom Moses, Colored Hero of the West,' '' Sam said. "Buster says it reads pretty good, but he don't hardly like the way I changed up his fight with Indians back in '64.''

"With the wolf-getter gun?'' Caleb asked, dredging up the recollections as if he had only read them in a book himself.

The author nodded. "I had Thom Moses shoot one brave and stab three others with the spike he built to stick that wolf-getter gun in the ground. Buster said that was just too much killin'.''

Ab's Chinese cook had been listening quietly in a cushioned armchair. "Next book you write, you call it 'Lee Fong, Chinaman Outlaw,' '' he said.

"Lee Fong,'' Dan Brooks said, "nobody'd have you as an in-law, much less an outlaw.''

Piggin' String McCoy laughed so hard that he spilled the coffee he was blowing in his saucer.

"Why must you always saucer your coffee?'' Amelia said, running for a towel.

"To cool it off,'' String said. "What else is a saucer for?''

"To rest the cup on, of course,'' she shouted from the kitchen.

"I thought that's what the coffee table was for,'' String said, leaving a ring on the hardwood. "Speakin' of outlaws''—he paused and drew back as Amelia worked furiously with the towel—"that Miss Wiley at the boardin' house in town told us about you killin' off a couple of bad ones in the territory.''

Caleb nodded vacantly. He didn't feel like going into that again. "Had some help from Long Fingers,'' he said. "That reminds me. The chief says he's comin' up in the spring, if the agents will give him a pass.''

"How old is he?'' Dan asked.

"I don't know. He still sits a horse straight. Tough old stob.''

"What's he comin' up here for?'' String said.

"Buster's been invitin' him for years.''

"What?'' Gloria said, wheeling on Buster as she carried a coffeepot among the guests. "You ain't gonna have no wild Indian stay with us!''

Sam tried to laugh and swallow at the same time. He sprayed coffee all over Dan and started coughing. He reached for the makings of a cigarette, as he always did when the fits of hacking came on him.

"Oh, woman,'' Buster said. "He ain't a wild Indian. Is he Caleb?''

Amelia went back to work with the towel.

"He ain't no wilder than Piggin' String."

"That's wild enough," String drawled. "Gloria don't 'llow me in her house neither."

The laughter of the cowboys rose and fell, and a shrill cry came from the stairway.

"That's Little Pete," Amelia said to Gloria. "I'll get him." She took the front of her skirt in hand as she sprinted up the stairs.

Sam licked the cigarette paper and rolled it around the tobacco.

"Looks like you're about to meet your nephew," Buster said.

"About time," Caleb replied. "It's a good thing you and Gloria had a boy, too, Buster. That way him and Pete can grow up playin' together."

"It sure is a good thing," Gloria said. "I couldn't stand to see no daughter of mine pushin' them plows."

"I wouldn't make a girl plow," Buster said.

"I don't know . . ."

Buster rolled his eyes at the men.

Amelia entered with her baby and put Little Pete in Caleb's arms. "Meet your uncle Caleb," she said, cooing to Little Pete. "Yours is sleeping like an angel, Gloria."

Caleb blushed and held the baby awkwardly in his arms. He put the stub of his left index finger in the baby's hand. "Good firm grip," he said. "I don't know if that's for holdin' onto broncs or makin' chords on a banjo."

"He could learn both, if someone would stay around long enough to teach him," Amelia said. She looked curtly at Caleb, ignoring the sudden silence around her.

EIGHTY-EIGHT

"How did you learn about these things?" Buster asked. He was holding the walnut box of a telephone against the wall of his Cincinnati house so Caleb could nail it in place.

"I've seen 'em used on some of those great big ranches down in Texas," he mumbled, gripping his nails with one side of his mouth. He was growing his mustache long again, and the little iron spikes looked like straight, square whiskers jutting from his lip. "They use 'em there so they won't have to send line riders out with messages all the time."

"What give you the idea I needed one?"

"That day the old man busted into your cabin and tore into you about not bein' handy all the time. I figured if we ran a few telephones between here and his office in town, he could put you to work about twenty-four hours a day."

Buster grunted. "That's probably just what'll happen, too. How come you didn't order more wire? You got to have a lot of wire to go between the boxes."

"Already got it strung," Caleb said.

"Where?"

With the palm of his hand he wiped the glaze of moisture from the inside of the cold windowpane and pointed at the nearest corner post of Buster's cow pasture. "Right there. Top strand."

"You're gonna hook it up to bobwire?"

"That's the way they do it in Texas. The corner of your pasture connects with the old man's south pasture. His south pasture runs right by his cabin and Amelia's house one way and dang near all the way to town the other way. No need to string new wire when we already got it runnin' all over the park."

"And that works?" Buster asked.

"Except when it rains," Caleb said, pounding in the last nail.

Gloria came in from Amelia's mansion to fix Buster's dinner. "What are you two doin' to my house?" she asked with no slight concern.

"Puttin' in a telephone," Buster said.

"Telephone? Are we gonna be able to talk to the folks in town?"

Buster nodded. "We're gonna hook it straight to Colonel Ab's office."

"Not that town! I was talkin' about the Springs. Ain't you gonna hook it up to Colorado Springs?"

"Woman, you don't know anybody with a telephone in Colorado Springs anyhow."

"If I had a telephone that would go there, I might get to know some of them! Why did you put it there by the front door? Why didn't you put it in the kitchen where I could use it?"

"You can use it here," Buster said.

"Next time you go messin' with my house, you better ask me first." She stormed through the parlor and into the kitchen.

Caleb grimaced and Buster rolled his eyes.

After dinner they drilled a hole in the parlor wall, despite Gloria's protestations. They ran two smooth telephone wires through the hole. One of them went along the side of the house and into the ground. The other ran out from under the porch roof and across the yard to the fence surrounding Buster's cow pasture.

Standing in the dirty slush of week-old snow, they attached a tall pole to a fence post to suspend the telephone wire high above Buster's front yard, over the heads of riders and wagon drivers. They ran the smooth wire down the high pole and connected it to the top strand of barbed wire on Buster's fence.

Buster looked down the fence line toward Ab's south pasture and saw that the barbed wire circuit wasn't continuous. "I guess we got to run a high wire over the gate, too," he said.

"I thought you didn't know nothin' about a telephone."

"Common sense," he said, shrugging.

"The most uncommonest kind of sense there is, ain't it? The world's shy on it, but you sure got your share."

They lashed a tall pole on either side of the gate, held tightly in place with twisted wire. They spliced a length of wire to the top strand on the fence, ran it over the tops of the tall poles, and spliced it again to the top barbed wire on the other side of the gate. Now the gate could be opened and wagons could pass underneath without breaking the circuit.

They hitched Buster's farm wagon and loaded a spool of wire, some poles, a few fence-working tools, and three other telephone boxes. They drove to the corner of Buster's pasture where it joined with Ab's big south pasture, inspecting the barbed telephone wire along the way for breaks. At the corner, they spliced the top strand of Buster's fence to the top strand of Ab's.

They traced the top strand of barbed wire around the perimeter of the big pasture and back toward the Holcomb Ranch headquarters. They encountered two barbed wire gaps and a gate and had to install more tall poles and splice more wires over the passages. Toward late afternoon they came to a corner where three fence lines met. One led toward Ab's log cabin. Another led past Amelia's mansion.

"Whose telephone are you gonna put in next?" Buster said.

"Well, I don't know. What's Gloria fixing' for Amelia's supper tonight?"

"Duck."

"Duck? You sure?"

"I shot 'em myself."

"Does Gloria cook a good duck?"

"Oh, she cooks 'em mighty good. She bastes that duck in butter and drippin's, then she stuffs it and serves it with 'taters, brown gravy, and greens."

"And biscuits?"

"No, Miss Amelia likes white bread."

"Doggone it, I guess I'll put in Amelia's telephone next, then."

They inspected the top strand of wire from the corner post to Amelia's horse stalls, where they would have to set several poles in the ground along a line running from the stalls to the mansion.

"Where are we goin' with the wire?" Buster asked, grabbing the posthole diggers.

"I don't know. I better go ask Amelia where she wants her telephone."

Gloria answered the door when he knocked. Before Caleb could get a word out, she said, "Miss Amelia said to hang it on the kitchen wall. She said there ain't nothin' ruder than somebody talking' on a telephone in the parlor when they have real-live guests sittin' in the room with them, or when somebody's trying to read the paper under the light. Captain Dubois had him a telephone in his parlor, and Miss Amelia made him move it to the kitchen."

"Wherever she wants it is fine with me," Caleb said.

"She told me to ask you if you want to stay for supper tonight."

"Why, yes, I would. I'd never pass up a chance to eat your cookin', Gloria."

She smirked. "I guess I better stuff another duck then." She turned into the mansion, closing the door in Caleb's face.

Gloria made Buster drive her home after the poles had been set and the telephone wires strung into the kitchen. The roast-duck dinner was on the table, so Caleb put aside the varnished walnut box with the polished black mouthpiece jutting from it like a blunderbuss. Holcomb Ranch's dawn of electric communications would have to wait until after supper.

When they sat down, Amelia asked Caleb to say the blessing. He turned red and felt a hot flush but said he would try. It was just Amelia there, after all.

"Heavenly Father," he began, "we thank you for these wild ducks and this garden truck and all. Not to mention store-bought things like salt and pepper and coffee." His tongue got mired for a moment, but he recovered. "And for the good friends and family to share it with, and the memory of them that can't be with us. In Christ's name we pray, amen."

Amelia smiled, her eyes glittering beautifully. "That was very nice," she said.

"Well, it ain't as good as Pete used to pray." He grabbed a fancy china bowl full of mashed potatoes. "I'm sure glad you asked me to supper tonight. This roast duck beats the likes of what I've been feeding on—poke salad and peckerwood eggs mostly."

She threw back the corner of a napkin wrapped around a loaf of well buttered bread. "Well, you look gaunt. You probably haven't eaten a decent meal in months."

"The last one I had was down in Long Fingers' village," he said, taking a slice of steaming bread. "Big victory celebration. They made the chief's favorite dishes."

"What would that be?"

"Roast dog and unborn calf!" He grew wide-eyed and grinned at Amelia.

She paused with her fork before her lips but choked back her protestations and ate. "Caleb," she said, sipping her tea. "I've been thinking of selling our cattle to make more pasture available to the horses. The Appaloosas are getting very popular among the people in town. Would you be available next summer to round the cattle up and market them for me?''

"Hadn't thought that far ahead," Caleb replied. He forked a load of roast duck into his mouth.

"I wouldn't ask, but I can't do it myself, you know. And I thought . . . if you were going to be here . . ."

Caleb grunted. His eyes shifted as his jaws performed some unusual mastications.

"Caleb?"

In a moment he put his fingers to his lips and removed a small lead pellet from the end of his tongue. He dropped it onto the floral china with a clink. "Buster's eyes must be goin' bad. He used to shoot 'em clean in the head every time."

After supper, Caleb insisted on hooking up the telephone as Amelia soaked dishes for Gloria to wash the next day.

"Now, see this wire?" he said, explaining the contraption. "That runs out there to the top strand of the fence and all the way over to Buster's Cincinnati house, and it's hooked up to his telephone. Now, listen, don't ever hold onto that top wire. Don't grab aholt of it if you're crawlin' through the fence or somethin', because if somebody just happens to crank on this handle, it'll send a jolt through you like lightning."

Amelia frowned over her shoulder. "Is it dangerous?"

"Well, it won't kill you or anything, but it won't tickle either." He hooked up the battery and the ground wire, made a final splice, and closed the hinged front of the telephone box.

"May I try it?" she asked, drying her hands on a dish towel.

"I don't see why not." He stepped back to let her send the maiden signal.

Amelia angled the blunderbuss upward and turned the magneto handle as if grinding a coffee mill for an army.

"Whoa!" Caleb said. "You're liable to spook Gloria up the chimney like that."

"Hello?" she said. "Buster?"

Caleb could hear the tinny strains of the Thompson household rattling from the earpiece.

"I woke the baby," Amelia said, making a pained face at Caleb.

"Oh, Lord, you're gonna catch it now."

"Let me speak to her, Buster. . . . Gloria?" She pulled the earpiece away from her chestnut tresses and grimaced. "Well, I'm sorry, I didn't know. The dishes?" She swept her eyes across the ceiling. "No, I'm soaking them. Yes. In the morning. Very well. Good night." She hung the earpiece on its spring-loaded cradle.

"She's about got you trained, Amelia." He noticed a strange look on her face.

"I just made the first telephone connection in Monument Park. Perhaps I should have thought of something more profound to say."

He shrugged. "Well, soakin' the dishes ain't just rat shot."

Amelia smiled at him and shook her head. "Pete always said you had the most picturesque ways of expressing yourself. He envied you for that."

Caleb felt his astonishment pull at his face. "Envied *me?*"

"Yes, for the way you talk, the way you sing, and . . . doing whatever it is you do out there."

"*Pete* envied *me.*" His skin was tingling. "That's swappin' ends for you."

"He always said, 'If I could just preach like Caleb sings.' " She lifted the coffeepot from the stove. "Go stoke the fire in the parlor, and I'll bring the coffee."

When she brought him his cup, she sat beside him on the sofa. "Caleb, what about next summer?" she said. "Will you round the cattle up for me?"

Caleb poured some coffee into his saucer. "It ain't really the cattle, is it?"

"What do you mean?"

"You could get Dan or Piggin' String to round cattle up for you."

She fumbled with her cup and stared into the roaring fire for a moment. "No, it's not the cattle. It's you. I want you to stay."

"What for?"

"For the sake of your nephew. He needs a man about, Caleb. There are things I can't teach him."

"There are men fallin' all over theirselves on this ranch," Caleb argued. "The old man, Buster, Dan, Piggin' String."

Amelia had put her cup and saucer down and was becoming agitated. "We've argued this before. The colonel is old and gruff, Buster has a family of his own, and as for Mr. Brooks and Mister McCoy . . . I know they're good men, Caleb, but they're just so dumb! They're ignorant, and they want nothing more out of life than to remain that way. They're not the least bit interesting, and I would rather have my son learn from his own uncle. He's your brother's son!"

He took her slender arm in his hand to calm her. She had toned muscles there from working with her horses. "Now don't get all headstrong." He looked into the round astonishment of her eyes and snorted. "There ain't nowhere else left for me to go anyhow. I've been thinkin' about stayin', but I didn't expect I'd have to come right out and tell everybody. It's embarrassing."

"Why on earth would that embarrass you?"

"I'm not used to goin' where folks tell me to go and stayin' where they tell me to stay. If you'd have just waited, you might have seen that I was stayin'." He put his coffee on the table. He had no stomach for it anymore. "Anyway, a fella can't ride anywhere no more for the fences," he grumbled. "There's roads now in places I went before there were even trails."

"Is staying here so bad?" she asked. "Why does it make you so bitter?"

"Because I'm twenty-nine years old and I don't have anything to show for it. If it's my fault, I don't know why." He fell back on the sofa and stared at the ceiling. "Lord, I remember comin' here as a kid, when we owned everything as far as we could see. I just knew someday this whole country was gonna be mine and Pete's and Matthew's. Now look at it. The whole park's plowed under and sectioned off with fences and roads and irrigation ditches so you can't ride from here to there without gettin' down to open a dozen gaps and stoppin' to say howdy-do to fifteen farmers."

"Don't feel so ungrateful," she lectured, no sympathy in her voice. "There are others with far less than you have. Your father still owns a substantial amount of property."

"It wouldn't matter if he owned it all. It's all changed now. It'll never go back to what it was when I came here." He sat up and looked at her, as if startled by a sudden revelation. "And you know what the worst of it is? I dug the first irrigation ditch myself. I built the first windmill, the first fence. Hell," he said, chuckling, "now I've gone and strung the first damned telephone!"

Amelia forced a smile. "It's still a beautiful place. The mountains are just as high and lonely as when you came here. The wildflowers are just as lovely. I didn't come here as early as you did, of course, but I have seen this land change, too, and I have changed with it. When Pete brought me here, I was still a squeamish little city girl. Now the ranch has changed me, and I've changed the ranch. But there are some things, Caleb, like those mountains, that will never change. You can hold onto them while everything else is changing around you. It gives you your place in the world."

He got up, walked to the window, and saw the snowy mountains under the moon. "You know, there's a place, right up on top of the hill, just the other side of Pete's grave. If you sit there in the grass beside the old Arapaho Trail and look west, you can't see a fence or a road or a windmill or a house. I remember the first time I climbed up there as a boy—the way I felt lookin' up the Arapaho Trail, where it winds up into the Rampart Range." He turned back to her. "I hope that's one of them things you're talkin' about that'll never change. It's the last place like that I know of around here."

She rose and joined him at the window, slipping her hand around his arm. "I'll tell you a secret, Caleb. One you've never learned on your own, because you've never stayed in one place long enough to learn it. If you look at something every day, then even if it changes, you don't notice so much. It doesn't come as such a shock to you. It's the same with people. You don't notice the wrinkles, or the gray hairs showing up, if you see them every day. And when you see the children every day, you don't even notice them growing. But if you see them only once in a while, you realize how much you must have missed. And it hurts you to have missed it. That's why people have homes. That's why we settle."

He nodded. "I've learned more than you think I have," he said. "The hard way, mostly." He stared at her a long moment and felt closer to her than he ever had before. He had seen her first wrinkles appear in this year since Pete died—tiny hairlines around the corners of her eyes. But there was no gray among the chestnut tresses. Amelia was still soft and smooth, and more beautiful than the day Matthew brought her home.

It had always shamed him to see her beauty. He usually looked away. He thought of her first as his brother's wife. But now he stared and felt no shame. Pete was gone. Dead a year, as a matter of fact. It had taken that long for him accept Pete's death and to see his widow as Amelia, instead of Mrs. Pete Holcomb. There was no dishonor in seeing her beauty now.

The logs shifted in the fireplace.

"Well, it's late," he said. "I better get back to the bunkhouse."

She walked with him to the kitchen door, gave him his hat, and helped him with his coat. Before he left, she put her small, warm hand in his and squeezed his fingers. "Good night," she said.

He stepped out into the dark Colorado winter.

He tried to clear his head as he trudged back to the bunkhouse with his hands in his pockets. "What did you say?" he said to himself. "Did you tell her you'd stay, or not? Nowhere else to go. Plenty of reasons to stay. That life's gone now, ain't it? The wandering? That's a hard life, and you know it. Why the hell don't you want to stay? The old man, that's why. How are you ever gonna get the nerve to speak to the old man? Not much of a ranch here now, either. You need room. Who's gonna listen to the music? My Lord, what did you tell her? Did you tell her you'd stay? You did, didn't you? You up and did it. You damn fool, you should have thought first!"

EIGHTY-NINE

THE BARBED WIRE telephone system sent tendrils all the way to town, where Caleb and Buster installed a box in Ab's office one day while he was out. They also put one in the colonel's cabin on the ranch.

Tess Wiley bought a telephone box with her own money and had Caleb hook her boardinghouse up to the system.

Gloria became so enraged with Ab ringing the bell in her house every night to talk to Buster that she made Buster tear the telephone out and put it in his old cabin. He usually went there in the evenings anyway, where he worked on various contraptions or played music with Caleb.

Piggin' String McCoy made a weekly inspection of fences, paying particular attention to the top strand on the south pasture. After Tess got her telephone, he started riding fences on Saturdays and would wind up at her boardinghouse in the evenings to wrangle an invitation for supper.

Tess stopped Caleb in the street one day as he was coming out of the general store. "What is Piggin' String's real name?" she asked. "He won't tell me."

Caleb chuckled. "When he first came here, he used to go by his initials—P.S. Said his real name was too embarrassing. We all just took to callin' him Piggin' String."

"I'm gonna find out what it stands for if it's the last thing I do," she said.

"He won't tell. I've tried for years to get him to tell."

The next Sunday afternoon, Caleb was saddling Whiplash, the stallion who had thrown Pete into Cedar Root Canyon, when Buster found him in the corral.

"Where you goin'?" Buster asked.

"Huntin'. Want to go?"

"No. What do you want to ride ol' Whiplash for? You tryin' to give the old man a stroke?"

"Oh, he ain't no outlaw," Caleb said. "Just a little high-strung."

Buster shook his head. "I just talked to Tess Wiley on the telephone. She was lookin' for you."

"What did she want?"

"I don't know. She wouldn't tell me. Said she only wanted to talk to you."

"I guess I better talk to her before I go," Caleb said. "Can I use your telephone?"

"Sure."

He rode Whiplash to Buster's cabin, got down, wiped his feet before stepping in on the burlap carpet, and took the earpiece off the side of the telephone. He gave the crank five short turns. Tess's was the fifth telephone on the system, so her signal was five rings. He waited a few seconds and gave the crank another five turns.

"Tess?" he said. "Buster said you wanted to talk to me."

"I found out," her voice said, crackling through the barbed wire.

"Found out what?"

"What *P.S.* stands for. Piggin' String's real name is Pendrake Sydney McCoy."

"My Lord!" Caleb said, laughing. "No wonder he wouldn't tell. How did you get it out of him?"

A mad whir of static came over the fence line.

"What?"

"I said that's none of your business!" Tess repeated. "Now, don't you tell anybody, Caleb. He might get riled at me."

"Lord, woman, if you don't want anybody to know, don't say it over the telephone. Gloria listens in on every conversation when she's at Amelia's house."

"I know, but this is her day off."

"Well, you can't be too careful. I have to go now. Tell Pendrake I said howdy."

"Caleb!" she said as he hung up the ear horn.

He chuckled as he went back out. But as soon as he got up on Whiplash, he heard the single ring that represented Buster's signal. He climbed back down and went into the cabin as the bell rang again.

"I was just jokin'," he said into the blunderbuss. "I won't tell nobody."

"Buster?" a gruff old voice said.

He stood in sudden surprise. "This is Caleb."

"Caleb? Oh. Tell Buster to get over to my house. I have some things for him to do tomorrow."

"All right."

They listened as the line hummed between them.

"Thanks," Ab's voice finally said.

"You're welcome."

There was a pause, and an empty drone of static, then a tripped switch broke the link between them.

Caleb hung up the earpiece, fascinated. His father had thanked him over the telephone. The old man had spoken to him with real civility. It had taken two miles of barbed wire to reach across the years of silence and anger. It was a precarious link, but Caleb felt the beginnings of a twist that he thought he might form into a solid splice. He felt an electric surge rise from his heart and travel up the back of his throat. The telephone was a wonderful invention.

NINETY

GREEN CAME TO the plains along the Washita, and patches of locoweed pushed blue-purple blossoms into sunlight. Long Fingers yearned for the timbered grades of the mountains. He left his canvas-covered house at dawn, wearing a broadcloth suit, a moon-white shirt, a flat-brimmed Stetson, and new moccasins of golden deerskin and multicolored quill work. He carried a leather satchel.

Walking slowly down the dirt lane of his village, he came to Red Hawk's farm, where the young chief was preparing the foundation of his house among stacks of rough-sawn cottonwood lumber. He stood silently and watched until Red Hawk noticed him.

"Where are you going?" Red Hawk asked, setting down the square-quarried stone he was carrying to a corner.

"I am going to see Man-on-a-Cloud."

"Do you want me to go with you to the agency?"

"No. I will go alone." He put his satchel on the ground. "Sit down, I want to tell you something," he said, and they both sank to a bench of stacked lumber. "When the white men come to break our land apart, it will be the first time since the Great Spirit made the Arapaho mother of all people that we will have no land to call our own. Just little pieces of land for different Indians. No longer a big piece for the tribe. It is the time of great change."

"I know."

"You have to hold the people together. I do not know how. It is for you to learn . . ."

As they talked, the sun rose higher, brighter, and threw light into a million dewdrops clinging to the fresh spring grass.

"You will be the last chief to remember the old ways," Long Fingers finally said. "You must remember the way you endured your test, and saw the vision of a Red Hawk in the morning sun. The others chose to fight, and now they are dead and are doing nothing for the people. You chose the right way. You must keep the old ways of the Arapaho in your heart, while you guide the plow in your hands. Remember the most important thing: the Arapaho tribe is the mother of all others on earth. It must never die."

He leaned forward and tried to stand on his tired old legs. Red Hawk stood quickly and boosted Long Fingers with a strong, gentle hand.

"I will tell you something else, too," Long Fingers said. "If you like a white man, and you want him to be a friend, give him an Indian name. Call him Standing Bear or Running Horse or something like that. Then he will be your friend."

Red Hawk nodded and smiled.

"Now, I am going to find a boy to put a saddle on my horse for me. Let your heart laugh when you see me ride away. I am going back to the old, sacred lands. I am going to see the mountains."

Red Hawk tried to let his heart laugh when the old man left, but it sank like a stone in a river and grew cold down in the beautiful murky depths of his sorrow. He sat on the cornerstone, hoping to see the bird of his vision quest soar into the red glow of the morning sun, but the hawk did not appear.

Long Fingers rode all day, plodding slowly on his paint mare. He reached Darlington that evening and stayed with the Indian agent of the Cheyenne-Arapaho reservation. He was a favorite of the agent for his long and steadfast friendship and cooperation.

"Here's your pass," the agent told him that night. "I'll see you off at the station in the morning. Remember, you'll have to ride in the immigrant cars."

The rails took him north to Wichita, where a black man he had traveled with out of Indian Territory helped him purchase his ticket for Pueblo, Colorado, and find his train. As he rode westward, the homesteads grew more scarce and the towns farther apart, until, beyond Garden City, he saw only the great, green swells of the prairie, marred occasionally by the sawtooth jags of barbed wire fences, zigzagging across the Great Plains.

Darkness came, but he did not sleep. He stared all night at the moon and the stars, their light streaked and smeared by the grimy windows. He could not feel the permanence of earth through all the gnashing steel pieces below him. In the morning he saw the homesteads lining the Arkansas. Too many of them to count. The cottonwoods planted in orchard rows around their homes were growing large now and casting ample shadows.

He searched the western horizon through the moist, hazy spring air. His heart rose until finally he saw them: the dark, purple faces of the sacred mountains. They were the same. He knew them. Some things didn't change.

At Pueblo he bought his ticket and waited for the regular afternoon run to Colorado Springs and, beyond, to Holcomb. As the rails carried him northward, he gazed with silent wonder at what the white man had done, in less than half his lifetime, to this place where the plains and mountains met. Everywhere he saw towns, houses, roads, fences, trash heaps, and huge square patches of scarred earth where once buffalo had lumbered in numbers too great to calculate and antelope had sprinted like light above the ground. He saw naked hillsides, once thick with timber. The power and stupidity of white men awed him.

The high ridge of Pikes Peak drew nearer. Long Fingers became almost hypnotized by its slow approach. He came to Colorado Springs and watched the rich white people come and go as the train sat in the station. Finally the cars jerked northward for the last stretch into Holcomb.

He was looking forward to the end of the trip. The constant rumble of the rails beneath him numbed his senses. He didn't like traveling in a box. He could hardly wait to get a horse under him on the Arapaho Trail.

The town of Holcomb approached. He felt the train slowing down. He recognized the country, but it had changed. It had once belonged to the Arapaho and the Cheyenne, who took good care of it, for it took good care of them. Now it was in the hands of a thousand greedy white men. He had signed it away to save his tribe. It saddened him to return after all these winters and suddenly see the changes, as if they had come overnight.

He turned his eyes from the window and stared straight ahead. He brought to mind the images of the plains and mountains before the white man. They came to him with more clarity than the memories of the canvas house he had left behind only two days ago. He longed for something old and familiar.

A murmur came from the rear of the passenger car. Someone spoke loudly. Someone laughed. Shoes scuffled across the aisle. Excited voices tittered and shrieked with surprise. Long Fingers came slowly out of his daze. He felt too weak to look around. The giggling came up behind him. Benches creaked under squirming thighs. Through the streaked window-pane he glimpsed a surge of whiteness. It seemed a cloud had come down to race the train into town. He turned his head slowly. His old eyes focused.

On the mast of the wind wagon, the billowing sail stood level with his car window. He saw Buster at the wheel, Caleb with his hand on the rope. They were bouncing on the spring seat, searching the passing windows as they gained gradually on the train. Long Fingers jerked a bandanna from his pocket and used it to polish the glass. Caleb saw him and pointed. Buster looked, grinned, waved. The black man's hat flew from his head in the wind. Above the rumble of the train Long Fingers heard Caleb hollering with the voice of a wild wolf.

The dirt road veered from the tracks to miss a shed and two houses. Long Fingers pressed his palms against the glass and watched the cloud flash between the buildings. Then Buster steered it hard against the tracks again. Long Fingers was laughing as the other passengers gathered around him to watch the strange vehicle run. The train slowed, and the wind wagon sped onward, out of sight, careening precariously on two wheels as it disappeared.

The Indian agent at Darlington had telegraphed ahead, and a crowd had gathered at the Holcomb Station to greet Chief Long Fingers. Colonel Holcomb came, as did Amelia and Gloria, each with a baby wrapped in her arms. Horace Gribble had made the trip from Plum Creek with his wife and children. Tess Wiley stood with Piggin' String McCoy. Dan Brooks sat on the highest board of the loading chute. Captain Dubois brought a brass band from Colorado Springs to announce the visitor's arrival with a fanfare. Photographers from Denver set up their cumbersome boxes. The wind wagon beat the train to the depot, and its crew leapt out onto the loading platform. When the train stopped, the band launched a march, and the crowd anxiously watched the passenger cars for some sign of the chief. Long Fingers came down the landing from a car near the caboose, carrying his leather satchel and regarding the young town with wonder.

"There he is!" Buster cried, pointing. He and Caleb went to escort the chief to the waiting crowd. But first Long Fingers had to play his harmonica along with the brass band.

"This is my wife and baby," Buster said after the fanfare ended.

Gloria drew her child close to her, afraid the old savage might scalp him before her very eyes. The chief smiled at her.

Horace Gribble was next in line.

"I am happy to see you again, Gribble," Long Fingers said. "Man-on-a-Cloud has told me that you refused to kill the Indians at Sand Creek. That was all you could do for us. I have remembered you well."

Horace swallowed hard and almost wept.

Long Fingers came to Ab. "Holcomb. You still grow the flowers for your wife's place in the ground?"

Ab nodded. "Yes."

"Good. I liked your wife. She gave us beef."

Before they left for the ranch, they posed for photographs, Long Fingers holding his hat over his heart as if singing the national anthem. As the crowd dispersed toward the coaches, he followed Buster and Caleb to the wind wagon.

"I am going to ride in this wagon with you," he said. "I want to feel the wind push me like a cloud."

They hoisted the sail and shot down the street. Most of the carriage horses wore blinders and didn't see the wind wagon until it had passed. But Dan Brooks's horse saw it coming just as Dan put his foot in the stirrup. The cow pony vaulted forward, kicking as he ran, leaving Dan in the dirt, stunned. Long Fingers laughed loudly.

Caleb trimmed the sail to reduce speed, and the wind wagon trundled smartly toward Amelia's mansion where a lavish dinner had been prepared in the chief's honor.

"Tonight we have to play some songs for the folks at the house," Buster said. "But tomorrow we can do whatever you want."

"I would like to ride one of the Nez Perce horses," he said.

"You can have your pick of 'em," Caleb promised. "Where are we goin'?"

"I would like to ride alone. Into the mountains. Stay there all day by myself. Maybe so camp there a night or two."

Caleb looked to Buster for approval.

"Whatever the chief wants to do," Buster said.

Caleb shrugged. "Chief, consider the mountains yours."

"I do," he said, nodding.

The guests at Amelia's mansion put up with the chief's discordant harmonica playing as long as they could, then found reason to depart. Long Fingers was worn out from traveling and asked if he could turn in, too. He was offered the guest suite but requested Buster's old cabin. The guest suite was upstairs, and he was afraid the mansion would catch on fire and trap him there.

"Chief," Buster asked, setting the old warrior's bag down on the burlap carpet. "Somethin' I been wonderin' about for years. Whatever happened to the Snake Woman. Did she ever have that baby?"

The chief searched the black man's face. "Caleb Holcomb never told you about it?"

Buster shook his head, then listened to the story Long Fingers had put together over the years by talking to Indians who had witnessed the Pease River slaughter. He remembered the spring of '75 and how Caleb had avoided his eyes. He knew something terrible had happened to Caleb out there but never suspected anything like that. Long Fingers assured him that no one knew for sure who had killed Medicine Horse but that Caleb was at the battle and had even led the charge.

He lay awake in the Cincinnati house that night and wondered why Caleb had never told him. But then Caleb was not the man for that kind of confrontation. That was the sort of thing that made him drift. Caleb was always looking for a warm welcome and an eager audience. When problems arose, he saddled up and rode on.

He wished Caleb had told him years ago, so he could have told Caleb it was all right. There was probably no way he could have avoided being in that battle. Anyway, if Buster had seen Medicine Horse drawing a bead on Caleb in the Pease River valley, he would have killed the young warrior himself. He would rather have destroyed his own flesh and blood than see Caleb dead. It was his own fault for not resisting Snake Woman in the dugout years before. He had always regretted that mistake.

NINETY-ONE

LONG FINGERS ROSE before dawn and carried his satchel out into the morning moonlight. He stripped naked and opened the bag. Inside he found a breechcloth, a pair of leggings, a deerskin shirt, and a single eagle feather, somewhat ruffled and crimped along the spine. He put the clothes on and wove the feather into his moon-silvered hair. Finally, he removed a straw-stuffed Arapaho pad saddle from the satchel and went to the corral.

Caleb got up at sunrise and found Long Fingers looking over the spotted horses. "Mornin', chief. Why didn't you wear that Indian outfit yesterday? Those photographers would have got a kick out of you in that getup."

"It is not for them to see. Only for you, and Man-on-a-Cloud, and the mountains."

"Oh." Caleb felt honored. "Do you want some breakfast?"

"No. I am not hungry. I am looking at the horses."

"Well, you pick any one you want. I'll go hurry Buster up. He'll want to see you off. I can tell you want to get an early start."

"Caleb Holcomb," the chief said. "I want to tell you something."

The musician stopped.

"You send my women the buffalo skins in the winter of the Red River war. You fight with my boys against Kicking Dog and the Comancheros. You have done many things for my people. Now I ask you for something more."

Caleb swallowed hard, slapped his palms against his thighs. "What is it?"

"The boomers are going to make my people have little pieces of land. They must learn to farm, or they will lose everything. When you go south, you help Red Hawk. You know how to make a farm. I know you don't like it. I don't like it either. But you please teach Red Hawk how to make a good farm."

Caleb's eyes became moist, and he heard the wind in the buffalo grass. He remembered the first time he rode to Indian Territory, a captive of the Snake Woman. "I will do that for you, Long Fingers."

"Good," the chief replied. "And now I want to give you something. I have thought about this a long time. Now you will have a new name, and it is White Wolf, because that is what you are like. I hear you make songs at night that way. Then you go."

Caleb tried to say the name but couldn't. He nodded, smiled, looked at the ground. He had to turn away then, a tear running down his cheek as if his pounding heart had pumped it out like a windmill.

* * *

When Caleb brought Buster out after breakfast, the chief had an Indian bridle and his pad saddle on a gentle old mare and was walking her around outside the corral.

"You picked a good one," Buster said.

"She is old and slow, like me," the chief replied. "But plenty smart."

Caleb looked at the Indian rig with some concern. "You can borrow one of our saddles if you want."

"I like this saddle." Long Fingers looked over the bald hill to the west. The sun had not yet risen beyond the Pinery but was bathing the high places in a fiery hue. "Man-on-a-Cloud," he said, "why are there so many wildflowers growing on that hill? I do not remember it that way."

"We plant 'em there every spring," Buster said. "Pete's buried up there. We throw the seeds around his grave."

"Do you have any seeds today?"

"I have all kinds of 'em."

Long Fingers straightened the reins in his hands. "I told you a long time ago that they will grow all by theirself if you leave them alone. Do you remember?"

Buster nodded.

"I have changed my mind about it. It is not a bad idea to help them grow a little bit. And to grow them where you want them. Get some of the seeds now, and I will help you and White Wolf plant them on the hill."

Buster raised his eyebrows at Caleb. "All right, chief. It's about time we planted 'em anyway, ain't it, White Wolf?"

"It's just the right time of year, Man-on-a-Cloud."

"Bring your fiddles and we will play a song or two before I go into the mountains," Long Fingers said.

They gathered their seeds and their musical instruments and climbed the hill. They cast the seeds first, pouring them into their hands from the old tobacco pouches and broadcasting them around Pete's gravestone. Then they sat on the ground and played "Old Dan Tucker" and "Camptown Races."

As they played, the ranch came to life below them. Gloria left the Cincinnati house and headed for Amelia's mansion. Lee Fong charged into the vegetable garden with a hoe. Piggin' String and Dan rode down a lane and let themselves into the south pasture through a sagging wooden gate. Ab went to the wildflower garden and cut some pink shooting stars to place over Ella's grave and some wild indigos to go over Matthew's.

The harmonica seemed to take the breath out of Long Fingers. He slipped it into a pocket on his deerskin shirt and straightened himself slowly as he got to his feet. "I am going to take the old trail into the mountains now," he said.

"You sure you don't want us to go along?" Caleb asked.

The chief led his horse up next to the grave marker and, using the stone to step on, climbed across the back of the docile Nez Perce mare. "You stay here and play some more songs together," he said. "I will listen to you when I go away." His feather wobbled in a sudden blast of wind. He raised his hand and turned the mare onto the trail.

"Let's play "Good-bye Ol' Paint," Buster suggested and bounced the bow on his fiddle strings to lead into the song. As Caleb sang, he saw a farm wagon, toylike with distance, creeping toward town on a dirt road. The railroad tracks shimmered, and the matchbox buildings of Holcomb, Colorado, wavered in the morning glare.

He finished singing, looked toward the mountains, saw Long Fingers pass over a hump in the trail, and sink out of sight. "What do you think he's gonna do up there?" he asked.

Buster said nothing.

The drifter looked down on the patchwork landscape and tried to remember his mother standing in the dream of dead grass. It was a vague and far-gone memory, dreamlike in itself. Suddenly his eyes were darting far across the ground below, and a hollow formed in his chest, like an old tree whose heartwood had died and rotted away. "Oh, my lord," he said.

"What?"

Caleb let the guitar lie flat across his thighs. "I can see every damn corner post on the ranch from up here!"

"So?"

"Well, hell, Buster. You remember the day when we had land to graze ten thousand head. Now look at it!" He gestured irritably with his free hand.

"Is it land you want?"

"Damn right! And should have had it!"

Buster chuckled.

"What's so damn funny?"

He flashed his honest smile at the sky and laughed. "You've left your tracks on more land than the ten biggest speculators in Texas. Why, son, you've done and seen things won't never come again!"

Caleb let his mouth hang open long enough that his tongue felt dry. "I know it, but . . . I'm the *reason* they won't never come again. I've kilt buffalo till there weren't no more to kill. I've turned grass under and seen the dirt blow off in clouds. I've seen dead antelope hung in bobwire fences I stretched."

Buster waved it all away. "If it hadn't been you, it would have been somebody else. You just as well get west of it and go on. Now, let's play some more songs like the chief told us. You don't know if maybe he can't still hear us. Them Indians have got better ears than we do. Play that one you made up yourself. The one you call the 'Shortgrass Song.' "

He turned back to the west and saw Long Fingers emerge as a distant speck on the switchback trail leading to Arapaho Pass. Left-handed, his fingers found their places on the guitar. He felt the chord under his calloused fingertips, caught the rhythm that lived forever in his heart. He began strumming in a vacant way as the sun warmed the stone over his brother's grave.

His voice struck the first words, and he felt their familiarity on his tongue. He shed his thoughts of Holcomb Ranch, his dread of its monotony. And as he sang, he began to feel release. The words rang from the hill in clarion tenor rhymes. The song grew larger than his soul and escaped like a vent of steam.

Singing, he looked down on the peopled fringes of the shortgrass plains. He felt as if he had blinked and missed the time of the frontier, and had only heard of it in stories and sung of it in songs.

He turned from sorrow to beauty, and his gaze crossed the face of Buster Thompson, holding the fiddle against his shoulder. Caleb's neck craned as he methodically changed chords, and his desperate eyes groped for the mountains, hoping to catch a last glimpse of Long Fingers climbing the Arapaho Trail. But the old chief was gone.

. . . and he camps there each year,
To tell his wild stories for his brother to hear.

All at once he knew. Everything in life had drawn him out onto the meandering trails. It all became instantly clear, and he owned, suddenly and finally, his destiny.

He had lied to Amelia. He was not going to stay. He was needed more on the lonely ranches and line camps than he ever would be needed here. Little Pete had Ab and Buster to bring him up. Buster had his work. Caleb had only a song, a story, and the trail before him. They would call him shiftless, say he could not take on responsibility. But what he did was not so bad. He brought music to lonely places, told stories to voice-starved ears.

He was going back out there. But this time he was not running away. He was riding toward something. His reason. He had children to visit in New Mexico, friends to help in the Indian Territory. There were songs to learn in remote corners. People would smile when they saw him coming. He would lope in long strides, like a wild white wolf, making music where he went, then vanishing like dust blown into darkness.

And he sang clearer and louder, with newfound purpose. The song was his truth, and he would spread it far. He needed no ranch, no cattle. He needed no brood around him. He existed to serve, to go out and find the quiet places and fill them with ringing song and laughter, to charge the legs of weary men and women with dance they would long remember.

He was gone. He saw a vision of himself riding west, up to the Rockies, away from the plains. He would walk beside the vision, become the vision. And they would look up and see him, one night every spring, sitting between the fire and the stone, telling Pete a story. And they would smile, then laugh, then sing and dance, then sow the seeds of wildflowers. He could never remain. It was his truth. Now he only had to find a way to tell them.

His voice echoed over the crags and chasms of the Rampart Range as he raked his strings with a trembling left hand. He touched the gravestone, looked up the Arapaho Trail, and turned to Buster.

His old friend was staring, smiling sadly. At least he wouldn't have to tell Buster. Buster already knew.